THE TWILIGHT OF COURAGE

A NOVEL

BODIE AND BROCK THOENE

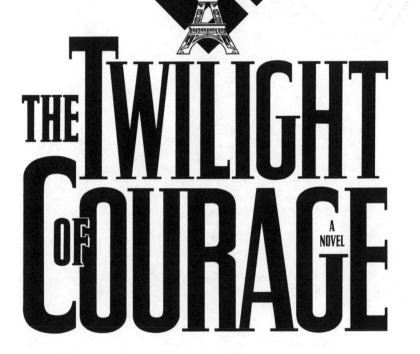

THE TWILIGHT OF COURAGE

A NOVEL

THOMAS NELSON PUBLISHERS

Nashville · Atlanta · London · Vancouver

Published in Nashville, Tennessee, by Thomas Nelson, Inc., Publishers, and distributed in Canada by Word Communications, Ltd., Richmond, British Columbia.

Scripture quotations are from the NEW KING JAMES VERSION of the Bible, Copyright © 1979, 1980, 1982, Thomas Nelson, Inc., Publishers.

Published in association with the literary agency of
Alive Communications
P.O. Box 49068
Colorado Springs, CO 80949

Library of Congress Cataloging-in-Publication Data

Thoene, Bodie, 1951–
    The twilight of courage: a novel/Bodie and Brock Thoene.
        p.   cm.
    "A Jan Dennis Book"
    ISBN 0-7852-8196-7
    1. World War, 1939–1945—Europe—Fiction. 2. Women journalists—Europe—
Fiction. 3. Americans—Europe—Fiction. I. Thoene, Brock, 1952– . II. Title.
    PS35701.H46T88   1994   94-26088
    813'.54—dc20   CIP

DEDICATION

—For Rick Christian and Jan Dennis

ACKNOWLEDGMENTS

The authors gratefully acknowledge . . .

. . . Research assistants Jake Thoene, Luke Thoene, Seth Townsend and Nathan Dahlen . . .

. . . Lowell Saunders, Communications department, The Master's College, for his help in arranging the internship program . . .

. . . The valuable information received from

        Association of Dunkirk Little Ships
        Christopher and Paulette Catherwood
        Dunkirk Veterans Association
        Imperial War Museum, London
        National Army Museum, London
        National Maritime Museum, Greenwich
        Royal Air Force Museum, Hendon
        Royal Geographical Society, London
        Royal Naval Museum, Portsmouth

        Musée de l'Armée, Paris
        Musée de l'Ordre de la Libération, Paris

        Bundesarchiv, Coblenz
        Institut für Zeitgeschichte, Munich

        National Archives, Washington, D.C.

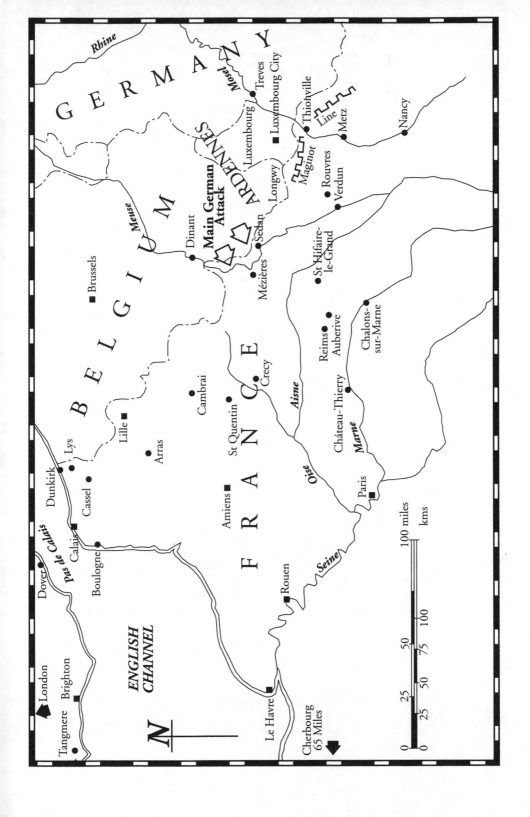

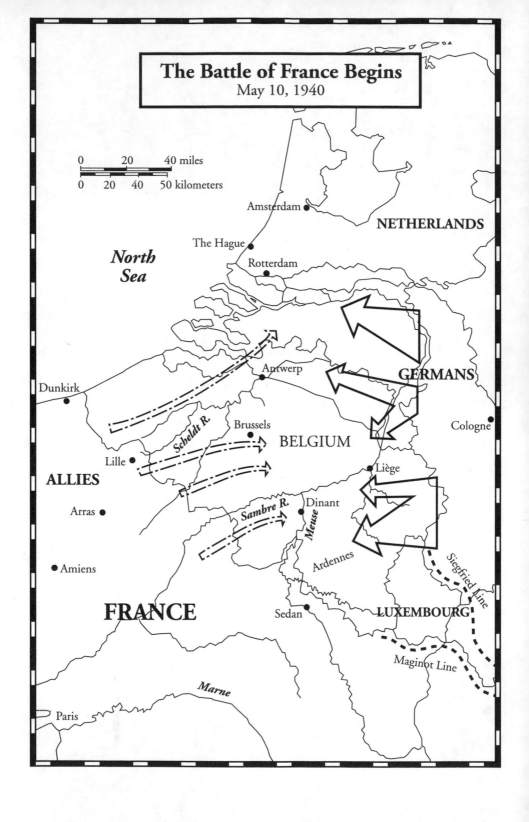

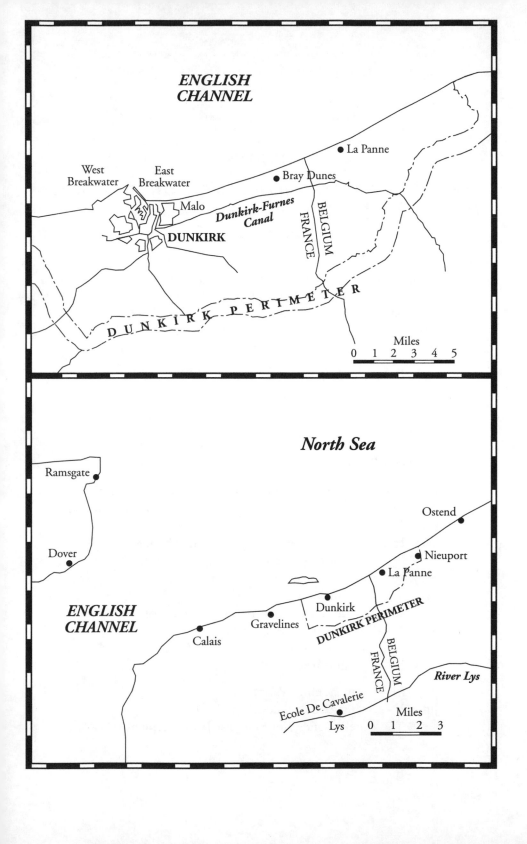

TIMELINE:

THE FIRST TEN MONTHS OF WORLD WAR II

1939

September 1—Nazi Germany invades Poland
September 17—Soviets invade Poland
September 27—Warsaw falls

October to April—"Phony War"

December 13—*Graf Spee* cornered in South Atlantic

1940

February 16—*Altmark* incident

April 9—Germany invades Norway

May 10—Winston Churchill becomes British Prime Minister
May 10—Germany invades Holland, Belgium, and Luxembourg
May 12—Panzers reach Meuse River
May 13 to 19—Blitzkrieg sweeps across northern France
May 14—Holland surrenders
May 16—Panic in French government
May 18—Germans capture Cambrai
May 20—Wehrmacht reaches the French seacoast
May 21—British counterattack near Arras
May 27 to June 4—"Miracle of Dunkirk"
May 28—Belgium surrenders

June 14—Germans enter Paris
June 22—Armistice concludes Battle of France
     Britain stands alone against Nazi Germany

PROLOGUE

September 1, 1870

The east wind smelled of dry, dusty, barren places. The Santa Ana breeze did not give moisture, it took it away. Even at sea, twenty miles out in the channel between Santa Cruz Island and the California coast, the air felt like the desert.

"Captain," Nicholas Smith remarked to the new master of the trading vessel *Argosy*, "it's fixin' up a blow; a real easter. We'd best run in behind San Miguel and set the hook. It'll be a rough day and night, I'm thinkin'."

Captain Reiss, no older than the mate Smith, was master of the *Argosy*, having won it in Panama at a card game. Just in from the East, Reiss knew little of sailing and even less about the California waters. "Nonsense," he said. "It's a fine, warm day and the wind is fair astern to push us on our way. By this time tomorrow we'll be 'round Point Conception and halfway to San Francisco."

"Sir," replied Smith with a tug at his forelock. Even when the skipper was dead wrong, one did not argue. The *Argosy* was a stout ship; perhaps it would be all right.

But the sense of apprehension did not fade. It grew even as the vision of Anacapa Island grew astern of them. The small isle, only three rocks forming a narrow spine above the water, swelled in the tempered air as if overtaking the ship instead of being left behind. It was a bad sign.

"Captain," Smith tried again. "The old Spaniards say that when 'Capa swells up like that it's a sure sign of a big wind out of the canyons."

Reiss studied the sight with his telescope. "Quaint superstition . . . interesting atmospheric phenomenon," he said. "Nothing more. Carry on with your duties."

Smith did carry on, but in addition to the regular chores of ship handling, he quietly went about doubling the rigging and checking the lashings all around.

By midafternoon, *Argosy* was in a patch of confused sea. The short, choppy waves held no rhythm, no pattern. They slapped against the hull from all directions as if unseen hands played with the planks.

The east wind filled in. Twenty-five miles away, Nicholas could at first point to an arroyo and see the current of wind that raced down from the hills to grasp the ship. Then, with an abruptness that defied belief, the shore, the foothills, and finally the dark green mountains were obscured by an ocean of dust that rose and engulfed the land.

Almost before Nicholas could order a reef taken in the sails, the full fury of the wind struck. Four-foot-high waves became six and then ten and then twenty. *Argosy* posed on the crest of a roller, trembling on the lip. Then down the wave's face she plunged, while Nicholas could only stare upward in fascinated horror as a thousand tons of seawater hung above the ship. Captain Reiss disappeared, huddling sick and frightened belowdecks.

Racing before the wind, they had a chance of escape. But on one of the downward drives, the bowsprit buried itself in the foaming green sea. The jib tore away with a crash and the helmsman panicked, letting the wheel spin out of control.

Argosy twisted sideways to the rushing sea, heeled over; masttips into the wave tops. The mountain of water astern rose above the hull, poised to swallow ship and crew. "God help us!" Nicholas cried.

PART I

"It is not by speeches and resolutions that the questions of time are decided . . . but by iron and blood."

—Otto von Bismarck,
speech to the Prussian
House of Delegates
September 30, 1862

ONE

Thursday, August 31, 1939, the full moon rose slowly over Jerusalem. British soldiers stood watch on the massive walls that surrounded the ancient city. Within that stone circle, Moslem, Jew, and Christian lived side by side in fragile and often shattered peace.

Tonight the spiked towers of minarets rising from the Moslem Quarter cast long shadows over the great arched rooftops of the churches crammed into the Christian Quarter and the synagogues of the Jewish Quarter. Around the holy shrines of three religions huddled the vaulted souks, tiny shops, and crooked houses of each community, separated only by twisting alleyways or flights of worn stone steps. From the perspective of the British guards manning the wall, the domed roofs looked like many yarmulkes crowning the heads of the pious. The streets stood deserted and iron grills covered the doorways of the empty souks, but in the moonlight and shifting shadows, the very stones of the Holy City seemed alive.

Rabbi Schlomo Lebowitz turned off the flame of the hissing Primus stove as his tea water came to a boil. In the winter, the three-legged kerosene stove served both to cook the old man's meals and to warm the tiny one-room flat he called home. But the days had been long and hot through August—too hot for him to heat even a cup of tea until long after sunset. *This is the best time of day,* thought the rabbi as he steeped the tea leaves and took two rough lumps of sugar from the jar on the shelf. A calico cat, the old man's companion, looked on.

"So. We are both awake. It is the best time for an old man and a cat to think and study and pray. Nu."

Heavy shutters were open wide. A cool breeze finally drifted up the pass of Bab el Wad from the sea to slip through the iron bars that covered the window of the stone room. Blue light reflecting from the moon added to the glow of a single beeswax candle sputtering on a rough wooden table.

The tea tasted strong and sweet. He gingerly sipped the steaming brew as he sat down to reread Etta's letter, dated August 1, which had just arrived from Warsaw this afternoon.

Propped against the stone wall was a gallery of photographs displaying the faces of his daughter's family. They smiled across the table at him: beautiful Etta, her husband Aaron, the children—Rachel, David, Samuel, the baby Yacov.

The old man had never met his grandchildren, but tonight, as he read the letter again, he was filled with the certain hope that soon they would all be with him in Jerusalem! He would bounce the baby on his knee. He would embrace the boys and touch the cheek of young Rachel, who was the very image of Etta at the age of twelve.

My dearest Father,

I know that the news you hear from Poland must be grim, but you must not worry. We are praying that there will not be a war. The Polish government seems to be working out its differences with Germany. None of it affects us, except that there are many Jewish refugees now flooding into Warsaw from Czechoslovakia to escape the Nazis there. We have set up a soup kitchen to feed them all.

Things are going well for us.

We are filled with hope that soon our documents and visas will arrive, allowing us to come home to Jerusalem. At least another six weeks, they tell us. Which is what they told us six weeks ago. But we are not discouraged. Aaron says he may send the children and me ahead, and then he will come later.

I have had new photographs made. They will be ready in a week or two. I will post them to you so you will not be surprised at how much the children have grown by the time you see us soon in Jerusalem!

It was a good letter. Full of hope, the old man lay down at last on the groaning springs of his iron bed and dreamed of grandchildren. The sweet dream lasted only until the morning, when news of the German invasion of Poland reached the gates of Jerusalem.

At ten minutes to five on the morning of September 1st, the radio message from German High Command reached a thousand portable Enigma decoding devices. On a front that stretched from the Baltic Sea to what had recently been Czechoslovakia, the troops of the Nazi Wehrmacht overran the borders of Poland. German battleships shelled the port of Danzig, Warsaw was subjected to a dawn air raid, and Stuka dive-bombers demoralized the Polish forces by attacking virtually unhindered and with surgical accuracy.

But after six days of almost uncontested gains, part of the German onslaught was in danger of grinding to a halt. Polish troops on the road to Lodz put up unexpectedly fierce resistance. Captain Horst von Bockman, leading the 3rd platoon of motorcycle reconnaissance, was sent forward to examine the situation and report. When he returned to the company headquarters, he found the Panzer regiment leader, Colonel Forster, impatiently pacing up and down inside the command post tent.

"The Poles are well placed behind the stone walls of their village. It is located on a hill that overlooks our approach," Horst informed the colonel. "We need tanks."

"We have outrun our tanks," Forster replied. "They will not come up until tomorrow. We have traveled so far in such a short time that the roads have worn out the tank treads and they must halt for repairs."

"With all due respect, sir," Horst resumed, "then we should withdraw. The Poles are using their temporary advantage to bring in artillery. We saw it moving into place."

"Withdraw!" snorted Forster. "Unthinkable! The only field pieces the Poles can muster were surplus twenty years ago. We will continue the attack."

"Perhaps we should at least call for air support," offered Horst's company commander.

"Agreed," replied the colonel, and the three men started for the radio in the colonel's armored half-track. Without any warning, Horst found himself flung backwards across the tent, which partially collapsed on top of him. Fighting clear of the heavy canvas folds, Horst hugged the ground as a rain of Polish artillery shells burst around the site.

As he crawled free of the tent, Horst came upon his company commander —dead. Next to him, propped against a tree trunk, Colonel Forster lay unconscious, his left arm shattered. Behind Horst was a thick line of trees and a tempting depression in the earth like a ready-made trench. Ahead, across an open space of some twenty yards, stood the command vehicle and the radio equipment.

The ground continued to quake as incoming shells straddled the targeted camp, but Horst moved steadily toward the half-track. The radio operators had bailed out of the open-topped vehicle and now huddled underneath it. "You!" Horst shouted to a shuddering communications lieutenant. "Get up there and call in the Stukas!"

The man, wide-eyed with fear, shook his head. "Are you crazy?"

"Do it!" ordered Horst, "before they pound us to pieces here!" He drew his Luger from its holster and waved it in the man's face. "Now!"

High explosive rounds continued to drop, each one threatening to be the direct hit that would end the matter altogether. At gunpoint, Horst forced the man out from under the half-track and back up into it. Spent pieces of shrapnel clattered all around from another near miss; the frightened lieutenant looked as if he might dive back underneath.

Horst was just behind the radioman when he felt a sharp pain. From the back of his leather glove protruded a steel splinter about two inches long. Horst waved his pistol, gesturing toward the dials of the radio and the wheels and keys of an Enigma encoding machine. As the man reluctantly put on the headphones and sat down in front of his equipment, Horst laid aside the Luger and yanked the jagged blade of shrapnel out of his hand.

"Get on with it," he ordered through gritted teeth. "Here are the coordinates."

Moments later, both Horst and the radio operator crawled back under the half-track. Five more minutes of explosions passed, some so near that the two tons of armored Kommando Panzerwagen bounced off the ground. Finally, unseen by the figures huddled under the vehicle, a trio of tiny black dots appeared high overhead. Diving earthward, the banshee scream of their sirens penetrating even the blasts of exploding shells, the Stukas swept toward their objective.

After releasing their five-hundred-pound bombs, the dive-bombers veered back toward their base. From a distance, the deep pitched crumps did not sound like much in comparison to the artillery rounds, but they did their job, silencing two of the Polish guns. The remaining cannon crew abandoned their position and fled.

TWO

A dull haze clouded the September sky with dust which rose off the unpaved road. The caravan of cars from the American embassy in Warsaw inched along the two-lane highway behind an unending stream of refugees in desperate retreat toward the safety of the Rumanian border.

Carts pulled by half-starved horses, hand carts, wagons, and even baby carriages lumbered under the weight of belongings. Polish soldiers, the survivors of divisions routed in the first assaults of the German war machine, abandoned their weapons and joined the retreat of the civilian population.

Behind the column lay the smoldering remains of the towns and villages they had called home.

In just a few hours five thousand Luftwaffe aircraft smashed the core of the Polish Air Force and then began terrorizing the civilian population. In Nalencczow, Dubno, Kuty, and Luck, German Messerschmidts made repeated low passes to strafe the open marketplaces and streets. Stuka divebombers followed in screaming swarms, killing with impunity. Military objectives seemed less important to the German strategy than inciting panic.

Such policy had been ordained at the planning table in the Chancellory at Berlin. Terror was the surest weapon of the Third Reich, assuring the quick defeat of Poland. The German Wehrmacht advanced almost unhindered while millions of refugees left the dead unburied and took to the roads, blocking the movements of Polish army divisions. Behind the German army, the Nazi Waffen SS units began the mop-up of any civilians who had been foolish enough to remain in their villages.

Eight staff cars comprised the American caravan. Each vehicle had the letters *USA* plainly painted on the roof. The lead car, containing Ambassador Anthony J. Biddle, Jr., and his wife and daughter, flew the American flag. Secretaries, liaison officers, assistants, and intelligence personnel followed with assorted American and Polish citizens crammed into every spare automobile inch. Under American diplomatic protection, the French Ambassador to Poland, Leon Noel, occupied the last car with Mac McGrath, the American newsreel cameraman for Movietone News. In the front passenger seat was a Polish Jew, Richard Lewinski; Mac assumed he was connected with the embassy staff.

The fleeing diplomatic corps had already been strafed twice. American flags and clear identification seemed to make no difference to the Messerschmidt pilots, who honed their battle techniques fighting for fascism in the Spanish Civil War.

Brakes groaned as the vehicles came to a complete standstill. The driver of the lead car leaned on the horn as the backs of the crowd pressed against the car's bumper. They were still thirty miles from the Rumanian border. Russian divisions were sweeping down from the north. In the distance, Mac McGrath could clearly hear the even cadence of exploding bombs.

Mac lowered his window. The back seat of the French-made Renault filled instantly with choking dust. Mac watched with amusement as Lewinski pulled the straps of a gas mask over a shock of wildly unruly hair.

Just outside the window stood a weary young peasant woman with two small, filthy children perched in a wooden wheelbarrow. The woman's angry face, framed in a bright red scarf, considered Mac with resentment.

"Why are we stopped?" Ambassador Noel asked the woman.

She shrugged as if she would not answer but then relayed the question forward to a stooped old man who passed it on. When the reply returned five minutes later, the convoy remained immobile.

"The Nazis strafed the road. There are many dead and wounded; their belongings are being moved out of the way," the woman reported with bland acceptance, acknowledging that the wounded would be left in the field beside the dead. "Two dead horses and an upturned cart block the road."

Mac chafed with impatience. The journey that should have taken only a few hours had stretched into days. The driver cut the engine of the vehicle to save precious fuel.

"Only thirty miles," Mac remarked. "We could walk faster than this."

The French ambassador eyed him patronizingly. "Impatient Americans." He jerked his thumb at the tangle of pedestrians. "No one is moving, Monsieur. Perhaps if you walk on the heads of the people you will arrive at the Rumanian border before me, but I cannot see any other way than that." Mac looked for support from the occupants of the front seat, but the driver only shrugged. Lewinski, still wearing the gas mask, ignored the discussion completely. With a loop of string and utter lack of interest in the events outside, Lewinski played the children's game Cat's Cradle.

Mac raised his hands in surrender then retrieved his DeVry Cine camera and cranked the key wind. A moment later he swung out of the side window and onto the bullet-riddled roof of the black Renault as the Frenchman shook his head in amusement.

Now able to see for miles, Mac focused on the ragged sea of heads stretching beyond the roofs of the eight official vehicles. Mac shot a few seconds of film and then walked forward, stepping from hood to trunk, until he reached the lead car belonging to Ambassador Biddle.

Haggard and unshaven, Biddle sat up on the window frame to see what Mac was doing on top of the car.

"You're going to want a record of this, Ambassador." Mac focused on the dead horses being dragged into the roadside ditch and fifty bodies laid out like rag dolls in a field of scattered baggage.

One hundred feet of film could capture only sixty seconds of action. Within the first five seconds of his shot Mac heard the distant buzzing of an airplane engine. He did not stop to wonder if the approaching craft was friend or foe. The mob of refugees stumbled off the road, leaving their bundles and plunging into the fields and ditches.

Mac stamped his foot hard on the metal roof. "Plane!" he yelled.

The doors of the vehicles burst open as men and women staff members poured out to join the headlong flight away from the road.

"Come on!" Biddle pounded the steel fender. "Get down!" He did not wait to see if Mac followed.

Mac remained rooted on the hood following the undignified scramble of the lanky American ambassador with the camera as the lone Messerschmidt circled and released a burst of machine gun fire. Handcarts disintegrated. A half dozen stragglers fell to the ground.

From the ditch Biddle shouted Mac's name as the trail of bullets stitched two straight lines toward the cameraman. Through the lense Mac saw baggage erupt, clothes and belongings whirled into the air. The screams of men and women blended into the roar of the engine.

The aircraft skimmed the road only a few feet off the ground.

"Get down!" Biddle cried.

Mac clearly caught the face of the pilot through the blur of the propellor, and the pinwheel cross of the Swastika. The guns stopped, but there was no doubt that Mac was still a target. The pilot nosed up only slightly, aiming to sever Mac's head with the prop.

Mac vaulted face first into the ditch, a bare instant before the craft roared past. Then it climbed and disappeared over the crest of a hill.

Cradled against his chest, the DeVry had knocked the wind out of Mac but was itself unharmed. Mac had twenty seconds of new footage in the camera. Fresh bullet holes scarred the car's American flag and the right front fender.

Mac sat up slowly as people climbed to their feet. Women searched for children lost in the scramble. Children cried for their mothers.

A half dozen refugees lay dead in the road, including the peasant woman and her two children still in the wheelbarrow. They were carried out of the way. Mac took his place in the rear vehicle across from the pale and shaken French ambassador. Workers completed the removal of the horses from the highway. Gradually the convoy began to creep forward again as an old man beside the road raised his hands and wept, pleading with the Blessed Virgin to save his family and Poland.

Mac figured the old man might make it to Rumania if he hurried, but he doubted even the Blessed Virgin could save Poland now.

It was the third morning since the German Army flooded across the Polish frontiers. As yet, no help had come from either England or France.

Sunday, September 3, 1939, Lt. Commander Trevor Galway sat between his sister Annie and his father John Galway in Westminster Chapel, Buckingham Gate, London.

The night before, as Prime Minister Neville Chamberlain rose to urge the House of Commons for patience in the face of the Nazi aggression, shouts of dissension met his pleas.

"Speak for England!" cried Mr. Amery from the Conservative bench.

The temper of the House was clearly for war. All the same, this morning England gathered once more to pray for peace.

Even the balcony of Westminster Chapel, parish of Reverend Martin Lloyd-Jones, was packed. Not a single seat remained in the long pews. Men and women stood in the aisles around the sanctuary. Children, giddy with the prospect of an exciting war, sat in the aisle and in front of the pulpit.

Hymn books opened, and the hall reverberated to the spiritual anthem of Martin Luther:

> *A Mighty Fortress is our God,*
> *A bulwark never failing . . .*

It occurred to Trevor as he sang that this was a German hymn. He wondered how many voices in Germany were likewise raised in the same melody at this very instant. The image of men and women wearing swastika armbands as they belted out Luther's words made him fall silent, made him angry.

Trevor's sudden unhappiness must have shown. Annie, who at nineteen was born just after the Great War with Germany, took his hand and gave him a chin-up look. Like all those too young to remember 1918, she had been storming about for two days, wondering why milk-toast Chamberlain continued to delay making a formal declaration of war. Many of the Pacifist Party sat in Westminster this morning. Trevor could spot them, smug and fervent as they warbled. Their presence now, in view of the damage they wrought to the cause of stopping Hitler's antics, added to Trevor's outrage. The Nazis might have been halted long ago, before the world had come to this moment. By allowing evil to eclipse central Europe unchecked, the shadow was about to fall across England and France as well.

As the organ boomed, a smallish, balding little man in a tweed coat too hot for the morning made his way through the throng waving a yellow slip of paper, much as Chamberlain had waved the little document signed by Hitler which the Prime Minister declared promised "Peace in our Time!"

The sexton climbed the pulpit steps and presented the message to Reverend Lloyd-Jones. The song continued. Second and third verses echoed through the chapel as the minister silently reviewed the message and the congregation watched his face reflect its content.

He stood as the music died away. Approaching the podium he raised his hand, and with a hard, piercing look, he said, "This message has just been broadcast by Prime Minister Chamberlain at 10 Downing Street . . ." He drew a deep breath and began:

Unless we heard from the Germans by 11 o'clock this A.M. that they were prepared at once to withdraw their troops from Poland, a state of war would exist between us.

John Galway tapped the crystal of his watch. It was 11:20.

I have to tell you now that no such undertaking has been received, and consequently, this country is at war with Germany.

A murmur rippled through the crowd. Here and there a few heads bowed, and the shoulders of mothers with military-aged sons shook with sobs.

John Galway grasped Trevor's hand. Annie put her arm around his waist and raised her chin defiantly. If Hitler dared stand in front of her she would spit in his eye!

You can imagine what a bitter blow it is to me that all my long struggle to win peace has failed. Germany will never give up force and can only be stopped by force . . . May God bless you all and may He defend the right, for it is evil things we shall be fighting—brute force, broken promises . . . I am certain right will prevail.

As the message ended, the prolonged, weird wailing of an air raid siren filled the air. Heads jerked up in sudden realization that German bombers might be approaching the coast of England at that moment.

The congregation was dismissed. As instructed, men in uniform reported immediately to their posts. Parents scrambled to retrieve children, and all were invited to make their way to the cellar beneath the church.

Trevor kissed Annie good-bye. He pumped the hand of his father. Then, without a backward glance, he left the church just as the siren fell silent.

Outside, nothing seemed changed. He stood for a long moment on the steps and listened to the silence as if he were hearing it for the first time. Above him on the cornice of the chapel, pigeons cooed and fluttered. He wanted to memorize this first moment of conflict; to remember it forever. It seemed no different than the peace of an hour before, and yet he sensed that from this hour his life was irrevocably altered. He closed his eyes for a moment and conjured up images of screaming bombs falling on London, of rubble and ruin and the cries of the injured. But when he opened his eyes again, there was only London, brick and stone and undisturbed tradition.

Just to his right, the spires of Parliament rose in the cool, light September morning air. He walked the long block and turned toward Victoria Embankment. He would need to fetch his duffel bag, extra uniform, and great coat. He would say good-bye to his dog, Duffy, and catch a water taxi down river to board his ship, HMS *Fortitude*. From there, who could say where he would go?

No German bombers passed overhead on his way to the Thames. As he strode along the embankment, thirty or forty silver barrage balloons slowly rose over the city like a school of fish swimming the breezes above London.

So this was war.

❧ ❧ ❧

The bells of the clock tower chimed twelve as the loudspeaker played *La Marseillaise*. After a respectful moment of silence, the doors to the enormous dining hall of the upperclassmen of the École de Cavalerie burst open, and 1,500 young cadets aged twelve to seventeen flooded into their places at the long tables.

Lieutenant Paul Chardon stood at attention with a half dozen fellow instructors behind the head table as the commandant of the school, Colonel Michel Larousse, entered solemnly through a side door. His left sleeve was pinned up, revealing an arm lost in the last war against Germany. He carried a communiqué in his right hand. As he stood for a long moment before ascending the platform to the head table, the Colonel observed his young charges with the weary eyes of a man who knew what war would do to the youth of his nation.

From the high walls, portraits of the great soldiers of France also looked down on the boys. Emperor Napoleon and his cavalry commander, Marshal Ney, stared across the hall at General Petain, who had led French armies to victory in the Great War.

Many of the best and the bravest leaders of the Republic had begun their education here in the junior school at age five. They had progressed through the ranks and supped at these same long tables. In a dozen different wars, brave comrades had gone from this place to die for France before they had a chance to grow up. Who remembered their names now?

Today the hall rang with laughter and boisterous conversation just as it had for 150 years. Paul Chardon glanced at Colonel Larousse and then at the cadets, dressed in the dark blue uniforms of the Cadre Bleu. It was as though the faces of past centuries looked back at him. France was at war once again.

The tradition of the military school had been broken only once in the 1914–18 war, when German troops had threatened to overrun Armentieres and the vast estate where Napoleon founded the school in 1805.

At that terrible time the cry had risen up, *"École de Cavalerie! France éternelle!* Not one inch of ground will we surrender! *Ils ne passeront pas!"*

But once again the École de Cavalerie was close to what must be the front lines of battle—only minutes from the Belgian border. Midway between Arras and Dunkirk, the school stood in the center of troop mobilization. The decision already made that the junior academy would be evacuated, what would become of these blustering, proud young Frenchmen?

Colonel Larousse cleared his throat and gave a nod to the bugler. The sharp flourish of the trumpet called the boys to attention: eyes forward, chests out, shoulders back.

"At ease." The colonel stood before a whining microphone. He cleared his throat. Silence. Here was the news they had all been waiting for, praying for! Perhaps they could fight! He began. "I hold in my hand a communiqué from Paris." He held it up to the light. The portrait of General Petain seemed to be reading over his shoulder. "Be it known . . . The recent attacks on our ally, the sovereign democratic nation of Poland, by the forces of Nazi Germany, violates all international laws and treaties. In view of this fact, this act of aggression is an act of war against the Republic of France. Therefore, the Republic of France is now at war with Germany."

A stirring of excitement rippled over the cadets. Paul Chardon saw their half-smiles, their winks, their delight at the prospect of putting into practice what they had learned in theory at the school. *To hold the defensive line against attack at the River Lys.*

Colonel Larousse likewise sensed their joy at the declaration.

"All cadets under the age of thirteen will be evacuated to the South . . ."

There rose a universal moan of misery among the twelve year olds. Winks and smirks and jabs to the ribs came from the older boys. Larousse held up his hand for silence.

"Those of the Cadre Bleu who are thirteen and older will remain at the school for the time being. We have nine hundred fine cavalry horses in our stables which will certainly be called to battle. It will be our duty to see that they pass into the hands of the Grand Armee in the most excellent condition and with the finest training. That will be our obligation as soldiers of the Republic and the future leaders of France."

His speech ended, and a great cheer rose up among the older boys. The twelve-year-old cadets sat dejected; near to tears. They were to be shipped off like little boys. They were to miss all the excitement!

A group of cadets due to graduate to officers' school in the spring jumped up on the table and led the cheer.

"Vive l'École de Cavalerie! Vive la France! France éternelle! They shall not pass!"

Then they sang *La Marseillaise* and ate lunch cheerfully, marking the beginning of the war for the École de Cavalerie.

THREE

Smoke rose from the inferno of Warsaw, blotting out the sun for a hundred miles. The ring of German fire and steel had encircled the city for three weeks. Although all of Poland fell, Warsaw refused to surrender. The boom of a hundred heavy guns resounded with the Nazi reply to this final defiance. Wave upon wave of Luftwaffe bombers dropped their cargos of incendiary bombs on churches and hospitals filled with wounded. Thousands of dead and dying littered the streets. The heat of the fires cracked the windows. Not one building in the city remained undamaged by the ceaseless barrage.

At 8:30 A.M. a frantic radio message reached Budapest:

> At this moment German heavy artillery . . . shelling Warsaw . . . German planes bombed Little Jesus Hospital only a few minutes ago. The left wing of the hospital . . . grave for hundreds of wounded soldiers, women, and children . . . Opera House, the National Theater, and the Polytechnic School are now on fire . . . German artillery now is concentrating its fire on the center of the city . . . Seventeen days of siege . . . difficult to keep order in a city of a million and a half people when death and destruction . . . Those still able bring what aid they can to the hungry . . . wounded . . . dying in the streets.

The broadcast ended with a desperate plea.

> We hold to hope . . . awaiting quick aid from our British and French allies!

In that same hour, France and England, who had declared war against Germany, still debated what help to send.

By late afternoon, Soviet Red Army troops closed in on Warsaw from the East, advancing toward the new Hitler-Stalin line carving Poland in two. Advance Russian units were within sixty miles of the city even as British

Prime Minister Chamberlain declared that the annihilation of Poland was "Fait accompli."

There would be no military aid from the West. Still, the last Polish army fought on in Warsaw. Soldiers gave the weapons of fallen comrades to civilians—women, old men, and boys who held the barricades. Pounded by the distant German artillery and the Stuka bombers, the defenders never saw the face of the enemy who slaughtered them. They simply died, still believing their allies would come. One hero at a time, Poland perished while France and England clucked their tongues and offered nothing more substantial than sympathy.

On the afternoon of September twenty-sixth, Josephine Marlow, the last remaining member of the Associated Press in Warsaw, covered her head as yet another explosion rocked the great edifice of the Cathedral of St. John above her. Ancient dust and flecks of mortar rained down on the carpet of wounded who lined the floor of the vaulted crypt.

The groans of four hundred sounded like one continuous moan. There was no more morphine for pain. The last of the disinfectant had been used the day before. Now bottles of vodka served as both antiseptic and anesthetic. The most severely wounded waited in the main hall of the cathedral where the priest moved from one to the other administering last rites. Here in the crypt were the women and children who might survive . . . if medicine could be brought for them in time.

Josephine followed Sister Angeline as she offered hope, cleaned the wounds, and changed the bandages of her patients. Carrying a precious bucket of boiled water, Josie ladled its contents into parched mouths.

Josie knelt to offer a drink to a young Jewish woman of about eighteen who had lost the lower part of her right leg in an artillery blast. She clutched Josie's grime-covered sleeve. Her dark eyes frantic, she cried out to Josie in Yiddish and would not release her grip.

"Sister Angeline," Josie called for help in French, the common meeting place between English and Polish for the two women. "What is she saying? What does she want from me?"

The young woman pleaded with the nun, who translated for Josie.

"She thinks you are French," explained the sister. "She wants to know when your French soldiers will come to save us from the Nazis."

Josie sat back on her heels and put her hand in despair on the young woman's hand. She looked into the face of Sister Angeline. "What do i tell her, Sister? What? That I do not think the French or the English will come? Do I tell her that I am American? That we are not even at war with the men who blew her leg off? That, as a member of the press, if I survive the shelling I can probably walk away from here to freedom with the blessings of the German High Command while all the rest of you . . ." Her voice faltered.

Eyes brimmed with helplessness and anger. She wired two dozen reports throughout the siege, each more desperate than the one before. She did not even know if her stories made it to the AP in Paris.

She had stayed too long in Warsaw and was now trapped like everyone else, though her plight was not an automatic death sentence as it must surely be for this young Jewess with half a leg. The SS had shot wounded numbering in the tens of thousands. What hope for mercy could there be for those in the crypt who reached up to Josie for an answer she could not give?

Josie covered her face with her hands, filled with anger and shame. With every bomb that fell, she found herself inwardly raging against the senselessness of this slaughter. Angry at the brutality of the Nazis, she was also angry at the useless courage of the Poles. Could the Polish High Command still believe that Chamberlain and Daladier would ride in to break the siege of Warsaw like the cavalry in a bad movie? Only one word, *surrender,* would stop the destruction! Why did the Polish High Command continue to hold out in the face of inevitable defeat?

Sister Angeline put a hand on her shoulder. "Josephine? Ma chérie," she said gently, "soon it must come to an end for us in Warsaw. We will stay and face what we must with God's help. We will each fight on in our own way. You must live. You must go from here and tell what you saw. Tell them . . . yes . . . we were afraid. But even so, we held out until the end. Perhaps it will help them to fight if they remember that Poland died alone, yet with courage."

"Oh, Sister!" Josie cried as the terrible roar of an artillery shell howled overhead, bursting somewhere beyond the church. Thunder succeeded thunder, drowning out screams as a dozen explosions followed the first blast. The ground shook. Sister Angeline threw herself across a patient as a section of wall collapsed on them both. The air of the crypt filled with choking dust. Josie crouched down and shielded her head as bricks tumbled from the pillars, and the ceiling at the far end fell in on fifty wounded.

Then there was silence. Josie sat up slowly. She was uninjured. Debris covered the place where Sister Angeline had been. Josephine crawled toward the heap, crying out the name of the sister. Her voice echoed in the shattered crypt. Outside, the distant rumble of artillery suddenly stopped, leaving only the voice of Josie.

The church sustained a direct hit. Into the night, Josephine worked numbly beside a priest and a few ragged soldiers to dig out the victims from beneath the rubble. The rough edges of the bricks tore and blistered Josephine's hands. Her clothing was shredded and soaked with sweat and blood. Josephine walked out into the night for the first time in over a week. She looked up and thought of words to describe what she had seen in this place. There were none adequate to the task. She tried to simply observe, to detach herself from the scene and mentally record the images of war. *Useless. Senseless. Waste.* These were the words which came to mind.

Two soldiers carried Sister Angeline out onto the pavement. Her wimple had come off in the blast, revealing short, greying hair. Covered with dust, her face was serene, almost joyful in death. Josephine stood over her for a moment and realized that she had told the sister everything about herself in the last two weeks. But what did Josephine know about Sister Angeline? Only that she fought a different kind of battle than the soldiers at the barricades.

The sky above Warsaw glowed orange with flames that enveloped the main buildings of the city. Josie shielded her eyes against the brightness as the Bristol Hotel, the Town Hall, and the Gothic edifice of the ancient castle burned. Acrid smoke billowed as if the earth opened and hell rose to engulf Warsaw.

They laid the dead on the shattered stone pavement outside the church. Row upon row. So many. So still. The fires of the fallen city shone in the lifeless eyes of the brave.

No one spoke. Only the fall of collapsing buildings punctuated the silence. The German artillery ceased. Was it finished then? Was the siege over? Had the last Polish child died defending the last barricade?

Josephine sank to the ground as the fires crackled behind her. She was thirsty. Somewhere she had lost the bucket of cool water with which she had comforted the condemned.

FOUR

Less than a month had passed since the German Wehrmacht streaked across the frontiers of Poland. Except for the final resistance in Warsaw, the German High Command considered the war a success. Wehrmacht troops were already leaving occupied Polish territory to reinforce the western front against the mobilized armies of France. Waffen SS, Hitler's own elite forces, rapidly filled the void left by the regular army.

Polish prisoners of war shuffling against the flow of Wehrmacht tanks, mobile artillery, and troop lorries packed the road leading from Lodz to Warsaw. Disheveled, bloody, and filthy, the captured Poles made a striking contrast to the victorious German troops.

Captain Horst von Bockman, now company commander in the 8th armored reconnaissance regiment of General Stumme's 2nd Light Division, watched the tide of conquered men divide and move into the roadside ditches as the heavy machinery of the Wehrmacht passed. The picture, he thought, perfectly summed up the war. The Poles fought using the tactics of the last century. The antiquated Polish divisions dug in along a border stretching for 1,500 miles. While the German Luftwaffe served as artillery, bombing airfields as well as civilian centers behind the lines; the highly mobile Panzerkorps of tanks and motorized infantry had broken through and cut the Polish units to pieces. Within ten days, General Guderian's tanks had covered 200 miles. In Zabinka they finally met a rare mechanized unit. Polish tanks being unloaded at a railway siding were destroyed before returning a single shot. Now, with the Polish Government fled to Rumania, no official remained to sign the surrender.

Horst von Bockman took pride in the performance of the men in his unit. As the commander of a motorcycle escort company, he led them through the Polish lines, often meeting enemy resistance before the main body of German troops reached the front. Unlike the Luftwaffe, which had been blooded in the Spanish Civil War, this was his first taste of real combat. Four years of hard work and sacrifice finally paid off. Though he found his first victory exhilarating, today, as he observed the herding of Polish prisoners by the SS, he felt ill at ease.

For a week von Bockman anxiously waited to leave Poland for the Siegfried Line. At first he explained away his misgivings as simple impatience to get to the Western Front, face the French, and finish what had been left undone in 1918. Rumors of mass graves—the results of SS execution squads —were every hour being confirmed as fact, and every hour increased von Bockman's desire to leave.

A motorcycle reconnaissance team happened upon an open grave filled with Polish officers. Reported to von Bockman and then up the chain of command, the grizzly discovery was dismissed as a burial place for Polish soldiers killed honorably in action. On the face of it, this answer seemed to satisfy all but the two men who had seen the site. It could not be, they explained; every Polish officer in the ditch was executed with a single bullet in the back of the head!

As their commander, von Bockman warned them to keep their mouths shut. Talking could get them into trouble. They performed their duty by reporting the incident; now they should forget it. In the hands of a higher authority than his own, the matter could no longer be his concern.

Now, as the distant rattle of machine gun fire echoed from the otherwise calm woods, von Bockman could not forget. For him and others in the German Wehrmacht, the glory of their patriotic war was rapidly dissolving into meaningless slaughter by Hitler's Waffen SS.

"We will be here until Christmas," he muttered to the fresh-faced young driver of his armored car.

"By Christmas we will be in Paris," corrected Lieutenant Fitz, the tank commander who arrived with the dispatch ordering von Bockman forward to General Headquarters outside Warsaw.

The line of withdrawing Wehrmacht troops stretched endlessly, disappearing into the smoky eastern horizon, marking the site of the continuing bombardment of the besieged city.

"With all the Wehrmacht marching to the Western Front, I suppose Poland will belong to the SS," von Bockman remarked bitterly as a group of six soldiers with the death's-head emblem on their caps emerged alone from the edge of the wood. Von Bockman did not go on to express his sense that the SS supermen aimed to be the only two-legged creatures left alive in the occupied territory.

Lieutenant Fitz inclined his head, acknowledging the harsh reality now facing the conquered nation. He shifted uneasily in his seat, visualizing the same unexpressed image of slaughter. Pretending boredom, he changed the subject.

"Well, Captain, you may be right. We won the war in a few days. It will take us until Christmas to pull the army back to fight the French. You are the reconnaissance expert. Is there another road to Warsaw?"

Two kilometers back down the highway, a narrow dirt track branched off and twisted through a string of deserted and ruined villages eventually leading toward Warsaw. Burned shells of buildings and collapsed roofs identified the arbitrary targets of Hermann Goering's pilots. Six milk cows lay bloated in a field where they had been machine gunned, no doubt for sport. Debris left behind by fleeing civilians littered the road. Von Bockman looked away and covered his nose and mouth against the sickly aroma permeating the air. This was what he would remember most about Poland. In practice maneuvers he never thought about what a battlefield would smell like after only one day in the hot sun. He imagined that Poland would stink for a thousand years; for as long as the Thousand Year Reich.

They passed the charred remains of a steeply gabled farmhouse. The fine stone barn across the yard stood intact. A dead plowhorse, still hitched to the plow, lay in the furrowed field where it had fallen. There was no sign of life. Von Bockman wondered what had happened to the family that lived there. Bits of furniture and clothing littered the gutted residence: a kitchen chair lay beside an overturned cradle; on the step, a woman's yellow calico dress;

across a rail fence, the trousers of a small boy; trampled in the dust, a doll with a broken porcelain head. They did not warn him about such sights when he was a cadet longing to see action.

Now, he only wanted to walk with Katrina in the sweet pine forest that bordered his family estate in Prussia. He closed his eyes for a moment and called up her image. At twenty-five, she was not what was considered fashionably beautiful. Dark haired and hazel-eyed, she was the opposite of the perfect Aryan vision of womanhood. She stood only 5'2", a full foot shorter than he. Fine-boned and fair skinned, she was a delicate contrast to his sunburned complexion, hawk-like nose, deep-set blue eyes, broad forehead, and jutting chin. She preferred riding breeches to dresses and Wellington boots to high heels. Her stride could match his in a hike through the forest. An excellent horsewoman, she could match him jump for jump on a cross-country ride. Her father owned one of the finest Arabian horse stud farms in the world. Katrina preferred riding above everything in life, she said, with the exception of making love. This she did with the same enthusiasm as a cross-country gallop.

In the beginning Katrina had been dangerously opinionated about Hitler and the National Socialist Movement. She openly displayed her contempt when Hermann Goering purchased a large boar hunting preserve in the Schonheide, north of Berlin and bordering the estate of Katrina's father. At a Christmas party she said she would love to see fat Hermann's head stuffed and hung on the wall of his trophy room with the rest of the Nazi swine. The comment was repeated, and neighbor Goering was not amused.

Horst had been privately warned. It was strongly suggested that, for the sake of his career, he keep company with a woman who had the correct political opinions. Dangerous was the emphasized word. About that time the arrests of dissidents, Democrats, Communists, and church leaders became commonplace. After that, Katrina kept her sense of outrage and her sense of humor to herself.

He married her in the summer of 1937 despite the official warning that she was a political handicap. His career was not harmed by the move. Horst believed that this was quite possibly because half the generals in the Wehrmacht secretly shared her opinion about fat Hermann and the Nazi barnyard. What would she say, he now wondered, if she could see Poland?

Katrina kept his mind occupied for another dusty hour until they turned onto a main road. Light traffic headed toward Warsaw. Joining a procession of a half dozen military vehicles, they were stopped at an SS roadblock on the outskirts of a small, still-smoldering village.

"Orders from General Guderian," said Lieutenant Fitz, presenting the papers to the arrogant SS soldier blocking the way.

"You will have to go back." The man barely glanced at the official docu-

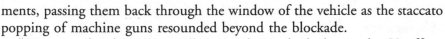

ments, passing them back through the window of the vehicle as the staccato popping of machine guns resounded beyond the blockade.

"We are ordered to Warsaw." Agitated, Fitz looked past the SS officer even as he argued. "You can see. The general himself . . ."

The SS officer cocked an eyebrow impatiently. "We receive our orders from SS-Obergruppenführer Heydrich. And our orders are that no one passes through the restricted area until mop-up is finished."

Von Bockman leaned forward. "Mop-up? Guderian's Panzerkorps took this area last week. Fifty thousand Polish prisoners were captured. I was here. What is left to mop up?"

"We receive our orders from Heydrich alone . . ."

"Then you should let SS-Obergruppenführer Heydrich and the general discuss their differences. In the meantime, I outrank you. The siege of Warsaw continues and you are blocking the way of officers ordered to battle at the front." A slight smile. "Lieutenant Fitz, check the identity papers of this SS whelp. Perhaps he is not German at all. He is willfully obstructing our progress."

Fitz drew his pistol and opened the door of the vehicle as the SS soldier stepped back. His eyes narrowed at the insult. He raised his hand, conceding that he had lost the argument. "Heil Hitler!"

They returned the obligatory salute and passed through the blockade and into the village.

On every corner, black-shirted SS with submachine guns guarded groups of terrified civilians: sobbing women, children, and old men. A few blocks beyond, thick black smoke poured from a gaping hole in the onion dome topping the village synagogue, drawing the gaze of von Bockman.

He peered out the window slits of the vehicle. What was going on? This village had surrendered to Guderian without a shot being fired.

"Pull up there," he ordered the driver as they neared a group of laughing SS who congregated near the fountain in front of the synagogue.

Smoke billowed out. Flames licked the frames of the broken stained glass windows. The wind caught the smoke, clearing a view to the open front doors.

Fitz gasped. "Mein Gott! Horst! Look!"

Von Bockman followed Fitz's gaze to a sight which made him reel.

Three men hung crucified on the heavy wooden doors of the burning building. First hidden by the smoke and then revealed for an instant by a breath of wind, they had been stripped bare to the waist and savagely tortured. They were, thankfully, dead as the tongues of flame shot out to touch them. The word, *Jude,* Jew, was scrawled in blood on the stone wall: a picture of Hell.

Von Bockman and Fitz leapt from the armored car interrupting the conversation of the dozen SS guards who stood as if there was nothing unusual about the scene.

"You!" Von Bockman rushed toward a sergeant whose smile faded at his furious approach. "What is this?"

The sergeant saluted as did the others. "Jews, sir. Caught hiding Polish soldiers."

Von Bockman grasped the man by his shirtfront, pulling him up on his toes. Bile choked off his voice. "Who . . . has done . . . this . . ."

"We act on orders. From the top. Such offenses against the Reich are punishable by death. And the death must be an example to others among the population who might benefit from such an example."

The SS sergeant's tone indicated his agreement with the reasonable nature of crucifixion as punishment for such a crime.

"Whose orders?" Von Bockman demanded, shaking the SS soldier.

An amused voice behind him replied, "Mine alone. Obergruppenführer Reinhard Heydrich. And you are?"

Von Bockman threw the sergeant back, then whirled to face the tall, slender, broad-shouldered figure of Reinhard Heydrich, general of the SS. Heydrich's sharp blue eyes narrowed with contempt at von Bockman's outrage. Thin lips twisted into a smile as the color drained from von Bockman's face. Horst realized that he was meeting the man known as The Butcher.

"Heil Hitler?" Heydrich intoned.

"Heil Hitler," came the submissive reply of Fitz and von Bockman in unison.

Heydrich nodded and considered the two with a new interest. "That is more like it." He walked slowly around the two men as a butcher might inspect a side of beef. "What are you doing here?"

Fitz fumbled for the papers. There was a rumble as a portion of the synagogue roof caved in. Fires crackled. Smoke swept across the square and touched them, making their eyes sting. "Trying to get to Warsaw, Obergruppenführer. We are under orders. You see?"

"This is a restricted area. You were allowed to pass at the barricade?"

"Yes, sir."

Heydrich glanced sharply toward the blockade, then, with a jerk of his head and a snap of his fingers sent two of his minions to arrest the guard.

"Sloppy. Careless. Not acceptable behavior in the Einsatztruppen," he said coldly. "So. You have lost your way." Rocking up on his toes he peered down his long nose at them. "An easy mistake to make, I suppose." He laughed and slapped von Bockman on the back. "It would be best if you get back into your car now and find another route to General Guderian, gentlemen. I will overlook your error . . . this time." He glanced at the papers.

"Company Commander von Bockman, is it? And Lieutenant Fitz? Be assured I will remember."

As the armored car sped away, Horst von Bockman did not look back at the synagogue as its doors were finally consumed by the fire.

FIVE

Seperember 24 was Yom Kippur, the Day of Atonement. The last letter from Etta remained unopened on the table of Rabbi Schlomo Lebowitz. The old rabbi was fasting. He would not allow himself the nourishment of reading what might well be the final correspondence from his daughter.

Ten days before, as the new moon rose over Jerusalem, the shofar announced Rosh Hashanah. The Jewish Quarter of the Old City celebrated the New Year holiday with the hope that the Polish army could hold back the flood of German invaders.

But throughout the Days of Awe which followed, the news trickling into Jerusalem from Poland had gone from grim to hopeless.

Now, on the anniversary of the siege and desolation of the Temple in ancient Jerusalem, Warsaw was in flames.

On this most holy Day of Atonement, two thousand years of Jewish culture in Europe were being irrevocably blasted to oblivion.

And what of Etta and Aaron and the children? Compared to their lives, even the destruction of a great city seemed of small importance to Rabbi Schlomo Lebowitz. Did they still live?

The old man made his way through the narrow streets of the Old City toward the Western Wall of Solomon's Temple. It was said that this part of the wall was built by the beggars of Solomon's Jerusalem. On the day of the Temple's destruction, angels linked their wings around the Wall and gave the command: "This, the work of the poor, shall never be destroyed!"

The Shekinah glory of God remained in this place, and at certain times the very stones wept for the destruction of the Temple. Would they weep today for the new desolation, the old man wondered?

A narrow space of only twelve feet separated the Wailing Wall from the shabby houses of the Muslims from the Moroccan neighborhood. Today worshipers packed that space. They covered their heads with prayer shawls and lifted hands and eyes to the sheer face of handhewn rock.

At a respectful distance, armed British soldiers stood guard over the assembly. In years past, more than one pious Jew had turned toward the Wall and found himself face to face with the Eternal, thanks to a well-aimed stone hurled from a Moslem rooftop onto a Jewish head.

Rebbe Lebowitz welcomed the presence of the English, even though he never worried about the rocks of his petulant Arab neighbors. He decided early in his life that there was no better spot for a Jew to die than in the posture of fervent prayer before the Holy Wall.

He turned his face up to the narrow slit of blue above him as he covered his head with his prayer shawl. He knew the prayers by heart, but still he turned the pages of his Siddur to the prayers of the High Holy Days. His voice joined the others in a dissonant song which somehow blended into the harmony of one voice and one prayer to heaven.

The Amidah was recited: "Blessed art Thou, our God and God of our fathers . . . who will bring a Redeemer with love to their children's children for His name's sake . . ."

The shofar sounded, reminding rabbi and congregation that in spite of their grief, the Eternal was sovereign in the world, that He remembered the deeds of all men and the Covenant of Abraham, that someday, He would send the Redeemer.

Was this not the time, the rabbi silently prayed? Would it not be best if Messiah would appear at this moment and bring home the children of the Covenant to Jerusalem? And the children and grandchildren of Rabbi Lebowitz too?

Where was Etta in the desolation? Where was her husband Aaron and the children?

They are in the hands of the Eternal, the old man reminded himself. *And He sees them just as He sees me.*

Was there a better place for Rebbe Lebowitz to remind the Eternal not to forget them? In all the earth this was the one place where a small chink remained open to the throne room of the Almighty. The old man had come with his petition written on a slip of paper. He reached up and urged his request between the blocks of stone.

As always, he was sure he heard the fluttering of angels' wings above him. Perhaps the stirring of their wings carried the prayer of the old man near to the ear of the Almighty. Did they wait each day to hear the same prayer recited by an old man? He felt the breath of angels on the breeze.

"With Your mighty hand carry Your children home to this place, this small piece of earth which is so near to Your throne. For the sake of Your

Name. For the sake of Your Covenant, call to the north and bring them home, that the kingdom of Messiah may be established and His throne endure forever in Jerusalem! Omaine."

The gathering of Yom Kippur was more solemn than usual this year. Everyone present had some link with the community trapped in Warsaw. The wealth of Poland had founded and supported many of the Yeshiva schools and synagogues here in Jerusalem. Now what help could they send back?

As the Holy Day passed, Jews flocked to the headquarters of the British Mandatory Government, each volunteering to be allowed to fight in the British forces against the Nazis on Polish soil. Politely turned away, they were not told that no British forces would go to Poland.

Josephine slept with her back against the sandbags that surrounded the shattered Cathedral of St. John. The still-raging fires illuminated Warsaw in a hellish light. Just after midnight on September 27th, 1939, the priest's gentle voice awakened her.

"Josephine? Child?"

She opened her eyes reluctantly. For a moment she could not remember where she was or how she had come to be there. Was this a dream? The face of the priest was pale and drawn. He smiled sadly. "The major has come to take you away from here."

She blinked in confusion and rubbed her burning eyes with the back of a blistered hand. Silhouetted against the backdrop of fire was a horse and a Polish officer. The horse was tall and sunken in the flanks. Flecks of lathered sweat dotted his dark hide. He snorted, eyes wide with resentment against the smoke and fire and smell of death. The Polish officer patted the animal's neck and spoke calmly to him.

The priest extended his hand, helping Josephine to her feet. "The Germans will be at the gates of Modlin citadel at sunrise. The major has come from Polish High Command to take you there. The streets are impassable to motor cars. You will have to ride."

Josephine nodded slowly in comprehension and wordlessly staggered to the officer and his mount.

The officer bowed slightly and clicked his heels. He greeted her in perfect French. His features were half-hidden beneath the shadow of his cloth cap. By his tarnished sabre, tall boots, and mud-caked spurs, Josephine knew that he was a member of the aristocratic Polish cavalry which had ridden out against the tanks of the German Panzer divisions in the first hours of the war.

"Your horse," she questioned, "I thought they had all been killed."

The animals which had survived the brutal cavalry charges had been butchered to provide food for the starving city in the last days of the siege.

"Not all, Mam'zelle." He bowed again. "We have a long way to go, if you please. It is dangerous."

She embraced the priest, who blessed her. "Remember us," he rasped. "Tell them."

Mounting, the major extended his hand and helped her up behind him. The horse danced nervously, iron-shod hooves sparking against the cobblestones. Somehow it seemed appropriate to Josephine that her last journey through the ancient city would be on horseback. Warsaw had always been a dream from another age. Trams and automobiles had seemed foreign to the grace and chivalry of the city. It was that grace and chivalry that had met the mechanized brutality of the National Socialist armies, only to fall forever.

"Hold tightly to me, Mam'zelle," the officer warned. "Press your face against my back and close your eyes. You must not look!"

She thanked him and leaned against him, closing her eyes. The rough wool of his tunic smelled of sweat and cordite and smoke. Then she remembered the admonition of the priest: *Tell them!* Her eyes snapped open to memorize the ruins of the city she loved second only to Paris.

Now it was almost unrecognizable. Great heaps of bricks spilled out across the streets, impeding the horse's passage. Once-stately rows of buildings looked like a comb with its teeth broken out in irregular intervals. Shards of glass protruded from the trunks of blasted, leafless trees in city parks, and everywhere lay the uncollected bodies of the dead.

Shell holes pocked the enormous stone citadel guarding the Vistula River. A torn Polish flag still waved where it had been run up on a shattered staff.

When Josephine arrived in Warsaw only one month before, the boulevards were brightly lit with neon signs. Sidewalk cafes were packed with people. Queues for theaters wound around the blocks. Now everything was still except for a skinny dog sniffing through the debris. There seemed to be no other living beings along the route to Modlin Fortress. No voices. No sign of life. No light on the broken theater marquees. Only the fires and the swirling smoke remained—swirling upward to cover the full moon in a veil of red.

Men and women slumped over the barricades of furniture and sandbags. Were they only sleeping?

Turning off the main thoroughfare, they carefully picked their way through a neighborhood of flats less damaged than the city center. The fire was behind them now. Above the roar of the inferno came a sound so startling that the major reined the horse to a halt.

From the dark hulk of a stone synagogue came the soft, sad voices of men singing. The melody drifted out through the empty window frames of the domed building.

"What are they singing?" Josephine spoke to the soldier for the first time.

"It is an old song," he replied, and then he translated the words for her.

> *Let the priests, the ministers of the Lord,*
> *weep between the porch and the altar,*
> *and let them say . . .*
> *Spare thy people, O Lord, spare them.*

It seemed to Josephine that they waited in the center of the deserted road for a long time, although it was only a few seconds. He spoke softly. "God is too high up to hear and France too far away . . . This is the end for them. We Poles may somehow survive for a better day, but when morning comes it means the beginning of the end for the Jews." He bowed his head and Josephine felt him shudder. Then he nudged the horse onward past the shadow of the synagogue.

The first light of approaching dawn leaked through the smoke when they arrived at Modlin Citadel on the outskirts of Warsaw.

Challenged by a young soldier, they passed beneath the arched gates where the remnant of the Polish army waited to surrender.

Josephine imagined a cup of hot tea. Maybe just a slice of bread. How long had it been since she had eaten? She figured three days at least. And it had been fourteen hours since she had even a drop of water to drink. She licked her parched lips and asked for water. A cup of cloudy liquid was handed to her. She thought better of it and handed it back.

"We have nothing left, Mam'zelle," the Polish major apologized. Then he explained that they had run out of food and ammunition at the same time. The last assault against the enemy had been made with bayonets fixed. They had no choice but to surrender or die. Maybe the Germans would give her breakfast when she was on their side of the line with all the other foreign correspondents who had no doubt been brought forward for the occasion.

"For your safety, it is best if your American press compatriots witness that you are alive and well when you leave us. The Nazis will treat you with courtesy and release you unharrassed to your countrymen if there are witnesses. No doubt they will even have hot tea for you, Mam'zelle."

He had not meant the statement to be an accusation, but Josephine was stung by guilt. What witnesses would there be to the Nazi treatment of the captured Polish prisoners after the international press was ushered back to Berlin? What of the Polish intelligentsia; professors, doctors, lawyers, and politicians who now were superfluous to a state which no longer existed?

And what record of the Jews of Poland who sang their hopeless prayer in the night?

In the soft morning light, Josie could see that her escort was in his early twenties. His eyes were grey. He had a shy, boyish smile, fair hair and complexion.

"I did not even ask your name."

"I am Count Alexander Riznow, Mam'zelle." He kissed her hand. "My family fled to London. If you could find them . . . my mother. My sisters. Tell them that you saw me and that I send my love."

"I will," she promised, accepting the torn scrap of paper with names and a London address hastily scrawled on it. In this way perhaps she too could be a witness that when she saw him, Count Alexander Riznow was alive and well.

The German demand for surrender was to be answered at six o'clock by a white flag flying over the Modlin Citadel. The German front lines were 250 yards from the gates. At six o'clock exactly, two Poles stood ready with the white flag. They were seconds too late for the impatient Germans, who fired one last barrage into the walls, sending everyone in the fort to their bellies and killing one last Polish defender.

Shouts and angry cries arose. When the dust cleared and Josephine raised her head at last, the flag was up. The siege of Warsaw was over.

Josephine walked unsteadily toward the line of German officers. The world was spinning as she heard her name spoken by the officer who escorted her.

General von Blaskowitz, looking very clean and untouched by the conflict, turned his gaze on her. "Fräulein Marlow."

"Associated Press," she managed to say as the scene before her became yellow and a border of darkness closed on her consciousness.

"Consider yourself liberated along with all of Poland." She saw his mouth twitch in a near smile just before she blacked out.

SIX

Of course this is Richard Lewinski! He may well be the most important person to have escaped from Poland! He is certainly the most important man in Paris! Including you, Bertrand!" Colonel Andre Chardon viewed the peculiar red-haired figure of Lewinski through the two way mirror in the Paris headquarters of French Military Intelligence at 2 bis Avenue de Tourville in the seventh arrondissement of Paris.

Colonel Gustave Bertrand scratched his head in amazement at Chardon's words. "I did not say otherwise, Andre. I only asked if this odd duck was indeed our Richard Lewinski. *The* Richard Lewinski."

Andre nodded. "Indeed."

"It is difficult to imagine, Andre, that the fate of France, as you put it so clearly, could rest in the hands of one so . . . unusual."

The two men silently considered the wild red hair, the blank stare on the pale thin face, the flannel shirt buttoned crookedly, the untied shoelaces, and the gas mask clutched in the right hand.

"He is deep in thought," Andre remarked.

"I would have said he was catatonic. Or worse. One of the living dead perhaps. When we bring him his food, he eyes it as if it is poisoned, nibbles a bit, and then consumes it with the enthusiasm of a hog at the trough. But the rest of the time he is as you see him now, a great lethargic zero. He has said nothing to anyone since he crossed the Polish border and left the care of the American, Ambassador Biddle, in Bucharest. He wept silent tears behind his gas mask when I boarded the plane to bring him here to Paris. He has scribbled this note." Bertrand handed Andre a slip of paper.

Andre read the childish scrawl aloud: "Attention! Nazi pigs, you have not deceived me! I will converse with no man but Colonel Andre Chardon." Andre laughed at the sentiment.

"Flattering, Andre?"

"A brave soldier, our Richard. Here is proof of the cause he believes in."

"Your old friend believes with all his heart that we are Nazi agents; instruments of Reinhard Heydrich in the employ of the German Secret Police. And so . . . there you have it," Bertrand shrugged. "I think he is quite insane, Andre. But I leave it to you."

"It is understandable that he should be suspicious, Gustave; that he should be cautious. First, he lost his parents in Germany. Then his wife and child were killed in Poland by a German bomb. He is fighting the only way he knows how to fight: by refusing to acknowledge anyone at all. Suppose he was right about you and yet proceeded in his work?"

"If Richard Lewinski were correct in this hypothesis, he would be dead."

"True."

"So." Bertrand spread his hands in a gesture of helplessness. "The fate of military intelligence may be in the hands of a lunatic, and the fate of the lunatic must be entirely in your hands. Shall I cover him in giftwrap before you take him home, Monsieur? Or is he colorful enough?"

✤   ✤   ✤

The German military victory review took place on October 5th in one of the few relatively undamaged neighborhoods of Warsaw. The Führer watched the goose-stepping parade of 15,000 troops from a hastily erected grandstand on Ujazdowski Allee where the foreign embassies and legations were located. On this street, colorful leaves still remained on the trees gracing the lawns of large Georgian mansions. Windows, rattled from bomb blasts, were dark with the grime of smoke but unbroken.

Horst von Bockman stood at attention beside his troops in the cool Autumn afternoon as Hitler addressed them.

"On September first, at my order, you lined up to defend our Reich against the Polish attack. Today I greet the troops sent against fortified Warsaw. This day ends a battle that has given evidence of the best that is in German soldiery. We stand closer together than ever, and we have cinched our helmets tighter. I know you, faithful to your belief in Germany, are prepared for any sacrifice!"

His words were greeted by a thunderous roar from the thousands of hand-picked troops who had come to meet him. Would they be required to fight again? The German Chancellor had been sending the West persistent hints that perhaps some settlement might be reached, now that Poland was in the pocket of the Reich. There was some feeling that once again the British Prime Minister Chamberlain would look the other way and that France would simply suggest the whole matter be forgotten and the war called off. Already the theaters and nightclubs of Paris had reopened and the wartime restrictions eased. The citizens of those allied nations worked to keep their daily routines as they had been in peacetime. In Germany, every man, woman, and child lived with the reality of war. The allies in the West lacked the determination to force a war over the dismemberment of a feudalistic nation like Poland, it was said. Having seen the gruesome face of war, Horst hoped now that Poland would be the last battle. He wondered what the citizens of Warsaw were thinking as they heard the cheers of their conquerors.

It was probable that even during the parade, not one Pole was aware of the presence of the German Führer in their conquered city. Cordons of German troops with fixed bayonets had closed off Polish access to all the buildings on the route from the airfield to Embassy Row. The houses and buildings had been cleaned out to rid them of any "suspicious elements."

The route took Hitler and Himmler past the devastated National Museum, the Polish Foreign Office, and the Hotel Europjeski. The downtown shopping area was demolished, with huge craters in the middle of the main streets and tram rails twisted like pretzels. Both in the suburbs and the center of the city, deep trenches and tank blockades made from overturned trolleys, automobiles, paving stones, and sandbags remained.

Horst von Bockman was among the honor companies that accompanied Hitler and Heinrich Himmler to the plane that would carry them back to Berlin. Impressed with the devastation he had witnessed, Hitler turned to the international press corps and passed along his warning. The words were clearly meant for publication.

"Gentlemen, you have seen for yourselves what criminal folly it was to try to defend this city. I only wish that certain statesmen in other countries who seem to want to turn the whole of Europe into such a shambles as Warsaw could have an opportunity, as you have, to see the true meaning of war."

Hitler then turned his attention to a pretty chestnut-haired woman who stood near the front of the crowd among the cadre of American reporters.

Lieutenant Fitz leaned closer to Horst and whispered. "The American woman trapped in Warsaw during the siege . . . A fräulein like her alone with 85,000 Polish soldiers. Not bad, eh?"

The weariness in her clear blue eyes reminded Horst of what he had seen in the faces of the conquered Poles. She met the gaze of the Führer fearlessly and without any trace of admiration for the leader of the German people.

He admonished her, as though she somehow represented all those who had resisted his will in Warsaw. "So, now you see how unwise it was to oppose German might. They were fools. And you were foolish to remain with them."

She did not reply but continued to look him full in the face. The silent defiance of her expression caused the ranks of troops and the journalists around her to stir uneasily. Horst imagined that after this encounter the American would be put on the next plane out of the Reich. Hitler prided himself in the adoration of women and his ability to charm them. This female journalist was clearly unmoved by his attention and unrepentant. Perhaps she had seen too much on the Warsaw side of the lines.

The Führer continued, raising his voice to the others in the crowd as he turned his back on the young woman. "These ruins stand as a lesson to all who seek war with the German Reich. Those Polish leaders who incited their people to violence have brought this destruction upon themselves. To defy the will of Germany is suicide."

The statement was a literal truth for those who had led the futile Polish opposition in hopes that France and England would deliver them. The mayor of Warsaw, Stefan Starzynski, was now reported to have committed suicide after the fall of his city. It had been his shaky voice that had broadcast messages of hope and courage, and finally, desperate pleas for rescue. Known as "Stefan the Stubborn" after he declined to accept the German ultimatum, he had organized the civilian brigades and inspired the populace to stand its ground. The claim of suicide was the official version of his disappearance. But Starzynski had been a devout Catholic, making suicide improbable. Horst had heard that the mayor met a different end at the hands of the SS.

As the silver tri-motor lifted off, carrying the Führer and his henchman back to Berlin, Horst caught a ride back to Pilsudski Square. The Centrale Hotel where junior officers were billeted was only slightly damaged by bomb blasts. The windows in his room were cracked and the brick facade was pocked by shrapnel. It was as if the artillery gunners had deliberately picked out this hotel as a kind of safe zone with the thought in mind that the German officers would need a place to sleep after Warsaw fell. Better to blow up a cathedral than a hotel.

Before the war Horst visited Warsaw a dozen times for the pure pleasure of it. Proud, joyful people had populated broad, brightly lit boulevards and stately homes. What he saw now sickened him.

Horst sent a wire to Katrina, telling her that he would be in Prussia for a short leave within a matter of days. He imagined her face when she got the news: ecstatic. But he felt no emotion even in the thought of home. He ate a tasteless meal in the company of officers who laughed too loudly and drank too much, then he walked past the armed guards in the lobby and out into the Warsaw twilight toward the Vistula River.

It was nearing curfew, so few Poles dared walk the streets. Here and there, beneath the watchful eyes of German soldiers on the street corners, small groups of people picked through the rubble, trying to salvage personal belongings. Without exception, the black armband of mourning adorned every Polish sleeve. He did not stop to ask if they mourned the loss of family members or the loss of their nation. Their sad, weary faces clearly displayed the privation they had endured during this descent into hell. They looked up at him with eyes full of hate and bitterness. He was no longer a man; he was The Enemy.

Horst walked quickly toward the bank of the river and sat down on a heap of broken bricks. At home, a view of the river had always comforted him . . . something about the slow current passing by . . . but there was no comfort here. Bits of debris bobbed on the flow. A small fishing boat drifted past, belly up, like a dead fish. The warehouses on the opposite bank were charred ruins.

He decided he would not tell Katrina about Warsaw. It had been one of her favorite cities. She shared with the Poles a love of the finest Arabian horses in the world. How many times had she struck up a conversation in a Warsaw cafe and ended up talking bloodlines until morning? If Katrina could see this, no doubt she would also wear a black armband.

His head ached. It had throbbed for days until he became accustomed to it. This was the first moment he had relaxed enough to identify the pain. He thought about the strong, gentle fingers of Katrina stroking his forehead. She would soothe away the ache he felt and make him forget what he had seen. The hands of Katrina would heal his inner wounds, and he would be whole again, proud again, a soldier for the Fatherland, ready to fight again without remorse.

He pushed his hat back and looked up at the sky. It was the only beautiful thing still in Warsaw. Pastel banners which faded into star-flecked purple in the east streaked the western horizon.

He silently watched as the last light deepened into night. The approach of footsteps went unnoticed until a woman spoke from behind him.

"Get up!" she ordered in broken German. "Slowly please, Herr Nazi. Herr butcher. I have a gun."

He stood, unsnapping the holster of his side arm.

She heard the click and warned him, "Try it and I will shoot! I have nothing to lose. Drop your weapon. Now."

He obeyed.

"There's a good little Nazi." She moved nearer. "Kick it over to me."

He nudged the weapon just beyond her reach with the toe of his boot. Her voice was young. Horst could hear the fear as she spoke, although he could not see her face. Her shadowed form swayed a bit as she debated how best to retrieve the Luger.

"What do you want?" he ventured.

"Shut up!" she snapped.

"Surely there can be no benefit in murdering me. You will only get yourself shot."

"Being out after curfew is enough to get me killed, Herr Nazi. What more can they do to me for shooting you?"

"Good point." He laughed aloud at the insane logic of her predicament. "So. Are you prowling around in the dark to ambush Germans? What is your name?"

"Sophia," she answered without thinking, disarmed by the innocuous question. She considered von Bockman silently for a long moment. "I have a child three miles from here near Muranow. I heard they were distributing bread near St. John's. I came for the bread. Night fell before I could get back."

"Did you get your bread?"

"Yes." She held up half a loaf as proof.

"Then perhaps we can be of some mutual service. I will see you safely to your home, if you will not shoot me."

Again the long silence of consideration. "Why would you . . ."

In that instant a powerful beam of light ruptured the darkness. The young woman cried out and shielded her eyes from the blinding glare. She had no weapon. Her precious bread fell to the ground. She dropped to her knees and scrambled to recover it.

"Halt, or we shoot," commanded a voice out of the spotlight's glare.

Crouching like a cornered animal, she covered her head with her arms. Horst heard her whisper, "Poor Jules! Oh, Jules," and then her words were choked by a muffled sob.

"Are you all right, Captain?"

"Of course. This was nothing. Nothing," Horst replied indignantly. "She came for bread for her child and was caught out after curfew. She is not . . ."

Two patrolling SS policemen stepped up, holding machine pistols at the ready, covering the Polish woman as if she were a rabid dog. "Thank you, Captain," one of them said smoothly. "We will take it from here."

"I . . . wait a moment," Horst said. "Surely she can be detained until daylight and then allowed to go home?"

"Of course, of course, Captain. If you will step aside, please."

Horst still stood, unmoving, between the SS patrolmen and the woman. The faces of the men seemed unconcerned; there was no anger or threat evident in their eyes.

"Come now, Captain, what do you take us for? Just stand aside, please. We will see that she is taken care of."

Horst nodded curtly, then looked down at her upturned face. Her expression showed a glimmer of hope.

"You hear them? They will not hurt you," he said.

"Thank you, Herr Captain."

Sophia rose to her knees as Horst reluctantly moved to the edge of the flashlight's glow.

In the same instant a blast of machine gun fire tore through the Polish woman, throwing her back down the embankment into the Vistula.

Silence. Horst stood wide-eyed and panting from the sudden violence of it. The black waters closed around the body. The loaf of bread, saturated with her blood, lay beside his Luger.

Two black-uniformed SS strode forward. One, a boy of eighteen, kicked the bread aside and retrieved Horst's weapon.

"It seems we were just in time, Captain," commented the young man. Smoke from the barrel of his pistol curled up, encircling his grinning face. "It is dangerous to be out after dark. Two of our fellows were murdered last night by prostitutes. The Polish women are as dangerous as the men, you know. Just as fanatic. By the way, thank you for your quick wits. You disarmed her suspicions completely. It is so much easier if they do not think of trying to run."

"That will be all." Horst cut him off sharply and retrieved his cap from the heap of broken bricks. "She only wanted something to feed her child." He pointed to the proof of her intentions then pushed past the SS guard.

"She should have gotten it in daylight."

"I will find my own way back," Horst said angrily, declining their offer of safe escort to the hotel.

SEVEN

Josephine Marlow committed an offense against the Reich and the Führer. For this reason she was detained at the great central train terminal in Berlin. Taking her to a small, clinically white room, a Gestapo matron searched her and relieved her of all written material. Confiscated with her notes was the precious scrap of paper containing the name and London address of Count Alexander Riznow's mother.

After that she was put on the first train out of Germany to neutral Holland. Following two days of much needed sleep in Amsterdam, she boarded a Dutch luxury liner to make the crossing to Southampton, England. The steamer would then continue on to New York. Josie would not be going that far, despite the frantic wire from her mother begging her to come home and settle down to a normal life again.

The craft was already packed double with somber Americans leaving Europe any way possible. How many more would be waiting in Southampton to jump on board?

"Droves of Americans," was the way *The Daily Mail* described the migration. And they all brought too much luggage.

"Where will you put them all?" Josie asked the ship's steward.

"They will sleep on the floor. We have mattresses stowed below." He was quite cheerful at this point, but the ship had not yet left the harbor.

Americans groused at the stewards about the baggage of other passengers. They complained about the rough sea in the Channel.

Within earshot of terrified mothers and cranky children, four British businessmen loudly discussed the danger of magnetic mines. A mine could not, after all, tell if a ship was neutral or not. Josie suspected the Englishmen had brought up the subject on purpose, like naughty boys stamping on an anthill to amuse themselves.

Such unguarded and pessimistic conversation had the effect of sending panicked parents scrambling for every available life vest on the craft. Any size would do. Tiny limbs and the tops of heads protruded from the bulky jackets. They waddled about like sacks of potatoes with legs. Older boys and girls alike whined about the tight belts tugging uncomfortably at their crotches. Would they have to wear these things all the way to the States? Sleep in them? Eat in them? Use the toilet? The adventure of war evaporated. It was all so humiliating.

Seasickness set in soon after departure, and the voyage became something like a scene from a Marx Brothers movie; a ship steward's worst nightmare. Who was going to have to clean the boat after the Americans left? Puking, hysterical children and pushy American parents fleeing the European war; it was a new chapter in maritime hell. Josie was relieved to be getting off in England.

There was no space to sit in the lounge. Every deck chair was occupied. A place at the rail was stand-at-your-own-risk considering the wind and the amount of regurgitation going on.

Josie had no luggage. She possessed only one ugly blue serge dress and a man's coat which Bill Cooper, the AP correspondent in Berlin, gave her. Not having a change of clothes, she stayed away from the rail.

Irritated by the unending trivia which seemed to send her fellow countrymen into fits, she suddenly desired to stand up on the Captain's table like a soapbox preacher and shout, "What's your gripe? Idiots! You should have been in Warsaw!"

But they did not see Warsaw. They did not want to think about Warsaw.

Nor would they want to hear the self-righteous Josephine Marlow recount the true life horrors of Warsaw. The *little* horrors of trying to get home were bad enough for the time being, thank you. Nothing about this crossing was pleasant.

Josie kept her mouth shut. When she spoke, it was only in French. She did not want the staff of the liner or the British travelers to think she was *one of those Yanks . . .*

An hour out, she made her way to the radio room to send a wire to London AP alerting them of her impending arrival.

"Madame," said the wireless operator kindly. "Of course we cannot send the actual time of your arrival." He pointed to the red lettered notice on the wall which listed the new rules of what could not be relayed in a wire. Time of arrival and departure were at the top of the list. It was clumsy of her; the last ship she had sailed on had been before the war. Things had obviously changed. Relating such details these days could get a person thrown into the brig as an *agent provocateur.*

What nonthreatening message to send in an economy of words and letters?

AP miss oo sumtin orful. Comin Lond 2day. Jo.

It would have to do. She shoved the form across the desk and counted out the precious few shillings which Bill Cooper left in the pocket of his coat. If Alma from AP did not pick her up in Southampton, she would be walking to London. Such was the state of her finances.

The crossing from the Hook of Holland to Southampton was memorable. Josie hoped she could forget it.

The sky over Southampton shone especially bright today, the air pleasantly warm. Two tugs nudged the ship against the dock as Josie looked down for some sign of a familiar face.

She spotted Alma Dodge standing at the opposite side of a chain link fence beyond the gangway. Roundfaced, round-everything little Alma! Thirtyish, brown bobbed hair, thick glasses, and a citric-acid sort of personality, Alma was giving a piece of her mind to a young man in the American mob waiting on the quay. Josie could not hear the words, but the expressions were unmistakable. One could not strike up a conversation with Alma and take an isolationist point of view without getting verbally clobbered.

The second party in the dispute looked vaguely familiar. Astounding! Alma was arguing with the eldest child of the American Ambassador to Great Britain. Sure enough, the whole Kennedy herd stood beside virtual mountains of luggage, waiting to sail back to the good old USA. So many children; Josie could never keep them straight. But no matter, the young man was either defending the pacifist fancies of his father, or perhaps he had tried to crowd in at the head of the line. Whatever the reason for the altercation, Josie could see that little Alma was putting him in his place. She was no respecter of persons. She had no particular fondness for the American ambassador; she did not think much of Henry Ford or Charles Lindbergh either. The lovely thing about Alma was that she would tell them her opinions face to face if she ever had the chance. So there she was, nose to nose with the Kennedy kid, and who cared who his father was. The discussion came to an abrupt end. Ashen, the adolescent Kennedy backed up a step and muttered something to his siblings. They collectively sneered and then laughed. A middle kid thumbed his nose at Alma's back. Josie wondered how cocky and confident the brood would be when they were crowded on the ship with the rest of their fleeing countrymen.

Josie called to Alma, but her voice was lost beneath the howl of the liner's throaty whistle. Alma glanced up, scanned the railing, and spotted Josie.

Unencumbered by luggage, Josie was first down the gangway and first through customs and out the other side of the fence.

"You!" Alma hugged her. "Look, look, turrible!"

"You were telling off that Kennedy boy."

"Is that who it was? Isolationist bugger, if you ask me! But then we've all been digesting too much of Chamberlain's milk toast these days. Makes me edgy. He's a bit bent, if you ask me." She skipped along. "Where's your luggage?"

"Warsaw."

A shrug, as if it did not matter. This was good. Alma would not allow Josie to feel sorry for herself, even if she might have wanted just a bit of sympathy.

"Well, Josephine, I suppose if you had clothes, the Gestapo would have torn out every hem and seam. Probed every orifice, as they say. Did they do that to you? They've been doing it to everyone. Oh, my dear! The stories I have heard in the newsroom!" She drew a breath and babbled on in Alma fashion. "Don't tell me another Poland story! I've heard them all. Bore me to tears. I know it was awful for you, but really . . . it *is* awful, isn't it? All of it? I'm just glad you're not bashed up or dead or something."

Josie was certain that Alma would eventually get around to pulling every detail of the ordeal out of her. It was a trick which Alma used to make people want to talk. She told them she did not really want to know whatever it was they had to say. It was effective in most cases.

"You got my wire?" Josie asked.

"Heavens, no! You sent a cable? Nothing gets through the censors these days. They've gone bonkers. Charlie telephoned your hotel in Amsterdam. They knew just when you'd be arriving. They knew just who you were. *That*

American lady who was in Warsaw for the siege. All you have to do to be a celebrity is survive something horrific. They told Charlie you slept for two days and ate like a horse when you woke up." A quick breath. "You'll never guess who has been ringing the office every day."

"My mother?"

"No! Mac McGrath! You've nearly killed the man with all this, you know. He said he thought you had left Warsaw on your own the night before. Then he ran off with his camera to film Biddle's escape and the rest and left you there! You know, he's mad about you. Charlie says we'll have to have him committed as a loon, if you don't ring him straight away when we get you back and tell him you're in perfect health."

So there it was: poor Mac. Josie had not expected to have to deal with him so soon.

"I want a proper bath first. Something decent to wear."

"Mac wouldn't care if you had nothing at all to wear. He just wants to see you and that's it."

"He'll have to wait a few days, Alma. Really. I'm not ruined by all this . . . but . . . I'm just really tired. I need to think."

"But my dear! My *very dear* . . ."

"Stop talking for a minute or so. Just a minute."

Alma lapsed into a silent pout.

Josie looked around her in wonder. Sandbags lined the buildings and docks. Men and women carried gas masks in little boxes on their shoulders as though they had some vague expectation that their lovely existence might be shattered. But their expressions and their conversations were so *lifeless!* They walked through the moment as if they saw nothing around them. They carried on their internal monologues, worrying about a million needless things.

Alma's mindless chatter grated like fingernails on a blackboard. The words of Sister Angeline echoed in Josie's mind. *No man limps because the foot of another man is injured. England will not come to help us, Josephine. They will not think of us again once we are buried. To do so would make them ashamed. But you? Leave this place with joy in your heart, daughter. You will never see the world as you saw it before. You will find God's presence in ways you had not imagined.*

They stepped out into the sunlight. For the first time Josie felt the glory of all that was ordinary: church steeples and slate rooftops standing as they had for hundreds of years, the tangle of chimney pots.

The unbroken skyline of the city gleamed in russet hues: brown brick, red brick, black brick. The day throbbed with color. A seagull cried as it soared overhead. The air smelled of ocean and the musty scent of leaves about to drop from the trees. Autumn would soon arrive in England. There was a wonderful living aroma. Had Josie ever really noticed it before? And if she had noticed, had she tried to define what made it so spectacular? She was suddenly filled with an exquisite joy.

"What is wrong with you?" Alma grumped.

"It's lovely here. So ordinary."

"Lovely warehouses? Lovely seagull droppings? Lovely screaming American tourists stumbling out of taxis?"

"Yes, I suppose."

Alma could not comprehend. She had not yet witnessed the world turned upside down. She had not breathed the air in Warsaw, and so she could not know that the sweet air of England, even in ordinary Southampton, was something holy. How could she understand what had happened to Josephine? Drawing a breath in safety had become an act of worship.

"I'm really thankful to be alive, Alma," Josie said in a tone so serious that it made Alma laugh. Her laughter did not matter.

"Well, so am I!"

Josie stopped her on the sidewalk at the end of the taxi queue. "No. I mean . . . I am *truly glad* I was in Warsaw. Glad I got left behind. That I met all those people. I must tell poor Mac. It's okay. I'm different, you know? Nothing to worry about. I mean . . . I am *thankful.*"

"Right. A new word. Can you spell that for me? I'll look it up in my O.E.D. whilst you sleep this off."

It was a quiet journey back to London.

EIGHT

As the autumn weather cooled, the war against merchant vessels at sea heated up. Not a day passed that a German U-boat did not plow a torpedo or two into some unarmed ship carrying goods to France or England. When the Scottish freighter *Coulmore* came under fire from a U-boat 200 miles directly east of Boston, a U.S. Coast Guard Cutter moved toward its rescue.

Vessels carrying British children to Canada or the United States were sunk with loss of life so tragic that the evacuation efforts were "regretfully" suspended by the British Government.

In the United States Senate, the debate on revising the Neutrality Act droned on. What kind of aid could be offered to the Western Allies? How should materials be paid for? Should the arms embargo be repealed? Colonel Charles A. Lindbergh, hero to millions, added his voice to the isolationist position: "I would not want to see American bombers dropping American bombs, which would kill and mutilate European children." In his view, not even Canadians, let alone Americans, should fight in a European war.

Despite the stature of the critic and the intensity of the debate, planes and supplies ordered before the war flowed north from the U.S. to Canada where they were loaded onto ships bound for England.

At the same time, a handful of young American airmen also headed to Canada. There, at the loss of their American citizenship, they joined the RAF, Royal Air Force. Some joined up in the idealistic tradition of the American LaFayette Escadrille which had flown for France in the First World War. Others came into the RAF with no other motive than the desire to fly the fastest planes in the world. Within days, each man found himself crossing the North Atlantic and in the middle of a real war.

Today, foaming green waves burst over the bow of the SS *Duchess of Windsor* and poured around the lashings that secured the canvas-covered Hurricane fighter planes to the foredeck. As American flyer David Meyer watched from his perch one deck above, the *Duchess* rode up the crest of another twenty-foot-high swell and dropped like an elevator into the trough beyond. Each breaker threatened to tear the aircraft loose from the transport ship and sink them in the North Atlantic, long before they reached combat.

For all the freezing blasts of air, it was still more pleasant up on deck than below. A week out of Halifax, Nova Scotia, the convoy seemed no nearer to England. David knew that the course carried them far to the north to avoid the prowling U-boats, but there were times when it seemed that such a prolonged crossing actually exposed them to a greater risk.

The night before, the seas around the *Duchess* had been empty of all other ships, so it was a surprising sight in the early morning to count two dozen laboring freighters. Ahead of and to either side of the convoy, a pair of circling destroyers cast about like hunting dogs after a scent.

The first night aboard the *Duchess,* the Canadian and American fliers slept in their clothing and their life jackets because of the likelihood of U-boat attacks. They remained dressed, although no one slept. On the second day out, David asked a sailor about the cargo which the *Duchess* carried in addition to planes and men. When he was told that the holds of the freighter were filled with live ammo, David had grinned, shrugged, and thereafter undressed for bed and slept soundly.

An enormous wave lifted the bow of the freighter and dropped it again. Forty feet of elevation were gained in three seconds and just as quickly lost. A sheen of ice from the frozen spray coated the railings and the safety lines and turned the decks into skating rinks. The fresh air was a nice change from his cramped quarters, but it was time to go below.

A bright flash south of the *Duchess* caught David's eye. A dark red flare rolled up into the sky from the black outline of a ship about a mile distant. A few seconds later the muffled whoom of a large explosion rolled across the seas. It was as if a giant hand lifted the unlucky freighter from beneath its steel belly while its bow and stern bent and drooped. To David's horror, the stricken ship broke in two. The forward section plunged almost straight down into the frigid water while the aft piece floated dismally, half on its side, like a broken toy thrown down by a petulant child.

Ahead of their route, a blast of black smoke erupted from one of the destroyers; it heeled sharply into the wind as it circled around. On the *Duchess,* strident alarm bells sounded. Under David's feet the freighter groaned and shuddered at the sudden demand for more speed. Sluggishly, unwillingly, the *Duchess* altered her course to the north and almost imperceptibly accelerated.

There was only a moment to note the tiny bobbing orange life rafts from the torpedoed ship, and then the tragic scene aft was hidden by the intervening swells.

All around the *Duchess,* other ships of the convoy were steaming northward, their churning wakes evidence of their panicked flight. But like wolves, the rest of the U-boat pack waited across the line of the fleeing ships. The guns of the second destroyer boomed as the knife-like form of a submarine's bow appeared on the waves ahead. Another freighter exploded with a shattering blast that knocked David's grip loose from the rail and temporarily deafened him.

Two fleeing ships, both seeking to avoid the path of a torpedo, turned into each other's course and collided. The arrival of the torpedo tore the bow off one and left a gaping hole in the side of the other.

Then it was time for the *Duchess* to receive the sub's attention. The cries of three lookouts shrilled, "Torpedo in the water! Torpedo on the port quarter!"

David watched with fascinated horror as the *Duchess* began an agonizingly slow turn *toward* the torpedo's path.

"More to port!" a lookout screamed. "Come on, *Duchess,* move your arse!"

The torpedo streaked into view, a lethal fish seeking to destroy the freighter and her cargo and crew. The *Duchess* swung sideways, the arc of its turn barely seeming to move.

David braced himself and ducked down below the rail, anticipating the hammer blow of the torpedo's warhead on the far side of the freighter. When a few seconds passed like hours of time and no explosion ripped through the ship, David cautiously raised his head.

Racing away aft, the torpedo's trail of bubbles was inscribed on the waves and led back toward the unharmed *Duchess* like an exclamation point.

Three hours and eighteen course changes later, the freighter made its way back across the stretch of ocean where the original attack had occurred. At a cry from the lookout, the *Duchess* altered direction one more time to intercept a floating life raft.

Aboard the scrap of safety were four men. Two were almost unharmed, although freezing and comatose from exposure. One more had bled to death and the remaining occupant had been blinded in the explosion.

It was that single moment, more than any other, which made David aware that he could actually get himself killed in a war that was supposed to be none of his business.

✣   ✣   ✣

For pilot David Meyer and the handful of other Americans who stepped off the transport ship in Southampton, the arrival at the Operational Training Unit at Aston Down made the RAF a reality. On that first cloudy evening after David's appearance at OTU, the RAF was also in for a shock at first meeting the Yank face-to-face.

While the rest of the new men lingered at the tables in the mess, David wandered out onto the grassy airfield alone to look over the object of his obsession. The Hawker Hurricane was larger than he had figured. It had a wingspan of forty feet and was thirty-two feet long. He reached up to touch the markings. Red, white, and blue concentric circles looked ominously like an archery target.

The Hurricane was not an all-metal aircraft. The front part of the fuselage and the wings were metal covered while the back of the body and the tail were fabric. The Hurricane had a reputation for being light and highly maneuverable with no bad quirks. The thick wing accounted for a relatively slow top speed of 340 miles an hour even with the powerful Rolls Royce "Merlin" V-12 engine, which produced 1,280 horsepower.

In spite of that, the wing construction gave it an amazingly tight turning radius of something near eight hundred feet at three hundred miles an hour. This fact alone would make the ship a match for nearly any German craft in turns. Three summers performing aerobatics with a flying circus made David eager to try her out.

He climbed up to peer at the controls. Inside, she was a single seater with an austere, unlined cockpit. At six feet one inch, it would be a tight fit for

David. He was glad that he was slender. At the mess tonight he had spotted two pilots who, much broader than he, would have a tough time fitting in. This could also mean serious problems if they ever had to bail out in a hurry.

David opened the canopy and, wanting to check the space for fit, slid in like a man trying to get the feel of a new car. He settled in easily, becoming part of the aircraft. He was instantly in love.

The Hurricane was controlled by a spade grip stick that moved laterally about halfway up. The reduced play from that of a straight stick provided better aileron control than David had been used to in the old Jenny biplanes. He grasped the spade grip, which was a circular ring about eight inches around and an inch thick. On the grip was a large firing button and a ring with which the pilot could arm the guns. There were eight .303 caliber Browning machine guns with fourteen seconds of ammunition for each gun and a precise concentration of fire.

David planted his feet on the rudder pedals. He peered through the gun sight and moved the spade grip until an imaginary ME-109 was dead center. And then he pushed the brass button on the spade grip.

What happened next was not imaginary. The still evening of Aston Down was shattered as a burst of machine gun fire tore into the rear fuselage of the Hurricane parked directly in front of the plane where David sat! Passing through the canvas structure, the .303 caliber bullets pierced a pattern in the wall of the mechanic's hangar one hundred yards further across the field.

The two-second burst sent men tumbling in terror out of the buildings. Heads craned back in search of the airborne enemy who had disrupted their evening meal. They scrambled toward the slit trenches, and then a voice boomed in outrage, "It's the Yank! It's the new boy!"

A string of curses followed from Arthur Cross, nicknamed "Badger," who was the largest and most gruesome assistant instructor at the OTU. "Look what the raving fool's done to my Hurry! I'll kill 'im!"

NINE

Rusted iron rings were set in the algae-covered bridges which crossed the Seine and the fortified stone of the riverbanks. A flotilla of boats and freight barges were moored to the ancient rings and to one another. There, within the shadow of the Louvre and Notre Dame and the opulent homes of wealthy Parisians, lived other citizens of the French Republic. Prostitutes, thieves, malcontents, and impoverished artists populated decrepit hulks moored close to the motor yachts of the rich.

Beneath Pont Neuf, between a garbage scow and an ancient tug, rested a narrow Dutch péniche which had hauled freight through the canals of Holland for fifty years. No one could remember how or when she had mysteriously appeared on the Seine. It seemed as if she had always been there. Her masts and sails had long since been lowered and tied off to the eighty foot deck. The giant rudder was secured to her starboard side. Those rare times when she moved along the river, it was by the power of a gasping diesel engine. The smoke from the exhaust had nearly covered over the once brightly painted name of some Dutch captain's favorite lady. Now only the letters *AIL* remained visible through the grime. In French, ail means garlic. Thus she was known along the Left Bank as the *Stinking Garlic.* The English interpretation of the word *ail* also seemed appropriate to the appearance of the craft. The *AIL* had obviously fallen very sick indeed. The final degradation had come when, during a game of cards, she became home to an infamous Communist clochard by the name of Jardin and his two ragged children. Hardly a day passed without some kind of a racket rising up from the *Stinking Garlic.* Today was no different.

"Jerome! Jerome, I say! Come here at once. You also, Marie. It is time for your lessons."

"Yes, Papa," came a small girl's treble from belowdecks. Six-year-old Marie appeared through the hatch near the helm station.

"Coming," agreed ten-year-old Jerome as he propped his fishing pole against the stern rail of the *AIL* and clambered over heaps of discarded rigging to sit on the stump of the mast.

Monsieur Jardin, his cast off dungarees tied around with a length of rope and his threadbare sweater and black béret, did not look like a famous philosopher. Neither that small matter nor his alcohol-fuddled brain, kept him from thinking highly of his store of accumulated wisdom. Not in the least.

Jardin stretched upward with an elaborate contortion, broke wind loudly, and proclaimed himself ready to begin the day's lesson. At his feet was a bottle of vinegary red wine, which he said had bravado and which he could get for twenty-five centimes a gallon.

"Now," he said, waving an instructive finger that was so dirty that the nail could not be distinguished from the rest. "Who remembers the name for the vilest and most flatuous of earthly villains?"

Jerome knew the answer, but he liked to give Marie a chance to go first. It pleased her when she got it right and did no harm to his standing with his father if he were called upon to help out.

"Cuttlefish," she said with a sight lisp.

Jardin laid his face sideways in the palm of one hand and stared reflectively into the grey Parisian sky. "Almost right," he allowed. "Jerome?"

"Capitalists," Jerome corrected.

"Bon! You both have the makings of scholars. But appearances are, as they say, discerning, so we must continue the lesson. Jerome, what is the greatest, most magnanimous fault man can possess?"

Jerome answered up at once, "Greed, Papa."

"Even so. Greed is a source of much triplication in the world. It is a whip hand held over the brow of the poor and downtrodden, never forget." After one of these profound statements, Jardin often helped himself to a swig from his bottle. Sometimes the length of the lesson depended on how much self-congratulation went on. Meanwhile, the volume of the instruction got louder and louder. Jardin took a drink, then wiping his mouth on his arm through a hole in his sleeve, he turned again to Marie. "Here is a tough one for you, ma chérie. What is another name for the wicked people who want to keep the poor always poor, in order to have them around to fight their wars?"

"Missionaries?"

"Well, that is a very fine answer, Marie. But I was looking for something else," explained Jardin grandly, taking another swallow of wine.

"Re-act . . . react-something," Jerome piped up.

Jardin snapped his fingers. "Bravo, Jerome. Also known as warmongerers. They are so busy looking backward that they cannot see the future when it hits them between the eyes."

Jerome was still trying to work out this metaphor while his father was already on to the next question. Such inattention was dangerous, to say the least, since a clout on the ear might result.

". . . who ever lived?" Jardin was concluding.

Jerome breathed an inward sigh of relief. He not only knew what the question had been, he knew the answer as well. "Stalin," he said promptly.

Jardin removed his béret with respect at the pronunciation of the Soviet leader's name. "Leader of the most processive nation on earth," he proclaimed loudly.

"You mean progressive," shouted a passerby from the quay, "or, more truthfully, repressive."

Jardin made an obscene gesture in the direction of the speaker and smiled proudly when Jerome and Marie both repeated the same arm movement.

"Papa," Jerome asked, raising his hand, "on the street they are saying that Monsieur Stalin has made a deal with Hitler. Did you not tell us that Hitler was the arch fiend incarcerate?"

Jardin scratched his scraggly beard, then beamed as the proper response came to him. "Monsieur Stalin knows what is best," he said. "Perhaps he has converted this Hitler fellow to see the error of his ways." This last observation made Jardin reflective. There was a slice of sun streaming through the clouds. Just enough for Jardin to sit and warm himself. "Now, that is all the lesson for today, I think."

"What are we to do for supper, Papa?" Marie asked. "We have nothing left in the cupboard."

"Jerome will go to the usual places . . . as usual . . . and catch something which might fall from the pocket of a capitalist. Or perhaps I will catch a cuttlefish." Jardin snapped his fingers in silent command for Jerome to fetch the fishing pole. "Now, Marie, go below and finish your chores. Jerome, I need to have a word with you."

Jerome wondered what sort of trouble he was in, or if the gendarmes had been around asking questions about too many handbags mysteriously disappearing on the boulevard. But this time it was his father who was in trouble.

"Jerome," Jardin said in a blast of vinegary breath, "I must tell you somthing in complete competence. The gendarmes are very angry that Hitler and Monsieur Stalin have made up their quarrel. It may be necessary for me to go away for awhile, without saying good-bye. You are not to worry, but you must promise me to take care of Marie."

"Of course, Papa."

Jardin held up his finger to emphasize the importance of his instruction. "Beware of the gendarmes and the priests. If ever I am away, you must not let on that I am away and you are still here even though I am not." He paused for breath and squinted at the water of the Seine. "They would lock you in an orphanage. Think of the disgrace if your sister grew up to be a nun."

Jerome solemnly shook his head in horror at the image. "I will not let that happen, Papa."

"That is my son. I knew I could depend on you."

❖   ❖   ❖

They shared a wonderful meal. Jerome stole a lovely eel which was on display on a block of ice in the fish market. He had put the thing down his pant leg. His escape had been slimy and cold, but the thought of such a feast made it worthwhile. Papa caught a catfish while fishing from the quay across from the Louvre. Old Uncle Jambonneau brought potatos and onions from the kitchen at the Hôtel des Invalides where he lived with the other old wounded soldiers.

Tonight the *Stinking Garlic* reeked of grease and fish and garlic from the cooking. It was a lovely aroma to Jerome. Marie had eaten so much she had a bellyache and had gone to bed in her tiny bunk.

Alone on the deck, Jerome scrubbed the crusted black skillet as Papa and Uncle Jambonneau discussed weighty matters belowdecks. Even in the darkness of the blackout, Paris was not entirely dark. There were lights sneaking out the slits of blackout curtains here and there. The gendarmes did not seem to mind the violations. Jerome could plainly see the outlines of the buildings on Ile de la Cité. A soft glow penetrated the cracks around the cargo hatch. The voices of Papa and Uncle Jambonneau were plainly audible to Jerome.

Jerome wondered why Papa burned the lantern since Uncle was blind. His eyes had been burned by poison gas in the Great War. Now he was a grizzled old relic who tapped around the City of Lights with a cane and a canvas rucksack slung over his right shoulder. A very large white rat perched on his left shoulder and whispered things in Uncle's ear.

Jerome had been warned that Uncle Jambonneau did not know that the rat was a rat. He believed it was a small dog with a long hairless tail. When some foolish tourist or Right Bank stranger gasped and screamed and called the rat a rat, Uncle Jambonneau became instantly offended. He assumed they were talking about him, not the thing on his shoulder.

Uncle Jambonneau named his dog, which was not a dog, *Petit Papillon*, which means small butterfly. All of this could be quite confusing to the uninitiated.

The boy peered down through the cracks at the top of the plank table as Papillon delicately held a bit of eel in his little hands and nibbled.

"There can be little doubt that my mother raised a fool," Uncle Jambonneau said to Papa. "Why did you have to become a Marxist?"

"I am content with what I am," Papa replied.

Jerome wondered, did Papa mean that he was content to be a fool or content to be a Marxist?

"Why not a Buddhist? The French government is not arresting Buddhists. Only Communists."

"That is true. But I know nothing about such things."

Uncle Jambonneau snapped his fingers and Papillon skittered up his arm to whisper something in his ear. "Well, little brother. You have one hope to stay out of prison, I think."

"What is that?"

"Perhaps you are not worth arresting. Not even the Communists of Paris will claim you. They say you are a fool."

"That may be true. But they are jealous."

"Of what?"

Papa could not think of an answer to that. He leaned his head against his palm and gazed around the cluttered cabin of the boat. "They are jealous of my property."

"Yes. I can see that," Uncle Jambonneau nodded his white head and scratched Papillon under the chin. "By owning this boat . . . you have violated one of the principles of communism."

"What right have they to constrain? I won the *Garlic* fairly at cards. She is mine."

"If Stalin invades France, you will have to give him the *Garlic*."

"If Stalin comes to Paris, by my honor, he may have her."

Uncle Jambonneau raised a gnarled finger in a gesture which looked much like an older version of Papa. "But will he want her?"

TEN

No one would have imagined that the two old sisters had not always lived in Paris in the big house behind the gate at No. 5 Rue de la Huchette. They looked like any grandmothers on the Left Bank: grey hair tied back in buns, aprons dusted with flour, rundown shoes, and navy blue dresses faded with many turns in the washtub.

They were spinsters: Rose and Betsy Smith of the Santa Barbara Smiths. That was Santa Barbara, California, USA. Rose was large, square built, strong, and was fifty-five years old. Betsy, tiny and frail-looking, was nearing sixty.

They were the daughters of a fisherman who, as a young sailor, had nearly drowned in a gale in 1870 off Point Conception. He had cried out to God as green water broke over the decks of the schooner. The masts snapped like twigs. The second mate was washed overboard and the situation seemed hopeless. When the young sailor looked up he saw silver angels moving in the sun-clipped clouds. A voice boomed in the thunder, and the sea became calm within moments!

Like the fishermen of ancient Galilee, he had heard The Voice of the Lord, and he loved the mighty sound of it! Every day he sang God's words as he worked his nets off the Channel Islands.

As his daughters grew he told them that except for the miracle in the storm, they would not have been born. In this way, the miracle came to belong to Rose and Betsy. Through the ears of their father they came to hear The Voice in the thunder. Through his eyes they saw the silver angels riding the clouds over Santa Cruz and Anacapa Islands in the twilight hours.

They believed there was some reason why their father had been spared; some reason they were born. They grew to womanhood certain that there was some larger purpose for their lives which they could not see.

And so they were not surprised when at a tent meeting in Ventura, in the

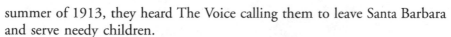

summer of 1913, they heard The Voice calling them to leave Santa Barbara and serve needy children.

But serve where? The dark continent of Africa was in fashion. The Voice was not specific. Rose bought a map of Africa and unrolled it on the kitchen table. She closed her eyes and plunged her finger onto the paper.

"Betsy," she called to her sister who was sipping lemonade in the yard and praying as she watched the sunset, "God wants us to go to Algeria."

They intended to do so. But the Great War of 1914 got in the way. Paris, the City of Lights, was far away from Africa. Their ship was sunk off the Canary Islands and they were brought to Paris. They could not recollect just why that was, but that was the way it happened; a true story.

There were needy children in Paris, too. So many little ones with papas killed in the trenches. The young fathers of France dissolved into the soil of Verdun and the Somme. So many mamas dead of the flu epidemic or simply dead in spirit.

The sisters started with one baby and then three and then seven, until they had thirty . . . so many in need in those early days! The need never ended.

One generation grew up. There were always more to take the empty beds and toddle in at night to be rocked and sung to . . . one child at a time, with different faces, different names. Twenty-five years came and went without celebration; without recognition by anyone beyond the Left Bank of the Seine. Day by day, needs were met by small miracles. Hour by hour, they dished out love in generous helpings to little ones whose souls were in danger of starvation.

Two spinsters: Rose and Betsy Smith. They were an unlikely pair in the Latin Quarter. After twenty-five years, they spoke the language like native Parisians. Nearly everyone thought well of them.

The Jews who lived packed in little houses above the tailor shops off St. Germaine believed that they were righteous, probably secret Jews.

The Catholics believed that they were perhaps doctrinally misguided, but still worthy workers for the Kingdom of God, possibly secret Catholics.

Paris had very few Protestants. Those who were there either did not know the sisters were Americans or were not aware of their existence. The pair served no church or ideology. They depended on God to provide their needs.

They also took in washing.

Over the years Rose developed muscular washboard forearms like a carnival strong man. Little Betsy did the ironing. She remained petite and, unlike broad-beamed Rose, she seemed to shrink as the years passed.

Their first children, all grown up now, often came back to visit. Some, who had done very well for themselves, now brought their laundry and their offerings to the sisters.

Ernest Hemingway was a friend. He stopped in regularly to pick up or drop off his shirts. No one starched the way Rose did, he claimed. When his first novel sold and he traveled to Africa, he returned months later to tell the sisters about the wonders of the Dark Continent! After he left, Betsy confided that she was still willing to go to Africa if The Voice so instructed them. But in the meantime she was very glad that they had been shipwrecked like the Apostle Paul and cast up on the shores of a city like Paris!

It was the children who kept them there in the hungry years of the twenties and into the thirties. And now, with a new war beginning, it looked as though the cycle was about to begin all over again.

Those first few orphans raised by the sisters were now called up to serve in the Grand Armee just like their fathers had done in 1914. Rose and Betsy prayed for each by name. They prayed for France. They even prayed for Germany, the new dark continent.

Mostly they prayed for the new generation of children who crowded into Paris from whatever country the Nazis crushed. It was always the little ones, the innocent ones, who suffered the mistakes of politicians and nations, was it not?

Old ladies now, the sisters had come to believe that God spared their father in the gale of 1870 so that they could be here in Paris in 1939. It was a very long-playing miracle. It was not finished yet.

✠   ✠   ✠

The French tricolor waved proudly over the great cobbled square in front of the main buildings of the École de Cavalerie.

The sun beat hot on the black uniform and two-cornered *lampion* hat of Cadre Noir instructor, Captain Paul Chardon. A darkly handsome, compactly athletic man of twenty-seven, Chardon began his education here as a small child and had eventually graduated to the riding school at Saumur. There, he had become a horseman of international reputation, winning gold medals in Olympic competition in 1932 and 1936.

Now he was *Écuyer-en-Chef;* Chief riding instructor of the school on the river Lys. Because of his Olympic triumphs, he was secretly called Apollo by the students. He also possessed authority that could not be ignored. It was Captain Chardon who had the power to recommend promotion to the great cavalry school at Saumur, an honor enjoyed by only a handful of students each year. It was his dream one day to return to Saumur as Chief Instructor, but his youth and ability to work with youngsters kept him here for the time being. Today, he inspected the long straight lines of miniature soldiers for the last time.

Two thousand grey-uniformed boys ages five to twelve stood with their backs to the left wing of the massive four-story building which had once been a summer palace for Louis XV. Facing them on the right were nine hundred and nine upperclassmen in dark blue uniforms of the Cadre Bleu. These older cadets would remain at the École de Cavalerie.

All of Northern France was on the move. Half a million civilians had been evacuated from military zones already. The train stations at Arras and Lille and Strasbourg were jammed with children being relocated. Some of these two thousand young cadets would be going back to their homes in the south of France or Switzerland or Monaco. The others would be resettled in a far less spacious school near Marseilles, where there were no horses or lessons in equitation. The majority of the staff were likewise being evacuated, leaving Paul with nine lieutenant-instructors to govern nine hundred cadets. No one seemed happy about the breakup of the school.

Head high, boots polished to a glossy sheen, spurs glinting in the sun, Paul Chardon walked among the little ones—Gulliver among the Lilliputian army.

At the end of a column the chin of a small pink-cheeked boy trembled with emotion. "Chin up, Jean-Claude." Paul patted him on the shoulder. "This will be over very soon. The Boche will be soundly beaten, and we will all be together here again."

Two rows back an eight-year-old named Pieter who had grown attached to a bay brood mare named Germain, sniffled uncontrollably.

"Be brave, Pieter," Paul enjoined.

"It is Germain, sir. Poor Germain. I have heard what they did to horses in the last war. Will she be made to haul a wagon? Will they kill her for meat?"

"She is in foal, Pieter. When you return she will have a colt at her side. The brood mares of the École de Cavalerie do not haul wagons. Ever."

At this the child brightened. And so it went on down the line. Colonel Larousse made a stirring speech, calling on each cadet to wipe his tears and serve France with dignity by being good students and thus good soldiers.

But they were leaving the horses behind, and that was hard to take. Their first week in school they had memorized the words of Marshal Soult in his message to the school in 1840. "Horsemanship is not everything in the Cavalry, but everything is nothing without it."

One hundred years later, the École de Cavalerie still ran on that principle. Therefore, without horses, everything seemed as nothing to the two thousand children with warrior's hearts who plodded onto waiting buses for the journey to the train depot in Arras. Suddenly they were mere foot soldiers.

In spite of the bright blue sky and the autumn colors in the trees, it was a gloomy day. The war was no longer exciting unless one was at least thirteen years old and dressed in the dark blue uniform of a Cadre Bleu cadet.

ELEVEN

The evacuation of two hundred thousand civilians from Northern France took place in the first forty-eight hours after the declaration of war. In Strasbourg, Alsace, each person was allowed only forty kilos of personal effects.

What to take? Old photographs or blankets? A precious heirloom or an extra pair of shoes? It was a terrible ordeal, and yet, they knew from the last war that the possibility of occupation by the Germans was a much more terrifying prospect. Not everyone left, but nearest the border entire villages now stood ghostly and deserted in the autumn haze.

The majority of the evacuees were placed in tiny farming villages like Perigueux. The Alsatian dialect was close to pure German. This problem was solved by double staffing in every store and public building. In the post office there were two clerks. One spoke Alsatian, the other spoke the local dialect. In the police headquarters there were Alsatian policemen as well as the rural French gendarmes. So it was in the schools and even in the churches.

But double staffing did not prevent personal resentment against the Alsatian intruders. The farm communities had not been asked how many evacuees they could take in; they had simply been ordered to prepare for their arrival.

So it was among the public and private charities in Paris. The nuns of St. Vincent de Paul were given a list of names of children arriving at Gare du Nord. They were ordered to make room in their orphanage to accommodate two hundred German-speaking Alsatian youngsters. Public institutions and private individuals were asked to open their doors to the overflow of Northern France.

Rose and Betsy Smith were visited personally by Monsieur Comperot, Assistant Minister of Civilian Relocation, who came to No. 5 Rue de la Huchette on a chilly afternoon in the fall.

He observed the ground floor of the three-story building which served as

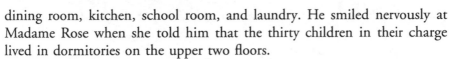

dining room, kitchen, school room, and laundry. He smiled nervously at Madame Rose when she told him that the thirty children in their charge lived in dormitories on the upper two floors.

"Madame," he began. "It is very difficult. You are American, it is true, but what I must say is as one human to another. *Comprenez vous?*"

Rose was always delighted to speak as one human to another. Frequently, however, it meant that one human had a favor to ask of the other human.

"But of course, Monsieur. We consider ourselves citizens of Paris and of France. How can we help?"

"There are certain children among the evacuees . . . difficult cases, Madame. We simply cannot place them."

"Difficult?"

"They are seven children who have been residents of a sanitarium in Alsace."

Rose gestured out the window of her cluttered little office to the happy squeals of children playing soccer on the cobbles. "Our children are very healthy . . ."

"These are not unhealthy, Madame. Not now." He swallowed hard. "They are crippled. Infantile paralysis. Polio as you call it. All of them affected in one way or another. Five in wheelchairs. Two manage on crutches. First they went to the community center in Perigueux. Farmers came in and picked children to take home. No farmer wants a child who cannot haul water or feed the milk cow. It is the same all over. We brought them by train to Paris. By then every place was full. There is some room at the insane asylum. But to put them into an institution would seem most cruel, Madame. They cannot climb stairs, which prevents them from being placed nearly anywhere. But as you can see, your facility is ideal. If you might make a place for them on the ground floor?"

Rose and Betsy shared a look of pleasant compliance. "But of course, Monsieur. We will make room for them. The other children will help us with them."

He mopped his brow with relief. "There are hundreds of others like them who are not so fortunate. They will be placed in hospitals for the duration." He drew a deep breath. "Of course the Boche will not pass the Maginot. Simply a precaution. But we all know what they did to unfortunate Polish children with physical limitations." He drew a finger across his throat. "Emptied the hospitals of useless mouths. Put them in a closed van and ran the exhaust fumes into it. They have no mercy, these Boche."

"Rest assured, Monsieur Comperot," Betsy puffed up her tiny frame in indignation. "Even if they got past the Maginot! Even if they came to Paris . . . If ever they came to No. 5 Rue de la Huchette, they would not pass!"

She held up her fist, which seemed a small and fragile weapon to wave in the faces of imaginary Nazis.

Still, the gesture was sweet. Monsieur Comperot seemed comforted. "Ah. You Americans! You must write your President Roosevelt and encourage him to come along with France again. Together we will settle the matter once and for all. You are not truly neutral. Not at heart." He thanked them and finished his cup of coffee with a flourish.

"And how long do we have to prepare ourselves for the arrival of our new children, Monsieur?"

He glanced at his watch and stood abruptly. "Within the hour, Mesdames." He gave a Gallic shrug and placed his bowler on his head. "The nuns at St. Vincent de Paul assured me you would not refuse."

TWELVE

Badger Cross did not forgive David Meyer for shooting up his Hurricane. The instructor dedicated himself to the task of making the young American's three weeks at Aston Down OTU pure misery. On every occasion, and to every newcomer, he introduced David as the best gunner in the RAF.

"Heartless, he is. Nerves of steel behind the gunsights! Or at least nerves of tin! The Nazis love this chap! He shoots up our own planes on the field!"

The combination of nerves of tin and heartlessness resulted in the moniker "Tinman" for David. Badger, who lived up to the ferocity promised by his name, meant this as an insult. By the end of the brief training period however, David was putting out his hand and cheerfully presenting himself as the Tinman. He took the ribbing with unfailing good humor. This increased Badger's hatred. Like a fraternity pledge, David determined that the moment would come when he would turn the tables on his tormentor. Badger Cross, who outweighed the American by forty pounds, seemed to welcome the prospect of finishing off the Yank who punctured his plane.

Three weeks of OTU was packed with formation practice, aerobatics, and night flying, all of which proved that Tinman was an excellent pilot. This fact disappointed Badger who would have liked to see the "cocky Yank" flounder miserably. But the hostility of Badger only served to strengthen David's friendships with the other pilots, like Hewitt and Simpson, who did not like the arrogant, acid-tongued Badger either.

On their first leave in London before being assigned to operational squadrons, however, David left the pub-hopping group of pilot officers. He struck out on his own after Badger chugged three pints of Guinness and declared, "I can whip any man here! Man of steel or . . ." He leveled his hot gaze on David. "Man of tin!"

David did not fancy spending his first night in London behind bars. One more pint down Badger's throat would mean that jail was a real possibility.

There were no affordable hotel rooms in the entire city, it seemed. When he inquired at the Savoy, the price of a single was too high after the wad he had just dropped on a new RAF uniform at Moss Brothers. So David spent the night in the opulent lounge of the men's lavatory at the Savoy Hotel.

An RAF pilot snoozing in an overstuffed chair within earshot of the urinals did not perturb the elderly men's-room attendant, who had himself fought in the last war in France. Running an officer out in the cold black streets of London would be positively unpatriotic, he declared. So David slept very comfortably until just before dawn when the rattle of a custodian's buckets and mops woke him up.

"Sir, wireless reports a contact with merchant ship *Collingwood.* It was attacked by a U-boat about two hours ago."

"Does it require assistance?" asked Lt. Commander Trevor Galway.

"Negative, sir. They were shelled, but escaped. They can make it into port. Request that we alert other ships in the area."

"We'll do better than that. Mister Fry, give us a course to the reported position of the sighting. Full ahead, if you please."

South of the Canary Islands, even mid-November had a pleasant, summery feel. Accounts like the one just rendered interrupted an otherwise quiet morning. Cruising along the coast of Africa, the destroyer HMS *Fortitude* patrolled the sea-lanes, protecting British shipping. And there was a great need for such protection despite the peaceful feel of the predawn air. Since the outbreak of the war two months earlier, over one hundred merchant ships had been sunk by German submarines, raiders, or mines. Over half were British.

An hour of steaming at top speed brought *Fortitude* to the freighter's location. From this point, the destroyer became a hunting dog, casting about over the surface of the Atlantic for any clues to the sub's whereabouts.

On the horizon a fishing boat headed northwest. "Attempt to contact that craft," Galway ordered. "Ask if she has seen any other vessels in this area."

The young officer studied the ship through his binoculars while he waited for a reply. The fishing vessel had two stubby masts and a jumble of nets heaped up on her stern. "She does not acknowledge, sir," was the report.

"Well, she must have passed through long after the U-boat," Galway pondered aloud. "She's only making five knots."

"Should we warn her?" Fry asked.

"I can't imagine a U-boat skipper wasting a torpedo on a fishing smack," Galway said, still gazing through the field glasses. "She rides so low in the water and . . . Mister Fry, sound action stations!"

Fry obeyed immediately, and the strident clanging of the warning gong shattered the stillness of the morning as sailors turned out of their bunks and into their battle gear.

Captain Pickering appeared at Galway's elbow, uniform blouse buttoned crooked and a glop of shaving cream behind one ear. "What's this, Mister Galway? Attacking a fishing boat?" he asked incredulously.

"Take a look, sir," requested Trevor, passing the binoculars. "I noticed how long and low the profile was, but when I studied the cabin amidships it became clear."

"It's a U-boat!" Pickering exclaimed. "Mister Galway, give the order to commence firing as soon as we have the range."

Fortitude carried four turrets of five-inch guns, two each forward and aft. Her gun crews needed no urging to rouse them to the attack; many had friends or relatives among the five hundred British lives lost at sea since the war began.

The two forward positions barked out their first rounds within a second of each other, vying for the honor of claiming the kill. The shots missed but bracketed the disguised submarine on both sides.

"What is the purpose of the deception?" Trevor asked. "To sneak up on victims?"

"Why would a vessel that can attack submerged need such a ruse?" Pickering said. "No, she must be damaged in some way and unable to submerge. She's hoping her trick will save her on the surface in daylight. Well done, Mister Galway. Your sharp eyes have seen through the camouflage."

The next shot from number one gun landed just astern of the supposed fishing vessel's cabin. The explosion blew one of the phony masts in half and exposed the grey metal of the conning tower. Movement was seen on the sub's deck; sailors running aft toward the pile of nets.

The heap of mesh was thrown aside, revealing the U-boat's own cannon. But before the German craft could fire a single time, another shot from

Fortitude made a direct hit, splintering the gun and catapulting its crew into the water. The sound of cheering from number two gun turret was heard clear up on the bridge.

"She's settling lower, sir," Trevor reported. The U-boat sank beneath the waves, but whether because of the harm done by the shelling or to attempt to escape was not clear.

Another round from the number one gun knocked the top off the submerging conning tower, and then the place in the sea was empty of all but ripples. "Cease firing," Pickering ordered. "Prepare to roll depth charges!"

The officer on the stern of *Fortitude* stood, stopwatch in hand, timing the rush of the destroyer to the exact spot where the U-boat had disappeared. When the clock's hand swept around the dial to the precise instant he shouted, "Roll one! Roll two! Roll three!"

Moments after the warship rushed past, fountains of water erupted from the ocean, spraying three times higher than the radio masts. Four times she charged over the spot, describing the figure eight pattern of the hunting dog who has run his quarry to earth. After the tenth explosion, the face of the sea was littered with thousands of dead mackerel, caught by the underwater concussions . . . and an oval-shaped oil slick that bubbled up from below. "Cease depth charge," was the command. "That's finished it. Well done lads, well done all. Helmsman, take us back to look for survivors of the German gun crew."

THIRTEEN

It was the dog that Pilot Officer David Meyer first noticed as he walked alone in London's St. James Park at dawn.

An enormous St. Bernard with a curving white plume of a tail, a black-masked face, and drooping jowls sniffed and lifted his leg against the white trunks of the plane trees, as if his aim in life was to mark every tree in the park. The animal was alone. Dragging his brown leather leash, he chased a grey squirrel and then proceeded to relieve himself beside a heap of sandbags surrounding an antiaircraft gun emplacement. This drew verbal fire from the gun crew on duty who cursed at David.

"Get that bugger out of 'ere, mate! Why look! It's lef' a stinkin' pile big as one of them cav'ry 'orses!"

Davis was about to deny ownership when the thing turned, wagged, woofed, and ran to him. It jumped up on his new RAF pilot officer's uniform. David pushed the beast down. Too late. A streak of muddy paw prints marred his trousers and white strings of saliva clung to his tunic. Thwarting a second joyous assault, David grabbed the leash and with a swift jerk ordered the St. Bernard to sit. Miraculously, the animal obeyed. With long dripping tongue lolling to the side, he gawked at David adoringly.

"Good dog." David patted the large square head firmly and looked around the wide expanse of the park for anyone who seemed to be missing a St. Bernard.

And then he saw her. Red hair pulled back in a single thick braid glistened in the morning sun. Petite and pretty, her face looked freshly scrubbed. In her early twenties, she was half-jogging, walking, and holding her side as she hurried up the gravel path toward David. She was wearing a man's topcoat which hung almost to her ankles. The hem of a white cotton nightgown peeked out over the tops of large black galoshes.

"Duffy! You're lookin' for a thrashin'!" she shouted angrily in a soft Irish brogue.

The dog's ears perked up. He glanced her way briefly but remained content and unconcerned at the side of the RAF pilot who held his leash.

David smiled and ordered his captive to heel. Duffy did so and the two walked calmly toward the pained and angry pursuer.

"Looking for something?" David smiled and extended the leash to the young woman who was flushed and panting so hard she could hardly speak.

"The *Thing!*" she managed.

"He's a Saint."

"Saint, indeed!" She gave the inattentive Duffy a whack on his hind quarters. "A devil is what." Clutching the coat to her, she spotted the paw prints on David's uniform. Her eyes were brown and warm and full of remorse. She gasped and scooped up a handful of leaves with which she attempted to brush the saliva from his jacket. "Were you layin' down when he did that to you?"

"Standing up." David enjoyed the attention.

"Aw. You're such a brute, Duffy! Look what you've done now to the officer's uniform!" She tossed down the leaves and put a hand to her head. "I can't tell you how sorry . . ."

"My name's David Meyer." They shook hands. Her hand was small and soft in his.

"Annie Galway . . . You've met Duffy, I'm afraid. So sorry, Officer Meyer."

"David."

"David. RAF is it? But you're a Yank, aren't you?"

He looked up at the leafless trees of St. James as if the answer was in the sky. "Guilty." He grinned down at her. She was beautiful. She had an oval face, wide eyes, and a pert nose. Her skin was fair and creamy smooth, and there was a hint of color on her cheeks. David thought how wonderful it would be to wake up to someone who could look this good with so little effort. "Has Duffy had breakfast?"

"No. I had just stepped out to bring in the milk when . . ."

"Bet he's hungry." Duffy wagged appreciatively as David patted his head. "Have you had breakfast, Miss Galway?"

"Not yet. This brute has kept me from it."

No wedding ring. Whose coat was she wearing? A large man, whoever he was.

"Neither have I. I know a little deli in the East End. All the cab drivers eat there. The only place in London where a guy can get lox and bagels. My dad told me about it."

Still clucking over the paw prints, she seemed to be missing the point. "You must let me take care of your tunic. It'll need a good cleanin', I'm afraid."

"Live far from here?"

"The *Wairakei*. Victoria Embankment. Do you know it?"

He did not, but he made an attempt at it. "Near the river?"

"Well done."

"I'll walk Duffy home for you if you'd like."

She surrendered the leash gratefully. "If you don't mind. He's Trevor's dog. Minds a man, but he has nothin' but contempt for me. I just stepped out for the milk . . . did I say that already?" They cut across the wide, leaf-covered lawn.

"And away he went."

"Exactly. I knew where to find him. Trevor always walked him here. St. James Park. Every mornin'. I just sort of flutter along behind on the end of his lead, and he tears about waterin' the King's shrubbery. I think he comes lookin' for Trevor."

"Trevor?"

"M' brother. He's in the Royal Navy."

Very good. The brother's dog. Annie must still live under the same roof with the family pet.

"Is that Trevor's coat?"

"My da's. I just grabbed it off the hook and out I went. And I'd best be gettin' it back to him." She smiled as an idea penetrated her brain. "Did I hear you say you'd not eaten breakfast?"

"Not yet. But I know this deli where we could go."

"The *Wairakei*. That's the ticket. We've got milk and we've saved some eggs. Would you like to eat with me and Dad, then? It's the least I can do. And I do mean the least. I'm a terrible cook, but Dad is a regular miracle worker when it comes to stretchin' eggs. Learned every trick in the Navy. You can put on Trevor's things and we'll get your uniform set right. Unless you have somethin' to do? What do y' say?"

"It's dinner time back home. This is the best offer I've had since I left the states." He let her think it was all her idea. He glanced down at the lumbering dog. "Thank you, Duffy."

The course of the River Thames was marked by barrage balloons which hovered over the river like a school of great silver fish, preventing the German Luftwaffe from mining the waterway. Duffy led the way out of the park along Birdcage Walk, through Parliament Square, beyond Westminster Abbey and the Houses of Parliament, before turning left along the riverbank at Westminster Bridge.

By the time they reached Victoria Embankment, Annie knew all about the Newfoundland retriever which David had owned as a child, and that he had spent his tenth summer as a cabin boy on a rum-runner named *Jazz Baby* off the coast of New York. Then he told her about the convoy crossing the North Atlantic and the U-boat attack and how there was more war going on at sea than in all of England, France, and Germany put together.

In that same time, David learned that Annie had been born in Ulster and had lived there until her father moved to Scotland to go into the shipbuilding business with his brother-in-law. The *Wairakei* was not an apartment block or a hotel, but a boat moored in the shadow of the Egyptian obelisque known as Cleopatra's Needle. Duffy had made his mark even on that distinguished relic, Annie told him.

A handsome, forty-two-foot, ketch-rigged motor-sailor of the Brown Owl class, the *Wairakei* had been built by Annie's father and an uncle at Rosneath, on the Clyde in Scotland.

"As a lad, Dad sailed 'round the globe. Said he never saw a place as fine as Waikiki and when he built his own ship, he'd name 'er Waikiki. Well, the painter, who was a drunken Irishman, got it all wrong."

Annie paused, leaned against the stone railing of the embankment and pointed down to the double masts of the well-kept ketch moored behind a row of deserted water taxis. The tide was up and the wind was up. The metal fittings on the rigging clanked a melody against the masts.

"Why didn't your dad have the painter put the proper name on her?"

"Ooooh! That's bad luck, doncha know that, Yank?" Those words were exclaimed in thick Irish brogue, as though they needed extra attention. "You never can change the name of a ship and have a thimble of good luck ever after. Would be like changin' . . . like changin' your own name! Someone would call you by the new thing and you'd not be able t' answer!"

He looked at her there in the soft morning light and thought that if he had a ship he'd name it *Annie*. He'd paint it on the stern in flaming red letters trimmed in gold. And then the words blurted out. "If I had a ship, I'd name her *Annie*."

She cocked an eye at him in amused disbelief. "Are all you Yanks so bold? Or is it all pilot officers?" She shrugged. He was blushing. She seemed not to notice. "Dad, Trevor, Duffy, and me sailed 'er down from Scotland through the Forth and Clyde canal, down the East coast to Chelsea, on the Thames. Dad's just got a contract refitting motor launches for the Admiralty. Patrol duty. Small wood-hulled ladies are less likely to blow up in a brush with those magnetic mines the Nazis have been seeding in the estuary. We'll be moving down to Dover when I finish school." She turned and looked back toward Parliament. "I'll miss this. London, I mean. She's a grand city even with the blackout and the air raid wardens and such. At night I lay in my bunk and the tide is coming in or going out. The lady rocks a bit as the riggin' rings like little bells. Through the porthole I can just make out Big Ben there. And I think what it must've been like in the old days. Before electric lamps. Charles Dickens and the like. It's quite nice, I think, unless you get run over by a taxi in the dark."

David recovered enough to tame his brain into thinking of suitable questions. "What do you do while your father is refitting patrol boats?"

"I'm studying to join the CNR, Civil Nursing Reserve. Last year I was at University of Edinburgh. Trevor was to have been Dad's assistant, but he joined the Royal Navy. Just what I would have done if I were a man. Lucky Trevor. He's on HMS *Fortitude*. I love the sea. It's in the blood I suppose." She smiled at Duffy. "I wanted to see the world. At least I've seen London. And what about you, David Meyer? Yank. What are you doin' in a war that's none of your business? Come to see the world, did you?"

He wanted to tell her that he would have traveled the world just to meet someone like her, but the impression of impetuous American had already been received with amusement on her part.

"I was barnstorming between terms at UCLA."

"Speak English, if you please," she warned him, as an enormous man with a bald head stepped out on the deck of the *Wairakei*. She gave him a playful wave which he returned. He did not seem surprised that his daughter was having a conversation with a soldier. She called to her father. "We'll be havin' a guest for breakfast, Dad!" The big man nodded and grinned up at her. Then she leaned closer to David. "Dad doesn't think much of Yanks. Says they speak gibberish and drink too much."

"Winston Churchill is half-American."

"Exactly. Dad cannot understand why thay've made him First Lord of the Admiralty. He says a man that talks so much ought to be Prime Minister."

David tried again. "I was a student at University of California in Los Angeles. Summer term I performed in a flying circus. The war started. I heard they'd be flying Spitfires and Hurricanes, so I went north to visit family in Montreal and I joined up. The RAF seemed pleased to have me."

She looked at him in astonishment. "You mean you've come all this way . . . put your life in danger . . . just so you could fly a particular aeroplane?"

He shrugged. "That was my original motivation, yes."

"And now?"

"Now it doesn't look real promising. The only reason the RAF is flying over Germany is to drop pamphlets. BUMF, we call it. Bum fodder; toilet paper; warning the Germans to be good little Nazis and stop this nasty quarrel. I think the war may be over before I get to France."

"What would you do then?"

"I don't know. What about you?"

"I suppose I'll go back to Edinburgh to University."

"Nice place, Edinburgh?"

"I suppose so. If you like old castles, bagpipes, and the history of John Knox."

"I'd like to see it. Maybe have a look at your school."

She shook her head. "All of this because my dog ran over the top of you?"

By the time breakfast was over David was convinced that if he never saw action in a Hurricane, he had come to England for one reason. And she was sitting directly across from him in the teak-paneled salon of the *Wairakei*. Annie was burned into his mind in bright red letters trimmed in gold.

FOURTEEN

For a while, Josie wore the borrowed clothes of a fellow newswoman. But she was hopelessly out of style in wartime London.

A cartoon appeared on the London news kiosks courtesy of *Punch* Magazine to sum up the autumn British fashion craze.

A tall, bony-kneed Highlander, dressed in his kilt, observed an English woman who was clothed in her new khaki uniform. The caption read, with thick Scottish burr:

"M'gawd, womin, ye look turrrrible!"

War had a curious leveling effect on ladies' dresses in London. Khaki on women suddenly became fashionable. Josephine Marlow had lost everything in Poland but the clothes on her back. Circumstances had elevated her title from foreign correspondent to war correspondent. And war correspondents, even from neutral countries, were all having military-style uniforms made up by the tailors on Saville Row.

Unlike her male journalistic counterparts, Josie did not have the funds for such extravagance, however. Gold braid and tasseled epaulets were beyond her means. The Mussolini-look just did not suit her. So she went to Moss Bros. & Co. Ltd., 20 King Street in London, where advantageous terms for uniforms had been arranged by the Associated Press. There, she was sensibly clothed on the AP expense account.

For a total of thirty-nine pounds, seven shillings, and threepence, she was fitted with two tunics, two skirts, a uniform cap, a greatcoat, four blouses, four pair of stockings, regulation shoes, tie, and gloves.

Undergarments were extra. Not willing to have some AP accountant know how many bras and panties she owned, she paid for those items out of her own pocket.

It saved the problem of picking out an entirely new daytime wardrobe, Josie told herself. It would simplify packing, would it not? And when news of this European fashion disaster got back to the States, surely every woman would rise up with one voice and declare that America must enter the war! The military might of the U.S. must make the world safe again for the fashions of Schiaparelli!

It was indeed possible that men would be more inspired to go to fight for a woman dressed in Schiaparelli than for a woman clothed by Moss Brothers!

Ah well. The whole world was topsy-turvy. She gazed into the mirror of the tailor shop and muttered the words of the Scot in his kilt. "Josephine, ye look turrible!" She now appeared identical, almost, to every other young service-age female in London. Large or small, buxom or flat chested, pretty or just pretty homely, in a dim room they were hard to tell apart. Josie stitched the press badges on the shoulders of tunics, blouses, and greatcoat. She was official, at last. She returned her borrowed clothes to Canadian newswoman Rhonda Grafton, who was now also decked out in Moss Brothers fashion. Rhonda, who had gained weight since she came to England, let Josie keep the cobalt blue evening dress: tight, low cut, and sexy. Rhonda informed her she must wear it in Paris if ever there was an occasion and if the French had not turned sensible like the English.

So. This comprised Josie's entire wardrobe: the uniform, the underwear, the cobalt blue evening dress. Pitiful, indeed.

It took a man with imagination to look through the khaki exterior which sashayed up Fleet Street and down Oxford Circus and through the revolving doors of Harrods.

Rich girls bought their uniforms from Harrods. They paid much more, but the extra expense was wasted. The effect was still khaki. Even the word seemed appropriate to the drabness of the color. Khaki. Khaki. Khaki. Say it fast and it sounded like someone retching.

Beyond the khaki, the sandbags in Picadilly, and the air raid shelters, except for blackouts and handbags containing gas masks, London seemed quite unaffected by the war.

The salon of London's Langham Hotel across from the BBC was crowded with radio broadcast staff taking afternoon tea. Josephine Marlow shoved her trembling hands deeper into the pockets of her greatcoat as the maître d' greeted her.

"Your reservation, Madame?"

"Thank you. I'm meeting someone. Mac McGrath." She looked past him, scanning the opulent room which hummed with conversation punctuated by the clink of tea cups.

At the mention of Mac's name, the expression on the face of the maître d' turned sour.

"Yes," he sniffed. "Mister McGrath. Indeed." Without further conversation, he regally led Josie through a mass of tables peopled by older men in

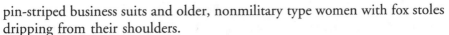

pin-striped business suits and older, nonmilitary type women with fox stoles dripping from their shoulders.

In the far corner of the oval room, Mac was seated at a small table behind a potted palm. The teapot and cups were already in place. He was out of sight of the elegant crowd, but clearly not out of the thoughts of the Langham staff.

Dressed in brown corduroy trousers, a blue tweed jacket and a turtleneck sweater with a comical bow tie, Mac looked decidedly out of place. Josie guessed rightly that he had come without the tie and had been fitted for that requirement with a spare from the Langham cloakroom.

Battling the potted palm, he stood awkwardly at her approach. He had the build and features of a prizefighter, but his usually cocky expression was filled with remorse as he held out her chair and said her name.

"Good to see you, Jo. I mean . . . I'm glad . . . really glad you're . . ."

"It's all right, Mac." She tried to console him with a smile, but she kept her coat on and her hands in her pockets. It would not help his tender conscience if he saw that her hands were trembling.

"Look," he lowered his voice and leaned toward her. "I didn't know you hadn't left or you know I never would've . . ."

"Please, Mac. Nobody's blaming you. And see . . . I'm okay." She took her napkin and shook it out, then laid it on her lap. But she clasped her hands together under the table.

He had to say it. "You told me you were leaving. I telephoned Mike at Warsaw AP. He thought you had gone on the night train. You know? I mean, Mike thought you were out of there before the first bombs dropped. He showed up at the embassy and we all made it out together. Except you. What happened? Where'd you go?"

"It doesn't matter. I just stayed behind." Should she tell him that she had decided to stay over in Warsaw one more day? That she had intended to call him in the morning and tell him she didn't mean any of the things she'd said?

"Well, look." He poured the steaming tea and then picked up his dainty cup in his large square hand. "I want you to know . . . Josie . . . I don't have any hard feelings. I know what I said that night. I was hurt . . . angry . . . I didn't have a right to be, but that's the way it goes. Anyway, I thought about it all the way to the Rumanian border. Nazi planes spitting bullets at us like mad hornets . . . anyway, you're right. This is no kind of life for me to inflict on somebody like you."

"Mac, please don't . . ."

He held up his hand. "No. Lemme finish. You're a wonderful dame . . . girl, I mean . . . beautiful and classy. You deserve something better than what you had. Danny used to say that. In Barcelona, the night before he was

. . . well, that night we got plastered. That was the night he pulled out your picture and told me about you. He said if anything ever happened to him, I should tell you to get hooked up with a banker or an insurance salesman. Anything but another journalist. He was right. But when I met you face to face, I couldn't help wishing that I was a banker instead of what I am." He tugged on the bow tie. "But I'm not . . . and I fell in love with you." His face was pained. "Then when I heard you were still in Warsaw, I just about went crazy. If I hadn't asked you to come . . ."

"I would have been there anyway. I had my own story to write, didn't I?" She did not dare pick up the cup. She was trembling so badly that the contents would have spilled. Josie looked away, trying to think about something besides Danny and Spain and Mac and Warsaw.

"I think you should go home."

"I will. Back to Paris. But I've got an assignment here. The evacuee children. Another month in England, Morris says, and then I can go home to Paris."

"Not Paris. I mean home. Back to the States. Back to teaching English Lit and living a quiet, normal life again. Get out of that getup . . ." He gestured at her uniform.

"I see you're not impressed by the latest style," she laughed. Of course Mac would hate what a uniform did to women. And from the look of his clothes, he would be the last journalist in Europe to visit a tailor.

He ignored her attempt to change the subject. "A girl like you . . . meet some nice guy and have kids."

Josie looked away. She smiled, hoping that he would not see what a knife his words were in her heart. "I've grown accustomed to this getup, as you call it. And Paris is home. And I . . . I'm not interested in meeting a nice ordinary guy and having kids."

"Why not?"

"I was happy with Danny. No one can ever replace that."

He inhaled deeply. Now she had slipped in a knife. "No. I guess not. I hoped maybe . . . For a while I thought maybe I could make you happy like he did." He shrugged.

She wanted to put her hand on his arm, to comfort him somehow, to let him know that maybe with time something might come of what she felt for him. But she would not answer him with hope that she could not find in herself.

"Maybe someday, but it's just too soon, Mac. I told you that."

"Well, we've come full circle, haven't we? I'm talking like a first-class chump. Sitting here pretending to like tea, when I should've met you at the Green Man pub with a pint of Guinness in my fist."

She laughed. "This does seem out of character."

"For me, maybe. But not you. This suits you. You know that. And I didn't mean to bring me into your life again. You were right and honest with me from day one. I know all that now, and I won't bother you about it anymore. I guess that's what I wanted to tell you. That and . . . that I'm glad you made it outta there."

"Me too."

He looked at his watch and tugged the bow tie loose. "Well. That's that. I gotta run. An appointment across the street at the BBC. The censor is looking at my film. They always cut the best stuff. Jack said to see if I can slip the guy a bribe. So. Maybe I'll see you sometime. Who knows, huh?"

He was on his feet, pushing his way out from the palm. Kissing her lightly on the cheek, he strode out of the room and tossed the tie at the maître d' without looking back.

FIFTEEN

The winter twilight dissolved rapidly into complete darkness as the battered Renault rolled down the long hill into the capital of the province of Lorraine. Mac McGrath squinted unhappily through the murky windscreen at the vague shapes in the blackness. His headlamps had been painted over until they were mere slits of feeble light.

One hundred and seventy-five miles east of Mac's permanent lodging at the Ritz Hotel in Paris, the medieval town of Nancy was a maze of crooked houses, twisted lanes, and narrow alleyways which climbed in almost vertical switchbacks. Charming in daylight, the town had become a treacherous place at night since the beginning of the war. As headquarters for the Operational Group consisting of the French Third, Fourth, and Fifth Armies, Nancy took the blackout seriously.

Mac cursed the night, cursed the cold, and cursed the Paris bureaucracy which had delayed his departure just long enough for him to arrive here after sunset.

Assigned by Movietone News to cover the French Army after his return from Poland, he had spent weeks maneuvering his way through the paper minefield of forms and interviews to obtain his permit to enter the forward areas.

Character references sufficient for sainthood had been required. Detectives of the Paris Surete, and officers of the French General Staff knew as much about Robert "Mac" McGrath as his own mother . . . Thirty-one years old. Graduate of USC. B.A. Photo-journalism. Specializing in Cinematography.

His hard-won *cartes d'identité* gave the following facts: 5'11" tall; 182 lbs.; brown hair; brown eyes. Beneath the official stamp his scowling photograph displayed rugged features . . . well, beat-up features, really. A one inch scar above his right eyebrow was the result of a sandlot football game in high school. His nose bent slightly to the left, souvenir of a fistfight.

These were only the most ordinary of details. French authorities now had a thick file that included his grades from grammar school and the precise length of his appendectomy scar.

More to the point: he had escaped the slaughter in Poland in the company of Ambassador Biddle with nothing but the clothes on his back, his DeVry Cine camera, and a rucksack full of film which had brought the war home to 100 million American theatergoers. And now because a rubber-stamp clerk had held him up thirty minutes too long in Paris, he was about to perish in the pitch black of a medieval town having never filmed the Western Front! All that paperwork for nothing!

He dropped the Renault into first gear and crept along the snow-slick lane. The scent of diesel exhaust and the rumble of a truck vibrated from somewhere on the road in front of him. Head and shoulders protruding out the side window, he scanned the blackness and spotted the dim taillights of an army lorry. Provided the lorry was not lost, not German, and headed into Nancy, Mac was in luck.

The truck led him to a shadowed mass which turned out to be the train station. From there he easily remembered his way to the Hôtel Thiers. Just across the square, it still took ten minutes to find the entrance to the hotel garage.

Behind the blackout curtains, the lobby of Hôtel Thiers was surprisingly well lit and comfortably warm after six frigid hours on the road from Paris. A parade of French and British uniforms tramped across the green marble floor while an old Frenchman with mop and bucket mumbled about paw prints and swept away their tracks in unending effort. The old man paused mid-stroke and cast a dubious glance at the American Press Corps patch sewn on the shoulder of Mac's well-worn Burberry's topcoat. With a sharp, suspicious look, the janitor glared at Mac's brown corduroy trousers, the blue turtleneck, the lapel of a grey tweed jacket, and finally the mud on the newcomer's shoes. He waited a moment until Mac stepped to the registration desk before he resumed his task.

Behind Mac through an arched doorway, male laughter and the aroma of garlic and hot bread drifted out of the brasserie. Mac's stomach rumbled. He was as hungry as he was tired. There was no clerk behind the registration counter. A woman's angry voice, engaged in a telephone conversation about the price of butter, shrilled from the back office. Mac rang the bell once and then again, impatiently.

A dark-eyed, heavy, middle-aged woman wearing a black sweater and skirt stepped into the doorframe. Her weary face betrayed disdain for his American Press Corps emblem.

"You are American," she said in the same tone she had used to declare the price of butter immoral and the dairyman a thief. Putting her hands on her broad hips in a defiant gesture she stated flatly, "Americans stay across the street at the Hôtel d'Angleterre, Monsieur."

"That may be. But I've been driving several hours in the blackout. I, myself, ran over three cows and a German saboteur on the road. It's too dangerous for me to walk across the street in the dark, Madame, even to get better hotel accommodations . . . I would like a room with a private bath. If you please?"

"We have private baths for our French patriots on leave from the front, Monsieur."

Mac arched his scarred eyebrow. "Do you have such a room available? Empty? Tonight?"

"Oui, but . . ."

"I'll take it. Since it is available."

She sighed. "Since it is unoccupied tonight . . . It will be ten francs additional."

He knew full well that across the road, the Hôtel d'Angleterre had only shared baths and toilets. American and British newsmen would be lined up in the gloomy hallways to use the facilities at all hours. Some would resort to bathing at three o'clock in the morning to avoid the rush. Others would stop bathing and simply rub themselves with Scotch once a day to kill the germs.

Mac smiled patiently and passed her the ten franc note.

"And when will you be checking out, Monsieur?"

"Noon . . . In a month or two." He knew he would be back and forth to Paris a dozen times between now and then. He did not want to suffer through registration more than once. He would keep the room on a long-term basis.

Pursing her lips, the woman looked at the old man with the mop who had paused to listen to the interesting exchange. With a disgusted shrug, the woman shoved a registry form and a police questionnaire across the walnut counter and then retrieved a room key from a row of pigeonholes. This she tossed onto the register. One last scornful look at the American patch, then in a regal gesture she rang for the hall porter and disappeared into the back office without additional comment.

The upper corridors of Hôtel Thiers were as black as the darkest street in Nancy. Whether this was a plan devised by the thrifty proprietor to save on utility bills or to keep German planes from spotting the Hôtel and blowing it to smithereens, Mac could not tell. Groping toward his room, he imagined that more hotel guests perished by falling over bannisters or tumbling down the stairs than would ever be killed by the Luftwaffe. Heart attacks brought on by the terror of bumping into fellow guests in the pitch black corridor might also be on some casualty list. Over all, the upper story atmosphere of the Thiers was something like the perfect setting for a murder in a Charlie Chan movie.

The black curtain in his chamber was drawn and the light switched on. His room, on the second floor and facing the square, was indeed equipped with toilet, tub, and sink in a tiny alcove which must have been a closet at one time. At least he would not find himself climbing into a bath with a perfect stranger from down the hall during a blackout. True, he would have to step over the toilet to get to the sink, and the tub was designed for one of the Seven Dwarfs, but it was his very own.

Painted pale blue, the sleeping area was small. Very small. Not made for entertaining. Beneath the window was a writing desk with a reading lamp and a straight-backed chair. Hôtel stationery was neatly fanned out on the blotter beside a pen. Against the right wall was a small, narrow bed with a dark blue coverlet and no pillow. Above the bed hung a poorly executed oil painting of the Alps. On the opposite wall towered a monstrous Victorian bird's-eye maple armoire. Along with a veneer of a thousand little maple eyeballs, it had carved ball and claw feet which made the thing look like it might walk out of the room in search of human flesh to devour. Mac would recommend that it dine on the desk clerk as first course.

"Just what I like," Mac muttered, tossing his canvas duffel into the belly of the armoire. "A room with personality." He ran a hand wearily over the coarse stubble on his cheek. "It ain't much, but it's home."

It was not home, certainly. No place was. Sleeping in the back of army lorries or under bridges in the middle of a rainstorm was no kind of life, but it was his living.

Nancy would soon be filled with journalists from New York and Fleet Street and a dozen other newsreel services. Most members of the Press Corps were old friends. Even the newcomers were aware that he had been here from the beginning.

The list of political blunders which had blazed across the screen in thousands of American theaters seemed endless. Terrifying!

He had recorded the landslide toward war with the dedication of a man who believed he had a mission . . . "Just show 'em the facts on film. They'll rise up with one voice and put a stop to this!"

His foolish idealism embarrassed him now.

Yes. Through his lens they had seen the German Luftwaffe in action during the Spanish Civil War. Hadn't Mac filmed the dead civilians in the streets of Barcelona after the bombings? That long, still row of slaughtered Spanish children laid out awkwardly on the sidewalk . . . Hadn't he captured the face of the mother holding her dead son in her arms? Did the audience think her tears weren't real? Did they imagine that the dead child would open his eyes and live again?

America and the free world were plenty informed, and yet knowledge that others suffered had not eased the suffering. Perhaps seeing it right there in black and white, squeezed in between the cartoon and the previews of coming attractions, had only made people numb. Maybe they observed death and tyranny with a detached interest as though it could never reach out and touch their lives with a personal horror.

Just another preview . . .

Spain was a preview of what happened in Poland. Poland was a preview for the show about to open in France. Now nothing could stop the Blitzkrieg from engulfing millions. It was too late.

Death waited patiently for spring just on the other side of the French Maginot Line. And so Mac had come here to wait as well.

He had survived the fall of Poland . . . a sort of personal miracle it had been. Yet tonight he had the sense that everything he saw there was child's play compared to what would inevitably arrive here on the doorstep of Hôtel Thiers.

In the meantime, this would be home. At least until the German offensive began in earnest.

Mac would make himself comfortable in this little room with the private bath until some Stuka divebomber unloaded its cargo on the roof . . . Just like a Stuka had done to the Bristol Hotel in Warsaw. Then Mac D. McGrath would pack up his camera and check out.

Spurs clicked against the floor of the Berlin Gestapo Headquarters as SS-General Reinhard Heydrich sauntered toward the film screening room.

Mousy and innocuous in appearance, Gestapo Chief Heinrich Himmler sat in his wooden rocking chair and cleaned his glasses.

"Heil Hitler, Heydrich." Himmler did not bother to look up as Heydrich entered the Spartan room. "Mein gott, Heydrich, take your spurs off. Do you think you are a cowboy?"

Heydrich sat down hard and raised his legs to imbed the spurs in the arm of Himmler's chair. "What is it you want, Herr Reichsführer?" Heydrich asked in a bored tone. "And this had better be worthwhile! I have plans tonight with a pretty Mädchen destined for great achievements in your breeding program." He tossed his gloves at Himmler. "So you see? This had better be important. I was about to make a significant contribution to Lebensborn tonight. Maybe create another little Reinhard, who knows?"

Himmler stared at him with amusement. Muscular, athletic, and brutish, Reinhard Heydrich was the exact opposite of the soft-looking former schoolmaster who now ran the German secret police. But Heydrich was also the German ideal of manhood.

"It is good to see that you are eager to populate the Fatherland, Heydrich. But here is one thing you may find almost as interesting as copulation."

"Impossible."

At that, Himmler raised his hand and snapped his fingers. Instantly the room was darkened. The ticking of the projector sounded from the projection booth like a time bomb. The silent images of an American newsreel appeared on the screen.

"It is the American Ambassador to Poland. Herr Biddle. He left Warsaw with a caravan of automobiles all stuffed with frightened people . . ." Himmler lightheartedly narrated the scene displaying a coatless Biddle helping to paint USA on the top of a vehicle. The next picture cut to the low approach of a Messerschmidt as it sprayed the road and scattered refugees in every direction.

"Yes?" Heydrich crossed his arms and sighed. "So the Luftwaffe chased the American ambassador. Amusing, but my Fräulein is waiting, Himmler. Will you get to it?"

Himmler held up his finger as if in readiness to make the point. The camera panned over the dust from the road and lingered on the broken bodies of slaughtered refugees. It caught the stunned and terrified expressions on the faces of the survivors, finally moving in on a bizarre figure wearing a gas mask. For just an instant the mask was raised, revealing the taut features of a man.

At this moment Himmler shouted to the unseen projectionist. "Halt!"

The eyes of the frozen image seemed to be staring in horror, directly at Himmler and Heydrich.

"Where did you get this?" Heydrich sat up with a start, his spurs clattering on the floor.

"Can your Fräulein wait now, Heydrich?"

"Richard Lewinski!"

"Quite." Himmler sat back with satisfaction. "Escaped from Poland under the protection of the Americans."

"But . . . his colleagues from the University in Warsaw informed my staff . . ."

"It is well known that men under extreme torture will say anything, make up any lie they think their captors wish to hear. His colleagues in Warsaw knew you wanted Lewinski dead. They said he was killed. It made their deaths quicker. You will have to teach your men more delicate methods of extracting information. It is the hope of life which makes a prisoner tell the truth when pain is inflicted."

"So Lewinski is alive." Heydrich breathed in amazement.

"Last seen in Budapest."

"How did you come by this film? Astounding!"

"The newsreel was shown in every theater in America, my dear Reinhard. Uncensored. Taken by an American newsreel cameraman. A member of our Bund in New York runs a moving picture theater there. He had the bright idea the film might be some use to us. It seemed worthwhile to know who was important enough to catch a ride out of Poland with the American ambassador. Your Lewinski was the only member of Biddle's entourage who remained an enigma, if you will pardon my double-entendre. I recognized him instantly, the first moment I viewed the film."

"He is still in Budapest?"

"We have a number of agents working on it. My guess is that he is back in America by now with his old friend, Albert Einstein. Possibly, as you said, he is no threat to our project. But who can say? I suppose his potential is enough . . . considering his outspoken opposition to the Reich."

Heydrich's mouth was a hard line of determination. "He must be liquidated."

"If he is in America, the matter is easily taken care of with such a brilliant idiot as Lewinski. He will step off a curb and under the wheels of a bus perhaps. Drown in his bathtub. Or perhaps slit his wrists?"

"That is best. Suicide. His wife and daughter died in Warsaw. That much has been verified. He had no other life except for his mathematics. Reason enough to kill himself. We have agents in America capable of carrying out this action?"

"If Lewinski arrives on the doorstep of his American colleagues from Princeton . . . if he wires them or telephones giving his whereabouts, he is a dead man. There are three men . . . American Jews . . . whom Lewinski worked with closely during his student days at Princeton. Each one is being carefully watched. Telephone conversations monitored. Everything that can be done is being done. Lewinski will one day make contact with one of his old American friends and then . . ." Himmler touched his hand to the hilt of his dagger.

"Keep me informed."

"That was my intention." Himmler smiled a tight-lipped smile. "So! Enjoy your evening, Heydrich. My compliments to the Fräulein. Heil Hitler."

SIXTEEN

Today was the visitors' day. Jerome and Marie waited patiently for Uncle Jambonneau beside the arched stone gateway which led to the inner courtyard of Hôtel des Invalidés.

The Invalides was an enormous building which housed the old soldiers of the French Republic. Napoleon himself had walked upon the very cobblestones to review his troops, Uncle Jambonneau had explained. It was a very proud and historical place.

The golden dome of Napoleon's mausoleum shone above the rooftops of the buildings. Last month Jerome and Marie had gone with their Uncle to visit the emperor's burial place. It was a wondrous monument of green and black marble towering up two stories from a huge round polished stone pit. Jerome thought that Napoleon Bonaparte must have been a very large man to need such a big tomb.

The building had been quiet and solemn. Jerome was suitably impressed. Uncle Jambonneau spoke to him about the great Napoleon and how the present honor of France was threatened by Hitler and his Boches, and Jerome had almost wept.

It had been a very good day until Papillon leapt from Uncle Jambonneau's shoulder onto the hat of an English woman. Who could blame a rat for wanting to taste grapes and strawberries? Even Jerome could see that the chapeau looked like a basket of fruit.

Unfortunately, the woman was one of those who did not know that the rat was Uncle Jambonneau's pet dog. Her ill-mannered English husband tried to kill poor Papillon with an umbrella. It was a very noisy and unpleasant scene. After the woman was carried off, Uncle Jambonneau, Marie, Jerome, and Papillon were escorted out and asked never to return. It did not matter. They had seen everything there was to see and a good deal more.

The incident gave Uncle Jambonneau many hours of pleasure as he angrily talked with the other old soldiers in his ward about the stupid and arrogant race known as The English. It was the English, said the old soldiers, who got France into this present war with the Boches.

"Now here we are. We have already made the great sacrifice, but we French must fight and die for England once again. They have no self-respect!"

Jerome could not think how Papillon jumping on the English woman's hat had brought about such prolonged discussion about war with the Nazis, but Uncle Jambonneau seemed extremely lively when it came time for Marie and Jerome to go home. Uncle Jambonneau had not been by to visit them at the *Garlic* since then, perhaps because of the bitterly cold weather. Jerome had missed him and Papillon too.

These once-a-month visits were perhaps the most wonderful thing about des Invalides. On this day the pensioners were allowed to have two guests for the noon meal. Some of the old soldiers had no guest to invite and so Uncle Jambonneau shared Jerome and Marie with them. There were old soldiers who had no legs or perhaps were missing a hand or an arm. All of them had smiles, however, when Jerome and Marie came to visit. This was perhaps the only place in Paris where they were welcome without suspicion.

In the enormous dining room they sat at long tables and ate delicious hot food and all the bread they wanted. Jerome usually stuffed his pockets full of rolls, and they had enough to last for several days after. They were also given free admission to the museums and even the Eiffel Tower. Of course, Uncle Jambonneau could not actually see anything, but he still had a good deal to say about everything. Papa called the monthly occasion with Uncle, "an educational outing." Papa also thought that it was very good that their trip did not cost anything. This was an event which Jerome and Marie never missed.

Last night they bathed in the big copper washtub belowdecks on the *Garlic*. Papa boiled their clothes clean and hung them to dry near the kerosene stove. The thin cotton of Marie's dress dried quickly. The waist of Jerome's trousers was still damp, but he wore them without complaint. He had not wanted to miss even a moment of the day.

But it was Uncle Jambonneau who was late today. Most of the other guests had already been admitted into the courtyard and then led beneath the columned porticos to the reception halls. It was cold out here. Marie was already shivering and soon it would be time for the meal to begin. Where was Uncle Jambonneau?

The uniformed poilu in the small guardhouse looked through his window at Jerome and Marie. He was a new fellow, young, with a pointed face and a thin moustache.

He leaned partially out the door because it was too cold to come out entirely. "What are you urchins waiting for?" He was an unpleasant man, Jerome decided.

"My Uncle Jambonneau is coming. He is a resident here. My sister and I are invited to lunch."

At the mention of lunch the poilu ran his tongue over his teeth and ducked back inside. He opened a tin lunch box and pulled out three kinds of cheeses, a thick sandwich piled with ham and chicken, two oranges, and a bottle of milk.

"I wish Uncle would come soon," Marie said through chattering teeth.

Jerome watched the poilu grasp the sandwich with both hands and maneuver his mouth around the bread and meat. Jerome's stomach was growling. If Uncle Jambonneau did not come soon, they might miss lunch altogether.

The poilu finished off the sandwich and licked mustard from his fingers. He guzzled down the milk. He ate the cheeses and then peeled his oranges one at a time.

Beyond the gate the courtyard was quiet and deserted. No visitors were walking about looking at old cannons or discussing Napoleon or the old wars.

Where was Uncle Jambonneau?

The guard finished his lunch and wiped his hands on a napkin.

Jerome approached the guardhouse. He tapped on the window. The poilu considered him with some irritation, then shouted through the glass. "What is it? Can't you see I am busy?"

Jerome called back. "My uncle is a resident here. My sister and I . . ."

The poilu held up his hand in impatience. He opened the door a crack. Jerome could feel the warmth of the little guard room as heat escaped.

"Now, what do you want?"

"My Uncle Jambonneau is a pensioner here. We were invited to come for the luncheon."

"Well, you have missed that to be sure. They have eaten everything and picked the bones clean by now, little beggar."

"I am no beggar," Jerome flared. "My uncle lives here. My sister and I have been waiting and he has not come for us."

"What am I supposed to do about it?"

"He is a patriot blinded by poison gas in the Great War. Perhaps he has fallen or become lost." Jerome doubted this because little Papillon forever whispered to Uncle Jambonneau which way to go and where he should walk.

"Well," the poilu was humbled a bit by the fact that Uncle was an old soldier and blind. "I will telephone the reception. His name and yours, if you please."

"Corporal Jambonneau Jardin. And I am his nephew, Jerome, and my sister who is shivering there as you see, is Marie."

The poilu nodded and closed the door. With Jerome's wary eye upon him, he telephoned reception and in a muffled voice repeated the names of all parties and the situation. He studied his nails as he waited for reply.

"Oui. I shall tell them." Down went the receiver. The door slid open a crack. "No free lunch today. Your Uncle Jambonneau Jardin is gravely ill. Pneumonia." This, he announced as if he were telling Jerome when the next bus would come. "He is in quarantine. Since you are infants, you will not be allowed to see him. Run along home now and tell whoever might be concerned that the old man may die very soon."

❧   ❧   ❧

"How do I look, Jerome?" Papa adjusted his blue béret in the dim mirror hanging beneath the hatch of the *Stinking Garlic*.

"Well," Jerome scratched his chin in wonder.

"Very well!" Marie piped. She had not witnessed the transformation and so did not know who the stranger was who looked into their mirror. "Now, who are you, Monsieur?"

"Papa," replied the fellow.

He had the voice of Papa, but looked entirely like someone else.

It was an amazing thing to see. Papa was clean. Not only had he washed his hands and face, but he had washed himself all over in the copper washtub. Also he had shaved his scruffy beard until only a pointed black goatee spiked his chin. He had Jerome trim his hair in the back. He smelled like soap and mothballs. The frayed white cuffs of his shirt hung out from the too-short sleeves of his old blue suit and there was a gap between the hem of his trousers and the tops of his shoes. All the same, it had been a long time since Jerome and Marie had seen Papa looking so good. Perhaps it had even been since the funeral of Mama. A very long time indeed.

"Now they will let you in to visit Uncle Jambonneau." Jerome said positively. "They will not even suspect you could be the same fellow."

Marie, perched on a stack of coiled rope, concurred. "You can tell the poilu at the gate that you are the other brother of Uncle Jamboneau."

"Jambonneau has no other brother than myself." Papa said sternly.

"But you do not look the same as that brother." Marie studied the face of her father. She could hardly see any resemblance to Papa. "Monsieur, you look entirely different from our other Papa who is Uncle Jambonneau's other brother. I suppose it will not make any difference to Uncle Jambonneau who you do not look like, since he is blind."

"But Marie! Uncle Jambonneau has only one brother! We have only one Papa," Jerome declared in exasperation.

"Oui, Jerome!" she replied in a haughty tone. "I have eyes to see that. There he is . . . the monsieur . . . only one person. But all the same, I shall miss the other Papa now that he is gone. He was very good, even though he smelled badly and beat us some times."

Jerome and Papa frowned down at her. Papa put his hand to his cheek and sighed. "She is too young to remember me, Jerome. It has been a long time since she has seen me as I was, I suppose." He knelt beside Marie and smiled into her face. "I will tell you a story which will help you understand that I am he." He looked upward as though the story was written on the cargo hatch. "When your papa was a boy on the farm he had a pig. He was a very dirty pig. Covered in mud from head to foot. Before we took him to market, Papa's father washed the creature. The skin of the pig was white underneath all the mud and suddenly your papa did not recognize him because he was clean. But, voila! It was the same pig! Soooooo." Papa dipped his head slowly. He held up his hands in a gesture which indicated that the story was finished.

"Oui," Marie thought it over, "So?"

"So, ma chérie! Think of it! I, myself, even I . . . am that pig!"

Marie pivoted slowly on the rope coil and eyed Papa with grave suspicion. "If you say so, Monsieur."

Papa smiled with satisfaction, clapped his hands once, and rose to his feet. "There. Take a lesson, Jerome. Speak plainly and you will not fail in your meaning."

SEVENTEEN

It had taken weeks for Josephine to track down the London residence of the mother and sisters of the Polish count. Alexander Riznow was the major who had spirited Josie away on the last night of the Warsaw siege.

She had made the young officer a promise to seek out his family, but it seemed to Josephine that perhaps the countess did not want to be found. Josie had made several inquiries at Whitehall asking the whereabouts of Polish Countess Riznow and had been questioned and gaped at as though she were a spy.

At last, at the suggestion of Alma, Josie put an ad in *The Times.*
"Seeking Countess Riznow. Son sends love.
Please reply. Confidential. The Times. Box 240."
After two days the reply arrived on monogrammed, watermarked, heavy bond stationery. The countess and her two teenaged daughters had taken up residence in a small flat not far from Sloane Square, at Number 3, Flat G, Cadogan Gardens. The note gave no telephone number, but offered an invitation for tea on Thursday afternoon.

It was raining when Josie stepped out of the Sloane Square tube station. She was twenty minutes early, so she wandered past the windows of Peter Jones Department Store before entering the tangled streets in search of the flat.

Cadogan Gardens was a lovely Victorian neighborhood; stately red brick houses topped with steep slate roofs and a forest of chimney pots.

Number 3, near the corner, overlooked the leafless trees of the communal gardens. The Riznow residence was on the third floor of the building and the lift was no longer running because of some war regulation.

Josie shook the rain from her umbrella in the lobby and pushed the buzzer to flat G.

Moments later, even as she raised her hand to knock on the door, it swung open. A young woman of about eighteen with red, puffy eyes greeted her in halting English.

"I speak French," Josie replied, knowing that most of the Polish aristocracy used French as their primary language. Then she introduced herself as the woman who had placed the ad in *The Times*.

The girl seemed relieved. She stepped aside and escorted Josie into a pale, cream-colored sitting room warmed by a small coal fire. Three banks of rain-streaked windows looked out at neighboring rooftops. Draperies were pulled back to let in the light, and yet the atmosphere was gloomy.

"Mother," said the girl cautiously, "this is Madame Marlow. She placed the ad. About Alexander."

A silver-haired woman wearing a long black dress of bygone elegance, the Countess Riznow sat beside the window. Looking out at the world with infinite weariness, she pivoted her head slightly, as though she was only vaguely aware of Josie's presence. She extended her hand in a regal gesture.

"How-do-you do?" Her English was much better than that of her daughter. "Won't you please sit down, Madame Marlow? We have no servants these days. But Danielle will serve us tea."

Josie took a seat, feeling awkward and not entirely welcome. "I have been trying to reach you, Countess. I have been back in London for several weeks."

The woman nodded one slow signal of acknowledgment, as if this meeting was a perfunctory duty.

Josie continued. "Your son, Alexander, gave me your London address, but the Nazis took it from me when I left Warsaw."

"Of course." She waved her hand and the daughter retreated into the kitchen.

"He was quite well when I saw him last." Josie tried to sound cheerful and enthusiastic. Could she penetrate the spell of despondency which permeated the little room?

"He was well." This was not a question but a flat unemotional comment, as if the memory was her own. "Alexander . . . *was well* . . ."

"Yes. I was at the Cathedral of St. John during the siege. He came to take me out on the last night before the surrender. He asked that I bring a message to you in London. He wanted me to tell you that he loves you all and that he is well."

"Is that all?"

"There was no time for anything else, Countess. Except . . ." She bit her lip and looked down at the toes of her black military pumps. "Your son is a wonderfully brave young man. He . . . and the others who held Warsaw . . . well, I cannot say enough. I was there, and they were extraordinary.

They held the city to the last bullet, Madame. I know that God will not desert such men as your son. He will survive. I just know it."

For the first time the Countess Riznow turned her face toward Josie. Her eyes were full of sorrow and some embarrassment. "Madame. It is kind of you to come. But . . . I cannot let you continue. My son . . . my courageous Alexander, is dead."

Josie blinked dumbly at her. In the kitchen the teakettle came to a hissing boil. She heard the muffled sobs of the woman's daughter. "I . . . I don't know what to say. I am sorry."

"You meant well to come. But have you not heard? They killed them all. All the professors. Doctors. They cleaned out every hospital of the sick and wounded. Then all the officers. All the aristocracy. Entirely, Madame."

"How can you be sure?" Josie asked in a horrified whisper.

"A friend, Jan Franciszkanska, escaped death with a bullet through his arm. My son stood beside him in a ditch as they faced execution. It happened quickly. The men waited. The SS fired machine guns. Alexander's body fell on Jan. He lay there beneath the corpses until the SS left. All night he waited. Then . . . he crawled out. He escaped from Poland." She shrugged. "I can be sure, Madame. My son is dead. My homeland is dead. But I thank you for coming all the same."

Throughout the days that followed the return of Horst von Bockman from Warsaw, the face of the murdered Polish woman haunted his thoughts.

Quartered at Berlin's esteemed Adlon Hotel with two dozen other junior officers who had distinguished themselves in battle, Horst had kept mostly to himself. This morning after breakfast, he pulled fellow officer Putzi Dietrich aside. Putzi had been a childhood friend. They had gone through Cadet School together and now shared the same rank, commanding different companies. If any man would understand the disillusionment Horst felt, his old friend would.

The two men walked slowly beneath the leafless canopy of trees in the Tiergarten. Horst began to tell Putzi about the three crucified Jews in the village and then about the young Polish woman at the river.

"Enough." Putzi held up his hand to silence Horst. "I do not want to hear this and you do not want to talk about it. Not to anyone, Horst. You understand? The war is over for us in Poland. We fought honorably and won. What happens beyond that is none of our business. We have careers to think about. Families." He leveled a chilling gaze at Horst as if the very mention of doubts was somehow treasonable. "You heard it. General Stumme has sent in commendations for us. That is why we are called to the Chancellory. Does that mean nothing to you? Do you want to risk all that because some overzealous SS shot a woman? It is not our business, Horst. Compassion has always been your weakness. You are too soft. This time compassion is misplaced, even dangerous. Hatred is a soldier's medicine. It makes us live; it inspires vengeance! Pity the enemy and you betray Germany."

This was the sensible response, Horst knew. He thanked Putzi as if this counsel had somehow relieved his conscience. But the words of his friend were no comfort.

This afternoon Horst stood ill at ease among the twenty-four newly promoted majors in the entrance hall of the Reich's Chancellory. Expensive carpets adorned the dark marble floor, and fourteenth-century tapestries showing hunting scenes hung on the walls.

The entrance hall was the only room in the Chancellory in which smoking was permitted, which made it the most popular room in the building for diplomats and government officials to congregate. But since Horst did not smoke, it was small comfort to him. At any rate, he was doing at least as good a job controlling his nerves as the other Panzergruppen commanders; they were smoking furiously.

The newly promoted officers being sent to join General von Rundstedt's Army Group A had been summoned to Berlin to meet the Führer personally before being given leave and then being dispatched to their respective assignments.

The Commander in Chief of the western front, General von Rundstedt, strode into the entrance hall from the curtained doorway to the diplomatic reception salon. Flashbulbs from a half-dozen cameras popped as the young men snapped to attention and then followed von Rundstedt through the salon into the chancellor's private living room.

On a dark leather sofa sat Joseph Goebbels, Minister of Propaganda, and high ranking Nazi leader Martin Bormann. A dozen other exalted officials of the Reich stood around the room. Among them was SS General Reinhard Heydrich, who spoke in low tones to fat Hermann Goering about the art of fencing. Horst looked quickly away from the SS General, in hopes that Heydrich would not remember their encounter on the road to Warsaw. Heydrich and Goering ignored the arrival of the majors, who waited in uncomfortable silence marked by the deep-voiced ticking of the clock over the Renaissance coat-of-arms on the fireplace.

Horst was perspiring as the door leading to the private rooms of Adolf Hitler opened. The Führer entered. All conversation stopped. Goebbels and Bormann stood to acknowledge Hitler's arrival. General von Rundstedt and the others saluted crisply. Accompanied by the probing lens of the photographer, the general presented each of the majors in turn.

Beads of sweat formed on Horst's forehead as Hitler walked slowly down the line toward him. Like a proud father, the Führer spoke to each man as Heydrich recited deeds of valor. But Horst heard neither the accolades nor the response of the German leader. Voices became inaudible beneath the pounding of Horst's heartbeat in his ears. The collar of his uniform felt as though it would strangle him. He stared ahead, catching the form of Hitler approaching down the line. Then Reinhard Heydrich stepped directly into Horst's vision. Heydrich cocked an eyebrow and smiled a tight-lipped, secretive smile. He silently mouthed the words, *Congratulations, Major von Bockman.* Horst swallowed hard and blinked back the sweat trickling into his eyes. So Heydrich remembered their meeting; remembered Horst's protests.

"Allow me to present . . . Major Horst von Bockman, Führer," offered von Rundstedt. "Distinguished himself several times in the early days of the battle . . ."

Hitler scrutinized Horst. He nodded and smiled at the recital of the young major's accomplishments. Yet when he smiled, cold eyes seemed to peer deep into the doubts and dread of Horst's most secret thoughts. Hitler patted him on the shoulder. "Relax, Major. Surely you did not tremble like this when you faced the enemy." He laughed and everyone in the room laughed with him.

Horst managed a feeble smile. "No, Führer."

"Well, then. We can trust that you will continue to do your duty for the Fatherland."

"Yes . . . Führer."

And so the personal attention ended. All that remained was to put the final touches on an event which would be published in the propaganda sheets.

Hitler stepped back by the fireplace to address them all. The flames behind him, he began to speak. "I have summoned you here to impress upon you the importance of the mission with which you are charged. You are soon going west to redress the unspeakable injustices inflicted upon the German people by the Versailles Treaty. Each of you has demonstrated in the recent Polish campaign that you have grasped the requirements of modern warfare: speed and unrelenting attack! We must not get bogged down in a war of attrition. When we strike, strike hard! You tank commanders and others of Panzerkorps Hoth, Reinhardt, and Guderian will be in the forefront of the Lightning War. We will not only even out an old score; we will teach the world a lesson about battle that it has never seen before."

Von Rundstedt thanked Hitler on behalf of the group for receiving them and for the benefit of his insight. "Perhaps, Führer, you would like to command a Panzer Division yourself."

"If only it could be," Hitler agreed without a trace of doubt about his ability to act in such a capacity. "Unfortunately I must remain where I can command a view of the larger picture of the war. But know this," he addressed the Panzer officers. "I will be following your progress with great interest. You are the future generals of our thousand-year Reich. One day you will tell your protégés of this meeting. And since you are soon to face the French, may I recommend that you study the best work on the use of motorized units in modern warfare?"

"That would be the work by General Guderian?" inquired von Rundstedt.

"No," Hitler corrected the general with an impatient wave of his hand. "It is written by a French colonel . . . his name is DeGaulle. Know your enemy well and you will defeat him." He turned back to the young majors. "Have any of you studied this book?"

Horst timidly raised his hand as did Putzi Dietrich and two others who had been students under Erwin Rommel. The work of the Frenchman evidenced his genius, but Horst was also aware that it had been largely ignored in France. Less than five hundred copies had been sold. Fifty of these had gone to cadets trained by Rommel in Germany.

"Then you shall continue to lead the pack," Hitler finished. "Now, I have a speech to prepare for my reunion with the Old Fighters in Munich. If you will excuse me." Chased by resounding Heils, he stepped from the room. Only then did Horst draw his handkerchief and mop his brow.

"Well, you survived meeting God face-to-face," Putzi Dietrich said.

Reinhard Heydrich stood just behind Putzi. "Major von Bockman is a survivor, I think. Aren't you, Major von Bockman?"

"Obergruppenführer Heydrich," Horst stammered. "It is good to meet you again."

"A little pleasanter surroundings than last time, eh, von Bockman?" he laughed. "Although it is always pleasant to do one's duty for one's country, is it not? One can sleep soundly at night knowing that duty is first. It is everything."

Putzi went pale. No doubt he was wishing he had not heard Horst's story about the SS action in the Polish village.

"Yes, Herr General," Horst agreed, although the nearness of Heydrich made him feel ill.

"I kept my promise to you," Heydrich smiled coldly. "I did not forget. You interest me, Herr Major Bockman. A man of such tender conscience and yet such courage. An odd mix for a soldier. Better suited for a priest perhaps." He laughed. "But then you are not interested in living the priestly life of celibacy. You are married I understand. Yes. A lovely woman. Tell me, does she share your enthusiasm to duty? Or only your tender conscience?"

Question followed question without a break for Horst to reply, and when Heydrich had asked enough about Katrina, he left Horst with the certainty that every answer would be found. And every answer had better agree with Reinhard Heydrich's concept of duty to the Fatherland.

EIGHTEEN

Georg Elser looked up and down the alleyway behind Munich's Bürger-bräukeller, exactly as he had each night for the past month. Seeing no one, he placed the carefully filed and oiled key into the lock on the delivery entrance door and slipped through into the dark interior. Elser had made the journey through the storerooms to the stairs so many times that he needed no help from the flashlight for him to find the way.

At the sound of a low growl, Elser stopped for a moment and fumbled in his coat pocket. "Here, Ajax. Good boy," he called softly. The noise of the watchdog's warning rumble changed to the thump of a friendly wag as the German shepherd recognized Elser's voice. A moment later, Ajax was happily munching a sausage, and Elser was taking the steps to the gallery two at a time.

The faint glow coming through the high windows in the beer hall's assembly room lighted the row of turned posts along the low railing of the balcony. Just ahead, in the center of the balustrade, loomed the brick pillar that supported both the gallery and the roof.

Now Elser switched on his flashlight. Its lens covered with a blue handkerchief, the faint glow seemed no more than an errant beam of moonlight in the echoing hall. Using his pocketknife, Elser pried free a strip of molding and then snapped open a cleverly disguised panel in the back of the column.

The pale glow of the flashlight probed into the hollow of the supposedly solid pillar as Elser bent forward to examine his handiwork. The onetime watchmaker traced the wires leading from the batteries to the alarm clocks and from the clocks to the dull gleam of the brass artillery shell into which Elser had stuffed fifty pounds of high explosive.

He read the numerals on the faces of both the primary and the backup clocks and compared the position of the hands to his wristwatch. "Running a touch fast," he murmured to himself. He did a brief mental calculation, then breathed a sigh of relief. "It is all right," he whispered. "By nine tomorrow night it will only be fifteen minutes ahead . . . perhaps that is even better."

Satisfied that all was in order, Elser carefully closed the secret panel and replaced the molding. On a sudden impulse he bent forward again and placed his ear next to the pillar. The faint ticking that reached his hearing was softer than the beat of his own excited pulse.

❈   ❈   ❈

The Sixteenth Reunion of the Old Fighters of Hitler's Brown Shirts promised to be a raucous affair. In the company of his comrades from the beer hall Putsch of 1923, the mighty Führer could relax, swap stories, and reminisce about the good old days. No foreign dignitaries to impress, no disapproving generals glowering around, nothing but pure adoration from the cadre of Hitler's earliest supporters.

Of course in November 1939, nothing was without political overtones, and each public appearance had its propaganda value. This night, Hitler's address to his old cronies would also be broadcast to the Reich and the rest of the world.

The beer hall, crammed to capacity, was saturated with a thick blue haze of cigar smoke and puddles of beer. The Old Fighters knew how to celebrate, and several foaming steins of lager had already sluiced down the throats of the party faithful before Chancellor Hitler made his appearance.

When at eight o'clock Hitler's booted step entered the room, all the chairs scraped hurriedly back and a disorderly forest of tan sleeves popped up in ragged salute. His entry, twenty minutes earlier than expected, caught the audience by surprise. The band on the stage hastily blared out the Horst Wessel song while everyone remained standing at attention. The Führer crossed the hall to the lectern just below the balcony, which was also packed with eager spectators.

Taking his place directly in front of the Nazi banner that hung from a massive brick pillar, Hitler approached the bank of microphones and began to speak. He recalled for the crowd those memorable days before the Nazi party had come to power, and he extolled the patience and faithfulness of the Old Fighters. Soon, many of them had tears rolling down their cheeks.

He had their full attention when he started to recite the list of German grievances against the Western democracies: "The German people have been injured, shamefully wronged. No redress has been offered to our suffering, no correction made of injustice. The British and French attack our unity of pride and purpose in the name of freedom. What hypocrisy! Where is the fairness in that odious document called the Versailles Treaty? Where is the freedom for the German people to fulfill our destiny?"

He paused to let the magnitude of the injustice sink in. "England and France bear a heavy burden for provoking Poland into attacking us . . . let them pay close attention to the consequences!"

A roar of approval went up from the crowd, and five minutes of *Sieg Heil!* laden with smoke and beery breath rocked the chandeliers. Even the Führer seemed overcome with the response, for he began to wrap up his talk after only fifty-five minutes instead of the customary hour and a half.

His cherished comrades-in-arms begged him to stay and drink with them, reliving more of the old days, but he would not be persuaded. By ten minutes after nine, the last salute had been offered and the last Hail to Victory shouted to the rafters. Chancellor Hitler, much to the disappointment of the Old Fighters, was in his armor-plated Mercedes and returning to the Munich train station.

Elaine Snow entered the lobby of the Insel Hotel on the German side of Lake Constance at 8:30 P.M. Hers was a simple assignment. Glued beneath the binding of a volume of Goethe was a Swiss passport for the man Georg Elser. She had been forewarned that Elser was a strange little man. The photograph on his forged passport showed a dark-haired, glowering face. He was missing his little finger on his left hand if she needed any other way to identify him. He would recognize her by the red cape and matching béret she wore. They were to meet here as if they were old friends. She would do most of the talking, as usual. The fugitives were nearly always too nervous to eat or converse with her, so she kept up a running dialogue about her daughter Juliette and their home in Luxembourg. It was like one long conversation which had stretched on for three years. If all her clients were somehow miraculously gathered together in the same room, they could each recite some small part of the history of Elaine's daughter from the age of two. After enjoying dinner and her own monologue in the converted cloister of the old Dominican monastery, Elaine would give Georg Elser the book with his passport sealed inside. She would bid him good night and then cross back over the frontier to Switzerland. From there the fellow was on his own. It was likely she would never see him again.

A train ride back to Luxembourg City and Elaine would be home by tomorrow night. It was that simple. She had done the same thing a hundred times in the last three years, always allowing German and Austrian Jews to escape to the neutrality of Switzerland with new identities.

Tall and fair, she had the look of purest Aryan breeding. The guards on both sides of the border liked to see her coming. Long ago she had offered the explanation for her frequent visits to Constance. "I have family there." No one guessed that her "family" included anyone on the run from the Nazis. Nor could they imagine that Elaine Snow was a Jewess born in the French province of Alsace just before Kaiser Wilhelm started the last war with France. Her grandfathers and two uncles had been killed in that struggle. When Hitler came to power, Elaine decided any enemy of the Nazis was a friend of hers. Her present occupation of courier paid quite well, but she liked to think that her motives were based more on conscience than money.

The work had become more difficult since the invasion of Poland and the declaration of war. This afternoon, Friedrich, the elderly German border guard who regularly stamped her passport at the crossing, warned her that soon the Gestapo would send a man to look over his shoulder. He was not happy with the intrusion. Life had been pleasant for him so far. He might ask to be transferred to the regular army if the secret police became regular fixtures at the little outpost he had manned for twenty-two years.

Perhaps the border guard did not know that the entire shoreline of Lake Constance was already crawling with General Reinhard Heydrich's brutal watchmen. The neutral Swiss side was just as contaminated as the German side.

Elaine sipped her wine and smiled toward the table where two men in dark suits ate their Sauerbraten without speaking to one another. Gestapo. Clearly. She could tell by the way they cast sideways glances at her. Sour-faced swine who had learned their uncouth table manners in a beer hall in Munich.

The radio played in the lobby. The growling voice of Herr Hitler penetrated the pleasant atmosphere of the Cloister Restaurant as der Führer vomited his hatred for the West at the annual gathering of the Old Fighters. Hitler's broadcasts were required fare these days on the German side of the border. Everyone had to listen, or at least pretend to be interested. Elaine raised her head as though every word was dear to her. When he reached the end, she nodded in approval at the resounding Heils.

The Führer had finished his anniversary tirade early this year, the announcer said. He was leaving the Munich Beer Hall well before schedule. Elaine was certain that this was a grave disappointment to the party faithful, but she was relieved to have the music of Bach replace the sounds of the reunion. She could enjoy her poached salmon in peace as soon as the absent Georg Elser appeared.

Twenty minutes later the waiter poured her another glass of wine and asked if she would still like to wait before ordering.

"He will be here," she replied pleasantly. "He is always late. I will order for both of us. I have a train to catch at ten." She ordered trout for Elser and salmon for herself, then sipped her wine as the radio concert was abruptly interrupted by a trembling voice.

"Just moments ago, as our beloved Führer drove away from the Bürger-bräukeller in Munich, a terrible explosion rocked the hall where hundreds were gathered to honor him. The toll of dead and wounded is unknown. Guarded by fate, the Führer is totally unharmed by the blast which was obviously designed to take his life! More news will be forthcoming. Heil Hitler!"

The Gestapo agents sat up in alarm. They whispered frantically to one another across the table. The shorter, more Neanderthal looking of the duo stood suddenly and, digging in his pocket for change, scurried off to find a telephone.

Elaine crooked her finger at the waiter.

"My friend is obviously delayed. I will eat without him. I have a train to catch," she explained again.

At her words, the ears of the remaining Gestapo agent perked up. Elaine sighed heavily. It was plain that this abortive attempt to kill the German leader was going to make her work as courier more difficult. Tonight the Bahnhof would be overrun with official slime, tearing out the lining of every coat and slitting open tubes of toothpaste to check for diamonds and secret messages. No one would escape the scrutiny. Perhaps if Hitler had died in the blast, she might consider the outcome worth the inconvenience. But at best, a few dozen Nazi drunks lay smashed in the rubble and Hitler was free to pursue his vengeance. Now Elaine would have to endure a strip search by some hairy-lipped Nazi matron. Most unpleasant.

She ate her salmon. The bearnaise sauce, which had been excellent before everything wonderful had been rationed in Germany, was mediocre.

The ape-like Gestapo agent came back to the table but did not sit down. He leaned over his companion and spoke in hushed, urgent tones. Then he turned toward Elaine and swaggered to her table.

"May I join you, Fräulein Snow?"

The salmon made a knot in her stomach. So here it was. So soon? She was not even trying to cross the frontier into Switzerland.

"It seems that you know my name, but I do not know yours."

"Allow me," he smiled. His teeth were stained with tobacco. "Herr Wachter."

"I am expecting a friend, Herr Wachter."

"Yes?" He sat down, not heeding her polite protest.

"He has been delayed."

"We have heard." He was toying with her now. Had he learned the information from the Cloister waiter, or was there something else? He reached a small, square hand out and placed it on the red leather cover of Goethe. "You enjoy fine literature I see."

"Herr Wachter, really." She blotted her mouth with the linen napkin and placed it beside the plate of unfinished salmon. "If my friend should see me here with another man . . ."

"Ah, but he will not, Fräulein Snow." He held the book up and flipped through the pages.

Her heart pounded faster. She tried to swallow, but could not. Where was Elser? What had happened to him?

"I have a train to catch."

"I do not think so, Fräulein. Not a train out of Germany, at any rate." Picking up a butter knife, he pried up the corner of the endpaper.

The room swam around Elaine. She feigned indignation. "What are you doing? A friend asked me to give the book to Herr Elser. What are you . . ."

"To Herr Georg Elser, Fräulein Snow?"

"Georg. Yes. The book is a gift from . . ."

The battered Swiss passport fell onto the table. "Well, well. Just where Herr Elser said it would be, Fräulein Snow." He narrowed his eyes and considered her with amusement. "We picked him up a few minutes ago at the Bahnhof. Frightened little fellow. He had a few clock gears in his pocket and a postcard of the beer hall in Munich which has just blown up. Naturally we were alerted to be on the lookout for anyone attempting to cross the frontier tonight."

"I do not know what you're talking about." She stood and tossed a few bills on the table to cover the cost of her meal. Now every head in the dining room pivoted toward her. The second agent approached, and with crossed arms, blocked any retreat.

"We have been watching you for some time. Hoping you would lead us to a trail of traitors. How long have you been at your work? A Jew, are you not?"

"I am a citizen of Luxembourg. I protest this arrogant . . ."

"You are in the Reich, now, Fräulein. It is best you come quietly," he whispered. "You are under arrest, I fear. There is a train waiting . . . to take us all back to Munich."

NINETEEN

The week-long Paris rain finally stopped. A thin glaze of ice coated the bare branches of the trees which lined the River Seine. Mist floated up from the water, shrouding the two islands in the river which formed the oldest part of the city of Paris.

Ile de la Cité, crowned with Notre Dame Cathedral and the crenelated towers of government buildings, resembled a great ship moored by bridges between the Left and Right banks of the Seine. Ile St. Louis, a quiet, residential island populated by wealthy Parisians, seemed like a smaller ship tethered behind Notre Dame. The two islands were linked together by the bridge known as Pont St. Louis. And together, the islands, known simply as the Cité and l'Ile, linked the distant past to the present.

At Number 19 Quai d'Anjou was a large four-story stone house on Ile St. Louis facing the Right Bank of Paris. First built in 1658 for the mistress of a bishop, it had in later years housed a succession of generals, poets, and the American statesman Benjamin Franklin. In 1849, the house became the Paris residence of a prosperous wine merchant named Chardon.

This afternoon, ninety years later, his great-great-grandson, Colonel Andre Chardon, looked out from the window of the study. A carload of policemen were just driving away, having returned Andre's houseguest. Andre turned to regard the thin figure of Richard Lewinski seated on a settee near the fire.

The pale man with the explosion of red hair was hunched over, playing with his loop of string. He looked like a woodpecker plucking at a stolen bit of twine. The gas mask, which he had been wearing while walking along Boulevard St. Michel, lay beside him on the couch.

At least Lewinski had been able to remember Andre's name when the gendarme stopped him for questioning. The police had returned Lewinski to the house on Quai d'Anjou, where Andre convinced them that the eccentric mathematician really did suffer from allergies and wore the mask against the fumes of Paris automobiles, not for some sinister purpose.

"Richard, you must wait for me if you want to leave the house," Andre requested, "or I will have my driver take you. You must think of your own safety."

Lewinski looked up from the complicated eight-sided figure he had just constructed from the string. "Safety, Andre? You have always made me feel safe here in Paris. You know that. Why, back in our days at the Sorbonne you . . ."

Andre interrupted the reminiscence. "That is what I am trying to say, Richard. I will see that you are protected, if you will not wander off."

From the halfhearted nod which was Lewinski's only reply, Andre knew that his message had not gotten through. He sighed heavily. What a responsibility, and all because Lewinski had specifically asked for Andre when he approached the French Embassy in Poland to request asylum.

Andre was still musing about his friendship with the gifted engineer when the housekeeper announced that Colonel Gustave Bertrand had arrived. Minutes later, Andre and his friend were with Colonel Bertrand in Lewinski's basement apartment.

A large wooden cabinet, open at the top and front, perched on a worktable. Trailing colored wires and black electrical cords and exhibiting shiny metal disks and a handcrank, the device looked like someone had set off a bomb in an organ grinder's instrument.

"The work goes well?" Bertrand inquired. "It progresses?"

Lewinski gave no sign that he had heard the question. An uncomfortable silence stretched into several minutes, finally punctuated by a piercing cackle from the scientist. "It is five! I knew they would not stop with three or four! Two more wheels gives them almost twelve million combinations instead of only eighteen thousand! Can you imagine?"

"Does this mean that your work is progressing?" Bertrand demanded. "Yes or no?"

"What? Oh, yes, yes, definitely advancing." Lewinski dismissed the inquiry with a flutter of his hand and was instantly engrossed again in his study of a fistful of wires.

"How does this thing work, anyway?" asked Bertrand, stretching out his hand toward the cabinet.

Lewinski glanced up from weaving his tangled filaments. "I would not touch that, if I were you," he said. "Curiosity killed the cat."

"Is he kidding?" Bertrand asked.

Andre could only shrug in reply. "We do not want to upset him," he said. The two men retreated toward the stairs, leaving Lewinski to continue

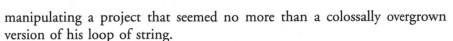

manipulating a project that seemed no more than a colossally overgrown version of his loop of string.

"Are you certain that he is a gifted scientist, as well as a crazy one?" Bertrand asked Andre.

"Bear in mind that SS General Heydrich wants Richard dead. Hopes he is dead. Richard was employed at the highest level of the factory that built the Enigma code machines for the Wehrmacht. That should tell us something about the value he had in Germany. If Heydrich knew Richard was here . . ."

"Wandering around Paris . . . lost . . ."

"No matter how it appears, Richard Lewinski is the best mind in the world at what he does," Andre soothed. "Remember, he worked at Princeton with Einstein."

"That does nothing to reassure me," replied Bertrand. "Have you ever tried to make sense of Professor Einstein's writings? But enough of this, Andre. I have another reason for coming to see you today. It is necessary for you to go to England."

"England? But how, Gustave? I can't leave Lewinski alone for more than an hour without him wandering off. Why just today . . ."

"I know all about it. I will supply some men to watch the house around the clock. If he gets out, they will follow and return him safely."

"Richard cannot work under scrutiny. He is like a child. He says his best ideas come when he's riding the Ferris wheel at the Tuilleries. You cannot put a guard around a mind like that. Richard will not have it. You will have to call my brother Paul."

"Will not have it?"

"He cannot be made to feel like a prisoner. We were children together. His father and mine taught at the Sorbonne."

"Right." Betrand wiped perspiration from his brow.

"What is so important in England?" Andre changed the subject as they entered the study.

"You know that British Intelligence is also working on Enigma. Colonel Menzies of MI 6 wishes to hear about our friend's progress and will share what they have. If your mad scientist produces the miracle we are hoping for, we will be able to read all the German transmittals . . . every battle plan from their High Command, every Luftwaffe deployment, every U-boat directive . . . but we must know how the machine has been modified."

"And the British?"

"They have two machines and are trying to reason out the modifications by taking those devices apart. They want to confer about it."

"They always do."

Bertrand cleared his throat nervously. "And there is something else, Andre . . . Sit down."

Andre obeyed, settling into a padded leather chair opposite Bertrand. "What is it, Bertrand? Am I being demoted?" He tried to joke, but something was terribly wrong.

"No." Bertrand patted his pockets, looking for a smoke. "I know it has been a long time since you and Elaine . . ."

"Elaine Snow?"

Bertrand nodded, then bit his lip as he searched for the words to tell him. "She has been arrested."

"Elaine?"

"Gestapo. In Constance, German side of the frontier. It was nothing, really. She was acting as courier. Taking a passport to a German. Well, the Gestapo caught up with her. Accused her of being part of the Munich Beer Hall plot."

"Ridiculous. She would not harm a fly."

"Hitler is no fly."

"What happened? What was she sent in to do?"

"It was a passport. Just like a thousand others, more or less."

"We've got to approach them. Pay a ransom."

"And if we do so?"

"Maybe there is some chance."

"She confessed."

"Confessed!" Andre bellowed. "What did they do to her?"

"If we approach the Nazis in this instance, all of France will be implicated. Herr Hitler has a keen interest in the case. He wants her shot. His ego needs to believe that there was a conspiracy. She has the perfect background he is looking to blame: a French Jewess. You see how it is."

Andre could hardly breathe. "You are telling me she is going to be executed? Just like that? She has . . . a child."

"Yes. We are aware. I am sorry. But there is nothing to be done. I wanted to tell you myself."

Andre covered his face with his hands. "Now you have done your duty. Leave me to mine. Go away, Bertrand. Just go away."

❧ ❧ ❧

From his window on the second floor, Paul Chardon looked out across the athletic fields and the stables behind the École de Cavalerie. It was not a very distinguished view, such as the commandant's office provided of the formal cobblestoned square at the front. Paul's panorama was less of the tradition and ceremony of the school and more of the boyishness of the students.

Just now, for instance, there was a wholehearted game of capture the flag in progress. A mound of horse manure, covered with a purifying blanket of snow, represented the besieged fort. The object of the struggle was an improvised flag made of toweling on which had been painted a blue cross of Lorraine. One team, marked by scraps of someone's blue shirt in their back pockets, defended the hillock against the red contingent.

The leader of the blue squad, seventeen-year-old Gaston, with his wrestler's build and personality, had sensibly deployed his troops in concentric rings around the base of the hill. Each of the three guarding circles had four piles of snowballs so that a supply of ammunition was within easy reach.

Opposing him as chief of the reds was a fellow cadet captain who was growing a scruffy beard to make himself look older: Gaston's best friend, Sepp. The forces belonging to Sepp launched their assault en masse across the open field against the south face of the embankment, ignoring the other sides of the hill.

From Paul's vantage point, it seemed that Gaston's defenders had a two to one numerical advantage. Why was Sepp's red team so small? He opened the window in order to hear as well as see.

There were yells of bravado and shouts of disappointment. Three of the reds went down, pelted by a quantity of snowballs from the higher elevation, but then Sepp's advance broke through the lowest line of Gaston's defense and killed three blues by ripping off their cloth pieces.

Commander Gaston, seeing his front threatened, called for the unoccupied defenders to shift around to the south side of the heap to help drive off the enemy. Paul noticed that Sepp did not press home his attack, content to stay at the extreme edge of the range and keep the blue team busy.

In another minute, Paul saw the full development of Sepp's strategy. From behind a tangled thicket of wagons and farm equipment furthest from the mound came a rush of the remaining reds. Led by good-natured Raymond, speediest and at sixteen, youngest of the cadet captains, the wave of new attackers were halfway up the hill before Gaston had seen the danger.

A furious battle ensued. The blues, caught between two foes, had to fight on twin fronts at once. Gaston bellowed for courage, for not giving ground, but his troops were forced backwards. Tangled with each other and unable to retrieve their supply of snowballs lower on the hill, they fell to well placed shots and the speed of the assault.

Raymond sprinted past the last ring of defenders, seized the flag and scampered back down the hill and out of reach of the angry Gaston. The game broke up into a free-for-all, in which everyone threw snow missiles at everyone else. Gaston wore himself out chasing a grinning Raymond, who taunted him with the flag, always staying just yards ahead.

❧ ❧ ❧

The oak-panelled and high-ceilinged mess hall bore numerous mounted racks of antlers, making it resemble an ancient hunting lodge. Paul Chardon gathered the cadet captains around him at the dinner table. "What did you learn from the game this afternoon?"

The three boys looked at each other. "Were we supposed to learn something?" Gaston blurted. "We thought it was just for fun."

"True," Paul nodded, "but it may be that even play contains valuable lessons. Sepp?"

"I suppose that I learned that strategy is as important as force," he said. "Gaston expected my attack across the most level ground where the approach was the easiest. He saw what he expected to see, which is why the surprise worked."

"Raymond?"

The smiling young cadet captain chose his words carefully so as not to offend his older and easily angered friend. "Even though we had to dodge around obstacles and started from further away, our speed made up for the advantages of the hill's defenses."

"Gaston?"

The young man with the pale green eyes and the fighter's crooked nose replied grudgingly. "I learned that a good defense is not enough if the enemy catches you off guard," he said.

Paul motioned for the boys to stack their dinner plates. When a space had been cleared on the table, he unrolled a map of northern France that showed the location of the school on the River Lys, the Belgian border, and part of the frontier with Germany. "Let us look for a little broader application of today's struggle. Here is the Maginot Line," he said, pointing to the well known ramparts that lined France's eastern boundary. "Here are the flat lands of Belgium. All right, Gaston, you are the German commander. Where do you attack?"

Gaston studied the chart. "I cannot risk a frontal assault on the Maginot, so I launch west against Belgium, ignoring their neutrality, of course, then swing south toward France."

"And what will be France's response to that thrust?"

"Move all forces into Belgium from this side."

"Does everyone agree with both statements?" Paul asked.

Sepp frowned and leaned forward over the center of the diagram. "What about this area here?" he said. "Between where the Maginot fortifications stop and the plains of Brussels?"

"The Ardennes forest?" Gaston argued. "Any force moving through there could not be significant. Everyone knows it is impassable to heavy equipment."

The discussion was interrupted by the arrival of a messenger with a telegram for Paul. "Excuse me, gentlemen," he said, opening the envelope. The argument continued over whether an attack through the Ardennes could be similar to the surprise movement in the game. "I must excuse myself," Paul said, apologizing. The cadet captains rose when he did and stood at attention. "I am called to Paris on military business and must leave at once."

"I bet he is being promoted and placed on active duty with a cavalry division," Raymond said.

Gaston looked unhappy. "They cannot do that to us," he said. "We will end up with some old geezer again like that retired colonel we had before Captain Chardon."

Sepp clapped his friend on the back. "You may have to put up with it, Gaston. Can it be that you are the only one who has not noticed: Captain Chardon wants active duty more than anything else in the world."

❊   ❊   ❊

It was generally agreed by the Fleet Street crowd that Josephine Marlow, widow of good ol' Danny, had left for Warsaw an unopinionated lamb and had returned a lioness. She had been, in the political sense, "Born Again." To the seasoned journalists in London, this change was infinitely irritating: little Josie spouting off like Winston Churchill just when American isolationism was at a fever pitch. Even the English were wondering if going to war over Poland was such a good idea after all.

The Great Debate between the young widow and Konrad Lock, of the Hearst syndicate, took place after the failed assassination of der Führer in Munich. The bombing aroused as much interest as *Gone With the Wind*. Everyone in Europe was discussing it. The arrest of French entertainer Elaine Snow, as a conspirator, made headlines. This afternoon the whole thing was rehashed by a troop of correspondents gathered for a very long lunch in the Savoy Grill. There was nothing else newsworthy happening, so why not eat and talk?

Starry-eyed with hope, Josephine started, "They'll get Hitler sooner or later. Even the German people secretly despise him."

Konrad puffed up in disagreement. "They adore him. He's another Caesar to the Deutschlanders."

"Then why try to kill him?" Josie insisted. "They know what he stands for. They're basically decent people."

Konrad considered her with a cynical twinkle in his eye. "You've forgotten Crystal Night already, my dear?"

There was nothing to say to that. She passed the baton to Ernest Ward of the *New Yorker*. He accepted, but ran the opposite direction from Josie's opinion. "They love the beast all right. He's built a bankrupt, starving, pitiful democracy into a thriving nationalistic dictatorship. The trains run on time. They've scraped the bums off the streets; wiped out the loonies; euthanized the sick, and turned the asylums into maternity wards for pregnant SS bimbos reproducing little Master Race replicas. What are a few Jews compared to that? What is principle compared to that?"

Josie sat forward and raised her chin in indignation. "But this Elser man . . . the bomb."

Konrad shrugged. "One little psychopath who likes to blow things up. That's all. The Germans love their Führer. They are as convinced that they are the Master Race as we Americans are convinced that we are one nation under God. In God we trust."

"Well, isn't it true?" Josie shot back. "We fought the last war for democracy, for freedom, for an ideal."

A number of looks shot around the table mixed with polite chuckles and a few groans.

Konrad, clearly Pope and chief apostle of the Doctrine of Cynicism, corrected her.

"We fought the last war because the Germans sank our ships and because we insisted on freedom of the seas. We fought the last war to protect our investments. This gag about making the world safe for democracy and God is propaganda which American politicians use to draw in the hillbillies who could care less about freedom of the seas or investment. Like the crusaders, those guys in the trenches needed some moral reason to leave home and die. And their mothers needed some noble cause to help ease the pain when the telegram came from the War Department."

"That is the ugliest thing I have ever heard," Josie said rather self-righteously. "Young men are not sent to die for other people's money! Everything we believe in; everything that is true and decent and honorable! That's why we were in the last one and why we must come into this one as well!"

Konrad was sure of himself. He continued as if she had not uttered a word. "The democracy thing is a terrible ruse; full of holes. You really think America can deliver God and democracy to the rest of the world? They don't really want either unless there is some economic benefit. They want their Hitler and their Mussolini and their Stalin and now Franco in Spain. As long as the trains run on time and there's a chicken in every pot, then people can just as easily take ideals, moral righteousness, and God or leave them."

This friendly discussion quickly disintegrated to outrage for Josie Marlow. She glared back at Konrad. "You're dead wrong. I was there, you know. I saw the faces of the Polish people. Watched them at the barricades. Heard their prayers. Prayed with them for deliverance."

"And were their prayers answered?" Konrad smiled smugly.

"Not yet. But it isn't over, is it? God will answer for the right. The Allies have gone to war over Poland."

"Leave God out of this for a minute. Poor God gets tangled up in the middle of all sorts of quarrels—blamed for everything. Now ask yourself. Do you think anyone cares about Poland, Josephine? This is not about Poland. It's about those idiots Chamberlain and Daladier finally drawing a line in the sand so that the entire economic wealth of Europe does not end up in the hands of Hitler."

"And the people? What about them?"

"The Jews you mean," he laughed. "As if anybody cared about the Jews of Europe. I mean, cared enough to do more than just talk, talk, talk, about them. Poor Jews. Not even the Poles like their Jews. England shut down immigration into Palestine. The Brits are still tossing illegal Jewish immigrants into concentration camps, both in the Middle East and here in England. Go down to Kent and have a look for yourself, if you don't believe me. They're behind wire down there, refugees from Nazi Europe. And good old America has closed the flood gates, slam-bang. All Roosevelt cares about is getting elected for a third term. America will get into this thing as soon as her economic interest is seriously threatened, not until, not for the sake of the downtrodden, certainly. There is no God but mammon in America. That is what the slogan means on our bills: In Money We Trust; For Money We Fight; For Money We Bury Our Sons. If God is interested at all, I don't believe human motives fit anywhere into His agenda."

So there it was. Konrad won the bout with a knockout. Josephine, who thought she had all the answers, backed into her corner. She listened politely to the rest of the conversation, which covered everything from the rifling of American mail by the British authorities to the lousy media censors.

Was Konrad right?

She was shaken by the logic of his arguments. She felt the whispers at her back as she left the Savoy. She saw the nudges and the winks, and she was embarrassed by her idealism. Was she foolish to hope that somewhere in the horror of war God still existed, still reached out, still changed the course of human events for the sake of righteousness and the value of human life?

She walked out into the grey afternoon and thought about the young Count Riznow. She flushed again at the trite optimism she had expressed to his grieving mother:

Surely God will spare such a brave young man!

Obviously God had not. Alexander Riznow had died . . . for what? And the others? All the young Germans on the Siegfried Line and the Frenchmen on the Maginot? Both sides declaring that God was with them.

Gott mit uns! Perhaps it was, as Konrad claimed, just a jolt of propaganda to ease the pain of dying.

TWENTY

It was snowing again. Horst drove carefully along the low ridge which led to the gravel drive of Arabian Nights Stud Farm. The snow covered pastures lay empty, an unbroken expanse of pristine white. The rail fences which in warmer months separated yearlings from weanlings and weanlings from brood mares were nearly buried.

In such a winter, Horst knew, Katrina would be exercising the horses every day in the shelter of the small indoor arena and lunging them in the round pen.

Like the horses she bred and trained, she hated the gloomy winter months in Northern Germany. Her father was purest Prussian, as hard and unyielding as a block of ice. But her mother was Italian and had passed on to Katrina the hot temperament and love of the Mediterranean climate. Often Katrina blamed her excessive love of Arabian horses on her Italian heritage. Horst had come to agree with Katrina that her personality did indeed match most of the characteristics which marked the best of that breed: fine boned, delicate features, intelligent eyes, a passionate disposition, and seemingly inexhaustible energy. And a love of warm climate.

Smoke rose from the chimneys at either end of the stone stables which joined the domed riding arena. Horst followed the recent tracks of a large double-axeled truck which was backed up to the arena doors.

No use driving past the barns and stables to the enormous Georgian style red-brick mansion which crowned a low hill overlooking the farm. Katrina would, no doubt, be with the horses.

He parked beside the canvas-covered truck. It bore the insignia of a Wehrmacht troop lorry except that the benches had been removed and horse manure covered the empty floor. A scarred wooden ramp leading from the truck into the dark interior of the stable evidenced that horses were either going or coming today.

Horst almost regretted that he had not warned Katrina of his arrival. She was in the middle of something. Now here he was, hoping she would be ecstatic about his surprise return.

The sound of unhappy neighing issued from the far end of the building. He strode in, grateful for the sudden warmth and the sweet familiar scents of hay and horses. Rows of alert Arabians looked out at him from behind heavy wooden stall doors. Small pert ears twitched expectantly and every equine face turned toward him. Placards bearing the names of Greek gods, ancient heros, and constellations hung above each stall, but Horst knew their names without the aid. Othello, black as a crow's wing, gave a familiar nicker as he passed. Venus, dapple-grey and elegant, pawed the floor and wagged her head impatiently as he walked on without stopping. Prometheus, muscled and impatient, stretched out his long neck to be touched.

Much was familiar, yet much had changed since last August.

He walked past what had been the tack room. Where were the saddles and bridles? A bed and a small chest of drawers filled the space. A heavy blue woolen coat hung from a hook which had previously held lunge lines.

From the upstairs quarters which had been the residence of two stableboys, the laughter of small children penetrated the planks. Children? The stable hands were unmarried adolescents. Perhaps the sounds were from the cook's grandchildren, he speculated, as delighted squeals followed him through the tall double doors into the arena.

Within the oval enclosure, twenty mud-caked, unkempt Arabian horses milled about in restless apprehension. Katrina, at the opposite end of the arena, studied the animals over the fence. Horst remained in the shadowed doorframe, watching her as she pulled herself up to sit on the rail. She wore a black jacket over tan riding breeches and tall black boots. Her expression showed some displeasure at the condition of the horses. Behind her, in deep shadows, stood a white-haired old man, a tall thin young man, and a mousy young woman about Katrina's age. All three appeared to be exhausted. The trio stood silent and grim as an SS lieutenant gestured toward the animals and spoke in low, insistent tones to Katrina. One quarter of the way around the arena were Hans and Adam, the two stableboys. A dark-eyed girl of about seventeen stood between them.

"Excellent brood mares . . ." said the officer. "General Goering is most anxious . . ."

Katrina did not reply for a long moment. "When I saw these mares in Poland last summer they were . . ." she turned her head and her words were lost to Horst but he could tell she was angry. "Now . . . just . . . prisoners of war . . . tell Herr General he shall have my bank draft, and that I will need to keep Herr Brezinski and his son and daughter-in-law in my employment to help get the animals back into condition."

At this the stooped old man looked down at the ground. Only in that instant did Horst recognize Walther Brezinski, the head trainer of Poland's finest Arabians. He was also a Jew. Brezinski had aged almost beyond recognition since his country was overrun.

"The General . . . not authorized . . . this Jew . . . Brezinski was only to assist with the mares until delivery."

"I cannot purchase the animals unless Herr Brezinski and his family members remain part of the agreement. You can see my stables are full. There are three mares in foal. The Reich has drafted my best help, including my veterinarian. I have all the stock I can manage now. The deal my father struck with General Goering was the horses *and* Brezinski . . . or nothing. The armaments industry of the Fatherland has six hundred thousand Polish war prisoners now at work in factories on German soil. Surely the Fatherland can spare me three in the interest of maintaining the most elite breeding program in the world. Either that or risk the production of Arabian horses inferior to those bred in prewar Poland."

Horst crossed his arms and leaned against the doorframe to wait until the scene was played out. *Bravo, Katrina.* If these SS imbeciles were obsessed with anything, it was breeding programs.

"Frau von Bockman . . . I have not the authority . . ."

"Then you had better telephone the general. I understand he is ten miles away at Karin Hall. He will not be pleased if you, by your own authority, violate his word of honor . . . the word given to my father in this transaction. The telephone is in the office." She snapped her fingers and called a stableboy to guide the officer to the telephone. "Adam!"

The boy sprinted to the side of the lieutenant and led him into the office as Katrina remained perched on the railing. There was silence except for the snorting of horses and the scuff of hooves against the turf. Brezinski did not speak or move. Horst dared not disrupt Katrina's resolve by suddenly appearing on the scene. She was doing well without him. She was strong and savvy. Hiding her long friendship with Walther Brezinski, his son Jan, and daughter-in-law Nadia, she pretended her only interest was in the welfare of the horses. Prove to a Nazi that a Jew was essential to the well-being of the mares, and then perhaps the Jew had some value. Nazis prided themselves in their love of animals, after all.

A few minutes passed. The officer emerged from the office. "Reichsführer Goering concurs that Herr Brezinski and his assistants remain in your service. He makes you personally responsible for their custody, however. He wishes to receive the bank draft at once."

"What else?" Katrina replied in a steely voice. Then to Brezinski she snapped an order. "All right. Get the mares groomed and fed while I attend to business. You will be quartered in the barn."

This seemed to please the SS lieutenant.

Walther Brezinski, who had often sipped tea with Katrina and Horst on the veranda of his fine estate in Poland, nodded silently without looking his savior in the eye.

Horst retreated back into the stables. He was scratching the soft muzzle of Othello when the SS lieutenant strolled past him alone. The man cast a startled look at Horst, who greeted him with an enthusiastic Heil! The SS lieutenant left without further conversation. Horst walked back toward the arena and this time stood beneath the flood light.

Brezinski wept as he led a sorrel mare from the small herd. Speaking to the animal in French, he called her "Ma chérie," and promised her she would not have to endure any further abuse since coming to the estate of his dear friends.

Katrina spoke quietly to Jan and Nadia, gesturing toward the horses and smiling with great relief. Nadia glanced up, spotting Horst at the far end of the arena. At her first sight of the uniform, her smile faded and she went pale.

"Do not be afraid, Nadia. It is only I," Horst called as he took off his peaked cap.

Katrina whirled around at the sound of his voice. With a little cry, she ran to him, calling his name.

"Oh, my darling!" She threw herself into his arms. "You are here! Oh, Horst! You would not believe . . . cannot imagine . . . what it has been like since you have been gone!"

❊   ❊   ❊

The quiet elegance of Arabian Nights Stud Farm was disturbed by the shouts of children playing in the snow. Horst was disturbed by the presence of so many strangers at his home. Katrina explained that they were children evacuated from Berlin, but Horst had not been aware that the panic about possible air raids had touched Germany as it had England and France. He watched them pelt one another with snowballs and then, at the call of a chaperone, run to their supper which was served each night in the stables.

He was glad when darkness fell and Katrina called up to announce that his dinner guests had arrived.

The oval dining room was large enough to comfortably seat fifty guests, but tonight the table was set for four. A white linen cloth trimmed in Battenburg lace covered the long table. Century-old Meissen china gleamed on sterling silver chargers, flanked by the Sheffield tableware which Katrina purchased on their honeymoon in England. Finger bowls and wine and water goblets glistened in the candle light.

For all this refinement, the dinner to celebrate Horst's safe return was simple German home cooking, just as Horst requested. The menu included roast pork with potatoes, spaetzel noodles, applesauce made with apples from their own orchard, and imported French burgundy wine.

Instead of a big celebration with little known acquaintances and party functionaries, Horst had insisted that they only invite Katrina's sister and brother-in-law.

"Kurt and Gretchen Hulse are company enough. Let us just be glad to be together without having to perform," he said wearily.

The war, and the fact that both men would soon be leaving again to rejoin their units, lurked on the fringes of conversation. Thus the atmosphere was pleasant yet restrained.

Horst stood and raised his glass in a toast to Kurt, who served as a reconnaissance pilot. "To my friend Kurt, the eyes of the Wehrmacht. And to the greater glory of Germany. May you continue to fight with honor and courage, and return from your service to our Fatherland in safety."

Suddenly, the atmosphere in the formal dining room of the Arabian Nights Stud Farm had more in common with the icicles hanging like bayonets outside of the picture window than with fairy tales and happy endings.

Standing beside his chair with his upraised glass, Horst felt as if he had accidentally spoken in some unknown language. Katrina, Gretchen, and Kurt remained seated, staring at him.

Katrina spoke up, trying to deflect what she saw coming. "Let us drink to your safe return, Horst, yours and Kurt's, and to your continued protection."

But no one raised a glass.

"What is it?" Horst sat down slowly. "Has something happened?"

"That is right, Horst," Kurt said. "You need to be sitting down for this." He glanced at Katrina. "It is no good, Katrina. We had better get this out in the open. The only three people I completely trust in the whole world are in this room, and I need to talk."

Kurt was dressed in civilian clothes, even though he was a military observation flier. In contrast, Horst was wearing his full uniform with his newly attached major's insignia. Horst had believed that being home, returning to a hero's welcome, and the congratulations for his promotion would revitalize his eagerness for the fight. Now, he wasn't so sure.

"I saw combat only from the altitude of my Henschel recon plane, but I saw enough! It wasn't what I expected, not the heroic defense of the Fatherland that I enlisted for," Kurt continued.

Visions of what he himself had seen in Poland flooded over Horst, but he could not let such a remark go unchallenged. War was never pretty, but Wehrmacht officers were expected to brace up, were they not? What kind of talk was this?

"Come now, Kurt! I know what you are saying, my friend. I too have been troubled in my thoughts. But to talk openly before the women will only make us sound like weaklings, or worse, cowards. Look at it this way: the overwhelming power of our forces meant that the war got over sooner. Probably lives were saved by the speedy conclusion."

Kurt's voice fell almost to a whisper. "It seems you have been reading Joseph Goebbel's propaganda, Horst. The King of Lies. But the truth is that war in Poland was quick, but not painless. The agony continues and grows each day for the conquered. Even propaganda cannot excuse murder."

Horst tried to shrug off Kurt's serious mood. "War is no pleasure cruise on the Rhine."

"I am not speaking of war. I am speaking of murder."

"Then perhaps you should not speak at all." Horst became suddenly irritated.

"Since when have we been afraid of the truth?" Kurt gave a bitter laugh. "I can answer that myself. Since Hitler became Chancellor."

"This is not the place," Horst flared.

"Where are you?" Kurt leaned forward and searched the face of his friend. "Horst von Bockman is . . . was . . . a man of honor. Do you want to be associated with murdering innocent women and children?"

Gretchen laid her hand on her husband's arm. She was an older reflection of Katrina, but quieter and more reserved. "Please, Kurt," she begged. "We cannot say such things to the ones we care about."

"This is important," Kurt argued.

"I agree," Horst replied. "To know the true feelings of those who are next to you in battle is essential. How could anyone trust you to come through for them, knowing that your sense of duty is halfhearted, to say the least. Duty has nothing to do with politics."

"Oh, yes, hide behind your precious belief in duty," Kurt said scornfully. "Hitler knows exactly what he is doing with his blood oaths and his voodoo ceremonies. You talk just like one of them!"

"One of whom?" Horst said coldly.

"You know what I mean . . . the SS! Ignorant, savage, murdering brutes, who hide behind their oaths of duty and loyalty when they commit acts of terror like a pack of wild dogs!"

Horst and Kurt rose from their chairs. They glared at one another across the table. Horst clenched and unclenched his fists as if ready to jump at Kurt's throat.

"Please, please," Katrina pleaded. "Sit down, both of you. Kurt, I am sure you did not mean to compare Horst to those horrible monsters, did you?"

Kurt ran his hands through his dark, slicked-back hair and fell heavily into his chair. "No . . . I . . . no. I am sorry, Horst. It is just that . . . I flew over too many Polish villages where the SS had been."

"And?" prompted Horst, though he already knew the answer. It was as if everything he had kept bottled up inside was now spilling from Kurt.

"You are right. Enough of this. I have ruined a perfectly fine evening. A man cannot weep for the entire world. Even Poland is too big. In days like these he must choose carefully who and what he may shed tears for. It is too dangerous to do otherwise."

Horst unbuttoned his tunic's top button in order to breathe better. He felt choked, so he reached for his wine glass, knocking it over. Red fluid splashed across the white tablecloth and drips of it spattered on Katrina's white blouse.

The discussion could not end yet. "It should not have happened," Horst managed to get out. "But it will be different in the West. It will be a real war, man to man, against an enemy that is ready for us. What is a man if he does not honor his oath, Kurt? Think of that."

Kurt raised his gaze from the slowly congealing gravy on his plate. "And what is a country that does not keep its promises, Horst? Do you think that all the pledges and guarantees and assurances coming out of the Chancellory will keep our tanks from rolling over Belgium and Holland? Neutrals, Horst! Neutrals! Innocent people who believe that not taking sides will keep them safe! Do you really believe Hitler will keep his sacred word of honor, Horst? Does anyone believe it anymore?"

"What will you do then?" Horst demanded. "Refuse to serve? Leave Gretchen at the mercy of the Gestapo while you rot in prison?"

"No," Kurt said quietly. "I am sending her out of the country, to Switzer-land first." Kurt glanced sharply at Katrina. "You have not told him your mother and father are not coming back from Switzerland?"

Horst sat back, stunned. To Katrina he stammered, "Not coming back?"

She nodded but did not look at him. "It is better. Father has friends . . . people who know. The Gestapo has a thick file on father. It was a matter of time."

Horst blinked at her in amazement and then turned his inquiry back to Kurt. "And what about you?"

"I mean to join them in Switzerland, if I can. But there is something I have to do first . . . I and a friend . . . we mean to convince Belgium that they are not at all neutral in the Führer's future plans."

"But how could you?"

"I fly over Belgium every day, Horst."

"That is not what I mean. I mean . . ." Horst tapped his finger to his heart. "This! To betray your country, your honor."

"I lost my country long ago. I seek to preserve my honor now," Kurt replied simply. "Even if my dearest friend should report me. I had to tell you, Horst. We will not likely meet again soon. I had hoped you would understand."

There was nothing more to say. Horst could not betray Kurt for his disloyalty because to do so would also condemn Gretchen. But by remaining silent after hearing such treason, he was himself condemned, and Katrina along with him. And as these thoughts were spinning around in his head, he was staring at the drop of wine on Katrina's blouse, so like a bullet wound, just over her heart.

❊ ❊ ❊

The moment that Captain Paul Chardon reached Paris, he went immediately to headquarters. He was told that Commander-in-Chief Gamelin wished for him to attend a dinner being given at the Hôtel Edouard VII on the right bank.

Paul was excited. The only reason he would be summoned to attend a soiree for the High Command was if he was about to be promoted and given an active duty assignment. Finally, it seemed, all those letters he had written about strategic concerns had come to the attention of someone important.

The chiefs of the Grand Armée had taken over the finest restaurant in Paris for their gathering. The Delmonico, located in the hotel at Number 39 Avenue de l'Opéra, was world famous for its oysters, caviar, and canard a l'orange.

When Paul arrived, the group had already collected for aperitifs. He immediately spotted the towering figure of Colonel DeGaulle, easily recognized because he was the tallest figure in the room. Paul joined the group surrounding DeGaulle and discovered that it included General Gamelin, and Gamelin's aide, Colonel Pucelle.

DeGaulle was expounding his theory of modern armored warfare. "It is absolutely essential," he said, "that armored forces operate as independent units capable of getting the most out of their firepower."

"But surely, Colonel DeGaulle," said Pucelle, "you realize that tanks and other armored vehicles are most effective when they screen the advance of the infantry. If they were to be concentrated into separate sections, they could not be used for scouting and for forward protection of the poilus."

DeGaulle snorted. "Just because we call tanks the cavalry does not mean they can be used like horses," he said. "The Germans . . ."

Pucelle drew himself up to look DeGaulle square in the chest. In a haughty voice he said, "You would quote the Boche in opposition to the views of your own commander-in-chief?"

DeGaulle bent his head and stared down his great beak of a nose at Pucelle. "I meant no disrespect to General Gamelin," he said, bowing to the general. "My sole motive is to insure that the Grand Armée remains the most modern and respected fighting force in the world."

"And following the guidance of the leaders who won the Great War will not accomplish this?"

Paul could see that DeGaulle was without support amongst the officers who were listening. Gamelin's protégé, Pucelle, was doing all the talking, but the aging commander-in-chief nodded his agreement.

DeGaulle had overstepped the bounds of protocol by writing a book criticizing all French army training and organization. But for all his arrogance, Paul believed that the big man was correct. "Excuse me," he said. "I concur with Colonel DeGaulle. The role for tanks in modern warfare has changed since they were used as mobile fortresses in 1918."

Pucelle gave him an icy stare. "And who are you, Captain?"

"Captain Paul Chardon, Chief Instructor at the École de Cavalerie in Lys. I was advised to come here to receive orders from the commander-in-chief."

"Yes, Captain. I am familiar with those orders," Pucelle said, drawing Paul aside and away from the higher-ranking officers. "Your brother, Colonel Chardon, is called away from Paris. You are needed to . . . I do not know exactly, but Colonel Bertrand of Military Intelligence asked for you to stay at your family home for the time your brother will be gone. You may go now, Captain."

Paul felt stricken. "That is all? Nothing further?"

"There was not time to put it in writing before this dinner, which is why I sent for you to come here. Good evening, Captain."

Paul saluted smartly, biting his lower lip. He bowed to General Gamelin and Colonel DeGaulle and left the restaurant feeling bitter.

Gamelin watched Paul's exit, then called Pucelle for a private word. "Make certain," he said, "that young Chardon never receives an active duty assignment. We do not want to give radical ideas like DeGaulle's any further support. Keep that captain back with the horses where he belongs."

"Exactly my thinking, General," Pucelle agreed.

TWENTY-ONE

Monsieur Pierre Mazur was not a religious Jew. He had been an active political campaigner back in the days when the French Socialists like Leon Blum were in power.

How quickly the flower fades!

In France, various popular political dogmas went in and out of fashion about as frequently as the Ritz arcade changed the dresses on their mannequins in the shop windows.

Mazur was definitely out of fashion. He turned his attentions to other matters.

He was a Zionist. He seemed about as Jewish in looks, belief, and habit as bacon on a bagel. The rabbis did not approve of him, and yet when the Jewish Quarter was close to bursting at the seams from newly arriving refugees, they grudgingly agreed to work with him.

The Jewish orphanages, both religious and nonreligious, were dangerously overcrowded. Soup kitchens fed many more thousands than could be properly cared for. Occasionally the French became irritated and threatened to burn down a synagogue or shoot a Jew for old times' sake. In those moments a man like Monsieur Mazur became an important intermediary between the religious Jews and the nonreligious Jews—between all the Jews and the hostile French population.

Today, in the Beth-el Children's Soup Kitchen, there was great upheaval. A conflict brewed between the religious children and the nonreligious group of five Viennese Goldblatt brothers who had just arrived via Warsaw and Bucharest.

It was obvious to all the religious males that the children from Vienna were more Austrian than Jewish, no matter what their surnames might be. They looked Austrian. They spoke with rolling German tongues and had arrived in Paris dressed in lederhosen and knee socks.

In the middle of lunch, which was strictly kosher, one seven-year-old

Goldblatt expressed too loudly that what he really missed and wanted more than anything was his mother's bratwurst, sauerkraut, bread and butter, and a tall glass of milk. Did they ever serve such things in this soup kitchen, he wanted to know?

One thing led to another from the religious side of the table. Phrases like "ham-eating goy" grew violently to insults like "pig-kissing Nazi."

A food fight ensued. The kosher soup kitchen was devastated. The non-religious culprits, who should never have been brought there in the first place, were deposited in the Zionist Office of Welfare.

Thus they came to the attention of Monsieur Mazur. They stood, covered in dried lentil stew, waiting for some more suitable place to be found for them, someplace where eating bratwurst and drinking milk at the same meal was not a transgression against the Eternal and an affront to fellow Jews.

Monsieur Mazur spent a long time on the telephone. Who in the Jewish neighborhood had even one square inch of space left for five little boys?

No one. No room at the inn, it seemed. The door of hospitality for these wild Deutsch-cluckers was unequivocally closed once word got around that they had done battle against fellow Jews with all the fierceness of miniature Wehrmacht troops. Spoons and tin plates had banged little Jewish heads. Not even the rabbinical students in attendance had been spared the indignity of black coats splattered with food.

"What am I going to do with you?" Mazur glared at them.

The five brothers were without remorse. They glared back. Mazur thought what very good pioneers they would be in Palestine. What wonderful soldiers they would make against the Nazis if only they were older.

Their papers were stamped with the large *J* for Jew. They were among those who had left Austria just in time. They had been sent to temporary safety in Warsaw and then managed to escape that siege as well. From Poland they journeyed to Rumania. Why had they been sent to Paris?

Mazur asked the question. They shrugged. "Where are we supposed to be?" replied the eldest, who was eleven and already bitter against life.

Mazur leaned his cheek upon his hand. He stared at the documents which allowed temporary residence in Paris for these stateless persons. His brain ached. He could not send them to the Catholics. Boys like this would turn the Catholics upside down, or die trying. Such a move would be bad politics; sending Jewish delinquents to the priests.

Who was strong enough to handle such a force? And yet softhearted enough to see the deep wounds in the soul of each boy?

A light came on in Mazur's mind. He held his finger up in mental exclamation.

"The American sisters! Madame Rose and Madame Betsy!"

He grinned as five sets of eyes narrowed in doubt.

Mazur picked up the telephone and dialed. He spoke to the defiant ones as the telephone of Rose and Betsy Smith buzzed.

"Madame Rose is an interesting woman. She has arms like a Titan. Once I saw her capture a thief who was attempting to steal the Mona Lisa at the Louvre. She tossed him to the ground and sat on him until he turned blue. I believe he died. In the 1924 Olympics she threw the shot put. After that she boxed a Russian bear in the circus for a living. She does not like boys, but perhaps she will accept you so you will not starve."

❊   ❊   ❊

Uncle Jambonneau was very ill indeed. He was so ill that Papa brought Papillon, the white rat, home in a box and gave him to Jerome to care for.

"It is Uncle Jambonneau's last request that you take care of his dog. Of course if Uncle Jambonneau does not die he says you will have to give Papillon back to him."

Jerome accepted the solemn responsibility. Now Papillon perched on his left shoulder and tickled Jerome's ear with his whiskers. Jerome could not understand one word that Papillon spoke to him, however. All the same, the dog which was a rat made very pleasant company for a small boy.

Marie got used to the new Papa, even though she often spoke wistfully about the old one. This Papa was very solemn and he was not often drunk and jolly. He combed his hair and stared into the mirror for long periods of time as though he was looking at someone he did not know. He reminded Marie of the self-portrait of the artist named Rembrandt, who Uncle Jambonneau said had cut off his ear and given it to a lady. When Marie pointed this out to Jerome, Jerome said that Papa did not look anything like Rembrandt. Rembrandt had red hair and his skin was yellow and green. Papa had black hair, white skin, and two ears. Marie replied that Jerome just did not know what part of Papa she was looking at.

After each visit to the hospital ward of Uncle Jambonneau, Papa came home and talked about things which he had never mentioned before.

"Do you know that your uncle, my brother, has very good care at des Invalides? And it is free."

Jerome and Marie had known this for a long time. They missed their free lunch visits.

And Papa would continue, "Did you know that when a French soldier is killed in battle, his wife and orphans also receive a pension?"

Jerome and Marie did not know that.

"So," Papa said, as Uncle Jambonneau grew stronger, "a French poilu receives fifty centimes a day. And there they sit. Warm clothes, new boots, socks, hot food, and grog every day. And what do they do for it, I ask you?"

Jerome thought about Uncle Jambonneau and his burned eyes and all the old soldiers without arms and legs and other missing body parts. "A poilu is a soldier, Papa. Soldiers go to war and get hurt and killed."

Papa wagged his finger in disagreement. "That is only when the war is real, Jerome. I have two ears, you know."

Jerome nodded and then gave Marie a look to remind her how foolish she had been to compare Papa with the crazy painter Rembrandt. "Yes, Papa. Marie and I have noticed your ears."

"These ears have heard some very interesting things about the funny war, Jerome. They say at des Invalides that there will not be a war. No one is killing anyone at the front. A very boring affair as wars go. Perhaps very soon everyone who is mobilized will be called down and then it will be over." He looked at his image in the mirror. "It will be over and everyone else will get pensions. Everyone else will come back wearing new boots and warm coats. When they are old and sick like Uncle Jambonneau, they will live in luxury at des Invalides and get free cigarettes and wine and food every day while I am here on the *Stinking Garlic* trying to catch a bottom sucking fish for my dinner."

Papa looked very sad at that thought. Jerome had never heard Papa speak so rudely about the fish he caught for dinner in the Seine.

"Marie and I will be here, Papa." Jerome tried to console him.

"No. You will be grown and gone. It is the way of life. A man must think of his old age. I will be fifty."

"When?"

"In twenty years, if I live so long."

"But you are only thirty now."

"Opportunity passes me by," Papa sighed. "Not even the gendarmes think I am a good enough Communist to arrest. Every worthy Communist is in prison for seduction against the government or fled. I have no employment. My children are ragged and hungry. If I perish now, where would you be?"

Papillon sensed the seriousness of the discussion. He ran up Jerome's arm and tickled his ear. "The same place we are now."

"This is what I mean," Papa scratched his head. "I could enlist and send you my pay. And then when they disband the Armée in a few months, I come home with the same rights as my brother. You see how it works, Jerome?"

"But what about Stalin?" Marie was very worried now at this crazy talk.

"He would only take our boat from us," Papa said with conviction. "It is a very difficult world we live in, Marie. There are times a man must join an army and fight for important things. Security."

"Like Uncle Jambonneau." Jerome said. "And the old men at des Invalides."

Papa took one last look at himself in the mirror. "They will not refuse my enlistment." He licked his palm and smoothed his hair. "I will look fine in the uniform of a poilu."

Marie's face puckered in consternation. "But who will take care of us if you enlist in the Armée?"

"Who indeed!" Papa scoffed. "I have given the matter some thought. Madame Hilaire has just been evicted from her establishment."

"Madame Hilaire!" Jerome and Marie blurted in unison.

"Well, what is wrong with her?" Papa frowned, although he knew the truth.

There were a million things wrong with Madame Hilaire. A former circus performer, she had been shot from cannons from her youth and was stone deaf by the age of thirty. Being deaf herself, she believed that the whole world was hard of hearing, so she shouted every word she uttered until one's head ached. Her hair, singed by constant exposure to black powder, stood out from her head in a permanent frizz. At the age of thirty-six she grew too large to fit into the cannon. She tried working in the concessions, but her shouting made small children cry, which was bad for business. After leaving the circus she took up the oldest profession in the world. Unfortunately, age, strong drink, and her ear-piercing voice made her unattractive to all but a blind man. Uncle Jambonneau was thus her only friend and customer.

Jerome and Marie sat in grim contemplation of living with Madame Hilaire in the small confines of the *Garlic*.

"It will not be so bad," Papa said. "I will send money home from the Armée and you will all eat well. Uncle Jambonneau says she is an excellent cook, and she is the only woman I know who is fond of Papillon. It will not be for long, my little chickens. You must remember that this is not really a war at all. We will all be better off for it."

There were few American war correspondents awake and moving in the lobby of Hôtel Thiers this morning. Enough champagne and brandy had been consumed in the brasserie press meeting the night before that Mac did not doubt that many of his fellow journalists had gone to bed still fully dressed in their splendid uniforms. Of course, the owners of those garments would not wake up until after lunch sometime. Blackout curtains had a way of making a man with a hangover believe that it was still the middle of the night when it was really high noon. Mac predicted that this would cause no end of grief for the hotel valet who would be expected to press dozens of pairs of wrinkled trousers instantly and restore slept-in jackets to their original crispness. No doubt there would be a lot of rumpled newsmen wandering around Nancy before the day was finished.

Only Ted Munroe, radio broadcaster for Mutual, had thought to have more than one outfit made for himself. His duds would have made Mussolini's tailor jealous. Last seen, Lou Frankovitch had spilled, or perhaps thrown, a plate of spaghetti on Munroe's tunic and Munroe was too far gone to notice. It had been an interesting gathering for the Eagles of Newsdom.

There were about two dozen survivors at seven o'clock in the morning when the croissants and fresh butter and steaming coffee were put out on the long table in the lobby for the French Armée press officers and the international journalists.

Mid-bite, Mac was relieved to spot one American among the other nationalities who was completely alive, showered, shaved, and dressed in plain tweed hunting clothes.

John Murphy, head of Trump European News Service (TENS) in London, looked up from lively conversation with a French officer. He waved at Mac, tugged his tweed lapel, nodded his head in approval of Mac's civilian clothes and raised his coffee cup in salute.

Murphy, as he was known to all, had been around Europe even longer than Mac. A congenial guy in his mid-thirties with a knack for finding trouble, Murphy had married a Jewish girl he met on assignment in Berlin. Such a union put an end to his days as a Berlin correspondent. The couple had one baby of their own and had adopted the two small sons of Hamburg journalist Walter Kronnenberger after Walter had been killed by the Nazis in 1938. Murphy was not the kind of reporter that Hitler approved of; he had a heart.

Lately Murphy headed up the central office of TENS on Fleet Street. It was an important administrative position which Mac suspected had been given to Murphy to keep him out of harm's way.

"What are you doing here, Murphy?" Mac asked. "I thought you big cheese bureau chiefs only sent the little Indians out to the trenches."

At that, Murphy pulled out his wallet. Showing snapshots of wife, Elisa, holding a baby, the two Kronnenberger boys, a pretty niece named Lori with an infant, a mother-in-law, and assorted others dear to his heart, he explained.

"They're all up in Wales. On a farm. Evacuated from London when the first alert sounded. So they're there until I can get them to the States. I stayed in London as long as I could stand it. It's a lousy, dark, lonely place when a guy's got a desk job. I got . . . irritable." He shrugged. "Fog. Coal smoke. Thought a little fresh air at the front might do me good."

"You forgot your uniform."

"Yeah. You too."

"Ted Munroe brought two."

A long pause. "We could borrow one."

"The one without meatballs. Divide it up. Epaulets, gold braid, and brass buttons. There's plenty to go around."

"I don't know. On second thought . . . If the Heinies spot us at the front with that stuff on, they'll shoot us down like generals."

A French press officer, who looked remarkably like the large half of Laurel and Hardy, announced pleasantly that the correspondents must be divided into teams of two men, with each team to be escorted to a different area of the Western Front. It had all the makings of a Boy Scout field trip.

Being the only two Americans who had underdressed for the occasion, it seemed natural for Mac and John to join forces. Assigned to a French Cavalry liaison officer for the day, Murphy and Mac shared the amiable understanding that there was no competition between them for whatever story they might discover. If there was a story . . .

Murphy studied the young, serious French captain who spoke in solemn tones to his superior officer.

"Our guard dog." Murphy remarked.

"This whole trip is canned ham. A tour of the factory."

The Frenchman scratched his head and read over a slip of paper which contained the destination of the day.

"We're a bunch of old ladies on a guided tour of Atlantic City. That's all."

"Where else do you want to go?"

"Elsewhere."

"We could get arrested . . . shot at." Murphy smiled slightly as though that was a pleasant thought.

"That would be a story anyway. Stick with our elegant friend here, and we might as well be climbing the Eiffel Tower. What about it?"

Moments later, pockets stuffed with croissants and cheese, the two walked nonchalantly down a corridor to the kitchen and then out the back door. They arrived at the garage in a roundabout way as a caravan of official government Citroens, loaded with official government guests, clattered off en masse toward the great concrete blockhouses of the Maginot Line. The battered Renault followed the tedious progress at some distance and then peeled off down a side road toward a village nestled in the valley sloping down to the Saar.

The lane passed through a series of snow-covered hop fields rimmed with sheaves of tall stakes stacked together like Indian tepees. Sunlight broke through the clouds and shone on the high peaks of the Alps which protected the eastern border of France. At first glance the countryside seemed like something lifted off a postcard, pastoral and undisturbed by the nearness of war.

It was too quiet. No smoke drifted from the chimneys of St. Wendel. No dogs barked as they entered the town. No people walked the streets. The black rubbish of unswept autumn leaves blocked the steps and doorways of homes and businesses.

"Nobody home," Mac whispered as the windows still displaying merchandise reflected the passing Renault. "Evacuated."

Mac pulled up in front of the Hôtel St. Wendel and stepped out. There was no sign of shell damage. No indication that this tiny fragment of France had been injured in any way. But a terrible dread permeated every brick and cobblestone of the dead village. A glance through the window of the hotel restaurant showed cups and plates of half-eaten food rotting on the red checked tablecloth.

Somewhere up ahead the distant thunder of artillery and the thin high scream of a shell sounded.

"Guess we're headed in the right direction," Murphy said wryly as he peered through the window at dusty bottles of wine and withered salamis hanging like stalactites above the bar. "Good thing we brought our own lunch." Then, he offered some explanation for the eerie discovery. "It's the German planes they're scared of, not German artillery, not tanks or infantry. Little St. Wendel is all tucked away safely behind the Maginot Line. And everyone knows the Panzers won't get through the Maginot Line."

"No. They'll go around. And they'll fly over," Mac added with the certainty of one who had seen it all before. "Too bad the French generals haven't figured that out."

Murphy looked up. Clouds scudded across the sky in close formation. Farther to the west the tiny dots of a fighter squadron passed somewhere near the Maginot. "But the people . . . they heard about the Stukas over Poland and so they've run away. Poor dopes. They can't run far enough away, can they, Mac?"

Mac gave a quick shake of his head. "No. Not far enough. Or fast enough. Might as well have stayed home and finished supper."

"France has the Maginot and England has the Channel." They climbed back into the Renault. "They'd better hold the Nazis here because England's got no place to run to. And it's twenty minutes by air across the Channel . . . sandbags and slit trenches all around London. You know we've got barrage balloons up over the Thames just waiting for the Luftwaffe. Paint faces on the balloons and the Thames would look like 5th Avenue and the Macy's floats at the Christmas parade. What I wouldn't give to have my kids there to see it. The Christmas parade, I mean."

He sighed, and Mac felt a wave of pity for Murphy. "I'm glad I'm not . . ." Mac thought through his meaning, choosing his words carefully. "This whole deal is tougher to handle when a guy's got a family to worry about, I guess."

John Murphy lapsed into a troubled silence. Doubtless he was thinking about his wife and kids all tucked away in Wales, which was not far enough or safe enough after all. He was wishing he had them on the other side of the Atlantic Ocean. Maybe that was the only safe place left to run to.

TWENTY-TWO

Admiralty Arch was almost buried under a twelve-foot-high thicket of concertina wire. The barbs were as wide as a man's hand and looked more like lance heads than thorns. Andre's identity papers and the orders directing him to consult with the First Lord of the British Admiralty were examined three times before he was allowed upstairs.

Escorted to Winston Churchill's war room by a secretary, Andre was asked to wait outside while Churchill finished his regular 6:00 A.M. consultation with his briefing officer, Captain Richard Pim. Pim came out carrying a stack of manila folders, each of which bore a red label reading ACTION THIS DAY.

Pim shrugged when he saw Andre staring at the heap of projects. "Go right in," he said with a cheerful grin. "I think he's cleared the decks for you now."

The rotund, dressing gown-clad figure of Winston Churchill studied a wall map of the North Atlantic. In it pins represented the whereabouts of British warships, merchant ships, and the last reported sightings of German U-boats. "Andre, son of my old friend," he said, drawing a black drape across the wall, "how good to see you again."

Andre looked around the room. All the walls were covered in dark curtains which presumably hid more maps and charts. It gave the office a very somber look. "A pleasure to see you also, First Lord."

"No ceremony," Churchill insisted, then with sympathy added, "I am aware of the situation with Elaine. I am sorry."

But Elaine was not the subject which had sent Andre to Churchill's office, and Andre said nothing except a muted thank you. "I am directed to tell you, without giving details, that the work on the German code is progressing, though slowly. We are hopeful of a breakthrough, but do not expect it to come soon."

Churchill stuck out his lower lip in thought, then walked over to the room's lone window and stood gazing down on Horse Guard's Parade. "It is of the utmost urgency," he said at last. "This delusion which your people call the Drôle de Guerre, and ours call the Bore War, is really a sinister trance! The fate of Holland and Belgium, like that of Czechoslovakia and Poland, will be decided by the next move. We must come upon concrete evidence of what follows in their infamous plan."

Andre wished that he had more positive information to offer. He wished he could reinforce the confidence of this man who was the backbone of British resolve.

Churchill continued speaking, now almost musing aloud. "The Nazis try to frighten us with their leather-lunged propaganda machine. But we are not frightened. Hitler tries to reassure the neutrals with solemn promises and guarantees . . . which is why they *are* frightened! They remember how he kept his other promises! I tell you, Andre, either Hitler and his minions will be destroyed, or all that Britain and France stand for will go down. And if that happens, the United States will be left to single-handedly guard the rights of man."

"You do not believe that it will come to that?"

The great head moved ponderously from side to side. "Only bullies and cowards support Hitler. The rest of the entire world hates the monstrous Nazi apparition. Once the Allies are awake to the danger, we shall not draw back until this business is finished once and for all."

"Then," said Andre, "we must hope that the slumber will soon be over!"

"You and I, and others like us, are awake already. If we do not fail in our duty, others will soon arise to share the burden," Churchill concluded. "But come along now, Clemmie would never forgive me if I did not take you upstairs for a visit. We recall with great fondness the times we spent on your family's villa in the south of France."

"How is your wife, sir? I heard about her automobile accident. Is she all right?"

"Bruised and shaken, but quite strong and willing to be on the road again. A bit like the national honor of our two countries, eh, Andre?"

Clementine Churchill sat at her desk in the pale yellow morning room, answering correspondence. Wearing a navy blue dress trimmed in white, she looked the female counterpart of the First Lord of the Admiralty. Her straight, Grecian nose and classic features were still beautiful in spite of her fifty-odd years.

Her face broke into a pleased smile as Andre entered the room with

Winston. She rose stiffly and only then did the aftereffects of her accident show.

"Andre! I was hoping you wouldn't get away from here without dropping in."

He embraced her gently and kissed her on both cheeks. "I was concerned for you, Clemmie," he said. "I read that you and your automobile have been tilting with brick buildings!"

"The driver swore he saw that nasty Hitler standing on the corner in Surrey," she laughed. "He tried to smash him like a bug, and I found myself sitting in a shop window like something on display."

"Sit down, Clemmie," Winston growled.

She ignored her husband and led Andre to a settee beside the bowfront window. Still holding his hands like a delighted auntie with a nephew, she looked him over just as she used to do when he was a child. He half expected her to proclaim that he had grown.

"Every time I see you, you look more like your handsome father at this age. He would have been proud of you, Andre. And your mother as well." She patted his cheek. "It's been too long since we saw you last. Summer seems like a century ago now. When Winston told me you were coming, I had the cook make up profiterolles just for you."

"A treat we cannot easily get in the patisseries of Paris, Clemmie. Merci."

Churchill cleared his throat and swooped up a prowling grey kitten which rubbed itself across his legs. "Well, you two don't need me for your tea party. I'll get back to work."

The cat under his arm, Churchill retreated down the stairs. Perhaps, Andre thought, Clemmie had warned Churchill that she wanted to have a personal word with her godson.

Tea and profiterolles were served. Andre felt more like a child in the presence of Clementine Churchill than any other woman.

"Do you notice anything since last you were in London?" she began.

"Apart from gun emplacements on the roof of Harrods, barrage balloons, gas masks, and sandbags everywhere?" he smiled. "It is the same in Paris, ma chérie."

"Listen." She raised her chin regally. "Do you hear it?"

He strained to hear whatever noise she was contemplating, but there was only silence and the ticking of a mantel clock.

"What is it?"

"Silence," she smiled. "London is as still as Chartwell. No churchbells. No taxi horns or train whistles. No sirens. No unnecessary noise. Winston says it was his idea. They let it out that the order for silence was to enable the air raid wardens to hear aircraft. But I think it was so Winston could tolerate living in London after years of peace at Chartwell."

"I would believe such a motive," Andre replied with a laugh.

They spent the next thirty minutes discussing the Churchill children as well as Andre's brother Paul. And finally Clementine came to the purpose of the tea and pastries.

Her expression became suddenly serious. "We were shocked to hear the news about Elaine."

"Luxembourg has appealed for her release," Andre stammered. "They offered to deposit a large ransom in a Swiss account if she might be released. Hitler will not hear of it. He is convinced that the plot against his life was either of British or French origin. And that Elaine . . . poor Elaine . . . had something to do with it."

Clemmie nodded slowly. She took Andre's hand. "What about the child, Andre? Have you thought of her?"

"I think of little else. The war . . . yes. It is almost a diversion to my troubled thoughts these days." He smiled grimly and shook his head. "She is with Elaine's father. An old and bitter man . . . I cannot think what to do."

"You will do the right thing, I am certain," she replied kindly. "How old were you when you lost your parents, Andre?"

"I was nine. Paul was five."

"Yes. I remember. A tender age, darling. A lonely time for you. But then, you had your brother and your grandfather." She let the memory of that time convict him.

"Grandfather. But for him it might have turned out differently for Elaine and me. For the child."

Clemmie rose and held up a finger, commanding Andre to wait. She retreated through a door and then returned a moment later, carrying a delicate porcelain-faced doll and a thin, green leather volume.

"These were your mother's. The doll she gave to me when she left for France to marry your father. She told me that one day I might like to pass it along in case she had a little girl. Until now I thought I should never be able to fulfill my promise to her. Of course she had sons, and so we held out for the possibility of grandchildren someday. This . . ." She placed the book into his hands. "Milton. *Paradise Lost.* We struggled through literature class together, she and I. All the notes in the margin are hers. Some lovely thoughts. I thought you might like these things. Perhaps you may wish to pass the doll along. Her name is Clementine."

Unable to reply, he nodded and held the doll in his hands. At last he spoke. "Well, she has your eyes, Clemmie. They look into a heart, do they not?"

"Perhaps, Andre, dear boy. But your heart is on your sleeve in this matter. Easy to see. It always has been."

❧   ❧   ❧

Wilhelmstrasse was as slick as an ice-skating rink as the staff car of Gestapo Chief Himmler pulled out from the curb of the Chancellory.

Reinhard Heydrich sat beside him, gazing out at the colorless day. The only break in the monotony was the red banners draped from the cornices of the building, indication that der Führer was in residence.

"He was in a mood," Himmler said without amusement.

Heydrich countered sullenly. "I thought you said he did not need to know about Lewinski. That it was better left untold until we have taken care of the matter."

"Nothing remains a secret from the Führer for long. Not even internal matters of the Gestapo."

Heydrich nodded. He swiped his finger through the fog on the windowpane. "Sometimes I think he has eyes in the back of his head." He arched an eyebrow. "Like my mother when I was a boy. She knew everything I did. Everything I said."

"There is no dark magic to it, Heydrich. Have you not figured out that we compete with everyone else with access to his ear? My guess is that Fat Hermann has an informer in my department who feeds him information . . ."

"Goering's appetite is healthy, to be sure."

"And from Goering's mouth to the ear of the Führer."

Heydrich tugged at his collar. "It is irritating. Lewinski is nothing. Nothing at all. I did not realize he was a Jew when he worked in the Enigma factory. I did not think of him at all. Just another engineer designing variations on the same theme. And when I found out, I sent him packing like every other Jew. Off to Poland. Dumped him on the Polish frontier with twelve thousand other vermin. How was I to know the rat would go underground?"

"You should have killed him."

"We were more careful in those days. World opinion mattered then. Lewinski is well connected in America. We still had some pretense of friendship with the Americans, Himmler." He laughed, "Before the Führer started calling Roosevelt 'the Paralytic.'"

Himmler opened the snap of his leather portfolio and fished out a clean handkerchief. He cleaned his glasses and then blew his nose loudly.

"I am catching cold," he complained. "Lewinski is not in America. That much has been confirmed. Not in Rumania. Every acquaintance has been followed."

"You will not call off the American agents, will you? I still believe he will show up there."

"We have the best men on it. Our fellow in the U.S. State Department has access to files which would indicate a change of identity." He sucked his teeth. "As I told the Führer, this is simply a matter for patience."

"It is a matter of cold weather. The army is stalled and he is bored, so we must amuse ourselves and him by tracking down some useless little Jew who may remotely be able to reconstruct our Enigma." He slapped his knee. "Even though the code cannot be deciphered without the exact and perfect combination."

"We will find him. It will disappoint Goering if we do so. It will please the Führer. We will bring in the Russian." Himmler shrugged as though the matter would soon be settled. "A man like Lewinski cannot be hidden for long."

Heydrich nodded and wiped away the fog again as they drove along the Spree. "He must be in the possession of one of the Allied governments. Or at least a neutral. Our enemies would not let a mind like that go free. They will feed him pastries and encourage him with praise as they keep up their hopes that he might be capable of doing us some mischief. But it is impossible. Enigma is invulnerable."

❧   ❧   ❧

Josie sat across the desk from Charlie Morris, London AP chief.

Heavy-set and white haired, he had a drooping moustache which reminded Josie of Mark Twain. A true southern gentleman, Charlie had been born in Valdosta, Georgia, in 1880 to the granddaughter of Confederate General Stonewall Jackson. He had covered the Spanish-American war in '98 and had come to London just in time to write the feature story on the funeral of Queen Victoria. Staying on nearly forty years, he was the principal European correspondent through the last war.

Charlie was a father figure to the younger members of the press. He had seen them come and go by the shipload. His Chelsea home was always open in the high standard of southern hospitality.

This afternoon he kicked the door of his office shut and leaned back in his cracked leather chair. He steepled his fingertips together and waited, as if hoping Josie would speak first.

She did not. After all, it was Charlie who had called her into the office. Was she in trouble?

He cleared his throat. "Heard you had a little problem with the boys at the Savoy."

She felt the color climb from the collar of her uniform blouse to her hairline. "Not much. I mean . . . a little."

"I heard Konrad cut you up, chewed and spit you right out like a chaw of tobacco."

"He's a cynic."

"That may be so. It *is* so. But he's right."

Josie put her head in her hand. "I give up, Charlie. I can't go over this again."

"Can't say I blame you, honey," he said gently. He drew a deep breath and continued. "You want to talk about what happened to you back there? Poland?"

"Something important." How could she explain? "I woke up, sort of."

He nodded and smiled. "I figgered. Lemme tell you, honey, I've seen folks wake up. I remember when I was a boy in Valdosta, there was a young man who died of typhoid. Back then you had to get them in the ground right away. Well, it was after dark when we all tramped down to the cemetery for the committal service. There we stood by lantern light around the headstones. Prayin' and preachin' and singin' and such. Just then, up on the road, there came the town's worst drunk! An ornrier drunk you never knew! He spotted us in the lantern light down there in the cemetery and thought the Lord had come and the dead had risen from their graves!" He laughed and slapped his knee. Josie laughed with him.

He continued. "It scared him so bad, that man was sober ever after! He was a changed man! And you know? He began to preach to everybody who would listen. Then he preached to everybody who didn't want to listen. He became a general nuisance, arguing with anybody about just about everything." He shrugged. "Folks in Valdosta liked him better as a drunk."

"Thank you, Charlie." Josie shot him a hard look. "The moral is loud and clear. Can I go now?"

"Now, now, honey. I don't believe you do hear me. I'm not saying you're like that fella. But here it is. Konrad was right in every cynical nasty thing he said."

"I was talking about ideals, moral obligation."

"You mention such things to newsmen and you'll be flayed alive. You think it's bad here, wait till you get back to that white-slaver Frank Blake in the Paris office."

"I have to go back, Charlie. Thanks for the care."

He looked at his hands as if considering his words carefully. "Danny won't be there."

"I know that."

"He would have been spouting off the same stuff as Konrad, you know. Your husband was a first-class cynic. He didn't die for a cause. He died because he was doing his job and got under a bomb."

"I have few illusions about Danny's nobility. But I loved him."

"Paris could be rough for you just now."

"I'll keep my mouth shut."

He mopped his brow and took a sip of tea. "God ought to smite a person dumb the instant the light comes on inside. That way there'd be no temptation to explain it. No argument about moral right or wrong or the existence of God. No way to let slogans substitute for actions. If only Christians couldn't preach on and on like that Valdosta drunk! Only way we'd have to tell other people about the love of God would be to show it, to live it. Give a cup of cool water to someone who is thirsty. Comfort some kid. It's not a church or a religion, it's a way of life. It's a different kind of war. It never ends."

Josie nodded, grateful that he seemed to understand. "That's what I want to do, Charlie."

"There are going to be a lot of kids in need of comfort before this is over, Josephine. There's no stopping it now. For all the reasons Konrad gave, this is likely to be a long, mean, ugly war. Whoever is left standing at the end will win. And if you get in the middle of it and live out the light as you see it, maybe nobody is ever going to say thank you. Maybe only God will ever know what good you do. Are you willing to face that?"

"I want to make a difference, Charlie. I don't want to just die without making things better by having lived. Isn't this the time . . . such a time . . . when the world needs people who measure convictions against God's love and then act on the best impulse they have? In Warsaw, up to the end, I saw people who lived and died just that way . . . And suddenly I saw how small and blind my own soul has been. What difference have I made? It seems to me I must be alive for some reason I don't know yet."

"That's what I thought you'd say. But trouble comes when you live out your convictions. You're young and full of hope, and you ought to be warned. I've seen souls wake up before, Josephine. You could get hurt." The old gentleman put his hand out to her. "If you need to come back to London, I'll have a place for you."

TWENTY-THREE

When Mac and Murphy arrived at the front, German artillery batteries on the opposite shore of the murky River Saar were hard at work. Above the trenches, 155 millimeter shells passed over with a head-splitting crack.

Mac ducked lower and considered the information the French artillery captain at the blockade gave him an hour before. The captain had smiled with some secret amusement as he examined the pink press passes which allowed Murphy, Mac, and his camera a front row view in the Zone des Armée. Had he noticed the surprise on Mac's face as a shell exploded on a hillside a half mile away?

"It is not really war up here, Messieurs. Only afternoon target practice. We send the Boches a gift and they return the gesture in kind. It is nothing. Really. This is not Poland."

Then the captain rapped his knuckles against the old style American army helmet perched awkwardly on Mac's civilian head. Here was a truly serious matter. "Your tin hat, Monsieur. It looks British. Keep your head down or the Boches will blow it off." He smiled apologetically. "If they think there are English soldiers in the trenches they are likely to get nervous and really start something." With that advice, he sent the journalists off like rats in a maze to capture the reality of life in the trenches.

The reality in 1939 was no different than it had been in 1918. Cold, filthy, and miserable, the trench system had been cut into the yellow clay of the bank which sloped a few feet above the level of the Saar River. The walls were lined with revetments of woven willow. It had been a hard, lousy winter. The lining was bellied out and the mud had broken through in places.

Mac and Murphy made their way through an unoccupied communications trench which zigzagged toward the main lines. At any point, Mac could have filmed the entire terrain, both German and French sides, by standing on a firing step and peering over the parapet. Murphy discouraged him from this by improvising the posthumous narration of his newsreel in thousands of American theaters.

". . . You are now seeing the last footage of the so-called Phony War along the French Front, filmed by the daring Movietone cameraman, the late Mac McGrath . . ."

Mac smiled appreciatively then paused a moment longer to listen to a hacking machine gun and the continuous popping of rifles on the other side. Then, remembering the German dislike of British-styled helmets, he resisted the temptation to stick his neck out and trudged on.

The duckboards on the floor of the trench were muddied and scarred from months of heavy boots and rifle butts. There were no visible bloodstains. A shell screamed past close overhead. Mac and Murphy plastered themselves against the sandbags until a loud crump sounded not far behind the lines. "Too close," Mac muttered as the acrid aroma of cordite filled the air.

Around one more corner, the support trench emptied into the front line. Mac unsheathed his DeVry camera and gave the key wind a crank.

There were ten French soldiers in this section firing rifles and sub-machine guns. They stood on the firing step and took aim through gaps in the sandbagged parapet. Mud caked their trench coats. The amount of firing along the line indicated a fully manned trench. As Mac raised his camera, a machine gun let off a clip almost in his ear. His knee-jerk reaction ruined the filming. He braced himself against the sandbags and began again.

Through the viewfinder he saw a lieutenant detach himself from the jumble of spattered uniforms and give a puzzled look at the camera and the two journalists. Lowering his rifle, he hurried toward them.

"Bonjour, Messieurs?" There was a definite question in the tone, as if a couple of tourists had lost their way to the Eiffel Tower and had somehow blundered onto the Western Front. This was a battle zone, after all.

"Good day," Murphy returned cheerfully as a deafening barrage roared over, drowning out his voice.

Mac gestured upward with the camera and then added in his best French, "The Heinies are really pouring it on!"

As if to confirm his statement, the shell exploded a few hundred feet behind their position, and the lieutenant forgot to ask either man for his papers. After all, what fool would be there if he was not required to be?

"What is going on?" Murphy shouted. The air was filled with surging tides of sound as the *thwap* of French guns answered their German counterparts.

A momentary lull and the lieutenant explained between rounds of small arms fire. "The Nazis have been at it for several days now. Last Thursday a

German captain went down to the river to smoke a cigar and hurl insults at the French army across the way, as was his custom every morning—to try our patience and show off to his men, I suppose. Our captain grew weary of this hairy Boche. He got on the loudspeaker and told this fellow to cease his obscenities and go back to his Nazi pillbox at once. More insults were exchanged. The Nazi cocked a snook at our fellows! He went too far, this Nazi. What can one expect? Our captain shot the Boche, who fell over, a very surprised dead man."

He glanced up at the sky with a pained look as yet another barrage whined over and then, after a series of rapid explosions, died away. "We were none of us happy that our captain shot the Nazi captain. It was like killing the lucky mascot, if monsieur understands my meaning. Every morning the Boche pig insulted us but nothing happened . . . now he is dead and the insults are more deadly. The Boches have advanced some on our territory. There you see, they have taken Spichern Hill. Captured French soil. Although it is in no man's land, it is listed in all the guide books as French soil. *Baedeker's Red Guide Books. Michelin Blue Guide.* It is most distressing. We have a monument to all the old battles up there."

Mac reloaded his camera and did not mention the names of the dozens of empty front line ghost towns in the guidebooks that were also listed as French although not one citizen remained in residence. The face of Lorraine had changed since September and would likely alter more as time passed.

The officer indicated that Mac and Murphy should stand on the fire step, look through the opening in the parapet, and see the disaster for themselves. The Frenchman handed Mac a pair of field glasses.

The black river twisted through the middle of a flat, snow-covered meadowland which rose gently to a sparsely wooded hill crowned with a pillbox and ringed with barbed wire. The concrete had been painted bright red and garnished with a number of black swastikas.

The captain clucked unhappily. "That hill has been like a soccer ball over the centuries, Messieurs. French. German. French. German. French. And now, as you can see . . ."

Spichern Hill was definitely German again. Well forward of the heavy concrete defenses and tank traps of the French Maginot Line, the loss of Spichern Hill did not matter much as a strategic position for the defense of French soil. For the Germans, it was more like winning a game of "King of the Mountain."

The French generals fervently believed that the great forts of the Maginot Line would keep the German Wehrmacht on their own side forever. The Nazis could sit on Spichern Hill and shout obscenities all they wanted, but they would not get past the Maginot. They could send artillery barrages until the end of time, but they would not pass the Maginot! This motto was emblazoned on the black bérets of the Maginot defenders, was it not?

Ils ne passeront pas!

For the French riflemen in the forward trenches of no man's land, however, the loss of Spichern Hill was a personal insult. Their fathers and grandfathers and great-grandfathers had died fighting the dreaded Huns over that mound.

The huge black-on-red swastikas emblazoned on what had been French concrete were somehow like the ghost of the dead German captain rising up to cock a snook at every patriot on the line, and their ancestors as well! For this reason, although there was nothing much to see and no one close enough to shoot, the Frenchmen were firing their rifles every time an artillery shell roared overhead.

"Why are your men shooting?" Mac focused the field glasses on the Spichern Hill pillbox.

"We keep the heads of the Boches down. We know . . . but of course . . . they are not going to attack! We know we shall go on sitting here and dying of boredom. We shall go on shooting our machine guns at soldiers who might as well be stuffed with straw for all the harm they will ever do to us! This is not Poland . . . We are not soldiers anymore, Monsieur. We are night watchmen. On duty till we die of old age, the way this war is going. We are the sort of guards they put outside bank vaults." He jerked a thumb in the direction of the Maginot. "Behind us is the great Maginot vault. *Ils ne passeront pas!*"

"They shall not pass," Murphy blanched and repeated the famed words of Field Marshal Petain in English as a succession of stretcher bearers approached. The two Americans stepped on the fire step and flattened themselves against the revetment as they passed by.

Mac turned on his camera and watched the procession from the safe distance of his viewfinder. There were nine young men on the stretchers. Two were alive. Their skin was a waxy yellow color. They licked their blue lips with greyish tongues. The color would not show in the black and white and grey footage of the newsreel. Some of the others may have been alive. It was hard to tell. Blood dripped from the ends of the litters onto the boots of the stretcher bearers and down to the muddy duckboards of the trench. Two bodies had been gathered up and loaded piecemeal onto the stretchers.

Mac gave the grim parade twenty-five seconds of film.

Not soldiers anymore . . . night watchmen . . . on duty til we die of old age . . .

Mac kept the camera rolling. He had seen this all before. For each of those nine broken French boys, this might as well have been the front lines of Poland.

How old were they? Eighteen? Nineteen? The prime age of all cannon fodder. They might just as well have faced the Panzer divisions bare-handed and shouted, "Vive la France," as they fell like heroes! Or galloped out across the field on war horses like knights of old to fight single combat against a German tank!

They were just as dead even though they had waited here patiently beside the Maginot with their rifles. They had believed that this war was not war, not Poland. They had wished they were home. They had talked about things young men talk about . . . *The Future!*

The Maginot Line had not saved their lives. Confidence and boredom and dreams of glory had all come to an end. Now who would tell their families that this war was supposed to be the Phony War, The Twilight War, The Sitzkrieg, the Drôle du Guerre—a joke?

Reports of light casualties were no comfort to the guy who got a shell bounced on his head. For that man, this was as much a war as any war had ever been. One man could die only one time, and after that he would not care who occupied Spichern Hill. And those he left behind would not care about the loss of the hill, but they would mourn all their lives for the loss of the man.

Mac tried very hard not to think of such things. Else how could he stand in this bloody trench and go on shooting footage to enlighten the civilians back home? He had given these dead and the dying twenty-five seconds of his life, and he would not give them more. He switched off the DeVry Cine camera and switched off his mind.

"I've got my lead paragraph," Murphy remarked grimly. "Greetings from Phony War. Your son is dead."

Mac and Murphy stayed long enough to eat lunch with the soldiers, who valued news from Paris. For three hours they talked about theater and women and philosophy and good food. They did not talk again about the war. No one ever asked them for their press passes. They could have been German spies sent by der Führer to mow all the soldiers down, and they would never have known.

❧   ❧   ❧

The terrible news had arrived the night before.

The wire from the Ministry of War came to the tiny studio flat above the bookshop at Number 26 Rue St. Severin just after 9 o'clock P.M.

Michelle Fain had put young Claude and Jean to bed. She sat down to write the weekly letter to her husband Jean-Paul, who served France at the Maginot.

There was a sharp, official rapping at the door. She called out to ask who was there. The reply was chilling.

"War ministry telegram for Madame Michelle Fain."

It was all so cut and dried.

"Madame Fain, we deeply regret to inform you that Private Jean-Paul Fain perished in an artillery attack . . ."

And so ended the life of her dearest Jean-Paul and all Michelle's hopes for happiness. Only last autumn she married Jean-Paul, who was a young widower with two small sons. They were good boys, but they were not her own. What would she do now?

This afternoon she packed a small wicker basket with the clothes of the children. It was the same hamper they packed with lunch and carried to picnic beside the Seine last summer.

Were they going on a picnic, little Claude wanted to know?

Michelle did not reply at first. What could she say to Claude, who was five, and little Jean, who at three was already so much like his Papa?

"I am going to be with your papa," she replied at last. "You will be well cared for."

Claude fought back tears. He was too old to cry, was he not? And little Jean did not understand, so he played with his blocks on the floor and paid no attention to anything.

After sunset Michelle led the boys by the medieval church of St. Severin, past the ancient well of the pilgrims and the gnarled tree in the courtyard. It was very dark, but they were not far from Rue de la Huchette, up one narrow lane and down the next, until they came at last to the heavy arched gate of No. 5.

"Why have we come here, Mama?" Claude asked, peering up at the black wood of the gate. He always called her Mama because his Papa said he should.

"There are lots of children here," she replied in a detached voice as though she were already somewhere else. "You will be happy here."

She put her hand on Claude's shoulder and her other arm around little Jean.

"When will you come back for us, Mama?" Claude asked.

She touched his cheek. "I am going to be with your Papa." She placed the basket on the ground. "Stand on the basket, Claude." She helped him onto the lid of the hamper. "Can you touch the rope?"

He reached up and grasped the frayed end of the bellpull. "Oui, Mama."

She kissed him and embraced little Jean. "Take care of little Jean. They will help you here." She tucked the hand of little Jean into the larger hand of Claude. "Count to one hundred and then ring the bell. Keep ringing until they open the gate. It will be good for you here. Better for you than with someone who has no money, no job. Adieu, chérie."

Claude began to count, "Un, deux, trois, quatre . . ."

She left them there and retreated along the dark street to a small space between two buildings. She hid and watched unseen, as Claude counted slowly. She should have told him to count to fifty. It would have been quicker.

"Quatre-vingt-dix . . . cent!"

"Good boy!" she whispered with relief when he skipped impatiently from ninety to one hundred.

The bell began to clang, loud and insistent. True to her instructions, he did not stop ringing until the latch of the massive gate clanked back and a sliver of light escaped, illuminating the two small boys on the street.

"What is this? Lord in heaven!"

A large woman stepped out from the courtyard and peered up and down the pitch-black lane in hopes of seeing some movement. Then she bent down very close to Claude.

"Are you lost, little man?"

"No, Madame. We are brought to you."

"Where is your papa?"

"At the war."

"Where is your mama?"

"Our first mama is gone to heaven. The other one goes to join Papa. She cannot keep us, Madame, she has no money."

Good boy! From her hiding place Michelle cheered him. The large woman clucked her tongue in sympathy, asked their names, and if they were hungry now. And then, with one more look out into the blackness, she turned and led them in behind the safety of the gate.

"You will be well cared for, Claude. And you as well, little Jean." It was a kind voice, raised just enough so that Michelle could hear her clearly.

The gate slammed. The iron bolt slid back in place. Michelle retreated alone back along the Huchette the way she had come.

✣   ✣   ✣

Trevor Galway and his ship, HMS *Fortitude,* were still off the coast of South Africa. Having successfully escorted a convoy of ships past the Cape of Good Hope and into the Indian Ocean, the destroyer was headed northward again. She kept company with a freighter called the *Doric Star.* For months there had been reports of a German raiding vessel operating in the South Atlantic, but the pocket battleship had not been located.

Captain Pickering felt relaxed. A coastal steamer had just notified the destroyer of seeing the British battle cruiser *Renown* a hundred miles up the coast. *Renown* was more than a match for any German ship afloat.

The British presence in the South Atlantic was increasing, and as a result, the losses to merchant shipping were declining. No matter that the land war was a hopeless stalemate, at sea the Allies were succeeding. A battle group including the cruiser *Essex* was operating off South America; soon the ocean from Brazil to the Ivory Coast would be as safe as a pond back home.

When the outline of another ship appeared on the horizon, Lt. Commander Galway studied her intently, as did the captain. "It's *Renown*," Pickering announced. "Have wireless contact her."

"Sir," the helmsman reported. "There has been an explosion of some kind." Pickering and Galway jammed their glasses back to their eyes.

A bright flash appeared on the other vessel. A billow of grey fumes drifted upward, from which the prow of the ship speedily emerged like the snout of a dragon coming out of its lair. Another flare of light and then another. "Where is that wireless contact?" Pickering demanded. "Mister Galway, go below and attend to it personally."

Trevor had just gone from the bridge into the alleyway that led sternward when a shell ripped into *Fortitude*. It struck the destroyer between the two forward gun turrets, shredding number one and leaving only the revolving ring to show where the second emplacement had been. The impact knocked Trevor off his feet and threw him against a bulkhead. From behind he could hear Pickering shouting to break out the signal flags; let *Renown* know about this terrible mistake.

The freighter sailing behind *Fortitude* was also being shelled. Trevor caught a glimpse of the *Doric Star* just after a blast amidships blew a gaping hole in its side. The steamer went dead in the water and a column of thick black smoke rose upward.

Trevor had only just regained his feet when another crash rocked the ship. This one penetrated the armor of the hull opposite the base of the first stack. Like twisting a dagger in someone's ribs, the piercing shell penetrated into the vitals of the destroyer, there to explode with devastating force.

The deck under Trevor's feet leaned away from him as *Fortitude* sagged in the middle. The stern of the warship rose out of the water, as if a giant hand were pressing down between her funnels and bending her into a *U* shape.

Clanging gongs and shrieking sirens mingled with the screams of men. Explosion followed explosion as the destroyer folded in on herself. Away aft, the cannisters of the depth charges fell from their racks, crushing the men caught on deck. The aft gun turrets pointed uselessly up at the sky, and their crews struggled to escape the confines of the steel cages.

Trevor knew the ship was doomed. He rolled down the passageway, jolting against the partition that was now more a hatch beneath him than a doorway. The loudspeaker was blaring, "Abandon ship! Abandon ship!" *Fortitude* was settling—sinking. In a minute more she would go to the bottom, carrying most of her crew trapped inside the hull. Trevor twisted the action that secured the hatch cover. He was trying to pull it upward, lifting the heavy weight while standing awkwardly on the frame around it when it suddenly dropped open and fell the other direction.

Wavering above a fall to where the ship's midsection had been, Trevor saw swirling blue water rushing over the hull. As he hesitated, still another blast ripped into the ship, propelling him through the opening and into the sea.

He saw the bridge and the bow of the ship poised like a giant shark leaping down to devour him, and he struck out swimming in frantic terror. More men were around him in the water, some paddling and others floating lifelessly. A sailor in a small raft beckoned to him. "Come on, sir, you can make it!" The young seaman pulled Trevor over the side of the inflated island of safety. Less than three minutes had passed since he left the bridge.

Together the two paddled away from the dying destroyer. For all the violence of the attack, the end came silently. *Fortitude's* bow and stern saluted each other, almost touching, and then the warship sank beneath the waves.

Thirty minutes later, Trevor and the sailor, whose name Trevor never learned, were plucked from the water by a boat from the attacking ship. Trevor could see that one of its smokestacks was a sham, and part of its superstructure was camouflaged to make it resemble *Renown.*

"What is that ship?" Trevor asked, in German, of the obviously German officer who retrieved him.

Thickly accented English answered him in a tone full of pride. *"Graf Spee,"* the Kriegsmarine lieutenant replied, "greatest commerce raider in the world."

TWENTY-FOUR

Stormy weather grounded the fighter patrol over the Kentish coast. If British aircraft couldn't fly, they reasoned, neither would the German Luftwaffe venture out in gale force winds.

David Meyer opened his umbrella as he stepped onto the West Canterbury train platform. The wind instantly tore the black fabric and twisted the frame into something like a featherduster. Pulling up the collar of his topcoat, he caught sight of Annie and Duffy laughing at him from the warm comfort of the depot. He tucked his head and dashed into the building. The door slapped open in the wind, refusing to close again until David leaned his full weight against it.

"Lovely weather we're havin'," Annie teased as his breath exploded with relief in the warmth of the station. Duffy rushed past her and jumped up to put his enormous front paws on David's shoulders in an eye-to-eye greeting.

"Lovely enough." David pushed the dog down and slapped the rain from his coat. "I'm not flying today and here you are. Very nice weather, if you ask me. Thanks for coming."

She kissed him lightly and let her hand linger on his cheek. "Yesterday they had all of us student nurses cleaning out the basement of University College Hospital for a maternity ward. Air Raid Precautions order. They say women will be having babies even in air raids and we should be prepared. Truth is, we all think the war will be over by Christmas. The hospital will be left with a very lovely basement."

"I'm glad you got it all done yesterday."

"I caught the first train to Canterbury the minute your wire came. I've missed you, Davey," she whispered quietly. They were not alone in the depot. Two elderly women observed the meeting with interest as they warmed themselves beside the coal fire at the far end of the small room.

The sight of Annie was enough to make him forget the bone-deep chill of the howling storm outside and the scrutiny of the old women inside. "You're famous. I've named my Hurricane after you. *Annie.* Painted in bright red letters. Trimmed in gold."

Suddenly shy, Annie inclined her head toward their audience. "Let's get out of here. What do you say?"

The torrential rain let up just long enough for the couple to make their way up St. Dunstan Street to the tiny Falstaff Inn in the shadow of the ancient West Gate of Canterbury. The sign above the heavy wood door of the inn rocked crazily in the wind, threatening to pull loose from the iron standard which held it.

The proprietor's head snapped up with surprise at the entrance of David, Annie, and Duffy. The beams above the bar were set low, requiring the tall barkeep to duck beneath each timber as he stroked the zinc-topped bar affectionately with a cloth. He was permanently stooped after years of duty at his station. With every step his head bobbed forward on a long, thin neck, giving him the appearance of turkey strutting in a coop. The dark oak-paneled room of the pub was nearly empty except for an English cleric who read *The Times* and languidly sipped his tea at a snug little table in the corner. What fool would venture out in such weather?

"A day trip," Annie explained as they took a table before the fire and Duffy curled up in contentment at their feet.

"Lousy weather for it," the landlord grinned. "Pilgrims come t'see the Cathedral, or just t'sun yourselves?"

"Picnic," Annie replied.

"Well, here's the place for it. Me missus makes the best kidney pie in England. Isn't that so, gov'?" He addressed the cleric, who seemed not to hear him or chose not to reply. "The old padre is deaf as a post. You can say what you like an' he'll not hear a word. Can I get you a bite to eat? 'Tis a slow day and I've got a bit of work to do in the cellar."

They ordered hot tea and a ploughman's lunch: heavy bread, Stilton cheese, and tart chutney. After serving them, the barkeep disappeared down the narrow steps, leaving David and Annie alone in front of the fireplace. Soft dance music played through the static on the enormous radio. Around the room etchings of Falstaff and scenes from Shakespeare's play *Henry IV* adorned the walls.

David leaned close to examine the fat, drunken character of Falstaff. "Did you ever notice how much this Falstaff guy looks like Hermann Goering?" he quipped. "Comforting to think that somebody who looks like that is head of the German airforce. A couple of Spitfires shot down a German bomber off the coast yesterday. Laying mines, most likely."

Annie's expression was sad and serious as she listened to him talk. "You're not in danger . . . I mean, not a lot of danger, are you?"

"Does this mean you lay awake at night and worry about me?"

"Of course. I can't help it. You're the only pilot I know."

"Are there other fellas who keep you awake thinking about them too?"

"Yes. Sailors mostly." At his look of disappointment, she added, "My brother Trevor and the crew of the *Fortitude*."

"In that case I'll let you in on a secret so you only have to worry about one of us . . . I haven't even seen a Jerry. The closest I've gotten is sitting here looking at Falstaff and wishing I could get a target that big in my sights."

She reached out and took his hand across the table. "I'm glad. I hope you never meet a German plane. I hope you stay here in England and that things go on like this forever."

"Me too." The hour passed quickly. David tossed a load of coal on the fire as Duffy snoozed. The cleric in the corner sat unobtrusively. Then the music on the radio was interrupted by the sound of the BBC Westminster Chimes. The pub owner reappeared at the top of the cellar steps. The reality of war suddenly intruded on the timeless peace of the rainy Canterbury afternoon.

"*The* BBC *has just received word that the HMS* Fortitude *has been attacked by a German raider and sunk with all hands. The urgent communiqué was received from the ship yesterday at . . .*"

Annie was ashen. "I've got to ring Dad. Got to get in touch with the Admiralty. They'll know about Trevor," she managed, looking around the room for a telephone.

"What is it, miss?" the pub man caught her alarm at once.

David answered for her. "Her brother was on the *Fortitude*."

The barkeep led the way upstairs to his apartment and pointed at the telephone as the news droned in the background.

"*The HMS* Fortitude *was the second British ship to be sunk within a week and the seventeenth ship to go down in the Atlantic since Saturday.*"

Winding the crank of the old-fashioned telephone, Annie raised the operator and asked to be connected to the offices of the Admiralty.

"*It is reported that she has been sunk in the South Atlantic. The presumption, therefore, is that she was attacked by the German Pocket Battleship* Admiral Graf Spee, *reported to be in that area.*"

The wait for the call to reach London seemed interminable. Annie wiped tears away with the back of her hand and stubbornly refused to sit when the pub owner's wife brought her a chair.

David stood beside her as the Admiralty secretary transferred her call.

"My name is Annie Galway. My brother, Trevor Galway, was Lieutenant Commander aboard HMS *Fortitude*. Yes. Yes. I'll wait." She closed her eyes and her lips moved in a silent prayer of hope. A moment later her eyes snapped open with alarm, and her ashen complexion grew more grey. "I see." Her voice was a barely audible whisper. "Yes. Thank you. My father

. . . you say the wire has been sent. Yes. Thank you . . ." She clicked the receiver and sank into the chair. There was no need for anyone in the room to question the outcome. She covered her face with her hands. "Ah, Trev," she sighed.

"I'll fix some tea," offered the landlord's wife.

"A spot of brandy would be better," argued the barkeep.

Annie looked up pleadingly at David. "Dad'll be needin' me in London. Can you come?"

David nodded. "For a couple days."

"You've just got time to catch the train, lad," said the landlord. He solemnly shook Annie's hand as though he stood in the reception line at a funeral of an old friend. The Missus was crying, wiping her tears with her apron. They did not even know Annie's name. "Our fine brave lads. I'm awfully sorry, Miss. Do come back on a better day, will you?"

The duties of patrol and intensified combat training did not afford David any time to spend with Annie.

David had been with her only once more, on the day of the remembrance service held at St. Paul's for the sailors of twenty ships fallen victim to German raiders. She clung to the hope that Trevor had somehow survived, that possibly he had been rescued. There was no word of hope, and yet she was resolute in her belief.

But now she was all alone on the *Wairakei.* Her father was burying his own worry under a mound of twenty-four-hour workdays in Dover while Annie stayed aboard the ship, still moored on the Thames, and worked toward the completion of her nursing studies. More than anything else, she seemed to miss David. Her letters, like the one inside his flight jacket pocket, were full of brave sentiments; but David could sense that she was terribly lonely.

Coming out of his turn, David looked down from ten thousand feet on the length of the railway line between Ashford and Tonbridge. He was on a refresher flight in cross-country navigation, and the next marker he needed to spot was the second branch line to the right. Locating it would anchor the Hurricane onto the last leg of the "Iron Dog" route that led directly to the Croydon Aerodrome; goal of this exercise. Miss the turn and he could end up over the coastal defenses, where some eager antiaircraft crew might put embarrassing holes in the Hurricane. They might even scratch the gold-trimmed red letters on the engine cowling that said *Annie.*

There it was, just where it was supposed to be. David guided the Hurri-cane into another turn, adjusting the throttle and correcting a little swing with a touch of right rudder. This flight had gone so well that David had a lot of time to think about Annie, and he realized that he missed her terribly. He also knew that there was nothing to be done about it. The young pilots were given almost no spare moments. If it wasn't flying patrols over the Channel, it was the endless repeated drilling: formations, attacks, evasive maneuvers, gunnery drill. It went on and on, and David got more and more withdrawn as he fretted about Annie. He was so on edge that he had quarreled with his mates, Simpson and Hewitt, and that was no good for a combat team. David had hoped that the long cross-country hop would give him a chance to think things through, but with the end in sight, he felt no closer to sorting it all out.

David roused himself to go through the mental checklist for landing: flaps, trim, propellor pitch, throttle—all as it should be. He took his left hand off the throttle knob to release the undercarriage lever. His eyes flicked over to the indicator lights, then looked again. Instead of a pair of green lights, one of the two continued to wink red.

David's first reaction was to grab for more altitude. Back up to 12,000 feet he soared, to give himself time to think things over. There was no other problem with the aircraft, and ample fuel, but this one snag was bad enough. After several futile attempts, raising and lowering the control mechanism, David radioed in for assistance.

"Croydon," he called on the radio, "I have a little problem here."

"Reach behind the gear release lever," Croydon instructed. "There you'll find a T-shaped handle. Pump it vigorously and see if the increased hydraulic pressure won't release the gear."

"Negative. I tried that already, Croydon."

"Try it again. It may take several minutes, but it should fix the problem."

It did. Less than five minutes later, David was rolling to a stop beside the Croydon hanger. As he got out he noticed a number of airmen looking at him curiously, but no one spoke as he went into the headquarters office and reported in. He filed an Incident Report and got a lecture on being more familiar with the equipment. It was two hours before he could get back outside. David was even more glum than before.

Since the second half of the mission was night navigation back to his base, David left the airfield and headed for the nearby King's Arms pub for a bite to eat. When he got there, some of the bystanders who had watched his landing were already present, and it was clear from the volume of their voices that they had two hours' head start on drinking. And Badger Cross was one of them.

The burly man came up to David. "So assassin . . . Tin Man," he said with a little slur to his words. "Heard you had a spot of trouble today."

"No, nothing to speak of," David replied.

Badger's face scowled. "Not surprised you couldn't manage it properly," he said with derision. "Didn't you learn anything? Why don't you go back home where you belong? We can get along without your help. Isn't that right?" he called over his shoulder to his fellows at the bar.

"Ah, pipe down, Badger," one of them responded. "Pay him no mind, Yank. He's tight."

"The gear was stuck," David said hotly. "It could happen to anyone. Now, let me by, please, I want to get something to eat." David slipped off his flight jacket, and as he did so, Annie's letter fluttered to the floor.

Cross beat David to it, snatching it up and holding it out of reach. "Ooh-la-la," he said, leering and waving the letter for all to see. "Lilac and lavender for the Yank. Where's she from, Yank? London postmark," he reported to his audience. "You Yanks come over here and wave a wad of dough about so all the women drop their knickers for you. Some poor sod off in the service will be pining away, while his girl is doing the dirty with the likes of you."

"Give me back my letter," said David. He could feel the prickle on the back of his neck that he always got right before a fight ever since he was a kid.

"Say pretty please," Badger taunted, mugging for his friends.

"Pretty please," David replied, and then he threw his jacket in Badger's face. While Cross was clawing at the coat, trying to clear his vision, David hit him in the mouth as hard as he could.

Badger spun half round, stumbling over a bar stool, then tried to respond with an overhand right that would have felled an ox if it had landed. But David ducked under the blow, landed two punches in Cross's ribs, and danced back out of the way.

"Get him, Badger," called one of the bystanders. "Don't let him do that to you!"

Badger nodded and came toward David, a thin trickle of blood running down from his nose and over his lip. David tried a couple more punches that bounced harmlessly off the heavier man's forearms. "Caught me when I wasn't looking," Cross said in a panting voice, "try it again, why don't you, Yank?"

David circled to his left, keeping the other man off balance. Tiring of the game, Cross gave up boxing in favor of grappling and forged straight in, trying to grab David around the middle.

David got in two blows that hammered Cross's eyes before being borne back against the edge of the bar. The force of the rush threw David down hard, and his head cracked sharply on the walnut counter. Cross raised both fists together over his head, preparing to smash them down on David's face.

Without an instant to spare, David thrust his right into Cross's throat. Badger gave a gurgling sound and rolled off. Outside there was a shrill whistle as the local constabulary came to investigate the uproar.

" 'Ere now, what's all this?" demanded the policeman, thumping his nightstick against his palm with evident relish. "Drunk and disorderly, are we? Brawling?"

"No, sir, constable," spoke up one of the fliers. "The Yank there was just showing Badger some new boxing moves, imported from the States."

"Uh-huh," said the policeman, eyeing the blood dripping from Badger's nose and the lump on the back of David's head. "And I suppose they both slipped and fell into each other's arms?"

"That's it exactly, constable," Cross pledged. "A friendly little tussle, in the interest of better foreign relations."

"Uh-huh. Well, see that your diplomatic efforts don't go any further, or I'll call the watch and you can take your tussle to the guardhouse."

When the policeman had gone, David yanked his crumpled letter from Badger's grasp. Cross moved as if he would renew the battle, but the stern look on the pubkeeper's face convinced him that this was not the time. "I won't forget you, Yank," he said. "I've got you down in my book."

TWENTY-FIVE

Rain fell on the hills cradling Jerusalem. Rivulets of water turned to torrents cascading down the dry ravines and filling the empty pools of the desert wadi.

It was night in the city. The shutters of Rabbi Schlomo Lebowitz were closed tight against the cold weather. Still, dampness seeped in through the cracks of the thick stone walls. The rain found its way through a hole in the roof and dripped a melody into the tin pot on the rabbi's floor.

He stretched his hands out to the warmth of the Primus stove and listened to the drumming rhythm above him.

"The dancing of an angel," he mused. "So again you have sent an angel to this old man, Lord?"

As if in reply, a drip landed on his cheek and coursed down onto his thick grey beard. "So. Maybe not an angel. Too bad. I would have liked some company tonight."

It had been two months since Etta's last letter. There had been no word. Loneliness settled into the void left by the absence of hope in his heart.

As he had done a hundred times before, he looked down at the photographs laid out on the table like a deck of cards in a game of solitaire. The silent faces of his family smiled up at him.

"Tonight, my angels, I am thinking of you again." He held each photograph up to the light of his lamp. Like a hallowed prayer in an often-repeated ritual, he recited each name . . . Etta, Aaron, Rachel, David, Samuel, Yacov.

"Etta. Wherever you are tonight . . . listen to the wind. Your papa sends you blessings." He closed his eyes and held the photograph against his heart. He said a prayer for little Etta as if she were still a child and not grown up with a family of her own.

"It is only a picture." He reminded himself of this and warned his heart that he must not hope too much for a miracle. All the same, her clear blue eyes seemed alive. They radiated warmth into the tiny flat and made him wonder what she was seeing now. Was her vision filled with some winter scene in Poland? Or was she somewhere far away from this world . . . beyond the grief of the war which had kept her from him?

A kiss and then he replaced the photograph in the gallery against the wall and picked up the wedding picture of Etta and Aaron.

"How young you were. Nu! How happy. That night you stood beneath the wedding canopy here in Jerusalem. If I had known . . . it is good that I could not see the future. It is better to live one day at a time with the blessing of the Eternal than to see the end of blessings."

He smiled as he remembered the music and celebration of that night so long ago. There in the group was the younger image of himself beside his wife, Rachel.

"A handsome couple, were we not, my angel?" He touched her face with his fingertip. "It is good we did not know how soon you would leave this earth. The mixing of joy and grief would have broken our hearts had we known." And again he said, "Nu. It is better not to see tomorrow."

For a long time he held the photograph of his wife. "My Rachel," he caressed the name. "You are in heaven. Nu. Maybe you can look down and see our Etta and Aaron and the little ones." He frowned and looked up. "What is it like? Can you fly to Poland and find them? Do you hear them speak to one another? Hear the children laugh? I envy you. You know I have never heard their voices? The children, I mean. Sometimes I think I hear them when I am sleeping. They are laughing—light and clear—like water running over rocks in a stream. It is a good dream and I hate to wake up."

Tears came to his eyes. "Or maybe you are all together already? Not in Warsaw." He looked up at the tapping on the roof. "Have they gone home to be with you? And have you all come to dance above me tonight?" He rested his head in his hands. "I would like such a visit, Lord. Or I would like to fly away. Catch the wind with you and fly away to Warsaw. To be with my family. To dance with them again."

He pictured them together while he remained in the tiny room in the shadow of the Western Wall.

"Can you hear me, my angel?" Only the dripping of water in the tin pot broke the silence. "If they are still alive . . ." He lowered his head. "Lord? A small request for one as strong as you, Lord . . . My family, you see. Just a little miracle is all I ask. Bring them here for me. Show them how to escape! And tell them I am still here in Jerusalem waiting for them to come home."

The note was slipped under the door of the Lubetkin family flat in Nazi-occupied Warsaw in the afternoon. Addressed to Rabbi Aaron Lubetkin of 30 Niska Street, the note was written in German by a trembling hand.

Verstecken Sie sich heute abend!

Hide yourselves tonight!

Snow fell all day, dusting the soot-blackened streets of Warsaw with a fine white powder. The grime of multiplied millions of coal fires was covered by early evening, and still it continued to snow. Steep slate rooftops, chimney pots, and wrought iron balcony railings took on the appearance of miniature Alps. Patches of white grew to heaps on the gables, then slid away in small avalanches onto the cobbled streets. Charred rubble from September's bombs and the freshly turned earth of mass graves were lost beneath the soft contours of new fallen snow. The all-pervasive stink of death which had hung over the city for three months suddenly vanished. Warsaw, once called the Paris of Eastern Europe, was beautiful again.

The heaviest snowfall in half a century covered the scars on the landscape and made the German soldiers playful.

It was no surprise to Rabbi Aaron Lubetkin that there would be a need to protect his wife, Etta, and their four children from some planned Nazi action against the Jewish community. During the first week of the Blitzkrieg the Lubetkin family had joined the flood of refugees. They had seen the ravages of the Polish countryside. They had run from the planes of the Luftwaffe as civilians were strafed on the roads. But Aaron had friends in Warsaw among the Gentiles; so he chose the lesser of two evils and turned back to the city. His decision kept them from being among the one and a half million Jews pushed out of towns all over Poland and Czechoslovakia and now living in fields, trapped between the Nazi onslaught and the Soviet invaders.

In September, their Warsaw home was destroyed, but they found a two-room flat across from the Jewish cemetery. From their window Aaron could see hundreds of new graves filled with old friends. The synagogue was burned. His congregation was scattered; decimated.

For weeks Aaron and Etta kept small bundles packed at the door for themselves and each of their four children. They slept fully dressed and ready for whatever might come in the night. They prayed and waited to hear from the priest who promised them forged passports. But tonight, the sender of the warning remained a mystery.

Hide yourselves tonight!

Etta cradled baby Yacov and stared glumly at the note in her husband's hand. "It could be a trick. You know the decree. If we try to leave without permits . . . if we are out after curfew . . . And if our new identity papers are not ready? The priest might know. Telephone him, Aaron. He might know."

Aaron let Father Kopecky's telephone ring twelve times before he hung up. The priest was not there, but somehow Aaron found comfort that the telephone still worked—an odd bit of normalcy in a world turned upside down. They were not cut off entirely. Not yet.

In October, forty-two-year-old Aaron, along with all Jewish men between the ages of fourteen and sixty, had been compelled to register for forced labor. When asked his occupation, Aaron had answered truthfully, "Mosaic Craftsman." The beady-eyed official at the desk made no mental connection to the Laws of Moses or Mosaic studies in this declaration. He simply listed Aaron as a tile worker and waved him on.

Already the German General Government had established twenty-eight labor camps in the Lublin district, twenty-one at Kielce, twelve in the Krakow region, and fourteen in the area around Warsaw. Men were conscripted daily off the streets to work in conditions worse than those of slaves. They disappeared without a trace, leaving families to grieve and wonder at their fate.

Aaron studied the note, then glanced in the mirror at his Semitic features. Dark eyes. High cheekbones above a black beard.

Verstecken Sie . . . Hide yourselves tonight!

There was no place in the world for Aaron to hide and not be recognized for who he was. "Good Shabbes, Rabbi!"

But Etta? Who would challenge such a beauty? Aquiline nose, cobalt blue eyes, shining black hair. The priest had told him, as long as Etta did not speak she could pass for a Gentile and a Catholic. Forged passports were being made for her and the children too. There were still ways to get out, even now. Bribes could be paid. There were officials who, for enough money, would look the other way as a woman and four children traveled south through Hungary and Yugoslavia, then by ship, perhaps, all the way to her father's home in Jerusalem.

Hide yourselves tonight!

Aaron had never told Etta of the priest's concerns. There were no forged documents which could transform Aaron's features. No bribe spread far enough down the line to stop some petty Nazi official in some obscure outpost from rightly suspecting Aaron's face and accusing his eyes of Jewishness. Then they would all be condemned, would they not?

He glanced out at the snow-covered cemetery. So peaceful . . .

"You and the children must go tonight to Father Kopecky."

"Not without you, Aaron." She was trembling.

He flared. She must not question. "Yes! Without me, Etta! Remember you are a Polish widow on your way to mass with your children. Nu! Just like we talked about. I will come after. Following. Always following. Never together! You understand, Etta. We must think of the children now!"

The children.

Rachel, at thirteen, was the oldest. Beautiful, like her mother, it had been months since she had worn a dress. Tonight she was outfitted in a boy's knickers, stiff-collared shirt, tie and jacket, woolen socks, and scuffed boots. Her long black hair was braided and pinned beneath a woolen cap. Etta wanted to cut it for the sake of safety. What if the cap blew off? But Rachel wept and Aaron relented. A few streaks of soot from the stove concealed the clarity of her complexion. Still, she made a very pretty boy indeed. Too pretty. She had learned never to look anyone in the face lest they notice her blue eyes and long lashes and suspect the truth . . . There had been too many young girls raped on the streets of Warsaw lately. It was a long road between here and the safety of Jerusalem.

"Keep your fists in your pockets," Aaron warned his daughter. Her gloves had been stolen last week. Disaster. Her delicate fingers lacked the squareness of masculinity. Surely even a detail so small could be noticed. "And keep your eyes only on the toes of your boots. You understand, daughter?"

"Yes, Papa." Fists were thrust deep into pockets and eyes looked instantly downward.

It pained Aaron that she understood the reason for this charade so completely. She was only thirteen, and yet, she had seen so much.

David, at ten, also understood. He raised his chin and mocked his sister. "I told you how to stand! Not with your feet so close together!" He demonstrated a masculine stance. Head cocked to one side, feet apart, toes slightly out, toothpick dangling from his lip.

Six-year-old Samuel joined the instruction. "Walk like this!" He strode past her; arms swinging like a miniature soldier marching to war. "See? You

walk that sissy walk of yours and it will be our own boys in the neighborhood who beat you."

"Papa said keep my hands in my pockets," Rachel protested. "How can I
swing my arms and . . ."

Aaron passed her his grey wool gloves. "Wear these." They dwarfed her
hands. The thumb was missing, but Samuel was right. The masculine effect
was better when she swung her arms, lengthened her stride, and marched a
bit.

Through this last-minute rehearsal, baby Yacov, called Yani, slept peacefully in Etta's arms. Etta sat in silence, sometimes looking at the sleeping
child and other times at the snow gathering on the windowsill. The scene
behind her was reflected in the glass pane but she did not watch it. She did
not want these images burned into her mind. Her eyes were full of other
memories; as though she were hearing other voices and seeing faraway moments of their life together. Did she suspect that Aaron would not . . .
could not . . . follow her and the children?

He tried not to look at her. He came close and touched the tiny hand of
Yacov. He kissed Etta on the cheek and then bent to brush his lips across the
soft brow of the baby. But he did not look into the eyes of Etta.

"He is too young to remember all this," Etta sighed.

"I am glad for that, at least." Aaron knew the child would not remember
him either, and he was not glad about that part of it.

"Are you?"

"Yes," he lied. "He will wake up in your father's house one day and think
that there has never been any place but Jerusalem. Only peace and joy.
Safety." He faltered. "I never should have brought you here. Or I should
have sent you home last year. Found a way."

"I am glad the other children will remember what it was like in Warsaw
for us . . . I mean before." She searched the face of Aaron. "You will come,
Aaron?"

"Yes," he lied again. He could not let her see his eyes. She knew him too
well.

"Aaron, look at me!" Her voice quavered. Behind them, Rachel marched
back and forth across the stuffy little room as her brothers coached. "Aaron! I
need . . . I need . . . you to look at me!" Etta whispered hoarsely.

He glanced at the windowpane, and his eyes met hers in that shadowed
reflection. In an instant he saw she had read his intention. How long had she
known he would not come? Such grief in the knowing! How much better it
might have been . . . so much easier . . . if they had gone on pretending!

She rose and turned to him, stroking his cheek. He caressed her face as the
baby slept cradled in her left arm between them.

"They will all remember . . . I promise . . . that it was good here for us. They will! And someday when this is over . . ." She bowed her head against his chest as words became small and died away in the face of truth. There would never be *a Someday* for them.

TWENTY-SIX

The Channel crossing from Dover to France was like a homecoming for Josephine. Now the world looked somewhat level again. The nightmare of Warsaw receded into a distant dream. Josephine's personal pain began to heal. No German bombs had dropped in London, and the evacuated children were trickling back to the city with the hope that perhaps no bombs were ever going to fall on Great Britain. The attention of the press had returned to France once again. American women wanted to know what effect the war would have on fashion, art, music, and culture, the AP insisted. Throw in a few human interest pieces on the work of the Red Cross and it was the kind of assignment that required almost no emotional commitment. Josephine wanted nothing more demanding than that. Traveling with her old friend Alma Dodge, who had just been transferred from Fleet Street to the Paris copy desk of the Associated Press, Josephine was eager to be back in Paris.

Dark waters blended with the low, slate-colored sky of the late afternoon. The windswept coast of England seemed peaceful; the white chalk cliffs of Dover looked like bedsheets hung out to dry.

Less than thirty miles across the English Channel was a different picture. Hundreds of sea gulls circled above the French Harbor of Boulogne-sur-Mer, screaming insults down at the human intruders on the docks. Gone were the herring boats and the ferry loads of tourists with their bags of bread crumbs to feed the birds of Boulogne. Of the thousands of khaki-clad men moving down the gangways of the big ships, not one even looked up at the gulls or seemed to hear them.

The din of officers' shouts and curses mingled with the roar of engines.

Quayside, shiploads of military lorries, tanks, and troops unloaded to join the swelling ranks of the British Expeditionary Force (BEF) in France.

Boulogne had been invaded by the English before. Henry VIII had taken the port in 1544. His son had given it back to France in 1550. In the eighteenth century it had become a convenient rendezvous for English duelists intent on killing one another in single combat. Then came the tourists, debtors on the run, and disenchanted British literati. The uniformed hordes appeared again in 1914 when the British arrived to help their French allies fight the war to end all wars against the Kaiser and his Huns.

Twenty-five years later, the BEF was back in Boulogne for much the same purpose. To hear Winston Churchill tell it, the issue might have been settled without disturbing the gulls of Boulogne if Herr Hitler would meet him in single combat. "Every bully is a coward beneath the skin. And der Führer is a bully in the first degree. Tweak the little paperhanger's nose and then we'll see!"

The problem of Hitler had, unfortunately, grown beyond the ability of one man to settle it. Now it would take millions of men and the armies of nations.

As Admiral Nelson had told the troops at Trafalgar, England expected every man to do his duty. Tweaking the paperhanger's nose was number one on the list of priorities for every soldier who arrived through the port of Boulogne. Second on the list was to get back to England alive. In the meantime, there were the pleasant prospects of meeting beautiful French women and seeing Paris.

The little Frenchman behind the bars of the train station ticket booth knew all these things about the soldiers who packed the trains out of Boulogne-sur-Mer on their way to Paris. This is exactly what he was trying to explain to the two young American women at the head of the line.

"Mesdemoiselles! You must not ride on the third-class car! It is filled with the soldiers of the British Armeé!"

"Merci. But we have obtained our ticket vouchers from the Thomas Cook Agency in London, as you see." Josephine fumbled with the leather ticket wallet. At a salary of twenty dollars a week, she could not afford to upgrade her ticket to second class. She pulled out the itinerary. "You see, Monsieur . . ." She put her finger on the line which read, *Night train. Boulogne to Paris. 3rd class. Arrival Gare du Nord. 5:15 A.M.*

"Mademoiselle." He ran his hand over his withered face in frustration. "So many soldiers, Mademoiselle! Common soldiers. On their way to Paris for a . . . for a good time . . ."

Behind Josie, Alma Dodge spoke up. "Tell him we don't care. Tell him we don't mind. Tell him we just want to get to Paris by morning!" Alma had been with AP for three years in England, and Alma had never been to Paris.

The marriage of a valued copywriter on the Paris staff had left the vacancy Alma had been waiting for. She did not want to wait a moment longer than necessary.

Josie drew a deep breath and thought through her response in her most refined French. "Monsieur. We do not have the funds to upgrade our travel to a first-class sleeping compartment. I have made this trip two dozen times. I do not mind third-class seats. We do not have funds . . ."

"What are they thinking of? This is a war, not high tourist season. I do not care how many times you have traveled on this train. It is not like it was before the war. Have you traveled to Paris since the war began?"

"I have been gone for four months, Monsieur."

He grimaced and tried again. "I, myself, am the father of eight girls, Mademoiselle. I tell you now that third-class travel these days is like riding in a cattle car . . . You are two lovely heifers. The rest are bulls. The journey takes twice as long these days. Nine hours to Paris with the young bulls . . . Understand?"

Josephine pretended to study the itinerary. "Oh."

"Oui. Yes," he said with relief. "You have come in the middle of a war. Which I cannot understand how two young American ladies are here at this time. You should have come last summer before this Hitler fellow got into Poland and started all this fuss."

"I am a member of the press . . . you see. Here to cover the effects of the war." Josie said distractedly.

"An American woman a journalist? In France?"

"For Associated Press . . . Well, what does it matter? It does not solve the problem. I am slightly impoverished at any rate. We have no funds to purchase space in a private compartment and . . ."

"Holy Mother!" The man raised his eyes to heaven. "I would not be able to go home with a clear conscience." His face puckered angrily. He closed his eyes and raised his hand for silence.

An English voice shouted up from the end of the queue, "What's that old froggie about, then? Makin' time wif them birds 'isself? I been practicin' me French for jus' such a chance meetin'!" The comment was cheered by fifty soldiers in the ticket queue. A string of French phrases about love were butchered in cockney enthusiasm.

The clerk shuddered. It was a nightmare unequaled since Henry VIII landed in Boulogne! Two women nine hours with this . . . He took the third-class vouchers, inked his stamp and clamped it down with a resounding VOID! At that he retrieved two new cards from the second class drawer and filled them out carefully.

"It is senile old generals and brainless politicians who ride first class in France. That would be the safest place for young ladies. Second class compartments are mostly reserved by officers of lesser rank. You will have to sleep sitting up, but at least you will be safe from the mob. I assign you to the compartment of a French Colonel. I only just issued his ticket," he said in a paternal tone. "He is older than the foot soldiers, but you must still be on your guard. You are a woman . . . two women . . . I must think of my daughters. If they were here . . . But the colonel, he is French, Mademoiselle. And in matters of love, one old French bull is, I am certain, the equal of a carload of these young English bulls. Only you will not be trampled in the rush." He sniffed.

Josephine smiled. "Merci, monsieur. One Frenchman will be easier for us to keep an eye on."

He slid the tickets across to her. "No charge. Vive la France! Next please."

A sea of British khaki parted as Josie and Alma lugged their baggage toward the train on platform three. Offers of assistance came from several dozen of the young British bulls. Josie, mindful of the ticket clerk's warning, pretended not to understand a word of English and pushed on without stopping. She spoke to Alma in French, warning her not to look, speak, or smile at the soldiers. In spite of Josie's instructions, Alma looked and smiled.

The French colonel already occupied compartment F. He was asleep, sprawled out to take up an entire bench seat. A copy of the Paris newspaper, *Le Journal,* covered his face. The headlines of the thin issue announced the execution in Munich of a former French singer who had been implicated in the November attempt on Hitler's life. The photograph showed a strikingly beautiful blond woman in a black dress with a plunging neckline, perched beside Maurice Chevalier on top of a grand piano. It was an old photograph. Josie glanced at the story. How odd it seemed that one woman would be given almost an entire page of rationed newsprint when so many had perished in obscurity. The French had a flare for the dramatic. Thankfully, however, as the two women settled into the coach, the reality of war was little more than a headline covering the face of a snoozing Frenchman.

Josie noticed the expensive riding boots, overcoat, and cap of the French officer stashed above him in the luggage rack. His clothing showed no sign of the hardships of life in the trenches. Perched on the back of his seat, a porcelain doll dressed in white lace gazed across at Josie and Alma with serene blue eyes.

Alma shrugged and gestured toward the doll as if to dismiss the concern of the ticket taker about the Lone French Bull.

Josie nodded in amused agreement, then opened the window to look out as the din in the train shed increased. The old man had been right about the matter of the third-class travelers.

It was still twelve minutes until departure, but the long, forest-green train to Paris chuffed impatiently. The red signal light glowered down like a disapproving eye at the scene in the station. On the tail end of the platform, swarms of soldiers cursed and pushed impatiently to board the third-class cars. The tin roof reverberated with angry shouts. Those first men on board began to pull their friends into the cars through open windows. A conductor fought his way out from the mob and hurried toward the front of the train. He had lost his hat. His coat was torn at the sleeve.

"We must depart immediately!" he shouted. "There is no more room in third class!"

"Stampede," Alma whispered.

Behind her a strong, resonant male voice replied from under the paper. "Riot, Mademoiselle. The window, if you please. Close it. Pull the shades. And lock the door."

But the colonel did not change his position. Josie obeyed, closing the window with clumsy fingers as the first group of soldiers broke off from the mob and ran toward the uncrowded second class cars.

" 'Ey mates! There's room up there!"

Suddenly three hundred men turned to the front of the train and swarmed toward them, leaping into second-class compartments as the whistle shrieked and the train lurched forward.

Josie locked the door but did not pull the shade as five men sprinted alongside them, gesturing and shouting to be let in. She and Alma watched the mad dash with horror as two of the men fell to the pavement. The other three kept coming as if they could race the train and somehow beat it.

"Come'on! Give us a lift, girlie!"

"Poor things." Alma put her hand on the glass.

They looked so hopeful and childlike. Josie's fingers were on the latch. For a moment she considered opening the door. Could it hurt? Three homesick boys who wanted only to get to Paris?

"Enough!" the colonel shouted. He sprang to his feet, throwing the paper to the floor, then with a small wave to their pursuers, he reached around Josie and pulled down the shade.

He remained standing in the center of the small space until the voices died away. Josie looked up at him, embarrassed somehow that she had not obeyed his command and yet angry that he had not opened the door for the young Englishmen.

The colonel was not such an old bull after all. In his early thirties, perhaps, and darkly handsome, he was something over six feet tall even without his boots. A small green leather volume of Milton's *Paradise Lost* protruded from the right pocket of his unbuttoned tunic.

He grinned at Josie and bowed awkwardly, with a gesture as if he had doffed his hat. He did not seem to notice that Alma was beside her. He swayed slightly. Was he drunk? The doll smiled placidly from behind him.

"Poor fellows missed the train. Well, war is hell, they say." He sat down hard on the padded bench and closed his eyes. "That is what they say." Using a leather portfolio as a pillow, he stretched out on the seat and reached up to touch the leg of the doll as if to make certain it was still there. Then he groped for his newspaper.

With an unconcealed expression of amusement, Alma retrieved the rumpled sheets of Le Journal and spread it over the face of the colonel as the night train to Paris rocked and gained a steady rhythm.

✢   ✢   ✢

The cold had settled over London tonight, but the nearness of Annie warmed David. In the moonlight, the Thames gleamed like a ribbon of tinfoil as it snaked past the wharfs and under Tower Bridge. David had not intended to go so far when they left the Wairakei to walk Duffy along the Embankment, but he was glad for the distance. Although David had not told Annie, he knew that this was their last night together for perhaps a very long time.

By tomorrow morning he would be nearly to Tangmere, the airfield twenty-five miles west of Brighton, between South Downs and the Channel. But he would not be there for long. POSTED TO FRANCE, his orders read. At Tangmere he was slated to join a formation of replacement pilots ferrying Hurricanes to the BEF. Once there he would belong to 73 Squadron body and soul. Tonight David realized that when they turned back toward the Wairakei, it would mean their final good-bye was near.

Duffy tugged David along to the next unlit lamppost and then to an ornate bench with camels decorating the ironwork. The pilot made no effort to slow the dog or turn him back. The further Duffy pulled them away from home, the longer the walk home would last.

Wordlessly, Annie took his hand, intertwining her fingers with his. It felt natural, as though their hands were meant to fit together. This gesture, which had become so familiar to him in their days together, made him ache inside. How he longed to tell her he was leaving and that he loved her. His desire was bigger than words. It dwarfed his thoughts until they were mere shadows of his feeling.

"You've been quiet all evenin', Davey." She stopped and leaned against his arm. He felt the roundness of her breasts through his sleeve. "What's wrong?"

He could hardly breathe. He could not answer her question about why he was quiet. She was the reason. There was the river and the moonlight and Annie. She tugged his arm and pulled him down to sit on a bench.

"Like a silver ribbon," David murmured, commenting on the shining river as if he were not thinking of her lying in his arms, yielding to his touch.

He was certain that he loved her. He wanted her as he had never wanted any woman. But if he loved her, how could he take her tonight and leave before dawn, maybe forever? She knew all the stories of the lines soldiers pulled on their "last night before going off to war." What could David say that would not sound like that?

Helpless in the face of reality, he remarked on the water, the shadows cast on the Thames by London Bridge and the shining dome of St. Paul's Cathedral. When he had finally run out of travelogue and was trying to think what else to say about the moonlight without repeating himself, he chanced to look down at Annie, who had curled up beside him on the bench. She was grinning up at him.

He caught on at once. "Rambling like an idiot, huh?"

"Blitherin'," she agreed, but with a dazzling smile that took the bite out of her comment. "Why don't you just say it?"

"Annie, I," David began and then paused. "I'd like to ask you to . . . marry me. I never would have believed that I could fall so much in love, so fast. You hit me like a ton of bricks."

She smiled again. "That's good is it? The ton of bricks, I mean?"

"More pain than I've felt in a long time . . . but as I say, I want to ask you, but I can't, not now. To ask you to wait for me, not knowing when or even . . ."

Her smile faded. She knew. "You're leavin' then. You've been posted to France?"

"Annie, do you know how much I . . ." He did not finish. Annie's father was in Dover. They could be alone on the little ketch tonight. The rising and falling of the tide. The rigging playing a melody against the masts. Her softness beneath him. He had imagined it all. He dared not speak it. Would she say yes? "I love you Annie. I won't ask a commitment from you that I may not be able to keep. If anything should happen . . ."

"Shhh!" she insisted hurriedly, putting her small hand across his lips. "Don't even be thinkin' that, Davey Meyer, not for one instant!"

They sat together in silence, both reflecting on what the unspoken words had been. The RAF casualty list for the first three months of the war had recently appeared in the London Times; 380 fliers had been killed since September, and everyone agreed that the fighting had not even started to heat up.

"It's just better for you to not get tangled up with me now," David said.

"David Meyer," Annie said with spirit, "don't you be tellin' me about what's better for me, without even askin' my thoughts!"

Duffy got in the middle of the argument, laying his great sorrowful head on Annie's lap.

"This is tough on me you know. Right now I wish I could change places with Duffy."

"I've been thinkin' the same thing." She laughed and he laughed, dissipating some of his anguish. "I'd be a liar if I didn't tell you I get a hunger when I think of you. I feel it now. I've never . . . been with a man, Davey."

He wanted to kiss her, but she turned her face away.

"It's a good thing we've walked so far from the *Wairakei,"* he ventured. "Or I'd . . ."

"I know. Me too." Annie lapsed into silence, staring across the luminous river and watching the way it flowed past Tower Bridge, as if she could see all the way to the Channel, all the way to France. "Do you see this river, Davey?" she asked. "Men and women have been sayin' good-bye on this spot for maybe a thousand years. It has always been a fearful thing to be waitin' for one you care about to come home. But sayin' that it's hard doesn't mean you can stop carin', even if you wanted to. Are your feelings like a spigot, that you turn off when you've a mind to? Or are they like this river, rollin' so strong that you cannot hold them back? I can wait. And you can leave me knowin' that I'll be true to you, because I'm true to myself. The river will be here when you come back."

David studied her eyes, her nose, her lips, memorizing her features in the moonlight. He took her face in his hands, and pulling her close, kissed her. She slipped her arms beneath his coat and buried her face in the rough fabric of his uniform jacket. David stroked the feathery texture of her hair. He buried his face in the nape of her neck and inhaled her sweet fragrance. He felt his pulse race as she pressed against him. He wanted to commit every sense of her to a forever part of his mind.

"I love you," he whispered to her. "Will you wait for me? Will you marry me when I get back?"

She nodded her head in reply.

She dared not let him walk her back to the mooring. And so they said good-bye beside the river like ten thousand others had done for a thousand years.

⚜ ⚜ ⚜

The night train to Paris had been quiet since the dining car closed some hours before. Blackout restrictions required that the passage be made in darkness in the unlikely event that a German Heinkel might wish to bomb the rail lines. The shade was up, and so the light in Compartment F was off.

Moonlight broke through the clouds, illuminating the snow-covered farmlands in a pale blue light. Josephine, her forehead pressed against the cool glass windowpane, watched the countryside slide by as Alma and the French officer dozed.

The world beyond the train seemed peaceful. Tiny villages dotted the valley. Steep-roofed houses with unlit windows clustered around tall, Gothic church spires. Rows of leafless poplar trees divided fields and defined the boundaries of roads and farms and lives.

In the moonlight, beneath the blanket of snow, the world seemed perfect; almost holy. *The calloused hands of the old man reached out for his wife in the darkness, and she lay against him as she had each night for fifty years.*

In those little houses, men and women raised their children together . . . ate their meals together . . . laughed and cried together. *The weary farmer sighed with contentment as his wife slid her hands along his back and said his name.*

Unseen by those on the speeding train, couples whispered secret things and made love in warm feather beds. *The clock on the nightstand hammered out the seconds as the impatient young husband pulled his bride to him and she yielded eagerly.*

Each day and night beneath those steep roofs, the sacrament of ordinary life was performed while the train to Paris passed by, changing nothing.

How Josie envied the people she imagined behind those darkened windows! Once again the ache of loneliness welled up in her, constricting her throat until she could barely breathe. Beyond the neat rows of poplar trees was everything that she had ever dreamed her life would be with Daniel. She had wanted nothing but Daniel. To share his bed and bear his children, to be young together and then grow old, one ordinary day at a time. He had not shared her dreams, however. In the first six years of marriage, they had spent a total of sixteen months together. While he had traveled the world on assignment with Associated Press, she had stayed behind to teach school. She had built her own ordinary life without him. In the summer of 1936 she joined him in Paris, and they fell in love all over again.

Less than a year later he died covering the Spanish Civil War. Something within her died with him.

A widow at twenty-seven, she had no job, no place to go. She longed only to remain in Paris, where she and Danny had the best of one another.

They were good to her at AP. She got a job as a reporter. Some said she was a better writer than Danny had been. More heart and soul they said, not knowing that whatever passion Josephine had put into her writing was born of her own personal grief. And so she had built a life without Danny after all.

The shadow of a cloud drifted across the face of the lopsided moon, blocking its light. The world was dark again and yet the image of Danny's face was clear and bright in her mind. The memory of the dead had crowded out all thought of living. She wanted to love again. There were moments when she thought she had found what she was looking for in Mac, but somehow she had let that die too.

"Beautiful, is it not, Mademoiselle?"

The quiet voice of the colonel startled her, but she did not acknowledge him. Instead, she snapped her eyes shut and pretended to be asleep. She wanted to think only about what she had lost. She resented this intrusion on her grief.

"Forgive me, Mademoiselle. I am afraid I gave you a bad impression this afternoon." He tried again. "I did not intend to be rude."

With a sigh, Josie raised her head and shifted in her seat, inching away from his outstretched legs. She was glad he could not see her face. "We thought perhaps you were . . . ill." She did not tell him that she really thought he had been drunk.

"In need of sleep."

"You missed the evening meal."

"You are . . . American. There are no tourists since September."

"My friend and I are with the Associated Press office in Paris."

"Yes? I know of it. P. J. Phillip is a friend of mine."

"P.J. is *New York Times,* but that's close enough. We eat at the same cafe and attend the same press conferences."

He frowned in consternation, trying to rectify his error. "Let me see. Associated Press . . . There was a fellow I knew some time ago. Daniel Marlow."

"My husband."

He blanched. "I am sorry, Madame. Clumsy of me."

"Quite alright. Danny had a million friends. Everyone knew him."

"You are working in Paris for a while?"

"For a while."

"You are not afraid of Nazis, Mademoiselle? That they will bomb Paris?"

She did not tell him that she had been in Warsaw. That her dreams were full of Stuka dive-bombers, the thunder of artillery, and the screams of the dying. "I hope that will not happen, Monsieur. I hope that France will not let that happen."

"Every able-bodied man is called up, Mademoiselle. The sandbags are heaped up everywhere. Notre Dame. The Opéra. The Louvre. Everywhere. A precaution, they say. But we have all seen the news films. What they did to Warsaw. Paris is crowded with the refugees from Poland. The Jews from Germany. Austria. Czechoslovakia. They would say there is reason to be frightened."

"You have family in Paris? A little girl?" Josie could just make out the silhouette of the doll behind the colonel.

He did not reply. Had he closed his eyes again? Drifted off to sleep? Or had she somehow intruded on his privacy just as he had done, unwittingly, to her?

"Duty calls me back to Paris," he replied after a long moment. Then silence settled between them. She did not ask what duty he had to face. She did not ask about the doll or Christmas plans or his family. Somehow she sensed that she had come too near to a painful place in the French colonel's thoughts.

Nor did he question her further. The only safe topic, it seemed, had been the war—the Nazis. Would they try to do to Paris what they had done to Warsaw? Who could say? For strangers on a train, nothing remained to be discussed.

Alma stirred and sat up. "How much longer til Paris?" she moaned.

"Four hours, Mademoiselle," the colonel replied in a voice so heavy that Josie was certain he wished he had more time before the train arrived at Gare du Nord.

"Merci," Alma slurred. "My neck will be bent like the hunchback of Notre Dame by then." Then she promptly went back to sleep.

For a time, the colonel sat silently across from Josie. Was his face turned toward her? She knew he was awake. She wondered if he would speak to her again. He did not.

A half hour passed before he slipped on his boots, stood, and wordlessly left the compartment. For a brief moment the moon broke through the clouds. Light shone on the pretty face of the porcelain doll in the white lace dress.

At last, Josie was lulled to drowsiness by the gentle motion of the train. Using her sweater as a pillow she settled into the corner and drifted into a dreamless sleep.

TWENTY-SEVEN

Katrina lay sleeping beside Horst in the enormous four-poster bed. She was turned away from him, lying half in a shaft of silver light that fell across the curve of her back. Her skin glowed with a sheen so beautiful that the sight made him ache inside. He wanted to start over again and pull her against him, awaken her with passion that could help him forget everything but her.

And that was his problem, he mused. In trying to make himself forget, he had somehow forgotten how to make her happy.

Tonight their lovemaking lacked the joyful abandon they had always felt when giving themselves to one another. He had been demanding and impatient. Once again he could see from the confused look in her eyes that she was troubled by the change in him. He had lain awake beside her, unable to sleep, until her breathing had deepened.

Now, lost in hopeless thoughts, he got up, wrapped himself in a down quilt, and moved into the sitting room to brood beside the window.

Their time together had been miserable. Perhaps his trip home had done more harm than good. Perhaps it was better for a soldier to steel himself for the horrors of battle, to build resolution on a foundation of hatred for the enemy, and not to allow himself the softer emotions. He should bottle up love and compassion, stick it on the shelf until everything was over and he could come home for good.

But that was not the answer either. He did not hate the Poles, much less the French, against whom he would next be engaged. Horst sighed heavily and pulled back the sheer curtain to gaze out at the night. He shook his head at the realization that the only hatred he felt was directed at the murdering SS swine. And he loathed himself. He detested the fact that he was connected to the death of the Polish woman by the river. What weighed most heavily on his mind was the fact that he had known the SS would not really let her go. It had been a convenient fiction, designed to save face and protect his tender conscience. But deep down he reckoned that he was a coward after all, since by standing aside he had let them kill her.

Katrina had more courage than he did, and his knowledge of this separated him from her. There were moments when he thought he saw contempt in her eyes when he talked of duty. Often he wondered if she would have gladly gone to prison except for the fact that she thought she could oppose the Nazis more effectively by remaining free. Her courage frightened him.

Thin wisps of smoke rose in the moonlight from the chimneys of the stables. Horst felt a flash of irritation at Katrina. Twenty-two little girls, supervised by two middle-aged women, now lived on the upper floor of the stable.

"Evacuees from Berlin," Katrina had explained.

Horst had not pushed her for details, but he had his suspicions.

Embers on the grate of the sitting room fireplace glowed deep orange. Horst tossed another spadeful of coal onto the fire and stirred them into flame.

"Horst?" Katrina called him as she entered the sitting room. She pulled on a silk robe which clung to the contours of her body. "Why aren't you sleeping?"

"I couldn't." He stabbed at the coals and then let the poker fall with a clatter.

She took a chair beside the window. Drawing her legs up under her chin, she looked childlike in the moonlight as she gazed down on her domain.

"Do you want to talk?" she asked.

"About what?" His irritation was evident.

"About whatever happened out there?"

He stood to his full height and stretched his hands out to the warmth of the fire. "I would rather you tell me the truth about those children down there."

"What about them?" she replied with unconcern.

"Are they Jews?"

"How should I know?"

"You should know!" His anger flared. "You're playing with fire, Katrina! Old Brezinski is one thing. You played that hand cleverly. Yes, he is essential to the welfare of the horses. When you have permission from Goering himself . . . Goering can change his mind and send the Gestapo out here to collect the old Jew whenever he likes. You will have to let them take him too! But those children and the women. Nuns, are they not? They cross themselves at every turn. They look like nuns even without their habits. Pious-faced crones. Turned out of their convent? Threatened with arrest? How can you expect to protect them? Do you know the penalty if you are caught?"

She jumped to her feet and matched his anger with outrage. "I told you! I do not know anything except that Father Johann asked if I had room for children from the city."

"This was just before they hauled the good priest off to Dachau, was it?"

"I do not know any more than what I have told you, Horst. I do not want to know more. I do not ask questions."

"You understand the penalty for keeping a collection of Jews beneath your roof? Little Jews though they may be. Even in your stable? Your punishment will be the same as theirs! Dachau! Sachenhausen! How long until one of your stable boys reports you?"

"You are no better than every coward in Germany!"

"I do not want to see you hurt."

"Only you have the power to hurt me. You use it very effectively."

"I do my duty."

"You do your duty?" She laughed bitterly. "Then do it. Serve whatever twisted evil god you must, and call it duty. But I also have a duty!"

"They will kill you."

"My life is the only weapon I have. If I am afraid to lose it, then I have lost the battle already. You . . . *Major!* . . . Surely you know this." The words rang with scorn.

"I have faced death with courage!" he shouted.

"You face death in battles against men who never were your enemies, yes? Then what is it you fear more than dying, Horst? You fear the disapproval of these Nazi monsters who call you brave and brother and comrade! You value their good opinion of you more than you value your own opinion of what is true and good! You fear their accusations of cowardice even more than death. And that marks the twilight of your courage. You have sold your soul to them, Horst, for a profane lie they call sacred honor. They own you."

"I have lost you," he said miserably.

She stood silently before him for a long moment. "No. It is you who are lost. What happened to you in Poland, Horst?"

"I . . . Katrina . . . I am . . . forgive me." He sank to his knees.

"You should divorce me, before I bring dishonor to your career. I want you to leave me, Horst." Her voice was without compassion. "You are not a cadet playing war games anymore. Poland was not military maneuvers."

"You think I do not know . . ."

"Then what are you doing?"

"What I must do! I have no choice. Where is the way out?"

She could not answer the deeper side of his question, but she raised her arm and pointed toward the snow-covered drive which led to the road. "There." Then she retreated to the bedroom and closed the door, locking him out.

❊ ❊ ❊

The soft nickering from the barn called to Horst as he tossed his valise into the back of the automobile.

Two sheets of black canvas tarpaulin formed a three-foot-deep entryway, keeping light from escaping, as Horst entered for one last look at the horses.

Old Brezinski was up in the lantern light, stroking the nose of a mare that was heavy with foal. His face expressed a moment of alarm at first sight of Horst's uniform, and then his shoulders sagged with relief.

"You are up early, Brezinski." Horst stepped to the stall door and stroked the soft muzzle of the old man's object of concern.

"Up late, Herr von Bockman." The old man did not look at the Wehrmacht uniform. Always before he had called Horst by his first name. Brezinski kept his gaze fixed on the soft intelligent eyes of the mare.

"I am leaving."

"So soon?"

"Katrina has asked me to."

"Ah. She has forgotten that politics has nothing to do with war. Is that it?"

"Something like that."

Brezinski shrugged as if the mind of a woman was unfathomable. "A pity you must go so soon. You will miss the foal. The mare is due any time. I could not sleep. Beautiful, is she not?" he said with tender affection. "Her sire was killed in your war. A Polish cavalry charge."

Your war, the words were not an accusation, but a simple fact in the mind of the old man. It was Germany's war. Horst's war. As if the whole matter had been something distant, a game played by only one team in which the spectators of Poland had been required to participate in the end.

"I am sorry," Horst said, sorry that such a fine animal had been forced to face the iron-hide of a German tank.

"No need to be sorry." The old man still did not look at him. "He was bred for battle. Brave horses to carry brave men to their deaths. It is a noble end. We will not see the like of it again."

Silence. The stirring of hooves in the stalls. The scent of hay and manure and horse flesh. All these familiar things which had been such an integral part of armies for thousands of years were now without significance. With those last heroic cavalry charges in Poland, a history as long as warfare had ended. Horst had seen the bloated carcasses in the fields where they had fallen. The horses of Brezinski had simply perished with Poland and had been ground to dust beneath the tracks of tanks.

Horst cleared his throat, breaking the stillness. "As a boy I loved stories of the cavalry. Alexander's army at Issus. Napoleon at Austerlitz. Waterloo. No matter which battle, it was the cavalry which fascinated me. I would have joined the cavalry of any nation, just to ride and fight."

Now Brezinski turned his head to look Horst square in the eye. "It was a noble profession. The cavalry. It was . . . There was something like love; a passion between the soldier and his mount. You know it. That is why I always liked you, young Horst."

"It was a game played on a level playing field. Man to man. Horse to horse. It was the noblest animal who carried his warrior to the thick of battle."

The old man nodded. "Not always the strongest, but the one with the greatest heart. It was the most courageous man who turned the tide and won the war. I have seen it with my own eyes. There was a horrible beauty in it. Death was not beautiful, but the dying! Now that is all changed. Everything is changed." He looked away down the row of stalls. "I always thought you were like one of these; like my Arabians. Bred for the sport of battle. When we were friends, before this war made us enemies, I said to myself, 'That boy is created to ride Orion into the line of waiting infantry!' It would not matter who you fought against or what you fought for, only that you would lead the charge."

"I was born one hundred years too late."

"You were born beneath the wrong flag," Brezinski chuckled. "Even in this modern age it could have been different for you. To have lived a few hours east of here . . . You would have ridden Orion into the final battle with the Polish cavalry. Just a few miles, an accident of birth, separated you from belonging to Poland. As recently as September you might have fought and fallen with the last men of valor."

Horst did not reply for a time. He smiled at the thought of what might have been. In the last century he would have ridden out with the Prussian cavalry to face Napoleon's army at Waterloo. And there would have been some honor in the terrible victory against the French. "I can still fight nobly against France, old man."

"Can you, Horst?"

"I must. In spite of the flag I am under."

Brezinski nodded. "I suppose it is true. A well-bred war horse knows nothing of politics. Of who is right or wrong. It knows only the battle. It lives only for the challenge." He extended his hand. "You are a man out of your own time, Horst von Bockman. An anachronism. Hitler hates you, but he will use you. I think you may well die before I do. I wish you . . . what? What can I wish a man who is so unfortunate to fight on the wrong side?"

"Wish me noble men to fight against, Brezinski. Opponents with courage and skill. There is nothing else left for a German soldier to hope for."

✱ ✱ ✱

Aaron Lubetkin stood at the darkened window and surveyed the cemetery across the road. Behind the high brick wall were ancient leaning headstones and broken monuments. Marble and granite markers once bore chiseled inscriptions . . . Beloved Father . . . Faithful Wife . . . Our Baby. Now scars from bullets marred those precious words. The stones had been machine gunned during the recent Nazi desecrations of Jewish graves. Tonight those eerie sentinels marked the path to freedom for Etta and the children. There was no other way out of the Jewish Ghetto. Since November the area had been ringed with barbed concertina wire. Only the field of tombs remained open on both sides.

In three days the population had doubled to over 300,000, as Jews from other parts of the city had been rounded up and herded into the already overcrowded neighborhood. The tribe of black-coated Orthodox was joined by thousands who had never read a word of Hebrew. Bank clerks, shop girls, nightclub singers, and taxi drivers suddenly found themselves thrown out of their apartments, trucked across town, and scrambling for a few square feet of space in which to live. For years they had blended in, purchasing clothing in the same department stores where the Gentile Poles had bought their garments off the rack.

The Ghetto district was a muddle now. Confused Nazis first singled out for persecution those who dressed in the fashion of religious Jews. Those who dressed in modern style were passed by. Then the invaders were reminded of the Aryan maxim that, "Everything that looks human is not human . . ." Yellow armbands marked with the Star of David were now required. In that way identification of the subhumans was easily made, no matter how they dressed or what their former station had been in pre-Nazi Poland. Those Jews who did not wear the obligatory badges and were caught suffered the severest consequences.

At a nod from Aaron, Etta slipped her armband off and then removed them from the children's clothing. Her hands were like ice. The cloth of the yellow badges trembled in her fingers. Did the children notice?

"A short walk. Just through the cemetery. On the other side we will be Catholics going to Mass. You remember . . . like we talked about." She tried to steady her voice.

Curt nods from all. Their eyes were wide, faces pale as they contemplated the penalty for walking out without the yellow band and trying to leave without papers. They had heard the stories and seen with their own eyes the punishment meted out by the enemy.

"Are you afraid?" young Samuel whispered to his bigger brother.

David replied with a single affirmative nod.

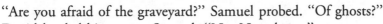

"Are you afraid of the graveyard?" Samuel probed. "Of ghosts?"

David leveled his gaze at Samuel. "No. Not ghosts."

It was not the fear of disembodied evil which shook them all, but the knowledge that all around, the darkest, cruelest evil had somehow possessed the flesh of living men.

The SS. Those human husks were empowered with inhuman brutality, and they were omnipotent over those who wore the condemning armbands. Hell had come to Warsaw to search out all Jews and destroy them as quickly as possible. Even little boys like David and Samuel. Even babies like Yacov.

David did not fear a walk through the dark graveyard. He feared those living dead—the soulless Aryan horde who dressed in handsome uniforms with lightning bolts on their collars. He feared the slap of their marching jackboots on the cobblestones and their proud voices raised in song together:

Crush the skulls of the Jewish pack
And the future it is ours and won;
Proud waves the flag in the wind
When swords with Jewish blood will run.

Even now those soldiers watched and waited on the other side. Yes. The boy was afraid. So were they all . . . except for the baby.

Aaron raised his hand and muttered, "Quickly now. Go." He turned back to the window as if to promise that he would watch them safely on their way.

A final glance of farewell. Then down the hall and onto the landing, quickly down two flights of stairs, and out past the closed door of the concierge. The sudden coldness of the air was like a slap in the face awakening Etta from the unreality of parting. She gasped, held the baby closer to her, and then stepped away from the shadowed alcove of the entrance.

The street seemed deserted at first, and yet Etta heard the faint voices of terror rustling in the shadows. How many, like themselves, had received the warning?

Hide yourselves tonight!

Fat, lazy snowflakes drifted down and landed on her dark shawl and flecked the coats of the children.

Three steps through the crunching snow and Samuel spoke. "Mama, I forgot . . ."

He was instantly silenced by a rough shove from David. What did it matter if Samuel had forgotten something? What difference could it make now? They had left their whole world behind. What was left of any value that Samuel could have forgotten?

Samuel persisted, his voice choked with sorrow. "I . . . forgot to kiss Papa . . . good night."

Yes. Papa. Papa. Left behind.

"You can kiss him when we are back together," Rachel soothed.

We will never be together again! No kissing Papa good night or good-bye, Etta wanted to scream! She fought the urge to run back to Aaron, to ask him if it was such a terrible thing for them to all die together? Could they not face the end together? To beg him . . . How could she go on living without him?

The sleeping baby sighed a ragged breath and turned his face toward her breast. She shook her head, as if to clear her mind for what lay ahead. For these she must live!

Pulling herself erect, she stepped from the curb and resisted one last look back at the window. The children followed. Crossing the street, Etta felt Aaron's gaze on her back. He was watching their retreat—willing them to go, yet longing for them to stay.

Little Samuel moaned at having forgotten the kiss. Rachel put her hand on his shoulder. "He is still there at the window. Blow him a kiss then, Samuel. Like this . . ." She turned and demonstrated. "You see? He is there. At the window. Good night, Papa."

Samuel imitated his sister even though he could not see Papa. Satisfied at last, they hurried beneath the rusted iron archway above the gate of the Jewish cemetery.

Then David balked a moment, spun in the snow, and ran back to the gate. He, too, gave a final, tentative wave in hopes his father would see him. After searching the dark eye of the window frame, he reluctantly ran after the others.

They wound quickly down a narrow pathway rimmed by snow-capped headstones. The gnarled branches of an ancient tree towered above them. Only now in the shadow, when she was certain Aaron could not see them, did Etta let herself look back at the dark brick facade of the apartment building.

Every flat and house in Warsaw had been fitted with blackout curtains before the outbreak of war. A precaution against German bombs. What a forlorn and foolish hope the black cloth represented! There had been no hiding from the Stukas.

Tonight, everywhere in Warsaw, blackout curtains remained in place like the black crepe of a household in mourning for its dead. No light shone from the window. There was no sign of life. But Aaron was there in the unlit room, she knew, still straining for one final glimpse of his family.

Just another window, she told herself, fighting again the desire to return to him. *No one there. He is not really there. Nothing to turn back for.* She steeled herself. *Think of the children! Of life!*

Etta tucked her head against the sharp wind howling down from the highest hill of the burial grounds. At the bottom of the slope they descended, snow had piled up dangerously deep. The paths had not been cleared since the first snowfall. Heavy drifts tugged at Etta's hem, holding her back like the dread-filled, grasping clutch in some terrible nightmare.

Behind her, little Samuel struggled on. He stumbled, fell, rose slowly, and stumbled again. Not bound by skirts or petticoats, Rachel moved more easily than her mother through the tomb-studded drifts. She grabbed the hand of Samuel, yanked him upright, and then, in marching stride, plunged on after Etta. David trudged along behind.

Rachel, panting, pointed up to the crest of the hill they must now climb. She called above the wind. "That way, Mama. Up there. Over the ridge. Past the Levy tomb and then out the gate to the Aryan side!"

Etta nodded, not sparing breath to answer. A dozen times in the last months Rachel had carried messages out to the priest using this route. It had spared her the questioning and the document checks at the barricades which guarded every entrance into the Jewish Ghetto. It still seemed a peculiar oversight that only rarely were Nazi guards posted at the cemetery gates. Tonight, she and the children would step from the Jewish side of this valley of death into streets where trams still clattered by and taxis blew their horns.

Father Kopecky's church was only a few blocks from the portals of the Jewish cemetery. The bells announcing evening Mass echoed across the landscape. They seemed frantic tonight, clanging wildly without their usual steady cadence.

Etta's stomach churned at the sound.

Were the bells a beacon to prayer? Or a warning?

The pealing died away. For a moment, only the scream of the wind joined the crunch of their footsteps as they began their ascent of the slope. Then another, more ominous sound penetrated the swirling snow.

Fifty yards from the top, Etta paused beside a headless stone angel. She leaned against the monument and put her hand out, stopping Rachel, Samuel, and David.

"What is it, Mama?" David asked, cocking his head toward the murmuring which undulated with the rise and fall of the wind.

Etta shook her head, demanding silence. She raised her eyes to the brow of the hill where grey light penetrated the veil of falling snow and silhouetted the tombstones. The glow flickered. Shadows of tombs and pillars lengthened and deepened. The light grew brighter—nearer! It spread out, illuminating the width of the ridge above them. A dog barked and then another. The murmuring became recognizable as the noise of men's voices and expectant laughter!

Terror and realization filled the faces of the children and their mother in that instant! *The soldiers were sweeping through the graveyard!* Men with torches and dogs entering the ghetto from the other side! They were looking for escaping Jews; they were blocking the route to freedom!

"Run!" Etta cried. "Don't look back! *Run!*"

No time to lose. Too late to consider the deep tracks they left in the snow. They clawed their way toward the gate which led back into the Ghetto.

Behind them the cry went up: "Footprints! Over here!" Hounds bayed as if in pursuit of a rabbit.

Rachel, dragging Samuel, was first up the path. Then David. Etta and the baby trailed twenty-five yards behind.

"It's Papa!" Samuel shouted and dashed ahead in a sudden burst of joy.

Coatless, Aaron had run from his outpost at the window. Ashen and tight-lipped with fear, he met them at the gate. "Where's your mother!" he demanded, shaking David. At that instant, Etta emerged from the shadow. She had no breath to acknowledge his miraculous presence. The thought flitted through her mind that she had gotten her wish. Perhaps they were to die together after all.

Aaron did not wait for her. "The torches! . . . Hurry, Etta!" Gathering the two boys into his arms, he sprinted back toward the apartment block. Rachel, bounding ahead of him, took the stairs two at a time. Etta, breathless from the effort, reached the flat only moments before their pursuers stormed the lobby.

The door was locked and bolted as two dozen men, following their wet tracks, swarmed up the stairs.

In the end it had been useless to run. They might as well have waited at the gate of the Jewish cemetery and surrendered there to the soldiers. The warning note, the clanging churchbells, the pain of farewell, the dash to freedom, and the frantic terror of the chase made no difference to the final outcome.

After all, the snowfall had made for a festive air, and the German soldiers were playful. It was they who had sent the note. The rumor was their own. They had spread the word in the Ghetto that some action was coming.

Verstecken Sie sich heute abend!

Hide yourselves tonight!

Like hunters flushing game from the brush, they had been ready for the hundreds who panicked and ran.

Locks and bolts were broken. The door was splintered by rifle butts and torn from its hinges.

And so, in spite of everything they were taken, this family of six, to await the train in the Umschlagplatz with fifteen hundred others. Together. They all went quietly with the enemy . . . except for the baby in his mother's arms, who finally awakened to wail in indignation that his sleep had been interrupted.

TWENTY-EIGHT

"Next stop! Gare du Nord! All passengers to alight! Paris! Ten minutes! Gare du Nord!"

Josie awoke to the sharp rap of the conductor's knuckles against the compartment door. The grey predawn light seeped in under the half-drawn shade. It was raining. Drops streaked the glass and drummed against the thin metal roof of the train. Swathed in blankets, Alma sat in numb silence for a moment. The seat which had been occupied by the French officer was empty. Boots, cap, coat, portfolio, and doll were all gone. The newspaper lay scattered on the floor and the small green volume of Milton's verse remained wedged between the cushions.

Josie retrieved the book, and, thumbing through the dog-eared pages, found whole passages underlined which might have been written about the conqueror of Warsaw.

> *Farewell, Happy fields,*
> *Where joy forever dwells! Hail horrors! Hail,*
> *Infernal world! and thou, profoundest Hell,*
> *Receive thy new possessor, one who brings*
> *A mind not to be changed by place or time.*
> *The mind is its own place, and in itself*
> *Can make a Heaven of Hell, and a Hell of Heaven . . .*

She read the words of Milton in a new light now. Who but one who lived through those days in Warsaw could understand the meaning?

Josie felt a renewed curiosity about the French colonel. How many Frenchmen read the works of the English poet? A vague sense of disappointment settled on her. He had gone without knowing she shared a passion for Milton's work. He had gone without saying good-bye.

Josie closed the book and tucked it into the pocket of her jacket.

"So when did tall, dark, and horizontal get off the train?" Alma asked, gathering her belongings.

"I didn't notice." Josie feigned unconcern.

"Really?" Alma looked at her own reflection in the mirror of her compact and grimaced. "I vaguely recall some conversation between the two of you. Did you tell him the story of your life?"

"You were dreaming."

"It wouldn't hurt, you know. A little male warmth and companionship."

"I'm not ready for that yet." Out of habit, Josie defended her right to remain lonely, to live in her own private hell.

"So you've told every eligible man who gets near."

"Every one of them journalists. One newspaper man is enough in a lifetime, thank you, and a man in uniform is just as dangerous."

"You have just eliminated every male in Europe under the age of sixty."

"I rest my case."

"You've been resting your case for too long, honey. You didn't even get his name? No wedding band, I noticed. But here he is taking the doll to some kid. Sweet. Sort of a tragic figure, I thought."

Josephine ran a brush through her tangled hair. "Maybe it was his doll. Think of that."

"Huh-uh. Not that guy."

"You meet your first Frenchman on French soil . . . drunk Frenchman . . . under a newspaper on a train to Paris, and you turn him into the hero of a Gothic romance novel. *Wuthering Heights* or something. If he had been old and ugly, you wouldn't have looked twice."

"Add rich to the mix and try me."

Josephine, in her best Snow White imitation, began to hum an off-key rendition of "Someday My Prince Will Come."

"Enough," Alma warned as the train slowed and slid beneath the enormous canopy of the Gare du Nord train shed.

Josie continued. "It doesn't matter how tall they are. Beneath the skin every prince is really just one of the Seven Dwarfs in disguise! If you ask me, our French captain was Grumpy standing on Sleepy's shoulders."

"Cynic."

"I'm just saying . . . All I'm saying, Alma . . . is that you should keep the dwarfs in mind when meeting men. Especially here. Then you'll never be disappointed."

"Or happy."

"I've tried Happy. Just another dwarf. Not that wonderful." Josie caught her own reflection in the window pane. She was lying. Happiness had been wonderful. It simply had not lasted. And what remained in the aftermath was worse than if she had never known Danny at all.

"As for me, I'm a realist. I'll settle for any one of the seven as long as he's taller than me and doesn't turn into a frog when I kiss him." Alma frowned, aware that the metaphor was flawed somehow.

"You're mixing fairy tales again," Josie corrected regally.

"You're the Lit. major, honey." Alma tapped the cover of Milton's epic. *"Paradise Lost,* huh?"

Yes. Paradise lost, Josie thought.

✾ ✾ ✾

The frigid morning air of Warsaw settled in the bones of the Jewish captives as well as the SS soldiers who guarded them in the open air of the Umschlagplatz. It was not mercy which led the guards to move the prisoners beneath the iron roof of the train shed, but their own quest for warmth. Oil drums were packed with scraps of wood and set ablaze around the perimeter. SS soldiers warmed themselves, smoked, laughed, and talked together beside the makeshift stoves. The fifteen hundred Jews inside the ring were forbidden to approach the drums. A boy in his early teens was shot dead for daring to come too near the blaze and stretch out his hands to steal Aryan warmth. When the boy's father ran to his dying son, he too was shot. Now the two lay embracing one another in death as a warning to the others that no violation of SS rules would be permitted.

Mid-morning of the day after their arrest, this was the hell in which Aaron and Etta Lubetkin found themselves and their children. They were thankful for one thing; the SS had not yet separated families. Husbands stood beside their wives. Mothers and children still huddled together against the cold.

The train scheduled to take them away remained derailed outside the city because of heavy snowdrifts on the tracks. The delay seemed a miracle to Etta. She held the baby, nursed him in the circle of her family, and prayed that someone would come to help them, that the Nazis would tire of their game and send everyone home. Surely the Nazis could not want to spend more freezing cold days guarding Jews in the Umschlagplatz. They must be as tired of this as their victims.

"The priest has heard by now," Etta whispered to Aaron when the guard looked away. "He must know. He will come, Aaron. I know he will."

Beyond the smoking drums, Poles walked cautiously past the group. A quick, guilty glance and then the pace would quicken. It was no good to look too long or let a guard spot a look of pity.

A prosperous man in a heavy topcoat stopped beside a guard and asked, "What did they do?"

"Attempted to leave the area after curfew without the proper permits, and resisted arrest," came the reply. "Expressly forbidden. Such an act makes them saboteurs against the Reich and the General Government."

"But the children?" asked the man.

"Their parents are criminals. Children suffer the same sentence as their parents. You know the penalty. It is the law. Everywhere it is the law. How else are we to keep order? If they think so little of their own children, then they deserve what they get. It would be the same for me in Germany."

This was true, Etta knew. In Germany, Austria, Czechoslovakia, and now in occupied Poland, the National Socialist law dictated that if one family member was guilty of breaking a law of the Reich then all members of the family suffered equally. Such a cruel edict had slowed acts of resistance against the Nazi state.

Accused saboteurs? Lawbreakers? No matter what the SS officer told the man in the business suit, the only real crime was that Etta and Aaron were Jews. Rachel, David, Samuel, and little Yacov were Jews. This crime received no pardon within the Reich. There was only one hope . . .

Etta gazed at the child sleeping in her arms. She brushed her lips against his forehead. Did she love him enough to let him go? Could she, like the mother of Moses, cast him adrift, knowing that she would never see him again? That she would die without knowing his fate?

Was there no hope of saving Rachel or David or Samuel? Older Jewish children were seldom taken in by Poles. If the priest did not come soon; if the SS would not accept a payment of ransom . . . then they would cling to one another and die together with thousands of others in some open ditch in the woods.

But Yacov was so tiny . . . Etta put her cheek against his cheek. She closed her eyes and pictured the daughter of Pharaoh rescuing a Jewish baby from the river, from the edict of certain death which her father had declared against the infant sons of Israel. The child had grown to be a prince among the enemies of his people until God called him back to lead his people to freedom.

The world had not changed in three thousand years. Were such miracles still possible? There was nothing left for Etta but this terrible, ancient hope. This was the miracle she prayed for now! *Oh, God!* That someone, anyone, would take her baby and walk away from her forever!

✳   ✳   ✳

Trevor Galway was imprisoned in the dank cargo hold of the *Admiral Graf Spee* for days before he was transferred onto the prison ship, *Altmark*, whose only purpose was to collect the human flotsam of British shipwrecks and transfer captives back to the Fatherland.

As senior British officer, Trevor had at first been questioned courteously about the mission and destination of HMS *Fortitude*. When he refused to answer he was lowered into a cargo hold with forty-five other men and the hatch had been battened down.

It was still an hour before dawn, and yet the tropical heat had already turned the prison hold into a steam bath. Trevor figured that the *Graf Spee* and the *Altmark* were somewhere near the equator, possibly off the coast of South America. He had not given up hope that the British Navy was tracking the German commerce raider with the diligence of a good pack of hounds after a fox.

Beside him on the bare wooden pallet that served as a bunk for eight men, Frankie Thomas, a Liverpool boy of seventeen captured from the British ship *Trevanian,* moaned and raised his hand toward the hatch. Even before his imprisonment Frankie had been thin and frail from his first voyage on a merchant ship. Captive's rations on the *Altmark* consisted of three thin slices of black bread twice a day and a pint of tinned potatoes. Now every bone was visible through Frankie's pale, stretched skin. He was like a baby bird, Trevor thought; all eyes and wide, hungry mouth. Unlike the other prisoners, Frankie had no beard.

The boy gasped and coughed at the stench of urine and human excrement overflowing from the waste bucket into the bilge. "I gotta breathe fresh air today or I ain't gonna make it, Commander Galway . . ."

"Steady, boy." Trevor tried to soothe him, although he also felt the pressure of filth, heat, and humidity bearing down on his chest. "You can't talk like that."

"Sure he can," barked the bitter voice of John Dykes from the dark pallet opposite. "And he can die if he wants. He probably will. You'd think the young ones would be the strongest, but they're not." Dykes had been on the *Altmark* longer than any prisoner in the hold. His freighter had been blown out of the water off the Cape of Good Hope at the end of September when the war was barely three weeks old.

"Shut up, Dykes," threatened Nob Jenkins, who was over sixty and had sailed in the merchant marine since he was the age of young Frankie. "Leave him be."

Dykes snorted in defense. "Just saying what I know. The young ones always die."

"Somebody open a window," moaned Frankie. "I gotta breathe."

"Window!" Dykes scoffed. "He's off his head. Thinks he's at his mum's house in Liverpool! I've seen it. He's a goner all right!"

"Not yet, he's not," Trevor spat.

Trevor put his hand on Frankie's forehead. The boy was burning with fever.

"Why d'ya suppose it's always the youngins?" asked the Australian.

"Mum used t' say only the good die young. Y'suppose it's because they ain't had time to live bad enough t' fear dyin'?"

"Shut up!" Trevor snapped. "That's an order."

It was still at least two hours before the hatch would open and fresh water and rations lowered. Frankie Thomas needed to be lifted out of the hold and placed in a doctor's care immediately or Dyke's prediction would be a certainty.

Trevor crawled out from the cramped space and groped in the blackness for the oil drum which held the discarded tin cans from the potato rations. Finding the drum, he grasped an empty tin.

George Daly was a merchant marine who spoke fair German along with a half dozen languages he had learned in ports around the world. Trevor woke him from sleep.

"We've got to get Frankie topside. I need you to translate for me."

George moaned. "I was dreaming, Commander. A good dream too."

"Stow it."

"You know the Huns can't hear us down here." At that he let loose with a string of insults in German at the top of his voice. "See there? If that wouldn't bring them down on us nothing will." This was followed by a chorus of curses from the other sleeping men. "You see? Nothing."

"Pick the worst of the lot and repeat it, George. Slowly and distinctly, please. Think of der Führer and spell out every word in German."

Trevor did not ask the meaning of George Daly's communiqué. He stood on the pallet and began to clang the can loudly against the hatch, reciting in Morse code each letter. Once, twice, three times, the message was tapped and heard topside.

Within two minutes the hatch was peeled back, allowing a blast of fresh air to penetrate the suffocating gloom.

Nob Jenkins touched the sick boy on his head. "Look, Frankie. The sky."

Frankie opened his eyes and blinked up at the square of star-flecked heavens. "Thanks," he breathed.

A cluster of German faces peered down angrily into the hold, pistols drawn.

"What'd you say to 'em, George?" hissed Dykes. "You was only supposed to make 'em a little mad."

George seemed pleased. "Just repeated a rumor that Hitler's mother's name was Schickelgruber. Sure to get us shot."

Dykes, a wild man with a long beard and matted hair, peered at him with eyes like two burnt holes in his filthy face. "The name of Hitler's mother?"

George had just opened his mouth to explain when the glaring face of Captain Thun appeared in the opening. A blaze of light stabbed the darkness, causing the men below to shield their eyes.

"Who has done this!"

Trevor held up the tin can as admission of guilt. "We have a seriously ill man here."

"What has that to do with this matter? Such slander against the purity of our Führer's Aryan blood is punishable by death in the Reich. Strictly verboten. Since you are ignorant of the ways of national socialism, however, we shall spare your life."

"We could think of no other way to get your attention. If this boy does not get help soon . . ." But it was already too late.

Frankie reached both spindly arms skyward as if to grasp the stars and pull himself up by beams of light. "Oh look!" He smiled. "Look at them!"

Nob clasped the boy's shoulder as if to hold him down. "Stay with us, Frankie. We're goin' home to England soon!"

"Home," Frankie murmured, and his arms fell in a limp tangle across his chest. The light left his eyes, sailing past the German captain to freedom.

"Dead," said Dykes. "Always the young ones."

"So, Mister Galway. You have the attention of the Reich." Then the German captain shouted the order to have Trevor dragged out of the hold for public flogging to precede the burial at sea of young Frankie Thomas.

❧   ❧   ❧

Hundreds of passengers who had been crammed on board the train emptied out into the vast, echoing *salle des pas purdus* of Gare du Nord. The station seemed almost tomblike. Unlike the teeming, noisy atmosphere of prewar train stations, the quiet was tangible. Chilling. Gone were the blue-bloused porters. Now all the station employees were old men in ancient, shabby uniforms which smelled like mothballs. Weary women in black dresses pushed brooms around the enormous hall. Things had changed, Josie noted, hoping that the early morning hour was partly to blame for the grimness of the place.

Formerly rowdy British soldiers disembarked like rumpled little Boy Scouts who had been roused too early by reveille. They staggered in confused bunches toward exits, stopped to peer at signs, turned, and wandered back the other way before finally finding their way to the taxi queue or out onto the street.

At the far end of the terminal, Josie noticed a French officer part a group of muddled Englishmen with a certain stride. Was it the colonel? Perhaps he had not gotten off the train at an earlier stop after all. Whoever he was, he knew how to get out of Gare du Nord. Josie nudged Alma in the same direction. Perhaps she could just get close enough to return his book . . .

He was gone by the time they stepped out onto Boulevard de Magenta. Rain sluiced down the cobbled pavement, overrunning the curbs and dripping melodically from the eaves. The air smelled fresh and clean. The boulevards were almost deserted. Streetlamps burned in the soft predawn light. Paris was still sleeping.

Josephine stepped into the rain and looked up the street for some sign of the tiny orange Citroen of her friend Delfina Periguex. Had Delfina received Josie's telegram asking her to reserve two rooms at the American House for their arrival this morning?

"Are you sure she's coming?" Alma asked as the downpour increased and the minutes ticked into half an hour.

"No," Josephine answered honestly, inwardly suspecting that the wire had not arrived. For the first time she worried about finding a place to live.

The line of cabs dwindled, and the bus came and went across the boulevard. Alma cast reproachful looks at Josie and, in halting French, queried the doorman about fares to the American House.

"The American House, Mam'zelle?" He seemed surprised. "It is a barracks now. All residence halls are requisitioned for the Armée as well."

Josie had sent the telegram to the graduate residence hall of the university where Delfina conducted research for her doctorate in child psychology. "Cité Universitaire?" Josie ventured.

"Requisitioned for the soldiers, Mam'zelle."

Josie hailed a cab, hoping that the AP office could help them find someplace to sleep out of the rain.

At that moment Delfina emerged from the entrance to the Paris Metro, the underground. Her normally perfect blond hair was tucked under a scarf. She had no makeup on her freshly scrubbed face, which made her seem younger than her twenty-five years. She looked as though she had just jumped out of bed. Still, she was the brightest spot in an otherwise gloomy morning.

"Here you are!" she gushed, embracing Josephine and then introducing herself to Alma. "I only just got your wire. Several days late. They've booted us all out of our rooms at the Universitaire to make room for the soldiers, and I spent the night in an air raid shelter. False alarm, of course, they always are. But no time to pull myself together this morning."

"Where's the orange bomb?" Josie asked about the automobile.

"Broken. We'll take the Metro." She hefted Josie's suitcase, leaving Josie with nothing to carry but her portable Olivetti typewriter.

"But where are we going?" Alma asked, lugging her baggage down the steep steps.

Delfina laughed, realizing that she had not told them the good news. "I've found you rooms at the Foyer International, Boulevard St. Michel. I'm there. Helene too. We'll have fun in spite of the war." Then to Alma, who was looking uneasy at having a stranger arrange her life, she said, "You'll love it, I promise. A walk to Notre Dame. A Metro ride to the AP office. Perfection. Almost perfection, anyway, except the elevators don't run anymore to save on electricity."

"We'll manage," Josie replied cheerfully.

"You're on the seventh floor," Delfina grinned. "But Madame Watson promises to put a chair on the landing halfway up so you can rest. Running down to the cellar in an air raid is the easy part. Getting back to bed is more difficult. This morning I just couldn't face it, and I'm only on the fourth floor. There are no bombs. None at all. I wouldn't even bother to go down, except that Madame Watson is a tyrant. She makes us all go every time the siren sounds."

Josie knew Adelle Watson by reputation only. An American who had come to study in Paris before the last war, she had stayed for twenty-five years, running a hotel reserved only for American women students. Josie was surprised that Delfina, who was from pre-Bolshevik Russia, and Helene, who was French, were allowed in. As if reading her mind, Delfina answered.

"Almost all the Americans have gone home, you know, so Madame Watson has become international. The Foyer is a regular tower of Babel. Poor Madame Watson. She can hardly understand anyone: Austrian Jews, Czechs, Rumanian, Polish, Bulgarian, and French. The rules are posted in eight languages. She will be glad to see you two."

The rest of the journey was spent with Delfina filling in the details of her life. No longer working with children, she was part of a program studying the psychological effects of stress on combat pilots. Delfina finished by stating that she was finding her current patients much more interesting than two year olds. The only thing the two groups had in common was that they were unmarried.

❧ ❧ ❧

The back seat of the gleaming black Citroen that met Andre Chardon at the Gare du Nord was already occupied by Colonel Gustave Bertrand. As they drove away from the train station, Bertrand said softly, "I'm very sorry, Andre. You know that . . ."

"I do not want to talk about it," replied Andre abruptly.

"As you wish, of course," agreed Bertrand. "What about the project then? Is there progress?"

Andre shook his head, but not in answer to the question. He gestured to the watchful eyes of the driver in the rearview mirror.

The inability to talk about Andre's mission to England and his unwillingness to discuss his personal affairs left an awkward pall hanging over the interior of the Citroen all the way to the Château de Vignolles, thirty miles outside Paris.

The large manor house, surrounded by its parklike setting of lawn and trees, was not a castle in the medieval sense. It had been built in the late 1800s for a wealthy Parisian family and a host of servants. It was now filled with an entirely different sort of family, all of whom were in the service of secrecy.

The operation going on at Vignolles was known to a select few officers in French military intelligence as *P. C. Bruno.* Seventy specialists in code-breaking were gathered in the château, including a dozen Polish refugees and a handful of Spaniards who had escaped from Franco's slaughter. The rest were French army officers.

Even though they were working with the same purpose, none of the cryptanalysts at Vignolles were aware of Lewinski's work. Security precautions dictated that each man know only what was absolutely necessary. In French military intelligence, only Bertrand and Andre had actually seen all three attempts to break the German code.

When a representative of each of the three nationalities had gathered in Bertrand's office, Andre filled them in on the progress of the effort in Britain. "MI 6 is convinced that the Germans have added two substitute alphabet wheels to the three on the standard Enigma machine. Not only can the setting and the order be changed, but any one or two of the three can be replaced with the extras. We, er, that is, we have had this conclusion confirmed by an independent source."

A Polish major sat back and groaned aloud. "That is it, then! It is hopeless! How can we devise a way to predict which three wheels will be used on a given day and to what position they will be arranged? Twenty-six letters on each—it is preposterous!"

"The British agree that the magnitude of the task has increased greatly, but they are not ready to give up," said Andre sternly. "They even have a suggestion for your section, Major."

"Yes, and what is that?"

"Realizing that you have radio intercepts going back to September or before, they suggest that you analyze the opening broadcast of each day. We have been informed that the Germans send test messages. It may be that they were foolish enough to use the same phrase more than once. If so, you might be able to discern a pattern in the repetition."

The Polish major brightened noticeably. "It is true!" he exclaimed. "We will get to work on it immediately."

"There is one more thing," Andre added, holding up a cautioning hand. "The need for secrecy has never been greater. The Germans obviously believe their encoding to be unbreakable, because they use it for everything from the highest levels of OKW communications to orders received at division levels. This means that as you approach a breakthrough, the Nazis must never suspect what we have achieved, or they would change methods entirely and all your work would be for nothing. Even now, the little we know might frighten them into a big alteration."

"We understand," replied the Polish officer. "But who could we tell? We are practically prisoners here anyway." Then with a bow toward Colonel Bertrand he added, "It is a most charming confinement."

On the way out to the waiting Citroen, Bertrand drew Andre aside. "I know you are disappointed that you did not have more to give them," he said. "But remember that they know nothing as yet about the project going on in your basement. Perhaps our friend Lewinski has come up with something definite. Perhaps there is good news waiting for you at home right now."

Andre gave Bertrand a bleak look. "I doubt it," he said.

The White Russian, Nicholi Federov, had every reason to disavow his association with the Gestapo now that Hitler and Stalin had become so cozy. And the Gestapo could have handed Federov over to Stalin's Communist government for a tidy sum, since Federov had been such an ardent and destructive force in the White Russian opposition to the Bolsheviks. But both Federov and Heinrich Himmler knew that such a move would be counterproductive.

Possessing a Nansen pass, the Russian could move with relative ease throughout the neutral nations of Europe. He was a well-known wine merchant with connections in Switzerland and France. Federov had first begun his work with the Nazi regime after being recruited in England by Hitler's foreign minister, Ribbentrop. Ribbentrop had also been a wine merchant before his rise in the ranks of Nazi power.

It seemed an innocent enough beginning for Federov. He was not particularly interested in the politics or the chaos of the German nation. He did not particularly like the strutting little brown shirts of the S.A., except that they hated the Bolsheviks. The Nazis feared and despised Lenin and Trotsky and the rest of the Czar-killers who had renamed the Russian cities after themselves. Leningrad. Stalingrad. Disgusting.

And so, although Hitler did not drink wine, he shared similar tastes with the Russian wine merchant. In those days, Hitler hated Stalin and all Communists with a passion which made him foam at the mouth like a rabid dog. This seemed an attractive quality when the Russian first observed the Nazi leader. Federov held to the old maxim, "The enemy of my enemy is my friend." Hitler, upon coming to power, had proceeded to smash the German Communist cells with impunity. Thus, an alliance was made between Federov and the enemies of his great enemy.

Federov knew everyone who either drank wine or sold wine in Europe. Since this grouping omitted very few people, he provided the Gestapo with a large quantity of information gleaned from various talkative sources. Which high-placed German diplomats had anti-Hitler leanings? Who had ties to certain organizations which would like to see der Führer dead? It was Federov who had been key in the apprehension of Elaine Snow as she attempted to assist the would-be assassin and probable-Bolshevik Georg Elser after his attempt to blow up Hitler in the Munich beer hall. The Führer had grown fond of the Russian. He was pleased to hear that Himmler and Heydrich had personally recruited him to handle the Lewinski matter.

Federov was informed that the Jew, Lewinski, was a notorious communist, certain to pull all of civilization down the drain after Russia if he were left to go free.

Since Stalin and Hitler were now allies, this should not have mattered to the Nazis on the face of it. Federov, however, understood the complex forces at work behind the extraordinary alliance.

With the unpleasant union between Hitler and Stalin, no one could imagine that Federov could have ties to German secret police. But the wine business was slow, and Federov had grown accustomed to living well. In addition to the issue of money, he justified his perfidious existence with the certainty that the treaty between the Nazis and Stalin was just a marriage of convenience. Soon enough, these strange bedfellows would wake up and notice that the other stank. By and by, Federov was certain, German troops would succeed in renaming Leningrad for St. Peter once again. The Communists who had destroyed his homeland would be slaughtered like pigs, and Imperial Russia would be restored. After some agreement with the Germans, of course.

Even now, after the war had begun, the Russian was welcome in Brussels, Amsterdam, Geneva, London, and Paris. He was the perfect choice to sleuth out the whereabouts of a certain brilliant Jewish mathematician working for one of these governments. Someone who drank wine would know him. And after one drink too many at some embassy party, the Lewinski beans would be spilled. Then Federov would simply dial the local fifth columnist thugs and the issue of Richard Lewinski would be settled for good.

This game depended entirely on who a man knew. Since Federov knew everyone, and was liked by most, he was very well suited to his occupation.

TWENTY-NINE

It was clear to everyone that the SS had every intention of carrying out some sentence against the criminal Jews and their families gathered at the Umschlagplatz. Rumor passed among the guards, and then the prisoners, that the Warsaw Judenrat, the Jewish Council, had spent all night and day negotiating with the authorities of the government for clemency in the matter of women and children. The authorities remained unbending. For the sake of *example,* the outcome was determined when the first runaway Jew attempted to enter Aryan Warsaw without permit or identification. Let all the population of Warsaw look at these lawbreakers and consider their fate.

In the interest of German mercy, however, and in consideration of the children, the authorities allowed a ration of bread to be provided to the prisoners by the Jewish community. The Judenrat sent a committee into the Umschlagplatz to pass out bread from the meager stores of the Ghetto. There was no milk, but weak tea was provided in tin cups from the Ghetto soup kitchen. The Judenrat committee was forbidden to speak to the prisoners. This order was obeyed even when one member of the committee spotted his son among the condemned. The father gave his son his allotted quarter loaf of bread, touching his hand in farewell. The two men spoke only with their eyes, embraced with a look, and parted forever after a few seconds.

When the kitchen committee left, they were allowed to cart off the two bodies shot earlier in the morning.

New SS guards had come in the afternoon. The train still had not arrived. A battered kettle, shielded from view by a blanket strung between two posts, served as the only toilet. Permission for use was granted at the whim of the soldiers. Permission was not always given. This seemed to be part of the sport.

By evening, small children slept in the arms of their parents. The older children and women slumped to the cobblestones. Men were forbidden to sit. They slept by leaning on one another.

Etta, who had dozed at Aaron's feet, now let him lean heavily against her back. His arms were draped over her shoulders and he slept. Rachel, still dressed like a boy, held the baby now. David and Samuel were mercifully asleep with their heads resting on Rachel's lap.

Etta scanned the perimeter for some sign of the priest. Surely if he came the guards would listen to him. Were they not all Christians like the priest? Would they not listen to a priest if he explained that there must be some mistake about the Lubetkin family? The Lubetkins were good people, he would tell them. Some mistake. They were Jews, but also friends of his. Etta kept this slim hope alive as the hours passed.

It began to snow again. The facades of familiar shops and buildings across the square were dim behind the veil of white. Etta could just make out the sign of the photography shop where the family once had pictures made to send to her father in Jerusalem. The photographer and his wife had been kind. The man had made the children smile. How long ago that seemed now. Etta was glad her father would have those photographs to remember them by.

The long sleek staff car of a Nazi officer drove into the Umschlagplatz. Guards came to attention as a black uniformed SS colonel emerged. Some among the prisoners stiffened to attention as well, almost as if they sensed that here was a man who demanded respect.

Aaron awoke as a harsh German voice crackled over the loudspeaker. *"Achtung! Prisoners will rise and form two lines, three abreast, for marching to board the trains. There will be no talking. All instructions are to be obeyed at once. Failure to obey will result in . . ."*

Etta shook her sons gently. Little Samuel could not wake up. Aaron gathered him in his arms as though he was going to take him upstairs and put him to bed. The child seemed unaware of what was happening. David stood slowly and glared at a German soldier who brushed past them, shouting for silence. Rachel passed the baby to Etta. She looked at the toes of her boots and shoved her hands into her pockets as she had been instructed. They took their places near the rear of the column.

The officer remained rooted beside his staff car. He observed the scene with disgust. His arms were crossed and his mouth set in a hard line. He raised his chin slightly so that he literally looked down his nose at the parade. Two civilian Poles, escorted by a guard, approached the officer. For a moment Etta did not recognize the man and the woman. They were smiling, nodding, talking cheerfully. The man held a large camera while the woman had a large wicker basket over her arm and she carried a tripod over her shoulder like a rifle. They were as pleasant to the officer as they had been to the Lubetkin family. Professional smiles. The officer smiled back at them. He waved his hand and nodded his head in agreement to their request. They had come to record the deportation of the criminal Jews. Perhaps they could sell the photographs to the newspapers?

A flashbulb exploded as the photographer snapped the officer's picture and then turned to face the prisoners beneath the train shed of the Umschlagplatz. The photographer moved quickly from the front of the line toward the back, taking photographs, changing film and replacing used flashbulbs from a pocket filled with new ones. Still smiling. How could he still smile?

Etta nudged Aaron, who followed her gaze to the couple. He shook his head, then looked away. The image of vultures came clearly to mind. They came closer. Etta heard the voice of the guard who accompanied them.

"There are whole cities now in Germany which are Judenrein. That is, free of Jews. You will see it here in Warsaw as well . . ."

The photographer smiled and nodded and snapped another picture of two bearded Jews who glared back at him. Then he lowered his camera and looked directly at Etta. The slim smile did not falter. He looked as he did when he greeted her at his studio: professional, very pleased to see her indeed.

His wife, a thickset woman with rosy cheeks, walked toward Aaron. She put a finger to her lips and winked at David.

Setting the hamper down near Etta's feet she turned to her husband and the young soldier. "This group?"

"Ideal," chirped the photographer. He took the soldier by the arm. "Would you give me a hand with the tripod?" The soldier cheerfully threw himself into the task of setting up the tripod, while the photographer engaged him in conversation.

Etta looked down. The woman stood planted in front of her, shielding her from view.

"The priest sent word," the woman hissed through clenched teeth. "Froi Lubetkin . . . The baby . . . hurry."

Etta's heart pounded in her ears. She could hear nothing, see nothing but the open basket between her and the broad back and full skirts of the woman. She felt as though she had been kicked hard in the stomach.

The ancient nightmare was real! She stooped and placed her baby into the wicker case. No time to caress him even one last time. She could not display her grief in any way.

Rachel gasped and choked back words of despair. A warning glance from Aaron silenced her.

The hamper was snatched up. The child was covered by a red wool blanket. The woman moved quickly away from them.

"Very good!" The photographer praised the soldier. "You know something about photography, I can tell!"

The soldier was pleased with himself. He spoke of the German-made camera he had carried everywhere with him since the war began. He talked and talked as the photo of Etta and Aaron and the boys was snapped and the smiling, nodding photographer moved down the line.

The baby began to cry. Etta moaned and closed her eyes and pressed her face hard against Aaron's arm.

Rachel looked back and whispered. "She is speaking to the soldier. She is taking Yacov back to the shop with her."

And so it was done. The SS guard never asked what was in the basket. Now he assumed the woman had carried a baby out of the shop and would take the same baby back.

Etta suddenly felt the emptiness of her arms. The column moved forward slowly. She did not allow herself to look back at the shop, lest some SS guard see her face and know the truth. Her eyes were dry. Her face was like stone. A prayer more painful than her own death had been answered. Her baby was gone.

❧ ❧ ❧

It was late before Andre completed his reports at Vignolles and returned to Paris. He was in a gloomy mood as he removed his luggage from the car in front of his home. Tucking Clemmie Churchill's doll beneath his arm, he climbed the steps slowly and looked back toward the frozen Seine. The thin blue strip of light from the staff car headlamps barely illuminated the pavement of Quai d'Anjou as the vehicle crossed the bridge. Paris seemed a gloomy place tonight.

Only now did he let himself think about Elaine. She was gone and that was irrevocable. The City of Lights had paid her homage in the newspapers. Her voice and her songs had been played all day on Radio Paris. It had been almost beyond bearing for him when he entered the staff lounge at Vignolles and heard her singing.

Mercifully, Andre knew that by tomorrow the city and the world would move on to other matters. Soon enough Elaine Snow would be forgotten. At best she would be a footnote in history, possibly remembered by a few Jews in Palestine as "the woman who gave me my passport in Constance one night . . ." But there could be nothing more. The human mind absorbed the news of another's death with a kind of surreal acceptance, as though the one who died had never lived at all. The faces of the dead became like that thin blue light—barely illuminating memory.

He entered the foyer of the great house. It was dark and quiet. It suddenly occurred to him that Elaine had been here only one time. That fact made the memory more difficult to deal with. There was no jumble of images to sort out. No past. Only the one, present, immutable vision of her standing there . . .

She wears the cobalt blue satin evening gown. Her hair shines golden in the light. Her eyes are clear, and more blue than the dress. She turns her face toward the door as I say her name. Her eyes hold me . . .

Too real! Too near! Until this instant he had been able to keep the finality of her death at bay. Now as the reality settled heavily on him, he wanted company. Anyone.

Peering down the stairs he saw that the lamp in Lewinski's workshop was out. Climbing the curving staircase he looked in on Paul, who was sound asleep and snoring. For a moment Andre considered waking his brother, but he did not. Paul would want to talk, to console him, but there could be no consolation tonight.

He closed the blackout curtains in the study, then snapped on the light, and tossed his valise in the corner. Placing Clemmie's doll on the bookshelf, he poured himself a snifter of brandy and sat down heavily in the leather chair facing the enormous walnut desk. He had sat in this very chair and faced his grandfather the day the news came about his mother and father. The old man had glowered down at him and Paul. The drooping white moustache made the picture even more grim. It was only that moustache which Andre could recall now, not tears or eyes or trembling hands. Only the white line curving downward above his lip. How it quivered as he spoke! All these years, Andre had imagined that the old man was furious at him.

"Have courage. Your father and mother were murdered by the Boche yesterday in Louvremont."

Andre stared at the white moustache which floated now before him in a blue haze of his memory.

"Have courage. Elaine was murdered by the Boche last night in Munich."

Andre sipped the brandy as the door opened. Paul, blinking at the light, entered the room.

"I thought I heard someone." Paul wrapped his burgundy robe around himself and sat down uninvited.

"Only me." Andre held the snifter up in salute. "Care to join me?"

"I just did," Paul yawned.

The two brothers did not speak for a long moment. The ticking of the mantle clock measured seconds at a ponderous pace.

Paul inhaled deeply. "I suppose you have heard the news. Elaine."

Controlled and cool, Andre replied, "Everyone in Paris has heard. The radio broadcasts."

"Yes." Paul considered Andre with hard eyes. "Is that all you want to say about it?"

"I am sorry. Of course." Emotion was choking him. He wanted to shout his rage, but he remained calm.

"You are a lot like the old man, Andre." A half-smile tugged at the corner of Paul's mouth.

"What do you mean?" It was an insult, Andre was certain. Paul had lost respect for him since the affair with Elaine Snow and the child.

"You do not remember the way he sat there and glared at us the day Mother and Father died?"

Andre did not admit that he had just been thinking of it. "Vaguely."

"He was telling us that his son was dead, and his wife with him. The grief of that! What he must have felt! To speak to us of courage at such a time . . . He spoke the words, and saying it made it true for him. Remember?"

Be brave. You must not weep!

Of course Andre remembered. Andre closed his eyes and thought about Elaine's child. What was to be done with her? What must he do? He rubbed his forehead and glanced toward the placid doll on the bookshelf. As though he was speaking to the child he thought the words,

"Have courage . . . Your mother. . . . Elaine is dead . . ."

Emotion burned in his chest.

Paul grinned and ran a hand through his hair. He shook his head as if he still could not believe it. "He was so cool, that mean old man. I grew up thinking he did not care that Father and Mother died, that we were left alone."

"What are you saying?"

"He was not really angry at us, you know. That day? I did not need to be brave. I wanted to be held." He shrugged. "You should at least try to see your child. Juliette. A beautiful name. A name Elaine chose from the great tragedy, I think."

"What would you have done in my place? With the old man like he was . . ."

"I would have married her." Paul tugged at the button of his pajama shirt. "I tried to, you know. After. I went to her and asked her. But she would not have me."

"I did not know you loved her."

"Of course not. How could you know?" His eyes brimmed with emotion. "My big brother." He waved his hand around the room. "Well, you have it all. Everything you thought was worth more than Elaine." He leaned close and put his arm on the desktop. His fist was clenched. "To you life is like a library full of first edition classics. Bound in leather. Gilt edges on the pages. Autographed by the authors . . . Only you are too busy to open the book and read the story. Pretty things without meaning."

"I did not ask you to intrude." Andre glared at him and lifted the snifter to his lips.

"No. You did not." Paul stood and raised his chin. "But, like Grandfather . . . you have missed the whole point, Andre. You give in just a little and think it does not matter. But it does! Add up all the times you have sold a piece of your soul, and all the times every other little man sells his, and soon all the world belongs to hell. That is what I think of what you did to Elaine."

"Hell possessed the earth long before I sold myself."

"But Heaven redeems the earth one soul at a time, Andre."

"It is too late now to make it right."

"If you really believe that, then I am sorry for you." At that, Paul left his brother alone.

PART II

"It's jolly to look at the map
And finish the foe in a day.
It's not easy to get at the chap;
These neutrals are so in the way . . ."

A.P. Herbert
Punch Magazine, April 1940

THIRTY

On a quiet afternoon in midwinter, in the neutral nation of Belgium, the peaceful life of farmer Leopold Dumas was about to be interrupted by the war.

The Belgian farmer scooped grain out of the gunnysack and into the canvas feedbag. An enormous draft horse put his great shaggy head over the stall and neighed with anticipation. Abruptly, the horse's ears pricked upward, and he turned his head toward the open door of the barn that framed a square of grey wintry light.

A moment later and the farmer noticed it also—an intermittent buzzing as if a mosquito were turning its shrill hum on and off. Leopold straightened up and listened, twirling one end of his bushy silver moustache in thought. "What can that be, eh?" he asked the horse. "What is an aeroplane doing around here, and in this weather also?"

The horse's curiosity about the unfamiliar noise ended, and he nickered again for his supper. Leopold shrugged and finished filling the feedbag as the humming receded.

The farmer was just slipping the leather strap over the animal's ears when the buzzing sound returned with a rush. It seemed to come from a great height, faint at first, and then increasing until the sputtering hum was directly above the barn roof.

There was a swoosh of air through the open doorway that scattered the chickens and swirled the dust. An instant later there came a sharp crack, as if a frozen treelimb had broken off, followed by more snapping noises and the rattle of breaking glass.

Leopold hurriedly retrieved his heavy coat from a wooden peg near the door and slipped the cap with the long earflaps over his head. At first he could see nothing amiss as he scanned the snowcovered fields of his farm, and then a man staggered into view at the far end of the pasture, climbing out of the culvert. Leopold started toward him.

A little closer and Leopold could make out the crumpled outline of a small plane. It lay half across the drainage ditch with its nose on one side and its tail on the other, but it had buckled in the middle as if the bug Leopold had thought of earlier had been squashed. A Nazi bug, judging by its markings.

A second uniformed man staggered up out of the ditch and joined his fellow. They appeared to be having a hurried conference involving a leather portfolio that the first officer waved excitedly. Both men patted their uniform pockets, looking for something.

They turned at Leopold's approach, and the man with the pouch spoke. "Sprechen Sie Deutsch?"

"I speak German," Leopold acknowledged. "So, your flying machine is broken, yes? Are you hurt?"

"No, no, we are very fortunately uninjured. I am Major Kurt Hulse, and this is Major Reinberger. And your name is?"

Introductions over, Hulse made an odd request. "Have you any matches, Herr Leopold?"

So, the search of the pockets was explained. "Yes," Leopold agreed, "why?"

"We need . . . that is . . . it is so cold. We need to build a fire, Herr Leopold."

"Come into my house," argued the farmer. "It is just beyond the barn there."

"Ah, no, we . . . we cannot leave the plane, you see . . . we must guard it."

"From what?" Leopold asked, looking around at the empty fields. A small car turned the far corner of the hedge-bordered pasture.

"Please," Hulse begged. "Our orders, you see. Could we build a fire here to keep warm?"

Leopold hesitantly produced two matches from his jacket and handed them to Hulse. Reinberger upended the portfolio, spilling a pile of papers onto the frozen earth.

A light snow was beginning to fall, and the first match sputtered and died without catching in the heap of typewritten pages. The auto pulled up across the hedge nearest the plane and slid to a halt on the icy road. A gendarme jumped out.

"Schneller," muttered Hulse.

The second match flared, and Reinberger cupped it against the wind and touched it to the corner of a page. The damp paper seemed to refuse the fire for a moment, and then a bright yellow flame jumped up just as the gendarme vaulted the ditch, pistol in hand.

Hulse turned to face the policeman, blocking his view of the scene as

Reinberger, in a sudden change of mind, stomped on the tiny blaze and hurriedly stuffed the papers back into the case.

"Leopold," called the gendarme, a man named Albert. "This plane . . . it is German."

"I know that," remarked Leopold with irritation. "It has chosen my field in which to crash."

Albert waved his pistol at the two Nazi officers. "You will move away from the plane," he directed. "Leopold, we will please go to your home to await my superiors. We saw this plane circle the village, obviously in difficulty. Others will be following me shortly."

Reinberger and Hulse exchanged a look, then complied with the policeman and started across the snow toward the farmhouse. Reinberger cradled the pouch under his arm as they went.

✳   ✳   ✳

Information about the German plane crash in Belgium and the attempted destruction of top secret Nazi papers reached French Military Intelligence two days after the event. By then the Belgians, and the Dutch, and the officials of tiny Luxembourg had already taken their turn interrogating the two German airmen. The suspect papers had been examined a dozen times and were the subject of grave concern in the governments of the neutrals. The trembling caused by the revelation of the German plan had somehow filtered down into the villages on the border, causing unconcealed suspicion of every stranger who passed through.

Andre Chardon, as French Military Intelligence Liaison Officer, was the obvious choice to travel to Belgium when the neutrals decided that it might be a good idea to let France in on the secret. In spite of the frigid weather, he elected to motor the route from Paris to Brussels and pass through the Ardennes along the way. The roundabout route was intentional: he wanted to review a growing suspicion about German objectives. Richard Lewinski grudgingly accepted Gustave Bertrand as a temporary guardian.

After a long uneventful drive, and a night in Luxembourg City, Andre left for Brussels early the next morning. A fine rain mixed with wisps of fog. The trip up through the rough terrain of the Ardennes was long and wet with plenty of time to consider the improbable possibility of German invasion by this route.

He passed through the frontier checks into Belgium without a problem, but upon entering the town of Arlon, he found that the hint of a Wehrmacht assault had sent a wave of panic through the Belgian populace.

The streets of Arlon were without markers. Barricades of logs lay across each of the main thoroughfares. These obstructions, Andre noted, were pathetic attempts by the citizens to block a German invasion of their town.

The heaviest obstacle could have been simply pushed aside or crushed beneath the treads of a German tank. The only result of the ramparts that Andre could see were crazy bottlenecks in intersections which were nearly impassable at the best of times. Driving from one side of Arlon to the other was something like trying to find his way out of a maze in the gardens of Versailles. If and when the Germans did decide to overrun Arlon, the town's pitiful fortifications would only impede the advance of friendly troops and artillery sent out to face the Nazi menace.

Finally reaching the center of town, Andre found further evidence of panic. All the men who might have manned the outer blockades were in the square listening to an inspiring speech by the mayor. Even here the word was, *The Boche shall not pass!*

It seemed that the townsfolk did not want anyone to pass, not even a French military officer with official business in Brussels. Andre was pulled to the side of the street. Military police came at the bidding of the metropolitan police who responded to the summons of the traffic police. Each group examined Andre's documents down to his French driver's license. Was he a spy dressed in French military uniform? Was he a fifth columnist out to take pictures of the little town of Arlon and pass information to saboteurs? Andre was held and questioned for two hours.

Finally cleared, he proceeded by a back road north toward Dinant and the bridge that crossed the Meuse River. There he was stopped by a cheerful captain of the Belgian military police who instantly read the irritation on the face of Andre.

"What is it, Colonel?"

"I might have been burned for a witch in Arlon. They have gone mad."

"It is the rumor, Colonel. No one knows where it began, but there is hearsay that the Germans will soon attack through Belgium and Holland."

Andre knew the source of the rumor would be the documents on the German plane. He did not know, however, how the information had escaped the confines of Belgian Military Intelligence to affect the intelligence of the ordinary citizens in Arlon!

"If there is a spy in Arlon, no doubt he has his papers in order and is carrying the briefcase of the town magistrate."

The captain laughed and passed Andre's documents back through the window. "Yes, and if there were a German spy in Arlon, no doubt he would have been the first to run and examine your papers, Colonel."

"Their hysteria is a bad sign. Frenzy and self-assurance do not go together."

"That is true. But poor little Arlon. Always the first to be invaded. But there is not much hysteria in Belgium. I, for one, do not believe the Nazis will attack us today. But who is to say?" He gestured toward the opposite bank of the river. "If they do, we will cut them to shreds without the help of either the French or English armies. You see this bridge? A German tank will never pass over it unless all of us are dead. We Belgians shall do it ourselves."

Andre did not argue with the Belgian captain, but he thought about the roadblocks on the main highways from France to Belgium. He shuddered at the difficulty they would cause for advancing French and English troops, should Belgium and Holland call for their assistance.

✻　✻　✻

The Ardennes. Andre pondered the rolling forest country as he drove toward Brussels.

The French High Command had simply looked at the hills of the Ardennes through the dim eyes of generals who had fought in the last great war. The conclusions reached were logical according to the tactics of 1918 trench warfare. It was not that the Ardennes was impassable to troops, but its narrow, twisting roads could not accommodate heavy siege guns. It was unthinkable to the old French generals that German infantry might be brought forward to fight without first having the advantage of artillery bombardment. Therefore, the German offensive against France would not come through the Ardennes. It never had. It never would. That territory was in itself a kind of Maginot. The French and the English were secure in that.

Who was Colonel Andre Chardon to question generals like Gamelin and Georges, or the British General Lord Gort? And yet, he found himself glancing up through his mud-spattered windscreen at the grey skies and thinking of Stuka dive-bombers. A new kind of artillery. The narrow roads of the Ardennes meant nothing to the Luftwaffe. The thought made him uneasy.

Andre found no comfort in the visible preparations of the Belgian defenses. There were, he knew, 700,000 men billeted in the beautiful hills of little Belgium. There were red signs on the fire lanes leading off the main highway which announced that the area was prohibited to all civilian traffic. Steel gates and armed guards blocked the bridge approaches. A massive red steel fence ran up hills and down valleys for the entire length of the country in hopes of catching stray German tanks. Just in case . . .

A few miles beyond Dinant, the drizzle turned into a serious downpour. Twilight and then darkness descended like a curtain. Andre drove slowly along the back roads. Belgian troops were coming forward one brigade at a time. The troop lorries tracked red clay onto the pavement until it was as slick as ice. Andre peered cautiously through the windshield and cursed the vigilantes of Arlon who had kept him from his journey too long for safety.

There were explosive traps set every kilometer along the highway from Arlon toward Brussels. Land mines recently set in place, they were meant to destroy the road and halt any enemy advance. Andre noticed trenches cut from the center of the road to the shoulder and filled again as though someone was laying a pipeline halfway across the highway. Beside every trench stood a rain-drenched soldier with a rifle, warning Andre to reduce his already slow speed.

He came to an intersection where the soil in the trench had been churned to thick gooey mud. There was a problem. Military vehicles had come to a stop on the crossroad. An angry officer was standing in the downpour trying to figure the best angle with which to turn tractors, supply trucks, and an enormous 155-millimeter gun around the land mine.

"Who put this so close to our turn! Stupidity!" he railed at the sky. "Dig the thing up!"

The sentry eyed the booby trap with respect. What did he fear more: the little trench or the officer?

"I cannot dig it up, sir. I do not know where the thing is. I am afraid to touch the string."

The string was a thin, feeble piece of twine set between two small sticks. Under slight tension, it held back the trigger of the land mine; a very dangerous thing for vehicles on the road.

The officer handled the inconvenience. He ran a tractor back and forth over the brush beside the road, cutting an alternate path for all his machines. Within minutes the bottleneck was broken.

Now, Andre thought grimly, *if the Belgians could so easily bypass their own traps, could not the German Panzer Corps think of the same solution?*

Andre drove on after the military equipment, rolling through mud which was nearly axle deep. He tried not to look at the little string. He made himself think about things other than the simplicity with which the trap had been bypassed.

Following military trucks all the way, he reached Brussels close to midnight. He spent a restless night in his hotel.

✿   ✿   ✿

Paul Chardon watched from the top landing outside the entrance hall. The brakes of the army lorry squealed as the vehicle halted on the slick cobblestones in front of the steps.

Watching with amusement, Paul saw his three senior cadet captains also observe the arrival from across the square. Their poses, arms folded across their immaculate uniforms and their weight leaned back on their polished boots, spoke of distrust and disdain. It was obvious that the idea of turning the École de Cavalerie into a hospital, and an English hospital at that, was repugnant to them.

The driver's door opened and a tall, very British doctor emerged. "You are

Captain Chardon," he said in very bad French. "I am Surgeon Officer Roberts."

Paul acknowledged the introduction. Roberts and his staff were to take over the now vacant wing of the Junior School, turning it into a casualty clearing station for the BEF.

"And this is Chief Nurse Abigail Mitchell," Roberts said, as a passenger slid across the seat of the truck and stood looking up at the imposing brick facade of the school.

Nurse Mitchell was tall, almost Paul's height, and dark brown of hair and eyes. Her complexion was ruddy, outdoorsy, and she had the lean, muscular look of a horsewoman. *Striking* was the adjective that came to Paul's mind. So striking in fact that he repeated it to himself, creating an awkward pause when he failed to respond promptly to Miss Mitchell's greeting.

"You are very welcome," he said, "I mean, I am also pleased to meet you."

Paul shot a glance at the three students who were studying him intently. Was his bumbling shyness around women that easy to read, even from fifty yards away? He gave a peremptory gesture to Gaston, Sepp, and Raymond to come forward and present themselves.

"I want you to meet the ranking student officers," he said, silently wishing that they would walk faster. By eye contact, he told each boy in unmistakable language to be on his best behavior.

When the three were introduced, each stepped forward, bowed stiffly, then stepped back to form an unbroken rank of disapproval.

"Right, I will leave it to you then, Captain Chardon," Roberts said. "Miss Mitchell will do the inspection, and you two can discuss the necessary modifications."

Paul saw the three boys exchange another look of disgust. Modify the school to accommodate a British female nurse? Unthinkable!

❖   ❖   ❖

Nurse Abigail Mitchell preferred the title Sister Mitchell. With great pride she wore the coveted scarlet cape of Queen Alexandra's Imperial Military Nursing Service. QAIMNS for short.

Paul Chardon learned early that she was a formidable woman. Aged twenty-eight on the day the war was declared, she had served in Calcutta, India, and then in Cairo. She had returned to England only two weeks before the Nazis invaded Poland and was among the first nurses to cross the Channel with the British Expeditionary Force.

Had she been a man, a Frenchman, she should have been a general, Paul thought as she strode through the corridors of the Junior School issuing orders.

All mattresses in the dormitories were to be cleaned, aired, and sterilized.

Every inch of window, wall, and floor disinfected. Little schoolboys carried germs, she said, and what a pity it would be if some brave British soldier was saved from his battle wounds only to die of some lurking measles bug. And so it went.

The kitchen of the Junior School, thanks to its tile counters and stainless steel sinks, was converted into an operating theater. Shadowless lights were rigged, and a generator installed as a source of backup power.

Because of her years in the warm climates of the British Empire, she had a morbid loathing of cold weather. At her command, tons of coal were laid in, enough to heat the entire Maginot for a year or more, Paul thought.

The CCS, Casualty Clearing Station, at Lys was set up to be the short-term holding component, receiving casualties from Field Dressing Stations and Advanced Surgical Units. Only urgent surgery would be dealt with in the field. All other cases were to be brought here, tended to, and then nursed until they were able to be transferred to the hospital ships just a few miles away in channel ports like Dunkirk or Calais.

Hardly a shot had been fired, but Sister Mitchell worked under the assumption that the École would soon be overrun with wounded men. With impunity, she recruited the school cadets to slave for her. There were complaints.

Big, muscular Gaston, his face smudged with smoke, his mouth turned down in indignation, and his uniform and tall riding boots filthy, reported to Paul: "Captain Chardon, I must protest the arrogant behavior of this arrogant Englishwoman! No wonder our countries have been so many times at war! The English women are much worse than the men, I think! Probably because they had a Queen for so many years! Today, Sepp and I were walking back from the stables to study for the calculus examination when she called down from the window which used to belong to the seven-year-old boys. You know the little boys sometimes wet their beds! Captain! What a job! She put Sepp and I to work hauling down the mattresses and burning them in the field! Look at my boots! My uniform! I am a cadet officer, not a janitor!"

Paul considered the muscular young man with a disapproving eye. "I have told Sister Mitchell that every young officer in the École is a gentleman and that we are all willing to help in whatever task she sets us to." This was not the truth, but Gaston was ashamed that he had complained. He apologized and went off to study calculus without further words on the matter. From that day on, he walked to the stables the long way around the Junior School.

Paul resolved to speak with Sister Mitchell about keeping cadets from classes and duties, but when he faced her, she beguiled him, thanking him for sending his "little chaps" round to help out with such an enormous task.

Well, what could he say? "Thank you, Mam'zelle . . . Pardon. I meant to say . . . that is . . . Merci, Sister Mitchell."

Andre would have handled it better, Paul thought. Under the guise of having pressing business to attend, Paul took refuge in the stables. There, he explored matters he knew something about. Bowed tendons and the difficult temperaments of mares in heat were discussed with the school veterinarian, Lieutenant Rappollo. Rappollo, Paul discovered, had also been nabbed by Sister Mitchell just the day before to paint the ceiling of the receiving room. Three cadets had likewise missed a chemistry test and had received demerits when the stalls of their horses had not been mucked out.

All military order had been disrupted by this woman. Everyone was angry, and there were only three patients in the CCS. One fellow had broken his leg in a motorcycle accident. Another had a very bad appendix. The third had the measles, contracted elsewhere, and was in quarantine.

Paul had sent in his request for transfer to active duty, he confessed to Rappollo. The request had nothing to do with Sister Mitchell. He had, in fact, made it before. But now that he had experienced the fearsome English-woman firsthand, he hoped to face the German army soon.

❧ ❧ ❧

Standing upright in his half-track, Horst von Bockman surveyed the encampment of his new command. To be the officer in charge of a recon-naissance battalion in the Seventh Panzer Division meant that Horst was responsible for over a hundred vehicles and the troops who manned them.

An armored car, bristling with radio aerials, pulled up alongside of Horst's location. General Erwin Rommel, the commander of the Seventh, got out and crossed to where Horst stood rigidly at attention. "At ease, Major," he ordered. "This is not a formal inspection. Not yet, at any rate. I want you to drill your men hard in rapid deployment through wooded countryside. Troops employed in assessing an enemy's strength on the field of battle must be able to get in, gather information, and return alive."

"Jawohl, Herr General," Horst agreed. "We'll start immediately."

"He talks like a textbook," observed Sergeant Fiske after Rommel had driven away. "Where was he when we were fighting our way across the Vistula?"

"That is enough, Fiske," Horst ordered. "No criticism of our command-ing officer, if you please."

Nevertheless, even in Horst's mind, Rommel was something of an un-known quantity. He had been the commander of Adolf Hitler's personal guard during the invasion of Poland and did not have a background in tank warfare. But Rommel had been convinced by what he saw in Poland that the onslaught of armored units would deliver the Allies into Germany's hands, and he wanted to be where the most glory was to be won.

Horst thought he knew what was coming. The Seventh was bivouacked near the town of Kalenborn close to the river Ahr; the Belgian frontier was only a scant eighty kilometers away. Studying topographical maps of the area, Belgium's Forest of Ardennes jumped to mind. Horst now knew that his brother-in-law Kurt was right. There would be no frontal assault on the Maginot defenses. The attack, when it came, would be through Belgium and Luxembourg, neutral or not.

The area of timbered terrain called the Ardennes was not fortified, because it had long been believed to be impenetrable to the movement of large numbers of men and equipment. That might have been true in the days of horse-drawn artillery and the painfully slow deployment of foot soldiers, but not in the mechanized days of 1939.

"Sergeant, contact the company commanders. Give them my compliments and tell them I wish to see them in one hour."

The boredom so prevalent amongst the poilus on the French side of the line was nowhere to be found in the ranks of the Wehrmacht. The Germans thought of themselves as the best soldiers in the world, and they were anxious to prove it, even if it meant continuous practice and drill.

Horst organized his command into recon patrols. Each unit had three armored cars and a screen of motorcycle officers. "Today's drill will be to cover the area from here to Staffel," he told his captains. "Each team will be assigned a route and an objective which are roughly equivalent in difficulty. The units will have to effect a crossing of the river; no using the highway, gentlemen! Sergeant Fiske will be in Staffel with the packets which represent the information you are to obtain and return to me here. Are there any questions?"

Captain Gruhn raised his hand. "And what will the winning team receive?"

Horst grinned. "Did I not explain that? The unit who returns the fastest without any demerits will receive five-day passes for Christmas!"

The day following, Horst was in his half-track, roaming the dirt roads of the practice area. He seemed to be everywhere at once, correcting mistakes and preventing cheating.

"No, Lieutenant Gelb," he scolded. "Go back and start over. You did not dispatch your motorcycles down that country lane about a quarter mile back. What if an enemy tank squadron had been waiting there to hit our main force in the flank? You are the eyes of the entire division; you cannot afford to have one eye closed!"

Horst managed to keep the tone of his reprimands light, even though the subject they were studying was deadly serious. In the back of his mind was the hope that all this practice warfare would never become real. Perhaps just the spirit and ability that they were demonstrating would convince the Allies that their only hope lay in embracing the bargaining table and avoiding the battlefield.

"No, Shultz! You cannot leave your artillery observer behind as a guard. Look, up in those trees, do you not see that enemy machine gun? It has pinned down the entire advance. Think, Shultz, think! You need that observer to call in supporting fire and you need him right now!"

In the end, it was the unit of eager Captain Gruhn who carried off the honors. Arriving back at a tributary of the Ahr a bit behind schedule, they found that the narrow bridge was blocked by a broken-down transport truck. Rather than give up, Gruhn reconnoitered upstream and found a bank of dirt that projected over the stream. The captain delighted his commandant by jumping his 500cc BMW motorcycle thirty-six feet to the other bank.

"Bravo, Gruhn," Horst applauded. "You and your men have carried the day. You win the holiday passes."

"Thank you, Major," Gruhn said. "What about yourself? Will you be going home for Christmas?"

Horst got a far-off look in his eye, as if Gruhn's question had reminded him of something. He shook his head to clear it before answering. "No, that is, yes, I will be away for a few days. Taking care of some business." Then, trying to recover some of the previous pleasant mood, he added, "By the way, you may tell your team that they especially deserve this victory."

"Why is that, Major?"

"Because, to make things more interesting, I am the one who arranged for the truck to 'break down' on the bridge."

THIRTY-ONE

Three francs a week arrived like clockwork for Jerome and Marie from Papa. Madame Hilaire was always on board the *Garlic* to accept the letter from the postman. She would open it up, cackle like a chicken which had just laid an egg, and then she would hold up the three francs in glee.

"A good man, your papa!" she would shout so every head along the Quai de Conti would pivot to stare. "We will eat well tonight!"

Each payday the old hag would indeed cook a wholesome meal. Fresh baguettes. Mounds of fried potatoes. A piece of cod. She would raise her wine glass and drink a toast after she screamed this sentiment:

"To the health of our dear Uncle Jambonneau, wherever it has gotten off to!"

Then she would drink another toast. "To your brave papa, who serves in the glorious Armée of France! May they raise his pay and increase his ration of grog!"

There were numerous other toasts. Some were drunk to the rat, whom Madame Hilaire said was the cousin of the president of the French Republic. As the contents of the jug decreased she would begin to weep copiously and raise her glass to various old circus performers who Jerome did not know. At last Madame Hilaire would drink the last drops of her gallon and lay her head down on the table to sleep in peace among the dishes.

But when the morning after came, Jerome and Marie would awaken to the quiet lapping of the Seine against the boat, and Madame Hilaire would be gone. The pattern was always the same. Jerome did not mind that the woman disappeared for six days and reappeared to collect the money and cook one meal a week. On the day that Papa enlisted, Jerome decided that he would rather live with a booming cannon than the shrieking voice of their guardian, Madame Hilaire. Good riddance. If she had not departed, Jerome might have done so himself.

This left Jerome to fend for Marie six days of the week, however. Some days the task was more difficult than others. This morning would not be difficult.

Jerome rose before dawn, stuffed little Papillon into his shirt and made his way to Rue de Buci. There was a break in the rain and the bitterly cold weather, which meant that the merchants would be setting up their stalls on the street. In the predawn light without street lamps, the place was easy pickings for a skilled thief like Jerome. He raised his hands in joy and blessed the blackout.

The air of Buci market smelled like fresh baked bread and flowers. The flowers had been shipped from greenhouses in the warm South of France as if there were no war at all.

Jerome passed the stall of the citrus seller. He nabbed an orange which he slipped into a canvas bag. What could be more simple? Would the merchant notice one missing orange? It could have just as easily fallen off the table and into the gutter where Jerome might have found it!

The loudmouthed wife of the baker was barking orders at her unfortunate little husband. He should move faster! The sun would soon be up and the housewives would come! He should cover the barrel of baguettes in case it rained!

When the baker argued that the sky was clear and that there was not a cloud, she roared and pointed upward. "How can you know what the day will bring? It has rained all week! Cover the baguettes!"

The baker bent beneath the table to fish among the boxes for something to cover the long loaves of bread which were packed upright like pencils in a pencil cup. At the same instant the broad backside of the baker's wife turned toward Jerome. Here was his opportunity! He reached out and grasped a loaf, pulling it out and breaking it in two. He dunked the two halves into his bag and hurried on.

Breakfast was taken care of. Now, what to do about dinner?

He gazed up longingly at the hooks in the butcher shop. Salamis by the dozen hung on the right of the open window. The hooks on the left held skinned rabbits and thin chickens. There was seldom any beef since the Armée of France got all the best meat these days. Jerome's eyes narrowed with intensity as he considered some way to snag a salami. A salami would be the prize of all prizes. He would not have to cook it, and it would last for days. But they were too far out of his reach. A pity.

A large American woman, the keeper of an orphanage, pulled her little wagon to the window of the butcher. She was out early. Jerome often saw her in the Buci market, pulling her wagonload of groceries from stall to stall and arguing over prices like a common Parisian. Perhaps if she would distract the butcher long enough . . .

"Bonjour, Monsieur Turenne," she called in a loud voice that hardly displayed any of the flat American accent.

The large butcher greeted her cheerfully. She was a regular customer and a good one. "Ah, Madame Rose!" he cried. "How lovely you look today, Madame!"

"It is too dark for you to know how I look, Monsieur Turenne," she laughed. "That is why I come early. I like your compliments."

"You are the light of Buci Market."

"If you look upon the soul, then I hope that is true, Monsieur."

"Ah, Madame." The butcher, who everyone knew was a lonely widower, lowered his voice. "To think that such a plum as you remains unpicked."

"Plum?" She laughed. "Coconut is more like it. Hard and tough."

"But sweet inside."

He was definitely distracted, although Jerome thought he would have to be as blind as Uncle Jambonneau to mean what he was saying. Madame Rose could have passed for a fair-sized side of beef in the dark. Maybe such a figure was what butchers were attracted to.

"Enough, Monsieur!"

Jerome inched forward toward the salami.

"How can I help you this morning, Madame Rose?"

Jerome was at her elbow, moving his hand up toward the hook.

"I need chickens for my children today!"

"Chickens, Madame! Fowl is very expensive these days. Rabbit would be better for the cost."

"No. Chickens. We have thirteen children down with bronchitis. Sister Betsy is not well either. Chicken broth, that is the thing. Four chickens, if you please. That should do very well for thirty-two little ones and two old ladies."

"Old! Madame! You are in your prime!"

Jerome wondered who the butcher could be talking to. Madame Rose was grey-haired beneath her scarf.

"Always you flatter me and after we argue about the price of the chicken you hate me. But I always come back."

Jerome touched the rounded end of the lowest salami. His fingers just grasped it at the bottom, but he could not get a firm enough grip to pull! He jumped, grabbed, and jerked the salami off the hook.

The butcher shouted. Madame Rose whirled around much faster than Jerome could have imagined such a large woman could move. She grasped his hair, jerking him back mid-stride and holding him firmly.

Thinking to terrify her, Jerome reached into his shirt and held up Papillon. The rat blinked at her with pink eyes and twitched his whiskers curiously.

Madame Rose was unimpressed. "You have a rat," she said, "Put him away or monsieur the butcher is likely to carve him up and grind him in his sausage."

Jerome obeyed her warning instantly. She still did not let go of his hair.

The great lumbering hulk of the butcher hurried out the door of his shop.

"Well, well, well! So, so, so! Madame Rose!" he cried. "You have caught the little beggar Jardin!" He yanked the sausage free from Jerome's hand and held it aloft triumphantly. "I owe you a debt of gratitude."

"Gratitude is nice, but I would rather have ten centimes off the price of each chicken."

The butcher grimaced. "Thievery, Madame. But . . . done. Now I shall call the gendarmes to haul this rat away."

The big woman leaned down and studied Jerome with one eye. She poked at his ribs. She pinched his cheeks. "He hardly weighs more than that sausage, Monsieur. If he were a fish I would throw him back in the Seine. Not enough to fry."

"He is a thief."

"I have seen him here in Buci. Perhaps he meant to ask you if he might borrow the sausage for a time?"

Jerome's hair hurt. He peered up at the large woman defiantly. "Borrow?"

the boy snorted. "I meant to eat it all. Monsieur the butcher has enough to go around. He is fat as a pig! AND . . . He has two large dogs at home to whom he feeds scraps. My sister and I would eat such scraps very happily. Are we not better than dogs?"

The butcher began making incoherent angry noises after the reference to the pig. He held the sausage like a sword, as if to stab Jerome with it. Madame Rose swung herself between butcher and boy in a series of moves which kept the butcher jabbing the sausage around her. Jerome yelped as he swung by his hair from side to side. Would not a thump on the head with a sausage be less painful than Madame Rose's fingers in his hair?

"Monsieur Turenne, you must stop this at once!" she cried. "I . . . I wish to purchase that sausage as well!"

"You may do so, Madame!" he huffed. "After I beat this boy with it!"

"No!" she shouted, putting her free hand up and shoving monsieur the butcher back. "I protest. Children do not beg unless they are hungry."

Jerome shot back defiantly. "I do not beg from the capitalist pig, Madame!"

"He steals!" the butcher bellowed.

"Not if I buy the salami for him."

The butcher stepped back and lowered his weapon. "If you do not allow me to call the gendarmes, Madame, then I shall have to charge you full price for your chickens and for the salami!"

Jerome peered out from behind the skirt of the American. The butcher had her there.

"As you wish, Monsieur Turenne, but it is not gallant of you."

He shrugged and went back inside to wrap the chickens. Madame Rose released her grip, letting Jerome free.

She bent low and put her nose to his. Her face was very fierce, and her mouth was straight and wide like a bullfrog's. "Do not move," she warned, then turned her attention to paying the bill.

Jerome did not stir. He stood at her back and petted Papillon through the gap in his shirt caused by missing buttons. The sun was coming up. The bunches of flowers in the barrels of the florist stall were bright and pretty. It would be too light to steal now, but at least he was not going to prison.

Now Madame Rose turned to him. "What is your name?" She took him by the arm and hauled him after her with the same determination as she hauled the wagon.

"Jerome Jardin."

"Now what am I supposed to do? I have paid full price for the chickens, and I have a salami I do not want."

"I am sorry, Madame." Jerome felt badly. The large American was a kind woman, after all. Everyone said so, except for Papa who said that Madame

Rose and her sister Betsy were only kind because they got something for it in return. Jerome could not think what Madame had gotten out of this act of kindness. The deal seemed quite a bad one to him.

"You do not have to steal, you know." She pulled the wagon out of the way of a gaggle of housewives and bent until her eyes were level with Jerome's. "You could have asked if you were hungry."

"I am not a beggar."

"I do not know what I will do with this salami." She extended it to him. It was wrapped in white waxed paper, but he could smell it through the wrapping. His stomach growled. He looked away.

"I am sorry," he said again.

"Would you like it, Jerome?"

"You are a religious person," he said in a lofty way as Papa had taught him. "Dangerous."

She laughed. Then she laughed louder as though what he said was the funniest thing she had heard in a long time.

"Well, I suppose that is a matter of opinion."

"You are a spider of the church. Papa says never take charity from the church. Charity is the web which catches the . . ."

This time her mouth twitched like she might laugh, but she did not. "So. You are a man of honor I see," she said seriously. But her eyes were laughing. "I would not entice you with a gift." She placed the salami back on the top of a heap of cabbages in the wagon. "But I suppose that if I turned my back and looked away, there might come someone who took the salami right off my cart." As she spoke, she turned slowly away from him and looked off at the vegetable stalls across the street. "If someone stole my salami, I would never know it."

Jerome gaped up at her. She was a giant silhouette against the sun. She was not looking. There was the salami. He picked it up. Then he picked up a cabbage and shoved it into his bag.

"Leave the chickens, Jerome," she warned. "If you and your sister are hungry, you may come eat with us. Our church does not look like a church, boy. It is inside our hearts. Get going."

Madame Rose was a confusing person. Their church was a church, but did not look like a church? Well, he could not think of that now. Sun would stream through the portholes of the *Garlic*. Marie would be waking up. She always called Jerome her hero when there was breakfast waiting when she woke up. Dodging through the trudging shoppers, Jerome happily took off toward the river. This sausage would be enough to eat every night until Madame Hilaire showed up again at the end of the week!

❖ ❖ ❖

The garret room at the top of seven long flights of stairs was ideal for Josephine. She alone occupied the floor of what had been an attic storage space. Tucked beneath the eaves of the Foyer International, two tall dormer windows looked out over slate and green copper roofs and the leafless trees of Luxembourg Gardens. To the left, the golden dome of Les Invalides marked the burial place of Napoleon. Above the tangle of chimney pots, the large square towers of Notre Dame marked the center of le Cité. To the right, the distant hill above Montmartre was crowned with Sacre Coeur.

In their time together in Paris, Josie and Daniel had climbed the north tower of Notre Dame a dozen times to overlook the city. They had picnicked on fresh warm bread with creamy brie and washed it down with red wine as they waited for the bells to toll. No doubt they had glanced toward the windows of this very room and yet had never imagined that Josie would be standing here alone one day waiting for the same bells to ring.

It was best, she thought, to hear them at a distance now, to turn her face to the north tower and imagine Danny there still, looking her way.

The room was small. A single iron frame bed rested against the wall beneath the sloping ceiling. Madame Watson provided a desk and chair where Josie could write. A tall chest of drawers was maneuvered with great difficulty up the stairs by two sweating delivery men who were past their prime. A blue floral rug Josie purchased at the flea market a week after her arrival covered the bare wood-planked floor.

Alma was quartered two floors below and down the hall from Irene and Helene. No doubt Josie's isolation had been planned by Madame Watson to protect the other residents from the clacking of an Olivetti typewriter at all hours. Whatever the reason, it was worth seven flights to be spared the constant borrowing and unending chatter of the lower floors which re- minded Josie of a college dorm. If someone needed a word with her or a telephone call came in, the message was relayed by banging on the radiator pipes which twisted up to her living space. No one, after panting up four or five stories, wanted to climb the rest of the way just to visit Josephine Marlow. Josie was grateful for the privacy and the view.

As a foreigner, she was required to register and be fingerprinted at the police station just around the corner in the Latin Quarter. But she did not feel like a foreigner. Her favorite café, Deux Magots, was a short walk. In spite of the cold, the *bouquinistes*—the booksellers—still displayed their wares in sidewalk bins. There were fewer students poking through the crates these days, but still the old Left Bank neighborhood had the look and feel of Paris before the war. It was good to be home.

Even so, Josie listened to the conversation of taxi drivers and waiters and shop girls, and she felt uneasy. She lunched with French government officials and visiting neutrals and fellow journalists at the Crillon and the Ritz, and she left each meeting with a heavy lump of foreboding. It was not the bitter cold of winter which made her tremble in her attic room, it was something else. France did not want to hear that what had happened in Warsaw was possible in France.

She had promised the little priest of St. John's Cathedral that she would tell the world what had transpired there, but no one wanted to be reminded of war. They wanted only to talk of politics.

Sitting in Café Deux Magots beneath the grinning wooden effigies of two Chinese Mandarin lords, the conversation was all politics.

Delfina, Helene, Alma, Irene, and Josie sipped their coffee and argued with an old waiter who had been pulled from retirement after the young waiters had all been sent to the front.

The old man winked at the young women and proceeded to enlighten them about The Great Problem Facing France. "Russia has a Man. Italy has a Man. Germany has a Man. If only France had a Man, we could beat them all." He shrugged. "But we have Daladier who gave Czechoslovakia to Germany's Man. England has Chamberlain, who did the same."

Delfina, who was Russian by birth and anti-Bolshevik by religion, flared. "If France and England were run by dictators, then what would make them different from Russia, Germany, or Italy, Monsieur?"

"If we had a dictator," said the waiter somewhat sadly, "at least he would be our Man . . . a French Man."

The waiter may have been a secret Fascist, a Socialist, a Communist, or simply a confused Democrat, but he expressed the longing of nearly every Parisian for a strong national government that could inspire national pride. Beyond that, government should leave the common man to live.

This desire, to be left alone to live according to one's convictions, was common to all French political positions. A strong leader was the one concept which united all parties. It was just that no one in France could agree whose point of view the Strong Man of France should represent. Each political faction believed that all the other camps should be brought into line with their own.

Confusion!

Helene, who worked as a seamstress at Redfern, simply shrugged. *"Mais que voulez-vous?* We French like our own politics, but we deplore those of everyone around who does not agree. It is not always easy, but we manage . . ."

"Oui," concluded Irene. "When the occasion demands it, we will put aside our differences, to be resumed at a more convenient moment. In the meantime, we all unite to defend our beloved France."

Josie remained silent through all of this. Her companions did not know, could not conceive, what it was they were defending beloved France against . . .

If the only requirement for an acceptable existence were to remain alive and relatively untroubled, then what difference would it make to the French if their government was Fascist, Communist, Socialist, or confused Democrat?

One was just as good as another, was it not? *Laissez faire.* As long as an individual was left alone to live day-by-day, one set of principles was as good as another, was it not? Provided that the Man at the helm of French government was French, perhaps even fascism could be tolerated.

Josephine had been too quiet. All heads pivoted toward her.

"Well, Josephine?" Helene probed.

Alma added with a laugh, "In England she could not stop talking politics. What's this? Run out of opinions?"

Josie sat back and drew a deep breath. "You sure you want my views?"

"This is France," Delfina remarked sharply. "Everyone has an opinion . . ."

"And every one is different," Josie interrupted. "All right, then. Unlike France, there is only one opinion in all of Nazi Germany, and here it is: Warfare is as sacred to men as motherhood is to women."

There was silence around the table for a moment and then a nervous giggle.

"Is that all, Josephine?" Helene laughed.

Josie shrugged. "They all agree on that. Or if they don't agree, they can't argue with it. Germans no longer talk politics on the Ku'damm in Berlin. They talk about war."

"Well, is that not what we have been doing?" Irene twittered.

"No!" Delfina shot back hotly. "Politics and war are not the same. It is war which ultimately decides politics, and religion, and what your life will be like day to day! Not the other way around. Right and wrong survive every battle. But only the victor has the privilege to choose between the two. The Nazis have known that from the beginning. Hitler . . . Stalin . . . they are all the same. They enslave their own people by giving them something that politics and religion can no longer provide. They give them belief in a meaning to existence beyond their own narrow self-interest. Give them a sacred war to fight! A reason to sacrifice! Some unity in a bloody cause! The real degradation begins when people realize they are in league with the Devil. But they feel the Devil is preferable to the emptiness of life which lacks larger significance. The Cause becomes their God. Right or Wrong? What is that? The Cause is everything."

Josie considered her friend with sympathy. Delfina's family had fled from Russia to France during the Bolshevik Revolution. Her carte d'identité was still the Nance Pass, the passport issued to displaced persons after the last war. She had suffered enough to know what she was talking about.

The others sat speechless at Delfina's outburst. There was an uncomfortable pall over them as she continued. "France is waiting for its French Hitler. The churches are empty. Lives are empty. What is your purpose for existence? Only to exist. To keep breathing and eating and . . . It all frightens me very much."

"War as sacred as motherhood?" Alma laughed. "Ask any French poilu at the Maginot how he feels about that! He'll tell you he much prefers making some woman into a sacred mother to making war! There's the difference between Germany and France!"

Helene shook her head in horror. "Dreary little Nazis! To imagine men who value fighting over making love!" She put a finger to her temple, indicating the madness of it. "Vive la France! It is them or us this time, girls!"

✤ ✤ ✤

Three days leave in Paris! The only way the prospect could have been more exciting was if it had been London, or if Annie had somehow managed to be in Paris too. Hewitt teased David when he said this. "The last place you want your regular girl to be is in Paris, Tinman!"

The train pulled out of Rouvres at noon; the trip would take only a few hours. David had never been to Paris before. He made a mental vow to store up sights and sounds to share with Annie. She had never been to the City of Lights either. He would bring her there some day and be her tour guide to the most romantic place in the world.

The countryside of eastern France rolled by. Hewitt and Simpson were asleep as the train pulled away from the platform at Chalons-sur-Marne. David leaned on the window ledge along the corridor outside the compartment looking at the Marne River. He compared the twin towers of the church of Notre Dame de Vaux to its description in a guidebook. *Romanesque nave,* he read, *Gothic choir and vaults.*

"What's this?" a gravelly voice belched. "Trying to improve your mind, assassin?"

A reedy, high-pitched tone agreed. "Sure he is, Mister Arthur. That's it exactly."

It was Badger Cross and his toady friend, Dinky Mertz. From the slur in both their voices it was clear that they had been drinking. David wanted to ignore them, hoping they would go away. The last thing he needed was to get into an altercation with Cross and maybe get put off the train.

Badger snatched the volume out of David's hands. "Too high and mighty for the likes of us, eh Tincup? Can't be bothered to speak to an old acquaintance?"

"Give it here, Cross," David said as Badger passed the guidebook to Dinky. "I don't want any trouble with you."

"He doesn't want any trouble with me? Isn't that sad, Dinky? Is that any way to speak to a comrade in arms?"

"No, not at all polite," Mertz hiccuped.

David tried to reach past Badger and grab the book, but Cross swatted his arm aside and put his beery breath in David's face. "Didn't know I lost me cushy instructor job on accounta you, did you, Teacup? Somebody ratted on me for the little tussle we had in the pub . . . was that you, Tincan, Buttercup . . . whatever your name is . . . was that you?"

"It wasn't me. Now get lost, Badger. I don't want to fight you again."

"Well, shall we let bygones be bygones, then?"

The meaty outstretched hand was regarded with suspicion. "Sure," he said at last. "Just as soon as you give me my book back."

"How thoughtless of me. Dinky, the book." Badger reached his right hand back over his shoulder as if to take the guide from Mertz. But when his fist reached shoulder height, he threw it straight forward, toward David's nose.

David had expected something of the kind, and that instinctive warning combined with Badger's drunken reflexes were enough to get David's nose out of the way. The punch did land on his ear, though, flinging him sideways into the window and knocking out the glass.

He lashed out with his leg as he fell and hooked Badger behind the knee. The big man also tumbled against the window, catching Dinky with a flailing forearm and whacking Mertz to the floor as well.

Quickly on his feet, David said, "Okay, so we still have something to settle. But not here, you idiot! Do you want to get thrown off the train?"

"Ha! Did you hear that, Dinky? The Yank has got no stomach, besides no heart. He's yellow."

"Sure he is, Mister Arthur," nodded Mertz, wiping his bloody lip with his sleeve. "But c'mon. He's right. We don't want to get put off."

"You little traitor. Just have to get the job done quickly then."

Badger put his head down and charged, more bull-like in his actions than his namesake. David caught him around the neck with one arm and brought an uppercut into the center of Badger's mouth. The force of the rush carried the pair down the corridor till they impacted the wall at the end, breaking out another glass panel.

Having Badger's twenty-stone weight behind the shoulder in the center of David's chest took all the American's breath away. Badger threw his head back and brought his hands together up under David's chin. "I'll throttle you good, Tinfoil," he said, squeezing David's throat. Cross braced himself against the motion of the train with a wide stance.

A mademoiselle came into the corridor from the far end. When she saw the struggle she screamed and ran back out the door. "Hurry, Mister Arthur," urged Mertz. " 'Fore the gendarmies get here!"

Though David's head was swimming, his early dirty fighting skills had not deserted him. He brought his right knee up sharply, into Badger's crotch.

Cross got a beatified look on his face, grunted once, and dropped his hands. David wound up his right hand and fired, smacking Badger in the eye and flinging him backwards into the just-arrived train conductor.

That worthy was knocked down, breaking his glasses and a gold watch. But the French damselle's screams had brought assistance: two stewards from the dining car and an off-duty policeman had come along as well.

Dinky Mertz disappeared.

When hauled before the magistrate in the town of Epernay, the judge was an understanding man. He was willing to let the two brawlers go, he said, provided they pay for the damage to the train, the glasses, the watch, and Monsieur the conductor's nose. Five hundred francs should cover it.

It was more than both had, put together.

"Trois jours," he said. "Three days in jail."

THIRTY-TWO

Luxembourg City. It was an anachronism; a hodgepodge mixture of architecture and ages which somehow managed to live together in harmony. It was the city where Elaine had lived. It was the place where Andre's child now resided with her grandfather, steel magnate Abraham Snow, in a tall gothic house overlooking the Petrusse River.

Andre's trip to Belgium was reason enough to make a detour into Luxembourg City. He spent the night at the Brasseur Hotel in the same room where he had often met with Elaine. The staff recognized him at once. Henri, the proprietor, and his wife, Agnes, greeted him solemnly. Did they sense that he had returned to their establishment on a sort of pilgrimage dedicated to Elaine? They did not mention her name. Henri simply handed Andre the key. Agnes, who sat knitting in the shadows beside the lift, turned her eyes upward in pity for an instant as he passed. The needles clicked like those of Madame Defarge watching the condemned climb the scaffold of the guillotine.

Her eyes seemed to ask, *Are you putting yourself through this ordeal willingly? Poor fool.*

He had taken his meal, *rôti de veau et asperge,* alone in his room. He had hardly been able to swallow. What little he ate was washed down with an entire bottle of Châteauneuf-du-Pap. It was a mediocre vintage, but he drank it all. The wine did not help him sleep as he had hoped. He lay on the bed and closed his eyes and saw Elaine.

Blue satin negligee. The thin straps slipped down revealing her shoulder. Her lips parted in a smile of expectation. He reached out for her, but she was gone . . .

He had hardly slept, and when he did his dreams were full of her. When she was alive he had still held some hope that one day they would be together again. Now there was nothing but the ache of longing.

At last his thoughts turned to the child—to Juliette. She was no more than a ten-minute walk from the hotel. Ten minutes away and yet Andre had never laid eyes on her. And so, in the morning, he got up, determined that he would see the child that he and Elaine had made.

It was raining. At eight o'clock Andre ate a croissant and gulped a cup of coffee in the small dining room of the hotel. He left his car in the garage and borrowed an umbrella from Henri for the short walk to Boulevard de la Petrusse.

He crossed the street and walked along the quay. With the river at his back, he stared up at the tarnished stone of the great house. Six smoking chimney pots topped the steep slate roof. The master was home, and yet the window shades were drawn as if the structure had closed its eyes in grief. The black crepe of mourning was hung above the massive door. Would Juliette come out and walk to school? Or should Andre go boldly up the steps, knock on the door, and ask to see the child? Should he risk being refused by Abraham Snow, who had good reason to hate him? That could mean a scene in front of Juliette. Hadn't she been through enough?

He could not make himself move toward the house.

Rain drummed hard on the umbrella, like impatient fingers drumming on a table top. It splashed up from the stones until the cuffs of his trousers were damp. How long had he been waiting? A lone man beneath a black umbrella on the riverbank. He must be a curious sight. He thought he saw the edge of a curtain of an upper story window stir and then fall back. Was someone watching him even as he watched the house? Perhaps it was little Juliette behind the glass.

He wished someone would raise the shades; could he have even one glimpse of Elaine's child, his child? But no one appeared at the windows. No one left the house.

It was almost eleven when he returned to the Hôtel Brasseur. The proprietor and his wife each glanced up furtively as Andre placed the umbrella on the marble top of the reception desk.

"Was your meeting a pleasant one, Monsieur Chardon?" Henri asked.

"It was very wet." Andre did not tell him that he had been standing several hours in the rain.

"Your trousers are damp, Monsieur Chardon," offered Agnes, setting down her knitting. "Perhaps you would like to have them dried and pressed?"

He shook his head and did not look her in the eye. "I have a long way to go today. It will have to wait."

He left Luxembourg feeling foolish. What had he accomplished except that he was more miserable than he had ever been? He felt the loneliness of his life more acutely than he had ever felt any emotion, and in the end what difference did it make?

✤　✤　✤

Andre's mission to Belgium had left him with a grim sense of foreboding about the defensive strategies of his own generals. Staying with Lewinski had left Bertrand grim and confused.

Andre sat silently beside Bertrand all the way to the Prime Minister's office at the Palais Bourbon.

They entered the building and went directly to Premier Daladier's suite. The group already present and waiting their arrival included Daladier, Supreme Military Commander Gamelin and Gamelin's aide, Colonel Pucelle.

The small figure of Daladier straightened his already squarely set shoulders and invited Andre to begin. "Everyone here is already aware of your mission, Colonel, and everyone knows its importance. Please proceed."

Andre opened his briefcase and extracted a crumpled sheaf of papers. These he fanned out across the table, carefully laying aside two pages that were partially charred. "You understand, gentlemen, that these are not all the contents of the German major's portfolio," he explained. "My Belgian counterpart has the rest, but we were provided with these originals so as to better judge their significance and authenticity."

"Can you give us a summary of what they are?" suggested Daladier.

"These papers purport to be the air fleet operation orders for the Luftwaffe division based at Cologne."

This much of the papers' secret was already known to the men at the table, but not what came next.

"And what are the orders?"

Andre drew a deep breath. "They direct the targeting of air attacks in connection with a German invasion of Holland and Belgium."

"Exactly!" said General Gamelin. "This is confirmation of what we have always said. The Germans would be fools to try a frontal assault on the Maginot Line. Therefore the attack, when it comes, must be through the low countries."

Andre frowned, but said nothing until prompted by Daladier. "You said 'purport to be.' Is there some doubt about their authenticity?"

Colonel Pucelle, in a tone that spoke of how anxious he was to curry favor with his commander, answered before Andre could speak. "Pardon me, Prime Minister, but what doubt can there be? The German officer carrying these orders attempted to destroy them, as we can see from the burned pages. In fact, we understand that he tried twice."

"Is this correct, Colonel Chardon?"

Andre acknowledged the accuracy of Pucelle's statement. "The gendarme who apprehended the two Germans did not see the first attempt to ignite the papers. Later, when they were waiting the arrival of the Chief Inspector, Major Reinberger made a second effort at their destruction, this time in the parlor stove in the farmhouse."

"But quick action on the part of the gendarme stopped him from succeeding," announced Pucelle with a triumphant tone. "Surely this proves that the papers are genuine. If the German scheme was to send us false information, why try so hard to eliminate what they wanted us to have?"

There was a murmur of agreement from General Gamelin and Minister Daladier at this reasoning. Andre still sat silently frowning.

"Colonel Chardon, you are still unconvinced," said Daladier reasonably. "Tell us what you see that we have missed."

Andre cleared his throat before replying. "It is directly contrary to the policy of the German High Command to ever transport top secret documents by air, in exact anticipation of what has occurred here. Secondly, the German majors stated that they crashed because they were lost and ran out of fuel; yet when the Me108 was examined, it still had enough fuel to have continued flying."

"A malfunctioning gauge, or ice in the fuel line," interrupted Pucelle.

"Please continue, Colonel Chardon," Daladier urged.

Andre nodded his head and spoke again. "Thirdly, the two attempts to burn the documents are suspicious, to me, anyway." He looked directly at Pucelle as he continued. "These are Luftwaffe officers . . . not fools . . .

carrying highly sensitive papers directly against orders. How many tries does it take to burn something so incriminating?"

"Bah," snorted Pucelle. "Colonel Chardon is striving to unravel a mystery where one does not exist. General Gamelin stated as long ago as 1937 that any future Nazi threat to our border would have to come through Holland and Belgium, and would precisely follow the German Schlieffen Plan. The same strategy they followed in the Great War, unsuccessfully, I might add."

There was a general air of agreement around the table, which only Andre and Bertrand did not share. To be fair, Daladier gave Andre one more chance to speak. "If this is an elaborate trick, Colonel, what could possibly be the intent?"

Andre cleared his throat nervously. "I do not believe this is a trick. However, I do believe that the German officers Kurt Hulse and Reinberger allowed these documents to come into the hands of the neutrals intentionally."

There was an undertone of surprise around the table. Daladier leaned close to drum his fingers on the documents. "Then you feel these Germans wished that we possess the complete details of Luftwaffe plans? They are traitors, in other words."

"They were reticent to speak with me, Prime Minister, because I am a Frenchman and the enemy of their Reich. But through a two-way mirror I observed a conversation between the German Kurt Hulse and a Belgian plainclothes officer who has befriended him."

"This Hulse will speak to the neutrals, then."

"I believe his plan was to warn them. But there is more." Andre drew his breath in slowly. What he was about to say flew in the face of all current military thinking. "At my urging, the Belgian asked this Hulse if he knew of any plans concerning the Ardennes . . ."

Pucelle snorted. "There could be none. Impassable to artillery . . ."

Andre continued in spite of the prevailing attitude of scorn. "Hulse said that it was just as easy for a Stuka dive-bomber to fly over the Ardennes as it was for it to fly over flat terrain."

"A dive-bomber could not carry enough explosives to make a dent in . . ." Pucelle began, but Bertrand leapt into the argument.

"You are forgetting Warsaw, Colonel! You are forgetting Barcelona!"

"Cities!" Pucelle retorted. "Vulnerable to air bombardment. But the entire French front could not be dented!"

"I tell you," Andre said quietly. "Hulse and Reinberger were warning the neutrals. But we Frenchmen should also be warned about the Ardennes."

Gamelin shook his head and stuck his lower lip out in disdain at the very idea. "A guess is not good enough, Colonel Chardon. I will not move whole divisions to sit idle before an impenetrable line because of an unsubstantiated guess." He slapped his hand down on the German documents. "This is what we go on. If these documents are authentic, and you believe they are . . ."

"But incomplete . . ." Andre began.

"What other information do we have? Show me proof and I may look at the Ardennes. But for now you waste our time with speculation!" The general stood and the meeting was at an end. Andre was dismissed like an errant schoolboy. He would not mention the Ardennes again until he had proof that his theory was correct.

On the way out to the waiting Citroen, Bertrand drew Andre aside. "I know you are disappointed that you could not convince them," he said. "But remember that they know nothing as yet about the project going on in your basement. Perhaps our friend Lewinski has come up with something definite."

Andre gave Bertrand a bleak look. "The truth, Gustave? I do not even know what he is up to."

December in the South Atlantic was hotter than any summer Trevor had ever experienced back home. Once a day the prisoners were allowed a ten-minute turn up on *Altmark*'s deck. It was an amazing relief, if only to have the temperature drop to a hundred degrees from the sweltering one hundred thirty of the hold.

Trevor realized that nothing in the Nazi's hearts had softened which caused them to allow this brief exercise. As Captain Thun had so grandly informed the prisoners, they were to be taken back to Germany and displayed. Britain's vaunted sea power was being humbled, and the parade of British sailors was the proof. As such, hostages to German propaganda had to be transported alive, if only barely.

The incident of the death of Frankie Thomas had resulted in a curious postscript. As additional proof that the Germans were still far more concerned with discipline than the welfare of the prisoners, an official proclamation had been posted inside the hold.

> Notice to Prisoners. On account of today's behavior of the prisoners, they will get bread and water only tomorrow. Further, I have given orders that the doctor will not make his regular round after this. Cases of severe sickness must be reported at the time of handing down the food.

But if the iron enforcement of German authority had not changed, something in Trevor's relations with the rest of the prisoners had. After Frankie's body had been unceremoniously dumped over the side, every Brit had taken the time to squeeze Trevor's hand in approval of his attempt to intercede.

When Dykes had complained about the loss of their rations, Nob had taken him aside. In a low, unmistakably menacing tone, Dykes had been informed that if he didn't shut up, his would be the next body going over the rail.

As the calendar slowly crept toward Christmas, the day finally came when *Altmark* was once again rafted up next to the *Graf Spee* to receive more prisoners. When the newly transferred captives were added to the crowd in the hold, each was quizzed for news of the outside world and the prospects of rescue. Trevor latched onto a tall machinist's mate named Dooley who had been on the freighter *Huntsman.*

"They've got the wind up about somethin'," Dooley reported. "Heard two Heine swabbies gabbin' about a big battle comin'. There may be nothin' to it, but they made a course change, sudden like."

Before Dooley had even finished speaking, orders were shouted and the lines securing the battleship to her smaller accomplice were cast off. Sirens blared on the battleship and the steam whistle of the prison ship shrilled a farewell. In the sudden confusion of the abrupt departure, no one had been commanded to shut the lid over the hold. To come out of the cell unordered would mean being shot, but Trevor risked standing on the ladder and poking his head up just far enough to get a narrow view of the sea across the deck.

At first he could not make out anything but the giant steel wall that was the hull of *Graf Spee.* But gradually the raider drew apart from the *Altmark,* and then Trevor could make out what had caused the sudden departure: two columns of smoke on the horizon were moving at high speed toward the German ships. As Trevor watched, a third smudge of dark fumes appeared a short distance behind the first pair.

The guns of the *Spee* roared. She carried three sets of enormous eleven-inch cannons, capable of throwing huge projectiles across miles of ocean. The crash of the guns reverberated within the confines of the hold, as if *Altmark* herself were under attack.

"What is it? What's happening?" came the urgent shouts from below.

Trevor had forgotten that he was supposed to be a reporter and not just an observer. "Can't make out the hulls yet," Trevor yelled back. "From the way they are coming straight ahead, they must at least be battle cruisers. Maybe the *Exeter.* "

"Get on with it, man," Dooley urged, "tell it all!"

"*Spee* has the range," he said. "The cruisers are firing, but the shells are falling way too short. Every time one of those eleven inchers hits it throws water two hundred feet in the air. Now I can see . . ." Trevor stopped awkwardly.

"What, man, what?" Dooley pleaded. "I mean, sir. Don't stop!"

"One of the cruisers has taken a hit," Trevor reported. "There was a bright flash and it's falling back now."

A groan went up from all the prisoners. "What about the other two?" Nob asked.

"They are zigging, making a smoke screen," Trevor recounted.

"To cover their retreat, the no-good cowards," Dykes muttered.

Altmark bore away northeast, leaving the battle scene behind as the *Spee* headed southwest. It was clear that there would be no rescue today; all the attention of the British warships was focused on the German raider.

The accidentally uncovered hatch was discovered, and Trevor was curtly ordered to drop down or face more punishment. Just before he complied, he hauled himself up on his hands and peered across the intervening water at the battle. He got a clout on his ear for his audacity and was knocked backwards into the hold.

"What'd you do that for?" Dykes muttered. "Tryin' to get us on bread and water again?"

Trevor came up holding the side of his head, but he was smiling. "Think what you want, Dykes," he said. "But it was worth it. The cruisers aren't running away. They are dashing in and out of that smoke like dogs after a lion. One of them closed to point blank range before plunging back into cover."

"And? Go on, man, finish!"

"I saw the *Graf Spee* take a hit on her bridge."

A cheer resounded in the cramped space of the hull that could not have been any greater if liberation had come. This behavior did in fact earn the prisoners another day on reduced rations, but not one, not even Dykes, complained.

❧   ❧   ❧

Mac and Murphy boarded the 7:00 A.M. train to Paris from Nancy.

The compartment was occupied by a man who snoozed soundly. A copy of the *New York Times* covered his face. He snored softly beneath bold headlines declaring the defeat of the German pocket battleship *Graf Spee* by the British navy at Montevideo Harbor in South America.

In unison, Mac and Murphy leaned forward to read the fluttering newspaper. It had been weeks since they had seen an American publication. The capture of *Graf Spee* had all of England waving the Union Jack as if the war had been won.

Photographs showed the proud German ship before its defeat and then the smashed hull as it sank slowly into the waters at the mouth of the River Plate. Proclaimed as a glorious victory for the British fleet, the sinking of the warship was an Allied public relations victory as well. The naval battle, fought an ocean away from France, had been the most exciting news event in the conflict for several months.

The *New York Times* rose and fell with the even cadence of the man's breathing.

A reprinted German communiqué beneath the photograph of the captain of the battleship announced:

> The commander of the *Graf Spee,* Captain Hans Langsdorf, did not want to survive the sinking of his ship. True to the old traditions and in the spirit of the Officers Corps of which he was a member for thirty years, he made this decision. Having brought his crew to safety he considered his duty fulfilled, and he followed his ship. The navy understands and praises this step. Captain Langsdorf has in this way fulfilled like a fighter and a hero the expectations of his führer, the German people and the navy.

Mac read the bit and let out a low whistle. "Really something. The guy went down with his ship."

From beneath the newsprint a familiar French voice bellowed, "Nonsense, Monsieur! Langsdorf was ordered by Hitler to shoot himself. Which he did in a hotel room in Buenos Aires." The figure sat up and extended the paper to Mac. It was the former French Ambassador to Poland, Noel, returning to Paris after a trip to Washington, during which he had personally informed Roosevelt of the events in Poland. He had taken along a reel of Mac's film as proof. "Bonjour, McGrath. We meet again. This time no one is shooting at us, eh?" He ran his hand through his thinning hair. "Your newsreel has been a great success back in the States. It had the president and Madame Eleanor on the edge of their seats. I suppose you have not had such exciting film since we escaped the Messerschmidts in Poland?"

For the next several hours Noel proved to be a prime source of real news. Having just arrived from the States, he was a fountain of information to the two journalists who had been living with the filtered, one-sided versions allowed by the censors. They sat like starved puppies waiting for the next morsel.

"And furthermore, the Royal Navy may have caught the *Graf Spee,* but not before she off-loaded several hundred British prisoners of war onto a German freighter called the *Altmark.* The British Admiralty is not printing everything." He yawned. "Oh, by the way. Did you hear that the Russians have attacked Finland an hour ago with Hitler's blessings? It is my opinion that Hitler wishes to let his friend, Stalin, wear out his army in the blizzards of Scandinavia this winter. Then Hitler will fight Stalin."

Poor Finland seemed very far away. Would England and Britain send troops to assist? Or would they simply be content to bluster and bellow and let the Finns fight their own war? Noel, who did not like the English, or his own government, believed that the fate of Finland would be the same as Poland. Enough said.

After that the conversation turned to news from home. Clark Gable had done a smashing job as Rhett Butler in *Gone with the Wind*. The German, French, and British ambassadors had all been at the theater for the Washington premiere. It made for added excitement during the burning of Atlanta. Noel rather enjoyed it.

The New York World's Fair was still packing in the crowds in spite of the cold weather. The German, British, and French exhibitions attracted all sorts of sinister characters who all ate at the same hot dog stand. Noel himself had enjoyed a beer from Munich under the watchful eye of two Gestapo men. They had even been bold enough to strike up a conversation with him about his escape from Poland. He had told them their pilots were very good shots. He was quite certain he had been followed everywhere he went, as if he knew anything of vital importance that the Nazis did not already know. He had not minded, he said. He found the whole thing amusing.

In conclusion, most people in America, including the resident Germans, French, and British, treated the war as if it were nothing more than a staring match across a concrete fence with a few muttered threats thrown in for interest.

Noel made a prediction. "How much longer can it last? A German captain ordered to shoot himself for the sake of tacking on a dignified ending? War without nobility soon becomes tiresome. We must hope that by spring some disenchanted German will shoot Hitler, and everything will get back to normal."

THIRTY-THREE

Y ou are looking at me strangely." Richard Lewinski tapped the top of his soft-boiled egg with a spoon.

Andre glared at him across the breakfast table. "You are tapping Morse code on your egg, Richard. You said, *Donnez-moi du sel.*"

"That is correct. So? Pass the salt."

Andre did so with some irritation then returned his attention to the newspaper. The tapping continued, this time against the egg cup.

THANK YOU and GOOD MORNING.

Andre lowered the paper and narrowed his eyes as Richard continued.

WHY ARE YOU CROSS?

"I will tell you why, Richard. Because it has been a long and difficult week. My superiors at Vignolle think you are a lunatic up to no good. Therefore they think I am a lunatic for continuing my support of you. You tell me virtually nothing about what you are doing in my basement all day. Therefore I have nothing to tell them."

Lewinski smiled and raised his spoon like a conductor's baton. "Tell them . . . I am building an organ. I intend to put a Nazi monkey on a chain and become an organ grinder in Geneva."

"You are mad."

"Yes," Lewinski nodded. "But there is method in it." He leaned his elbow against the table and gazed intently at Andre. "Tell them . . ." He smiled. "Tell them this is all a child's game."

"Deciphering enemy codes is no game for children, Richard."

"But it is." He blotted his mouth and smoothed his napkin out on the table. "Remember when we were children? Remember the code?"

"No."

"Yes, Andre! You must. We made up a list. Every letter in the alphabet was substituted for another letter." He began to write on the napkin.

H=T, E=Q, L=Y and P=N. HELP=TQYN

"Yes. A child's game. I will give you that. We have an entire team working to decipher the German substitution codes."

"Too simple. *E* is the most common letter. One progresses from there. We learned that from Sherlock Holmes. Remember, Andre? *The Case of the Dancing Men.*"

Andre had lost his appetite. There was nothing in this that he did not know. "Richard, the problem is that we are deciphering German codes too late. It takes months. They change their ciphers every day."

"Exactly. Enter ENIGMA. The original commercially marketed machine has three wheels, each of which contain connections for 26 letters of the alphabet."

Andre nodded, hoping that there was some point to Lewinski's lecture. "This we know was sold on the open market as a business encoding device just after the last war."

"The machine is no secret. When the operator types the letter *A* the setting of the first wheel might change it to the letter *R.* The second changes the *R* to a *Y* and the third changes the *Y* to an *H.* Which is the first letter of the word *HELP.*"

"Richard, Intelligence is aware of the problem. What is the solution?"

"Someone who knows how to set the wheels could read the message running the H back through the machine to the letter A, to decipher it."

Andre stared glumly at the word *HELP* on the napkin. "Changing one of the wheels changes the outcome. Changing all three of the wheels changes the outcome by possible millions of combinations. And the Nazis alter the setting each day."

Lewinski added cheerfully, "It is much worse than that, Andre. I have discovered . . . The Nazis had added two additional interchangeable wheels to their ENIGMA machines. There are billions of possible combinations."

Andre was speechless. If this was true, then the code would be virtually impossible to break by any human.

"You see why the Nazis are not afraid to send thousands of these machines up to the front lines of battle. Why they are on every ship and every command car. They are supremely confident that all your work is too little, too late. And it is. Your cipher experts are ants in combat with a bull elephant."

Andre's brow furrowed as the implications became clear. Accurately coding and decoding messages depended on three things. Using the right three wheels, putting them in the Enigma machine in the correct order, and setting all three wheels to the correct starting position.

"Is this what I am to report to Bertrand at Vignolle? That Lewinski says it is hopeless?"

"Indeed not, Andre. What is needed is another machine which can duplicate and electronically interpret the impulses of the Enigma transmissions."

"And where is this miracle?"

"In your basement." Lewinski picked at the shell of his egg as though they had just been chatting about the weather.

"Richard . . . Is it possible?"

"A child's game. Multiplied a million times. But still, a child's game."

"When will it be ready?"

"When it is finished." He salted his breakfast and the conversation ended.

She was somewhat a celebrity since her return. Men of the press corps who had known her before as "Danny Marlow's widow" looked at her with a new respect since Warsaw. Then there were others who proclaimed that a woman had no place at the war.

"Stick to human interest stories!" ordered Frank Blake at AP when she expressed a desire to interview French Prime Minister Daladier. It had been Daladier who, with British Prime Minister Chamberlain, had handed Czechoslovakia over to Hitler in exchange for the promise of "peace in our time." Josie simply wanted to ask the diminutive French politician what his thoughts were on the matter since the fall of Poland.

The AP Paris chief left little doubt that such questions were the domain of the male journalists. As some recognition of her ordeal, however, Josie was given a raise of five dollars a week and sent out to interview dressmakers about the scarcity of French silk. Josie took the story an extra lap by tracing the sale of French-made silk to neutral Belgium, which in turn sold it to Nazi Germany to be made into parachutes. Was it possible that the German Reich intended to return the silk to France one day?

The question and the reply were cut from the story. The conclusion was that in the French textile industry, it was business as usual.

This morning Josie finished her work in the gloomy AP office. Most of the male staff, resplendent in newly tailored military press uniforms, had headed for a guided tour of the Maginot Line. Alma Dodge manned the switchboard and gathered up the tape streaming from the wire. Josephine was just wrapping up a story about the care and feeding of millions of soldiers. True to the stereotype, the French army had drafted civilian pastry chefs first. This army of bakers, equipped with mobile stone bake-ovens, filled the trenches daily with the aroma of fresh-baked French bread. Nothing like it. Josie had toured the mobile kitchens this morning and had come back ravishingly hungry. No doubt this was some sort of new mental warfare against the German troops. The Wehrmacht was, by now, faced with the threat of mass defection unless the German bakers could learn to make French baguettes . . .

Since an army was as good as its food supply, Josie presumed that this was meant to be evidence of the superior quality of France's divisions. It was, as Frank Blake reminded her, clearly a human-interest piece. Such a story would have no difficulty getting through the tribe of French government censors who had taken over an entire floor at the Hôtel Continental on Rue de Castiglione.

"I'm taking this to the Continental," Josie called to Alma as she gathered her coat and handbag. "You want to meet someplace for lunch?"

Alma glanced at the clock. "Café Deux Magots? One?" Then her eyes widened as the door to the AP office swung open and a tall, handsome man entered.

It was the colonel from the train. Dressed as a civilian today in an expensive double-breasted brown suit, he held a brown fedora in his hand as he leaned against the counter and smiled at Josephine.

"Madame Marlow?" he began. "You probably do not remember me. We met . . . briefly . . . on the train from Boulogne to Paris some time ago. Colonel Andre Chardon."

Of course Josie remembered the nameless colonel. The awkward conversation in the dark compartment. The doll. The volume of *Paradise Lost*.

"Oui," she replied. "I have something of yours. A volume of Milton. I did not have your name or I would have . . ."

He snapped his fingers. "I was hoping someone had picked it up. It belonged to my mother."

"The notes are hers, then."

"Oui."

"She must be a very special lady."

"Yes. She was . . . Madame Marlow. A dear friend of hers gave me the volume as a gift. I have not yet had the opportunity to . . ."

"Lovely thoughts." Josie felt herself color. It was natural that she would have looked through the book, but somehow she felt as though she had been snooping. "She must have been a fan of Milton."

"Perhaps she was." He glanced at his watch, obviously in a hurry. "You have the volume here, Madame Marlow? I am grateful."

"I've got to get my story through the censors at the Hôtel Continental, and I'm afraid your book is at my lodgings. If you would like to drop by tomorrow . . ." It would be nice to see him again. Share thoughts on Milton's *Paradise* over a cup of coffee.

"You are staying at the Hôtel Continental?"

Alma laughed. Josie shrugged. "Nothing that upscale, I'm afraid. Foyer International."

"Foyer International. On St. Michel." He made a note of the address with a slim gold pen. "May I send a courier by to pick it up this evening?" So coffee and *Paradise* had not occurred to the handsome Frenchman.

"I'll be out this evening."

Alma chirped. "You can leave it with me, Josie. I'll make sure he gets it. Tell him to ask for Alma Dodge."

More scribbles and then he snapped his notebook closed. "Done. My deepest thanks to you both." The colonel seemed pleased. He retrieved a fifty-franc note from his pocket and laid it on the counter. "The book is of great value to me. A small reward, Madame. Please. For your trouble."

"I wouldn't think of it!" Josie protested.

He left it there, backed up a step, and said cheerfully to Alma, "Take yourselves out for lunch on me." With that he bowed slightly and exited the AP office without a glance back.

In silence the two women watched him step into a sleek new Citroen and disappear into traffic.

"I'd rather have lunch *with* him." Alma scooped up the fifty-franc note.

"How could you take that?"

"Of course, lunch *on* him might be nice too." She tucked the bill into her pocket.

"He's not your type."

"Apparently we're not *his* type either. I thought these Frenchmen were interested in American women. Not even a glimmer."

"We've just met a man who loves his mother." Josie gathered up her papers.

"We'll have to settle for lunch. Deux Magots? One o'clock."

❧ ❧ ❧

The richly appointed corridors and rooms of the French censors at the Hôtel Continental were crowded with the junior staff of press agencies filing stories wired in from their frontline correspondents in Nancy. Former guest rooms decorated in delicate floral print wallpaper and lace curtains were the backdrop for conflict between the censors and the members of the press. Josephine was at the back of the queue.

A lively argument ensued from a suite just up the hall. Josie recognized the voice of Mac McGrath as one of the combatants.

"What do you mean . . . won't do?"

"It simply will not do, Monsieur. For the sake of morale . . ."

"Morale! These guys died up there fighting for France! Well . . . they died anyway. Don't they deserve . . ."

"It is the decision of the committee, Monsieur McGrath. The footage has been confiscated."

"I've driven all this way from Nancy to bring this . . ."

"You were in a forward area without an official Press Officer, in a place where you had no business to be."

"So that's it, then?"

"Oui! As you say it. That is it."

Josie looked for a place to hide. The linen closet was locked. She tried to squeeze into the nearest room but was warned off by angry glares from a crowd of male journalists who had been waiting for hours.

Too late. Mac left his oppressor with a string of uncensored American expletives and exploded red-faced and grubby into the corridor just a few feet from where Josie waited.

For an instant she thought he would storm past without seeing her. No such luck. He stood for a long moment, unshaven and rumpled. He had come straight from the front to the censors' offices at the Hôtel without stopping to clean up.

He glanced her way, did a double take, and then ran his hand through his hair. He looked like a kid caught with his hand in the cookie jar.

"Hello, Mac."

"Hullo, Jo." His expression displayed clearly that he would rather not be seeing her right now either.

"Quite a ruckus in there."

He shrugged and changed the subject. "So you made it back to Paris."

"You were right. Things have changed since the war began."

"Lousy censors. Herr Josef Goebbels in Naziland is easier to deal with than these French poets and literary critics turned officials. Give 'em a little power and . . ."

"When I said things have changed, I was thinking more of other things."

"Yeah. I haven't slept in a couple days."

"I meant the restaurants. They're only serving half a cup of coffee and there's no more butter on the tables."

"War is hell. I'm glad that's all the trouble you've had." He gave a bitter laugh. "Where're you staying? I heard they requisitioned your block of flats for the French Armée."

"Foyer International."

"Yeah?" he grinned. "With Mama Watson? Like being an inmate in a girls' school, isn't it?" His breath exploded in a sigh as his tension dissipated. "Well. Nothing I can do around here." He laughed and wiped his hands on his muddy coat. "Except take a bath and sleep for a week. And I'm hungry. You had lunch?"

"I'm meeting . . ."

"Never mind." He interrupted her sharply. "I look like something the cat dragged in. I know."

"You could use a bath. But I was about to say I'm meeting Alma Dodge at Deux Magots if you'd like to come. If you want to go upstairs and bathe, we'll meet you there."

Josie blurted the invitation without thinking. What could be more awkward than sitting across from Mac and pretending that there was nothing between them? His nearness only sharpened her loneliness, making her nights longer. No more journalists! Why had she opened her big mouth?

He looked down at the toes of his boots for a moment then stepped closer to her. "I wanted to see you alone, Josie. Tonight?"

"Tonight . . . there's that Polish thing at the Ritz," she said too cheerfully.

"Right. The Polish thing." Mac took her arm and put his face next to hers. He lowered his voice as though he was in pain. "Look. I can't do this, you know? Pass you in a crowded hallway and end up sitting across from you with a teacup in my hand. I hate tea. I don't know why I mentioned lunch just now. You know what I want when I'm with you and it isn't a ham sandwich. Last time we were together at the Langham I told myself I wouldn't ask again. Better for me, I think. Sorry." He ran his hand across his cheek. "Guess I need a shave. See you around."

❊   ❊   ❊

Darkness descended on Paris like a black curtain.

The interior of the Ritz Hotel on Place Vendome was as bright as ever. The lobby of the Ritz was a blaze of holiday lights which reflected endlessly on and on in the massive gilt mirrors. A string quartet played Mozart as eminent men in dinner jackets and dress uniforms accompanied women in satin and jewels. The guests moved familiarly through the corridors and sitting rooms furnished with Louis XIV chairs and tables. A long arcade lined with shops lured browsers with diamonds and designer fashions. It seemed as if there were no war at the Ritz, and yet it was the war which drew such a distinguished crowd tonight.

The Society of the Friends of Poland had spared no expense in their reception for the former American ambassador to Poland, Anthony Biddle. The tables were laden with a buffet personally supervised by the head chef of the Ritz. An ice sculpture of the Eiffel Tower rose from the center of the buffet table; hors d'oeuvres were assembled to create a replica of Warsaw's Cathedral of St. John. Polish flags draped the walls and a banner stretched across the room proclaimed in French, FORGET NOT POLAND!

In spite of the sentiment, the general attitude among the non-Polish guests in the crowd was that they would very much like to forget Poland. Invitations had been sent to every ambassador on Embassy Row. Of all the top diplomatic officers only William Bullit, the American ambassador to

France, attended. The majority of the ambassadors from neutral nations had felt it was more politic to send their assistants. How would it look to Berlin, after all, if the top representative of a neutral nation nibbled caviar and drank champagne beneath a sign imploring them not to forget Poland, which had just been incorporated into the Reich?

Even the newsmen in attendance viewed the occasion as a very fancy wake for a very cold corpse. But the food was excellent, and here was opportunity to eat well and drink freely.

"Remember the Alamo," Mac McGrath said as he raised his champagne glass, gulped the contents down in one go, and then took another from the serving tray of a passing waiter.

"A first-rate spread for a third-rate cause," said Frank Blake, the squat, balding tyrant of Paris AP.

John Murphy eyed him disapprovingly. "Cynic. I should have stayed at the Maginot. At least there they think there are some things worth fighting for."

"Right, Murphy. Ol' bleeding heart Murphy!" commented Blake, as he took another hors d'oeuvre off the steeple of the Cathedral, giving it an ominous, bombed-out look. "I'll tell you what they fight for. The English fight for tea, crumpets, and mother. The French fight for sex, a good table in a restaurant, and the right to a pension. Sensible people, the French. Trust me. I've been here long enough to know. First Kraut the Frogs see bobbing across the Meuse and they'll cut and run."

Murphy had enough of Frank Blake. It did not take much. Angry, he grinned, thumped Mac on the back in farewell, turned, and wandered off into the babble of the crowd, leaving Mac alone to argue the point with Blake. Blake was already half drunk, and the evening had only begun.

"I saw Josephine Marlow at Hôtel Continental today." Mac tried to turn the topic to something he cared about. He had not stopped thinking about her. "How is she getting along?"

"That is one lady I do not talk politics with! I keep her covering the Paris bread lines. It's safer, if you know what I mean." Blake snorted and consumed another glass of champagne. "An idealist, that one. Raving lunatic when it comes to Poland and the Nazis. She was a lamb before she left Paris last August. Lovely little political cretin, she was. Now she's Winston Churchill and Joan of Arc in one pretty package. Bonkers. Too bad. The whole thing spoiled a very nice gal, if you ask me. Good writer, though. Gets the job done. Good as ol' Danny was that way."

"Is she here?" Mac had been looking for her since he arrived thirty minutes before. He wanted another chance before he returned to Nancy. He needed to talk to her again.

"Josephine Marlow? You think she'd miss this? Bleeding heart Polish."

Blake jerked his thumb at the shrinking edifice of the Cathedral, then at a table across the room. "What say we go over there? They've built the Belvedere Palace out of smoked salmon."

"Go on. I'll catch up." Mac watched him weave through the mash of Polish uniforms and tuxedoed bankers and oil magnates to the replica of the Belvedere Palace. Oblivious to the platter of smoked salmon and Melba toast surrounding the sculpture, Blake thrust his fork into the dome and removed the roof, toast and salmon slices, onto his plate. A little Hitler, that one, Mac mused. He did not know how Josie could get along with him in the same office.

Knowing Josie, this would be a perfect topic of conversation. He mentally framed the hook for his lead paragraph. *"Hi, Josie. Frank Blake is a real putz, isn't he? He just ate half the caviar off the Cathedral of St. John and now he's attacking the Belvedere Palace. How can you stand working for this guy? What do you say we get out of here? Talk it out over coffee somewhere . . ."*

Mac made his way through the crowd in search of her.

❖   ❖   ❖

The reception at the Ritz was a logical place for Federov to continue his search for Richard Lewinski. Nearly everyone who had anything to do with his escape from Poland was in attendance.

Federov was certain of this fact because, as a member of the Friends of Poland committee, he helped make out the guest list. His firm had supplied the champagne. The bill, along with the rest of his expenses, would be submitted to the Gestapo.

His niece accompanied him on the social rounds, and then wandered off somewhere while the Movietone film of the dramatic footage of the American ambassador's escape was shown.

Federov made certain that he stood beside Mac McGrath during the showing. McGrath was on the downhill side of sober. He seemed distracted, disinterested in the whole affair.

"Magnificent footage, Mister McGrath." Federov spoke to him in English so there could be no misunderstanding. "An exciting trip, was it?"

"The last decent film in the war."

The clip moved on toward its climax and the figure of Lewinski in his gas mask appeared in close up. He pulled the mask up and mopped the perspiration from his brow.

"An odd looking fellow," Federov probed, taking care that McGrath could hear the amusement in his voice. "Who is he?"

"Some character taking up room in our car." The cameraman looked over his shoulder toward the door as if searching for someone.

"He has to be something more than just a character if he escaped with the ambassador."

"I suppose. Just another pretty face to me. Ask Biddle." The American excused himself and walked to the entrance of the dining room. He looked to the right and the left and then disappeared as applause from the appreciative crowd swelled.

Federov decided that Mac McGrath knew more than he was saying. There was, of course, no way to ask Ambassador Biddle about Lewinski. Biddle certainly knew everything or he would not have spirited the Jew out of Poland. Therefore Biddle would have nothing to say about his identity and less to say about his current whereabouts.

As for the cameraman, Federov would put his Gestapo contacts to work on him. There were ways to find out what McGrath really knew about Lewinski.

"Americans," Federov sighed as the lights came up. He pondered his problem. It seemed obvious that the neutral Americans were holding all the cards in this matter. Probably they were also holding Lewinski. Or had they allowed this film past the censors to throw the Gestapo off the trail? Who else rode in the automobile with Lewinski from Warsaw to Rumania? McGrath would answer that after a little sensibly applied pressure.

There was only one way to confirm what he suspected. An active branch of the Friends of Poland was lobbying in Washington even now. Friends of Lewinski would doubtless also be active in the organization.

THIRTY-FOUR

It was the color of the dress which first caught Andre's eye. Cobalt blue satin, cut low in the back, it was worn by a tall woman with a graceful neck and thick, plaited chestnut hair done up on her head. If the hair color had been blond, Andre might have mistaken her for Elaine from behind. He could not help himself; he stared at her, wishing that she would turn around.

Attractive from the back, she apparently was worth looking at straight on as well. A semicircle of four male guests stood like smitten adolescents in front of her. Andre recognized Johnson who had served as assistant to the American Ambassador to Poland; at her right was the Polish Count Radziwill, grim and intense; and Clive Blackwell, the London journalist who had championed Chamberlain's pacifist policies before the war. Finally, crowding in at her left hand, there was Federov, the White Russian wine merchant, whose main interest in life was not commerce, but social functions and beautiful women.

And then the blue dress turned enough so that Andre could see the face in profile.

Madame Josephine Marlow. This was the first glimpse of her out of that khaki press uniform. Impressive. Unlike the other women in the crowd, she wore no jewels, no furs; she did not carry a beaded handbag. She was just there in the blue satin dress. Her face was fresh as a farm girl's. Nose straight. Forehead high. Classic. And she was beautiful.

Andre had noticed that much about Daniel Marlow's widow before, but he had not given her much thought. Perhaps it was the sight of the Russian, Federov, lusting after her like a third-rate museum curator lusts after the Mona Lisa. There was something about this woman, like a rare piece of art, which was out of reach.

Andre excused himself from the mindless buzz of conversation and moved toward her.

"Marlow," said the London journalist. "Marlow? Any relation to Daniel Marlow?"

"We were married."

"I was in Paris with him for a year in 1934 before I left for Ottawa, and I never knew Marlow was married. How long were you married?"

"Six years."

Blackwell counted on his fingers. "You mean he was married . . . ?" There was an accusation of the late Daniel Marlow in the comment. Everyone knew the reputation of the American journalist. He never behaved as a married man. But why bring that up now? Blackwell was a soul entirely without tact.

Andre sauntered up and patted the journalist on the back. "Well, Blackwell, good to see you back in Paris. Did you just arrive?"

"Yes."

"Did the fresh Canadian air do you some good?"

"It's the best air in the world, Colonel Chardon."

"Your tuberculosis is better these days, I take it. Very good."

The journalist gaped at Andre. What was he to say? "But I didn't have tuberculosis."

"Whatever it was . . . terrible thing. We all thought you would die. All the same, my congratulations that you are out of the sanitorium, Monsieur."

Andre crowded in beside the speechless Canadian and kissed the hand of Josephine. "Madame Marlow. We meet again. A pleasure."

The others in the group cast concerned glances at the London journalist, bid Madame Marlow adieu, and sauntered off to less contagious parts of the room.

Andre took her arm and led her away from the stunned Blackwell.

"That was a slick piece of work." She smiled as they halted beneath a Polish flag. "No wonder you are a colonel."

"He is ridiculous, this British journalist. Ungallant."

"It's all right, Colonel. Blackwell doesn't shock me. I was aware of my husband's reputation."

"It is difficult to imagine that Monsieur Marlow would have had a reputation when one sees you."

"We were apart for a long time."

"That is also difficult to imagine. To be apart from you by choice?" His eyes flitted to her throat, her hair, her mouth. "Very difficult."

"When I came here two years ago I intended to divorce him."

"And when he saw you again he would not let you go? That I believe. At times it takes a second look and a man knows he was first blinded by the sun."

The wall was at her back. "Why is it that I feel like I've just jumped from the frying pan to the fire?"

"The frying pan?"

"And old American saying. It means that you are . . . skilled at conversation, Colonel." She eyed him with doubtful amusement.

"Just Andre, Madame."

"Well then, just Andre." She pointed to herself. "I will be just Josephine."

"No. Josephine the Just, I think . . . or Josephine the Gracious. Or the Beautiful."

She laughed, great uproarious laughter the way American students on the Left Bank laugh when they have consumed too much wine. It embarrassed him.

"What is it?"

The laughter subsided and she patted him gently on the cheek, the way a sister pats a little brother. "You're just so good at it, that's all! And I thought you were such a gloomy person the first time. Then today in the office, I might as well have had a bag over my head. Now this!"

Wasn't that just the picture? Mac watched them at a distance: Josie in the blue dress with her back pressed against the wall; the French colonel in his dress uniform and tall boots . . . one hand in his pocket, the other hand touching her hand. The colonel stood close in front of her like a fraternity man making time with a freshman coed.

She laughed at something he said. The kind of laugh that made a guy feel as clever as William Powell with Myrna Loy.

Mac wanted to break the Frenchman's handsome face. He wanted to thump his chest like Tarzan and hit this clown over the head with a Louis XIV gilt chair. He wanted to drag Josephine off to his cave and . . .

"What's with you?" John Murphy pounded him on the back.

"What do you mean?" Mac snarled and looked away from the too-cozy scene.

Murphy spotted Josephine and the colonel, then studied Mac. "Oh. I get it."

"Get what?" Mac controlled his urge to pop Murphy in the kisser for being nosy and for knowing too much before Mac even said anything about it.

"You should marry her," Murphy said in a nonchalant tone, as if he were saying, "Hey Mac, you should get a new shirt," or, "Well Mac, it's a nice day we're having."

"It's not that easy, so mind your own business, Murphy."

"What's tough about it? Just marry her. You love her."

"It takes two."

"Yeah. The colonel's got that figured all right. She is as ripe for picking as a peach in June." Murphy mimed the plucking of succulent Josephine Marlow from the tree.

"Look at her. All soft and fluttery over the uniform. Dames! They go for all that stuff." Mac caught his own reflection in a mirror. His tweed suit was wrinkled. His red tie, which he had owned since his college days, was tied something like a red rag around the neck of a big dog. He needed a haircut.

"Yep. They do go for it," Murphy agreed. "Good thing I married Elisa before all the journalists were out getting fitted for uniforms. Course, if it was now, I'd visit Mussolini's tailor if I thought it would make Elisa look at me. Man, she is something." Murphy got the faraway look of a hungry man dreaming of ripe peaches.

"Yeah," Mac said miserably as Josie left with the colonel. "She is."

Andre Chardon brought Josie to the Casino de Paris, and with a bribe to the head waiter of fifty francs, procured a table on the first balcony. He then ordered champagne at a cost which exceeded an entire week of her income. It was obvious to her that he was living on something more than the pay of an army colonel.

Back home in America, Josephine had been content to crowd into the movie theater like everyone else for a black and white glimpse of Maurice Chevalier. Now here he was in the flesh.

It had taken the war to bring Chevalier home from Hollywood. Cheeks rosy and lips red in the footlights, his white straw boater was pulled down over one eye as he sang the most popular song in France. Called "In the Maginot," it was set to the tune of La Marseillaise. It provided a complete picture of the democratic army of France.

> *The colonel was in finance*
> *The major was in industry,*
> *The captain was an insurance man,*
> *The lieutenant had a grocery.*
> *The adjutant was an usher at the*
> *Bank of France.*
> *The sergeant was a pastry cook,*
> *The corporal was a dunce,*
> *And all the privates had private incomes . . .*

Josie smiled at Andre across the small round table. He sipped his champagne.

"Everyone in the army was something before the war," she asked. "What did you do?"

"I kept myself busy with horses and wine." He raised his glass to her. "And beautiful women."

"Back home we would call that a recipe for poverty."

He laughed. "It is not as bad as all that, Madame Marlow. Josephine . . . As a young man I trained as a cavalry officer at Saumur. Thus the horses. My brother, Paul, carries on the tradition."

"And the wine?"

"My family owned vineyards in Bordeaux, which Paul and I inherited."

She smiled and thought, *Thus the money.*

His gaze moved to her throat, her ear, her cheek and then lingered on her mouth. "As for beautiful women? I suppose they are also family tradition . . . one which, with your assistance, I may carry on in spite of the war."

What could she say to that? *Very smooth, Colonel Chardon? Top of the class, Colonel Chardon?*

Chevalier belted out his melody as sequined show girls strutted their stuff around him.

> *. . . D'excellent Francais!*
> *D'excellent soldats . . .*

And all this makes fine Frenchmen,
fine soldiers . . .

Josie did not look at Andre. "I suppose you are highly skilled at what you do."

"I manage. I am out of practice in some things." His look warmed her. "Equestrian pursuits, for instance. And I find that my palette is not as sharp as it used to be. As for other matters?" He gestured toward the entertainer as though the words to the song provided some answer to his final pursuit.

Qui marchent au pas;
Marching in step;

Ils n'en avaient plut habitude;
They'd got out of the habit, but

Mais tout comm' la bicyclett' . . .
Like bicycle-riding you don't forget!

It occurred to Josie that in the mind of the colonel, she was the bicycle. It was an interesting idea, but it also frightened her. Soldiers were as bad as war correspondents. Shiny medals and brass buttons attracted bullets. She had had enough of that for a lifetime.

"I am not sure I want to get to know you, Colonel Chardon."

"Call me Andre, please." He seemed undeterred by her frankness. "And then tell my why you feel that way when we know each other so well."

"Not so well."

"We slept side by side on the train. You know I do not snore. Usually women do not discover such things until it is too late. Even when a husband snores, it is difficult to divorce him in France. There are laws. So. I do not snore. I am rich. I ride well. What more can you ask?"

She laughed. "You must have some flaws."

The amusement in his eyes faded. There was the look she had seen on the train. The look of a lonely man.

He nodded curtly. "Many." He turned to stare at the act. The song ended to thunderous applause. The game was over. What had she said to kill his pursuit so entirely?

"I should take you home." He crooked a finger at the waiter and asked for the check.

The image of the doll jumped to Josie's mind. She blurted, "Did she like the doll?"

He looked at her as though she had read some small line in his thoughts. "How do you know . . . ?"

"I saw it on the train. I assumed you were taking it to someone."

He drew a deep breath. "I have a daughter."

"And did she like it? A beautiful thing."

"She has not seen it. Nor has she ever met me." He shrugged as though the words had escaped unbidden. "My greatest fault." An embarrassed smile. He counted out the bills to pay the check and had to count again.

Josie felt suddenly tender toward him. "I like you much better when you are not trying so hard."

"I suppose I am out of practice with beautiful women as well. It has been a long time since I could look at anyone else." His words trailed off.

"Anyone else?"

"The child's mother. She is dead now. It was hopeless long before she died. And yet I hoped. I noticed you tonight. Beautiful. Aloof. Intelligent. But . . . I have forgotten how the game is played."

"Not really. It is just that I prefer honesty to the game. I have had too much of the first and not enough of the other."

He bit his lip and leaned closer, like a man wanting to share some secret plan. "She is only five, my little girl. Living with her grandfather in Luxembourg."

"A beautiful little place."

"A dreary life. He is a grim and bitter man."

"Well? Have you thought about bringing her to Paris?"

"I know nothing at all about little girls. Children."

What was that in his expression? A plea for help? Josie sensed she was coming near to a dangerous situation. Here was a man who wanted to bring his child into his home, but how could he manage? Was he looking at Josie as some sort of potential nursemaid? Sweet, but no cigar.

"They are something like puppies. Feed them, love them, teach them manners, and they usually grow up to be quite decent."

"I have no experience with puppies either."

"You are deprived."

The spark returned. "Do you know about such mysteries?"

"Puppies. Kittens. Colts. Six brothers and sisters. You name it."

"Would you share your advice with me? If perhaps I went to meet the child?"

She considered his request for a long moment. "Is that why you asked me out?"

He tucked his chin. "Honestly?"

"I told you how I feel about honesty."

"Well then . . . no. Honestly. You have a beautiful face. I noticed your eyes even when you were wearing your press uniform. But this color blue suits you better. Now I find there was much beneath the khaki that I had not seen before." He took her hand and lifted her fingers to his lips. "Beneath your tunic, I see, there was a fountain of maternal instincts waiting to be uncovered."

His appreciative gaze made her want to reach for her coat and button up. On the other hand it had been a long time since any man had looked at her this way. She was enjoying it, but she did not give him the satisfaction of knowing how much.

"All instincts aside, Andre . . . Common sense is what is required here."

He sat back and drummed his fingers on the table. "You are right, of course. What do you suggest?"

"If I were you, I would wrap that beautiful doll for Christmas and make a trip to Luxembourg."

"I was considering it." He frowned down at his hands in thought and then raised his eyes to meet her gaze. "Thank you for saying it. Would you go with me? I may need a friend to hold my hand."

⚜ ⚜ ⚜

Mac felt the presence of danger even before he could see the vague shadows of the two men following him. It was a short walk through the darkness from the Ritz Hotel to Hôtel Continental, but Paris was entirely without the benefit of street lamps. Muggings were again as common in the City of Lights as they had been during the dark times of Charles Dickens. Every alleyway and narrow space between the close-packed houses and arcades could be hiding places for thugs. Not even the blue-uniformed gendarmes were immune from being robbed; they traveled in pairs these days.

So who was on Mac's trail? He listened for voices, but heard only the heavy footfalls of two men. They slowed when he slowed and speeded up when he began to walk faster.

Other shadowy forms slipped past him in the dark. The drunken laughter of a group of revelers echoed across the square and reverberated beneath the portico.

The footsteps did not stop when Mac turned on Rue de Castiglione and quickened his pace toward his own hotel three blocks away. A cold wind blew up from the Tuileries, carrying on it the dank scent of the Seine and the sewers which emptied into the river in the night.

He pulled the collar of his topcoat up around his ears and clutched his keys so that they protruded from his fist like spikes. He carried only ten francs in his wallet, hardly worth dying for. But his hard-won clearance papers were worth a fortune on the black market. To anyone interested in buying and selling false identities, the papers of an American were certainly worth killing for. There were a number of unidentified bodies fished out of the river every week. They were laid out in the morgue until someone recognized them. They were never found accompanied by their documents.

Mac wished he had a revolver. There were a number of men in the press corps who carried sidearms just for such occasions. Benny Morris could get anybody any kind of weapon he wanted. It had been foolish for Mac to refuse. He had told Benny that the DeVry camera was enough to shoot. Now Mac would have been glad just to have the DeVry to hit one of these guys over the head. Too late for that now.

A car roared past on the street, driving too fast in the darkness. Blue light glimmered feebly from the slits in the head lamps. Mac attempted to glimpse the features of the men he was certain would assail him. Black, bulky silhouettes stood out in momentary relief against the white stone of the building, but he could not make out their faces.

The Rue de Castiglione was deserted. The voices of the drunks died away behind him. He was still a full block from the corner of Rue de Rivoli; he remembered that somewhere along the block was the side entrance of the Continental. But where? He groped for the door like a blind man in unfamiliar surroundings.

The footsteps quickened, closing the gap. Mac stopped and plastered his back against the hard stone wall. At least he would face them when they jumped. Nobody would club him from behind and dump him, unconscious, to drown in the river!"

"Hey!" he shouted. "I'm ready for you!"

The footsteps halted abruptly. Silence. Right. It was two men the size of prizefighters.

Mac challenged them again. "I've got ten francs, pals. If you think it's worth a try, come ahead."

"Don't say?" The accent was American. "Is that you, Mac?"

It was John Murphy and Ambassador Biddle.

Mac wished that the interior of Hotel Continental was not so bright. Biddle and Murphy said his face was as red as the lantern on a caboose. He glowed even in the dark. There was no escaping the ribbing. At least it got his mind off Josie and the French colonel for a while.

The elevators were not working at the Continental, so he plodded wearily up to his room. Inserting the key, he turned the lock and entered.

He swayed in the darkness for a moment, making certain that the blackout curtains were drawn. They were not. The notion that something was wrong rushed back. Or maybe he really had gone paranoid as Murphy suggested.

The window onto the fire escape was open. Cold air billowed in. Mac crossed the room in the dark, while something crunched underfoot.

Drawing the curtains, he turned on the light and stared at what he saw. The mattress and pillows had been slit. Every bit of his clothing was dumped onto the floor. Toothpaste was squeezed out of the tube . . . soap smashed . . . safety razor taken apart, the blades scattered like leaves on the bureau top.

He could live with all of that. Only one thing mattered. The rucksack containing his film was gone. And his DeVry camera was smashed. It lay in pieces on the floor.

THIRTY-FIVE

Cold weather hit Northern France with a fierceness which sent all brave soldiers on both sides of the line burrowing into their bunkers. Apart from the daily ritual of artillery rounds at the Maginot, the war was very slow indeed.

There were no wounded soldiers in the Casualty Clearing Station at the École de Cavalerie. There were, however, about one hundred patients with either bronchitis or pneumonia. The entire wing reeked of linseed, antiphlogistic poultices, and camphor steam inhalations which clung to the clothes and skin of the nurses.

Including Sister Abigail Mitchell.

Paul smelled her before he saw her. As was his custom, he strolled through the stables after dinner, not so much to check the horses, but because he found comfort in the warm earthy scents of horseflesh and the quiet of the place during the study hour.

This evening he was troubled by what had passed between him and Andre in Paris. He was right, he felt, but perhaps he had spoken too frankly. It was a fault of his; speaking too frankly. The same fault had put him into disfavor with General Gamelin when he had argued on behalf of DeGaulle's military strategy.

So here he was: acting headmaster of a cavalry school, and here he was likely to stay until the war was over one way or the other. He stroked the soft nose of a brood mare and felt sorry for himself.

Suddenly there was that aroma of camphor. He turned too late to escape the smiling greeting of Sister Mitchell. She was quite pretty, even though she had an Amazon personality, Paul thought.

"Bonjour, Captain Chardon!"

This meant good day and it was evening. Her French, as always, was very bad. Paul decided to speak English which he managed very well.

"Good evening, Sister."

"You speak English very well."

"My mother was English," he explained, and suddenly she looked at him as if he was forgiven for whatever it was he had done.

"I thought there was something different about you." She pulled her coat tighter around her and leaned against the stall door.

"Different?"

"Polite. Like an Englishman. A gentleman. Not like the rest of the . . ." She faltered. "Oh. I didn't meant that . . ."

"What did you mean?"

"The very thing I came to discuss with you. It seems that one of your officers has been seeing one of my younger nurses."

"Yes?" Paul nodded, casting through his mind for the right match. Probably Jules Sully, the chemistry instructor, and that cute little thing from Jersey. The Channel Island women were beauties and spoke decent French as well.

"It is that Chemistry teacher and Miss Bremmer from Jersey."

"A very pretty couple."

"No! I forbid it! He actually wishes to marry her and it simply cannot . . . We must put a stop to it."

"Mam'zelle." Paul had heard quite enough. "I am only half English. I do not admit it often, and in matters of the heart I am entirely French, I assure you. As was my mother, who, even though she was raised in England, was French to the core. A woman of great passion and understanding in such matters as affairs of the heart. Therefore, do not assume, though you yourself have no understanding of love, that I will allow you to direct heaven in the matter of a man and a woman who wish to be married. I am not so cold as that."

Her jaw dropped. She blinked at him in amazement. "But you cannot mean it."

"Mam'zelle. Sister . . . whatever. You may direct your CCS. You may scrub your little life away and tend to your camphor poultices, but there is more to life than that. I will grant my permission when the request is made. I would suggest you do the same, lest you reap the disdain of every citizen in Lys and every feeling heart at the École de Cavalerie."

"Well!"

"Very well, indeed." He bowed slightly. "It is no wonder you require so much coal to warm yourself . . . Now if you will excuse me. The smell of camphor has opened my head in ways I had not imagined. I bid you good evening, Mam'zelle Sister Abigail Mitchell."

⚜ ⚜ ⚜

The École de Cavalerie was empty of students when Paul Chardon left to spend Christmas with Andre in Paris. It was an odd homecoming. Andre was even more on edge than usual.

Richard Lewinski's hair gleamed like copper beneath the lamp which hung from the ceiling of his basement workshop. Laboring over a mass of wires and gears, he barely looked up as Andre and Paul walked down the steep steps.

"Bonjour, Richard," Andre called. "Paul is back in Paris, my friend."

"Merry Christmas, Richard," Paul called cheerfully.

Lewinski replied with a grunt as he continued his work. Sometime later, Andre suspected, his absentminded guest would ask where Paul had been and for how long. Of course, Andre had to admit the possibility that Richard Lewinski had not even noticed Paul's absence.

"He is no trouble, really," remarked Andre with a shrug. "Although he is more vacant than in the old days, I think. Not one word of conversation. We played a game of chess two nights ago and he was winning, too. Suddenly he got up and ran down to the cellar. Odd. I never see him eat, but Cook takes him his food and when she returns later it is gone." He laughed.

"What is he up to, anyway?" inquired Paul.

"The mad scientist," Andre avoided the question. "You know Richard has never been happy unless he is tinkering with something."

"Something from a Jules Verne novel, I expected—a time machine. Perhaps he will vanish and return with Napoleon at his side."

"An excellent guess." Andre clapped his brother on the back as they entered the study. "France could use another Napoleon these days."

Paul laughed. "Some of our generals are so old that I would swear they knew him personally."

A porcelain doll dressed in white lace was perched on a bookcase bearing red leather first editions autographed by the author, Jules Verne, and another set signed by Victor Hugo, both of whom had visited this house in former days.

Andre's younger brother warmed his hands by the fire.

"Will you try to see your daughter on this trip to Luxembourg with your pretty American friend?"

"I thought I might take mother's doll to give to her. A Christmas gift."

"Have you thought of bringing her to Paris?"

"I have thought of it." Paul's straightforward questioning made him uneasy.

"You should keep Lewinski away from the child. He's apt to frighten her. The way he peers through that gas mask and prowls around at all hours."

Andre sighed and shook his head. "This is crazy. I doubt that her grandfather will even let me see her. And if he did? How could I manage with the war on?"

"As a gentleman, do you have a choice, brother? There is really nothing else to be done under the circumstances. Elaine left the child in your hands. Her last bequest. Rightly so, I think."

Andre did not acknowledge the opinion of Paul about his personal affairs. The comment irritated him. What could Paul know about it? Andre fell silent, pretending to busy himself with unopened mail.

At last Paul broke the stillness. "So how is the political side of the war?"

"The British are ecstatic about the destruction of the *Graf Spee,* the German battleship. Full of self-congratulation, as if the British navy had won the war. Winston Churchill, as First Lord of the Admiralty, is quite the celebrity. We would all be better served if he headed the government of England, I think. Hitler hates him. That's a good sign."

"It will not be like the last war," Paul countered grimly.

Andre nodded in agreement. "I saw Charles DeGaulle last night at a party. Swaggering giant . . . He is arrogant and outspoken as always, but he's right. Tanks, he says. Tanks and planes. Mobility. But our generals are from another century, Paul." He smiled and half turned to gaze at his brother, who still wore the uniform of a cavalry officer. "We still have the finest horses in the world."

Paul bowed slightly. "Horses and French courage will defeat the Boche. My cadets are convinced of it. If only every poilu had the courage of my boys . . . They are certain that the Boche will melt in the face of our bravery."

"It must have been the opinion of the leaders of our Republic as well. Or why would they have gone to Munich with the English to give Hitler Czechoslovakia and the Skoda Arms Factory?" A bitter laugh. "I hear the Panzer Divisions are now driving Czech-made tanks of French design."

"But we have our eighty-year-old generals to inspire, do we not? General Petain, the hero of Verdun. He glares down at me from the dining hall of the École de Cavalerie, accusing me of being too modern for a cavalry officer. Petain, good horses, and courage. The Nazis cannot overcome such a combination."

The brothers fell silent. The fire crackled. Andre looked at the doll on the bookshelf.

"The English have evacuated their children from London. I have considered speaking to Juliette's grandfather about sending her to England. Perhaps it would be best if she does not stay in Paris."

"So. She is the reason behind all this talk of war." Paul laughed. "It is easier for you to consider mass destruction than fatherhood."

"That's not it."

"There are a few months until the offensive will begin. Trust a horse soldier in that. Hitler will wait until the roads dry out. Try to bring her here to be with you until then. She needs someone."

Andre nodded. "I was thinking that it might be better if she does not become . . . attached." Running his hand across his face he muttered, "Should I give her the doll at once? Should I go alone to the house to meet her? Or will it be better to bring a woman with me? Josephine seems fond of children."

"How do you know such details about women after so short a time? They are inscrutable to me after months of conversation. You amaze me, brother." Paul shook his head in amusement and turned toward the fire.

A sleek black limousine drove across Pont Marie and onto the island. The vehicle turned left on Quai d'Anjou, slowed and pulled to a stop in front of number 19.

"Josephine Marlow is here, Paul," Andre announced quietly.

"Shall we go?" Paul turned, rocked up on the toes of his boots, and added a word thick with sarcasm, *"Papa?"* He tugged at the tunic of his cavalry uniform in a nervous gesture. He looked past Andre as Josephine Marlow emerged from the vehicle. "Very nice. I am disappointed in only one thing."

Andre's brow furrowed. "Yes? What is that?"

"I should have met her first."

❧　❧　❧

Old Brezinski perched on the top rail of the stall as the spindly-legged colt stooped to probe his mother's underside in search of supper.

"He is a beauty," Katrina von Bockman said softly, taking a seat beside the Polish Jew.

"He will be black as a crow's wing by the time he is a yearling," Brezinski observed with pleasure. "His father was the same at this age, and look what came of it—Othello—black as night and the most magnificent stallion in Poland."

"Shot out from under Count Gratz in the battle of Krakow." Katrina brushed her hair back impatiently. What was the use of talking about what had gone before? It had all vanished now.

"The stallion was bred for battle, Katrina. Perhaps it is not wrong that he should have ended his life in such a way."

"A waste."

"So it always seems, except that courage in battle . . . of men and horses . . . is the stuff legends are made from."

"Legends. We would be better off to have Othello standing at stud right now, passing on some of his legendary qualities to his offspring."

The colt found the faucet and latched on with an enthusiasm which made the mare stamp her rear hoof three times.

"Starbright has taken to motherhood," said the old man. "She was such a flighty thing. It always settles them." He did not look at Katrina as he spoke. "It will be good for Horst to see her and the colt. It will cheer him."

"He is not coming home for Christmas." She raised her chin regally, as if expecting an argument.

"That is a shame. I would have liked for him to see this one."

"You are too kind, considering."

"Considering?"

"What he is part of."

Brezinski pushed his cap back on his head. "Horst is like Othello, Katrina. Have you not noticed?"

"I have noticed, all right. I have asked him to leave me, to gallop off and fight his war, even though he does not know what he is fighting for."

Brezinski contemplated her bitterness in silence for a while. "He is fighting because he must fight."

"For the Nazis?"

"For us, perhaps."

"You are a Jew. How can you say such a thing?"

He gestured broadly and turned his eyes upward at the sound of children's footsteps. "Your husband is a Wehrmacht hero, Katrina. His loyalty is unquestioned. Though the Nazis do not have his heart, they have his oath as a soldier. And as long as he continues to fight well for the Fatherland? Well then, we might remain relatively safe. If there is any safety for a Jew in Germany, it is only that he might be useful in the service of a German hero."

She blinked at him in astonishment. "But, Brezinski . . ."

He turned his gaze on her. "Your brother-in-law? Kurt Hulse? His plane down in Belgium? Lucky fellow. Your sister and parents are in Switzerland. You think the Gestapo is not watching you now?"

"How do you know this?"

"Everyone from the kitchen to the stable knows it. The little girls whisper about it. The nuns pray. Are you leaving the Reich as well?"

She frowned down at the back of the colt. "I had no plans to leave."

"Why?"

"This place . . . all of you."

"You are fighting in your own way then, instead of running. If you leave us, you know they will come for us."

"Yes."

"And if Horst is disloyal to his oath?"

Her eyes narrowed. "He is not fighting for us. He is fighting because he loves it."

"Not every man in the Wehrmacht is evil, Katrina. You know the Nazi law. If one family member commits a crime, all are punished." He took her hand. It was ice cold. "So now the only honest men left in Germany are in concentration camps. Holy places, those prisons. Full of saints and martyrs. Everyone else? Either hostages, true fanatics, or terrified liars . . . or fools who rage at a wind that will blow them away."

"It has become so complicated. I can't sort it out anymore."

"It is simple for me, because I am a Jew. Hitler made the decision for me. But what about you? And Horst?"

She sat sullenly considering the old man's words. "We should have left before the war."

"And what would have become of us? My family . . . the others you hide here?"

"I cannot guarantee your safety even now."

"Nor can you guarantee your own. But at least we are still breathing."

"Why didn't you leave Europe?"

"I wanted to go to America. I was there for a short time with the Kellogg Arabians. But I could not get visas for my family, so I returned, even knowing that this was a possibility. You see? For the sake of my family."

"That is different."

"Is it? Horst loves you, Katrina. Love sometimes calls for a peculiar kind of duty." He shifted his weight on the narrow rail and rubbed his chin. "I used to think of it when I was young. When my wife, Tanya, was alive and the pogroms were so fierce against the Jews in Poland, here was the question I put to myself: A man comes up to me on the street and puts a gun to the head of my wife. He tells me he will blow her brains out if I do not break into the house of my neighbor and steal his gold. What will I do?" He shrugged. The choice seemed obvious. "For the sake of her life, I will become a thief." He looked away as some terrible image crowded into his mind. "In Poland now the Nazis have made Jews to be policemen to arrest their fellow Jews. Good men are made to be traitors to their own friends. Their wives and children are hostages. The Gestapo learned that trick first in Germany, did they not?"

"What can I do?"

"You are doing all you can. You have put yourself at risk for all of us. So be smart. But you must have mercy also on your husband. They hold a gun to your head, and he loves you."

* * *

It was a chance meeting with a major in a Wehrmacht artillery regiment which turned Horst's interest back to Poland.

"Holiday leave?" The major swirled his glass of whiskey and soda like an Englishman. "I'm taking my pay back to Poland. Why should the SS swine get all the profit, while those of us who fought and won the war end up buying Polish goods in Germany for double the price? I tell you, von Bockman, there's a profit to be made in Poland in everything from lace doilies to horseflesh. The best for practically nothing!"

The wealth of Poland was finding its way into Germany. Coal and grain flowed west with antique furnishings, tapestries, and art. Jewels, furs, china, silver, and gold which had been smuggled out of Russia during the Bolshevik Revolution were now in the coffers of the Reich, or for sale at bargain prices for Christmas.

The trains ran unhindered across former Polish territory into Danzig and East Prussia and the now humbled, broken Polish cities of Lublin, Krakow, and Warsaw.

Enterprising merchants with the permission of the Reich General Government traveled east to examine the possibilities of establishing manufacturing centers manned by slave labor.

Major Horst von Bockman presented his request to enter the occupied territory to a minor clerk in the offices of commerce in Berlin.

"Yes, Major von Bockman. You say you wish to examine and purchase livestock from the General Government of Poland?"

"That is correct."

"What is your purpose?"

"In private life my wife and I own a stud farm. Arabian horses. I understand there are still many more to be had in Poland. The Poles are slaughtering horses and selling the meat on the black market. It is a waste beyond contemplation."

It had occurred to Horst that somewhere in the horror of the stock pens of Poland were the finest Arabian horses waiting to be butchered and hung on hooks in a meat shop. If he could purchase a dozen of the best and return them to the farm for Christmas, Katrina would have to speak to him again.

"How much cash do you intend to take into the General Government?"

"Five thousand Reichsmarks."

"A considerable sum."

"We purchased a number of Polish horses from Reichsmarshall Goering.

The amount seems modest for the quality of animal I have in mind to bring back to the Reich."

At the mention of Goering's weighty name, the eyebrows of the clerk raised in respect. The rubber stamp bearing the eagle and the swastika thumped down on Horst's travel permit.

THIRTY-SIX

Andre had clumsily wrapped the doll in red tissue paper and tied it with string. His efforts at packaging his daughter's gift embarrassed him as did the fact of his paternity. Driving Josephine north from Paris along the Chemin des Dames, the highway named for the daughters of Louis XV, he felt awkward.

To the wonder of Josephine, who had not been able to secure passes into the Zones des Armée, his documents gave them unhindered admittance through the concrete chicanes which blocked the roads leading toward the border of Luxembourg. Sentries saluted him, bade him good day, and sent him on his way.

He spoke little, although there was much he wanted to share with the beautiful woman beside him. She sensed his uneasiness and filled the silence with conversation, answering his questions about her life in America.

Born in Fort Smith, Arkansas, she had moved to California with her family when the drought and the Depression withered their world in 1930.

She confided, "We lived in a tent beside a river until my father found work in the oil fields. I was sixteen, gangly, and self-conscious. The girls made fun of me because of my Southern accent. Like the teasing done to the evacuated children from Alsace who are billeted in Paris; just the same. In California, the more of us who came west, the uglier things got. Compassion wore a little thin."

Andre wished he could have known her then. He glanced at her. Thick chestnut hair was plaited and pinned up. A strand curled at the curve of her cheek. Her face was clean and scrubbed-looking. Her eyes matched the shade of her hair color. Her gaze held knowledge of sorrow too great for her years.

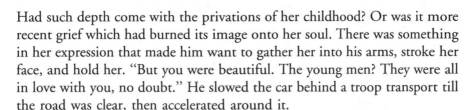

Had such depth come with the privations of her childhood? Or was it more recent grief which had burned its image onto her soul. There was something in her expression that made him want to gather her into his arms, stroke her face, and hold her. "But you were beautiful. The young men? They were all in love with you, no doubt." He slowed the car behind a troop transport till the road was clear, then accelerated around it.

She laughed at him in genuine amusement as she had laughed the first night they met. "Plain brown hair . . . brown eyes . . . ordinary . . . too tall. I'm glad of it now, but back then? I hid in the library and read until my eyes crossed. I excelled in French class. When I spoke French, no one noticed my Southern accent, you see? I spoke as well as . . . better than . . . the other girls in French class. In the summer I worked as a laborer in the vineyards outside a little shanty town called Arvin. See how much we have in common, Andre? You own vineyards in Bordeaux, and I once harvested grapes in Kern County, California." She laughed again. "But I was good in school. I got a scholarship to UCLA."

"And your husband?"

"We met in a literature class. Danny was the first man I ever loved. The only man up until then. I thought when two people were in love they got married, had children, worked, and went to church on Sunday. Danny surprised me. He married me, got a job with AP, and left for Europe."

"And you followed him."

"Not for five years. I taught in a little one-room school in the mountains above Bakersfield. When I came to Paris, I thought it was finished. But I fell in love with my husband all over again . . . and then I lost him."

Rows of leafless poplar trees slid past like a picket fence bordering snow-covered fields.

There was so much Andre wanted to know about her. She was different than any woman he had ever met. From a childhood of poverty she had a nobility of spirit and a strength untainted by bitterness. She was far from ordinary, and yet she accepted his compliments only with amusement, as if she had never really looked at herself in a mirror; as if his attentions were simply empty attempts at flattery.

"You have loved other men?"

"One." Rubbing the fog from the window, she looked out at the countryside.

Her silence made Andre wonder if she still loved the other one. "Where is he now?"

She smiled. "Probably out here somewhere chasing a story about the war, wishing he could befriend some French colonel who would get him through the roadblocks as easily as you! He is a newsman; cameraman. I promised myself after I lost Danny that I would not get involved with another journalist. So. Common sense prevails over love and he's gone."

"But you are a journalist."

"Danny didn't believe in life insurance. I have to eat. I love Paris. No one in Paris minds the fact that I was born in Arkansas. No one in France even knows where Arkansas is. America is just one big dreamland to the people over here. Writing for AP beats harvesting grapes in the vineyard of Colonel Andre Chardon."

He looked at her with surprise. It never occurred to him that she was actually working because she had to. She was smiling, but her words seemed like a rebuke. Driving into the courtyard of a small inn, he shut down the motor and set the brake. He turned to face her as sleet began to fall. Taking her hands, he raised them to his face. For the first time he noticed the remnants of callouses on her palms.

She eased her hands from his grip and closed her fists, suddenly self-conscious. "Everyone in France did something else before the war, Andre. How does the song go? *The colonel owned a vineyard. The correspondent tended vines . . .* Something like that. *Like riding a bicycle you never forget . . .*"

He pulled her against him and touched her cheek. "I would make you forget, if you will let me." Then he kissed her as the sleet drummed on the roof of the car.

※　※　※

The road into Luxembourg City climbed out of a canyon and across a narrow ridge known as "The Bock." Since Roman times this had been the main approach to the heights of ancient Luxembourg.

Like a broken tooth against the sky, the ruins of a tower marked the remnants of the city's original ramparts. Legends about the founder of Luxembourg claimed that Count Sigefroi sold his soul to the devil, who built the fortress for him in a single night.

As the evening mists swirled up from the Alzette and Petrusse Rivers to drift among the sloping medieval streets, it was not hard for Josie to imagine that the legend might be true. Here in this tiny neutral nation, other pacts were being made with the devil. The city was full of Gestapo agents, she had been told. Deals were struck, and military information bought and sold as commonly as vegetables on market day.

Andre had changed into civilian clothes at the border. Any military uniforms made the citizens of Luxembourg nervous. They preferred the "see-no-evil" approach to the war. Trusting in their policy of strict neutrality, they crossed their fingers and closed their eyes to the fact that they were snug against the borders of France and Germany.

As for the state of their own army, Luxembourg kept a troop of 350 men. Who would want to overrun the Grand Duchy, they reasoned, when it was such a useful meeting place for spies of both sides?

Andre knew the city well. This fact surprised Josie, since while his little girl lived here he had never been to visit her. With the certainty of a homing pigeon he made his way past the gothic cathedral of Our Lady of Luxembourg and the Grand Palace and the National Museum, finally stopping at the Brasseur Hotel.

The place exuded the faded grandeur of the last century. The lounge was draped in deep red. A portrait of the Grand Duchess Charlotte hung over the mantel of a large open fireplace in which the logs blazed cheerfully. In the stone of the mantel beneath Charlotte was carved the national motto of Luxembourg:

Mir woelle bleiwe was mir sin,
We want to remain what we are.

Was the motto merely wishful thinking?

There was a large Christmas tree in the corner behind a heavy square grand piano. A thin-faced man in an old fashioned cutaway coat played Mozart. The lounge was populated almost entirely by middle-aged men with grim eyes that darted from the pages of their newspapers to look at other grim men. With the piano providing the mood, the setting reminded Josie of an old silent movie she had seen about Mata Hari.

Andre knew the proprietor of the Brasseur, who peered up at Josie with interest as Andre signed the register for two rooms.

"Adjoining, Monsieur Chardon?" His inquiry was discreet, but heads turned all the same. Had Andre been here with other women? Perhaps with the mother of his child?

Against her will, the color rose to Josie's face.

"No. Merci, Henri," Andre replied. "My regular room for me. A suite for Madame Marlow."

There was no need for a bellman. Josie had brought a small carpetbag with one change of clothes and the blue dress. Andre carried the red-wrapped doll and a small, expensive leather valise.

Her suite was on the second floor near the stairs. His was on the third floor at the end of the corridor.

"Is an hour enough time?" he asked. "Dinner at eight-thirty. The small dining room. I'll come by and we can go down together."

"I'll meet you," she said, not wanting to take the chance of asking him in. He stooped to kiss her mouth. She turned her face away and his lips brushed her cheek. "Please don't," she whispered. "Not now. Not . . . tonight. I am . . . vulnerable."

He backed up a step and inclined his head in a slight bow, like a junior officer coolly accepting a command.

She closed the door of her room and turned the lock without thinking. Was she locking him out, or locking herself in? The last thing she needed was to get involved with a French colonel. At this moment she wished they were each staying at different hotels. In fact, the way she was feeling, separate cities might be the only real margin of safety.

❀   ❀   ❀

It was bitterly cold in Warsaw. With some relief Horst von Bockman noted that the snow covered some of the scars of battle. Trams had been righted and the rails repaired from the Umschlagplatz to the hotel. On the streets, open-backed lorries transported prisoners to shovel snow or to work on repairing the roads. Horst did not look at their gloomy faces as they passed.

In the late afternoon Horst retraced his steps to the river. There was no sign of what had transpired there some months before. Sections of the Vistula River were frozen, and yet black water lapped around the pilings of the bridge which joined the right and left banks of the city. He imagined the body of the woman Sophia still beneath the water. Or, in death, had she escaped Poland and drifted down to the sea? It seemed so long ago now. Why could he not forget her face? Why did he hear her repeat the name of her child each night as he lay down to sleep?

"Jules! Oh poor Jules."

He thought about the child of the dead woman. Once again he replayed the incident in his mind, wondering if he could have done anything different. Would the SS have arrested him if he had not stepped aside? Would they have shot her regardless? And if Katrina had been there with him, would her courage have brought about a different ending to the tragedy?

Katrina. She had a way of changing the world by her will. Perhaps that is why she believed that her will would change him now. How he ached for her approval and her love, and yet her self-righteousness angered him. She had known he was a soldier when she married him. Why had she chosen to reject him now when he needed her more than ever?

"Herr Major!" A ragged boy of about eleven approached from behind a heap of rubble. His coat was thin. Dark circles framed his eyes. He had the look of malnourishment. His German was barely passable.

"It is almost curfew, boy. You should get home."

"You look lonely, Herr Major. I have a pretty sister for you to spend time with." He took a cautious step closer.

"Little beggar," Horst scoffed, even as he wondered how evident his loneliness was in his expression. "Any sister of yours would not be something I want to spend time with."

"Oh no, Herr Major!" the boy blurted eagerly. "She is not like me! A beauty, I assure you!"

"I am not interested in Polish women or Jews, boy."

"We are not Jews!," the child spat. "She is very Aryan. Blond. Blue eyes. Young. Pretty. Better than the whores in Berlin." He moved his hands in the shape of an hourglass. "And she does not cost much to make a major very satisfied indeed! Come see! It cannot hurt to look. There is a gramophone for music. Vodka to drink. A pleasant way to pass a lonely evening. If you do not like her, you will leave. But you will be well pleased, I promise!"

To forget. That seemed the primary concern of Horst this evening. He was in need of diversion, he told himself. And what harm was there in just taking a look at the merchandise the boy was selling?

The sky was steel-grey as a thick fog descended over the city. Horst followed the beggar, keeping in mind that German soldiers had been led to ambush by partisans with the promise that a pretty woman waited at the end of a short walk.

"I will be discreet, Herr Major. You must not seem to be following me."

The boy was cheerful, walking a few paces ahead of Horst like a native guide. On deserted streets, he pointed at the windows of shops and flats which were patched together with lead and putty out of pieces of shattered glass. Those spaces too large to be repaired were simply boarded up, the boy explained. It would not matter until summer when the weather turned hot. Maybe by then everything would be back to normal. Maybe by then there would be no more war and the Germans would see that the Poles were really their friends. There would be whole panes of glass in the windows of Warsaw again.

They crossed a bomb-pocked street and passed a small knot of a half dozen sullen Poles who separated at the sight of Horst, retreating into shadowed alcoves as if they did not know one another.

At twilight they entered a building which had been moderately damaged in the bombardment. The stonework of the five-story building was scarred by shrapnel. The cornice work was broken and the windows here were more boarded up than patched.

The door into the lobby had once been glass. Now it was completely covered by bits of scrap wood. The interior of the entryway seemed entirely without light. Holding the door wide, the boy looked past Horst into the fog and hissed, "Come on, Herr Major. No one will see you."

Horst unsnapped the leather flap of his holster and rested his hand on the butt of his Luger. For a moment he hesitated and then stepped in after the boy. The door swung shut as the child leapt onto the narrow stairway. A small glimmer of light from a single light bulb identified the spiral of the staircase and each vacant landing. Other than that, there was an oppressive gloom. Horst listened for the sound of any footsteps besides their own. He glanced at each door as they passed, half expecting an ambush.

"It was a very nice flat before the war, Herr Major," the boy chirped as they passed the landing on the second floor. "Maybe next year . . ."

Horst was sweating by the time they reached the third floor. The climb had been uneventful, but he still felt the presence of danger as the boy knocked softly and called, "Smyka?"

There was a long pause and then the sound of a Schubert waltz penetrated the wood of the door.

"She will just be a moment." The boy turned apologetically. "You know . . . these females."

Horst kept his hand on the Luger. How stupid it would be to have survived battle and be murdered on a gloomy back street in Warsaw. "Of course."

The doorknob clicked, the hinges groaned slightly, and the door opened. A stream of light spilled out on Horst and the beggar. Silhouetted in the light was a girl with blond shoulder-length hair. Dyed, Horst reckoned, to make herself more appealing to the German clientele who were fixated on all things Aryan. Her eyes were wide and blue in an oval face and reflected her nervousness. Or was it fear? She was not much more than eighteen, if that. Wearing a flimsy light blue cotton robe, she was small and thin. She was not as starved-looking as her brother. Nevertheless, the spector of hunger was in her eyes.

"I have brought someone, Smyka," said the boy in an urgent tone, as if he was warning her to keep a bargain.

She did not smile or raise her eyes as she stepped aside. *"Guten abend,"* she said timidly.

Horst brushed past her into a small, musty-smelling room. The windows here were boarded. Fresh air would have been a relief. There was a neatly made bed in the corner. A small kerosene stove on the opposite wall. A curtain provided partition for what might have been a second room, but there was nothing else.

"He is a major, Smyka," said the boy. "I have told him you are very nice. That you have music and vodka too."

The girl's eyes darted up. "I am out of vodka, Herr Major. But if you like, my brother can get some."

Horst nodded, and looked toward the curtain.

"Oh that," the boy said brightly. "It is nothing. Just clothes and things."

Putting out his hand, he said, "If you want vodka you will have to pay in advance, Herr Major."

Horst dug in his pocket and retrieved a handful of change. "Yes. I would like a drink."

The brother and sister exchanged a look. The girl leaned in close and murmured some instruction in Polish. Then the urchin was out the door, clattering down the stairway. Schubert played on, skipping and scratching through one waltz and popping onto another.

"You will want to remove your gun and your tunic, Herr Major."

The girl looked at the bed and began to take off the robe.

"Wait until your brother comes back. I want to drink first."

She managed a weak, self-conscious smile and tied the belt again. Was she relieved? "As you wish, Herr Major. Would you like to dance then?"

The curtain stirred. Someone was behind it. Horst felt the hair on the back of his neck prickle. He stepped away from her as she put her arms around him.

"Who is there?" he demanded hotly.

"It is nothing, Herr Major. Nothing!"

He pushed her away roughly and drew his Luger as if to shoot through the cloth. The girl shrieked and stumbled, throwing herself between the muzzle of the pistol and the curtain.

"No! It is nothing, Herr Major! Do not shoot! Please! I beg you!"

Horst flung her aside and tore away the fabric, revealing not an enemy waiting in ambush, but a small crib with a child of about twelve months standing, clutching the bars.

The girl wept and clung to Horst's boots. "Please! I told you! You see? Only a baby, Herr Major! You cannot hurt him!"

A wave of dread enveloped Horst. Suppose he had fired?

The baby began to cry.

"Why did you hide him away?" Horst shouted at her. "I might have killed him!"

"I thought . . . you would not . . . want me! I need the money, Herr Major! Please! Do not leave me! I will do anything you want!"

Horst's breath exploded from his lungs. "Is the child yours, girl?"

"My baby brother."

"How old are you?" He grabbed her arm and pulled her roughly to her feet. "Do not lie to me. How old?"

"Sixteen." She cried. "Please . . . It is only me to care for them! For my brothers! Don't leave yet! There is no other way! You can see! No kerosene. Nothing left to eat! Please stay! I will make it up to you, Herr Major!" She sank to her knees and covered her face with her hands. "God, help me! God help us!"

The record bumped to an end. The ticking of the needle against the label marked time with her sobs. Horst shoved the Luger back into the holster. He reached into his pocket and pulled out a one hundred Reichsmark note and handed it to the baby.

Then he strode out of the room and out of the building into the foggy streets of Warsaw.

THIRTY-SEVEN

Hot water. Josie lay back in the tub and let it wash over her in delicious waves. She almost regretted her promise to be ready in an hour. How wonderful it would be to simply throw on her nightgown and climb between cool sheets, cool off, and sleep for a while!

The telephone rang. She wrapped in a towel and answered it on the fifth ring. The tone of Andre was too cheerful. "Chérie! I've met some old friends who are staying here. I hope you don't mind. We are invited to join them at their table. I could not refuse without compromising you to gossip."

She suppressed her vague sense of disappointment with the knowledge that there was safety in numbers. The way she was feeling, dinner by candlelight with Andre could be fatal. "Of course, Andre!" Did her too-cheerful tone match his?

Dressed in the cobalt blue evening dress, Josie entered the lobby of the hotel. Andre had already seen her in the gown, and she felt as though she was a caterpillar among the butterflies which he must see around Paris.

"Fantastic," Andre uttered, as if seeing her for the first time.

Escorting her to the dining room he explained that a number of foreign nationals would be at the table tonight, including an American oilman and a Polish colonel in exile.

"All men, I fear. Most English-speaking." He leaned close to her as they entered the small dining room. She felt his breath on her shoulder and his nearness warmed her. "You said you were vulnerable tonight. I have taken you at your word. I have provided you with, I hope, an entertaining diversion, but I cannot always say that I will be such a gentleman."

His frank gaze made her blush again. Suddenly wide awake, she could feel the color climb from her throat to her cheeks. He smiled at it, and she imagined that he said such things on purpose. There was a kind of power in a man who could warm a woman with a look. Was it an acquired skill, she wondered, or just some inherited talent peculiar to the French? She forced herself to remember the wizened old face of the railroad ticket clerk in Boulogne. What was it he had said about the French bulls?

"May I speak frankly?" she asked.

"But of course."

"On our first meeting on the train to Paris? I am relieved that your eyes were closed and your mouth open most of the way from Boulogne. Otherwise I might think you were a dangerous man."

"Oh, but I am! You'll see when you know me better." He laughed, but Josie had the distinct feeling that he was no longer joking.

The large round dining table was set before a fireplace at the far end of the salon. Four men rose in unison as they approached.

Andre introduced Josie. "This group will be all politics and war. The food is the best in Luxembourg, and this was the personal table of the German Kaiser in the last war." He pulled out her chair. "This was the Kaiser's chair."

Introductions passed clockwise around the table: the American oilman, Hardy, thickset and sunburned, with a Southern accent; the Polish colonel, Wolinska, fine-boned, grim, and steely-eyed, as though thinking about Christmas misery in Warsaw; a Canadian journalist, Tibbets, who had arrived on the continent too late to make Christmas on the Western Front with his colleagues; and Medard, an elderly French Assistant Minister of Commerce, who looked like a librarian.

The Canadian squinted curiously at Josie. "Marlow. Marlow? I knew a Marlow. Quite a ladies' man. Put us all to shame. Danny Marlow. Any relation?"

So here it was again. Right out. "My husband."

The Canadian swallowed hard. He scratched his chin and took a sip of wine. "I never knew Danny was married."

Andre glanced at her and smiled that inscrutable smile. Was he enjoying the fact that she was blushing again? Thankfully, the conversation rushed past her and the subject of Daniel forgetting to tell anyone he had a wife back in the States. The Canadian murmured words of sympathy, and then the topic leapt to offensives, defense, the Germans, the English, politics, and war.

"Neutrality," spat the Polish colonel. "Americans call themselves neutral, safe on the far side of the Atlantic. I say Americans are another yellow race."

The face of the oilman grew redder with the affront. "I'm in Europe to put French tankers under the protection of our flag. France will be in need of American neutrality in shipping if this goes on a long time."

"The last war was a long one," said the French commerce minister, "and we won it. Therefore this will likely be a long war and we will win."

"History repeats itself," agreed the Canadian journalist. "Time won for the Allies. In 1914 the Allies were disorganized and unprepared. But time, working for us, assured our victory."

Andre Chardon remained silent, complacent, as if the topic bored him.

The French minister went on. It was apparent he was a well-read man. He quoted every government newspaper and magazine and arrived at his version of the truth about the inevitable outcome of this war. "An impregnable defense cannot be taken. The Maginot Line constitutes an impregnable defense. The Belgians also have their own Maginot between them and Germany. Belgium is on our border and is impregnable. And Luxembourg! A maze of mountains and valleys. Impassable to artillery. Therefore France cannot be taken. We wait it out. And if France cannot be taken, Germany is beaten."

"That may be true," commented the American oilman. "But suppose Hitler has some secret weapon? I sent my family home at the thought of it."

The French minister scoffed. "He has nothing but the tanks and dive-bombers he used against Poland, a very weak and unprepared nation."

The Polish colonel bristled. "You are wrong! It was not the tanks or dive-bombers we were unprepared for. It was the way the Germans used them. It was not history repeating itself, but something new and terrible. A war of movement!"

The French minister wagged his head at the naivete of the Polish colonel. "Of course they moved across the Polish plains. But through the Maginot? Never. Through tank traps and barbed wire? Through the Ardennes and Dutch floods and the Belgian defenses? In the face of our air force? *C'est ridicule,* Monsieur! France is impregnable. If we cannot be beaten, then Hitler is beaten."

For a moment it looked like the table might come to blows. Josie shifted her gaze from one debater to the next as though she were watching a tennis match. Andre Chardon said nothing at all. Josie found his calm demeanor disquieting. Did Andre have any opinion? Was he unmoved by the terrible fate of Poland? For the first time she saw him as cold and detached. She smoldered inside as she listened to empty prattle which could not alter what she had lived through in Warsaw.

The Polish colonel, a cavalry officer, was the only man among them who had tasted battle. He now found himself in what he considered a group of ignorant café generals. He became increasingly sullen as the minutes ticked past.

Dinner was ordered. Colonel Wolinska recited tales of horror to the unimpressed French minister, who babbled about the need to maintain the French economy. The oilman agreed that commerce must be protected.

"While France delays converting commercial factories into armament facilities for fear of harming a peacetime industry, the German nation puts all its energies into preparation for war," said the Polish colonel. He narrowed his eyes in disgust. "You are talking politics. There is a difference between politics and war. The Nazis know that. The Allies do not. France talks and talks while the Germans march and kill. That is the weakness of France, why France remains unprepared."

The Canadian replied in a patronizing tone. "Unprepared? The French fortifications are unlike any the world has seen before, my dear colonel."

"The only defense for France is to attack first. But even now it may be too late for that. Poland is destroyed. The Germans are moving their armies again. This time they gather at your precious invincible Maginot." The first course was served.

The colonel was calm again for a moment. He had angered the complacent allies at the table and so had won a small battle in his own bitter eyes.

"Defeatist!" spat the French minister.

It was evident that Josie had been meant to somehow restrain the potential volatility of the dinner guests. At least the Polish colonel and the French minister had not yet thrown the goose liver paté at one another. But Josie was falling down on the job. The conversation moved on to poison gas which might humanely murder all of Paris in its sleep, or possibly peel the population alive like so many ripe bananas.

Then the inevitable question arose. What was this all about, anyway? It was no longer about Poland. Poland was gone. So why the naval blockade against Germany? Why the blustering on both sides?

"And what do you think, Colonel Chardon?" asked the American. "Is this a righteous war?"

Andre turned his gaze first on the Canadian journalist and then on Josie. "Some poet said it. That boys and girls and women who would groan to see a child pull off an insect's leg, all like to read of war. It is the best amusement of our morning meal. Until we face death ourselves, until it touches someone we love, the death of strangers is an amusement we savor in the papers. Other people's sons. Other people's brothers, husbands, and fathers. Hitler says war is about honor—dying with courage. I think it is more about breaking the tedium of ordinary life . . . a terrible game of chess between Hitler and every other government in Europe, and we are all caught on the playing board."

Outraged, the Polish colonel tossed his napkin onto the table. "Not for me, Monsieur Chardon! It is about my homeland! The national honor of Poland! There is cause enough to die for!"

Andre touched his fingers to his brow in salute. "And yet, when Hitler invaded Czechoslovakia, Poland darted across the border like a hungry little mongrel dog to grab the Czech province of Teschen! Hitler let you have it too, Colonel, because he knew all along he would take it back. Check and checkmate. Where were all our high ideals when Austria went under and Czechoslovakia was overrun? Do ideals only apply when what *we* value is stolen? I, for one, am still hoping, as General Gamelin says, that France will not be bled white again. Not for any cause or nation beyond our own borders."

"You would negotiate with Hitler after what has been done?"

"I would negotiate with the devil if I thought there was a chance that this could all be stopped."

"But Poland!" The colonel sputtered with indignation.

"No matter who wins, I fear, your nation will be lost. Spoils to be divided among the victors. A point on the negotiating table. The war is no longer about Poland."

Red-faced, the Polish colonel leapt to his feet, wavering a moment as if he would like to strangle Andre. Then he stormed from the dining room.

Josie, her expression matching that of the Pole, simply stared hotly at Andre for a long moment as if she could not believe what she had heard. He smiled at her but she averted her eyes. While the others recovered easily from the rage of the Polish colonel, Josie finished her meal in stony silence. Whatever warmth she had felt toward Andre had completely vanished by the time coffee was served.

❊   ❊   ❊

Horst stayed on the snowy bank of the Vistula until almost dawn, then leaving the river, he walked through the deserted streets until he came to the Cathedral of St. John. The broken spire was profiled in the predawn light. He entered through a side door which hung from one hinge. It seemed a dead place. Holes still gaped in the ceiling. Morning stars shone through the vaulted stone. Rubble had been cleared from the floor in front of the altar where a colony of red votive candles burned beneath a crucifix in the otherwise dimly lit interior. He removed his cap and crossed himself, more out of habit than conviction. Some years before he had visited the magnificent Warsaw structure with his red *Baedeker's* guidebook in hand. Now, there was little left that he recognized.

As he turned to go, a man called in German from the shadows.

"We are inconvenienced, but still in business, for the moment." There was a sharpness in his voice. "It was five centuries old, this cathedral."

"Yes," Horst replied. "My wife and I were here before . . . very old. I remember."

"This *building* you have destroyed, but you have not . . . cannot . . . destroy the truth."

"You Poles have one truth. We Germans another. So? What is truth?"

The voice was nearer. "Curfew is not lifted, Herr Officer. I knew you had to be a German officer. Your friends are shooting Poles and Jews who are only looking for wood to warm their families for being out past curfew; shooting them as children shoot sparrows in an orchard, and leaving them in the snow." As he spoke, the popping of a rifle sounded distinctly. The priest crossed himself. "As I was saying."

Horst could not reply to that. He closed his eyes briefly and saw the young mother being hurled into the oblivion of the Vistula. He was suddenly ashamed that he had come here.

"I did not mean to intrude, Father. Forgive me." Horst inclined his head as the priest struck a match and lit another candle a few feet from him. He was a tiny, dark-eyed little man.

"Forgive you?" The priest held up the light as if to study the uniform of Horst. "Well, you are not SS." He sounded relieved. "I thought . . . I have been expecting the SS."

"No, Father. Major Horst von Bockman. Seventh Panzer."

"You are Wehrmacht. I thought most of you had been withdrawn. To leave us to the vultures."

"I came back . . . on business."

"You are a Catholic?"

"I was. But I only meant to . . . I have brought something." Horst retrieved an envelope from the pocket of his overcoat. Giving it to the priest, he shifted his weight nervously. "I have heard . . . You feed people here."

The priest opened the folded paper and looked at the crisp new Reichsmarks. His expression displayed neither surprise nor curiosity as to why so much money would be given to feed the hungry.

"You must carry a heavy burden of guilt, Major."

"Yes." Horst did not argue.

"God is not some sort of court magistrate who accepts a fine in payment for the crimes of men."

"I did not know where else to turn."

"The condition of your soul is between you and the Almighty. No one else. Not the church. Not a priest. The only hope for any of us is that God alone is good and merciful. It gives Him joy to forgive us freely. Even the angels rejoice at the turning of one sinner's heart toward heaven. So says the Scripture. But then we must be willing to live as if we are forgiven. Showing mercy to others."

"Where do you see mercy or goodness in Warsaw?"

The priest held up the envelope as though it was some small proof. "The Almighty is also a pragmatist, I think. There is more at stake here at St. John's than your peace of mind, Major. The sun and the moon do not orbit around your guilty conscience. There are other, more helpless lambs in the flock who also need mercy . . . So many Reichsmarks will feed many hungry children. We were down to the last of our provisions."

❧ ❧ ❧

Andre awoke before dawn and lay in bed impatiently waiting for the hours to pass before he could telephone the home of Abraham Snow.

He showered and ate breakfast early without ringing Josie to join him. Then he retreated back to his room and placed the call to Elaine's father. There was a long silence on the other end of the telephone when Andre announced his name.

Then the gruff voice of Abraham Snow replied, "Colonel Chardon, why do you bother me? My daughter is . . . Elaine is gone. There is no changing it. Leave us to our grief."

"I wish to see Juliette."

"Why are you suddenly interested? She is getting along as well as any child might who has lost her mother in such a way. Your sudden appearance in her life would simply disturb her mind. She has never known a father."

Andre glanced at himself reproachfully in the mirror. His eyes flitted to the red wrapped package on the bureau.

"You are right in what you say, Monsieur Snow. I mean nothing to her, of course. But I have brought her a gift. Something for the holidays."

"A gift? It will only be a gift from a stranger—meaningless. Why not send it with a messenger, Colonel? What purpose can it serve to meet her? If she knows you are her father it can only hurt her. I must refuse."

"Please don't hang up. I wish only to see her. I would not hurt her for anything, Monsieur Snow. I will not tell her. I have something which belonged to my mother . . . a doll. I wish only to give it to her."

A bitter laugh emanated from the telephone. "Yes, I know these kinds of presents. You do not bring it for Juliette, but for yourself. To ease your guilt? To satisfy your curiosity, perhaps? Or do you hope to see what Elaine must have looked like when she was five? To see the child is to see the mother. Well, then?"

He was right, of course. Andre had brought the gift, thinking somehow that to behold the child would be to recognize some tangible part of what he had lost when he lost Elaine. His motives were selfish, and yet . . .

"Five minutes is all I ask. You will be there. I will be discreet. I will tell her I am an old friend of her mother's who has just dropped by. I implore you."

Abraham Snow considered the request a long moment. "Bring your gift, then." The phone clicked hard in his ear as the old man slammed the receiver down.

❅   ❅   ❅

Josie was not in her room. The door was open when Andre stopped. The hotel maid was already hard at work, stripping the linens from the bed.

Clutching Juliette's package, he did not wait for the groaning lift but ran down the stairs to the lobby. Josie was taking coffee with the Polish colonel in front of the fire. The two were speaking in low and sympathetic tones. The Pole glanced up, caught sight of Andre approaching, and stiffened. He muttered something at which Josie turned. Her expression was less than friendly. Clearly she had not forgiven Andre for insulting the Polish colonel with the truth.

"Bonjour." Andre was unintimidated by their dour expressions. The morning was too full of hope to be ruined. "I am glad you have found pleasant company to breakfast with, Josephine. I had a telephone call to make."

"A success, I take it," she replied.

He held up the package as indication that he was going to be occupied for a while.

"We finished breakfast some time ago," Josie said. It was apparent that she had not approved of Andre's end of the discussion last night. Now here she was in the lounge conversing with the very man whom Andre had insulted. Andre was certain that he was meant to feel this as a kind of unspoken chastisement.

At the moment Andre did not care if she approved or disapproved. He did not mind that she was sipping coffee with a vain peacock of a man like the Polish colonel. Water off a duck's back, as the English would say. Andre was about to have five minutes with his daughter! To meet his child face-to-face for the first time! It was not much, but it was something. Perhaps a beginning.

"Take as long as you like, Andre." Josie seemed pleased that he was on his way. The reserve in her eyes was unmistakable. "Colonel Wolinska and I are going to the cathedral to have a look around. Regular tourists. Do you mind?"

Andre glanced at his watch. It was nine.

"I thought we would leave for Paris by eleven o'clock this morning."

It was clear that his timetable was not hers. She had come all this way for one very unpleasant dinner at the Kaiser's table and not even a full morning in Luxembourg City.

Her smile was forced. "You are the man with the travel pass."

⚜ ⚜ ⚜

This morning the blinds were drawn and the sunlight shone through the tall windows of the great house on Boulevard de la Petrusse. Andre glanced up at the facade and for an instant caught sight of a small figure dressed in red looking down from an upper story window.

"Juliette!"

He said her name, and in that instant the face vanished. The broad steps of the house were guarded by two stone lions, blackened by time and the all-pervasive coal smoke of the city.

Andre hung back just an instant as some twinge of apprehension knotted his stomach. He could not touch the door or cross the threshold without the awareness that this had been the house where Elaine had lived. How vast and empty the rooms must now seem without her.

He swallowed hard and prayed that he would say the right thing; that he could remain calm, even though he wanted nothing so much as to wrap his arms around Juliette and tell her everything!

He rang the bell and waited. Behind him, a cloud passed in front of the sun. The door was opened by an elderly butler in formal dress. Chin high, expression aloof, the man did not step aside to admit Andre.

"Monsieur Snow told me to expect a messenger." The servant looked at Andre with surprise.

"No. I am . . . Colonel Chardon. I am expected by Monsieur Snow. I have come to pay a call on Monsieur Snow and his granddaughter Juliette."

The man still did not budge. He considered Andre with a look of pity. Perhaps he was fully aware of the identity of Andre. Perhaps he knew as much as anyone about Elaine Snow and her child.

"I regret, Colonel, that Monsieur Snow and his grandchild have only just left for a long trip to Belgium." He raised his hand regally to indicate the back bumper of a large, black American Buick fast disappearing around the long curve of the boulevard.

"But I only just spoke to Monsieur Snow! Twenty minutes ago from my hotel. He told me to come."

"Be that as it may. They have gone."

Andre looked up at the windows. "I just saw a little girl in the window upstairs."

"You are mistaken, Monsieur. That is the daughter of our cook." The man wagged his head in dignified refusal to accept Andre's protest.

So that was it. Even if they were in the house, Andre was not to be admitted. He could not charge past the servant. Nor could he make demands. Abraham Snow had simply decided that he and Juliette would not be at home when Andre came. There was nothing to be done about it.

The shadows around him deepened. He glanced down at the gift in the rumpled red paper.

"I am sorry, Colonel," the butler suddenly blurted in a voice thick with sympathy. "Shall I take that for you? Give it to Mam'zelle Juliette?"

Beaten, Andre nodded. "I was in hopes of giving it to her personally. I have not written a note. Will you see that she knows the gift is from me?"

"Of course, Monsieur Colonel." He looked past Andre as if the sight of him there on the doorstep was painful. Like a lost puppy in the rain.

Andre fumbled in his pocket for a pen and a small notebook. What to write?

> *"Merry Christmas, dearest Juliette,*
> *I give you a beautiful little girl*
> *in search of a loving home. Take care*
> *of her.*
>
> *Best regards,*
> *Colonel Andre Chardon."*

He tore the paper out and placed it in the outstretched hand of the butler. Andre looked at the dignified face of this man, and it suddenly occurred to him that this servant knew Juliette very well.

"What is she like?"

The brown eyes softened still more. "She is very sweet, Monsieur Colonel. Beautiful as her mother was at that age. Except . . ." he almost smiled. "She has brown eyes. Much like the color of your own. And she sings like a lark. You would be proud."

So he knew.

Andre handed over the gift. "This belonged to my mother. If she ever asks, tell her I was . . . a dear friend of her *maman*."

"Yes. My solemn oath, Colonel."

THIRTY-EIGHT

B flight of the 73rd RAF Fighter Squadron completed its early morning patrol and winged in toward the base at Rouvres. All six planes touched down safely, none showing any sign of having been damaged, or of having even been in battle.

Terry Simpson examined each returning plane's unscarred outline and sighed heavily. "Right-o, chaps," he said. "Our turn to 'ride boldly ride' . . . Death to the Huns." He flicked the butt of the Players cigarette onto the ground and crushed it beneath his heel.

"More likely we'll footle around with nothing to show for it," growled his wingman, Hewitt. A sly look crossed Hewitt's face and he tossed the next remark casually into the circle of men that made up *A* flight like a nonchalantly dropped hand grenade. "Unless we jump some Messers, like Tinman here."

David Meyer colored up to his hairline until his freckles glowed.

"Put a sock in it, Hewitt," ordered Simpson, watching both men for signs that combat might erupt on the ground.

"Aw, he knows I'm just havin' him on a bit. Right, Tinman?"

David gave a negligent wave of his hand to indicate that he had taken no offense, but as he walked toward his waiting Hurricane, his ears were still burning. Three days before their just completed leave, in an excess of zeal born of frustration, he had spotted and attacked a formation of what he took to be German aircraft. He pulled up abruptly when he discovered that they were French Morane fighters, but not before the French section scattered in all directions and a startled French pilot had loosed a string of machine gun fire. *And a string of obscenities too,* David thought morosely. The incident had brought a vociferous complaint from the French squadron's officers and a severe dressing down from his own squadron leader. David held his breath during the reprimand, fearing that they would lose their furlough, but the captain had let him off with a caution.

David settled into the cockpit of the Hurricane with a sigh and adjusted his parachute harness. After the engine roared to life and David checked the gauges on the runup, he throttled back and looked over toward Simpson, getting a nod and a wave. He gave the thumbs-up to his groundcrewman to pull the chocks, and moments later the Hurricane was speeding toward the end of the runway and leaping up into the clear blue French sky.

A flight orbited at twenty-five thousand feet and, as Hewitt had forecast, "footled about" looking for nonexistent targets. "Right," came Simpson's muffled voice through David's earphones. "Let's have a look-see southwest."

The new course carried the flight across Verdun. David looked down over the snow-covered hills and thought again how five miles of altitude could hide a lot of tragic history. Verdun had been the setting for the ten bloodiest months of the Great War. Close to a million men . . . French and German . . . had been killed or wounded there. And after close to a year of attacks and counterattacks, the line of battle had ended almost where it began.

David peered over his right wing at the wintry calm below and was brought up sharply when Simpson's voice crackled in his ear. "Meyer, what's that black spot at your nine o'clock low?" David's head snapped around and he grimaced at his inattention. Too much of that would get a man killed.

Red section, Simpson, Hewitt, and Meyer, broke off from the other three planes of the flight and dove southeast to investigate. A few moments passed and then Hewitt gave a yelp of exultation. The long, pencil-slim silhouette and twin tails identified the craft as a Dornier Do 17. It was probably heading back to Germany after a reconnaissance mission, although the twin-engined planes were also used as bombers.

"Right!" Simpson's voice was crisp. "Form line astern . . . Attack from dead aft . . . I'll lead and we'll break left, right, left. Here we go!"

The orders called for the three Hurricanes to change from their V formation to a line with Simpson in the lead, Hewitt next, and David following last. They would attack the Dornier from directly behind it, since that area of the bomber was not protected by machine guns.

The crew of the German craft spotted them at the same moment the Hurricanes formed their line, because the top turret machine gun opened up. A streak of tracers reached across the void toward Simpson's plane, and his guns responded as if the two aircraft were trying to tie each other together with lines of deadly fire.

Simpson dove below the cone of defensive bullets, stitching the fuselage of the Dornier before flashing past. He broke abruptly left before his plane came within the sights of the bottom turret gun.

As David watched, Hewitt repeated the maneuver, scoring hits on the left engine of the German plane. Then it was David's turn.

Matching his craft's position to that of the bomber, David also matched the German pilot move for move. The Dornier jostled abruptly from one side to the other, like an animal trying to shake off a predator that has landed on its back. At two hundred and fifty yards, David watched as his sights slid along the body of the twisting Dornier, raking its length.

When the Hurricanes reformed, the left engine of the Dornier was in flames, as was the plane's midsection, and one of the rudders flapped raggedly. As the three RAF pilots closed again from astern, the Dornier made a lazy half roll and began a vertical spiral toward the ground.

"Shall we give 'im another go?" Hewitt inquired.

"No," came Simpson's sharp rebuke. "He's done for. Give them a chance to get out . . . poor sods."

As red section circled overhead, one German appeared at the hatch of the doomed plane and launched himself out. In quick succession the white blossom of parachute appeared and then, only an instant later, the German aircraft slammed into the countryside, a black and flaming meteor against the white hills.

❅   ❅   ❅

This afternoon Lewinski carried his gas mask in a canvas shopping bag. He was less likely to be noticed without the thing on his face, he decided.

It was Christmas. Lewinski had not bought gifts for either Andre or Paul, so now he strolled beside the open book stalls on Quai des Grands Augustins, searching for some last-minute prize. The scent of roasting chestnuts filled the air. Lewinski bought a bag and munched them as he browsed through rare volumes in hopes of finding something which was not already on the shelves of the Chardon library.

American titles would be most appropriate. Herman Melville and *Moby Dick*? Washington Irving and *The Legend of Sleepy Hollow*? During his years of study in America, Lewinski had read every volume of the works of Mark Twain. *Roughing It* and *Huckleberry Finn* were not among Andre's classics; pitiful oversight. Andre needed help. Now that he was spending time with an American woman he would certainly desire some rudimentary knowledge of the American literature. He could not talk to the lady all day about wine and horses, could he? Well, yes, perhaps it was possible with Andre. But Lewinski had never found it possible to speak to a woman about anything unless he had prepared well ahead of time. Literature and art were always safe topics. If he spoke of physics or mathematics, nearly everyone but Albert looked at him as if he had dropped off the moon.

Albert. Lewinski wished Einstein were here to discuss the enigma of Enigma with him. Together, their two minds were flint and steel. The sparks would fly and the riddle would be solved in no time!

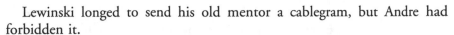

Lewinski longed to send his old mentor a cablegram, but Andre had forbidden it.

"Happy Holidays, dear Albert! I am not dead! I am Richard Lewinski!"

He laughed loudly at his own joke. Heads turned to see what was so amusing. They did not hear it and so did not know.

He jingled his change. Enough for *Roughing It* but not for a cablegram too. Too bad. Such a message would cheer poor Albert up. No doubt he was also depressed over there in America. So many minds like his and Lewinski's had been extinguished here in Europe.

Lewinski found Andre a copy of Twain. He dipped into his pocket and fumbled with his change again. French money. So confusing.

"May I help you, Monsieur?" asked a young lady. She was a student from the look at her drab clothes and rundown shoes. But she had a pretty round face, brown eyes, and thick black hair beneath a blue beret. He smiled at her.

"Are you fond of the American author Mark Twain, Mam'zelle?"

She gazed up at him as if she had not understood the question.

Did he ask the question aloud or only think he said it? "I said . . ." he began again.

"You are . . ." She unsheathed thick glasses and put them on. "Doctor Lewinski!" She said this very loudly.

Richard reached for his gas mask as heads turned. Two tough-looking fellows with determined expressions pivoted in unison to glare at Lewinski.

"You are mistaken. I am not."

"Pardon! But you *are* Doctor Lewinski! I heard you lecture at University in Berlin. Four years ago. A moment! My boyfriend is just there! He teaches mathematics now at the Sorbonne! He attended your lectures each week . . . Oh, Jan! Look here! It is Doctor Lewinski!"

"No, it is not." Lewinski backed away as panic welled up in him.

She turned aside for an instant. "But I remember . . ."

Lewinski slapped down his payment for the book and hurried off. The young woman called after him. The two toughs put their hands in the pockets of their overcoats as if they had guns.

The woman smiled and waved as she shouted down the quai, "Merry Christmas, Doctor Lewinski! I am so glad that you are not . . ."

"Dead." Richard finished her sentence as he rushed across Pont Neuf and forgot to turn toward home.

❈ ❈ ❈

Jerome was desperate. He thought of the two American sisters. Madame Rose and Madame Betsy. He remembered the salami and the cabbage and imagined chicken boiling in a very large stew pot today.

Something would have to be done.

"I should throw you into the Seine and let the fish of Paris eat you!" Jerome gave Marie a threatening shake as he pulled her up the stone steps beneath the bridge that spanned the river. The rat balanced precariously on his shoulder. Compared to life with Jerome, surely Papillon's life had been a dull existence with Uncle Jambonneau.

"No! Jerome! Please do not kill me," Marie wailed. She had been wailing all morning about her empty stomach, and Jerome was sick of it. She was picking up noisy habits from Madame Hilaire.

"I will use you for fishbait if you do not shut up! I will catch myself a big fish with your toes. And then I will only have myself to feed!"

"I die anyway with the hunger!"

"Ingrate!" He shook her again and came very near to carrying out his threat to throw her off the steps of Quai de Conti. A man riding his bicycle across Pont Neuf looked down from the bridge with disapproval, and Jerome controlled his anger.

Jerome had done the best he could with breakfast. It had been raining early this morning when he left the barge for the market. The vendors had not wheeled their pushcarts onto the sidewalk of Rue de Mazarine lest their baguettes grow soggy, their cabbages mold. The capitalists had remained inside their warm shops where bells tinkled a warning above doors whenever anyone entered or left. It was difficult to steal a croissant when all the bread was inside the patisserie and under guard.

This morning at the patisserie, the little bell dinged and the overstuffed wife of the baker looked down her long nose to see that it was Jerome who entered the shop. She announced his arrival very loudly to a dozen customers. They had all turned at once to stare at him as if he was a cockroach swimming in a bowl of soup even, though Jerome had left the rat at the boat.

"Look here, Papa! Is this a stray cat dripping on the clean floor? What sad brown eyes! Soaked clear to the skin! I will bet it is hungry, too!"

"Look again, Madame! It is no cat, but a small, scruffy, river rat and the son of a rat! Mesdames and messieurs, hold tightly to your purses, if you please! Meet Jerome Jardin, unfortunate offspring of that drunken Communist clochard who would rather sit on his filthy barge moored beneath Pont Neuf and read the works of Karl Marx than work an honest day! But of course! Little Jerome is here to rob us rotten Capitalists again! You want to eat something, little rat? Go to the soup kitchens! We serve only honest citizens here! Out of my shop, if you please!"

On days when the street market was open Monsieur le Baker had no opportunity to humiliate Jerome. He was too quick for the fat man. It was easy enough to hide behind the baskets of the florist and wait until Madame and Monsieur were each busy with a customer and then . . . he would dash in, steal a baguette, and be gone. But it had been a long time since the days had been warm enough for that.

Now Madame Hilaire was gone again . . . somewhere. It was three days until Papa's letter would arrive and Madame Hilaire would make dinner. Jerome was not worried about this, not much. But it had been three days since Marie had eaten anything but stale crusts which Jerome had gathered from the garbage bins behind the Ritz. She was getting on his nerves. She did not appreciate that he had to scramble even to get bread from the garbage. They were not the only hungry Parisians these days. Refugees had crowded into the city making it more difficult to scrounge.

"Where are you taking me?" Marie shrilled as he led her toward Pont Neuf and Quai Augustins, which followed the left bank of the Seine.

"We are going to eat," he said firmly, fixing his eyes on the great statue of Henri IV which towered above the center of the bridge. The old king had been melted once during the Revolution and had become cannons for Napoleon. Later, someone had melted down a statue of Napoleon and made a new King Henri. Now he was back on the bridge overlooking Ile de la Cité.

Last summer, the old king attracted tourists who posed for photographs on the parapets and were often careless with wallets and handbags. Jerome had been a better provider in those days. The head and shoulders of King Henri also served as a roost for pigeons. Pigeons were easier than fish for Jerome to catch. Being fed by tourists, pigeons had no concept that they could themselves be eaten. But today there were not even pigeons cooing on the head of Henri.

A crisp wind assailed the two children as they trudged beside the river. Marie's spindly legs turned pale blue beneath her ragged coat and her wail diminished to a whimper. Jerome took Papillon from his shoulder and handed him to Marie.

"Put him in your shirt. He is cold." He said this not because the rat was bothered by the cold, but because Papillon's extra warmth against Marie's belly might help her.

"He will be warm there." She cradled the creature. "Thank you, Jerome. Where will we eat?"

"The soup kitchen," he replied with the stern authority of a young man of ten. Just then, across the river, the towers of Notre Dame came into view beyond the buildings of the Préfecture of Police.

Marie balked. "No! Not the church, Jerome! Papa says they poison people there!"

"Poison in the head, Marie." He tapped his finger against her temple and softened a bit at her terror. Papa had been arrested many times and taken to the fortress of buildings which flanked the cathedral. Sometimes Jerome thought that Marie did not know the difference between Notre Dame Cathedral and the Police Headquarters. Papa hated both places with equal fervor. He was always talking against the charity of the soup kitchens. Always he spoke about the priests as spiders waiting to pull the unsuspecting person into a web of religion by feeding empty bellies.

"I do not want my head poisoned!"

"If you do not eat, you will die of hunger before Madame Hilaire comes back with potatoes. Or I may kill you to shut you up. You will eat where I say, or I will leave you somewhere terrible and not come back."

"Papa says the church is . . . the . . . something. . . . of the people!"

"Opiate." Jerome glanced at his little sister with respect. Not bad for a six year old. Marie had been learning her Marxist catechism well. Papa had taught them both to read and cipher. He told them that the schools of France were corrupt. It was better to stay home and learn the truth than to attend public school and be filled with lies.

"What is op-i-ate?"

Jerome ran a hand over his face in frustration. Papa had taught the words, but not entirely the meaning. It was something terrible he knew. Something worse than death, according to Papa.

"It is . . . something . . . I don't know."

"They will lock us in cells because we are Marxists. Then Papa will beat us because of the charity soup kitchen," she sighed and shuddered. She was confused again. "I am scared." Papillon clambered up and poked his head out of her collar to have a look around.

"Are you more hungry than scared? Or more scared than hungry?" Jerome stopped in resignation at Pont St. Michel, the bridge which would take them to Notre Dame. He leaned against the parapet and stared off toward the twin towers of the cathedral—the great spider web of France. How Papa hated the towers and the bells which rang out morning and evening! How he cursed the priests when the bells sounded!

"The people will not be free until every priest is strung up and Notre Dame is a gymnasium."

He often spit on the sidewalk after a priest walked by. He taught Jerome to spit as well. He seemed very pleased when Jerome spit first.

Marie was right. When Papa came back he would beat them if he found out where they had gone. And surely someone would tell him. Maybe even Madame Hilaire, who often ate there when times were bad. Ile de la Cité was a small place. No doubt someone would see Marie and Jerome go into the soup kitchen. Someone would see Jerome there maybe talking to a priest or a nun about the soup and bread. How could he spit on the floor of the people who fed him? Everyone knew how his father felt about the church.

Jerome could not see the line of people waiting to go into the Cloisters

Soup Kitchen, but it was there, on the far side of the cathedral. Once a day at this time a line of people formed along Rue du Cloître, waiting to go into the cloisters where the long tables were set and the nuns ladled out bowls of hot soup.

The wind cut through Jerome's thin cotton coat. Marie rested heavily against the stone wall and lay her head in her arms, careful not to crush Papillon.

"All right." she said miserably. "All right."

Jerome put his hand on her shoulder in a wave of pity. For Marie to agree to go to this place meant that she was very hungry indeed. "Maybe there is somewhere else. Another kitchen where no one will know we are the children of the clochard. If no one knows us, he will not hear about it. We can eat and . . ."

"But where, Jerome?" She raised her head slightly but did not try to stand without the help of the wall.

"Can you walk, ma chérie?" He asked in a voice so kindly that he surprised himself. He had not done well by her. He had eaten the best stuff himself. He had not cared for her as he should have.

"Very far?"

"Quai d'Orsay."

"So far?"

It was a long way for small legs carrying a hungry belly to go. "Only four kilometers back along the river. There is a place . . . they feed refugees and ragged people bread there. Beside a Université. American . . ."

"But Papa hates the Americans."

"Those people do not even know how to speak French. How could they tell him we were there?"

Some hope filled her eyes. "Yes? And so?"

"There is a building which looks like a church. But it is not. We will go into the building which is not a church even though it looks like one outside. So you will not have to be afraid. And there, we will eat."

Marie nodded as he took her hand, more gently now. She had never been into any church. She would not know the difference if he did not tell. Her face was set. Her small mouth turned down slightly and her dark eyes fixed on the farthest bridge she could see across the Seine. It was a long way.

"*Je marche!*" she said again solemnly as they set out.

❖   ❖   ❖

The Paris shops were closing early because of the holiday. Traffic began to thin out as men and women hurried to get ready for family gatherings and midnight mass. It seemed that all of France had become religious again since the war. Jerome had not remembered that everything in the city closed up tight on Christmas Eve. From the great Louvre to the lowliest butcher shop, the signs were hung and the doors were locked. This fact worried Jerome. It seemed that he and Marie were the only two in Paris who were headed away from home.

"How much longer? I am tired, Jerome." Marie looked like a half-drowned cat. Brown hair hung in limp strands around her face. Ears protruded like the open doors of a taxi. Her clothes were soaked through, which was unpleasant for her and poor Papillon as well. Shoes that were already too large got bigger with every puddle. Her feet shuffled on the sidewalk, and she lagged further and further behind her brother.

Jerome stopped in front of a closed bakery. He put his hands on his hips and tried to look stern, but she was so pathetic that he could not. "You need to walk more quickly, Marie."

"Why are the shops closed?" She bit her lip and looked at the display of pastries in the unlit window. "Where is everyone?"

"You can see that all of Paris is closing and going home for roast goose. It is the night before Christmas. The food at the soup kitchen will be better than every other day. We should hurry." He looked up at the threatening sky. Soon it would begin to snow. Night would surely come before they got back to the *Garlic*.

Marie leaned against the stone facade of the shop for a moment. "Can I wait for you? You can run ahead and bring back roast goose for me and Papillon."

"No," he snapped and took her by the arm and pulled her along. "I never said that we would have roast goose. Other people have it on Christmas. We will have . . . something else. I do not know what. But you will be glad we walked so far. It will be warm there and the food will be good. You'll see."

He was talking now just to keep her on her feet and moving. She did not reply. Her eyes were dull. It was too cold for her to be out without a coat. Her sweater was drenched as well.

Jerome looked up and spotted the ornate spire of the American Church rising above the buildings. "There it is, Marie!" he shouted. "It only looks like a church, but it is not," he lied.

Marie lifted her face and blinked against the raindrops. Jerome thought that maybe now it no longer mattered to Marie what the place was. As long as she could eat and be warm.

"Good," she said, and at last her numb legs began to move a bit faster.

The last two blocks were not as difficult. Marie did not ask to stop and rest even one time.

There was no line of hungry people winding down the street like at the cloisters of Notre Dame. "Everyone is already inside eating," he told her.

There were no sandbags heaped up outside. Jerome explained that this was because the Americans were not at war with Hitler and so their building would not be bombed.

Jerome helped Marie up the broad stone steps. For a moment they stood before the bronze doors, deciding where to go in. Jerome pushed hard on the biggest door. It swung back easily and the two tumbled onto the hard stone floor of the lobby. Beyond them, the church was dimly illuminated by the soft colors of stained glass windows on each side.

Jerome had sneaked into a church before and he knew that this was just how a church was supposed to look. Very old. High arched ceiling. Stone columns. A large cross behind a big table at the front which had things covered up with a red velvet cloth. A bright red banner hung down from the ceiling. It had golden words on it inscribed in English. Candles in golden stands stood in front of rows and rows of benches and red cushions on the seats. In an alcove behind the pulpit was a large oil painting of a kind looking man. It was very serene and beautiful. This was all part of what made it so dangerous, Papa said. Today, this church was also very empty.

"Keep Papillon out of sight," he warned as the head of the rat protruded from between two buttons of Marie's dress front. "Soup kitchens are very strange about pets like Papillon. They will think he is a rat."

Marie shuddered. "Where are the people? The food?" Her voice echoed hollowly.

"Maybe in the cellar." Jerome bit his lip. He hoped he had not made a mistake. Where was the cellar? He pointed at the steps leading down at the far end of the foyer. "There." He held her hand and guided her down the stairs.

"It is nice here," Marie said hoarsely.

"Warm," he agreed, hoping they had not arrived too late for the food.

At the bottom of the steps was a long corridor with dark wooden doors on either side. Jerome tried all the latches, but all the doors were locked. At the far end of the corridor was another set of stairs leading up. The two ascended, only to find themselves in the very front of the large auditorium. There was no soup kitchen, no roast goose; only this big, peaceful, empty building.

Marie sank down on the front pew and began to cry very softly. "I was too slow," she moaned. Her tears mingled with the water dripping from her hair. She was shivering through her wet clothes in spite of the fact that the interior of the building was much warmer than outside. "They ate without us."

Jerome sat beside her and stared numbly up at the red banner and the golden English words written on it and the red velvet cloth on the long table at the front. He sighed. "It is my fault. I brought you all this way for nothing." He glared at the picture of the kind man in the alcove. The figure had a beard and a long white robe like a nightshirt. One hand held a lantern and the other knocked on a door which looked very much like all the locked doors downstairs.

"This is why Papa hates you," he lifted his voice to the vaulted ceiling, "and now I will hate you forever also. We come all this way, my sister and me and Uncle Jambonneau's dog, and you are not really here. We will go away cold and with empty bellies from this place which looks like a church but is not a church."

"It is . . . a church . . ." Marie trembled harder now. Her teeth chattered. She could not get warm even with Papillon snuggled inside against her. She had nothing in her stomach to help her get warm. She needed a blanket. For the first time it occurred to Jerome that she might die if she was not warmed and fed very soon. He felt afraid.

"I am sorry I brought you here, Marie," he said bitterly. "Yes, it is a church. I thought you would not come if you knew. It doesn't matter. Now you see Papa is right."

"What is your Papa right about?" asked a muffled voice behind them.

Jerome whirled around to face a creature as horrible as the gargoyles which gaped down from the facade of Notre Dame. Marie gave a little cry and covered her face with her hands. The thing looked something like the head of a locust attached to the body of a man. The tails of a heavy red-checked flannel shirt stuck out from baggy corduroy trousers held up by suspenders.

Jerome leapt up and doubled his fists in defense against the monster who cackled wildly. Then Jerome realized that the thing was not a thing, but a man in a gas mask.

Unruly red hair like wire protruded from the rubber thongs of a mask. With an odd sucking sound, like water going down a slow drain, the man pulled the mask back on his head.

"What are you doing here?" he asked Jerome.

"We just came to eat something." Jerome was defiant.

"Yes." The man stared around the place as if he was looking for something. "Where is supper?"

"But there is nothing to eat in your church."

"Not my church. I'm Lewinski." He cackled again as if his name explained everything. "No one is here. I was hoping to use the telephone, but there is no telephone that I can find." He walked slowly up to Marie, who peered up at him in terror through her fingers. "What is wrong with her?" Lewinski asked, glancing at the alarm clock tied around his waist by a length of twine.

"She is hungry and wet," Jerome said, "leave her alone."

"Why do you not feed her and get her a blanket?" Lewinski looked over his shoulder as he said the words, giving the odd impression that he was addressing someone behind him. Then he bounded up the low steps to the altar at the front. He looked upward and touched the gas mask on his head as if in salute. "You can plainly see the little girl is cold and wet."

Like a magician in a performance at the Tuileries Gardens, he pulled the red velvet cloth from the altar. Marie gasped from behind him.

"Jerome, look! Look what is here for us!"

It was like magic. Marie applauded. On the marble table, three braided loaves of bread were heaped on a large brass plate. Beautiful loaves they were, with golden brown crusts, baked to perfection. Had there ever been such beautiful loaves of bread?

"How did you do that?" Jerome cried. He had always been impressed with magicians.

"Well, I do not know." Lewinski seemed surprised by his trick. "But dinner is served." He scratched his head and tossed the red cloth to Marie. "You will look very nice in that color, Mam'zelle. And warm. Well, well! Put it on!"

Jerome gaped at the feast for a moment and then with a whoop, he joined Lewinski, who tossed a loaf into Jerome's arms. The boy ran to Marie. "Get up! We have to get out of here quick before he changes his mind!"

Marie had an odd smile on her face. As if she knew some wonderful secret. She stood up on unsteady legs. She raised a face ever so slightly toward Lewinski. "Thank you, Monsieur," she whispered. Then, "Are you . . . a priest?"

The hall reverberated with Lewinski's laughter.

"Well then . . . an angel?"

Lewinski howled and fell to the ground at the humor of such a question. Tears streamed from his eyes, then suddenly he stopped laughing and stood up.

"I am lost," he announced in a very serious tone. "I went out shopping and suddenly I realized that I was somewhere else."

"Somewhere else besides where?" Jerome sniffed and looked at him suspiciously. He was almost certain that this fellow must be an inmate escaped from the lunatic asylum. If so, he was quite far from his place of residence.

"Andre will be looking for me. Last time they called the police. Or the police called Andre. It is very dangerous for me to be out alone, they tell me. But you two look harmless enough." He bowed to Marie. "And you look very pretty in your red blanket, Mam'zelle. Also you have a rat climbing out of your collar."

She giggled as Papillon emerged and leapt from her shoulder to the arm of Jerome. Jerome nudged her in the ribs for silence.

Yes. So it was the asylum, after all. Jerome took Marie firmly by the arm and stepped back. "We have to be going now."

Lewinski frowned. "Do you know the way to number 19 Quai d'Anjou?"

"Oui! On l'Ile!" Marie clapped her hands, obviously carried away by the clownlike appearance of the lunatic Lewinski. "We will take you home."

"No, Marie," Jerome hissed.

"Yes, we will!" Marie tore free from Jerome and ran to the side of Lewinski, who cackled with relief, looked at his alarm clock, and replaced the mask.

"Marie! You heard him! Police!"

"Oui! He is magic. He got me a blanket and made the bread appear." She took Lewinski's hand as he slid the mask back over his face. Lewinski tore off half a loaf of bread from his hoard and presented it to his guide. She broke off a piece for Lewinski, who could not eat it because of his rubber mask. Together they marched up the center aisle and out onto the street, with Jerome trailing at a safe distance behind them.

❋   ❋   ❋

It was a strange entourage that paraded through the streets of Paris. Jerome followed ten paces behind Lewinski and Marie. She was wrapped in yards of bright red cloth stolen from the church. Wiry red tufts of the madman's hair protruded through the straps of the dark green rubber gas mask as if Lewinski's head were a flowering weed.

Jerome thought about calling out for help. After all, their route to Quai d'Anjou led right past the Palais de Justice. Normally, all the gendarmes in the world stood around under the awnings on the Ile de la Cité smoking their *Gauloises* and chatting. But today, what with the showers and the cold wind sweeping down the river, there were no blue jacketed figures in view.

Sighing heavily, Jerome thought that perhaps it was just as well. He and the law were not on the best of terms anyway. How could he explain about the altar cloth? Jerome's father had taught him that the police were the arm of the oppressive power of the privileged classes, whatever that meant. Something to stay away from, no doubt.

But how to get Marie free from what was obviously a lunatic? There she was, clinging to Lewinski's hand and chattering away like a magpie. Jerome could have strangled her.

Following the rain slickened pavement led the little procession across the Pont St. Louis. The red-haired figure pushed the gas mask up on his forehead and divided another chunk of the magic bread with Marie. They seemed to have forgotten that Jerome was still behind them, fretting and worrying.

At last the Quai de Bourbon became the Quai d'Anjou, and Lewinski pointed to the curve up ahead as if he recognized a landmark. Now what?

Lewinski and Marie were walking very carefully, staring down at the paving stones. Jerome could see that they were being very cautious about not stepping on any of the cracks in the sidewalk. It made Jerome watch where he was stepping too, until they had passed the bend in the road and Jerome suddenly looked up.

There, not a half a block away, was a police car. It sat in front of the house to which Lewinski was leading Marie. It was a trap!

"Run, Marie!" Jerome yelled, sprinting up behind his sister and yanking her hand loose from Lewinski's grip. "Run, I say! He is trying to turn us in to the police!"

Jerome dragged a stumbling Marie away from Lewinski and back down the block. When they came to an alleyway, he ducked in, pulling Marie in after him.

Marie was blubbering again. "I did not get to tell him thank you for the bread."

THIRTY-NINE

Andre and Josie followed the course of the Meuse River. Once again his military pass and rank gave them easy access through the barricades and checkpoints along the road. He spoke little, but his expression reminded Josie of her first impression of him on the night train to Paris. A sort of tragic figure, she told Alma. What had happened when he went to see his child? He had not spoken about it, and she did not ask. She was certain it had not gone well.

She was angry with him last night and this morning, but her anger cooled when she saw the pain in his eyes. Now there was something else. It was as if he had a secret he wanted to share with her.

They passed through the tiny, empty village of Bras and then turned away from the river onto a road that was little more than a cart path. The trees were young, with slim trunks and unscarred bark. The contours of the hills and ridgelines were ragged and uneven as though some giant spade had dipped down, turned the earth in great chunks, and dumped it in useless heaps. Josie could see beneath the undergrowth that there were lines of trenches and broken barbed wire mired in the mud.

"Where are you taking me?" she asked, even though she knew this was a battlefield.

The line of his mouth hardened at her question. He did not reply but turned off on a winding, rutted side road which climbed a hill crowned by the slim beech trees. At the crest of the ridgeline, he stopped the car and sat staring through the windshield for a long moment. He gestured with his hand at the sign beside the road.

Louvemont, village detruit.

"There was a village here when I was a very young child," he said in an almost inaudible voice, as though he had entered a cathedral in the middle of mass.

There was nothing beyond the sign, no houses, or shops, no parish church, or cobbled square; only the heaps of earth and scattered stones which might once have been a wall or a foundation.

"My mother was born here." Andre cleared his throat to clear away the emotion. "My grandparents lived here." He pointed toward the next ridge. "It was a beautiful place. They were good people. They left when the war began in 1914. My mother came back to see my father here, near the front in Louvemont, and so now, together, they are the dust of Louvemont."

"You do not owe me an explanation."

"You think I am a coward."

"I do not! No, Andre! I just think . . ."

"You think!" he said fiercely. "But you cannot know what France was before. You ridicule Gamelin for saying that we will not be bled white again. But you cannot know whose blood watered this place! How can you know? There are too many to count. But I can see the faces of some just as clearly as I remember that the village of Louvemont was here. My mother and father died in one day at this place." He shook his head.

"I am sorry, Andre. I had no intention of prying into your life."

"It is not only my life, Josephine. There is more for you to see if you will understand what this war must mean to France."

He started the car again and drove on slowly through the emptiness as though there was something to witness. On each side of the road, signs were posted in short intervals: *TERRAIN INTERDIT,* forbidden ground.

"The woods and fields are still littered with unexploded shells and cannisters of poison gas. A million acres and more, the land cannot be farmed or grazed. No couples can picnic or make love. These are fields of death for any who walk here even now."

He glanced at her, gratified somehow that she was pale and unhappy with his macabre revelations. "For eight months it was quiet here. The sons of France waited in their muddy trenches, praying that the Germans would wear down through the long winter. And all the time they were building up. Time was not on our side. The Germans were waiting for spring. As they wait now."

There was no stopping him. It was as though he had to tell her, had to make her see the peace of these fields and know what ghosts still lingered here. "My father was a colonel. Mother often came here to Louvemont to be with him. It was his birthday. They had a friend in the high command who secured her a pass." He swallowed hard. "She would not let Paul and me go with her. Maybe she sensed what was going to happen . . . just as I am certain that hell is coming again to France, Josephine."

His knuckles were white as he gripped the steering wheel. "Look at it. On the day before the German offensive began in 1916 there was snow on the forests . . . on the fields and rooftops of the village. I have seen such days as a child . . . beautiful . . . peaceful. They must have awakened in an embrace and smiled at the sound of a lark outside the window. Who could imagine what would come? Just past dawn it began. The artillery shells fell like so many drops of rain. The church exploded. The houses exploded. Pits erupted across the fields like the craters of the moon. Trees and animals and barns and men . . . gone. The heat melted the snow everywhere. By noon, peaceful Louvemont had vanished."

"And your mother? Your father?"

"Gone. They were never found. There was not enough left to bury. A million people died here in this place. One man in love . . . like me. One woman, beautiful and passionate . . . like you. Here! Look around you, Josephine, and know what war is . . . what it means to France. My mother and father? They are only two who died on the first day. A million lives were swallowed up right here. Only 160,000 bodies of that million were ever identified."

He fell silent again as the road wound up the slope of a long hill crowned with two granite monuments which stood at the empty crossroads and overlooked the killing fields. For a moment he waited, as if thinking whether to take her all the way to the center of his knowledge.

"Come," he said, opening the car door for her.

The wind was biting as they stepped out and stood in the center of the road between the two facing monuments. One was a granite structure of blocks topped with the bronze helmet of a knight. On it was carved,

AUX MORTS DES CHARS d'ASSAUT 1916

The other was a simple stone crucifix inscribed with the words,

Ossements qu'animait unfier souffle naguere,
Membres épars, débris sans non, humain chaos,

Pêle-mêle sacré d'un reliquaire,
Dieu vous reconnaître, poussière de héros!

"Say it in English, Josephine, and then you will remember."

She stood shivering before it. Around her, the fields seemed to awaken with the ghosts of a million young men who barely lived before they died; who disappeared into the maw of war without leaving even a trace of themselves to bury.

She began to read. Her voice was carried away on the wind and sounded to her ears as though it was some other voice.

> Heaps of bones once moved by the proud breath of life,
> Scattered limbs, nameless debris, chaos of humanity,
> Sacred jumble of a vast reliquary,
> Dust of heros, God will know you!

Silence. The wind. The distant memory of a day like Armageddon. The thunder of artillery mingled in her mind with the screams of dying men.

She turned to Andre, who searched her eyes and then held out his hand to her.

"Time levels all men. Good and evil alike. A century will pass in the blink of an eye and who will sort the particles of dust? *God will know you!* I look in my mirror each morning and say to myself, Andre, one day everything you think you believe about yourself will be put to the test! Then there will be no more empty talk over the dinner table. Honor? Love? Faith? Courage? They will become suddenly tangible truths which stand before you and require you to make a choice. You will live out your Truth even to the death, or Truth will die inside you even if you survive. Do you see what I am saying?"

"Forgive me." She did not look at him. Leafless branches reached up to touch the grey sky. She felt suddenly ashamed of her empty talk about principles and courage. In the face of reality, such talk was hypocrisy. She had seen the reality in Warsaw. Could she forget so soon? "I have made this into a philosophical debate."

"Perhaps debate is the beginning of courage. There are no righteous wars. There is only, regrettably, sometimes the necessity to fight. I would negotiate with the devil to stop what I know will come. But there are no words left to stop him. So I will stand with France and fight the devil for the sake of my own soul. Now we wait. When the waiting ends this spring, I know what real war will mean. When it comes to this place . . . to France, to us . . . you and me." He pulled her against him. "I have already made so many wrong choices. Hurt so many others. Thrown away so much. Everything important, wasted on my own selfishness. Now I may lose my life, when living is precious to me at last. But for the first time in a long time, I think have found something . . . someone to live for."

❊ ❊ ❊

David navigated the borrowed 1928 Citroen Cabriolet to the village nearest the snow-covered field where the Dornier had crashed. From there, a narrow icy track led out into the countryside. They stopped the car when they caught sight of a lone soldier standing guard beside an opening in a hedgerow. The trio of fliers piled out gratefully from the battered car's narrow single seat and stretched.

As the three approached the short-statured French poilu, he came away from the hedge, shook his fist, and waved the bayonet on the end of his rifle in their faces. "Easy, mate," instructed Hewitt, pointing to the RAF badge on his cap. "We're the ones who shot down the German."

David looked past the guard, through the gap in the fence, toward the skeletal wreckage of the German bomber. What he saw chilled him worse than the wintry air. "Shut up, Hewitt," he urged. "Look!"

Though the rolling hills were barren for miles around, the falling Dornier had crashed on top of a farmhouse. The nose had struck the roof dead center and punched a hole into the structure. Then both plane and farmhouse had burned together. Only two stone walls remained upright around the gutted interior.

The French soldier's head pivoted in the direction of the debris; when he turned back around he was crying. "La famille entière," he said. "Toutes ensemble."

"What'd he say?" whispered Hewitt.

"He said, the whole family," Simpson muttered back.

Outside the charred hulk of the house lay a row of bodies. They were all wrapped in tarps. Three of the bundles were very small, only half the size of the others.

Hewitt was violently ill and had to be helped back to the road by David, who felt far from well himself. The three pilots packed into the Citroen and drove away without speaking.

David and Simpson decided between them that they would drive to Nancy instead of returning directly to Rouvres. "If we go back to the base too soon, everyone will want to know what we made of the crash," David suggested.

"Too right," Simpson agreed. "Besides, it's Christmas Eve, and we've need of some good cheer."

Hewitt shivered, but offered neither argument nor support for the plan; he only sat with a stunned look on his face and stared out at the French countryside.

David pushed the protesting Citroen to its maximum speed, wanting to reach Nancy before the darkness and the blackout restrictions made travel more difficult. The icy roads were deserted except for one farmer and a wagon drawn by an ancient draft horse. The car swung through the wrought iron-encircled Place Stanislaus and into the crooked medieval lane named the Grand Rue, just as the sun was setting.

"Here we are, then," Simpson pronounced grandly, trying to lighten the mood. "The Excelsior Brasserie—finest food and drink in at least . . . five kilometers."

Hewitt shook his head as if just waking up from a long and especially unpleasant nightmare. He looked at the number of impressively uniformed men going in and out of the Excelsior and finally spoke. "I don't know," he said doubtfully, "there's a lot of blokes about. Can't we find someplace a bit quieter?"

"Nonsense," Simpson reassured him. "None of these are our chaps, Hewitt. Most of them aren't even soldiers. They're either North American correspondents or South American dictators. Either way, they're no concern of ours. Come on."

Three bottles of the local red wine improved the spirits of the group, and their returning appetites led to the consumption of enough potato-and-rabbit pie to have served twice their number.

David was relieved when Hewitt leaned back in his chair and looked much more his usual self when he patted his stomach and belched. An extravagant stretch backwards brought one of his large hands into abrupt contact with the back of an American correspondent's head.

At Hewitt's apology, the correspondent scooted his chair around to the table with the pilots. "RAF," he noted. "I thought so. Two English and one American? Fighter pilots."

"Right," David agreed.

"What gave us away?" Simpson inquired. "Our keen eyes and deadly serious expressions?"

The correspondent laughed. Hewitt's eyes looked anything but keen, and the goofy grin on his face was not at all serious. "Yeah, that's it exactly. Anyway, you three look in a lot better shape than the other fliers I bumped into tonight."

"Is that so? What was wrong with them?" David asked.

"Couple German prisoners out of a plane shot down by some of your boys. One's busted up pretty bad and the other's burned. They got brought here for treatment before being sent on to Paris."

David and Simpson were suddenly all attention, and Hewitt was struggling to follow along. "Did you catch what sort of craft? That is, where did this happen?"

"A Dornier. Shot down between here and Verdun."

"Quick, man! Where did you meet these two?" Simpson demanded.

"They're under guard upstairs, not that they could . . ."

David tossed a few franc notes onto the table and was halfway to the stairs as the newsman called after them.

"Hey, what's the rush?"

Hewitt staggered to his feet, but even so was only a few steps behind David and Simpson. "Because," he remarked over his shoulder in a rush of slurred words, "we're the lot who put paid to that beggar."

David had no difficulty talking his way past the guard outside the door at the top of the stairs. Apparently this poilu had been making a profit by charging admission to many who wanted to view the Nazi aviators, like the keeper of a small menagerie of dangerous beasts.

But the first sight of the two prisoners gave David no impression of menace. He eyed them with an unexpected and unwelcome sense of guilt. As if he had accidentally injured an opponent in a football game and needed to find a way to apologize. What could he say to these two young men, his enemies?

A thick shock of dark hair stood up on the head of the first German. His thin face was boyish and worried. He was still wearing a ragged flight suit from the waist up, but his legs were in plaster casts from ankles to thighs.

The other man was wearing a bathrobe. His head was completely swathed in layers of bandages showing only a pair of glaring, bloodshot eyes. His hands were similarly rolled in white gauze, and it occurred to David that if it were not for the bare feet that showed below the robe, he would have seemed to be a very thoroughly wrapped mummy.

David, who had a rudimentary grasp of the German language, became the spokesman for the group. "I don't know if you understand English or not," he began, then he introduced himself and the others in clumsy German. "We are the Hurricane pilots who shot down your Dornier. We are glad that you made it out all right."

"I speak English," replied the man with the broken legs. His mastery of English was much better than David's attempt at German. "I am Unteroffizer Hammel. Klinger is here." He gestured toward his companion. "We . . ." He searched for the words. "Parachute . . . three others in our crew did not."

"We . . . we know . . ." The vision of the wrecked Dornier and the lingering odor rose fresh in David's imagination, causing his stomach to churn. "How did two of you survive? We only saw one chute."

"Ja," answered Hammel with a shrug, "I carry Klinger. His hands so burn . . . jump we together. The weight is too great and my legs . . . who can think snow will be so hard?" Tears welled up in his eyes. "But we will not have lived if you . . . continue shooting. We are told you English fire on parachutes."

"We would not do that!" Simpson remarked with horror.

"We would!" snapped a voice from beneath layers of gauze. David had supposed that the burned man spoke no English, but now it was apparent that he spoke it well and that he had plenty to say.

"We do not believe in letting an enemy escape!" Klinger added with venom. "If we had been in a Messerschmidt, the outcome would have been far different!"

"You feel this way too?" David asked Hammel.

"I . . . it is hard to . . ." Hammel caught a ferocious glare from Klinger and subsided in misery. "War is a terrible thing," he concluded lamely.

"Come on, Tinman," said Simpson, moving toward the door and pushing Hewitt ahead of him. "We've done what we came for." Halfway down the stairs, he remarked, "Officer Hammel probably has family back in Germany."

✤　✤　✤

The organ of the Cathedral of St. John was miraculously intact. With the steps leading to the organ loft blown away, Horst watched an old man in the robes of a musician climb a ladder to reach his instrument. Two boys who would tred the bellows followed. The bellows wheezed a few moments before waking, then the building filled with the joyous strains of Bach's chorale, *Nun danket alle Gott,* Now thank we all our God. The music resounded through the shattered windows to the outside, drawing in still more worshipers from the streets until the place was packed. Still, there was room enough on each side of Horst for several more to crowd in.

The melody of Bach formed a sharp contrast to the somber congregation. In all the vast sea of people, Horst could see no spot of holiday color in their attire. Black dresses, shawls, and scarves adorned old and young women and girls alike. Old men and young boys wore black coats and sweaters. Their complexions all reflected varying degrees of the same shade of grey.

Horst's grey-green uniform made him stand out from everyone. The presence of a German officer at the mass seemed as inappropriate to the prevailing mood as the music of Bach. He caught the fearful glances of the Poles who worshiped there. Why did he not go with his own kind, their eyes seemed to ask? Was it not a fact that the German military had their own army of priests and pastors who preached the doctrines of the Reich and spread their poison even on this holy day? Why, then, was this German major disturbing what small comfort the faithful found in this sacred place?

How could they know that he was not the one they should fear? Horst knew he was not the only German attending the Christmas Eve Mass at the cathedral. He easily spotted the plain clothes of the Gestapo agents among the congregation. While men and women knelt in prayer, the Gestapo looked on with disdain and scribbled notes and phrases from the priest's sermon in small black notebooks. From the diligence of these agents, Horst was certain that the days of the diminutive priest were numbered.

And what was the priest's crime? Today he preached the old sermon; the same story Horst had heard every Christmas Eve as a child growing up in Germany. Yet now, in the context of Poland, the story of the birth of a Jewish baby in a manger took on a new and irritating significance to the servants of Hitler. Horst knew their questions:

Was there some political reason why the priest dwelt on the jealousy of King Herod and the murder of every baby boy in Bethlehem in an attempt to destroy the foretold messiah? What did the priest really mean when he spoke about the desperate flight of Joseph and Mary from the slaughter? He used the word refugee. Was he drawing parallels, perhaps? Why mention the death of the tyrant of that age and compare it to the victory of the one life which began in the degradation of a stable? Was he intimating the treasonous hope that the Führer would perish? And why did he mention that the child was a Jew descended from Abraham? Surely he knew the edicts of the Führer on the unfortunate matter of the Jewish heritage of Christ. Why did he read aloud those promises of Old Testament prophets whose writings were now banned in all churches of the Reich?

Horst saw suspicion and judgment in the faces of the Gestapo as the crowd filed out. The priest had condemned himself, not because he had uttered one word different from the Christmas story told in all previous years but because the story itself was the ultimate reproof of all tyranny. The ancient tale could be taking place at that moment in Warsaw, could it not? Simply substitute Nazis as the antagonists determined to slaughter every Jewish child in Poland.

Horst considered that perhaps he had never really understood the story before now. Like the minions of Hitler who had mingled today with the faithful of Warsaw, he had also listened with a new interest.

Thinking that he would warn the priest about the hostile members of the congregation, Horst lagged behind as the crowd filed out. The booming organ fell silent. The organist descended from his perch in front of Horst. Nearing the high arch of the foyer, he noticed three of the Nazi officials conferring beside a massive pillar pocked by shrapnel. Horst looked away quickly before he drew attention to himself. Leaving the building, he determined that he would come back later and inform the priest of the danger.

❊   ❊   ❊

Tonight, at the appearance of Horst von Bockman in the foyer of the Cathedral of St. John, the old custodian leaned against his broom and stared fearfully at the heap of dust on the floor. He crossed himself as if he was in the presence of great evil.

"I am looking for the priest," Horst said, stamping the snow from his boots before proceeding across the newly swept flagstones.

The old man cleared his throat nervously and probed at his ear with a bony finger. He did not acknowledge Horst.

"It is important that I see your priest, old man." Horst had no time for guessing games. "For the sake of his safety."

The swish of the broom against the stone was the only reply. The custodian nudged the heap of debris toward the entrance as though he was the only one there.

"You must believe me. I am a friend of his." Horst tried again. "Will you take him a message? Tell him Major Horst von Bockman has come to say good-bye. I leave for Berlin tonight. Tell him it is urgent that I speak with him."

The thin face looked up slowly. Beneath bushy eyebrows, dark eyes glinted with unconcealed hatred and mistrust. The old man leaned his broom against a stone column and without a backward glance, padded down the long aisle and vanished in the shadows of the auditorium. Horst heard the creak of heavy hinges and then a strange metallic rattle, like sabres clashing, before the unseen door slammed shut again, blocking out the sound.

There was no heat in the building, and Horst's breath rose in a steaming vapor. He blew on his hands and stamped his feet against the cold. Pacing the length of the foyer and back again, he considered how meaningless this visit was. What difference would it make if he told the priest that he had been watched; his words recorded in little black books? The priest's voice turned him.

"Merry Christmas, Major von Bockman." The priest was alone. "We will have no midnight Mass tonight. The curfew, you know."

"I did not come for that, Father. I wish it was that simple." The cleric was coatless, yet smiling as though he did not notice the cold breeze blowing through his church. "I was at the afternoon mass."

"I saw you. I could not help noticing. You were the only one not dressed in mourning." The priest shrugged. "I was glad you came."

"There were three Gestapo officers there as well."

"Only three?" He was not surprised, nor was he alarmed.

"Probably more. But I saw three myself. There is no mistaking their kind, although they attempt to blend in."

"The presence of the secret police is to be expected these days, is it not? It is cold here since we lost the windows. Would you like to go where it is warmer?" Taking Horst by the arm, he led him through the cathedral to the maze of vaulted corridors in the cloisters. Before a heavy wooden door he stopped and looked up at Horst. The odd clacking sound penetrated the wood. "I knew you would come tonight."

"How could you know that?"

"I knew." He pulled down the latch to open the door. The corridor was filled with light and warmth and happy voices which bubbled up from a steep stairway. The priest made no move to enter, but stepped aside so that Horst might look down into a deep storage cellar which now served as a dining room. Long tables set among the pillars were packed with several hundred children who laughed and talked over tin plates filled with thick stew. It was the banging of spoons against the plates which had reminded Horst of clashing swords. Horst spotted four nuns carrying pots and ladles. The sisters glided behind the benches to cheer the diners and refill empty bowls. The din was deafening.

"Three hundred and twenty-six children. Each has lost mother and father. Some were brought to us, but many made their way here on their own. Some from Warsaw. Others from a great distance. Look at them Horst . . . Look at their faces."

Horst gazed down at a table packed with small boys who wagged their spoons in conversation and laughed at some joke which was lost to Horst beneath the racket.

"I am glad to see happy children on Christmas Eve. I am cheered by it . . . by your good work for them."

"Yes." The priest's voice was not so joyful. "I want you to remember them. Think of it. Any one of them might be the child of one of the men you saw crucified or the woman who sank into the Vistula."

Horst's pleasure vanished. "Why do you say such a thing to me?" He stepped back from the doorway as though he had been kicked.

The priest closed the door on the scene and shrugged as if the reason for his cruel statement was obvious. "Each of them has a story much like the one you told me. They are only children, yet have come here along the path of grief and brutality. They are not here by their own choice. Others made this choice for them. German soldiers."

Horst snapped. "I did not come to hear this. What can I do to change that now? It is not my responsibility . . ." He caught himself and began again. "At some risk to myself . . . I came to warn you. The Gestapo . . . The SS."

"Thank you. I am warned."

Horst stared bleakly at the black door. "You do not care if you are arrested . . . But what about the children? What will become of them?"

"You know the answer."

The vision of the future exploded in Horst's mind as though it was already the past:

The priest was tortured by the Gestapo and hung. The sisters imprisoned. They died of hunger, dysentery, and typhus. Those little boys who laughed and talked over their tin bowls that Christmas were herded into a room and stripped naked. They were sorted like animals being prepared for market; Jew from Gentile. This was easiest with male children because of the practice of circumcision among the Jews. Those confirmed or suspected of being Jewish were liquidated. The Polish children were placed in Nazi detention centers where they were abused and starved and taught to read a few necessary German commands and trained in the proper attitude towards the Reich, the Führer, and their Aryan masters. And most of them perished too before it was over . . .

Horst covered his face with his hands to shut out the images. "What do you want from me? I cannot undo what is past!"

"It is in your power to change tomorrow. I knew you would be here." The priest put his hand on Horst's shoulder. "Come with me now."

Horst followed him down the shadowed corridor, although he wanted to turn and run the other way. The children were singing in the cloister now. Christmas carols. Happy voices pursued the priest and the major until they turned a corner and entered a warm and quiet room with ten cribs and a dozen sleeping infants. Christ, crucified, looked down from the wall above them.

An elderly nun sat in a rocking chair near the coal fire. She held a baby boy in her arms. She curled his dark hair around her gnarled finger. He sucked milk from a bottle and kicked one foot free of the blanket as if in time to the old woman's lullabye. She touched the tiny toes and pulled the blanket over his foot again. The slurping sound stopped a moment as the infant looked up at the old woman with trusting blue eyes and gurgled in happy response to her humming.

The priest glanced up sharply at Horst. Was the future clear in his mind as to the fate of these little ones as well?

"Enough," Horst whispered, staggering back to lean against the wall. His stricken face reflected in the glass of a picture of Christ and the children.

"You are here tonight as one of God's footsteps," the priest replied quietly. "You came tonight because tomorrow may be too late."

"There is nothing I can do to help these . . ." Horst waved his hand over the room as if it were already empty.

"You can save one."

"Save?"

"It is in your hands now to change the future of one."

"How can I . . ."

"I have a plan."

"You're talking nonsense, Father."

"You must do exactly as I instruct you. It came to me clearly as I prayed."

"How can anyone choose which of all these? It is impossible to save one while the others . . ."

The priest looked at a painting of Christ encircled by children. "Jesus said . . . anyone who welcomes a little child in my name welcomes me . . . Don't you see, Horst? How God loves them! Their angels are constantly before His throne. To have compassion on a child . . . There is no act so holy. It is as if you carry the Christ child in your arms!"

Horst raised his eyes as the baby leaned his head against the old woman's shoulder. Heavy eyelids began to droop in contentment. A drop of milk dripped from the corner of his mouth and clung to the black fabric of her habit.

The priest took the child from her and laid him in Horst's arms. "It is Christmas, little one. The sword of the tyrant is poised above all the children of Israel again . . . You must go." And then to Horst, who cradled the infant with awkward gentleness: "To save one small life, Horst. Perhaps one day the world might be saved by that life . . . His name is Yacov Lubetkin."

✳   ✳   ✳

Horst carried Yacov Lubetkin from the Cathedral of St. John in a small wicker laundry basket packed with diapers, one baby bottle, and two cans of milk. The aged sister warned Horst that the seven-month-old baby was teething and that if he should fuss, the best thing for it was straight rye whiskey smeared on the gums.

But baby Yacov did not fuss. Wide awake, he smiled up at Horst. In the Warsaw train station he squealed happily as an SS colonel leaned over the basket and tickled his chin. It was, Horst thought grimly, something like a lamb being licked by a tiger. Then the child took the colonel's finger and pulled it to his mouth. This pleased the SS colonel. He roared with laughter.

"He is teething." Horst looked away uncomfortably.

"Yes. I feel two teeth coming through on the bottom." The SS colonel displayed his patience and affection with Aryan children. "Your child, Herr Major?"

"A strong child, I am pleased to say," Horst said cheerfully. He controlled the revulsion he felt at the hand of a murderer so near the baby's face. How many Jewish children had that hand slaughtered?

"I can see the resemblance. The eyes. Beautiful blue eyes, Herr Major. Where is his mother?"

"I am taking him home."

"A son?"

"I do my duty for the Fatherland. This son is the only gift an honorable soldier can offer the future of the world in such a dark time."

"Indeed! So says our Führer. If a soldier might lose his life for the Reich, he has left behind a legacy in a child. And this boy will be the best to come from Germany, it is plain to see. Very bright. I can spot a future general. This grip! A child who will sink his teeth into life!" He laughed at his joke and held up his wet finger. "What is he called?"

"Can you guess?" Horst gulped as the name escaped him. "Named for a great leader, Herr Colonel."

"Adolf! Well done! A well-mannered infant. A handsome German son. I, myself, have four sons in the Hitler Youth. There is nothing like sons. You have done well for the Fatherland."

"Thank you, Colonel. And now we are off to Berlin."

The SS colonel offered advice for dealing with the ordeal of teething . . . *whiskey on the gums.* With a pleasant pat on Horst's back, the tiger strolled away without suspecting the truth. Reeling, Horst hurried off to hide with Yacov in his first-class sleeping compartment.

On this, the night of all nights, the train from Warsaw to Berlin was nearly empty. Except for a handful of drunk soldiers heading home for the holiday, everyone was already wherever they were going.

Horst was grateful for this. There would be no grandmotherly types to croon over the baby. They were an hour out in the dark Polish countryside before his hands quit shaking and he turned his thoughts from the SS colonel to the child who slept beside him in the basket. The priest's plan for his escape seemed fantastic, and yet it might work.

"It is good that you are too young to know what all this is about, little one. You sleep on the edge of a flaming abyss and yet you are not troubled. What voice whispers peace to you?" He looked out at the star-flecked sky. "The priest says your angels ascend constantly before the throne of God and back to you again . . . If there are angels who follow you, boy, they descend into the center of hell tonight."

Horst tucked the blanket around the child's chin. His gaze lingered on the pink cheeks and the long lashes. Here was contentment: Yacov's tiny fist was clenched and his thumb placed in his mouth. Touching the velvet-soft head, Horst considered the story which the priest had told him about Etta and Aaron Lubetkin. Where were they and their other children now? What kind of world was this which made mothers and fathers thrust their infants into the arms of strangers, then turn away forever?

"I can make you no promises," Horst whispered as though the parents of his ward could somehow hear him. "I cannot even promise that he will survive. But on my own honor as a soldier and my very life, I vow . . . I will do everything I can to see your child safely home." He closed his eyes. "I am so sorry . . . God? Hear me."

He took the hand of Yacov, so small and soft and perfect, into his big fingers. The child stirred and breathed a ragged sigh.

What man could think of stopping such sweet breath? What kind of national government could call for the crucifixion of such innocence—to drive spikes through hands like these? What sort of people could allow it?

Had Horst known all along what was being done? Like everyone else in Germany, the truth of Nazi racial doctrines had lingered like a dark shadow in the back of Horst's thoughts. But tonight he was certain of what Hitler meant when he threatened the annihilation of the Jews of Europe if there was war! The threat was not merely rhetorical!

The vision of the future loomed before Horst tonight in the image of a million nameless children. His eyes stung with tears of rage and shame. *So many! How many are there? Too many to count!* And it was only just beginning! This is what Katrina had tried to tell him. This is why Kurt had chosen to warn Belgium that their hope of neutrality was vain. The shadow must not reach any further beyond the borders of the Reich!

"I must do this," Horst whispered. "But I cannot think of the others. Too many . . . too much . . ."

So it came down to the life of only one child in the mind of Horst von Bockman. For this one life he could risk everything! Exhaustion swept over him. With his fingers closed gently around the hand of the baby, he leaned his head back and for the first time in months, he slept soundly.

FORTY

The mess hall of the Maginot Fortress echoed with the sounds of shouts, laughter, and loudly sung, off-key Christmas carols. Mac had to lean close to Murphy's ear and yell to make himself heard. "Do you 'spose these guys would even know if they were under attack?"

"Not unless they took a direct hit," Murphy shouted back. "They're making more noise than an artillery barrage now."

The scene inside the underground French fortification was one of raucous merriment. As Mac and Murphy looked on, one corner of the room erupted with men pelting each other with pieces of bread. Across the huge, concrete-walled chamber, another set of four soldiers climbed up on the table and began an impromptu can-can, accompanied by whistles and lewd suggestions. "How long will this go on?" Mac bellowed, giving the can-can dancers ten seconds of film time.

"Til dawn," Murphy replied, "except for a short interruption at midnight for Mass."

Mac took a step back to change the way the scene was framed in the viewfinder of his new camera and stumbled over an empty wine bottle underfoot.

Murphy caught him by the elbow to keep Mac from falling. "And they better pray for a hangover cure at that mass. If the Germans attack tomorrow, these guys'll will surrender at the sight of an aspirin bottle."

Mac turned at a tap on his shoulder. A French artillery captain started to say something to the two journalists, then shrugged because of the noise and gestured for them to follow him. When the three had gotten into the corridor and closed a steel door on the merrymaking, the officer tried again. "The colonel would like you to join him for Christmas Eve supper," he said.

Up two flights of concrete steps and down two long corridors that echoed with the passage of their boots, they arrived at the officers' dining room. Once there, Mac and Murphy were introduced to Colonel Benet, the commandant.

To Mac, Benet looked like a Marshall of France from the time of Napoleon. He was an elderly man, but tall and straight; he carried himself with ramrod correctness. The shock of white hair combed back from his high forehead was matched by the gleaming sweep of an elegant moustache. Among the medals and ribbons on his uniform was the Croix de Guerre.

"Please be seated, gentlemen," the colonel urged. "We have just enough time for an aperitif before the meal."

A junior officer rapped on a connecting door and a nervous-looking soldier dressed in a white apron entered, pushing a serving trolley. "I must apologize for the poor quality of our hospitality," the colonel said, "but there is a war on, you know." The soldier-waiter offered each officer a choice of whiskey, sherry, port, madeira, armangac, or any of a dozen other liqueurs.

"I am a banker in civilian life," Colonel Benet explained over the first course of the supper, steaming bowls of vichyssoise. "But old soldiers never die, as they say, so I dusted off my uniform from the Great War and returned to duty."

"And are you expecting to have to fight the Great War over again?" Murphy asked.

"The Germans are without imagination," the colonel maintained, carefully brushing the ends of his moustache with a linen napkin. "Right now they are holding back because they realize what an error they have made to come to blows with us at all. Sooner or later, Herr Hitler will have to launch an attack, to save face, of course, and when it is repulsed, then the politicians will settle things."

Mac accepted a plate of roast pork with cauliflower in cheese sauce from the waiter and allowed the colonel to swallow a sip of wine before raising another question. "And your men are ready to face a German attack?"

Spreading his broad hands, the commandant gave an expressive shrug. "But of course! You have seen for yourself what good spirits they are in. Here we are, on our own soil, behind the greatest fortifications in the history of the world. How could we be more ready?" The colonel studied his platter of food for a moment, and then in an abrupt change of subject said, "Our cook is just like the Boche . . . completely without imagination!"

When supper concluded, Mac asked, "Has there been any activity by the Germans in your sector? Could we go to one of your lookout posts and get a peek across the line?"

Colonel Benet cleared his throat with disapproval. "I was going to suggest that we adjourn to the auditorium," he said. "The enlisted men are putting on an amateur musical performance. It should be very droll."

"With respect, Colonel," Murphy added, "Just a quick look at what the other side is up to."

"Very well," Benet grumbled, "but you will not see anything. Nothing going on tonight, I can promise you."

The observation platform of the fort was four stories above the mess hall and directly above the outpost's armament of 75mm cannon. The sentry on lone guard duty stamped his feet against the wintry air that swirled in through the open small arms ports. He snapped to attention as his commandant arrived, and Mac wondered what crime the man was being punished for to draw this duty tonight.

"Anything to report?" asked the colonel.

"Nothing, sir," answered the guard, "except that it has been snowing again."

"What about that light over there?" Mac asked, pointing to a faint yellow glow that dimly outlined a knobby hill about a half mile off.

"Ah that," snorted Benet. "That is Spichern Hill. Until recently it belonged to us, but a patrol of Boches crept round behind it and captured it." His tone sounded as if he thought the Germans had done something unfair. "We will retake it, never fear."

"There seems to be some movement going on there now," Murphy observed. "In fact the light is brighter now than it was when we first looked, and it seems to be moving toward the top of the hill."

"Shall I ring the battery and give the order to fire?" asked the sentry, stepping toward a telephone on the wall.

"Absolutely not!" corrected the colonel, his moustache quivering with indignation. "How can you think of such uncivilized behavior? They are enjoying a quiet Christmas celebration the same as we. Why should we do something so antagonistic? Come now, we've seen enough. Let us adjourn to the auditorium. I am sure the singing is already in progress."

A soundless snowfall dropped onto the outlines of Spichern Hill. Sturmann Geiger hunched his shoulders against the cold of the Western Front. It was a mistake; the movement caused a tiny avalanche to cascade off the back rim of his steel helmet and into the collar of his greatcoat. A thin stream of icy water trickled down his back, adding to his misery.

Sentry duty in the Saarbrucken sector was not enjoyable in December of 1939, especially not on this cold and sodden Christmas Eve. The tree trunks below the ridge commanded by the pillbox were black skeletal forms against the snow. Geiger had seen dead men that looked like that: Polish soldiers killed by machine gun fire and abandoned by their comrades, left hanging over fences to rot.

The quiet Western Front was different, to be sure, but in the lonely darkness, it was easy to conjure up all the spectres that haunted Geiger's dreams. Even the pride which the German soldier felt at taking part in the capture of this tiny piece of French soil had frozen into a corner of his mind. He could take it out and examine it, but it refused to give warmth or comfort.

Instead, he tried to shake off the oppressive dread by thinking about his home in Munich. His family would be gathered for a festive meal in a house filled with light, food, and warmth. But try as he might, he kept seeing phantoms lurking in the darkness and the reproachful stares on the remembered faces of the dead. He frowned and shook his head, reminding himself that just to the west, no more than a half mile or so away, a live French sentry was also standing guard, along with ten thousand of his fellows.

Wondering if the French would send out a patrol on this darkest night of the year made Geiger peer through the swirling flakes toward the French lines.

Counting off ten paces to the end of his duty area, a slow pivot faced him back toward the concrete pillbox that guarded the unremarkable chunk of French territory called Spichern Heights. Geiger snorted with the contempt shared by his entire regiment at the French defenses. This machine gun emplacement was impressive enough in its solidity, but there was one major flaw: like the entire strategy of the Maginot Line, its designers were so convinced of its invulnerability that its guns faced only toward Germany. There had been no allowance of either men or equipment preparing the French for the encircling German infantry patrol that looped through the woods to attack Spichern Heights from the rear.

But that triumph had been some time before, and it was back to business as usual on the Western Front. Another hour to go before his relief showed up.

It was difficult to judge the passage of time on the lonely walk, and it dragged all the more because Geiger stopped to listen to the night. The squishing of his boots made thin echoes that sounded as if someone else were marching when he marched and stopping when he stopped.

He made five circuits of his post and drowsiness began to replace his earlier terror. It was a cold, miserably wet night after all, nothing more. Geiger stopped again to listen, but it was more out of habit than expectation.

That was when he heard the footfalls . . . real ones that continued on though he stood rooted in place, and his heart raced as apprehension flooded over him again. He tried to call out a challenge, but his voice was only a harsh croak of meaningless noise. His fingers fumbled with the safety catch of the rifle, but were so numb that he could not tell if he had moved it or not.

Geiger forced himself to look down at his weapon, to visually determine what his sense of touch could not confirm. Yes, the catch was off. He raised the gun to his shoulder and sighted along its barrel . . . into a hazy yellow glow that had not been in front of him a moment before.

"Halt!" he cried, finding words at last. "Who goes there?"

An advancing mass, black against the frosty background, resolved itself into separate dark shapes approaching his position. "Halt!" he ordered again, "or I will . . ."

"Achtung, Sturmann Geiger!" The voice of the company commander demanded, "We are coming to inspect the post!"

The captain and four other figures moved with the glow of a shielded lantern to join the sentry on the ridge. Whether because of his earlier fear, or because of the stiffness induced by his hours on guard, Geiger was slow in lowering his weapon. When he allowed its muzzle to drop, it slid across the form of a short man clad in a black leather coat.

A low chuckle came to the young man's ears. "Would you shoot your Führer?" a familiar rasping accent asked.

The Führer! Sturmann Geiger snapped to attention, or did his best, but the leader of the Third Reich paid him no further heed. Instead, Hitler addressed the men in his entourage. There was a tone of smug satisfaction in his voice as he said, "In 1918, I vowed to never again stand on French soil until I could give it to the Fatherland! Tonight that promise is fulfilled! You and your men, Captain, have made it possible."

The captain made a modest rejoinder that the emplacement was a very small attainment in the scope of the war, but Hitler interrupted him. *"I* am Germany," the Führer said, "and the ground where I stand is symbolic of *all* of France." His voice rose in pitch and trembled with excitement, "Of the whole world! I stretch out my hand toward the west, so . . . and it is as if it were already taken!" The Führer swung a Nazi salute over the hilltop at Spichern Heights; over the whole of the darkened earth.

✣   ✣   ✣

Had Katrina gotten his message?

Horst spotted her as the train chugged beneath the dome of the Friedrich Strasse Bahnhof in Berlin. Wearing a loden green wool skirt, sweater, and beret, she leaned against an iron pillar which was draped with red swastika banners.

The baby was wide awake. Fed, washed, and changed, he perched on Horst's arm and watched the world slide by with interest. Horst stepped from the compartment onto the nearly deserted platform with the last huff and shudder of the train. He left the wicker basket behind, carrying only his valise and the baby.

Enormous posters of the Führer glared down at them from every wall. Katrina glanced, unseeing, toward Horst and then away. Her expression changed with the startling realization that the man walking towards her was indeed Horst and he was not alone. She looked back again, held her astonishment in check, and pretended that the strange child in Horst's arms was fully expected.

"You made it! Merry Christmas, my darlings!" She hurried toward them.

Well done, Katrina! How beautifully she improvised in a world where the expression of surprise could be cause for official investigation.

Horst spotted the ubiquitous Gestapo agents lounging around the lobby of the uncrowded depot in search of any traveler who displayed even a glint of apprehension. Two plainclothes officers near the stairway. Another was beside the news kiosk, while a fourth pretended to read the paper.

"There is Mama!" Horst said loudly, pointing toward Katrina. It seemed a very ordinary reunion. The Gestapo barely glanced up as Katrina kissed Horst and took the child from his arms with delight.

There was other quarry to be sniffed out. A small dark man with a haunted look walked too quickly toward the exit and glanced over his shoulder as if he were being pursued. Two of the Gestapo exchanged knowing looks and strolled after him.

The charade of Horst and Katrina played out. "Look at you! How I have missed you!" She kissed the baby and held him up over her head. Yacov frowned down at her and for an instant seemed as if he might break out in tears. "No, my angel! What is it? Are you hungry? Horst, where is her bottle?"

"Teething," Horst replied.

The light banter went on with Katrina calling Yacov *she* and *her* until at last they passed through the portals of the gleaming marble edifice of the Friedrich Strasse Bahnhof and settled into the car with Horst behind the wheel and Katrina holding Yacov. Two policemen on the sidewalk with crossed arms seemed not to see them.

Horst started the engine and ground the gears, his only sign of nervousness.

Katrina eyed him coolly. "So. Hello, Horst. I am a mother, am I?"

"He is a boy."

Katrina shot him a look. "Polish?"

"From Poland. Jewish."

"A Jewish boy?" Katrina kissed Yacov on the cheek and brushed his hair with her fingers. She studied him for a moment, and he smiled curiously at her and batted her nose. "Very pretty. But Horst, a boy? He is circumcised."

"Yes." Horst pulled from the curb and drove down the deserted street.

"Well, well, little one," she said. "We must not let a Nazi change your diapers."

"With any luck he will not be in Germany long enough to need a change of diapers."

"It is already too late for that. Do you have any clean things?"

"The valise."

She fumbled with the latch and retrieved a diaper. Changing the baby on her lap as they drove toward the suburbs, she said with a touch of wonder in her voice, "You might have told me about this."

"I did not know about it until last night."

"The Gestapo could have seen how surprised I was and then . . ."

"You are a good enough actress, Katrina. I was counting on it."

She was silent for a long moment as they passed the new Chancellory building. The enormous Nazi flags were on display, indicating that Hitler was in residence. Katrina shuddered and instinctively held the baby nearer.

"Where are we going, Horst?"

"Home."

"That is not what I meant. I mean . . . us. Where are you and I headed? What has happened to you since you left me? Why have you done this? Brought this baby to me . . . Is it because you thought it would change my mind about us? To pacify me somehow?"

Horst thumped his hand angrily against the wheel and swore. The baby began to cry. "An arrogant thing to say, Katrina!"

"Look now. You have frightened him!" She caressed Yacov and tried to quiet him, then fumbled in the bag for a bottle.

Horst pressed his foot down hard on the accelerator and sped across the bridge over the Spree River. "I have done this because . . . because I must! That is all! It has nothing to do with us . . . with where I stand with you! Or whether I remain a soldier or abandon my men in a fight because I do not agree with the politics of my country." He ran his fingers through his hair. "What is the use? The child will be out of Germany soon enough. Safe. I need your help with him for a day or so. No more than that. It has nothing to do with whether or not you still care about me. It is his life and my soul! For once it has nothing to do with you. Can you understand that?"

Katrina stared straight ahead. Her jaw was set. "Good. That is all I wanted to know. Because . . . I wanted to tell you . . . You need not do anything to prove yourself to me . . . But this . . . Well," She turned toward Horst and put her hand on his shoulder and slid her fingers down his arm to touch his hand. "I have missed you, darling."

❧ ❧ ❧

He was home again. Really home.

Horst and Katrina lay together beneath the warmth of the down quilt, and it was as it should be. He was drowsy and contented beside her now. He felt somehow healed by her touch; whole again as though they had never argued, never been apart. She kissed his neck and traced the line of his shoulder with her fingertips. Afraid to move, afraid she would stop, he pretended to sleep.

"Touch me," she murmured impatiently and took his hand, bringing it to her lips.

He wanted her again. Pulling her against him, she yielded with the gentle, urgent desire of familiar love.

"I knew you were awake," she laughed.

"I never really sleep when I am with you." He kissed her mouth and felt her heartbeat quicken to match his own.

"And when you are not with me?" Her voice was tremulous, but still teasing.

"Then I sleep only to dream of you."

"Horst." Her breath was sweet. Whispered in his ear, the words made him dizzy. "I want us . . . to make a baby. Part of you to stay with me when you are away."

There was a kind of magic in her request. It charged him through with tenderness for her like he had never known. He could not speak to answer.

He wanted to see her face, but it was too dark. He wanted her to look in his eyes . . . to know how much he loved her.

Her lips moved against his ear, but he could not hear her voice beneath the drumming of his own pulse.

It did not matter what she said. He would agree to anything, everything she asked him. He nodded as she ran her fingers through his hair, then strummed his back in rhythm as though she heard music playing.

FORTY-ONE

This time Madame Hilaire came back on board the *Garlic* with a man in tow. He was dark-eyed, unshaven, and ominous in the way he wandered around the cabin picking up everything as though he was shopping in a flea market. He looked at Papillon, who was perched on Jerome's head, as if he might crush him.

"Who are you?" Jerome demanded of the man. After all, this was Jerome's home, and what right did Madame Hilaire have to bring a stranger onto the *Garlic* without asking? And what right did this ragged character have to examine everything so closely?

"Who am I?" The man acted like he might strike Jerome for asking. Then he shouted to Madame Hilaire. "He wants to know who I am?"

She snorted at the impudence of such a question. When Jerome tried to get an answer from her she did not look at him. She reeked of sour wine. Her hair was even more unruly than usual. She stood with her hands on her hips and stared with proprietary satisfaction past the children at the bed, at the table, the dish cupboards, and the pans stacked in the dry sink.

The man lifted the hatch and peered into the engine compartment.

"What are they doing, Jerome?" Marie asked. She was troubled, even frightened, by the intrusion.

Jerome took his sister up the ladder and onto the deck. He instructed her to sit on the rope coil and hold Papillon. The sun was bright and beautiful over the buildings of the Concierge. The stone faces on Pont Neuf bridge gaped at the two children. Jerome took a seat beside the open cargo hatch and leaned down to listen to the conversation. With the shouting of Madame Hilaire, it was not hard to understand the intent.

"Well, Captain, what do you think of it?" she screamed.

He shouted back, enunciating each word. "She is a reeking *Garlic* all right, Madame!"

"But what will you pay for her?"

Marie jumped to her feet. "Pay? Does she mean buy? Buy the *Garlic*?"

"Stay here!" Jerome ordered. Then he bounded down the hatch. "Monsieur." He was panting as he stood at the elbow of the man who ignored him. "I do not care what Madame Hilaire tells you. Our ship is not for sale. It is not hers to sell. She is our guardian only."

He turned and laughed, throwing his head back and opening his mouth wide to reveal blackened teeth.

"She is your guardian, boy?"

Jerome put his hands behind his back so the man would not see how he was shaking. Something terrible was happening, and Jerome did not know how to stop it.

"She is meant only to watch over my sister and I, Monsieur. The *Garlic* is ours. It belongs to our father who is a poilu at the front."

Again the laugh. Madame Hilaire looked at Jerome as she would regard a fly to be swatted or brushed away. She shrugged.

Jerome knew that his words were of no consequence. The scheming hag was up to something.

"Look, boy." The man shoved him back. "Let me tell you something. Madame Hilaire has this paper, see? It is from your Papa. He gives her the power to tend to his affairs while he is gone. Do you understand, boy?"

"But Papa did not mean . . ."

"She has the paper. He has signed it. Madame Hilaire is authorized to sell this tub. Of course the money will be used to care for you and your sister."

The hag nodded broadly and grinned in agreement with whatever she thought she heard.

Jerome rushed at her ferociously. He grabbed her arms and pushed her back against the wall. "Thief! You cannot do this to us! I will tell my Uncle Jambonneau! I will write Papa, and he will have you thrown into jail!"

"Get the rubbish off me!" she wailed.

The man picked Jerome up by the back of his shirt and held him aloft. Jerome swung his fists, but the man was out of reach.

"Look boy, your father was in debt. This is the only way his debts can be paid. What can he do? Settle his accounts on fifty centimes a day?"

Madame Hilaire brushed herself off in indignation. She tugged up her sleeves and waddled to where Jerome dangled. She spit on the floor of the cabin and then slapped Jerome hard across the cheek. Much worse than the slap was the way she lowered her voice and spoke to him in a sinister whisper for the first time.

"Little beggar! There are plenty of charity wards for scum like you and your sister. You think I can support myself and you on what Jardin is paying me? Now get out of here! I have the paper! I can do what I like! I am selling the *Garlic,* and there is nothing you can do about it! When the war begins, your father will die anyway. They always put the stupid sheep in front of the cannons. A charity ward is all you have to hope for."

Jerome heard the sobs of Marie from on deck. The eyes of the stranger turned up. He guffawed. "A pitiful thing, this is, Madame Hilaire. Tragic. That a man does not even care for his own children properly. Ah, well. This way they will begin life with a clean slate . . . with nothing at all to encumber them."

✳   ✳   ✳

It was as if something had turned on a water tap in Marie's eyes and Jerome could not turn it off again. She was not blubbering or making even a sound, but every time Jerome looked at her face there was an unending stream of new tears trickling down her cheeks. Very quiet and troubling. The noiseless suffering of his sister made him feel even more miserable inside. He felt bad enough already. Madame Hilaire tied up some clothes in a bundle and threw them from the *Garlic* onto the quay. She told Jerome and Marie that if they came back she would call the gendarmes and have them sent to a charity orphanage. Jerome would be conveyed to a home for boys. Marie would be dispatched to a home for girls, and they would never see one another again!

"Do not feel badly, Marie," Jerome said. "We will go to the hospital. We will send word to Uncle Jambonneau. He will know what we should do."

Marie nodded and sniffed. Even her nose was dripping. Marie was like a sponge, Jerome thought, oversaturated with liquid. It was as though Madame Hilaire had stepped on poor Marie and all the juice was squishing out of her at once. Could there be so much dampness in one so little? It was a pathetic sight. Even Papillon was worried. Sweet little rat Papillon; he had the kind heart of a dog, even if he was a rat. Sitting on Marie's shoulder, he patted her salty tears. Putting his paw to his mouth he tasted her grief and twitched his whiskers in concern. When Marie finished this weeping, would she be all shriveled and dry like a raisin?

The entrance to Hôpital de la Charité, where Uncle Jambonneau now lived, was in the Rue Jacob among a warren of little shops and old buildings. The hospital was itself a dreary place. Its stone facade was black with years of exposure to coal smoke.

Marie stood on the steps and craned her head back to peer up at the sooty windows.

"Stay here," Jerome instructed her firmly. He tried to sound like he was not really worried at all about her. "There are nuns and nurses inside. They will think Papillon is just a common rat. They will not like him in their establishment, ma chérie. So you will have to stay out here with him."

She nodded wordlessly. Jerome, in an impulse of compassion which surprised even him, leaned down and kissed her quickly on the head. Papillon leapt up and clung to his shirtfront.

"No, Papillon, dear little dog. You must stay here with Marie. She is afraid of the nuns, you see." He pulled Papillon loose and replaced him in Marie's pocket.

Marie would watch over Papillon. Papillon would watch over Marie.

The inside of the hospital smelled like antiseptic and mold. The plaster of the ceiling was flaking. The green linoleum squares of the floor were chipped. Two long benches in the foyer held grim-faced men and old women cradling cranky children. Above their heads was a crucifix. On the opposite wall was a large framed photograph of the Pope. In an alcove was a statue of Mary and the Christ child. This was familiar to Jerome because his mother had died in this place. He remembered sitting on the long bench and wondering when it would be time for lunch. Even now he could recall the red, swollen face of his Papa. From that day on, Papa had blamed the sisters, and the priests, and the doctors, and especially God, that Mama was gone. Jerome wished very much that Uncle Jambonneau was in a different hospital than this one.

There was a nun behind a very tidy desk. She was talking on the telephone when Jerome approached her. She smiled at him as she spoke to someone else. She winked at him and held up a finger to ask him to be patient. And then . . .

"Yes, young man? How may I help you?" She looked at his cap to indicate that he should take it off.

He snatched off the cap and kneaded it in his hands. "My Uncle Jambonneau?"

"Your uncle's name is Jambonneau? You call him Uncle Pigs-knuckles?"

Jerome scratched his cheek. He could not remember Uncle Jambonneau's real name. He had always been called Pigs-knuckles. "He has the same last name as me, Sister. It is Jardin. He is an old soldier from des Invalides who has pneumonia. He is here. I must get word to him."

The nun busily pored over her book. "Jardin. Jardin . . . Oui. Jacob Alfred Jardin. He is here, but you may not see him. He is better, but still a very sick man. Children are not allowed. But I shall see that he gets a message that you have come by."

Jerome twisted his hat in his hands. How could he tell this woman who wore the black garb of the enemy that he and his sister had no place to go? That he needed help? Surely she would swoop down like a terrible black crow and lock him and Marie into a room until they could be deposited in an institution for homeless waifs. Papa would not like it. Marie would die from terror.

"Madame," he addressed her quietly and respectfully. "Please tell my Uncle Jambonneau Jardin that his niece and nephew, Marie and Jerome, have come by to wish him well. Tell him also that his dog, Papillon, is fat and happy. Everything is fine and he must get well because we all miss him very much."

She copied Jerome's words. "I will take him the note myself," she promised.

"Uncle Jambonneau is blind," Jerome warned her. "You must also read the note to him aloud or he will not know what is on the paper, Madame."

She agreed and he hurried out of the hospital with his head spinning. What could he tell Marie? What were they to do now?

❖   ❖   ❖

Horst placed the telephone call to the Associated Press office in Berlin at nine o'clock on the morning of December twenty-seventh as the priest instructed him. A German receptionist answered the telephone. In English, Horst asked for Josephine Marlow.

"Marlow?" the receptionist was puzzled by the request. "She is not in the office."

"When do you expect her?"

"Expect Josie Marlow? Well I can't say. She doesn't work in Berlin, you see. She might have gone home to America."

Horst glanced down at the baby, who was crawling happily around a small space which Katrina had hemmed in with furniture. The priest had not told him what to do if the American journalist was not there!

Attempting to remain businesslike, he asked for some member of the staff who might know how she could be reached. A few moments passed before a man came on the line.

"Bill Cooper here."

It was a friendly male American voice. Horst breathed a sigh of relief. "I am trying to speak with Fräulein Josephine Marlow, you see."

"Josie Marlow? Sorry. She's on Paris staff."

Paris. There was no hope of Horst speaking with her directly. It was still possible to send wires to Paris which were routed through Holland or Belgium, but those were subject to strictest scrutiny by the Gestapo. Any

German attempting to contact someone on the outside could be arrested at the whim of the secret police and charged with treason.

Horst was certain that even this call was being monitored by the Gestapo. To say more now could cast some suspicion on Bill Cooper, as well as make the reentry of Josephine Marlow into the Reich very difficult when and if the time came.

"Is there something I can do to help?" Cooper asked.

"No. Herr Cooper, is it?" Horst wrote down the name, thanked the man, then quickly hung up the telephone.

Katrina did not speak English, but she clearly understood the disappointment in her husband's expression.

"The woman is not in Berlin?"

"Paris."

She shrugged and smiled down at the child, who was picking at the bows on her black pumps with tiny persistent fingers. "I will keep him here," Katrina scooped Yacov up. "He is a fine baby. And I will just keep him."

"No, Kat. Not a boy. It is dangerous enough what you have here. How many little girls learning to act like good Catholics? If it is possible, for your safety and the child's, I must do as the priest instructed."

"But if the woman is not in Berlin, then she is not in Berlin."

"If I could speak privately to Herr Cooper. He knows her. He could get word to her."

"Horst! You cannot dare go to the office of the foreign press! Every door is watched by the Gestapo. You know that! Such an act could land you in Sachenhausen tommorrow!"

"Yes. Maybe if the baby can stay with you awhile . . . I must go to the Führer's speech in Berlin on New Year's Eve. There is always good attendance by the foreign press. If I can find this Bill Cooper among them . . . Perhaps there is some hope to contact Fräulein Marlow after all."

"And if you contact her, what will the message be? There is no passage from France into Germany. How can she come here?"

He sat down hard in the rocking chair and scooped up the baby. "How can we send you on your way to Jerusalem, little man?"

"I will keep . . ."

"No, Katrina! I forbid it! He has a grandfather who no doubt would not think kindly of a Wehrmacht major keeping his grandson. Now help me think!"

Resenting the command, Katrina began to think. "There is my Aunt Lottie's house in Treves. It is just across the border from Luxembourg. Luxembourg is neutral so . . ."

He snapped his fingers as if that was the solution. "She is a journalist.

Treves is full of neutral journalists. The Porta Nigra Hotel is crawling with journalists."

"And Gestapo?"

"Of course. The Gestapo is everywhere. Like fleas. Treves is no different. But it is right on the border. She can enter Germany over the Wasserbillig bridge. That is it! I will contact this Bill Cooper and he will carry the message to her. We must give her time to get the proper documents for him of course. American documents."

"Can she do that?"

"If she cannot, then we will have a son."

✣　✣　✣

Jerome hoped that Marie would not ask him any questions for a while because he needed time to think up answers.

They trudged silently back along the Quai Voltaire. The water of the Seine seemed very dark today. No longer like home.

Two large women, heads covered with scarves, walked past them. They nudged one another and made unkind comments about Papillon and the fact that Marie was skinny and her shoes were much too large for her feet.

Jerome turned and glared hotly at their retreating backs. He cocked a snook at them and muttered savagely that women who were fat as pigs should not say unkind things about such a little girl as Marie.

Marie's head went down. She looked at her shoes. "What will we do, Jerome?" she whispered.

The moment of truth. He did not yet have an answer.

"Uncle Jambonneau said . . ." He hesitated. "What do you think he said?"

Marie shrugged. "How should I know?"

"Guess." He was stalling for time.

"Tell me, Jerome. I am too tired to guess."

"Come on. I will surprise you. He has a very good solution. You know Uncle Jambonneau. He always has good ideas. He is a very smart man. He told me to take you . . . someplace . . . and surprise you." He held his head up as if he knew where he was going. "But do not ask me any more questions, Marie. And you must stop leaking all these tears."

She stopped crying. She did not ask any questions. Finally Jerome found himself back in Buci market, leading her among the stalls of flowers and vegetables and patisseries and the open shop of the butcher. Only then did it come to him. Like a flash of lightning, his dim brain lit up.

"Stop here." They halted beside a basket of blue flowers. "This is what Uncle Jambonneau told me to do, ma chérie."

"He told you to bring me to Buci? But we have no money to buy food."

"Listen." Jerome took Papillon from her. "Uncle Jambonneau says that you must go to the window of Monsieur Turenne, the butcher. You must ask him where Madame Rose lives."

"Who is Madame Rose?"

"A friend of Uncle Jambonneau."

"On no!" she wailed. "Not another one like Madame Hilaire! What more can happen to us?"

"No! No, Marie, ma chérie. Listen! Madame Rose is American. Nothing like Madame Hilaire. She does not drink."

"Not ever?"

"I do not think so. But anyway, go ask the butcher where she may be found. It is like a treasure hunt, Uncle Jambonneau says. When we find this Madame Rose we shall find our treasure! Chicken to eat, maybe, like in the old days. Like visiting day at des Invalides! A happy ending, Marie!" He nudged her forward as the great hulk of the butcher appeared, framed in his window by naked poultry and rabbits and loops of sausages.

Jerome ducked down behind a handcart of flowers as Marie walked cautiously forward. He did not dare to look, but he strained his ears to hear.

"Pardon, Monsieur Butcher. My Uncle Jambonneau says I must find Madame Rose. The American."

"And how should I know where such a Madame Rose person is?"

"Uncle Jambonneau says you will know where she is. Like a treasure, Monsieur. And so I am sent to ask you."

"Why should you want to know?"

"Because he says I must."

Silence. "You look like something that would interest Madame Rose. Something the cat would leave on her threshold."

"What cat, Monsieur?"

"Never mind. If I give you her place of residence, you must say I sent you to her. She will like that, I think. She will think well of me."

"Oui, Monsieur Butcher."

"All right then. She lives with her sister and the urchins at Number 5, Rue de la Huchette. The house is a large one behind a heavy wood gate where the coaches used to go in and out of the courtyard. Ring the bell, little one. Wait beside the gate even if it seems like no one is home. By and by someone will come and let you in."

Jerome cheered behind the bunches of petunias. He kissed Papillon on the nose! He congratulated himself for the brilliance of his idea! Marie came back smiling. It was the first time she had smiled since they left the *Garlic*.

"Number 5, Rue de la Huchette. I heard. Well done, Marie!"

"Now what?"

"Now we go there. It is all so simple. Uncle Jambonneau says this is the kindest of all ladies in the Latin Quarter. She is nothing at all like Madame Hilaire. She is a large woman and has a mouth like a bullfrog, but you must not be frightened of her. She also has a sister who is scrawny. Her name is Betsy. There are many other children who are there. They eat chicken sometimes for dinner."

Marie caught Jerome's excitement! Madame Rose with a mouth like a bullfrog! Beautiful Rose! The treasure of Uncle Jambonneau! Chicken for dinner!

Located one block from the Seine, Rue de la Huchette was a short, narrow street bordered by Place St. Michel to the west and Rue St. Jacques on the east.

It was a close-packed, narrow street, lined with houses which Uncle Jambonneau said were several hundred years old. A single gutter ran down the center of the cobbles. This had been used as a sewer in the old days when the contents of chamber pots were tossed out of the upper-story windows. But now Huchette was a much cleaner place, though still quite poor. Napoleon himself had lived in one of the houses when he was impoverished. This fact had always been used by Papa to remind Jerome that even poor boys could make good and end up with a nice tomb like the one Napoleon now occupied at des Invalides.

The neighborhood was ideally situated for student riots, rebellions, barricades, and bloody battles. Such events came around every few decades on the Left Bank and the Huchette was a very popular street in those times. Beneath the buildings were deep cellars where the unfortunate prisoners of the Reign of Terror had been confined and tortured. Devices of torment were still to be found in some of those basements. Uncle Jambonneau had cheerfully informed Marie about this historical fact, which made her hesitant at first to walk down Rue de la Huchette.

But it was getting on toward dinner time, and the scent of cooking food wafted through the air. Jerome wisely talked about Madame Rose and chicken dinner and how well liked the place was by all the children who lived there. And besides, Number 5 was only just a few houses from the corner. Jerome told his sister that it was a newer house and that it had no skeletons in the basement.

"How can you know this, Jerome?"

"I know this because the house has no basement." He lied because it was easier than arguing. By the time Marie found out that this was one of the oldest houses and also that it had a cellar which was deeper than all the rest, it would be too late. "Number five. And there it is."

An enormous arched wood gate sealed the house off from the street. The stone around the portal was rounded and chipped from the days when wagons and carriages had turned into the courtyard and clipped the edges with iron hubs. The heavy wood planks of the gate were black with age and scarred from ten thousand small encounters over four hundred years. It was a venerable gate which had experienced the knocking of Latin scholars, pilgrims, prostitutes, musketeers, and the angry fists of the Revolution's mob in search of priests or terrified aristocrats hiding within.

This evening, as twilight closed over the narrow strip of sky, Jerome added the rapping of his small knuckles to the history of the gate.

He waited patiently for some minutes. No one came. It was dark.

"Monsieur the butcher said to ring the bell," Marie insisted as the smells of garlic and fried potatoes made her stomach growl.

Jerome could not see a bell. A frayed red rope dangled from a hole in the wood. He pulled it violently and a bell rang inside the courtyard. More waiting. Another pull.

A woman's gruff voice called, "Patience! I am coming!"

The clank of a heavy metal latch sounded and the gate swung open a tiny sliver. The aroma of food escaped like a strong current of water. Jerome could easily see Madame Rose framed in the light behind her. She was peering out into the street at an angle much above the heads of Jerome and Marie.

"A prank!" She spat and slammed the gate.

"No! No! Madame Rose!" Jerome grasped for the cord and pulled hard. He held tight to it as if it was a lifeline thrown out to someone drowning.

The hinges groaned back again and the big face of Madame Rose peered out now at his level. The thin lips of the wide bullfrog mouth curved up in a smile. "Who is there?"

"It is me, Madame Rose. Jerome Jardin . . . Salami?" He attempted to jar her memory without giving away to Marie that Madame Rose did not know Uncle Jambonneau.

Silence. The crack widened. "Salami?"

"The butcher told us where to find you, Madame Rose." Marie interjected eagerly. "And Uncle Jambonneau says you will feed us if we come here."

The gate was wide. The two stepped in. Madame Rose studied Jerome in the shadowed light. "But of course! Jerome Jardin! Did you bring your rat?" She closed the gate.

"And my sister, Marie, also."

Marie giggled. "You know Papillon too!" Such relief. Such joy. "Papa is at the war. Uncle Jambonneau is in hospital. Madame Hilaire has sold our *Garlic* and now we have no place to sleep. But you do not have devices of torture in your cellar because you do not have a cellar. So I am not frightened. And Uncle Jambonneau says you are a treasure, and Monsieur the

Butcher says you will think well of him since he told us how to find you! And you will also have chicken sometimes for dinner."

Jerome did not need to say a word. Marie was doing all the talking. Very little of it made sense to Madame Rose, but she put her big hand on Marie's scrawny shoulder and nodded and made contented noises as though she was interested in everything. Jerome was relieved. Marie babbled on gleefully.

The house was three stories high, with open terraces, built in a U-shape around a cobbled courtyard. Young children gaped and twittered down at them from between the slats of the bannisters. Laundry hung on lines like colorful flags above their heads. Blue shirts. White shirts. Red dresses. Calico dresses. Clean, white underthings. Knickers. Bloomers. Long and short socks of all sizes tiptoed in the air above the courtyard.

Even in the faint light, Jerome could see that the walls were clean, white, and like new. No doubt the building was very old beneath the facade, but it did not show its age. The two sisters had fixed it up beautifully! Jerome remembered that some French king had demanded all the wood framed buildings be plastered over after a great and terrible fire and swept through the city some centuries before. Number 5 Rue de la Huchette would have been around in those days. But tonight the building seemed quite bright and cheerful even in its ancient coat of plaster of paris. It was not anything like what Jerome had pictured an orphanage would be. The courtyard smelled like whitewash and spring flowers. It also smelled like cooking food, of course. A pleasant combination.

"We are not too late for supper?" Marie blinked up at Madame Rose.

Madame Rose laughed a big, boisterous, American laugh and called to her sister. "Do not put the leftovers away, Betsy dear! We have two more for dinner!"

FORTY-TWO

A record cold gripped Berlin this New Year's Eve. A coal shortage compounded the wartime gloominess of the holiday. To add to the edgy
mood of Berliners, Himmler revoked permission for the bars to remain open
all night for the celebration. The Gestapo chief further warned against excessive drinking and requested that German citizens greet the New Year with
sober thought and consideration of the Führer's upcoming speech. In spite
of that, the Kurfurstendamm was crowded with drunks who drowned their
troubles beneath the watchful eyes of thousands of Himmler's police.

Above the packed pavement of the Ku-damm, in ludicrous contrast, loudspeakers broadcast the grim New Year celebration of the Nazi Party as it
unfolded in the great Sports Palast. It was a very sober affair.

The floodlights ringing the stadium produced streaks of brilliant white
light alternating with bands of deep black shadow. The view of the crowd
from the high platform resembled a thickly timbered forest; thousands of
brown-uniformed human trees were brightly lit, and thousands more remained in darkness.

Ten men to a row across one streak of illumination . . . ten tens to an
eagle standard . . . ten hundreds filling a strand of radiance to the far side
of the stadium . . . a hundred bands of light and dark.

The crowd was mostly still. There was some jostling in place as necks were
craned to see what privileged celebrities gathered on the stage. Any comments made were spoken in hasty, reverent whispers. The highest podium
was empty, unoccupied except for a row of microphones that guarded a
vacant lectern.

At a unseen cue, a barrage of drums crashed into cadence. The tempo was
deliberate and measured, but the volume was so overpowering that the air
itself seemed likely to split apart. A hundred thousand men found that they
were breathing in time to the drums, their heartbeats mimicking the rhythm.

When the throbbing of the drums so reverberated through the bodies of the crowd that they no longer heard the sound but felt it, at that exact moment a legion of trumpets burst into a fanfare and an encircling ring of spotlight beams jumped upward into the sky from the rim of the stadium to tower over the scene like pillars of ice.

Between the sky and the assembly, a cloud of red and black banners unfurled, fluttering in time to the trumpet blasts. The expectation of the gathering had reached a feverish pitch, exactly the right moment for their object of worship to appear.

As if controlled by a single switch, all light and sound vanished. The arena was plunged into absolute blackness and total stillness with such suddenness that thousands believed they had been struck both deaf and blind in that instant.

And then . . . a single spotlight reached out from the back of the stadium, stabbing the highest podium. As if by magic, the lectern was now occupied by the stern, brooding figure of Adolf Hitler.

Hitler extended his arm and swept a salute across the crowd. *Sieg Heil* burst from a hundred thousand throats, repeating and reechoing until equal in volume to the now silent trumpets and drums.

At last the Führer motioned for silence and the ecstatic adoration died away. He then began to speak. Angry denunciations of the democracies flowed from the Führer in an unchecked stream. The hundred thousand Nazi party members hearing him speak in person were ready to march against Western Europe at that very moment if Hitler so ordered.

"We are about to enter the most decisive year in German history. In 1940, the Jewish capitalistic world wants to destroy us. I have repeatedly asked France and England for peace. But Jewish reactionary warmongers and their puppets like Winston Churchill are unwilling to cancel their plans to destroy Germany."

Hitler stopped speaking and regarded the audience sternly, with folded arms, like a father who is about to make an unpleasant demand of a child for its own good. "Sacrifices will be required . . . sacrifice of ease . . . sacrifice of comfort . . . sacrifice of personal choice for the greater good of the Reich . . . yes, even sacrifice of blood . . . but we will go on from victory to victory . . . unflinching and unstoppable . . . to secure the rightful place of the German people!"

Thunderous applause greeted these words, as if the speech were concluded, but Hitler had something else to add. He waited patiently for the outpouring of patriotic spirit to subside before speaking again.

Now he addressed them in a more measured tone, the voice of a father who dotes on his children. He called upon their loyalty to him personally, not to their patriotism or devotion to the Reich, but to himself as the living embodiment of the spirit of Germany. "You see me before you tonight,

uniformed as your Führer . . . not in the simple garb of Citizen Hitler
. . . not in the trappings of state, such as Chancellor Hitler would wear
. . . but as your Supreme Commander . . . to lead you ever forward,
until final victory is achieved! I pledge this to you: you shall not see me in
any other form than this until our goal is reached—Germany everywhere
triumphant and all its foes crushed!"

The *Sieg Heils* reverberated. The tide of emotion burst out of the stadium
and echoed over the loudspeakers in the street. The revelers barely raised
their heads to acknowledge the racket. Like people who lived near a train
track, they had learned to ignore the predictable clamor and were even
comfortable with it.

Unaware of the lethargy of the general populace toward his oration, Hitler
acknowledged the accolades with humbly bowed head, as if in deep reflection, then he turned and made his way down from the high platform.

And yet, a closer look revealed that not every arm in the Sports Palast was
raised in praise of der Führer. Among the rank of dignitaries gathered at the
foot of the stage were the uniformed generals and officers of the the Wehrmacht. They exchanged looks with one another. Their expressions spoke
volumes without uttering a word. They had warned Hitler not to press his
luck. Poland was one thing. France was quite another. Russia had attacked
Finland with Hitler's blessings and was now was taking a beating from the
cold and the Finnish army. German resources could be stretched only so far.
Why not quit while they were ahead?

This was the hope of the German High Command as the bells tolled the
coming of 1940.

✤   ✤   ✤

Horst stood as the Nazi party dignitaries marched out. He marked the
thinly veiled expressions of disgust as Himmler and Heydrich and Goebbels
passed the officers of the High Command. Admiral Canaris, Chief of Military Intelligence, was well known for his disapproval of Gestapo and SS
tactics. A man small of stature, but of great heart, Canaris raised his hand for
an instant as if in heil and then he wiped his nose instead.

Located four rows behind the distinguished group of generals, Horst kept
his gaze locked on them. Men of true valor, these few represented all of the
Fatherland to Horst: von Bock, von Brauchitsch, Canaris . . . for these
brave men, Horst would walk through the fire of hell itself. Each of them
was under suspicion by the Gestapo. Each was monitored and scrutinized by
the inner circle of Hitler's black-shirted elite. And yet they attended the
speech tonight. They prepared their troops for battle. They listened silently
to the rantings of the madman. They stood at attention when he and his
minions passed. And if the order came to "sacrifice," they would do as

commanded. But their faces spoke volumes about their contempt for the tyrant who now controlled Germany. Were they holding on, hoping for some chance to take the nation back?

This remote possibility seemed real to Horst tonight as he observed their subdued behavior. They filed out as a group, leaving junior officers like Horst to brave the massive crowd inching for the exits. Horst craned his neck, searching for the tribe of foreign press who always sat in a reserved section near the front.

He spotted them and fought his way toward them against the current. There were dozens wearing press badges issued by the Ministry of Propaganda, stamped with the approval of the Nazi Reich.

This thought halted Horst in his tracks for a moment as he moved toward a small cluster whose American accents penetrated the rumble of retreating voices. What if Bill Cooper, the American AP journalist, was a man who favored the Nazi policies? There were such political abberations among the foreign press, Horst knew. Many actually approved of Hitler's conduct of racial oppression and conquest. As if in confirmation of his fear, Horst noticed the Englishman, William Joyce, who broadcast German propaganda to England under the name of Lord Haw-Haw. He was laughing and engaged in animated conversation with a young man wearing the badge of a Belgian journalist.

Horst pressed on.

"I am looking for an American," he ventured to a thin, stoop-shouldered man with a balding head and thick glasses. "Bill Cooper."

The man squinted with amusement at Horst's uniform and pointed to where a small, round man in a dark suit chatted at the foot of the podium with an American photographer.

The aisles were clearing. The noise had quieted down.

Horst approached Bill Cooper, who looked something like the round monk on a Munich beer stein. The men fell silent when Horst appeared, as though his uniform had taken the humor out of their private joke.

"Herr Cooper?" Horst ventured.

Cooper turned unsmiling to face him. There was a flash of curiosity in his eyes, but this was tempered by caution.

"Ja. Ich bin Cooper." His German was quite good, but Horst felt uncomfortable using his native tongue here.

"Mister Cooper," Horst began again. "We should speak English."

"Sure," Cooper shrugged and then shook hands in farewell to the photographer, who said he planned to get good and drunk tonight and wanted to get started.

"Mister Cooper," Horst lowered his voice and looked away. "I was trying to reach Josephine Marlow."

A moment of recognition and then Cooper's cautiousness erupted into curiosity. "You're the guy who telephoned." He said this too loudly and then, catching the look of fear on Horst's face, lowered his voice. "Sorry. How can I help?"

"I have something for Fräulein Marlow. She was in Warsaw."

"Right. Barely got out, thanks to the efficiency of your army." There was an edge of bitterness in the comment. This was a good sign.

Horst continued. "I have recently been in Warsaw. I have a message for her. From the priest at St. John's Cathedral."

"From her priest?" Cooper seemed pleased. "She talked about him. I thought he would be dead by now."

Horst leveled his gaze on Cooper. "Not yet. But it cannot be long. Please, Mister Cooper. Can you take a message to Fräulein Marlow? I must trust you in this . . ."

Cooper looked over his shoulder instinctively, as if he felt the probing eyes of the Gestapo on his back. "I'll see her in Paris next month."

"A month?"

"That's the best I can offer. You know the rules. I'll see her face to face, and that's the only way to carry a message out of Germany these days."

Horst nodded in agreement. What choice did he have? Katrina could manage for a while longer. There was no hope but this.

And so, in the shadow of the Führer's podium, Horst told what he had seen at the Cathedral of St. John—the doomed children and the one child. Cooper listened intently as the stadium fell silent and the last of the crowd dissipated into the streets. Walking slowly out of the arena, Horst explained to Cooper about Josephine Marlow and the plan of the little priest in Warsaw.

✤   ✤   ✤

Madame Rose was a kind person. She noticed things. Like the fact that Marie squinted at everything, lost her shoes and socks regularly, and could not read letters on the blackboard.

The sisters arranged for Marie to be examined by an oculist and get a free pair of glasses to wear. Now she could see everything! Blades of grass and minutiae of every description became objects of wonder! She seemed almost intelligent at times. This surprised Jerome very much.

The gift of Marie's miraculous vision was paid for by the American rich man named Dupont who stayed at the Ritz Hotel. Mr. Dupont had met Madame Rose by accident when he was lost and looking for St. Chapelle. She cheerfully guided him to the holy chapel of St. Louis and personally conducted him through the jewel-like building. "We have a child in our orphanage who simply cannot see anything but the colors of these exquisite stained glass windows," she told Mr. Dupont. "And we do not have the funds to get her glasses."

Her assistance, in the end, cost Mr. Dupont a pretty penny, Madame Rose later told her sister. By the time the tour was finished, he had agreed to donate Marie's eyeglasses as well as other items. New shoes were ordered for everyone, a necessity since there were so many more children now at la Huchette.

Jerome considered that if Madame Rose had not been working on the side of Heaven she might have made an excellent escroc—a con man.

All the new shoes arrived in boxes brought on a delivery van. Children lined up and were allowed to try them on and chose whatever pair they liked.

It was this great occasion which made Jerome believe that, if there was a God, Jerome would want God to be something like Madame Rose . . .

There were five boys at la Huchette who were in wheelchairs. Jerome was allowed to guide the chair of Henri whenever they went on outings. Because of this he had become good friends with Henri, who was ten years old and very bright.

On the day the shoe truck arrived, Henri was in an unhappy mood. He stayed in his room and told Jerome not to bother him because the present from Monsieur Dupont was not meant for boys who could not walk. Henri pointed to his brown leather shoes. They did not have even one scuff mark, and Henri said he had owned them for a long time.

"I used to wear out lots of shoes," he said. "My mother was always saying she never saw a boy wear the sole off the way I did. I could run faster than any boy in Kroulouse before I got sick."

It was difficult to know how to answer. Jerome had never imagined what it must be like to be able to run one day and then be stuck in a wicker chair with wheels.

Madame Rose came in.

"Henri! We have been looking for you! Is your tire flat?"

"Not my tire." His chin went down.

"Are you out of gas?"

"No."

"Well, then! You are missing the party."

"It is not for someone like me." He pointed to the clean, unmarked leather.

She said the American word "Fiddlesticks!" She stuck her lower lip out in a pout and grabbed the handles of the wicker chair. She made the sound of an engine revving up and tilted Henri back almost to the ground before she roared out of the building with him.

Among the boxes and boxes of wingtips and oxfords and patent leather were seven boxes bigger than the rest. Five for the boys in the chairs and two for the boys who walked with crutches.

"Riding boots." The old woman raised her chin and snapped her fingers, and the gates of Rue du la Huchette swung open.

A great long-legged bay horse stepped in beneath the arch. On his back was a tall, handsome Frenchman dressed in the old fashioned uniform of a cavalry officer from the last war. His chest glittered with medals. The iron shoes of the horse flashed sparks on the cobbles. The rider pulled his animal up in front of the rank of wheelchairs.

On cue the animal bowed before them, executing the courbette.

The children gasped and applauded. The officer doffed his hat. It was then that Jerome recognized the man. Jerome had seen him only last Armistice Day as he led the parade on this very horse! He was the great hero François Monceau, who had lost both his legs fighting the Boches in the last war! This was an amazing thing.

The officer saluted, then rapped his knuckles loudly on his wooden legs. The little girls shrank back in horror. "Gentlemen," Monceau said, "Madame Rose has asked that I come here today to teach you a few fundamentals of horsemanship. Rule one is that you must always wear proper footgear before riding. Ah! Yes. I see you have fine boots. Well then, you are almost ready. Rule two is that you must never be afraid. And rule three is that no matter what circumstance befalls you, you must never, never, give up."

The rest of the afternoon was spent with the hero of France riding up and down la Huchette. The children held on behind him. Sometimes two or three at once. Jerome was on the very tail and did not much like it. He broke rules two and three instantly. At the end of the lane he slid off and walked home.

But there was Henri and the other Special Ones, as Madame Rose called them. They wore their new riding boots and rode just in front of the brave French cavalry officer who had much less in the way of legs than they had.

The experience cheered Henri up considerably. He began to believe rules two and three were possible even for a boy in a wicker chair with wheels. Polishing his boots every day, he made plans to own his own horse after he invented something and became rich.

After that first day, the officer rode by at least once a week to retrieve a mysterious package from the two sisters. He often gave the residents of la Huchette rides and let them pet the nose of his horse, Alexander. He said it made him happy to do so.

The question was asked, where did Madame Rose meet this famous fellow?

She had been washing his shirts for years.

FORTY-THREE

When Paul Chardon unrolled the map on his office desk, the three senior cadet captains found themselves looking at a detailed chart of the Lys River of the École de Cavalerie and the immediate area around the school.

"More war games, Captain?" Gaston inquired in a tired voice. "With respect, sir, my command is exhausted from just juggling their studies, the care of the horses, and the demands of Miss Mitchell."

Paul said with exasperation, "Gaston, the military education at a military school does not stop because you are tired, overworked, or underappreciated!"

Gaston exchanged questioning looks with Sepp and Raymond. The fictitious defense of the school and the banks of the stream had been enacted every year that the boys had attended.

It was said that the same simulation had occurred every year since the school's founding, except 1918, when it became actual fact. In that last year of the Great War, the Kaiser's forces had made a push toward the sea. A Herculean effort by the Allies had stopped them near that very spot, but only after the cadets had been evacuated.

The same thought struck all three student officers at the same moment. What if history repeated itself and the École was again in the path of the Germans?

Paul read their minds. "I am not saying that it will come to that, but it is possible. Certainly an invading army would want to seize the Channel ports, and Lys is right on one probable line of advance. My intent is to develop the plans for defending this sector, so that the Regular Army will have them to study should the need arise."

Gaston, whose interest had been sparked by the thought that the war might be coming to him, looked crestfallen. "We practice the resistance for someone else to perform?"

Paul almost gave an angry retort but caught himself and addressed the three boys in a kindly tone. "We all have a role to play in defending France," he said. "What does it matter if you actually fire the shots, so long as the strategy we have worked out succeeds?" He looked around at the faces, getting a ready smile from Raymond, a quick understanding nod from Sepp, and a grudging squint from Gaston.

"Look now," he said, directing their attention back to the map. "I have already made unit assignments, and it will be your duties to work out the detailed plans. Gaston, to you is given the area of most immediate danger—the direct assault on the town from across the river. You must develop the defense of the bridges and their demolition if opposition is no longer possible."

The fact that Gaston had no comment to make convinced Paul that he had gotten through to him about the seriousness of the responsibility. Besides, Paul remembered, in the history of the school, no war games had ever included demolishing the bridges; no one ever built a retreat into their plans.

The artillery barrage at the Maginot was called the "The Salute Matins," because every dawn about the time of morning prayers, the heavies began to murmur explosively on the wind.

The booming was distant and mellow. Mac commented that they were probably howitzers, judging from the dullness of the reverberating echo. Mac and Murphy felt no urge to flop out of the car and dive for cover.

There was no other sound or sight of activity along the line. The highway passed between two green mushroom turrets on the hilltop that identified strongpoints of the fortifications. Mac and Murphy drove onto a narrow plateau in the highlands of the Moselle River. From there they could plainly see the muddy yellow military roads that branched off into the openings of Maginot tunnels. At each entrance were gates painted like barber poles that indicated no unauthorized visitors were allowed. All around were piles of rusted metal and dumps of weathered concrete left over from the construction of this new Wall of China. Beyond the bastions was a thicket of tank traps. Known as "asparagus patches" because they sprouted up in stalks, these were painted a harmonious green to match the landscape. But there was no sign of life, no indication that anyone was really inside the turrets or beneath the mushroom buttons which topped the hills.

"It's too cold for them to be out," Murphy shuddered in the car. "It's a whole lot better than the last war when our guys were left to shiver in the rain, isn't it?"

They left the restricted military area and drove on along the Thionville highway. Coming to a control point, Mac geared down and moved slowly through a barbed-wire chicane. A surly French lieutenant with a stubby Hitler-fashion moustache examined their passes as if they were spies.

Fortunately, the lieutenant was too wet and cold to argue. He waved them on to the muddy barrier of Evrange, their last stop before crossing into neutral Luxembourg.

The rain poured down. The road leading to the frontier came to a stop at a lonely concrete barrier. A single guard manned the sandbag-enfolded blockade. Sloppy spirals of concertina wire ambled off down the hill.

It was Mac who first commented on the carelessness of this outpost. The Maginot simply stopped somewhere back down the line. It was as if no one in the French government imagined that the Germans might possibly come through little Luxembourg to cross the border.

"Is this it?" Mac said incredulously.

Murphy nodded. "And it's pretty much the same all the way along the Belgian border too. I asked Prime Minister Daladier's assistant why the Maginot only went part way along the frontier. He told me that the French didn't want to insult the Belgians, didn't want the Belgians to think that France didn't trust *them*. The nation of Belgium is the rest of France's line of defense. Get it?"

Mac rolled his eyes and shook his head in frustration. It was as if the minds of French politicians were also made of concrete.

A man in a heavy oilskin coat stepped out of the door of the customs shack and crooked his finger at Mac and Murphy. Would they please enter the office? And would they bring their luggage?

It was at this outpost that France had stationed her toughest three officials. Perhaps it was believed that if the German Army breached Belgium and Luxembourg, the French customs officials would stop them at the border. Perhaps it was true.

These three men were dressed in blue serge uniforms trimmed in silver braid. Before the war, their kind had made the lives of tourists miserable at every entrance and exit of France. Now, with a war on, they exercised their duty with a double dose of diligence. They refined the harassment of tourists to high art. Their lives were dedicated to increasing the mental anguish of every traveler to a level matching the Queen's court officials in *Alice in Wonderland.*

Stained moustaches drooped over teeth yellowed by smoke from years of confiscated tobacco. And this trio knew well how to strip a suitcase to the lining in search of smuggled chocolates.

As the shadows of afternoon lengthened, they provided Mac and Murphy with in-triplicate forms. Private life, military status, reasons for traveling to a neutral nation were all scrutinized. Authority for leaving France, the right to drive an automobile, and the permit to take petrol out of the country all received careful examination.

Sharp-eyed from years of searching for illegal cigars and contraband liquors, the eldest of the officials caught a flaw in the documents of Mac and Murphy.

"You will notice that your papers state that you are to leave France by the route of Sierck. This is the gateway of Evrange. That is not in order."

"There is a slight battle in Sierck," Murphy offered.

The customs official looked stunned. "Is that so? And how do you know this, Monsieur?"

"We were turned back and unable to enter Sierck," Mac explained.

The officials conferred. "This is military information which you ought not to have, Messieurs. Yet you expect to be allowed to pass out of France and into a neutral nation where the enemy also has access?"

The Queen from *Alice* lurked in Mac's mind. At any moment he expected them to begin shouting, *"Off with their heads!"* He drew himself up and addressed the clerk as "Chief," in hopes of using flattery to turn the tide. "If the French are fighting the Germans at Sierck, then surely the Germans know it very well and the information is no longer a military secret."

It made sense. Did it not?

Mac and Murphy were taken to a small anteroom heated by a pot-bellied stove. The door was shut and the lock turned. There they baked slowly for three hours while the customs officials, bastions of the gates of France, checked their story.

"I have telephoned Paris. Your papers are now in order."

At last they were set free with a slight apology. They had to repack their clothes and reinsert the insoles of their shoes. The cuffs and sleeves of their top coats had been carefully slit. They were given the name of a tailor in Luxembourg.

It was after dark when they entered the Grand Duchy of Luxembourg. They were tired and almost convinced that at the French outpost of Evrange perhaps the Germans would not pass after all. At least not easily.

❧   ❧   ❧

Perhaps the best view of the war was in the Luxembourg village of Remich, on the terrace of the Hôtel Bellevue. The Bellevue was owned by a former vaudeville performer named Lucien Klopp. After the last war, Klopp had retired from the London stage for peace and quiet. The quaint establishment he managed was in the area known as Luxembourg Corners, where a point of the Grand Duchy jutted out to touch the border of France and Germany.

Klopp's terrace looked out over a valley so picturesque it might have been lifted from a fairy tale. An ancient castle with turrets, moat, and drawbridge topped a ridge on the left. Vineyards for creating sweet Moselle wine climbed the blueish hills. Along the river in both directions clustered little white villages surrounded perfect white church spires rising against the cloud-studded sky.

The river wound gently in the sunlight, a shining ribbon of light, before it left Luxembourg and flowed away. Beyond the border of the neutral country, the Moselle River divided France and Germany. From Klopp's patio, tourists could see the beginning of the purple mass of the Maginot fortresses and the Siegfried Line across from it in Germany.

With the aid of binoculars the batteries of both sides were plainly visible: barbed wire, earthworks, and machine-gun studded pillboxes. Right there, on display from the peaceful promenade, was The War.

Mac and Murphy came out onto the terrace. "They've taken an intermission," said Larry Beavers of *The Post*.

Four other newsmen leaned on a stone wall, looking off to where the Schengen bridge crossed the wide blue river.

Mac could hear birds chirping in the cleft of the hill. He saw no artillery, no smoke. The peace of little Remich was tangible.

Bill Cooper, the stout, round-faced AP correspondent from Berlin turned his field glasses skyward. "You guys missed it. We had five airplanes up there a while ago. Two of Hitler's and three of Chamberlain's. Nothing happening now, though."

Murphy laughed and patted Bill on the shoulder. "So, Bill! Things must be boring in Berlin too, huh?"

"Deadly dull. The Führer's off in Bavaria with his band of Merry Men. If you ask me, I'd say everybody's about to forget about this war business and sign an armistice. Any takers?"

There were a few comments about the lack of news. Everyone standing in Klopp's garden had come here hoping to pick up at least a small story. Hôtel Bellevue had ringside seats, but the bout appeared to be called on account of weather.

"It's too cold to fight," Murphy shuddered, pulling up the collar of his coat. "It's too cold to stand here and wait." He retreated sullenly into the drafty breakfast room of the Bellevue.

Mac guessed that about now John Murphy was longing for foggy old London town and his wife sitting by the fire. The war, the separation, and the evacuation were turning out to be a lot of bunk. Not one bomb had fallen on London, and yet Murphy had endured being apart from his family for months. The strain on this normally phlegmatic guy was definitely show-ing . . . now all the trouble of crossing from France into Luxembourg with probably nothing to show for it but days of groggy conversation with a bunch of rheumy-eyed journalists.

Bill Cooper cocked his head slightly and peered at Mac with interest. "Hey, Mac! Weren't you . . . Are you still seeing Danny Marlow's widow?"

"Josie? Occasionally I see her." Mac shifted uncomfortably at the question. He could have said that he wanted to see her more than anything in his life, but he hoped Cooper would move on to other topics.

"Where is she?" Cooper looked around Mac's shoulder as if expecting Josephine Marlow to stroll out onto the terrace.

"Paris." Mac did not add that she was most likely breakfasting with a French colonel.

"You're going back to Paris?"

"I might as well. There's no war here."

Cooper's round, ruddy face lit up. He lowered his voice. "Listen, I was supposed to pass along an important message to her, from a German Wehrmacht officer I met in Berlin. He brought something out of Poland for her . . . from that priest she's so fond of. I thought I was going to be in Paris to give her the tale in person, but my kindhearted little Nazi press officer advises me that if I go to France I may not be allowed back into dear old Deutschland. And this isn't something you can put in a letter. The French authorities in the Anastasie would pounce on it like ducks on a bug. You know?" Cooper was correct about the French postal service. The censors had been named after Saint Anastasie, the woman who had her tongue cut out on orders of the Emperor Diocletian. The tongue of every letter which entered or left France these days was cut out, leaving the reader to wonder just what it was that the original document meant to say. Important matters like this could not be trusted to good fortune and the mails.

Cooper checked over his shoulder, as if Klopp's terrace might also be a hangout for Gestapo spies. He was right to be concerned. Luxembourg, Holland, and Belgium were packed with German "tourists" these days, many of whom had more sinister reasons for traveling in the neutral nations than sightseeing.

Cooper took Mac by the arm and led him to a path which wound down the face of the cliff toward the river. Out of range of prying ears he told Mac about the German major, the Catholic priest from Warsaw, and an old rabbi in Palestine. At last he opened his wallet and removed a photograph of a small baby. A half-smile flicked across his face. "This year in Jerusalem," he said.

❋   ❋   ❋

War games at the École de Cavalerie were like an elaborate contest of King of the Mountain. For the exercise, two-thirds of the cadets were to play the part of the German army. One third, under the command of Paul Chardon, were to defend the school and the north bank of the Lys River as part of an examination in military strategy. But was it only a game?

The town of Lys, little more than a mile wide along the river of the same name, narrowed to a point as it climbed the hill north of the stream and ended against the military school.

From a knoll above the village and the river, Paul pored over a topographical map of the area which showed each point of defense in the battle that had taken place here during the last war. Officer Cadet Raymond was at his side.

"Our responsibility," Paul said, "extends from the bridge at Rozier downstream to a mile upstream where the banks are too steep for armored vehicles to climb out."

The chart showed the island in the middle of the river, over which the main road into Lys passed. Connected to both shores by bridges, the island was the first line of defense against attack. "Gaston is planning the protection of the island," Paul said, "and Sepp will figure the coverage for the banks of the stream in front of the town."

"And me?" Raymond asked, knowing that there was a reason why his assignment had been saved to last.

Paul reflected a moment. "This is just for practice," he said. "You understand that it will probably never be needed, and certainly would never involve you actually in the defense."

Raymond nodded.

Paul stabbed his finger on the downstream crossing of the Lys, five miles away from the school. "This bridge must also be defended," he said. "But if a withdrawal had to be made, it is a long way back. For that reason, I want your plan to include the horses. We will need our vehicles elsewhere, but I do not want to leave you . . . the defender . . . without a means of escape."

Raymond looked Paul in the eye. The young man was the finest horseman at the school. The assignment was an honor. "Understood," the cadet replied as Paul struck out to inspect the positions of Sepp and Gaston.

Halfway down the hill toward the river, Paul and Raymond spotted Sepp with four younger cadets of his command. They were outside the church of St. Sebastian and embroiled in an argument with Father Perrin and the mayor, Jacques Fontain.

"But Father," Sepp appealed, "we must climb the bell tower of the church in order to see across the river."

"You are spotting landmarks on the far bank to use for range finding," complained the priest. "I forbid it."

"I too forbid it," said the mayor, an elderly man who shook his cane in Sepp's face. "I will not have Lys turned into a battleground." Then spotting Paul's approach, the frail, bent man said angrily, "You are the cause of this, Chardon!"

"I did not start the war," Paul defended.

"No, but you will bring it here," the mayor replied.

"It is only an exercise in strategy. Like every other year," Paul soothed. "A way of preparing the cadets for some future situation."

"Lys wishes no future situations with the Boche. Ever," spat the mayor.

"Of course. Certainly. Only for military theory, you see. What would you have our cadets do? Welcome the Boche with open arms? Invite them to take all the wounded in the hospital as prisoners?"

The mayor appeared to think that over. Was this really just the game of a few hundred students at the École? "It is a British hospital," he said. Even Father Perrin looked shocked at the mayor's statement.

Paul stepped between the mayor and the cadets. "We are simply making a study of how the town can be defended if need be. None of us wants . . . or expects . . . that to happen. But you remember 1918, Jacques. Should we remain unprepared?"

The mayor fell silent. "No," he said at last. "I thought we taught the Boche a lesson when they called here twenty years ago, but perhaps they are stupid and will try again."

Sepp and his group gained entry to the church tower, and Paul and Raymond continued across the stone bridge to the island. Gaston, sounding like a drill sergeant, barked orders to a dozen subordinates about the placement of the school's two anti-tank guns. "One here to cover the bridge," he said. "The other further back to guard against the loss of the first."

"How is it progressing?" Paul inquired quietly.

Gaston jumped at the sound of his commander's voice. "I did not see you coming." He thumped his broad chest in a gesture of relief.

"It is a good thing we are not Germans, Gaston," Raymond teased and then ducked as Gaston cuffed him.

"All right then." Paul broke up the tussle. "Your situation, Gaston, if you please."

"Hardly enough heavy weapons. Any chance of adding tanks or artillery to this plan?"

"Nothing we can count on."

"What about the 75mm piece up at the schoolyard?"

Raymond laughed. "You mean the one Colonel Larousse was afraid to fire even as a signal gun for fear it would blow up?"

"You are doing fine work, Gaston," Paul encouraged. "Keep it up. Take good notes. If the enemy were to advance this far their defeat might depend on the information we could supply to our army."

"Captain," Gaston said as Paul turned to leave. "According to the Principles of Modern Warfare, how many defenders are required to guard this length of river?"

Paul thought a moment. "Fifteen thousand," he said, "provided they have adequate artillery support."

"And how many cadets remain at the school?"

"Nine hundred," Paul replied.

⚜ ⚜ ⚜

The engine that would carry John Murphy to the coast of Belgium chuffed impatiently beneath the ornate train shed of the Luxembourg City terminal. Murphy was just as impatient to be on his way back to London.

Mac extended his hand in farewell. "Kiss Elisa and the kids for me."

"Her wire says she'll be waiting at Victoria Station when I get there." Murphy's eyes were alive with anticipation. "I may take a few days off. It's been four months." He glanced at his watch as if even the minutes were too long to wait now.

"I envy you," Mac said, and he meant it. "Someone to come home to."

"Well, then? Get busy. I told you what Trump said. He's ready to open a new section: TENS Newsreel in London. He needs a good man to head it up. Why not?"

"I'm not cut out for a desk job. Anyway, Jo is otherwise occupied with that French colonel from what the rumor mill says. Blake at Paris AP says she's with him every day."

"That might be because you're not around."

"Five months ago I would've believed it . . . before Warsaw. She might've said yes if I'd had the sense to stay put, gotten a job editing other people's stuff. But I didn't. And it's too late."

"Some American you are, Mac!" Murphy laughed and thumped him on the shoulder. "Gonna let the competition win by default, huh? Just roll over and play dead?"

"My real competition was with a guy who's already dead. I couldn't win against Saint Danny. She already had his memory bronzed when I came along. No matter that her memory has nothing to do with reality. You know, Murphy, Marlow was my friend, but he was a genuine bum when it came to Jo. So what is it with these women? Attracted to guys with all the loyalty of a lone bull in pasture of Jersey heifers. So now she takes up with this colonel, in his fancy dress uniform, and a list of female conquests as long as my arm . . . French accent . . . shiny boots and gold braid. How can a guy fight that?"

Murphy shrugged. "Better get yourself a uniform and boots and take her to lunch. You know what they say about love and war."

Mac waved his hand in front of his face, as if the thought was a fly to be brushed away. "Never mind love. It'll kill me for sure. All I care about right now is the war. It's safer. Talk to Churchill for me when you get back to London, will you Murphy? See if you can't get me and my camera on a Royal Navy ship."

✤ ✤ ✤

The two large men standing near the serpentine wrought iron of the train station lightpost were in no way remarkable in either looks or actions. To any but a trained observer, the raincoat-clad figures, one in brown and the other in navy blue, would have been indistinguishable from hundreds of other middle-class businessmen.

But Mac was a trained observer. The watchful eye of the camera never captured interesting scenes unless Mac had noticed them first. And these two men, both wearing fedoras pulled low across their foreheads, were interesting. Mac was certain that they rode the tram to the train depot with him and Murphy. But they had not boarded a train themselves, and now, after Murphy's express had pulled out, they were still lounging in apparently idle conversation.

Mac's mind flashed back to the destruction of his hotel room. He still couldn't fathom the reason for the vandalism, but these two gave him a clue as to the identity of the criminals. This pair had Gestapo written all over them. Mac toyed with the idea of going straight up to them and demanding that they pay for his busted camera. Better to verify his suspicions first, though; even if they were German agents, they might not be interested in him. And if they weren't, it was better to leave it that way.

One way to check. Mac turned sharply and boarded the tram that waited to return to the center of the city. Sure enough, when Mac seated himself and looked out the window, he saw that the conversation had come to an abrupt halt and the two men were hurrying toward the tram.

Just as the first of the two, dark-eyed with a prominent nose, entered the car, Mac stood up and pushed past, back onto the sidewalk. "Changed my mind," he said to the conductor. "Sorry."

Mac wanted to see how they would handle this. For both to get out again right behind him would be suspicious to a blind man. Both figures took a seat. The one nearest the window had a heavily jowled face which he pointed everywhere in the tram—ceiling, walls, floor—everywhere except out the window at Mac. The tram pulled out.

Knowing that he would now recognize both sets of features again wherever he next saw them, Mac's need now was for alternate transportation back to his hotel. No taxis presented themselves, and when the next tram pulled up, Mac boarded it.

There were no stops between the Gare Centrale and the ancient battlements that towered over the Petrusse River. The coach slowed as it crossed the viaduct that rose on long spindly iron legs over the chasm. The heights of the rock wall were shrouded in mist, but eventually the coach crossed the ramparts of the medieval fortifications.

At the stop above the cliff face, Mac recognized his mistake. The man with the prominent beak had gotten off the earlier coach and was waiting in the fine rain. The last thing Mac wanted was to lead these thugs to his hotel and risk another spree of destruction, so he tried to make the train station trick work again. Mac waited until the big-nosed man seated himself and the tram door had closed, then popped up and said apologetically that he had almost missed his stop and needed to be let off.

The raincoated figure stood and also demanded to get out. At the now deserted tram stop, Mac found himself face to face with his pursuer.

"I don't know what you want," Mac said, "but you are one ugly customer."

"Was ist?" replied the figure, whose wide-mouthed grin revealed that he was missing his front teeth. "Come now, Mister McGrath. There is no need to be uncooperative. We just want to speak with you about a matter of great importance. You will come with me." The last sentence was punctuated by the sudden appearance of a small Mauser pistol from the raincoat pocket.

Mac's protest died unspoken and he raised his hands. "There is no need for that." A casual wave of the pistol accompanied the instruction. "Please walk on slowly, a pace ahead of me. And you will not try to run. Having your knee destroyed would be very unpleasant for you, and I could scarcely miss at this range."

"What do you want?"

"All in good time."

Turning aside from the tram line, they paced the damp stones of the walk that skirted the edge of the precipice. Sheer rock walls fell away into the depths of the narrow gorge. The slender path followed the line of the ancient fortifications, which were themselves carved out of the solid rock of the cliff.

It was a very lonely spot. There were no others out walking on the cold and damp day, and they had come away from the tracks so that a screen of brush blocked the view. "That is far enough," the man said.

"Look, what's this all about? I know you're Gestapo, but I don't know why you want me. And why'd you tear up my room in Paris?"

The thickset agent smiled his gap-toothed grin, but said nothing. He gestured for Mac to back up until his legs were against the rain-streaked boulders of the parapet.

"Is this just for fun? 'Cause I got news for you, pal. I'm an American journalist. My country won't like you strongarming its citizens. Your boss won't be happy either."

"Enough chatter! Where is he?"

"Where is who?"

The German agent lunged with his pistol hand, striking Mac across the side of the face with the barrel. Mac's head snapped back, and the skin over his cheekbone split. Clenching his fists, Mac crouched into a fighting stance. But another motion of the pistol forced him to relax and drop his hands again. A trickle of blood ran along the line of Mac's jaw and dripped onto the paving stones.

The German leaned close. He put the muzzle of the Mauser under Mac's chin, lifting Mac up on his toes. In evil-smelling breath loaded with onions and herring, he said, "Coy is not your style, Herr McGrath. We know you were with Lewinski getting out of Poland. Where is he now?"

"Wait, hold on. Let me think." Mac's mind was racing. Where had he heard that name? He really did not know what this thug was asking about. But he couldn't say that. The image of the flight from Warsaw scrolled itself in Mac's mind. He saw a replay of Ambassador Biddle and the staff people and a weird character in a gas mask. "Do you mean the strange duck who wears the gas mask and has the curly red hair?"

"Of course! That's Lewinski!" A backhand rake of the pistol barrel across Mac's mouth burst his lip open and knocked him to his knees. "Quit stalling! Where is he?"

Now what? Mac could not say that he didn't know this Lewinski character's whereabouts, even though he didn't. He'd never be believed. "Yeah, sure. I know where he is. He's in . . . Paris," he said, naming the first city that popped into his head.

The Gestapo agent hefted the pistol as if weighing it. "So, you are telling the truth? Lying to us can cause great pain."

"So what do we do now? Stay here until the other bully boy runs over to check my story? Can I get up?"

The dark eyes stared down the bulbous nose and into Mac's bloody face. He put the pistol back in his coat. "Of course," he said, extending his hand to help Mac get up. Mac knocked the offer away and unsteadily rose to his feet. "There's just one problem."

"Yeah? What's that?"

The burly man suddenly grabbed Mac by the neck and his belt. He hoisted the cameraman onto the wall and pushed his head downward over the dropoff. "The problem is, I don't believe you. You would never give away a secret as vital as Enigma so lightly. Where is he really?"

Mac was truly terrified. Blood from the cut on his cheek was now running down into his eye. And below Mac's eye was a cloud that concealed a two hundred foot drop. "I really don't know. Don't you think I'd tell you if I did?" he gasped.

"Probably," the agent grunted, and he momentarily relaxed his grip.

It was the opening Mac needed. His hands, which had been down by his waist, burst apart the grasp. Mac kicked the man in the midsection, knocking him back a pace. But before Mac could get clear of the wall, the Gestapo thug charged in again, anxious to get his hands back on Mac's neck.

The agent's damp shoe slipped on a loose rock underfoot, turning his lunge into an unexpected sprawl. Mac slid down. Grabbing the lapels of the raincoat as he dropped, Mac pulled upward as hard as he could.

With a startled cry that turned into a long-drawn-out scream, the Gestapo agent plunged over the edge of the precipice, hurtling into the canyon. The shriek made less noise than the sirens of the Stukas Mac had heard in Poland, and stopped abruptly.

Mac picked himself up slowly, wiping the blood from his cheek and lip. He resisted the desire to see where the man had hit. Instead he turned his thoughts to a more immediate problem: what to do now.

If he went to the authorities, what would he say? How could he explain that he had just killed a Gestapo agent who had been threatening him over some secret that Mac didn't have? What was that all about, anyway? And what about the guy's partner? Where was he?

In the end, Mac slipped into his hotel through a side door and checked out immediately to return to Paris. A sympathetic clerk exclaimed over the condition of his face. "Yeah, well, those slippery rocks are dangerous sometimes," he said.

FORTY-FOUR

Josie had spent the night in the bomb shelter beneath the Foyer International after two German bombers had flown lazily over Paris just to have a look at the Eiffel Tower. No air raid alarm sounded, no bombs dropped, but the harsh crack of antiaircraft fire erupted from eager batteries across the city. It was a French shell which rained down near the Metro in the Montmartre District. Two men were killed and one woman suffered an amputated leg. After the damage had been done, air raid sirens sounded just before midnight, but there were no enemy planes overhead.

The morning paper offered no apologies to the families of the Montmartre dead and maimed, nor for the loss of a night's sleep. The headlines clearly blamed the victims for their own bad luck and offered this word of warning in the headlines of the front page:

Citizens of Paris!
When You Hear the Sound
of Antiaircraft Guns
Go to the Nearest Air Raid Shelter!

Josie had spent the morning at the Ritz Hotel covering a fashion show staged for the benefit of French soldiers. In the hotel, there was no discussion of the incident of the previous night. The lobby of the Ritz bustled with overdressed ladies eyeing the latest fashions in the shop windows. Nearly every one of the shoppers wore a tricolored ribbon with a paper rose pinned to the lapel. This was a sign that they supported the drive to beautify the Maginot Line for the soldiers of France by planting rose bushes at the front. The explosion near the Metro did not concern them at all. After all, none of them were the sort who rode the Metro anyway. Limousines were their style, Josie thought, as she passed two women walking their beribboned Pekinese dogs. Something in their manner made Josie believe that these grand dames of society could not imagine a stray shell having the impudence to land anywhere near their domain.

"Did you hear it? It hit just outside the Metro station, my dear."

"But of course! It had the good sense to avoid the Ritz! Can you imagine what a scandal that would have been! What a racket last night. It woke me up, and then I could not get back to sleep."

Josie tucked the newspaper under her arm and passed through the oblivious mob. She took the Metro to meet Mac McGrath at the Café Voltaire on Rue de l'Odeon and noticed that the faces of subway passengers were not smiling and carefree this morning. Who on the train this morning had not recently climbed the steps of the Metro station at Montmartre? Nearly all on board had been there at one time or another. The incident had a sobering effect on the ordinary men and women who could easily imagine themselves in that place when the errant missile hit its mark.

Josie found herself looking up at the patch of blue sky and imagining planes and artillery as she ascended the stairs to the street. She comforted herself with the old adage about lightning never striking twice.

She walked quickly to the café, which was crowded with a mix of professors and political types, who gathered each lunch hour to rehash theories about the war. A blue haze of cigarette smoke hovered over the noisy room. Josie spotted Mac at a small table in the far corner. He wore dark glasses and was miraculously dressed in the uniform of an American Correspondent. He looked very handsome, Josie thought, in spite of a small bandage on his cheek. Mac sipped a glass of wine and looked sullenly out the window at the teeming crowd of pedestrians on the sidewalk.

She was at the table before he noticed her. His smile of greeting was almost guilty, as if he did not want her to suspect that he was brooding about something.

"You made it," he said, regaining his pleasant exterior instantly. "I didn't think you would come."

"I told you I would." She smiled at her reflection in the dark lenses. "Clark Gable in sunglasses."

He raised them enough to reveal that his right eye was nearly swollen shut. "Gable would've fared better. Some drunk in a bistro didn't like Americans. I showed him what a friendly bunch we are." He let the frames slip back into place.

"All the same . . . You look . . . really wonderful, Mac."

He flipped his lapel absently, as if his tidy appearance embarrassed him. "Oh, this. I had to give in."

"What have you done with your tweed coat and your lucky red tie?"

"I've still got them. The war won't last forever, you know."

Same old Mac. The uniform was only a temporary aberration.

"You look swell all the same, even if it won't last."

"I've hitched a ride with the British navy. John Murphy put in a good word with Churchill for me. They're old friends, you know. Murphy and the First Lord of the Admiralty. But I had to get myself a regular uniform, he said. The Brits wouldn't have me on board otherwise. Maybe going to get some real action on film." So he was leaving France. "The sea. That's where the real war is. This whole Maginot thing is . . . well, you know how it is. The Phony War."

"I'm glad you called, Mac."

He put down his wine glass and took her hand. "Are you, Jo? You mean it?" He was too hopeful.

"Yes, really. I wanted to talk to you about something."

"It doesn't sound good already. Why do I always feel this way when I see you? Like I'm fifteen or something?" Mac looked at her with an expression that resembled a sorrowful puppy.

He needed a haircut. He needed someone to look after him like a mother. He was not the navy type. Hadn't he told her that he spent his first, second, and third transatlantic crossings with his head in a bucket?

"You'll do fine," she replied, as if he had already expressed his concern about unending weeks on one of Mister Churchill's big boats.

"We're always saying good-bye, aren't we, Jo?"

"That's the problem all right. Hello and good-bye. I should be flattered, I guess. That you want to see me before you sail away."

He grinned sheepishly. "That's not why I called you."

"Leave me with my illusions, will you?"

"I can't. I saw Bill Cooper in Luxembourg. You remember Coop?"

"Of course. How are things in Berlin?"

"Dull as here unless you're on the Führer's bad list. But Coop has had some contact with a friend of a friend of yours—that priest in Warsaw."

Suddenly charged with energy, Josie knocked Mac's wine glass over, splashing red Bordeaux on his tunic. "Oh no! Mac! Your new clothes!"

He gaped down at the mess and dabbed at it with his napkin. "That's all right. It needed something to break it in." He snapped his fingers at a passing waiter and ordered soda water for the stain and another glass of wine. "As I was saying. Cooper. The priest sent a message through a German Wehrmacht officer. More than a message really." Tapping his temple, he said, "I carried it up here to avoid having it pinched by the Gestapo in Luxembourg or the French Anastasie. Then I wrote it all down for you." He pulled an envelope out of his tunic and placed it between the salt and pepper shakers. "There's this kid. A little Jewish kid. A baby actually. The Polish priest sent him out of Warsaw with this German major. Coop says he's not a

Nazi. A really nice guy, Coop says. So this major has the kid. The priest says you're supposed to go get him."

"Get him? Where?"

"The Reich. Treves."

"In the middle of a war?"

"Not much of a war, Jo, you have to admit. Anyway, it's all there in the envelope. The place. Your instructions. All figured out except the date. That's up to you. You'll have to get papers for the kid."

"Papers?"

"Travel documents."

"Where do I arrange that?"

"This is out of my field of expertise. Neutral American newslady crosses the border in Luxembourg. Grabs kid and scrams back. Happens all the time, doesn't it?"

She picked up the envelope and stared thoughtfully at it. "If the priest says it can be done, I suppose it's that simple."

The moody look returned. "Your Frenchman should be able to help you with the papers. Great for cutting through the red tape, these colonels."

"My Frenchman?"

"Don't play coy, Jo. I know, okay? The guys in the press room at the Continental are taking bets on whether you marry the guy."

"And how did you bet, Mac?"

"I didn't."

"Why not?"

"My daddy taught me never to bet when my own horse is running."

"Thank you for that jewel of wisdom, Mac. I'm sure the meaning will come to me in the middle of the night." Her bouillabaisse arrived. She was not hungry.

Mac poked his smoked salmon with his fork. "If I bet that you marry him and you do, then I win, but I lose."

"What has that got to do with your horse?"

"Never mind. I thought it made sense when I said it. You want to confuse me? The point is, I did not bet, although this may be the sporting event of the season."

She tasted the fish stew. "Why didn't you bet against the proposition?"

"Because. You're ripe as a peach at harvest time. Murphy said so." He mimed the plucking of a peach. "And I'm not the lucky guy beneath the tree. I'm the guy outside the orchard fence. Story of my life. Look but don't touch."

Josie watched as a steamer chugged up river with a load of British soldiers. "Yes." She turned her gaze on him. "Like Danny. Always the observer. Never the guy who gets involved. I've been living like that too, Mac, and I hate it."

"Spend my time binding wounds and I'd have to lay my camera down. That's for medics, nurses, and missionaries. I make my living telling about stuff that happens to other people. I get up every day hoping I'll be there with lots of film when the sky falls in. You, on the other hand? Still the Sunday school teacher from Fort Smith, aren't you? Never got over wanting to make the world a better place."

"I fell into this job when Danny died. But it isn't me, Mac. I can't sit back and just watch the world anymore."

"Is this what you wanted to tell me?"

"Yes."

"There is a possibility of a opening in London . . . Murphy told me about a position with TENS." He put his hand to the bruise on his cheek. "I've been thinking about living a life with a little less edge to it. I admit it. I have been thinking. But I won't get in your way . . . throw a wrench in the works. You love this Frenchman?"

"I . . . maybe."

"Do you love me?"

"I thought I did. I followed you to Warsaw . . . to tell you. But even if you took a job in London." She hesitated. "Would it change anything? About you and me? We're so different, Mac."

"Well, then. I'm not going to hang around Paris and hope. I wasn't going to hang around Paris anyway. Looks like there's going to be an armistice, and I want to get a few clips of the war before it goes away."

They ate in silence. The clatter of dishes and the murmur of other conversations went unnoticed.

"When will you be back?"

"End of May." He took off the glasses. His eye was painfully swollen, and his lip looked puffy too. "You've made up your mind. You're right, I think. I'll always be outside the orchard wall looking in."

❊   ❊   ❊

The dining room in the Adlon Hotel at Number One Unter den Linden in Berlin was full of eminent Wehrmacht officers and Nazi party officials. Even though they outranked everyone else in the room, Heinrich Himmler and Reinhard Heydrich occupied an undistinguished table in a corner.

Himmler was fussing over a plate of noodles in a bland cream sauce, taking small bites and frowning at the plate. "This has too much garlic," he remarked to Heydrich.

Heydrich was halfway through a heaping mound of a fragrantly spicy stew. "How unfortunate, Herr Reichsführer," he consoled. "Why don't you try what I'm having? It's excellent."

The slimly handsome Heydrich was baiting his boss and he knew it.

Himmler had such a delicate stomach that the sight of blood from an underdone steak upset him. It was a dangerous game to play with the mousy little man who was the second most powerful figure in the Reich, but it helped Heydrich's ego. Working for a former fertilizer salesman was tough on Heydrich's self-image.

Heydrich stopped eating to smile broadly at a pair of fräuleins seated across the room who were openly studying him with interest. Heydrich's constant womanizing was another activity of which Himmler did not really approve.

"What progress have you to report in the Lewinski matter?" Himmler asked, knowing exactly how to burst his aide's self-satisfaction.

"We're working on it, Herr Reichsführer," Heydrich pledged, turning his attention back to his meal. As head of the Main Office of Reich Security, Heydrich was under pressure to get results and he knew it. "We are pursuing contacts at all the universities where Lewinski is known to have connections: Oxford, Princeton, Stanford, even the Sorbonne in Paris, although that is most unlikely."

"Does it seem that this investigation is rather slow to produce results?" Himmler said, squaring his sloping shoulders. The Reichsführer SS also knew how to needle an opponent.

"I assure you, Herr Reichsführer, that we are proceeding with the utmost greundlichkeit," Heydrich said. "Thorough in every detail."

"If the secret of Enigma should get out . . ."

"Let me reassure you. Since the code setting changes every day, and the method of establishing the new settings is quite secure, the most that is at risk is that a mind like Lewinski's might unravel one day's code . . . but certainly too slowly to be harmful." He gave a dismissive wave of his hand. "But let me say, Herr Reichsführer, so that you will not lose a moment of sleep over the matter, that we are closing in on the fugitive even as we speak."

Himmler paused to polish his already spotlessly clean spectacles, then put them back on his pinched, narrowly placed eyes before replying. "That is most comforting," he said. "For your sake, I hope you succeed quite soon."

✽　✽　✽

It was an amazing thing when Madame Rose rolled her eyes towards the sky and said, "With God, all things are possible."

Jerome soon discovered that Madame Rose did not mean that she should sit quietly at Number 5 la Huchette and wait for God to do some impossible thing. On the contrary, this meant that she went to work at impossible tasks and simply expected that because she was well acquainted with the Almighty, those things would become possible to accomplish.

This seemed to be true.

Was the orphanage low on potatoes? Low on funds? Low on beds as twenty new children arrived?

Madame Rose had a scripture promise for every emergency. These promises were drawn upon and recited back to heaven regularly.

"Lord, you have promised to care for the widows and the orphans . . . therefore, we need potatoes. A few plump chickens thrown in for good measure would be kindly appreciated . . ."

Then she would go out to Buci in search of potatoes and chickens. Always she would get what was needed and a little more besides.

She expected miracles each day. Jerome suspected that the miracles were the result of a very strong personality. When he said as much to Madame Rose, she laughed and said that if it was so, Jerome should thank God for giving her such a personality.

There was no way to argue with her without feeling confused.

Enough of this, Jerome thought. If Madame Rose believed that with God all things were possible, he decided that he must ask her to ask God if it would be possible for Jerome and Marie to get in to see Uncle Jambonneau at the hospital.

Madame Rose went alone the first time. Carrying Papillon in a paper sack, she walked to the hospital on a Sunday afternoon to visit Uncle Jambonneau.

She came back very cheerful and brought a note that the old man had dictated.

Dearest nephew Jerome and niece Marie,

Madame Rose has told me what terrible thing Madame Hilaire has done by throwing you off the Garlic *and stealing it. However, I, your dear Uncle Jambonneau, am certain that you are both better off with Madame Rose than with Madame Hilaire who has a voice like a cannon and a personality like a crazed anteater . . .*

Jerome knew that Uncle Jambonneau had mentioned the anteater because it was Jerome's least favorite creature at the zoo. Always sucking helpless ants out of their houses. Terrible. Jerome had experienced nightmares about anteaters sucking him out of the porthole of the *Garlic,* and so it was appropriate to call Madame Hilaire an anteater.

The note continued:

Please take care of my little dog. I have missed his little whiskers at my ear. I miss you both also. Be good children and obey Madame Rose. Your beloved Uncle Jambonneau.

The next week, Jerome and Marie followed Madame Rose to the back door of the hospital. She waited until Rodrigo, the Spanish laundry delivery man, arrived with a white canvas cart filled with towels.

Madame Rose knew everyone who did laundry on the Left Bank because she had taken in washing for so long herself. She and her sister were very good friends with Rodrigo. She told him about Uncle Jambonneau and then about Marie and Jerome.

Rodrigo emptied the canvas cart and Jerome and Marie got in. Towels were piled on their heads. Madame Rose gave Rodrigo the room number and said she would meet him there in five minutes.

In this way the impossible was accomplished. Jerome and Marie were trundled up the freight elevator to the floor where Uncle Jambonneau shared a ward with twelve old men. Madame Rose drew a curtain around the bed and Marie and Jerome popped out of the towels like cabaret performers out of a cake.

Rodrigo stood guard. The other old men in the ward said they heard the voices of children. Madame Rose opened the window, peered out and said. "You certainly do! Spring is in the air!"

Five minutes only. There were hugs and whispers, and Jerome told Uncle Jambonneau about Henri and the horse of the French hero with the wooden legs. Marie let him touch her glasses, and he said that it was a very fine thing to be able to see. He was very pleased for her.

Uncle Jambonneau stated that Madame Rose was a very well connected woman. She knew some very important personages who were able to achieve impossible and wonderful things.

Jerome agreed that this was true.

FORTY-FIVE

As a pleasure cruise, travel on the *Altmark* left much to be desired. Under any other circumstances, this observation would have been feeble humor at best, but to the prisoners in the hold of the German freighter, it was uproariously funny.

Trevor Galway spent the better part of each day dreaming up ways to keep up the mens' morale. Over two months had passed since his capture. The steady northward progress since the brief glimpse of the battle involving *Graf Spee* meant that the chances for rescue were decreasing. If the prison ship were not intercepted soon she would be inside protected German waters and would have accomplished her purpose.

For the past two weeks the prisoners had lived with increasing cold. From the roasting tropic conditions of their capture, many of the men now suffered the opposite agony in the unheated hold. Perversely, the Germans had finally decided that the captives needed more fresh air, and they left the hatch ajar just enough to admit a frigid draft.

Now the crowded conditions were a blessing, without which some of the sailors would have frozen to death. As it was, the cramped space they had formerly complained about was now warmed solely by the packed bodies.

Trevor had worked out a shuffling spiral of motion. The activity kept the men moving, keeping their circulation going. It also made sure that every one got a fair turn at being near the center and warmed on all sides.

But even this effort only lasted so long. Eventually they became too tired to do anything but sleep, though the men had nothing but their thin and ragged clothes with which to cover up. In their exhausted hours, the sailors kept up unconscious movement, like a herd of sheep in a snow storm. One would worm his way into the center of the pile of sleeping bodies, only to find himself rooted aside again later and shivering against an icy steel bulkhead.

It was during one of these semi-awake sleep periods that the forward motion of the freighter slowed and then stopped. "Do you think we're in Germany?" Dooley said. "Even a nice warm prison camp would be better."

"Shh," Trevor warned. "Listen!"

There were shouts from alongside the *Altmark,* answered by replies from her deck. Trevor could barely make out the exchange. "George," Trevor hissed. "Wake up and translate this."

"One of them is speaking Norwegian," Daly replied. "Wait, now he switched to German. That one is demanding to come aboard and search . . . something about neutrality."

"Everybody up!" Trevor shouted. "Make all the noise you can! There are Norwegian officers alongside. It can only mean that we're inside their territorial waters. Bang on the walls! Yell your heads off! Do anything you can think of to make noise!"

Norway was officially one of the neutral nations. As such, she was entitled to see that the ships of the belligerents passing through her national zone carried no arms or other war material. The prohibition included prisoners of war. If the British could make their presence known, the Norwegians could demand their release.

The men stamped their feet, banged tin cans together, yelled obscenities, and even sang snatches of songs. "How can they not hear this?" Dooley wondered.

From overhead came a shrill whining sound, joined by the thump of an engine, then another engine noise and a long-drawn-out squeak. The air filled with what sounded like a thousand out-of-tune violins scraping and sawing. "It's the cargo winches," Trevor groaned. "They've started up all the engines to drown us out."

The *Altmark* shuddered into motion again, carrying its discordant noise away from the Norwegian patrol boats. A short time later the hatch was uncovered and Captain Thun appeared with several armed guards. There was a clatter in the darkened hold as tin cans dropped to the decking. "I have been too lenient," he said. "Stricter measures are now required. You, Mister Galway, and you, and you." Thun pointed his flashlight at twenty of the prisoners who had been standing closest to Trevor or who were caught still holding things to make noise. "All of you, come out of there."

"What are you going to do with us?" Trevor demanded.

"New accommodations," Thun said without humor. "Hell hole."

✳   ✳   ✳

It was an American story. Two aging American ladies in Paris taking in a load of kids and a lot of laundry; human interest. It was just the sort of thing that could spice up the back page of America's newspapers during the Bore War. It would make U.S. citizens feel better about themselves . . .

"Read this here, Bertha. Us Amer'cans ain't isolated-whatevers after all! Amer'ca's still got heart, don' it? That's Amer'cans like us over there takin' care of them waifs! Just so long as they don' bring the filthy little things back here!"

It was the sort of story which would be quoted in Congress. Senator Borah and the rest of the anti-foreign-devil mob were dedicated to keeping immigration to a trickle.

"It is noble American volunteers over there in that Paris slum! Proof of the grrr-eatness of the American spirit. But the average American citizen does not want more refugees coming to our great nation and bringing their slums to our grrr-eat shores. We've got trouble enough!"

Frank Blake assigned the story to Josie. Who else? Nobody else on staff could stand to write bleeding heart material. Too depressing. But Josephine Marlow? She actually felt this stuff, was moved by it! Every day she frowned down at the blank sheet of paper in her Olivetti and grieved over what she was about to write, as if she was that Robert Frost guy or that Steinbeck troublemaker. She pondered internal questions and agonized over content:

Will this story make a difference? Am I capturing the essence of it? The heart of the people?

Frank Blake always let the literary drama play out. He smiled and thanked her when she presented her piece, then told her to go take a break. In less than one minute, starting from the bottom up, he cut the article in half and wired it to the States. That was good clean journalism: heart surgery with a red pencil as scalpel. Slice it up. Toss out the heart. She never knew the difference. No doubt it would be cut in half again and altered by every editor in the syndicate. Let the little woman have her illusions. She was really just a high school literature teacher, after all.

This was the cold and reasoned scenario that brought Josie to the door of Number 5 Rue du la Huchette for the first time.

It was cold, but a few of the book stalls were open on Quai des Grands Augustins. Josie was early for her appointment with Betsy and Rose Smith, so she browsed from stall to stall in search of her own copy of *Paradise Lost.*

It was not easy these days to pick up English volumes on the quay. There were no more English-speaking tourists, and the average British soldier who came to Paris on leave was not interested in reading. But there were lots of tinted postcards of the Eiffel Tower and Notre Dame and etchings of the bridges across the Seine looking toward the cathedral from Pavillon de Flore. The troops of the British Expeditionary Force purchased such things and sent them home by the bagful.

"Hullo, Mum. Wish you were here!"

Of course they were quite content that their mums were on the other side of the Channel so they could sow their wild oats. The German troops did not seem so youthful as the British, nor as old as the French. That fact was worrisome when Josie stopped to consider it.

There were a half dozen young BEF soldiers browsing the open air stalls this afternoon. They stopped at the booth of Monsieur Lemoine, who was a veteran of the last war and had the empty sleeve of his coat pinned neatly to the shoulder. The soldiers did not notice the bookseller. They could not look at such a withered old man and imagine that he had once been in an army himself.

Ignoring the bookseller's amused gaze, they winked at Josie and spoke to her in clumsy French. *"Parlez-vous l'anglais?"* The words were flat, without any pretense of correct pronunciation; as if they were being read from a guide book. English-French. French-English. Barely recognizable.

She shook her head politely, shrugged and smiled apologetically.

They nudged one another and made suggestive remarks about her in their native language, thinking that she really did not *parlez.*

She knew the old bookseller well and asked in distinct American, "Bonjour, Monsieur Lemoine. If you please, I am looking for a certain volume of the works of Milton."

"Oui! Madame Marlow!" He held up the index finger of his one hand in exclamation. He had just the thing.

"Blimey!" exclaimed the fairest boy. "She's a Yank!" He noticed the press badge on her topcoat. "A journalist!"

"What would your mother say if she knew you spoke this way to a lady?" Josie raised an eyebrow regally.

The boys blushed. British males were usually stolid when it came to women, unless they thought they could get away with something. And these were very young. Probably this was their first time out of their Yorkshire village. Tipping their service caps, they wandered quickly in the opposite direction.

"Well done, Madame," exclaimed the bookseller. "One hopes these English will learn something about women while they are in France, but they do not even know how to speak. I hope they know how to fight the Boche."

"Let's hope the whole thing will be finished before it matters, Monsieur."

"Oui, Madame." He accepted 50 centimes for the volume, then with his solitary hand, deftly wrapped it in newsprint and tied it with twine. Josie held her finger on the center of the knot. "Are you working today, Madame?"

"An interview with the American sisters on Rue du la Huchette."

"Madame Rose and Madame Betsy?"

"You know them?"

"But of course! Everyone knows them."

"How long have they lived here?"

He shrugged. "Since before I came home from Verdun. For a time they cared for the son of my dear sister who perished from the influenza in '18. The boy is at the front now. I hope he comes back in one piece." He flipped the empty sleeve in a gesture which indicated he knew much about war. "Take the ladies a gift from me, Madame." He counted the 50 centimes back into her hand then added an additional 20. "The church is rich enough. Bonjour, Madame! Merci! Good day!" He turned to a new trio of customers.

❧   ❧   ❧

Josie pulled the bell rope, announcing her arrival at Number 5 Rue de la Huchette.

A small, thin girl with straight, bobbed brown hair and thick glasses opened the gate and peered out curiously like a strange little bird. She wore a coarse, handknit red sweater and a high-collared yellow dress. Her shoes were scuffed. One blue sock was up and the other down, revealing a spindly leg.

Behind her in the confined space of the courtyard a group of boys played at baseball. The noise of cheering was amplified against the high white walls of the building. Chalk squares drawn onto the cobbles served as bases. Beside each base was an umpire, a boy in a tall, old-fashioned wheelchair being pushed by a second, much smaller boy. An orb wrapped and bound by burlap and twine served as the ball. A tennis racket was the bat.

The girl at the entrance screwed up her face at Josie and shouted. "I am

Marie Jardin. Do you like my new glasses? I can see everything very well now, thank you. I did not know I could not see before. But now I can. You see? Who are you? You have a nice face."

"I have come to see Madames Rose and Betsy."

"They are playing baseball." She stepped aside and swept an arm up to point to two old ladies in the thick of the fray. "You would like to watch? Madame Betsy launches the ball. Madame Rose is at la batte. My brother Jerome is the catcher of the baseball, which is a common potato all wrapped up. Jean Marlotte, the boy who rides in the chair with wheels is the vampire, but he does not drink blood. Vampire. It is something you have in American baseball, no? You see him there? He holds Uncle Jambonneau's dog, who is a rat. Papillon is on his shoulder."

Josie spotted a rat riding on the shoulder of the grinning, wheelchair-bound child beside first base. "Very interesting, Marie." Josie determined that she would steer clear of the kid with the rat.

"The game, she is a tie. Last inning. Two outs. No one on base and two strikes on Madame Rose."

Josie stepped around her just as the scrawny sister Betsy wound up and tossed the wrapped potato over home plate. Rose swung hard and connected. The twine around the burlap broke and the ball flew into pieces. Part of the potato struck Rose as she ran for first. The catcher, a thin-faced, male version of the little bird-girl, clawed at bits of the tuber in an attempt to find enough potato to throw her out. Madame Betsy called for time and shook her bony finger at her laughing sister. This required a judgment from the umpires. It wasn't fair, Betsy declared. Half of the potato had touched Rose and Rose was out! She had broken the ball and she was out! The wheelchairs rolled together for the umps to discuss the situation. The four boys mumbled and nodded their heads as the rat looked on seriously. Finally they judged against the base hit. Madame Rose was definitely out. Remaining on first, Rose blustered her protest. She was promptly warned that if she argued further her team would be penalized one run. Josie concluded that in this French version of baseball, the rules must be very fluid and unpredictable, something like French politics.

Pursing her lips in obvious disagreement, Rose dusted herself off as if she was Babe Ruth and stalked from first back to home.

Thus ended the inning and the game, with a tie. Thirty-one to thirty-one. Both teams, the umpires, and the spectators lined up to congratulate one another beneath the banners of laundry drying above the courtyard. Jerome plucked the rat from the shoulder of the ump and placed it on top of his head. He danced around in joyous circles, then fed the rat a bit of potato left over from the ball. Josie was taken firmly by the hand and guided to the center of the mob by Marie, who blinked happily through the lenses of her glasses.

Madame Rose, who did indeed have a grip something like Babe Ruth, pumped Josie's hand. "Hello, hello!" Her cheeks had bright spots of color. "You are Josephine Marlow. We have no room for a *terrain de foot*—a soccer field—so we play baseball. My team usually wins."

Betsy pouted. "Rose cheats . . . makes up her own rules."

"When in Rome, as they say, Betsy dear!" Rose retorted cheerfully. "You have Papillon as mascot, don't you, Jerome? That draws all the best players. If I did not cheat a bit, how could I ever win?"

All good-natured, the hands of the children reached up to pat their coaches in congratulations. It was a good game. The best kind of ending: nobody lost.

"We do not want you to enjoy yourselves too much! School work!" Rose clapped her hands, and Betsy spread her arms like a hen herding her chicks into the coop. There was an audible groan. The crowd, with curious looks at Josie, dispersed to trudge up the outside stairs which led to the upper stories. The four umpires in their wheelchairs were piloted toward the wide door of a ground floor room by Austrian boys in lederhosen who growled like race car engines and charged over the rough cobbles in competition. The catcher and his rat beat everyone up the stairs to the landing where he thumped his chest and yodeled like Tarzan.

"How many children?" Josie asked, looking after them as they disappeared from balconies into a half dozen doorways.

"Seventy-two," Betsy replied. "From the tiny ones to age twelve. More than twice as many as usual."

"And the rat?" Josie asked.

Betsy put a finger to her lips, letting her in on a secret. "They all think he's a dog with a long hairless tail. He belongs to Uncle Jambonneau and Jerome is taking care of him," she confided, as if this was an answer.

"How ever do you manage?"

"We are never without help," Rose explained. "Students from the Sorbonne come to tutor the children in exchange for meals. Grandmothers come to help us cook and help with the babies. The older children help with the younger. And with God's help, over all, it is not difficult, Madame Marlow. He brings us little miracles every day."

"I'll bring tea." Betsy excused herself as a half dozen volunteer cooks banged on the gate.

Josie remembered the seventy centimes which had been sent by the bookseller. She fished in her pocket and presented the coins to Rose.

"From Monsieur Lemoine, the bookseller. He says you cared for his nephew years ago."

"This is why it is not difficult. Every day God reminds our friends that we are still here. Like Monsieur Lemoine . . . his nephew Jacques, all grown up now and old enough for it to happen all over again. France has enough empty sleeves from the last one." She shrugged, mopped the perspiration from her brow and led Josie to a cramped and cluttered office. Framed needlepoint Bible verses hung on the wall. "Do unto others . . ." She moved a stack of hymnbooks from a battered wooden chair and gestured for Josie to sit. "And now, my dear, how can we help you?"

Bells and whistles were going off in Josie's head. She remained serene and hoped that Rose would not see the sparks flying out of her ears. Could it be that this was not just one story, but an entire series? Tomorrow she would submit a newsy little human interest article to the bloody knife of Frank Blake for AP. And then? Then she would write something new and wonderful each week and sell it free-lance to *Harper's* or *Ladies' Home Journal*!

Josie calmly took out her notebook. "Would you mind starting at the very beginning?" The tea arrived and Betsy joined them. "How did you come to be here?"

The sisters exchanged looks as if they had been waiting the longest time for someone to ask.

"You see, my dear. Josephine, is it?" Betsy began. "It started with a miracle that took place in 1870. We would never have been here at all, otherwise . . ."

Rose got a faraway look in her eyes as if she heard another voice speak to her. "Our father, Captain William Smith, was a sailor . . ."

Somewhere in the telling of the miracle, the thought hit Josie that Madame Rose was just the woman who could help in the making of another miracle.

She took out the envelope with the photograph of the baby from Warsaw and slid it across the desk of the old woman.

"I need help. I don't even know where to begin. This child is in the Reich . . ."

The eyes of Rose brightened as she studied the photograph. "And you want to bring him out?"

"Yes. I have approached the American Embassy about the proper documents. They are intractable. The waiting period for immigration to the States is years. No Germans are being allowed out of the Reich. Especially not Jews."

"Of course. Unless he is your son. A handsome little fellow."

"Can that be done?"

"Certainly." She grinned and opened a cluttered file cabinet to remove the forms.

"Is it difficult?"

"Heavens no! I'll hand carry the letters myself. We'll have to pretend he started out here in Paris." She winked. "A little larceny for the sake of a child. God doesn't mind a bit. We're an orphanage, you see. A matter of two months and you will be a mother. I know an excellent bookbinder who can conceal the documents for you to cross the German border. A simple matter. Done quite a lot these days."

⚜ ⚜ ⚜

The dark-eyed beauty with the long black hair batted her lashes at Professor Alan Turing of Oxford University. Her passport indicated that she was Portuguese by birth, and everyone knew that Portugal was a neutral nation, so her presence at Oxford as a student of literature was no surprise.

What was amazing was her sudden interest in mathematics. She attended one of Turing's lectures on games theory and stayed around after class to inquire further. "Ees eet true that the great Einstein lectured here and that hees blackboard notes are still preserved?"

Turing was so delighted by her breathy accent and her way of leaning toward him when she asked her questions that he promptly forgot what she had said. Noting the way her breasts filled out the silk blouse she wore did not help his concentration either. Turing blushed up into the roots of his thin brown hair. "I'm sorry," he said. "What was that again?"

"Einstein," she repeated simply.

"Oh, yes," Turing confirmed. "He was here . . . let me see . . . clear back in '31. His notes are still on the board in the basement lecture hall."

"Can we see them?" Miss Francesca Pereira asked.

Turing loved the way she said *we.* "It's a bit of an old dusty room," he said. "But perhaps I can arrange it sometime."

"Why not now?" she asked, pushing out her lips in a pout to go with her disappointed frown.

"Now? It's after hours and there would be no one about," Turing said, inwardly groaning after his objection.

Miss Pereira fluttered her eyelashes again and inclined even closer to the mathematics professor. "But this way you could geeve me a private explanation of what eet means," she purred.

Turing found himself walking rapidly along the curve of the Sheldonian Theater. He was vaguely uncomfortable to be under the disapproving gaze of the thirteen giant stone heads known as the Emperors. Miss Pereira talked incessantly and actually pressed against Turing's arm. "And you know Professor Einstein personally?"

"Yes," Turing agreed and then waxing brave added, "and other important thinkers as well."

"Really?" Francesca said. "Who else? You don't know Lewinski, do you?"

"Richard Lewinski?" Turing repeated. "Certainly."

"Ooh," she said. "I just adore hees ideas on a universal calculating machine . . . fascinating, and so ultramodern."

"Richard and I have discussed his theory many times. In fact, we worked on it together while he was here at Oxford."

"You don't mean eet?" Francesca's voice rose in amazement. "But this ees fabulous . . . eet will be the foundation of a whole new world. But tell me, where ees Lewinski now? Why has he not published his work?"

Turing wrinkled his forehead, worried that he might somehow fail an exam for which he had not properly prepared. "I don't know. I lost track of him after he went to Warsaw." Turing could tell that Miss Pereira was unhappy with the answer. "But I know where he isn't," he added. "He did not go to America, because a colleague of mine from Princeton wrote and asked me the same question. It seems someone from Poland was trying to locate him about some money he had coming."

"But you must be concerned for heem," Francesca urged. "Can't you think where a great mind like hees would go to continue hees work?"

Turing thought a moment. "Lewinski always said that he loved Paris better than anywhere on earth. I should think he is in seclusion there."

Francesca's eyes widened. "Does he have something to be frightened of?" she asked.

"No," Turing laughed, tired of so much talk about Lewinski. "He's just like that; solitary and reclusive. Anyway, I would bet on Paris if I were trying to find him. Shall we press on to the classroom now?"

Francesca looked at the watch on her slim wrist. "Oh, my goodness," she said with alarm. "I'm late already, but we can do eet another time, yes?" She planted a quick kiss on Turing's cheek and hurried away.

"Yes," he called after her. "Another time, then!" Turing looked at his own watch. How could he have been so inattentive? He also was late to his secret work at Bletchly Park where he oversaw the MI 6 attempt to unravel the German code device known as Enigma.

FORTY·SIX

It was a fact which Trevor Galway doubted would be believed at home. There was a young navy chaplain named Gabriel Horne who shared the space of the men in hell.

Being a tiny, dark-eyed Protestant from County Tyrone, Chaplain Gabriel had more the look and sound of a leprechaun than an archangel. It was observed, however, that the little man did not possess the power of either being.

The area in the hell hole of *Altmark* was even more confined than the cargo hold had been. It was not possible for those imprisoned there to do anything other than stand up. Trevor thought it was amazing what humans could cope with and keep going; he and the others in the small cubical enclosure leaned against each other to sleep.

The hell hole was below the waterline. When the ship rolled in the waves of the North Sea, icy, foul, oily water from the bilges sloshed around the legs of the prisoners.

When the hatch was shut, absolute darkness clamped down. While it was literally true that Trevor could not see his hand in front of his face, that was far from the worst of it. Left without any ray of light to register on the senses, the mind soon conjured up images to replace the lack. At first the figures were simple, like sunbursts and fireworks. But as time passed, Trevor imagined that he could see flowers and trees, and recognize people in these pleasant outdoor scenes. It made him wonder if he was losing his mind, but everyone in the confinement experienced the same thing.

Chaplain Gabriel, being shorter than the others, suffered from salt water ulcers on his legs. And yet he coped with his suffering without curse or complaint.

To deal with the physical pain and the gnawing possibility of going crazy, Chaplain Gabriel encouraged the others to tell stories. Every man in the bowels of the ship remembered more than he thought he did: sights from travel in distant lands, or more homely memories. It was decreed that they would not talk about real food or sex. Chaplain Gabriel declared that discussing mother's home cooking or the girls they left behind was the surest way to drive each other crazy. They should think of this enforced fasting, two crusts a day, as a sort of spiritual purification. This pronouncement was at first harshly booed by the boys in hell. But when Dooley began to conjure up fresh strawberries and cream and a pot of hot tea for breakfast with Greta Garbo sitting naked across the table, Chaplain Gabriel battled the phantoms using bits of song alternated with Bible verses.

"Seek ye first the kingdom of God and his righteousness, and all these things will be given unto you."

This sentiment caught the attention of every man in the hold.

Dooley was silenced. The discussion began:

"Seek the kingdom of God and I'll be given Garbo?"

It was a beginning, at least.

Chaplain Gabriel did not explain everything to his captive congregation, but from strawberries and Greta Garbo came great debate about the nature of heaven and the chaplain's belief that the power of heaven could be summoned and miracles could happen when people pray and speak the word of God.

"Even here in hell?"

"Were there ever fellows more in need than we are?" Chaplain Gabriel asked.

And so even the doubters decided to give it a try. Nob, who had not spoken aloud to his creator since childhood, when he asked lightning to strike his Yorkshire schoolmaster, asked exactly what a fellow said to God, anyway.

"Just have a nice chat. That's all. And then listen for a while."

Halting, childish prayers began to be uttered by desperate men. It was a time when prayer became reality, not the egocentric petitions of the well-to-do self-righteous, or the frantic prayers of the drowning man, but something altogether different. The men in the hell hole prayed for each other.

"Lord, let Nob's cough be better tomorrow than it is today."

Then came the listening part, "Seek the Lord while he may be found. Call upon Him while He is near . . . I will never leave you or forsake you."

"Jesus, take the ache out of Chaplain's legs."

"Father, protect our children from ever having to go through anything like this, ever."

And Gabriel spoke the promises, "Though I walk through the valley of the shadow of death, I will fear no evil . . ."

There was resistance when Chaplain Gabriel suggested that they pray for their captors.

"Pray that they get caught out in the open and shot to bloody ribbons you mean!" The normally softspoken Nob was not buying this "love your enemies" line.

"Nob," the chaplain asked, "where will you be in a hundred years?"

"What nonsense are you talking? I'll be dead, a course."

"And where will the guards be?"

"In a hundred years? They'll be dead too."

"Can't happen soon enough to suit me," someone grumbled in the dark.

"But think," Gabriel replied. "Suppose you could change places with the guards right now, but doing so meant that you had to be in their place a hundred years from now." There was sober reflection in the hell hole. "To stand before a righteous God and give account? I'd rather stay right here in this stinking hold for a while than stand in the shoes of Captain Thun on that day, thank you sir!"

A point well made.

Later, as Chaplain Gabriel slept, it was quietly discussed by the boys in hell that one hundred years from now heaven was sure to be filled with women who looked like Garbo and all the steak and strawberries a man could eat. It was a great comfort to them all.

❧   ❧   ❧

Norway's craggy coastline jumped up from the dark grey sea in front of Mac. The snow-covered outcroppings offered only tiny amounts of level shoreline. It seemed as if the Norwegian fiords wandered through a drowned country where only the tops of the mountains remained above water.

A glistening coat of ice sheathed the forward rigging of His Majesty's Ship *Cossack*. The destroyer had been Mac's home for the past several weeks. It, and the rest of the squadron, patrolled the North Sea, pouncing on German merchant shipping and unwary U-boats.

Right at the moment, the kind of action Mac had often witnessed was unfolding against the backdrop of the Norwegian coast. Minutes before, *Cossack* had intercepted a small freighter gliding along just outside Norway's territorial limits. When her skipper caught sight of the destroyer's knifelike prow cleaving the waves, he put his helm hard over and ran for the Norwegian coast.

It was a game of sorts; intercepting German shipping was part of war. If the steamer was not armed and carried no military cargo, international law permitted her to seek refuge in neutral waters. The game turned more interesting by the deceptions practiced by the German officers. It was made infinitely more complex by the ability of Adolf Hitler to intimidate the neutral nations.

Cossack accelerated to more than twenty-five knots, rapidly overtaking the merchantman. "Put one across her bow, Mister Longbow," Mac heard Captain Vian order.

The gunnery officer relayed the command, and moments later the destroyer's forward five-inch gun barked a command to halt. The shell exploded a hundred yards in front of the steamer, now straining to turn out eight knots of speed. But rather than heaving to, the German ship steered even more sharply toward Norway and safety. Her shuddering frame and lone funnel streaming black smoke proclaimed her resistance to surrender. The name on the stern which waved defiantly in *Cossack*'s face announced her to be the *Schwartze Himmel* out of Hamburg.

"I'll have another round closer in, Mister Longbow," Vian ordered coolly. "Mind that your crew do not blow off her bow, like they did to that trawler last week."

"Practice makes perfect, sir," returned Longbow with a grin.

The next shot fired landed just under the freighter's nose, and she abruptly pulled up and turned broadside to the warship. It was clear to the German vessel, as it was to Mac, that another shell would not be a warning.

"Bravo, Mister Longbow. Nearly clipped her anchor chains! Mister Perry, hail the captain."

But the master of the *Schwartze Himmel* got his words in first. "Ve are loaded mit hospital und relief supplies only," he called over the loudhailer. "Und ve are inside Norvegian vaters. Let us proceed, if you please."

"Tell him, 'right after we verify his cargo,'" Vian said.

When this was relayed to the *Himmel,* there was no further reply. The deck of the freighter was littered with cable spools and canvas-covered stacks of crates. It was difficult for Mac to see anything warlike in her appearance.

The destroyer put down a boat and First Mate Perry led the inspection team. He and his men would become the prize crew to sail the freighter back to England if the German captain's story proved untrue.

There were groups of sailors clustered on the deck of the steamer, studying the progress of the launch. As Mac watched, they slowly resolved themselves from an aimless mass into two distinct formations. One set of men stood near a heap of crates forward, the other around a netting shrouded pile amidships.

"Captain," Mac muttered.

"I see them too, Mister McGrath. Longbow, order those sailors to back away to the far rail. And tell them to step lively."

It was as if the command was the signal the Germans had been waiting for. Instead of retreating, the two teams of seamen pulled the tarps from the supposed cargo, exposing a pair of antiaircraft guns. At the same moment, the *Himmel* belched a sulphurous blast, and shook herself into motion again.

"Sink her," Vian ordered. And to the helmsman he commanded, "Put us between the launch and the target."

One of the rapid-firing German guns opened up on the small boat. Whether this was planned as a way to force the *Cossack* to save her own, or simply murderous intent, the result was the same. The quick chopping noise of the antiaircraft shells had not reached Mac's ears before the launch was splintered along with the men in it. Three figures were seen diving over the side into the icy water, and then Mac had to duck as the other antiaircraft gun fired into the bridge of the destroyer.

The five-inch gun boomed again, crashing into and silencing *Himmel*'s midship's weapon. The chatter of machine guns coming from both vessels added to the sudden chaos of noise. From hearing only the keening of the wind and the slap of the waves a few minutes earlier, the torrential blare of war now broke over Mac.

A shell exploded against the bridge, knocking the helmsman away from the wheel. Captain Vian took his place, aiming the destroyer's bow directly at the fleeing German craft. The marksmanship of the Germans proved no match for the Royal Navy; first the other antiaircraft position, and then the machine guns fell silent. "Put over another boat to pick up our survivors," Vian ordered, "then we'll finish this business."

Into the carnage of the bridge rushed a young officer that Mac vaguely recognized as the radio operator. He was waving a yellow cable form. "Urgent message, sir," he said to Vian, who was silently urging the rescue operation to hurry as the *Himmel* limped slowly out of range of *Cossack*'s guns.

"Not now!" Vian snorted. *"This* battle is not finished yet."

"But sir!" begged the communications officer. "It's the *Altmark*! They've located the *Altmark*!"

Against this piece of news, even the treacherous ploy of the *Schwartze Himmel* no longer mattered. As soon as a handful of remaining sailors were retrieved from the frigid sea, the *Cossack* shifted her course south. Soon all that remained of the deadly encounter were a few floating bits of debris and a smudge of the freighter's smoke on the horizon.

❉   ❉   ❉

On the chart in *Cossack*'s ward room, Jossing fiord looked like the head of a cobra. Less than a quarter mile across at its mouth, the inlet expanded just inside the rocky opening, then narrowed again until it pinched out one and a half miles back from the headland.

The skipper of the destroyer *Intrepid* conferred with Captain Vian about the situation, as Mac listened in. *"Altmark* was spotted by a patrol plane as she made the passage between Iceland and the Faroes. I caught up with her a dozen or so miles offshore, but she made the run into the fiord before I could overtake. You see where our Norwegian friends have positioned their gunboats . . . that's when I contacted you."

Through the shrapnel blasted shutters of the bridge, Mac could see the two Norwegian patrol craft. Their low profiles and ugly, blunt snouts reinforced the image of Jossing fiord as a nest of vipers. Drifting ice floes bobbed in the current, but an unobstructed swath in the center of the channel showed that something larger than a gunboat had recently entered the gulf.

Captain Vian explained the importance with which the *Altmark* was regarded. "The freighter accompanied the *Graf Spee* during the battleship's rampage in the South Atlantic. When the *Spee* was surrounded, the *Altmark* eluded capture, carrying away with her perhaps as many as two hundred British sailors."

"So she has remained at large ever since the *Spee* was scuttled? Nine weeks ago?" Mac asked.

Vian looked chagrined. "Not for want of trying on our part. She has been the subject of an intensive search. We believed that she would try to return the prisoners to Germany for the propaganda value of such a move. And from her position here, she almost made it."

"How do the Norwegians figure into this?"

"Commander Riks, the ranking officer of the gunboats, is arriving now to answer that question," Vian said, pointing at an approaching small boat.

The Norwegian skipper was a stocky man with sandy blond hair and pale green eyes. He looked uncomfortable from the moment he boarded the *Cossack,* saluting the British colors as he did so.

"Captain Vian," Riks began. "I must request you to take your warships out of Norwegian territorial waters at once."

"We have reason to believe that the German vessel sheltering in this bay carries British prisoners of war. As such, she is clearly a belligerent and has violated your neutrality."

Riks stared at the floor. When he spoke again, the words came slowly as if dragged from him against his will. "We have already searched the craft in question," he said. "There are no British nationals on board, nor is the ship armed. She has requested and been granted asylum in our waters."

"Asylum!" Vian exploded. "You can't mean it! Do you think we will let her escape to take our people back to Germany? I'll board her and see for myself!"

"Regrettably," Riks said softly, "I cannot allow that. As you can see, the torpedo tubes of my gunboats cover the entrance to the fiord. I have been instructed to use them against any unauthorized attempt to enter the strait."

Vian looked disgusted, as if he had bitten into an apple and found Riks inside. "You have delivered your message and may return to your ship, Commander," he said tersely, "while I confer with my superiors."

When the Norwegian had left, Mac stopped Vian on the way to the radio room. "Does this development discourage you, Captain?" he asked.

"Not in the least, Mister McGrath," Vian said. "First Lord Churchill will be responding to the situation personally."

❖   ❖   ❖

As always, the waiting was the hardest part. The torpedo tubes of the gunboats stared at *Cossack* like the muzzles of 2,000 caliber guns. Mac supposed that the Norwegians did not want to fire on the British; he knew that they despised Hitler and all the Nazis stood for. But more importantly, they feared the Führer's intentions regarding their skinny, poorly defended shoreline of a country. Fragile neutrality depended on not offending the master of the Third Reich, not giving him any excuse to invade.

Besides, U-boats and mines had already sunk over 200,000 tons of supposedly neutral Scandinavian shipping. "So sorry," the Kriegsmarine replied. "Better keep your ships out of the sea-lanes used by the Allies. Let them only trade with the Reich and they'll be safe." As extortion, it was not very subtle.

Mac imagined the discussions taking place in the Admiralty offices back in London and the response from 10 Downing Street. It was like Czechoslovakia and Poland all over again, only on a scale where everything could be taken in at once. Mac was certain that Churchill's response would be belligerent: "Show the Norwegians that we mean business and they will stand aside . . . show the Germans that the sea is still a British possession and its freedom will be defended."

But Mac was equally certain that Chamberlain's reaction would be one of dithering and fretting. "What will the Norwegians do? What will the world say about us if we blast our way through neutral ships defending their own territory? What if the *Altmark* has already disposed of its captives?"

And what about those captives? Mac knew that some of the prisoners taken by the *Graf Spee* had been in custody somewhere for as long as nine months already. Had they given up hope of ever being rescued? Were they even still alive?

The hands of the clock silently registered the political wrangling going on in London. Its hands swept around the dial several times before reaching 1600 hours and a reply from the Admiralty was received. "Good old Winston!" beamed Captain Vian waving the cable. "He says we are to ask the captain of the *Altmark* what he has done with the prisoners!"

Mac accompanied Vian to meet Commander Riks on the gunboat *Kjell.* "Are you prepared to withdraw from our territory, Captain?" Riks asked.

"Not exactly. My government has ordered me to place two proposals before you, either of which will be satisfactory. The first is that we jointly escort the *Altmark* to port in Bergen, where an international inquiry will be made."

Riks was already shaking his head before Vian had finished. "You know I cannot fall for that," he said. "It would mean effectively giving an unarmed ship into your control. What is the other proposal?"

"The second option is that you and I proceed to the vessel and inspect her together. Just in case your earlier visit . . . missed something."

Mac sensed the difficulty with which Vian was restraining his temper. But if the warning signs were present, Riks did not heed them. "I'm sorry, Captain," Riks replied. "That is not in my power to agree to either."

"In that case, sir," Vian said coldly, "we are prepared to take action without your cooperation."

Riks pointed to the uncovered warhead of a torpedo ready for launch. "We will be forced to resist such an attempt," he said.

"May God have mercy on you, then." With that the British captain and his followers returned to the destroyer.

✳ ✳ ✳

When the rolling motion of the *Altmark* stopped again at last, the men confined in the hell hole began to pound on the walls and shout. Trevor tapped Morse code messages on an overhead pipe. The feeling was that the effort to alert someone to their condition might not do any good, but they could scarcely be treated any worse for trying.

A strange grinding that came from outside the hull of the freighter replaced the vibration of the engines. It was the noise of metal being scoured with wire bristles, or the shriek of fingernails on a chalk board.

"Sounds like the bottom is getting torn right out." Trevor said.

Dooley chuckled. "You never sailed the North Sea afore, did you, Commander? That's the sound of ice floes rubbin' alongside the hull. We must of turned into a fiord to hide out or somethin'."

The imaginations of the men went wild. Hiding in one of Norway's icebound waterways meant two things that spanned the gamut of emotion. The first was the despairing realization that their unwilling journey to Germany was almost over. If the *Altmark* passed the Skagerak passage between Denmark and Norway, then hope of rescue was done.

On the other hand, stopping to lay over in a fiord this near to her destination must mean that *Altmark* was closely pursued.

No one answered the clamor made by the prisoners, nor did the engines start up again. The ice continued to creak and growl against the hull like that Coleridge described in the *Rime of the Ancient Mariner*.

Presently a new fear crept into the hell hole.

"What if them Nazis have cut and run?"

"What if this tub is stuck in the ice and no one finds us afore we freeze to death?"

It was in fact getting noticeably colder. With only the thickness of the metal hull between the ragged men and the ice-covered sea, the temperature dropped as did the spirits of the prisoners. It had been a long while since the last meal, though there was no way to judge the passage of the hours in the deep hold. The gnawing in Trevor's stomach alerted him that at least one issue of rations had been missed.

"That's it, then," Dooley said at last, voicing the despair the others all felt. "They've left us here to rot."

"Don't give up hope," Chaplain Gabriel urged. "Maybe all this means is that rescue is near."

"Sure, padre," Dooley said. "I just don't want to get rescued after I'm already dead."

A tremor ran along the spine of the *Altmark*. "What was that?" Trevor remarked.

"What was what? I didn't hear nothin'."

"Not hear, felt."

"I didn't feel nothin' either. Course, I haven't felt my toes in about three hours."

"There it is again," Trevor said, as a shudder coursed through the freighter.

"I felt it too," Nob agreed.

"You're both dreamin'," someone challenged. "It's just more ice buildin' up outside. Like as no they'll find us froze inside a iceberg in a hundred years or so."

The bilgewater in the hold started sloshing from side to side. "They started up the engines!" Nob exulted. "We aren't abandoned after all."

The freighter rumbled with the returning life of her powerplant, but she did not get under way immediately. "What are they playin' at?" Dooley wondered aloud.

The senses of the prisoners in the hell hole were so tuned into feeling the rumble of the ship that they did not notice the hatch being opened until it was thrown back.

"Achtung, tommies," Thun's guttural voice ordered. "We are about to be attacked by a British warship."

Loud cheering greeted these words, but Trevor was instantly suspicious. Why was the German captain telling them this? The answer was not long in coming.

"Shout while you still have voices," the Nazi officer said. "Here is a little something to keep you company." He dropped into the hold an oilcloth-wrapped parcel, which was caught by the Chaplain. "If we get away, I'll take that back from you, otherwise it is yours to keep."

"What is it?" Chaplain Gabriel asked.

"I will scuttle the *Altmark* here in the fiord, rather than let her be captured," Thun said. "That is the time bomb to do the job. It will go off if you unwrap it, or in thirty minutes if we do not escape." The hatch clanged down, shutting off the horrified protests of the men in the hell hole.

"Shouting will do no good, lads," Gabriel counseled, "but God can hear our prayers."

✳   ✳   ✳

Even after all the time he had spent on board the *Cossack* in the high latitudes of the North Sea, Mac was still surprised at how abruptly and how early the sun went down. It was barely late afternoon, and already a curtain of blackness replaced the grey veil of the daytime sky.

The destroyer prepared for her entry into Jossing fiord. Her gun crews stood by their weapons. The orders they had received were understood, but no less difficult to accept: they were not to fire unless fired upon. "Blimey!" the loader in a heavy machine-gun team burst out. "Let them blokes what thought of that one come here and go eye-to-eye with them torpedos!"

Cossack's sister ship *Intrepid* was to stand by and assist in defeating the gunboats when the shooting started. It was also understood that she would inherit *Cossack*'s mission if the lead destroyer was blown out of the water.

Captain Vian ordered the huge incandescent searchlights lit. Beams millions of candlepower strong blazed across the dark water. "Like givin' them torpedoes a track to run on," muttered the loader, earning himself a cuff on the ear from his crew chief. Vian wanted to leave the Norwegians no doubt as to his intentions. *Cossack* would proceed directly into the mouth of the fiord, daring the gunboats to fire. It was Churchill's precise instruction.

The blazing lights pinned the gunboats against the snow-covered walls of the narrow entrance. Their lethal black forms were perfectly outlined in front of the icebound shore. They squatted like the lifeless stone guardians of an ancient temple, but Mac knew they could spring to life at any moment with the deadly animation of a coiled snake.

Cossack swept closer and closer to the entrance of the bay. At this distance, there would be no escape when the torpedoes were launched; no room to turn with only unyielding cliffs on either hand. Mac saw that the helmsman's grip was white on the wheel. So was his own on the iron ring of the bulkhead by which he steadied himself. Only Vian seemed undisturbed at the peril. He murmured instructions to the helmsman in a calm, quiet voice.

It was a staring contest at point blank range. The stillness of the gunboats

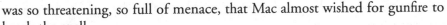

was so threatening, so full of menace, that Mac almost wished for gunfire to break the spell.

Then suddenly they were past the mouth of the fiord and into the widening reach of the bay behind. The Norwegian warships lay astern of *Cossack;* they still had not moved. A chorus of excited exclamations echoed off the towering walls of the canyon.

But if Captain Vian had been unmoved by danger he was no less implacable when it had passed. "Belay that noise," he ordered sternly, "this mission is far from over."

The gleaming cakes of drifting ice closed in around *Cossack* as her searchlights probed the recesses of the gulf. At slow speed she glided almost silently around the bends of the fiord, alert for her target.

"There she is," Vian observed at last.

Mac could not immediately make out the *Altmark* against the shore. He saw a pale, two-story building that stood on top of a cliff of black stone; then realized that he was looking at the superstructure of the freighter above the dark mass of its hull. The stabbing light beams swept the deck of the German steamer, but no movement was seen from the cargo masts amidships to the heap of netting on her bow.

"She looks deserted," gunnery officer Longbow observed.

"All the more reason for us to look sharp," Vian countered. "Helmsman, lay us alongside." The British ship slipped through the water toward its objective as if being pulled along on the searchlight beams.

Cossack's bow, which pointed directly toward the center of the freighter, swung to port as the destroyer edged up next to the *Altmark*.

When the warship's flank was opposite the merchantman's bow, a blasting siren from the German ship ripped the night apart. *Altmark* jolted awake and her bow swung toward *Cossack*'s side. "Ahead full," ordered Vian calmly. "She is trying to ram us. Mister Longbow, give the order to fire."

The heavy bow of the freighter swung after the destroyer with ponderous but inexorable motion. It was like being chased by an iceberg; there was no speed to speak of, but any collision with so massive an object would be shattering. Even the lines of tracers that reached out from *Cossack*'s machine guns seemed a puny attempt to ward off such a crushing blow.

Altmark's starboard quarter swung across the fiord's width to swat the *Cossack* like a bug. At the last second before impact, the freighter's stern grounded on the shore of the inlet. Her movement suddenly stopped with a rasping noise and a shudder.

"Now, helmsman, hard to starboard," Vian commanded. "Mister Longbow, rake her deck. Boarding party!" Vian's voice elevated to shout a command that had not changed in a thousand years, "Grappling irons away!"

In an instant, the two ships were wedded together by barbs and cables of steel. "Come on, lads," second officer Beard led the charge over the rail, waving his pistol.

In the superstructure of the steamer, shots were fired from ports looking down on the deck. A heavy machine gun pivoted upward to shatter an entire row of the openings, and the shooting fell silent as quickly as it had begun.

Mac saw a group of German sailors break out of a hatch amidships and make a dash for the netting-covered objects on the deck. But *Cossack's* earlier experience with camouflaged weapons had taught them well; not a single figure even reached the gun emplacement before all had been cut down.

Racing from the bridge, Mac found himself across the rails and onto *Altmark's* deck before he was even aware of what he was doing. He was as caught up in the excitement of the rescue as were all the others in *Cossack's* crew.

Mac sprinted toward the gangway that led below. The clatter of *Cossack's* machine guns kept the Germans pinned down as the British tars swarmed over the deck. Halfway to the ladder, Mac tripped over a coil of rope and sprawled at length. As he fell, a trio of shots splatted against the metal of the *Altmark's* superstructure, showering him with chips of rusty paint. The point of impact was just where his chest would have been.

Each gunshot was a blossom of radiance in the darkness. The blazing searchlights swayed across the surface of the steamer, pinpointing knots of armed Germans. The rapidly firing heavy weapons of the destroyer swivelled to follow the path of the beams, making it seem as if the rays of light were doing the killing. The whole of the deck was a stage performance gone berserk: brilliant illumination, pitch darkness, popping sounds and screams, and rapid, rushing movements followed by crouching stillness.

More German sailors emerged from the cabletier at the far bow end of the freighter. Attempting to take the British from behind, they came out of hiding firing MG 34's from the hip and spraying the freighter with bullets. Two Englishmen went down, and the rest knelt to take aim at the new threat.

One of the Germans drew himself up to lob a grenade. At the peak of his motion, a searchlight pierced him and a single shot rang out from the bridge of the *Cossack*. The German clutched his side, bobbling the toss. The explosive clattered on the metal of the decking, bouncing amid shrieking men. Mac turned his head aside at the instant of the explosion. The crump of the grenade was followed by a renewed chorus of agonized groans.

Mac saw a handful of remaining Nazis throw themselves over the side of the ship, but whether into the water or onto the shore he could not tell. He had reached the stairway down and was rushed along with a knot of British sailors intent on freeing their countrymen.

The interior of the *Altmark* was absolute blackness, and though a few of the men carried electric torches, they were afraid to use them for fear of drawing a shot. The charge slowed abruptly, as suspicion of an ambush took hold.

A muffled shouting and a riotous clanging noise reached the ears of the rescue party. "That's more shooting up on deck," someone called.

"It's water gurgling in the hold," yelped another. "The Germans are scuttling the ship"

"Shut up and listen!" ordered Second Mate Beard.

In the silence that followed his command, the din of metal on metal continued, but over it could be heard voices yelling, "Help us! Get us out of here!"

"Come on, men!" Beard shouted. "It's this way!"

They met no more Germans on the descent into the *Altmark*. The hatch of the first hold they came to was dogged shut from the outside, but Beard still opened it cautiously, his Bren gun ready. The portal was a dimly seen silhouette that led from blackness to even deeper shadow. No sound came from the interior. "Are there any English in there?" Beard called out.

There was a momentary silence and Mac held his breath, then, "Yes, mates, get us out of here!"

"Well," Beard offered by way of explanation. "The Navy's here!"

Hatch after hatch was flung open to reveal scores of British prisoners crammed into unlighted, poorly ventilated iron cages. Out of every cargo hold came sailors who had been imprisoned for months. By the improvised lighting of handheld flashlights and torches, Mac shot film of the emotional scene. Total strangers fell on the necks of their rescuers, shaking hands and hugging, offering their gratitude over and over. Painfully squinted eyes blinked against the unaccustomed glare and trembling hands clutched bearded faces in an agony of fear that the deliverance was not real.

Mac backed up against a bulkhead to frame another shot when a small square hatch under his feet rang with the sound of repeated blows.

"That's the hell hole!" one of the rescued shouted hoarsely. "Get 'em out of there!"

The hell hole was an unused fuel tank. It stank of bilge, diesel fuel, and human waste. When the lid was raised, the muffled calls of "Hurry! Hurry!" increased instead of subsiding. Instead of men climbing out to freedom, a small parcel wrapped in oilcloth was passed up first. "Quick!" someone said as the object was handed to Mac. "It's a time bomb! Over the side with it!"

Like a child's game with disastrous consequences for the loser, the bomb was passed from hand to hand out of the hold of the ship and up to the rail. "It's a bomb! Get rid of it!" The device was launched over the rail of the *Altmark* to sink in the depths of the fiord, and no one ever knew whether it would have exploded or not.

The fifteen by fifteen foot steel cube disgorged twenty men. Their oil streaked, pasty complexions and bony frames made Mac think of Jonah, half digested in the belly of the whale. He helped lift them free of the pit.

"When did you get captured?" he asked one young man, no more than age twenty-five, who nevertheless looked about seventy.

"I don't know what day this is."

"It's mid-February."

The emaciated form was racked with coughing. When the spasm subsided, he replied, "Two months?"

"Does your family even know you are still alive?"

The face narrowed in thought. "I don't know . . . I doubt it. How could they?"

"What's your name?"

"Trevor," the figure replied. "Trevor Galway."

* * *

Adolf Hitler was in his office in the Chancellory when he got word of the fate of the *Altmark.* "And how many British destroyers were sunk in this action?" he demanded.

The Kriegsmarine officer swallowed hard. "None, Führer."

"None!" Hitler shouted, a speck of moisture flicking onto the naval officer's face. "No resistance? No courage?"

"Five sailors did die, Führer, and five more . . ."

But Hitler was not even listening. "All the way back from the South Atlantic. Two months of concealed movements. Nearly returned with all the prisoners, and then this! To give up without a fight! Shameful! Despicable!"

The officer knew better than to argue the point. "The Norwegians are to blame, Führer. They permitted the British destroyer to enter their waters and attack the ship after granting *Altmark* their protection." He saluted crisply and exited from the office. Hitler barely acknowledged his departure.

"Get me von Brauchitsch," Hitler bellowed into the intercom, demanding the immediate presence of the Wehrmacht's Commander-in-Chief.

Heinrich von Brauchitsch was a quietly intelligent soldier, widely respected for his ability. But his will was no match for Hitler's, and he had long since given up trying to oppose the Führer's wishes.

"Have you heard of this outrage in Norway?" Hitler demanded without preamble when the general arrived. Von Brauchitsch barely had time to nod before Hitler launched into his orders. "We will not wait to attack Norway. The assault on the French will take place as planned, but I want the invasion of Norway moved up a month. A whole month, do you hear? Norwegian collusion will allow the British to use the North Sea ports against us. We will not permit it!"

PART III

"Now storming fury rose,
and clamor such as heard in Heav'n till now
was never, arms on armor clashing brayed
Horrible discord, and the madding wheels
Of brazen chariots rag'd: dire was the noise
of conflict; overhead the dismal hiss
Of fiery darts in flaming vollies flew
And, flying, vaulted either host with fire . . ."

—John Milton,
Paradise Lost

FORTY-SEVEN

Rain tapped gently on the glass panes above Josie's bed. Miss Watson had warned her against sleeping directly beneath the skylight becuase it had leaked last year and she was uncertain if the maintenance man, a notorious drunk, had fixed it properly. But after the first rain of winter, when the seal had held, Josie moved her little iron bed beneath the square of glass so she could see the sky at night and the light of morning before the sunrise. Only then did Miss Watson confess her real purpose in warning Josie about sleeping below the skylight.

"Suppose, my dear girl, that we are bombed without warning in the middle of the night? Or suppose that those idiot French antiaircraft gunners shoot off a round that misses the Huns entirely and lands smack on you?"

"Even if the round missed my skylight but came through the roof, being in the attic, I would be the first to go. Don't worry, Miss Watson. This way if any Germans fly over Foyer International and aim at my skylight I will see them and be able to give the alert."

Josie's reasoning satisfied Miss Watson completely.

And when it rained, the rhythmic patter only made Josie sleep more soundly.

Josie was the first in Foyer International to know that spring had arrived. Larks began to build a nest on the windowsill. They chirped and argued with one another about the placing of this twig or that bit of string. And then they were finished and Madame Lark laid four eggs.

This morning, from the tall window of her garret room, Josie looked over the wide expanse of the Tuileries Gardens. The gravel paths were flanked by color. The chestnut trees were in bloom. The air was fragrant and rain-washed. The cobbles of the street below were shiny after the rain. Then vendors with their wood-wheeled carts rattled slowly up the narrow lane selling precious rationed items like milk and eggs and sugar.

War seemed remote, impossible.

She had gotten two brief letters from Mac. The texts had been run through with the black censor's pen of the French Anastasie. She had learned more about his adventures with the *Altmark* from the newspapers and the wire service than she had gleaned from his notes.

Consistent in both messages was the sense that Mac McGrath loved what he was doing too much to ever willingly give it up for a desk job in London. What was the use of kidding herself? Mac had already made his choice.

And then there was Andre. Each hour she spent with him was better than the last. He talked openly about his longing to see his child, to get this dreadful war over with and settle back into a comfortable and ordinary existence. To enjoy the spring days of Paris without thinking of the clouds on the Eastern horizon.

Josie had fallen in love, in spite of his uniform.

❧   ❧   ❧

The grounds of the École de Cavalerie were bright with the colors of spring. The U-shaped four-story brick structure also had a freshly scrubbed look to it after the hard winter. Enormous red crosses had been painted on the roof tiles between the dormer windows and the tall rectangular chimneys.

Andre pointed to the top story windows of the section which was now a hospital.

"I spent the best years of my life dreaming out that view," he laughed.

"When you are not listening, I want Paul to tell me everything there is to tell about you." Josie squeezed his hand.

"That wing is now an isolation ward for measles patients," Paul Chardon observed. He inclined his head toward the figure of the head nurse, Miss Mitchell. "And there is the woman most deserving of isolation."

As if she heard Paul's remark, Miss Mitchell cast a hard look in Paul's direction and then turned away coolly.

Paul Chardon extended his arm to Josephine. "If you will allow me, Madame Marlow," he said. "I will escort you to the Chardonnet where the Carrousel will take place."

With Andre following her, Paul led Josie through the wrought iron gate with its top rail of gilded spearheads. Past the thickly planted row of tall elms was the grandstand beside the riding arena. After Josie and Andre were seated, Paul excused himself to go to the reviewing box and a microphone at which he became the master of ceremonies.

"This arena is called the Chardonnet . . . thistle field? Like your family name?" Josie asked.

She saw Andre smile. "I think I may have mentioned that our connection with the school goes back quite far. A multi-great ancestor donated this field to King Francis the First for use in jousting tournaments. My forebear was made a baron for his generosity and changed his surname to remember the occasion."

"Mesdames and Messieurs," Josie heard Paul announce over the squealing microphone. "The Carrousel will commence." Paul waved to two lines of riders at opposite ends of the arena.

With Sepp leading one column, and Gaston the other, the senior students and their mounts elicited exclamations of approval from the crowd. The horses were harnessed in the gold and purple trappings used only on ceremonial occasions, and their manes and tails were braided with gold silk ribbons.

The boys themselves were also fittingly attired. They wore the brass helmets and shining metal breastplates of the cavalry of Napoleon's day. Each carried a lance with a gleaming brass head with a tiny gold and purple pennant fluttering from it.

After a slow pass of the reviewing stand with the lances held stiffly at attention, the two lines of riders completed their circuit of the arena. When they began the second lap, the mounts leapt to a gallop as one. The spearheads flashed in the light as the columns met and swerved aside at the last instant, weaving a high speed crisscrossing pattern. The slightest miscue would mean a terrible collision or an impaled rider, but such was the precision of the performance that no flaw was evident. The audience, and Josie, broke into enthusiastic applause.

She watched as Gaston wheeled his troop apart from the others who retired to the corners of the ring. Under his shouted commands, the group of a dozen equestrians put their chargers through a series of maneuvers that dated to at least the time of King Francis. They executed the croupade, that leaping kick backwards in midair designed to destroy a pursuer, and the nimble, goat-like jumps of the cabriole. When the exhibition was completed, Gaston led his command into a line in front of the stand. Then as the lancetips were lowered to the ground, the row of horses also bowed their heads in a courbette in unison.

When Sepp's troop reentered center stage, Josie saw that they had removed the ceremonial costumes and wore their black dress uniforms with the red piping on the collars. Barricades and rails were dragged away from the walls of the ring to form a steeplechase circuit. From a standing start, a dozen of the best riders flashed around the loop, leaping over fences, widely spaced bars, and stacks of wine barrels. Josie added her groan of dismay to the crowd's when Sepp's black horse caught his back hoof on a rail. Sepp tumbled forward over the mane, but he recovered his seat and spurred the mount to even greater speed. With only one quarter lap to go, Sepp caught up with his fastest opponent so that the two horses flashed across the final fence exactly even. In the last split second before the finish, Sepp's charger spurted ahead, giving him the victory by a neck.

Josie clapped wildly and joined the others in shouts of "Bravo!"

Andre leaned over smiling. "Does it make it more impressive or less if I tell you that the entire performance, including the near fall, is part of the act?"

Each year the senior students were allowed to perform a finale of their own choosing. Josie realized that no one, not even Paul, knew what to expect from this display. Curiosity and amusement rippled through the crowd as Sepp and Gaston and their lieutenants carried a table and four chairs into the center of the ring. There they laid out a perfect picnic, including bread, cheese, apples, a bottle of wine, and five glasses.

With expectation growing, Josie craned her neck to watch the action. Confused laughter erupted as Gaston drew the cork of the wine bottle with a flourish and poured four glasses of red Bordeaux. In a loud voice he proposed a toast to the École de Cavalerie, and his three comrades stood and raised their glasses together.

At that exact moment, over the wall at the far end of the arena leapt Raymond on a charging bay. Directly at the table he spurred, as if he did not even see it. The horse neither swerved nor shied. At the last possible second, the four boys sat down in their chairs just as Raymond urged the bay into an enormous leap. Horse and rider sailed over the group of cadets who made a great show of clinking their glasses under the horse's belly.

And then, when a gasp of relief rose from the crowd, Josie saw Raymond pull up the mount at the far end of the field and spur back again. As the cadets calmly ignored the thundering horse bearing down on them, they again toasted each other with the red wine.

Gaston refilled the glasses and, this time, also filled the empty fifth goblet. Timing his movement to match the jump, Gaston stood and thrust the glass into Raymond's hand. The cadet captain downed the liquid before the hooves of his mount crashed again into the soil of the arena.

The four young men at the table rose as Raymond circled his horse to come up behind them and all faced the reviewing stand. Wine glasses in hand, they saluted Captain Chardon and their guests. Said Gaston in a resounding tone, "We hope you agree, mesdames and messieurs, that this year is a truly excellent vintage possessing style and grace!"

✤   ✤   ✤

Two months to the day after the rescue of the captured British sailors from the holds of the *Altmark,* Mac was in Greenwich, on the Thames east of London. He was there to visit Trevor Galway, to check up on the young officer's recovery.

Trevor was seated on a lawn chair, his lap draped in a blanket. It was a soft spring day in April, and although Galway was clothed like an invalid, his physical appearance was greatly improved.

"What have they been feeding you?" Mac asked as he crossed the wide expanse of green. "You look like you've gained thirty pounds."

"Two stone, to be precise," Galway corrected, smiling. "Five pounds heavier than before I enjoyed the hospitality of the Nazis." He stood up in his bathrobe and slippers to shake Mac's hand.

"Don't get up," Mac said. "You'll get me in trouble with your nurse."

"Never fear," Trevor laughed. "I'm quite recovered. So well in fact that I go back on active service next week. I've been assigned to the *Intrepid*."

"Congratulations! Does that mean you'll be going to Norway?"

"I can't really discuss that, sorry. But speaking of nurses, here comes mine now."

Mac turned to see a pretty red-haired girl with a radiant smile. Accompanying her were a balding older gentleman and an enormous St. Bernard. "Team of specialists, too?" Mac questioned.

"Mac McGrath, meet my father, John Galway, and my sister, Annie. The long haired horse there is Duffy." Duffy lay down on the green grass and rolled over like a puppy for all of his two hundred pounds.

Annie, Mac found out, really was a nurse. "My applause, Miss Galway," he said. "Your brother looks fit. Your care must suit him."

"Pooh!" she scoffed. "He is the worst, most uncooperative patient ever. If he gets well, it is in spite of me. But I must thank you, Mister McGrath. Trevor tells me that you are the man who pulled him out of that dreadful hole."

"Aye, that's why I remember the name. Give us your hand again then," demanded John Galway. His fist engulfed Mac's and pumped it vigorously. "I'd still like to lay hold of them Nazi . . ." He caught himself because of Annie's presence.

"Easy, Da," Trevor and Annie both cautioned. "Besides," Trevor added. "I'll be doin' my own payin' back after next week. My orders have come through and I got *Intrepid*."

Annie looked worried. "Oh, Trev," she said. "Back to the war so soon?"

"At least it won't be to Norway you'll be goin'," John Galway muttered, waving his meaty fists in agitation. "A hopeless muddle! Jerry has troops at Trondheim and Narvik and Oslo, and we can't budge 'em. Too little, too late, I say. You mark my words, our boys'll come home with their tails betwixt their legs, and it'll be the end of this Chamberlain and his mealy mouthed bunch of . . ."

"Da," Annie scolded with a wink at Mac that her father did not see. "You must not get Trev excited now!"

"Do you really think this failure will bring down the government?" Mac said. The Phony War had already claimed French Premier Daladier as a political casualty. Was Chamberlain next? A movement on the hill behind the Navy buildings at Greenwich caught Mac's eye. The red time signal ball was hoisted to the top of its staff.

"Has to, laddie," John Galway concluded in a calmer tone. "The P.M. has been wrong once too often, and this time our people have suffered for it. He'll have to go. It's just a matter of when."

On the top of the cupola of the observation tower, the red ball descended from the peak, accompanied by the firing of a signal gun.

⚜ ⚜ ⚜

It was the first of May. A warm, pleasantly balmy spring day bloomed over Paris like the unfolding of a delicate flower. But no matter how hard he tried, Andre could not dispell the obsessive sense of gloom and anxiety that weighed on his thoughts.

There was a German invasion coming; he could feel it. The rains had stopped and the fields were drying rapidly. Soon there would be no barrier to the free movement of tanks and armored vehicles, no fear of their bogging down.

Even worse, military and political figures alike were distracted. The high command was not focused on France. They were bemoaning April's debacle when the Wehrmacht swept over Norway. After delaying a week, giving the Germans ample opportunity to land troops all along the Norwegian coast, the Allies had sent too little help. In ten days the campaign was lost, and those that were not dead or captured came out again. Chalk up another victory for the undefeated Führer. How much longer would he hold back Blitzkrieg from France? And what reason had the West shown to make him hesitate: None!

Generals blamed politicians for not committing to help Norway sooner. Politicians blamed generals for their ill-prepared troops. Both groups blamed the British; after all, Norway involved maritime forces and the landing of troop ships. Wasn't that the subject where the Royal Navy claimed unmatched expertise?

The upshot was, French politics was in one of its perpetual crises. Prime Minister Reynaud was rumored to be fed up with General Gamelin and his cohort, Defense Secretary Daladier. But if Reynaud fired those two, it would certainly bring down the government. Meanwhile, English Prime Minister Chamberlain was also on thin ice for the failure in Norway. It appeared that both administrations might collapse within the week. It could not have come at a worse time. Everyone was already bored with predictions of a German invasion that never really materialized. Now it was impossible to get anyone in authority to listen. Andre was more of an outcast than ever, since he was still convinced that the main Nazi threat was not where the aging leaders from the Great War said it was.

He sat on the second from the bottom tread of the stairs leading down to his basement and studied a back view of Richard Lewinski. The carrot-topped engineer was enmeshed in the bowels of his reconstruction of Enigma, as if the giant machine was swallowing him. It was difficult to separate the wild explosion of wiry hair from the profusion of tangled wires encircling the cabinet. If it were not for the thin khaki-clad legs that protruded below the circuitry, Andre could not have distinguished Lewinski from the machine.

A decision born of frustration made Andre call out to Lewinski, "Richard, are you making any progress?"

The Polish Jew's form did not change position; his backside was answering the question. "Of course. I now know the wiring of the first three wheels. If there were only three, we would be done."

"Can you do anything to . . . speed up the process?"

Now Lewinski emerged, looking childishly peeved. His face puckered into a pout. "I am working as hard as I can, Andre . . . all alone, and from memory. Can you think of a way for me to work harder?"

Andre waved his hands to sooth the engineer and head off a potential tantrum. Then he reached inside his coat pocket and removed a pair of twice-folded sheets of paper. "Richard," he said at last. "I am not supposed to have this, let alone show it to you. But desperate times call for desperate measures."

Lewinski came over to sit beside Andre on the step. His bony knees stuck up, and he looked like a stork awkwardly perched on a wire. "This is a coded transmission," he said. "Where did it come from?"

"Where is not important. In fact, the reason you did not, could not, know about this is that if you were . . . It is just better for you to not know any more than you need to."

"So, spy games and paranoia. What is this?"

"These are intercepts of two Wehrmacht radio transmissions from last September; the first page of each. A team of cryptanalysts have been studying them for patterns to find clues to the settings of the dials."

"Is there a starting hint?"

"Not really, just a guess. The British think that the Germans use rhymes or cliches as test messages. If they were so stupid as to use the same test phrase more than once, we might catch the repeat . . ."

"And be able to unlock the settings of the dials," Lewinski concluded. "Andre, I should have seen these long ago. Now, what common German sayings are short enough?"

Lewinski was already lost in thought. Like a child absorbed in a riddle, he pored over the pages, squinting at the meaningless words and counting letters. "Four, five, three . . . and over here four, five, three . . . no, that's no good. The next word is six on one, three on the other."

Scanning the documents with the intensity of a hawk soaring over a field that contained a hidden rabbit, Lewinski suddenly pounced. "Ha!" he said. "Here it is. It is the same sequence, only backwards on one page."

Andre looked over his shoulder. "If it is backwards, how do you know it is the same?"

Giving his friend a withering stare, Lewinski asked, "Do you think the radio operators have time or intellect enough to make up new phrases every day? Of course not! Now, let's see, what proverb is six, six, three, five, five . . . how absurdly simple."

"What?" Andre said breathlessly, unable to believe what he was hearing.

"You know how the Deutschlanders like to hang posters and paint slogans? Well, I could hardly miss this one. It was printed in red and black letters over my workbench in Berlin. Look here," he said, pointing a crooked forefinger at a line of type. "This can be nothing but 'Morgen, Morgen, nur nicht heute, sagen alle faule Leute.' Tomorrow, tomorrow, never today, say all lazy people."

"That is it? Just like that?"

Lewinski looked offended.

"Not that I doubt your brilliance," Andre hastily reassured his friend. "It is just that . . . the others have been working for months. How did they miss this?"

"Were they Poles?"

"Yes," Andre cautiously agreed.

"That explains it then. When I worked in Germany I forced myself to *think* in German. Besides, they have probably never studied Gematria."

"Gematria?"

"The Jewish practice of numerology. It helps one recognize patterns like nothing else."

"And now?"

"Now I go to work seeing how the patterns changed from one paper to the next and I will know how to set the wheels. Can I get more of these; something current, so we can test the hypothesis?"

"Anything you want," said Andre, jumping to his feet and running up the stairs. "You are a genius!"

Hugging his knees, Lewinski rocked with a satisfied grin on his face. "I know," he said.

✻   ✻   ✻

"You see," Lewinski said to Andre and Colonel Bertrand, "once you find a pattern in the way the coding changes, you can deduce the method to predict future changes."

"And have you done that?" Bertrand insisted. "Can you decode all the messages? Tell us how it works!"

Lewinski looked disappointed. He wanted to spin out this yarn in his own way, milking to the fullest the story and his role in the discovery. "Yes," he sniffed. "I took as my premise that the change from one day to the next would have to follow a simple model. That way the superiors of the field operators of the Enigma machines would always know the correct settings for the wheels. Just think, if they had to follow an instruction book for each day's changes, what would happen if that book were lost or stolen? It is much simpler for a communications officer at, say, the division level, to have the guide memorized and radio the new setting as the last message encoded on the old setting."

"Yes, yes!" broke in Bertrand impatiently. "Get on with it!"

Andre laid his hand on Bertrand's shoulder, silently urging him to contain himself. Temperamental geniuses cannot be rushed. He said soothingly to Lewinski, "You are explaining this so well, Richard! Please go on."

"It is simple really. The shift of the dials depends on the date, the day of the week, and the cycles of the moon. I just consulted a simple almanac, which I got from the newsstand at Place St. Michelle, and there it was."

Bertrand looked stunned. In a low tone he said, "Are you telling me that the Germans change the wheels based on an elementary calculation? That you can decode their messages?"

"Not only can; I already have," Lewinski said proudly. "My machine, though not as polished looking as theirs, is every bit as functional. See for yourself: here is something I fed in this morning."

Bertrand gave Andre a sharp look. Lewinski was not supposed to actually decipher communications. His role was only to reach a conclusion about the encoding pattern. "I felt there was no time to waste," Andre said by way of explanation.

"All right, what do these messages say?"

Andre took over at this point. "Most are routine transmissions regarding resupply and logistics; except for this one. It reads 'Fall Gelb will commence 10 May. Sichelschnitt must reach Meuse by 12 May.' "

"Plan Yellow and the Cut of the Sickle? It still does not tell us anything."

"Yes, it does!" Andre insisted. "I have studied the maps. The only operation of any kind that can reach the Meuse River in two days is an armored attack through the Ardennes!"

"We must see Gamelin at once," Bertrand said.

Lewinski brightened. "Do you suppose I will get a medal?"

"Richard," Bertrand said, trying to sound kindly. "You cannot go. It is more important than ever that you be protected. You can imagine how valuable this information would be to the Germans. They would change the whole system if they knew. Not only would all your work go for nothing, but you would personally be in great danger."

Lewinski deflated. If compared to a balloon, he had never resembled more than a very skinny one. Now he looked like the remains of one after it has been popped. "Find me a new project then," he said. "I am already bored."

FORTY-EIGHT

I am really sorry, Chardon, but the C-in-C cannot see you today after all. He is incredibly busy with really important matters."

Colonel Pucelle's tone laid a thick stress on the word *really*.

"When *can* the General see me? It is extremely important!" Andre was ready to punch General Gamelin's assistant in the mouth for his superior attitude and manner.

"Why do you not just give the message to me, and I will deliver it to the general."

Andre exchanged a glance with Gustave Bertrand. The very last thing the two intelligence officers wanted to do was to put sensitive material in Pucelle's hands. Lewinski's breakthrough was too important to be filtered by a man whose most prominent ability was currying favor.

Maybe there was still a way. "Look, Pucelle," Andre tried. "You remember the earlier discussion about where the focus of the German attack would be? We have new evidence that the invasion of Holland will primarily be a diversion."

"Oh, no!" Pucelle groaned with dismay. "Not again! Really, Chardon, this horse will not run. The general has studied all the possible invasion routes from the Sedan gap to an airborne offensive on Rotterdam. No more idle speculation, please!"

"Pucelle," Andre said, "just suppose that there is something to this. Suppose that the Germans *are* planning an attack through the Ardennes. If you suggested to General Gamelin that he reinforce Corap's Ninth Army and Huntziger's Second Army by shifting over part of Conde's force, you would look like a genius."

Pucelle's face twitched. It was a feline expression, like a cat narrowing his eyes when he spots a bird within reach. Pucelle never wanted to disagree with anything on which Gamelin held convictions. But a chance to pull off a strategic coup and get all the credit was too good to pass up. Even so, he was not about to stick out his neck too far.

"Since you will not reveal your source," he said, "I have nothing on which to base such a suggestion except your opinion. Get me some concrete evidence that you are correct, and I will consider broaching the subject with the general. Now I really must go, gentlemen. You will have to excuse me."

❦　❦　❦

Rocking the plane from side to side enabled David to see over his shoulder as the flight of Hurricanes proceeded up the valley of the Meuse River toward Belgium. The swaying motion used up more fuel, but it was necessary as a means to watch for enemy fighters that might be sneaking up behind. Only two days earlier, Benny Turpin, a new boy with the 73rd Squadron, had not paid careful enough attention to his six. Benny had ended a promising flying career in a ball of flame at the hands of an Me 109. It only marginally lightened David's thoughts to recall that he had personally dispatched the Messerschmidt just moments later.

David's mood was also darker than usual because of the plane he was flying, or rather, because of the aircraft he was not flying. *ANNIE* had taken a bullet through the oil cooler in the engagement with the German who shot down Turpin. She was out of service for another day, so David was flying a spare ship. He felt no connection with this aircraft. It almost seemed that the controls were not as responsive to his touch, even though the mechanic assured him that it was all his imagination.

Hewitt's voice barked over the radio. "Cluster of black dots at my two o'clock high."

"Roger that," Simpson agreed. "Could be Heinkels. Let's go."

The section went into a steep climb to position themselves above the intended targets. The number of enemy bombers seemed to be increasing as the Hurricanes got closer. "I count twenty," Simpson reported. Then a moment later he amended the number to thirty and then again to forty.

Black dots seemed to be materializing out of thin air. The range was closing rapidly as Simpson prepared to initiate the dive that would lead the three fighters swooping down on the intended victims, when suddenly he announced. "What a duff play this is."

From his position guarding the rear of the formation, David had not yet figured out what Simpson meant.

"Flaming onions," Hewitt growled. "Take a closer look at our targets; those are ack-ack bursts."

And so it proved. The magically increasing numbers of enemy bombers turned out to be the black puffs that marked the explosions of antiaircraft shells. "Let's get out of here before someone throws one of those our way," Simpson ordered.

"They must be shooting at something," David observed. Scanning the sky as the Hurricanes turned back to their original course, his view from twenty-five thousand feet covered a lot of territory. "And there it is," he continued. "Dead ahead. A flight of Dorniers at angels twelve. Two pairs of Me 110's flying cover. All heading northeast, back to the Reich."

"Full bore now," Simpson said.

"Even into Belgium?"

"Didn't stop the Nazis, did it? We'll chase them into Germany if we have to. Hewitt, you and I will take the two on the right. Meyer, you have a go at the other pair. If we can scatter them, we'll come back after the bombers. Let's go."

The plunge onto the German fighters took them completely by surprise. Not as maneuverable as the 109, the twin-engine German fighter/escorts were nevertheless tough to knock down. When they were in service with Franco during the Spanish Civil War, they were known as Destroyers.

David's attack slashed toward the inner of the two German planes from an angle on its stern. A short burst from his machine guns was followed by another, longer stream as the 110 broke to the outside. David noticed the line of his fire saw through the rudder of the craft, part of which tore completely free. A portion of the tail surface was severed as well. The German pilot banked sharply, trying to control his now erratically plunging machine. David followed in a tight spiral, hoping that a final salvo into the nearside engine would finish the battle.

That was the instant when David chanced to look groundward. The aerial combat had carried him very near the German border. And what a view of western Germany it was. On the roads leading back from the border were countless parallel rows, nose-to-nose like elephants heading for a watering hole, of German tanks, armored cars, and half-tracks hauling artillery pieces.

There was a moment in which David thought about the significance of this sight, when there was an enormous explosion and the plane began to shudder and lose altitude rapidly. Over his shoulder, David could see the pursuing form of another Messerschmidt. It was the partner of the one just downed. David's fighter had taken a blast of twenty millimeter cannon fire at close range.

He went into a steep dive, twisting the damaged Hurricane around and heading it back toward France and home. The maneuver successfully evaded the Messerschmidt, but the right wing made a whining complaint, and the craft felt sluggish and heavy, as if lifting more than its accustomed weight. When the engine burst into flames that hungrily licked at the cowling, it was time to kiss the airplane good-bye.

David eased the ship out of its dive and hoped that any other nearby German pilots had better things to do than chase parachutes. He opened the canopy just as the engine conked out. Once clear of the radio cable and the oxygen tube, the pilot dove over the side into space.

When the chute popped, the sudden uplift yanked him away from the fighter. It dipped its nose and raised its tail, almost as if waving good-bye.

David barely had time to observe his surroundings before his hurried exit from the aircraft. But drifting silently toward the ground, he used the opportunity to examine the forested hillsides below, confirming his earlier suspicion. It was the wrong side of that river that seemed to be slowly twisting below him; he was coming down in Belgium.

As David watched from his floating perch beneath the canopy of the parachute, his Hurricane streaked earthward. It was headed toward the church steeple of a village on the horizon. Now trailing a column of thick black smoke, the aircraft was a flaming arrow on a colossal scale. The fighter struck the ground a couple miles from the village and a fiery pillar shot into the air. The dull roar of the explosion followed a few seconds later.

As grateful as he was for the safe descent, David wished that it would get over quickly. The detonation and the bonfire blazing above the territory of the Ardennes forest would attract some unwelcome attention. The Belgians, as citizens of a neutral nation, were not at all happy about the Germans and the Allies using the skies above their country as a battlefield. They not only shot at the airplanes of both sides, but they interned captured pilots for the duration of the war.

The Belgians, like the Dutch, were being very short-sighted and ungrateful, since the presence of the Allied army was keeping der Führer off their necks. With all the German armor poised on the edge of Belgium, the security gained by Belgium's fragile neutrality was not going to last much longer anyway.

Perhaps David could parlay information about the terrifying buildup into freedom and safe passage to France. But he couldn't very well surrender and then ask the Belgians if they would please let him go. Better to stay out of their clutches and save the barter plan for a last resort.

He was drifting onto a timbered hillside. There were no buildings in sight, except for a farmhouse on the far side of the knoll. A clearing with a small creek at the bottom presented itself as a likely possibility. So did a patch of bare grassy slope covered in white and pink wildflowers. No such luck; the light swirl of wind chose that instant to die away completely, lowering David directly toward the tops of the pine trees that crowned the hill.

Trying to coax the chute into another course by pulling on the straps met with no success. Plunging between two sixty-foot-high trees, the edge of the silk bubble caught on one side, swinging David across the open space. Partially tearing, it dropped his shoulders while his feet swung up again like a pendulum. He was hanging almost upside down, one leg tangled in the shrouds, suspended a dozen feet off the ground.

Groping awkwardly in a zippered pocket on the leg of his flight suit, David searched for the small knife carried for just such an emergency. He reasoned that if he could saw through the cords binding his leg, then it would lower him enough to cut free from the rest and fall the short remaining distance.

David removed the knife and opened it, taking care not to drop it because of the strange angle at which he was working. Half of the lines were severed when he first heard a dog barking. The sound of the animal's deep voice echoed from just over the hill toward the farm. It was still far away, but definitely coming closer. He began to saw even faster, anxious to get down and find a place to hide.

The dog bayed again, a real bloodhound noise in the experience of David's childhood years spent in Arkansas. Not a good sign if the beast were accompanied by the Belgian police.

Two cords remained to be cut when the knife slipped from his fingers. David made a frantic grab for it as it fell, touched it, and succeeded in batting it into a high arc that gleamed in the afternoon sun. Arching through the air, it stuck upright in the grassy soil and mocked David from twelve feet below.

The barking dog was still coming. David began to yank on the almost detached leads. Once more he gave a sharp tug and the strap parted. His weight pivoted on the remaining tether and swung him sideways at the same moment that the rent in the parachute expanded.

Just as the hound crashed through the brush surrounding the trees, David's head smacked into the trunk of the pine. Despite his leather flying helmet, the impact stunned him. The animal was almost on top of him and there was nothing he could do about it. Into David's upside-down view bounded the biggest black dog he had seen since his childhood companion, a Newfoundland named Codfish. "Good dog," he called, trying to keep his voice calm and friendly. The dog's tone changed to a suspicious growl. Its hackles rose and it walked stiff-legged toward the strange apparition hanging in the tree. "Good dog," David tried again. "Bon chien. That's it, bon chien!" The dog continued to snarl menacingly. "Gute hund! Gute hund!"

The coal black shape made a leap that carried it directly up to David. The pilot put up his arms in an effort to protect his face from the mauling he was sure was coming. He felt the animal's hot breath on his neck, and then it began to lick his ear.

Cautiously, David inched his hands apart and peeked out. The dog, still regarding him with curiosity, was wagging. *"Gute hund!"* he repeated, heaving an enormous sigh of relief. "Now, if you could only help me get down from here."

"Are you speaking to the dog?" asked a gruff voice in French. "Have you always been crazy, or does it happen when you fly planes?"

David pivoted around again and focused his eyes on a pair of rough country boots. From these he scanned upward over heavy corduroy covered legs, a bulky torso, muscular arms and a face framed in salt-and-pepper beard. One of the hands was holding a pitchfork.

"Can you get me down?"

"You are English?" the farmer asked.

"American flying for the RAF."

"That was your air machine that crashed over by Couvin?"

"Yes, I am sure it was. Could we discuss this after you cut me loose?"

The farmer pulled an enormous jackknife from his pocket and sliced the remaining shroud lines in one stroke. Tumbling free, David scrambled to his feet. "Thank you, Monsieur," he said. "Where is the French border?"

The grizzled farmer shook his head. "The police will be searching for you. You must hide until nightfall when it will be safer. They do not want to find you, you understand. It is not as if you were German." He spat out the word as something incredibly distasteful. "But there are those in the village who favor the Nazis. They would make trouble if the police found you and then let you go free. You must come with me. I will hide you until dark."

"Good idea," David agreed. Then a worrisome thought crossed his mind. "Tell me, why does your dog understand German and not French?"

The man looked amused. "He is a refugee. Showed up on my doorstep two years ago. Ask him, Monsieur. He hates Nazis."

David spotted his pocketknife sticking in the ground. Picking it up, he offered it to the farmer. "I am grateful for your kindness. May I give you this knife to say thank you?"

The man scowled. "I take no pay for helping someone who fights the Boche! But perhaps I will make a trade." The two men and the dog started over the hill toward the farm. "My knife for yours?"

"Done," David said. "But your knife is so much bigger and sharper. What will you do with mine?"

Winking at David, the farmer laughed, "Give it to my grandson for a toy."

The Belgian farmhouse was modest but built of stone and sturdy-looking. It nestled in a ravine between two shoulders of the hillside and overlooked a marshy pasture in which a few tawny milk cows were placidly grazing. "I will show you where to hide," the farmer said to David, "and then I must return to my chores. If I am not at work at this time of day, the authorities will find it suspicious."

"Fine," agreed David. "In your barn or in the house?"

"Neither will serve. The police may wish to check them. But there is a place which I can vouch for as safe. Come with me."

On a small hill at the edge of the pasture stood a wooden structure whose appearance left no doubt as to its function. David hesitated at the doorway. "How long will I . . . ?"

"Get in quickly," the farmer urged. "I'll come back later and take you into the house." Whistling at the dog, the man shut the door behind David and turned toward the field.

If the farmer intended to betray David to the authorities, then they would all have a good laugh when his location was revealed. It was a warm, late spring day, and the atmosphere in the hideout was ripe.

It was not long before the issue was decided. The black dog barked a warning, and soon the jingle of a bicycle's bell announced an arrival. Peeping through a crack in the outhouse wall, David saw a blue-coated gendarme waving to the farmer. The policeman was accompanied by a second bicyclist; a fat man in knee britches and a waistcoat.

"Bonjour, Dennis," called the gendarme to the farmer. "Did you see the crash of the airplane?"

"You mean the machine that went over my house like a duck with its tail feathers on fire? Of course I saw it! Scared my cows with its great roaring sound. Probably soured their milk. What brings you out here, Joseph, you and Monsieur Navet?"

The fat man, wiping his flushed face and panting to catch his breath, answered for the gendarme. "Did you see a parachute near here? We have heard that one floated down in this direction."

"Do I have nothing better to do than watch the sky for falling Englishmen?" Dennis scoffed.

"How did you know he was English?" The fat man pounced on the farmer's words like a cat on a mouse.

"German then, or French. What is it to you, Navet?"

"It is a matter of extreme importance! Just last week two English airmen escaped from the jail at Dinant. How long do you think Belgium's neutrality will be respected if we aid the Allies?"

"And how long even if we don't? Go away, Navet, you annoy me. Search if you wish, but why would a man who has just fallen from an airplane run to where he would be captured? Don't you think he would remain up in the hills until dark?"

"Come along, Monsieur Navet," the policeman urged. "Dennis is right. We must start hiking if we expect to locate the flier."

"We should search the house and the barn first!"

"Fine," the farmer agreed. "Search away."

The fat man motioned for Joseph to follow him as he bustled importantly into the farmhouse and reemerged moments later looking disappointed. He then examined the barn and came back covered in dirt with straw in his hair.

"Sorry to have bothered you," the gendarme apologized.

Monsieur Navet looked around suspiciously. His eye lit on the outhouse. "Wait," he said. "There is yet one more place to look."

David tensed up at the words and braced himself to make a run for it. "It's a good idea," Dennis said. "Leave nothing unchecked. I would not want you to come back later and accuse me of something, Navet."

Navet's eyes narrowed in his fleshy face, disappearing into swinelike folds. "I think you are toying with us. Why are you being so agreeable?" He squinted at the sinking position of the sun. "Let's go, Joseph," he said. "We've wasted enough time here already."

Dennis turned his back and returned to tending his cows. Several minutes passed, and then he went into the barn and brought out a sack of grain. He fed the hens, tossing handfuls of corn on the ground, and wandering toward the outhouse. In a low voice, with his head down as if addressing the chickens, he said, "That Navet! He is a Gestapo agent that one! Fat pig! I hope he busts something pumping his bicycle up and down the hills!"

"When can I come out?"

"Not before dark. Be patient."

As soon as the shadows of the surrounding pines lengthened enough to cover the little valley in the Ardennes, David was released from his odorous refuge and brought into the comfort of the farmhouse. Dennis provided fresh water for bathing and a change of clothing, then sat the pilot down at a rough-hewn plank table in the kitchen. The farmer produced a heaping platter of jambon ardennais, a half dozen boiled eggs, an entire loaf of fresh bread, and a pitcher of cold buttermilk. David protested that it was too much, but proceeded to devour it all.

Then it was dark and time for David to leave. During the long hours of waiting, he had heard the sounds of passing aircraft overhead. He thought about his buddies who would not know what had become of him, and how some raw recruit would be filling his spot, flying *ANNIE*, if he didn't make it back fast. It was time to rejoin the war.

"The border is 10 kilometers southeast from here," the farmer said. "I will give you my bicycle for the journey. As long as you speak to no one, you will be safe . . . your accent is atrocious! When you come to the river, get off the road. You should have no difficulty finding a rowboat that you can borrow and then you will be back in France. But if you cannot cross tonight, find somewhere to hide and try again tomorrow night. There are others like Navet, who volunteer to guard Belgium's neutrality by watching the border crossing for escapees. Trust no one!"

"I want to thank you again," David said, "and the best way I know is to warn you: the Boche are coming. I have seen a huge army forming just across the frontier, and they will be coming straight at you."

The farmer shrugged. "The Germans have come before, twenty years ago, and earlier than that, in the time of my grandfather. The Spanish against the Dutch, the French against the English, the Romans against the Francs . . . the armies of many nations have found it convenient to fight their wars on our soil, rather than on their own. But you see, the good God is very good indeed . . . we remain."

"It will not be like any other war in history," David warned. "From what I have seen, if the Nazis break through, they will go all the way to the Channel."

The Belgian looked sad. "Then, my friend, it will be a long road back. May God protect you until we meet again. Now go."

A broken spoke on the bicycle made a continuous clicking sound. The handlebars were loose and the frame wobbled from side to side. David had to struggle to keep from either shooting abruptly across the center of the lane or crashing into the ditch. But the narrow country road had no turnings and was easy to follow even in the inky blackness. The smells of flower blossoms filled the cool evening air.

When he came to the village, everything was still. A dog barked as he clicked by, but all was in darkness. David stopped at a fork in the road just outside of the town and struck a match to examine a road sign. One fork led toward Mariembourg, the other indicated Rocroy. Neither pointed the way toward the river and France. As he stood studying the problem, the noise of an automobile engine reached him coming from the Mariembourg road. The car was coming fast.

Bare, grassy swards fell away from the highway on both sides. There was no place to hide. Running across the fields was out; all he could do was go on as if he had a perfect right to be cycling down a road in Belgium.

Remounting the bicycle, David peddled stoutly toward Rocroy with his back to the oncoming car. As he came within its headlight beams, the vehicle slowed momentarily, as if looking him over. It then picked up speed again until it pulled up alongside and then passed him without stopping.

Breathing a sigh of relief, David set himself once more to the task of keeping the bicycle on the road when suddenly the car braked at the curve just ahead. The gears clashed as it shifted into reverse and began to back up toward him.

"Do you need a ride? I am going to the border crossing," called a nasally voice from the dark interior of the car. The question was followed by a sneeze.

Thoughts about sitting out the war in a Belgian prison raced through David's head. His French was bad; there was no way he could be mistaken for a native. What to do?

"I said, do you want a ride?" came a strangled sounding voice again, impatiently.

"Sorry, I do not speak French," said David in English.

The car, which had been pacing David's progress, squealed to an abrupt halt. "Who are you and what do you do here?" questioned the driver, replying in English. "You are . . ." The man sneezed again, loudly, "American?" David agreed. "I thought so! I pride myself on how well I can distinguish accents. Tell me, did you see anyone else along the road? An Englishman, a pilot, perhaps?"

David shook his head. "Nobody but me. Why?"

"The impertinent British think they can fly over our country to make war on Germany. But we always catch and imprison their fliers when they are shot down. I myself have been searching today for just such a one. We are very careful of our neutrality. Do not many in *your* country favor the French and the English?"

David got into the car. "Most folks figure Hitler for a bully and a blowhard. Personally, I don't pay attention to politics much. I do like a place where everything works, though. I hear the Germans are very efficient."

"You have not been to Germany in your travels? You would like it. Of course, it is difficult just at present to get freely across the border. But soon it will be put right again."

Navet and David passed several minutes in one-sided conversation, with the Belgian explaining how the west should be grateful to the Nazis for standing up to Stalin, and how it was only the Communists, the Jews, and the English who had forced France into a war.

Finally, around a curve in the road, the headlights gleamed on the flow of the river. The lights of the bridge and the border crossing were visible just a half mile ahead. "Say, would you mind stopping? Need to answer a call of nature." David was already opening the car door, and Navet instinctively slowed down. "Just be a minute," David called, hopping out and jogging into the bushes that covered the slope of the riverbank.

Where were those boats that the farmer had described? David slipped and fell on the muddy incline and kicked a rock into the stream with a splash. "Are you all right?" called Navet's voice from the road.

The first rowboat was chained to a log. The second had no oars. The third was half full of water and one of its oars was broken. "Where are you?" Navet yelled again. "Have you injured yourself?" The sound of another sneeze boomed down from the road and echoed along the water.

The last dinghy in the line was tied to a tree stump. The oars rested in the oarlocks and it was clean and dry. David yanked out the jackknife he had gotten in the trade and slashed the rope. Pushing the boat into the fast flowing stream, he jumped in and began to row for the far shore. "Good-bye, Monsieur," he called. "Thanks for the ride. Maybe the RAF will give you a medal for your assistance."

FORTY-NINE

Frank Blake, Associated Press Bureau Chief, was cranky.

". . . So! What do I find this morning? A wire from New York! From Larry, no less! *Come on, Frank,* he says! *Send us The War!*" He blew his nose loudly and kicked the overflowing trashcan beside his desk. "Like I can control this! Like I can inspire Hitler to get moving! That's it! I'll just send der Führer a wire. *Dear Hitler, please attack at dawn. The American public is bored with the war!*"

Alma, leaned over Josie's desk and whispered, "A little too much oo-la-la for Frankie last night. Quite a little tart from what I hear. She stole his wallet."

Josie nodded and continued typing as Frank went on with his tirade.

"This is the most boring war I have ever . . ." He stopped mid-sentence and turned toward Josie. "Hey! Marlow! Yeah, you! What are you working on?" Without waiting for reply, he snatched the paper from her typewriter and held it up to the light. He began to read. "Champagne is now added to the ration list. It is available in Paris only three days a week!" He screamed out the lines, then pounded his fist on the desk of Henry Merkle. "Do you think this matters to the American people? Champagne is rationed! Who cares? You know how many Americans have champagne three times in their whole dreary little lives? Let alone three times a week! Is this appropriate? What possible difference can it make how many bottles of champagne . . ."

Furious, Josie stood and squared off with Blake. "Frank, you are a cretin. You are the one who gave me this lousy assignment yesterday, and now . . . you may take your bottle of champagne and place it wherever you feel is most appropriate."

There was applause from a half-dozen other reporters at their desks.

Blake sneered and spun around to glare back at every face. "Mutineers!" he spat.

More applause. The chorus chimed in.

"You're a really scary guy, Frank."

". . . When you have a hangover."

"Or when some French beauty steals your wallet!" Much laughter. Blake actually blushed.

"We ought to send you to Berlin. You'd get the war going in no time!"

Blake blew his nose again and tossed Josie's lead paragraph back on her desk. He rubbed his forehead and plopped down hard in his chair.

"Okay. Gimme some help here, fellas. And mesdames. What I need is some American story. I mean this place is the morgue. We got ladies knitting socks for the poilus. We got little collection boxes on the bar at the Crillon for the Help-Beautify-the-Maginot Fund!" He shook his fist in frustration. "Somebody gimme some human interest or I'll be on the next boat back to New York for a permanent position doing obits on a daily!"

The telephone rang. Alma passed it to Josie with a shrug.

Madame Rose was on the other end of the line. Josie could hear the happy shouts of children echoing off the courtyard walls of Number 5 Rue de la Huchette.

"Josie, dear! Dear, dear girl! Good news! Your adoption papers are complete. You must . . . must . . . pick up your baby boy on the eighth of May. Do you understand, my dear? The stamp specifically designates the eighth of May."

Josie considered the implications. The papers of Yacov Lubetkin would be smuggled into the Reich beneath the end pages of a German book. But it was imperative that the child's documents be stamped ahead of time with the forged imprint of a Reich visa and the date as though he had crossed the border into Germany at Wasserbillig bridge with her at the same time. This narrowed the possibilities for her own journey into Germany.

"May eighth," she repeated the date. "Yes. I'll arrange it. Should make a very good story."

She replaced the handset and smiled at Frank Blake, who was still grousing.

"Well, Frank, I've got your war for you. I've been invited to see the German Siegfried Line firsthand."

Blake's jaw dropped. He considered her with grave suspicion. "How did you do that?"

"I've been working on it for some time."

Two hours later, after the office emptied out for lunch, Josie sent a wire to AP Amsterdam, to be conveyed to Bill Cooper at AP Berlin, who would then pass the date to Katrina von Bockman as arranged in Cooper's instructions to Mac.

The message said simply: *HAPPY BIRTHDAY BILL. HARD TO BE-LIEVE YOU ARE 58. SIGNED JO.*

Of course Cooper was at least ten years younger, but *5* was the number of the month and *8* marked the day of the month when she was to cross the Wasserbilling bridge from Luxembourg into Nazi territory.

❊   ❊   ❊

Following his instructions, Andre boarded the bateau mouche named the *Vert Galant* at the platform below the Hôtel DeVille on the right bank. He stood near the bow, letting the warm spring breeze flow over him with its scent of peaceful renewal. The little steamer was not crowded at this hour of midmorning. The clerks and shopkeepers who used the river for their commute to work had long since arrived at their destinations.

Scanning the few other passengers, Andre saw no one he knew, nor did anyone seem to be showing any particular interest in him. The boat passed under the bridge adorned with the carved leering caricatures said to be Henry IV's comic revenge on his ministers. It swept downriver to its stop below the Louvre where most of the travelers exited and a handful of others got on. There was still no attempt made to contact Andre, and he was getting impatient.

The steamer released its moorings for what was only a short move downstream to the wharf leading to the Tuileries. At the last moment before casting off, when the stern line had already been released and the gangplank slipped ashore, Gustave Bertrand jumped aboard. He spotted Andre at once but strolled nonchalantly around the ship before joining him in the bow. He asked Andre for a match to light a cigarette, as if they were total strangers.

"What is the meaning of the cloak-and-dagger act?" Andre quizzed. "Could we not have met at my home, or your office, and without all the theatrics?"

Bertrand looked wounded. "Do you think that I do this for fun? I have been followed, Andre. Gestapo, I think. It would be extremely dangerous for your houseguest and his work if I were to be shadowed to your home, or if you were pursued after meeting with me. Believe me, this is necessary."

The top of the obelisk in the Place de la Concorde slid by as Andre considered the weight of what Bertrand had said. "Perhaps I need to move Lewinski out of Paris. To Vignolles?"

Bertrand nodded thoughtfully. "That may be the answer. We'll look into it as soon as you return."

"Return? From where? Not another trip to England, Gustave? Paul cannot be recalled from his duties just now."

"Calm down, Andre. This is not another trip to England. In fact, you will be back the same day. And it *is* vitally important."

Sighing heavily, Andre asked, "There is no escape, I suppose. What is this about?"

"I knew I could count on you. I want you to go to Mezieres, to the aerodrome there. There is a young American fighter pilot, David Meyer. He was shot down on a mission a few days ago. Just before bailing out, he says, he spotted an enormous buildup of German armor—tanks and troop carriers."

"How does this involve us, Gustave? Shouldn't it be reported to General Headquarters?"

"That is exactly the point. It already has been, and no one is taking him seriously. You see, the area over which he was flying is the Ardennes."

Andre gripped his friend's arm with a sudden squeeze. "You mean that what we have feared is coming to pass?"

"It appears so. Now you understand. I need someone with your reputation to talk to the man. If, in your judgment, he is correct, there is still time to shift some of our forces to meet this threat. But only if we hurry."

"I will leave tomorrow!"

"I thought you'd say that. Here are your tickets."

The *Vert Galant* pulled alongside the quay at Pont de l'Alma with its stone figure of the soldier in the uniform of a Zouave. The water swirled around the knees of the statue's baggy trousers. "I will leave you here," Bertrand said. "It would be best if you ride another stop or two before you disembark." He took a step toward the gangplank, then paused and gestured at the statue. "You know how Parisians watch the level of the river? If it reaches to his waist, there will be a disasterous flood. Let us hope the rest of our army is in no such danger."

※　※　※

Andre studied the young American. "I realize that you have repeated this story fifteen times," he said. "But tell me again, exactly what you saw."

David looked disgusted. "Will it make any difference? All right, here it is. I was engaging an Me 110 that was flying escort to a squadron of Heinkels returning to Germany from a raid."

"And this was . . . ?"

"Just north of Luxembourg, where the Ardennes plateau crosses from Belgium into Germany."

"So you were over Belgian territory?"

"Yeah. We are spread so thin, we can't catch all the bombing runs on the way in, but we don't like to let them get back to Naziland unpunished."

"And were you alone?"

"No, my section mates Simpson, that's Flight Lieutenant Simpson, and Pilot Sergeant Hewitt were there too."

"Did they see anything like what you report seeing?"

David shook his head and frowned. "No, unfortunately not. They were busy. But that doesn't change what I saw," he finished belligerently.

"Calm down, Meyer. I didn't say that I doubted your word."

David sagged visibly in his chair. "Sorry. It's just that no one seems to take me seriously! I even volunteered to fly a recon mission myself to get proof. They said no! Said for us to stay away from Belgian territory after this." The flier stood up abruptly and pointed to a map on the wall. "Right there, not a hundred miles from where we are right now. I'd say at least two divisions, maybe more. Tanks and all the support equipment to go with them."

"And how do you know the objective is the Ardennes? Perhaps they were being moved further north, where the main body of the German force is known to be?"

David pounded his fist on the topmost point of the triangular outline of Luxembourg. "Aimed straight into Belgium! Not loaded on rail cars either. Those big grey monsters were on their tracks, Colonel. I may not know much about tanks, but unless somebody gets in their way with a lot of firepower, those babies could be in our laps in about two days."

"And you realize the importance of this information?"

"You bet I do! We've already been told that our unit will be pulled back when the Germans launch their attack. Problem is, the High Command says the invasion will come through Holland . . . two hundred miles in the wrong direction!"

❖   ❖   ❖

Andre slammed the door of his study and paced the room as Josie explained about Yacov Lubetkin and the planned rendezvous in the German city of Treves on May eighth.

Andre was angry with her.

"You will get captured and killed!"

"It is already arranged," Josie countered. "I am going with or without you, Andre."

"I forbid it!"

"Forbid? What right have you . . ."

"You will not cross the French frontier into Luxembourg if I put a stop to it!"

"And if you do, I will catch the clipper and fly out of Paris and out of your life tomorrow!" she stormed.

He took her arm and spun her around. "Listen to me! I lost one woman I loved to the Nazis . . ."

"You lost Elaine through your own . . . stupidity!" she shot back. "You lost her long before the Gesapo got hold of her! And they killed her for the same reason you let her walk out of your life! The same reason, Andre! You let some bigoted old man ruin your life and hers! Destroy your love! You let it happen!"

He stepped back as if she had struck him. "What do you know about it?"

"Only what you talked about. And your brother Paul."

"What did he tell you?"

"Everything. About your grandfather. About you being more afraid of that wicked old man than of losing the woman you loved, and losing the right to be a father."

"This has nothing to do with you crossing the Wasserbillig bridgehead on the eighth of May! It is too close!"

"Too close to what?"

"You think the Germans are camping out over there for fun? There will be several hundred thousand Wehrmacht, SS, and Gestapo between you and that baby in Treves!"

"I have faced them before."

"Not on the eighth of May!" he roared. "Not Luxembourg! It will be the Nazi highroad into . . ."

Josie glared back at him. She tossed her head defiantly. "You have a daughter in Luxembourg. Have you forgotten?"

Parting the curtains, he raised his eyes slowly towards the twilight gathering east of Paris. The Eiffel Tower stood silhouetted against a backdrop of lavender hues. Like the watercolor painting of a Montmartre street artist, the pastels faded to purple and then to black.

So few hours remain before the darkest nightfall . . .

"Juliette," he said softly, all the fight gone out of him.

"What do you think the Nazis will do to the half-Jewish daughter of a French colonel when they march across the Wasserbillig bridge into Luxembourg?"

"You know what they will do."

"Yes, I do know. And there is another Jewish baby waiting for me in Treves. All he needs is for one of those Aryan hags to change his diapers over there and what do you think will happen to him? And to the people who care for him?"

"You do not even know him." His argument was feeble.

"And how well do you know Juliette?"

Andre was beaten and he knew it. "Then . . . we will go to Luxembourg together. You cannot . . . must not . . . go alone, ma chérie. If they should attack . . ." He nodded, arguing with himself. "Across the bridge on the eighth. Back the morning of the ninth. You must promise me."

"Yes. And while I am gone will you speak with Abraham Snow about Juliette?"

"Even if he will not see me . . . I will make certain my daughter will not remain behind in Luxembourg to face the Nazis."

※   ※   ※

Mac McGrath and John Murphy took their seats in the Reporters' Gallery of the House of Commons. The two friends viewed the Hall from above and behind the Speaker's chair at the north end.

Murphy had been tipped off that the debate offered on Saturday, the seventh of May, would be important, perhaps even critical, for the Chamberlain government. Only three weeks after the British mobilized to combat the Nazi invasion of Norway, the battle was lost and the troops had been withdrawn. Just as John Galway predicted, Mac remembered.

Prime Minister Neville Chamberlain entered the House of Commons. He was greeted with unenthusiastic applause from his allies and scathing rebukes from his political enemies. Mac heard someone call out, "Missed the bus!" Other voices took it up, until the oak-paneled chamber rang with shouts of "Missed the bus! Missed the bus!"

Mac knew that the sarcastic wisecrack came from an unfortunate remark made by Chamberlain himself. The Prime Minister had told the House that Hitler could have attacked France right after Poland, but now the Allied positions were too strong, so Hitler had missed the bus. Now that the campaign in Norway was a disaster and a clear-cut German victory, Neville's quote came back to haunt him.

Mac wondered who would replace Chamberlain if the government fell. He hoped it would be Churchill, but Halifax or David Lloyd George were possibles. One thing was certain: Chamberlain was fighting for his political life . . . and he might be the only one who didn't know it.

Neville Chamberlain opted to speak first. He droned on at length about how the country really did not want war, was unconcerned and complacent about events outside England. He got roundly hissed for that. As Mac laughed to himself, Chamberlain gave a very prissy, effeminate gesture of exasperation. "I still have friends," he pouted, and the hissing turned to jeers. "Now that Germany controls harbors in the North Sea, I fear that our country does not realize the gravity of its peril," Chamberlain suggested.

"Do you?" mocked a voice from the back bench, and a new round of catcalls and "Missed the bus!" erupted. Chamberlain sat down, looking dejected and tired.

Clement Atlee, head of the Labour Party, and Sir Archibald Sinclair, leader of the Liberals, both gave speeches criticizing the handling of the war. But in Mac's opinion, the fireworks didn't really get started until Labor M.P. Josiah Wedgwood gave a speech in which he accused the Royal Navy of cowardice.

Just as Wedgwood was finishing, Murphy nudged Mac's elbow and pointed. Into the chamber walked Admiral Sir Roger Keyes. Someone Mac did not recognize handed a note to the highly decorated officer.

The face of Keyes got as red as the ribbons of the medals on his chest. He cursed and then demanded and was granted the right to immediately reply.

Mac expected the admiral to be called to task for his language, but no censure was offered, and the naval hero of the Great War launched into his speech. "I have repeatedly offered to lead a fleet of warships into the fiords," he said, "and just as repeatedly was told that the army had the situation well in hand. How can our troops be expected to advance along a narrow shore-line under constant and undeterred fire from the German ships? It is not a lack of courage with the sailors! It is a failure of leadership in this govern-ment!" Cheering from the Opposition was greeted with stony silence and deep frowns from the government side of the House; Sir Roger had been one of their own.

Mac wondered if Churchill, as First Lord of the Admiralty, would get tarred with the same brush as Chamberlain.

David Lloyd George, the Opposition statesman who had led England during the 1914 war, rose to speak. Adjusting his pince-nez, he theatrically ran a hand through his mane of silver hair and attacked. "This country is in greater peril now than during the whole of the Great War," he said. "What is the good of sea power if it is unused?"

A chorus of "Hear, hear!" sounded from both sides of the aisle.

"But I do not think that the First Lord is to be blamed for the mistakes," Lloyd George continued.

Churchill popped up from his seat beside Chamberlain. His brooding pose had made Mac think that Winston was scarcely following the debate, but his sudden spring proved that idea false. "I take my full share of the responsibility, sir," he said.

"Admirable," Lloyd George replied, "but I hope that the First Lord will not become an air raid shelter to keep splinters from hitting his colleagues!" Applause followed these words.

It was unexpected support. Maybe Churchill could surface from the sinking ship after all.

Leo Amery was called on to speak next. It was Amery who had attacked Chamberlain's conduct of the war clear back in September; his views had not moderated since then. "We must have men in government who can match our enemies in fighting spirit," he said, "in daring, resolution, and thirst for victory."

Mac saw Amery study the faces of the members, obviously thinking about what he was about to say, judging its timing. "I quote certain words of Oliver Cromwell spoken to a government he judged no longer fit to rule. I do this with reluctance, because those to whom it applies are old friends of mine, but this is what he said." Amery stopped and looked squarely at the top of Chamberlain's bowed head. "He said, 'You have sat too long here for any good you have been doing. Depart, I say, and let us have done with you. In the name of God, go!' "

As the speaker called for order to be restored, Mac thought that there was no longer any question whether Neville Chamberlain could remain Prime Minister. The resultant vote of confidence on the conduct of the war produced a Conservative victory, but only a margin of eighty-one votes. Every single uniformed member of Chamberlain's party deserted him and voted with the Opposition. Clearly, it was time for him to go.

FIFTY

Lewinski stared at Bertrand with disdain.

"What do you mean, you can't read them anymore?" Bertrand snapped.

"Was I not speaking plainly enough, Colonel Bertrand? I mean, the pattern for setting the wheels has changed. It no longer follows the formula I deduced a week ago."

"Could you have miscalculated?"

Lewinski gave Bertrand a withering look. "I never miscalculate," he said. "I *never* miscalculate! What this must mean is that the invasion is really on for tomorrow. It makes sense to change the pattern when strategic orders are about to be replaced by tactical ones. You know, when a division commander calls for help or some such operation, if your enemy has even the slightest clue about what you are up to, then it would be disastrous."

"I know!" Bertrand exploded. "Like this alteration is disastrous for us! How long will it take to uncover the new procedure?"

Lewinski's look changed to one of pity. "I suppose that depends on what they changed it to, now doesn't it?"

"Could this mean that they know we've cracked the first setting?"

"Possibly, or perhaps they had always planned this change to occur simultaneously with the invasion. But there is one sure way to tell."

"What is that?" Bertrand asked, desperate for a ray of hope.

"If they know that we know, they'll change the routine so drastically that it may be months, even years, before we crack the new one."

❧   ❧   ❧

As instructed, Josie left the Brasseur Hôtel carrying only her passport, twelve dollars worth of Luxembourg francs, and the precious volume of Goethe's *Faust* with the travel documents of Yacov Lubetkin sealed beneath the end sheets. Nothing else.

Driving the car into the village of Wasserbillig, she parked at a bier-stube with windows overlooking the river and the bridge into Germany. She gave the dubious barkeeper a slip of paper instructing him to turn the automobile over to Andre Chardon if she should fail to return from her trek into the Reich.

A charge of excitement went through her as she walked up onto the Wasserbillig bridge. Below the metal girders she could see the slow-moving river which divided Luxembourg from Germany. Pontoon bridges were built halfway across from the German shore. Terminating just in the center of the languid current, the pontoons punctuated the border at one-hundred-yard intervals both up stream and down. Even if the little army of Luxembourg blew up their half of the Wasserbillig bridge, how long would it take the Nazi engineers to slip the rest of the pontoons into place for the crossing? Then how long would it be before the Panzers would overflow the Luxembourg side of the riverbank?

Midway across the Wasserbillig bridge was a gatehouse and customs office festooned with warning signs and capped with the swastika flag. A handsome young Wehrmacht sentry stared through Josie without curiosity as she approached the barrier. He stopped her with stiff formality and demanded her passport.

He seemed unimpressed by the American document, but not at all surprised that an American journalist was walking on his bridge and entering Germany.

"Your destination, Fräulein?"

"Treves."

"Purpose?"

"Sightseeing." This she said in a matter-of-fact tone, as if the Siegfried Line was not between her and Treves . . . as if she was a tourist out for a day trip and there was not a war on.

Without comment, the youth directed her to an anteroom in the customs office where the Nazi officials took on a much more sinister tone and appearance. The manner of the questioning was far from friendly.

A poster bearing the likeness of the Führer glared down on a small assembly of civilians: two men and three women who had crossed the bridge just ahead of Josie. They were returning to Germany by order of the Reich. They all seemed unhappy about it. One portly, middle-aged woman wept continuously without any attempt to hide the reason for her tears.

"She is sad because we have to leave our little grandchildren," her pale, frightened husband kept explaining over and over to the interrogators. "She will feel better when we get back home. We have not been there in ten years."

The resident Gestapo agent was unimpressed. In his eyes something was definitely wrong with a German citizen who had stayed away from the Fatherland so long and who wept so copiously at the prospect of returning. As Josie waited in line behind the woman, the official tore through the couple's luggage. He ferreted out a bar of chocolate, held it up in triumph, stripped it of paper and broke it into tiny pieces as the woman's weeping became louder.

"Do you not know it is illegal to smuggle contraband chocolate into the Reich?" He roared his displeasure as if her crime was a personal offense! With a wave of his hand he summoned a white-uniformed Nazi matron who forcibly hauled the unhappy woman into an examination room while her meek husband was escorted to a second room.

The woman screamed as the door was closed. Then it was Josie's turn at the declaration counter. Oblivious to the howls of the captive, the officer snapped open Josie's passport and examined it without comment for a long moment.

Hard, cold eyes pivoted up to study her press uniform. Then back to the passport photograph. Then to her face and the press badge on the shoulder of her jacket.

"Fräulein Marlow, is it? An American journalist, are you? Anything to declare today, have you?" He smiled, but his eyes were dull and hard, like the eyes of a copperhead snake Josie nearly stepped on as a child in Arkansas. He gave the impression that he could kill her without a twinge of emotion simply because she put her foot wrong.

"What is the purpose of your visit to the Reich, Fräulein Marlow?"

"Sightseeing." She tried not to look at the conspicuously posted sign which listed the names and photographs of foreign travelers who had been convicted and executed as spies in the last twelve months.

He closed the passport. "Have you anything to declare?"

"Thirty Luxembourg marks. Nothing else."

"Empty your pockets."

She did so and placed the copy of *Faust* on the counter. Heaping coins and cash onto the cover of her book, she slid it across to him.

He picked up the bills, one by one, as if checking for counterfeit currency. Stacking the cash neatly to one side he retrieved the volume of Goethe.

The rush of Josie's blood pumped in her ears. She focused her eyes on the small rectangle of Hitler's moustache as the agent examined each page with the same intensity with which he had checked the bills. What was he looking for? A code? Some message pricked into the paper with the point of a pin?

"What is this, Fräulein?"

"A copy of *Faust.*"

Suspicion hardened the line of his mouth. Josie resisted the urge to turn and run out the door; to escape back into the safety of Luxembourg.

"Why do you carry Goethe's work into the Reich?"

She shrugged. "Something to read on the ride into Treves. *Faust* is not among the banned books. Germany is quite fond of Goethe, I understand."

He thumbed through it as the wailing of the woman prisoner in the examining room diminished to a whimper. Beads of sweat formed on Josie's brow. The prickle of fear crept up the back of her neck. Her mouth tasted like iron.

Would he notice the thickness of the baby's forged papers sealed beneath the end sheets?

"Why exactly did you chose this volume, Fräulein?"

"Because I was certain I would not be inconvenienced if I carried approved reading materials into the Reich. If I was wrong, then keep it for yourself." She glanced accusingly at the splintered slab of chocolate. "You can see I have come here emptyhanded just to avoid any waste of time at the crossing. One volume is not worth it. I can buy myself a dozen more just like it."

He furrowed his brow and silently read through a passage. "It is not to my liking." Snapping it shut, he passed it back to her along with the neatly stacked bills. "Heil Hitler." He thumped the stamp down on her passport and dismissed her, turning his reptilian gaze onto a sallow old woman who brooded in line behind Josie.

As Josie emerged into the spring warmth, the old woman argued with the official without fear of Hitler or his splendor or his might. The words were bitter and loud. Josie could hear the curses as she walked unsteadily toward the German end of the Wasserbillig bridge.

❀　❀　❀

The taxi driver waiting for Josie on the German side of the Wasserbillig bridge was the last fool still roaming free in Hitler's Reich.

A squat, muscular little man with swarthy skin and big ears protruding from beneath a Jaeger's hat, he smiled broadly with gapped teeth and waved at her approach. He leaned against the bent fender of an ancient taxi. Tires were worn down to the fabric. Windows were cracked. The engine had a knock which made the vehicle shudder like a dog shaking water from its fur. But it was clean. The cracked windows had been polished. The metal of the rattling fenders shone through what had been black paint.

"You are the American. Ja! It is plain to see. Guten Morgen, Frau Marlow. I am Hermann Goltz," the Fool said joyfully as he opened the back door for Josie and bowed slightly like a chauffeur as she entered. He waved happily at the sentries who stared at the scene from their posts on the bridge. "You see, I promised I would be here. Although I had to wait. I thought perhaps you would not come, but I waited here all the same. Where do you want to go?"

"To Treves. Porta Nigra Hotel." Josie gestured broadly eastward where the forward blockhouses of the Siegfried Line were in plain view.

"Very good, Fräulein. As we travel I shall point out all objects of interest along the way. Americans like to see the sights. I have always enjoyed guiding Americans. They do not come here often enough these days." He closed the door and hurried around the car to slip in behind the wheel.

Josie believed that she was quite possibly the first American that he had seen in many months.

The taxi lurched into motion, but turned off the main highway to Treves. Instead, their route followed a secondary road which skirted a high bluff and led away from the river. This road was clogged with military traffic. Motorcycles roared past. Armored cars and troop lorries rumbled off along snaking side roads to isolated blockhouses and rows of mobile artillery set to face France as well as little Luxembourg. It was clear to Josie within minutes that she was seeing what she was not meant to see. She pictured the poster commemorating the execution of foreign spies by the Reich. She imagined her own face smiling serenely out at future travelers. She felt the sick chill of apprehension.

"How is it you are able to get a pass to move so freely through this zone?" she dared to ask.

"A pass?" he chortled. "I have no pass, Fräulein!"

"Then how . . ."

"They do not ask me. Who would be here unless they were allowed?" Another laugh which ended in a contented sigh. Then he continued pointing out items of interest while Josie sat grim and pale in the rear seat. "Americans enjoy the backroads. Unusual sights. I know this well. How else will you see unless I guide you? This first line is six miles deep," instructed the taxi driver over the engine. "The second line behind Treves is much deeper. Many more troops. Much more going on. But you can see. They are all moving forward!" This information was expressed with the same enthusiasm Josie had heard in the voice of a beefeater conducting tours of the Tower of London. But this military zone was no tourist trap; no point of interest found in a guidebook. Josie knew that she was witnessing some terrible and momentous force being set in place like the pieces of a chess game. And yet the taxi moved with absolute freedom through the forbidden region of the German West Wall!

Hermann Goltz greeted military sentries cheerfully. He expressed to them his delight in the beauty of the spring day. They smiled back. Perhaps it was his audacity which kept him from being stopped and challenged. No one driving such a contraption could be a spy.

He pulled to the side of the road as a convoy of troop lorries blocked the way in front of them. Through the spiderweb pattern of the cracked glass, Josie looked out on an erratic field of green concrete barriers which traced the folds of the hills and valleys on and on into the lovely spring haze. A sentry beside a roadblock fixed his gaze on the taxi. But he did not move forward to question Hermann.

"This," the driver exclaimed loudly and within hearing of the sentry, "is a tank trap. The French call them asparagus beds. The French are very amusing." Hermann laughed. The sentry laughed. Only Josie remained unamused. Her mind was racing with the dreadful implications of what she was seeing. Enormous artillery pieces on carriages with rubber wheels were being hauled toward the Meuse River, toward Belgium, toward Luxembourg. Not toward France. She had observed enough to be shot as a spy a dozen times over. She would tell Andre everything she had witnessed, but she did not want to see any more. Her only desire was to get the baby and then to get out of the way of the Nazi steamroller poised to flatten everything on the other side of the river.

"Is there a quicker way to Treves?" she asked.

"Ja. But very uninteresting. Americans like to see the sights."

With that, they were waved on through the chicane by the sentry. The highway ran parallel to an obviously occupied trench punctuated by a series of large gun emplacements.

"Fräulein Marlow! Look there," shouted Hermann as he pointed to a cliff wall which rose from the side of the road. A half dozen sentries observed him with a fascinated curiosity but made no move to stop him. "It is a fort. You see there where the colors change from green to brown? Very good, is it not?"

And then Josie saw that the rock was no rock at all, but a heap of concrete piled up and painted to match the cliff face. No reconnaissance plane could pick it out. It was nearly invisible even close up. The Nazis had intended that this place be kept a secret, otherwise they would not have gone to all the trouble of making it a secret.

Josie looked quickly away. "Please, Herr Goltz. Take me to Treves now. The shortest route."

He was disappointed. The tour had only just begun in his eyes. Still, he agreed and pointed the taxi toward the city. There were still plenty of sights if one knew where to look, he explained. There were antiaircraft guns in haystacks; 88 millimeter artillery pieces were concealed inside steep-gabled little farmhouses and barns.

"Just think of it," the Fool said brightly as they passed a house that looked like something out of *Snow White and the Seven Dwarfs*, "What the French air force would not give to know that there is an .88 millimeter long rifle hidden under that roof! When it begins to send its shells into the French troops, the French generals will not even know where to look for it. They will not know where to drop the bombs to stop it, will they? The French will be very sorry they did not drop their bombs first." He turned and winked at Josie. "I think it will begin very soon now, Fräulein. Perhaps within days. The Sitzkrieg is about to become the Blitzkrieg."

⚜   ⚜   ⚜

"But Monsieur Snow is not at home I tell you!" Andre pushed past the butler into the spacious foyer of the mansion.

"Then I will wait for him."

"You must ring for an appointment, Colonel Chardon," the man pleaded. He glanced nervously over his shoulder at a pair of heavy mahogany double doors.

"His office?"

"No, Colonel." The man stepped between Andre and the path to the doors. "If you do not leave at once I shall be forced to telephone the . . ."

The panels slid back, interrupting the threat. Abraham Snow, a dignified presence with white hair, drooping moustache, suit and waistcoat from another era, stood framed in the arched doorway of the study. He viewed Andre for a long moment and then glanced up at the landing of the grand

staircase. Andre followed his gaze, hoping to glimpse Juliette, but the stairs were empty.

"Thank you, Pascal. You may show the colonel in. That will be all."

The servant bowed, clicked his heels like a Prussian aristocrat, and stepped aside. Pivoting with military precision, he hurried down the corridor.

Silence reigned as the two men contemplated one another for the first time. An enormous grandfather clock counted the seconds.

"You are Colonel Chardon," Snow nodded once. "She has your eyes."

"I had to speak with you."

"We may be a very ancient house, but we do have the modern conveniences. You might have telephoned."

"Like last time? To give you opportunity to go to . . . where was it?"

"Belgium." Snow's eyes narrowed. "We will be able to speak more freely in here."

Andre entered the large, high-ceilinged room with tall windows overlooking the Petrusse River. It was lined with bookshelves which surrounded an alcove where three original paintings of haystacks by Monet hung side by side to capture the full effect of the changing light.

On the wall behind an enormous, ornately carved desk, was a full-length portrait of a woman in a long yellow gown of Victorian fashion. She looked much like Elaine. Andre's eyes lingered on the woman's features.

"I see you are a man who appreciates beauty."

"She looks so much like . . ."

"She was Elaine's mother. She passed her perfection along to my daughter. And ultimately to your daughter as well."

"Monsieur Snow," Andre began. "I must speak to you about Juliette."

"She is at school, or I might have had you arrested at the door. You have been here before, have you not? Standing there on the riverbank?"

"Yes." Andre glanced at the light streaming through the window. Snow had watched him from here.

"Won't you sit down, Colonel Chardon? I suspect I know why you have come." There was resignation in his voice. He took a seat in a tall wing-backed leather chair opposite Andre. "I hear that the Nazis are collectors of great art." His gaze lingered on Monet's haystacks. "Hermann Goering, is it? He has had a palace built in Berlin just to house the paintings he has stolen." He inclined his head as if bowing to the inevitable. "Do you know the haystacks in the fields just across the river from us in Germany now conceal machine gun emplacements?"

Andre inhaled deeply with relief. It was true that Abraham Snow had good reason to hate Andre, but he was a realist. "That is why I hoped to speak with you today."

"Of course." Snow smoothed his moustache. "We in Luxembourg are protected by an army of 350 soldiers, Colonel. I am no fool, although others in the Grand Duchy may be. How long do you think we have?"

"It is spring. The ground is drying out."

"I drove to the Meuse yesterday. The Germans are observing our neutrality in a peculiar way. They have built their pontoon bridges halfway out from their side of the river to the center of the stream." He gave a bitter laugh and reached for a box of cigars on his desk. He offered one to Andre, who refused it, then took one for himself. "You are a soldier, Colonel. How long would it take them to construct the other half of their bridges into Luxembourg if der Führer is so inclined?"

"No doubt the parts are prefabricated."

"How long?"

"An hour."

With much thought, Snow trimmed the end of his cigar and lit it. "A single hour. And Luxembourg would go up in smoke."

"It could be. Yes. And that is why I came. If the Germans come through the Ardennes and Luxembourg . . ."

"If? Is it not inevitable?"

"There are some who think not."

Snow laughed. "Well then, they are in for a surprise, are they not, Colonel?"

Andre did not express his own certainty. "I am concerned for your welfare."

"And the welfare of my granddaughter?"

"Of course."

Snow let the ash on the end of his cigar grow. "It has occured to me, of course, that I may be at some disadvantage considering my social status. That is, if Hitler turns his eye on Luxembourg." He held up his fingers, ticking off logical reasons for danger. "I am, first of all, a Jew. A very unpopular thing to be in the eyes of the Nazis. Secondly, I own the highest producing steel manufacturing plant in the Duchy. And thirdly, of course, I have a collection of fine art which would be highly prized by Hermann Goering."

"Good reasons to get out of the way. Just in case."

"I considered Switzerland. But it is rumored they will move against Switzerland at the same moment they strike Belgium, Holland, and our little corner of the world."

"I cannot speak to that. Only to the fact that Luxembourg is likely to be a very busy intersection in a long German highway before long."

Now he tappd the ash delicately on the edge of the ashtray. "All of this does not mean that I do not despise you for what you have done. However . . . even in your folly you accomplished one good thing in your life. There is Juliette. My last real treasure, Colonel. The Nazis do not like Jewish children any more than they like steel magnates and art collectors, I am told."

"Let me bring her to Paris, to my home. You will both be welcome . . . safe there. Two million French soldiers stand between Germany and Paris, Monsieur Snow. I cannot think that line will be broken. And . . . I will not . . ." He faltered, unable to finish.

"You will not tell her who you are?"

"It does not matter. Her safety is my only concern now."

"In that we see eye to eye. Otherwise you would not be here. When will you take her?"

"Tonight. But will you not be coming with her?"

"I will follow later. If there is a later."

FIFTY-ONE

With a promise to pick up Josie at seven o'clock the next morning, the Fool let her out at the ancient Black Gate in Treves. The Porta Nigra Hotel, named for this Roman wall, was a grand old pile built in the Victorian splendor of the 1890s. Swastika banners draped the gingerbread cornices. Tall, arched windows looked out on a small quaint square, which bustled with men in uniform. The staff cars sporting the flags of officers from the German High Command arrived one after the other in front of the hotel. Josie recognized them from photographs and her brief stay in occupied Poland. Arriving first was the chief of Army Group A, von Rundstedt, and his Army commanders, Busch and List, also Army Group B's chief, von Bock, and his subordinates, Reichenau and von Kuchler. Following after these were the lesser lights: division leaders Erwin Rommel and Heinz Guderian.

Josie watched them enter the Porta Nigra with the sense that she had somehow stumbled into the hub of the Wehrmacht universe. There was a tangible excitement in the atmosphere. This gathering of eagles held the portent of momentous events.

Not one head turned her way as she ascended the steps and entered the hotel among the less vaunted members of the general staff. Josie brushed shoulders with plainclothes Gestapo agents, uniformed secretaries, and young adjutants all crowding into the lobby. Like a school of tiny scavenger fish, they swarmed after the sharks, oblivious to everything but the proud backs of their masters.

No one checked her documents. Would she be at the Porta Nigra without permission from Berlin? Impossible!

Josie hung back as they tramped en masse down a wide corridor to the double doors of a meeting room. Was Major Horst von Bockman among them, she wondered? Who of all these sycophants would have the courage to bring a Jewish child into the midst of such a congregation? The undertone of conversation sounded like a gaggle of geese. Coats and gun belts hung on a long polished coatrack in the hall. Here was proof of the superiority of the German nation. No one in the Reich would dare to steal the gun or the coat of a general.

The doors banged shut. The roar subsided to a murmur. Josie remained alone in the foyer and was at last approached by a wizened little doorman in the long green coat of a turn of the century hack driver.

"May I direct you, Fräulein?"

"I have reserved a room."

With this revelation he handed her over to the desk clerk who confirmed the fact that American journalist Josephine Marlow was indeed expected and most welcome in Treves. So far so good. He picked up a dusty book entitled *Rules for the Entertainment of American Tourists,* and rang the bell to summon a porter. She had no luggage, but she was escorted to her small hotel room where the red fabric of the Nazi flag blocked the view out onto the square. There, as instructed, she settled down to wait.

❀   ❀   ❀

Horst emerged from the staff meeting at the Porta Nigra Hotel in the late afternoon. The ever-present Gestapo agents lounged in overstuffed chairs in the lobby. They pretended to read the *Frankfurter Zeitung* as they observed the comings and goings of everyone who was not one of them. Wehrmacht officers made quiet jokes about Himmler's goons, citing the fact that this race of weasels had completely disappeared when the real action started in Poland. They only resurfaced when the bombs stopped falling. Soon enough they would scurry back to Berlin and hide in the Chancellory bunker once the offensive against France began.

In the meantime, they were here in Treves and were as dangerous as an .88 millimeter rifle. Horst resisted the urge to climb the stairs and knock on the door of number 221. He had spotted Josephine Marlow instantly among the crush of the crowd this morning. The American had arrived safely, at least, and moved easily through the confusion of the meeting as Horst had hoped. But things were quiet now, and he dared not push their luck. He decided to wait until after supper to go to her room. By then most of Himmler's agents would be full of sauerbratten and half drunk on good Muenchner beer.

He escaped the cloud of tobacco smoke, emerging onto the steps of the hotel. The morning had given some promise of warmth, but there remained a chill in the air.

Thousands of soldiers strolled along the narrow, twisting lanes of medieval Treves. By tomorrow night, Horst knew, they would be called back to their units in preparation for the offensive. Today they cluttered the sidewalks and bargained for mementos to send their families back home. Inkwells, cheap fountain pens, lead paperweights fashioned in the form of the cathedral all bore the legend, "Souvenir of Treves." By the end of the week it was quite possible that the fresh-faced private waiting patiently to purchase a pink comb for ten times its worth would no longer have a head.

And all the while, on the other side of the line, French and British soldiers, destined to die, were also being lovingly cheated by the merchants of their homeland. Just boys, all of them. Horst could not help feeling pity for them. The day was so beautiful. How many beautiful days did the world have left? He could count what remained of peace in hours now.

Horst inched his way through the throng and turned up an alleyway in a shortcut to the house of Katrina's aunt. The echo of youthful laughter pursued him. The living voices of the condemned already seemed a distant memory.

By tomorrow afternoon the shops will be empty . . .

The windows of the half-timbered home on St. Helena Strasse were open wide to let in the fresh spring air. Katrina was playing the piano. Horst could hear the music of Mozart, *Für Elise,* as he rounded the corner of the medieval lane. Window boxes overflowed with red and yellow blooms.

By tomorrow afternoon Katrina will be on a train to Berlin, and I will be gone . . .

He quickened his pace. He was grateful that the baby had given her reason to come to Treves. Pastel banners in the sky began to deepen to lavender and purple as he looked up through the steep gables. He took the stairs two at a time.

Katrina was here, he knew, but it seemed like a dream. The reality loomed terrible and dark over the beauty of Treves. How many years would it be before there was another spring day like this one in Europe?

✤   ✤   ✤

Katrina was alone in the house when Horst entered the small sitting room. She did not look away from the piano until the baby playing happily at her feet squealed and crawled quickly to Horst.

Horst stood awkwardly gazing down at the child as Yacov reached out to bat his reflection in the highly polished boots.

Katrina stopped playing. She smiled at the scene. "Pick him up, Horst. He wants you to pick him up."

The tall man scooped up the infant and raised him high overhead. Yacov chuckled a deep and rollicking baby-laugh, which made Horst smile in spite of all the news he had heard today.

"You should be a father," Katrina said wistfully.

He held Yacov in the crook of his elbow and sat in a delicate pettipoint chair beside the window of the bric-a-brac cluttered room. "When things are different we will have children. When our world is not controlled by madmen and morons and sadists."

"When will that be?"

He ignored her question. "Where is Aunt Lottie?"

"I took her to the train station. She will stay at Aunt Margarethe's until . . . I don't know how long."

"We are alone then." Yacov drove his finger into the side of Horst's mouth as if to disagree with the last statement. "Almost alone," Horst corrected himself.

"Yes." Katrina folded the sheets of music. "You did not tell me if the American came."

"She did."

Katrina lowered her head. "I see."

"You are sorry she came."

"He is a good baby, Horst." She did not look at her husband or the child. "I was hoping . . ."

"He is not a lost puppy."

"That was a harsh thing to say. Please . . . I only meant that I will miss him."

"I suppose his mother feels the same. If she is still alive," he remarked bitterly.

She glared at him. He wanted to argue with her, it was obvious. "What happened to you between this morning and now?"

He rubbed his forehead, attempting to push away the ache. "We are all being called up. Every unit. You know what that means."

Her eyes lingered on the baby. "It means . . . he must go with her. Must." Then her gaze flitted to Horst's face. "It means this is our last night . . . it means . . . let us not waste what few hours we have left. Not argue. Look at me, Horst. Please."

He nodded and stretched out his hand to her. She came to him and cradled his head. "I am sorry," he whispered. "For myself. For you. For this child, and ten million others. For everyone. And there is nothing I can do. There is no changing anything."

❧ ❧ ❧

The Snow mansion was built in the grand style of the nineteenth century with a formal staircase leading up to a large sitting room with Louis XIV furniture and a massive concert piano in the corner. French doors opened onto a broad balcony which overlooked the Petrusse River.

It was nearly 8:00 P.M. but the sky was still light behind the rain clouds when Andre arrived and was directed by the sad-eyed butler up to the sitting room.

At the top of the stairs was a portrait of Elaine in the blue dress. She smiled down at him. Her tranquil gaze followed him with the same tolerant amusement he had seen in her eyes a thousand times when they had been together.

You have been a fool, Andre, she seemed to say. *You missed the best of everything. You lost me and nearly lost Juliette! But now you have another chance. Take it!*

Those words thrummed in his head with every step. *Another chance! Another chance! Another chance!*

He entered the pale yellow room which displayed the stamp of Elaine's good taste. Monsieur Snow stood beside the piano Elaine had played. He wore a dark burgundy smoking jacket. The dourness of his expression and darkness of his form and clothing seemed to clash with the brightness of the space.

Andre's breath was coming fast as he looked around for Juliette. She was not there.

Snow did not move as Andre entered. He pivoted his head slightly in acknowledgment and nodded to the butler in some unspoken signal the two men understood. The servant gave Andre a half-smile as if to indicate that he had kept his promise and had given the doll to Juliette. He was an ally, silently cheering Andre on.

"You are very prompt, Colonel," Snow said stiffly.

"I hope not too early."

"Juliette is not yet here." He inclined his head slightly. "Ballet class. Like her mother at that age." There was infinite sadness in his voice. "We are losing our whole world. But little girls must have dancing lessons."

How to reply? Should he promise that Juliette would forever have ballet lessons? Piano lessons? Ride the carousel in the Tuileries every Sunday?

Should he tell Monsieur Snow that his granddaughter would live in a world as perfect as if there were no war?

"Shall I collect her luggage before she comes back? Perhaps it will make the parting easier."

"There will be time for that. Grundig will see to it."

"How did she take the news that she is leaving?"

"She does not know yet." The old man's shoulders sagged for just an instant. "I could not bring myself to tell her everything; only that she would be leaving with a friend of her mother's for a short visit."

It was clear in his expression that he did not believe he would ever see the child again. This was more than just a temporary parting for him. It was a final farewell.

Andre took a step nearer and extended his hand palm up like a supplicant begging for forgiveness. "Please. You must come with her. Elaine would approve if . . . after everything . . . we were to become friends. You come to stay in my house in Paris until this business is over."

"We will never be friends, Colonel. We may be allies out of necessity for this time, but we will never be friends." His cheek twitched with emotion. "Why was it you were unable to marry Elaine, Colonel?"

Carrying two brandy snifters, the butler entered the room, interrupting Andre's reply. Snow raised his glass. "Napoleon brandy." He swirled the amber liquid. "Eighteen-sixty. I was saving the bottle to share with the man who married Elaine. If it might have been. I will have to content myself to drink with the father of my grandchild." The servant left and closed the double doors behind him. "Now you must explain to me. Why did you not marry my daughter?"

Andre studied the brandy. This was the question he had dreaded. "My grandfather . . . threatened to disinherit me if I . . ."

"If you married a Jewess?" Snow finished and inhaled deeply of his brandy. "Is that correct, Colonel?"

"It is." Did his voice betray the shame he felt in that admission?

Snow raised his brows slightly in a gesture of understanding. He looked from Andre to the faint light emanating through the window. "Ah well, it does not matter after today, does it? Our lives, our individual folly, all evaporate after today."

"This war . . . this Great Folly . . . is made up of insignificant fool-ishness, Monsieur Snow. Each minute evil committed or allowed by ordinary men has evaporated into the air like water in the hot sun. We thought it did not matter, but now it has come back in a cloud to cover us with darkness— with storm and flood and thunder. My little sins? Joined with those of other men, they may now wash us all away." He placed his snifter on the table. "I

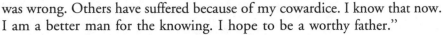

was wrong. Others have suffered because of my cowardice. I know that now. I am a better man for the knowing. I hope to be a worthy father."

"In that case . . . pick up your glass, Colonel. I will drink with you. I should have liked you I think, if there had been time."

They drank together.

The servant knocked softly on the door.

"Mam'zelle Juliette has just arrived, Monsieur Snow."

"Thank you." And then to Andre, "Have you seen her?" He held back the curtain and let Andre look down on the street.

Andre watched as the grey-uniformed chauffeur circled the car and opened the back passenger door. Reaching in, he extended a gloved hand to assist his passenger. A moment, and then a five-year-old girl emerged. Miraculously, she held the doll that Andre left for her so many months before. She was dressed all in blue: blue coat, hat, and toe-shoes. Very pretty, and yet she was a picture of the unhappiness she surely felt. The child was not in a hurry to climb the steps. Turning her oval face up toward the house, Andre could see that she was frightened. She blinked as drops of rain began to fall. Turning to the open door of the vehicle for a moment, it seemed as if she would step back in.

The chauffeur, Rene, was a man with seven children of his own. He bent at the waist until his face was level with hers. He said something cheerful, gestured toward the house, and then took her hand. She nodded, one downward thrust of the chin only, then walked slowly up the steps beside the chauffeur.

"She is small," Andre said under his breath. "So small."

The bell rang. Andre watched her enter the house. Conversation drifted up the stairs; the too-cheerful voice of the housekeeper asked Rene about the weather and the roads, muffled replies, and then questions about dance class.

"I almost missed you standing there behind fat Rene, Mademoiselle! Pardon!" the housekeeper teased. "Come here. Let's have a look at the costume. Ah, very fine. Beautiful, wouldn't you say, Rene?"

Rene agreed with a laugh and then excused himself to get the young lady's valise and move the car.

Andre felt his throat constrict as he and the old man stepped out of the sitting room and stood on the landing to listen. The child's voice was soft. Some words were lost to him. He looked over the banister but could not see her face. She seemed even smaller beside Rene's six-foot-three frame. She blended into a sapphire square of marble on the checkerboard floor of the foyer.

Boot heels clicked on the polished tiles. For an instant Andre wished that Paul was here. Paul may have envied Andre's ability with women, but Andre's younger brother was a master with children. Dumb animals and innocents were charmed by his cheerful nature and openness. Andre had always considered those traits to be foolish, but today he envied his brother.

"I will go down first," said Monsieur Snow in a forced tone.

The child said hesitantly, "How do you do, Grandpapa?"

"I am very well indeed, despite the rain. Our guest has come."

She had come home early to meet the old friend of her mother . . . She had come to meet Andre, who was standing frozen above them on the landing, wishing he was elsewhere.

Monsieur Snow looked up. His eyes locked on Andre's face. A flash of compassion. Was Andre coming down?

Andre nodded curtly, drew a deep breath, and hurried down the broad, curving stairway.

"Here he comes now, I think, Juliette." Snow put his hands on her shoulders and gently pivoted her toward the staircase.

For an instant her eyes flitted upward toward Andre. Brown eyes. More like milk chocolate than dark. Like Andre's eyes . . . She looked quickly down at the toes of her shoes. Her cheeks flushed. She had dark eyebrows and long lashes. Andre could not see her hair color beneath the snug-fitting cap, but she looked like a miniature version of her mother. Darker of complexion perhaps, but there was no doubt that this was Elaine's child—a beautiful child.

He and Snow exchanged looks over her head.

"Bonjour, Mademoiselle Juliette." Andre extended his hand palm up. Still unable to meet his gaze, she touched her tiny fingertips to his. He quickly kissed her hand and then stepped back.

"Bonjour," she whispered.

"I am . . . I was . . . I knew your mother very well, Juliette." Andre looked at his own reflection in the gilt mirror. Today, he looked older than his thirty-two years. There were dark circles under his deep brown eyes. His normally elegant and erect frame seemed stooped a bit. He had shaved, yet his face seemed dark. "I am sorry about what has happened to your maman."

Juliette did not answer. Her chin trembled. She looked at his highly polished shoes, at his gold cuff links, at his hands and manicured nails, but never at his face.

Had Elaine told the child about him . . . about them?

"Do you know who I am, Juliette?"

"Yes, Monsieur. You are Monsieur Andre Chardon. You were my mamere's friend a very long time ago. And I am to stay at your house now for a short time. Grandfather says so."

So she was unaware. It would make it easier for Andre if she did not know; no messy sentimentality, no expectations. He began to talk as though he were discussing the sale of a thousand cases of wine.

"Very good, Juliette. We have a room prepared for you, Monsieur Paul and I and a fellow named Richard. We are three bachelors in a very big house and know very little about children. Monsieur Paul is an officer at a military school . . . and away from Paris much of the time. I have duties with the government now. And there is a gentleman, Richard, whom you will meet . . . he is a guest there. You may think he is odd . . . He may seem to ignore you, but he is only thinking all the time. He may not even know you are there. A very beautiful lady from America will ride with us to Paris."

Now she looked up at him fiercely. "Maman kept your photograph on her dressing table." The statement was an accusation. Why had he never come to see them? If he was such a good friend before, why did he not help Maman when she needed a friend? Eyes brimmed. She bit her lip to hold back tears.

Andre was not handling this at all well.

"I was sorry to hear about your maman, Juliette. Truly I was. She was very beautiful. Bright and happy when I knew her." Andre dropped the business-like tone. Silence. "Are you hungry? Have you eaten? I made a reservation for supper and then tomorrow we can go to Paris. There is a carousel at the Tuileries if you like."

Silence. She clasped her hands and looked at the enormous front door as though she wanted to run away. Thankfully, Snow put his hand firmly on Andre's shoulder in a gesture of support.

"Juliette, it was Colonel Chardon who gave you Clementine, your doll. You will enjoy being with him. Rene will drive you to your hotel."

Juliette clung to the hand of her grandfather. "Will you not come too, Grandpapa?"

The old man shook his head firmly. "We have been over that. I have business." Although his tone was abrupt, Andre saw the shine of moisture in his eyes. He stooped and embraced the child briefly, then turned wordlessly and climbed the stairs to pass out of her life forever.

FIFTY-TWO

What if nobody comes?

The thought occurred to Josie a hundred times as the evening deepened into night. It was after nine o'clock. She was hungry, but she dared not go down to dinner. She sat beside the window in the unlit room and tried to see into the square. The breeze caught the red banner and lifted it, then let it fall again.

Tinny music from a phonograph playing military marches penetrated the walls. Voices and footsteps passed in the corridor. No one knocked. Would the German major bring the child to her? The instructions had seemed so simple:

Enter Germany through Luxembourg over Wasserbillig Bridge. A taxi will be waiting for you there. Bring nothing but your passport and American documents for the child. Treves. Porta Nigra Hotel. A room will be reserved in your name. Wait there.

And so she waited. She waited for hours. She had not yet cut away the end sheets from the book to remove the child's identity papers. She would not do so until she had the baby safely in her arms. To be arrested with forged identity documents and no infant to go along with them would be proof of intention to defraud the Reich. The volume of *Faust* remained on the night table.

Now it occurred to her that perhaps there was no more German major, no Jewish baby from Warsaw. All this might be an exercise in futility. A German officer determined to risk his safety for the sake of one child might already be tucked away in one of those prisons the Western democracies kept hearing about. If that was the case, she would simply meet the taxi driver in the morning and head back to the Wasserbillig Bridge.

She was about to kick her shoes off and climb onto the bed when soft rapping sounded on the door.

She did not switch on the lamp, but stood in the darkness with her hand on the doorknob and her heart beating a tattoo as she remembered the Gestapo agents downstairs. She wondered if her ride through the Siegfried Line had somehow caught up with her.

"Who is it?" she asked stupidly in French.

"Frau Marlow?" The response was whispered—urgent.

She opened the door to the dim blue light of the corridor. A tall, lean German officer pushed past her, shut the door behind him, and snapped the bolt in place. She could not see his face. He did not attempt to turn on the light.

"Horst von Bockman. Guten abend. Bitte, take off your clothes, Frau Marlow." He was already unbuttoning his tunic.

"Take off my . . ." she stammered and backed away. Either this was some kind of joke or the major was drunk. She could see the outline of a bottle in his hand.

"I have been followed. Gestapo. Do as I say, Frau Marlow, or we are dead! Take off your clothes and get into bed." She fumbled at the buttons of her jacket and blouse. He flung his tunic carelessly across the back of a chair and kicked off his shoes, then pulled the blackout curtain tight across the window, mussed his hair, and turned back the sheets. "He may come to this room. You and I have been lovers since Warsaw."

She obeyed him; stripping to her camisole, she climbed into bed with her skirt on. She pulled the blanket tight around her chin and lay there with her teeth chattering. He left his trousers on and stood barefooted in the center of the room to wait.

The blare of the military march seemed a strange counterpoint to the pounding of her heart. Why had he been tailed?

Only moments passed before a fist hammered on the thin wood.

"What do you want?" Horst bellowed angrily.

"If you please," came the polite reply. "A message for you, Herr officer."

"I am busy! Go annoy someone else!"

"It is most urgent, I assure you," the voice whined.

Horst leaned close to Josie. "We met in Poland, you and I. Remember we are in love."

Then Horst cursed loudly for the benefit of the intruder and fumbled with the bolt before he opened the door a crack.

Blue light spilled in, followed by the rough shove of a massive man in a long leather coat. There was an instant of struggle in the blackness. When the light was snapped on, a gun was at the head of Horst von Bockman.

"Well, well. Heil Hitler." The Gestapo agent beamed at Josie. "Two birds with one stone, it seems."

"What is the meaning of this?" Horst growled through clenched teeth as the muzzle of the weapon steered him toward a chair and guided him to sit.

"Come now, Major von Bockman." The heavy-set, dark-eyed man seemed very pleased with himself. "While every other member of my force has been scampering after the great men, I, alone, have been observing. It was you who arranged for a taxi to be at the Wasserbillig bridge this morning, was it not? That half-wit of a taxi driver told me everything."

No use denying the fact.

"So what?"

"So . . . You bring this American woman here through the Western defenses. You take me for a fool? She is a spy. And you are a traitor."

Horst stiffened at the accusation. The hammer on the pistol clicked back.

"Does this look like we are involved in treason?" Horst waved the brandy bottle clutched in his fist.

The ponderous head of the official pivoted to consider Josie, who peered out with wide, terrified eyes at the scene. She attempted to blurt out the words from the impromptu script which the major had given her, but she could not speak.

"A little pleasure with your business, Herr Major?" the agent smirked.

"Americans are neutrals, have you forgotten?" Horst remarked coolly. "And you are taking your idiotic games too far for the approval of the Reich or the Führer or your own superiors." He gestured toward his tunic which bore the decoration earned for bravery in Poland. "You call me a traitor? I will see you are shot for this, Herr whatever your name is."

"Herr Mueller," replied the agent with a click of his heels. He was not to be so easily convinced.

"Then, Herr Mueller, I would suggest you remove your weapon from my head and telephone General Rommel to ask his opinion of my loyalty. He is staying in this hotel."

For the first time Josie saw the fixed smile of Herr Mueller twitch with doubt. "The general should not be bothered with matters of security."

"He will wish to be consulted in a matter so serious, I assure you. A matter involving harassment and false accusations against one of his front line commanders."

Mueller stepped back from Horst, still keeping the barrel level on his head.

"Shall *I* call the general then?"

Mueller's smile vanished. The taint of fear crept into his expression. He stepped back one more step.

"Please summon the general, Herr Mueller. I insist you do, unless you wish to be strung up by piano wire. Frau Marlow and I have known one another since Warsaw. You may check that fact if you wish." His rebuttal was hard steel and ice, the voice of a leader not to be questioned. "Frau Marlow is an American journalist. She was trapped behind the lines in the siege. We met and have been good friends since that time. Her documents are quite in order." He reached over and snatched up her passport, opening it to display the visa stamps of Poland, then the Nazi occupied territories of Poland, after that the Third Reich and finally the stamp of the customs officials at the Wasserbillig bridgehead. "All in order, Herr Mueller." Horst tossed the passport to Josie.

It fell on the bed beside her. She merely nodded. She had gone mute.

The Gestapo agent also seemed to be suddenly struck dumb. He lowered his weapon a fraction, and for an instant it looked as though Horst had defeated him. Then he threw a hard look at Josie's jacket and blouse. Something was wrong. His mouth curved in a half-smile. He reached out and tore the blanket off the bed, revealing that Josie was still wearing her skirt and her shoes.

He threw back his head in laughter at the attempted deception. "Very good! I was almost convinced. In quite a rush, major?" Then to Josie as he pressed the gun hard against her temple, he said, "Get up, Frau Marlow." He menaced. "Gestapo headquarters will be interested to hear you explain that Americans make love with their shoes on. I remain unconvinced, however." He ogled her form, leering at her as if her obvious terror heightened his own pleasure. "You are both under arrest for espionage and conspiracy against the Reich. Heil Hit . . ."

The heavy glass of the brandy bottle crashed down on the back of Mueller's skull. The force of the blow propelled him face first into the wall at the head of the bed. Josie gave a shriek, putting both hands up to her face to stifle her own scream. The gun flew up in the air and landed on a pillow as Josie rolled across to the opposite side. Mueller fell heavily across the bed. His mouth hung limply open and a heavy, sonorous sound rolled from it as if he were sleeping off drunkenness.

Josie pressed against the furthest wall, wide-eyed and panting. She clutched her jacket to her like a life preserver. Horst examined Mueller and looked down at the brandy bottle still swinging by its neck in readiness.

"Well, Frau Marlow," Horst said. His words were calm, but Josie could see his eyes darting around the room, keeping pace with his racing thoughts. "We are very fortunate . . . all things considered. The gun did not go off, the bottle did not break, and we do not have a dead Gestapo agent in your bedroom to explain."

"But what will we do now?"

Horst uncorked the brandy and splashed some on the recumbent Mueller. "I have a car in the alley behind the hotel. With your help I think we can take our drunken friend here for a ride."

"It is too dangerous for you to remain in Treves until morning," Horst warned Josie as he began to sift through Mueller's pockets. He shredded every scrap of identification and proceeded to flush the paper down the toilet. "We must take you directly to Wasserbillig. Do you have the documents for the baby?"

She held up the copy of *Faust* in reply. "Here."

"Listen carefully." He took her arm and glared into her eyes. "You must not take the child back to France."

"Belgium or Holland then?"

"No!" He emphasized his vehemence by gripping her arm painfully. "Get him off the continent. To England first. Do it immediately. Do you understand me, Frau Marlow? After tomorrow it will be too late. Take a train from Luxembourg, then a neutral ferry to England from Ostend. Soon there will be no neutrals."

"But Holland . . ."

"You witnessed Poland. I need not tell you more. Get him out of Europe!"

His warning was so stern and frightening that Josie knew instantly there was far more at stake here than the life of one child.

Not Holland! Not Belgium! Soon there would be no neutrals!

Horst checked to see that the corridor was clear, then supporting Mueller between them, Josie and Horst staggered down the back stairs of the Porta Nigra. A Wehrmacht staff car waited in the alley.

The blackout in Treves facilitated their moves. Horst bound and gagged Mueller, then crammed him into the boot of the vehicle as Josie climbed in.

It took her a moment before she noticed she was not alone.

From the back seat, the soft voice of a woman startled her.

"He is a good baby, Frau Marlow. No trouble. You will see."

Josie gasped and whirled to peer into the dark shadows. She could see only the vague outlines of someone directly behind her. "Who are you?"

"I am Katrina von Bockman. The major's wife. I have brought Yacov to you."

Josie wished her mastery of German was better. There was so much she wanted to say; so many questions to ask; but the words escaped her. In an instant Horst was behind the wheel and they were inching through the narrow lanes of Treves.

"There was trouble." Horst explained to Katrina.

"Gestapo?"

"Yes."

Katrina was calm. "He is dead?"

"Not yet."

"What will we do?" If she was worried, the tone of her voice did not betray it.

"It is tragic how many drunks stumble in the dark." Then to Josie he said,

"It is time now to take out the travel documents of your son, Frau Marlow. You have been a delightful guest for me and Katrina. We hate to see you go."

Josie peeled back the end sheet on the copy of *Faust* and removed the dated document for infant Daniel John Marlow. They rode in silence for several miles, finally coming to a roadblock guarded by a drowsy sentry who shone his flashlight in through the window at each of the occupants. This was the first glimpse Josie had of the baby who was supposed to be her son. He slept in the arms of Katrina. He was fair skinned and plump. A blue knit cap covered his head. He sucked his thumb in contentment. A beautiful child.

With seemingly detached boredom, Horst passed their documents to the sentry who gave then a cursory glance and then waved the vehicle through. A number of rumbling lorries pulled up to the gate behind them. Horst speeded up and turned onto a side lane beside the berm of a rail line. Switching off the engine, he sat in silence.

"Herr Mueller is about to attempt to stop the train to Luxembourg." With that he set the hand brake, retrieved a tire iron from beneath the seat, and left the car.

The baby sighed in Katrina's arms. The sweet scent of spring flowers drifted in through the window. Josie heard the trunk lid open and the moan of Mueller through the gag. This was followed by what sounded like a metallic clank against a ripe melon. Silence. Horst von Bockman had left nothing to chance. Josie felt ill.

"He has done what he must, Frau Marlow," Katrina von Bockman defended her husband in a hoarse whisper.

The vehicle swayed a bit as the major pulled the heavy body of Mueller out of the trunk. And then above the calls of the night birds came the sound of the body being dragged through the gravel and up the berm to be deposited on the tracks.

How cool von Bockman seemed! He returned to the car. He acted as unruffled as if he had just stepped on a cockroach instead of killing a man! Josie was not sure she liked him. She should thank him for saving her life. She should admire him for rescuing the baby. "I am . . . grateful," she stammered unconvincingly.

"Do not waste pity on a creature like Mueller."

"You are efficient," she replied. It was his efficiency which disturbed her most about all of this.

"I know it is hard for you to understand, Frau Marlow," he replied to her unspoken question. "Perhaps later you will see. It is necessary. When an unpleasant task is necessary then emotion is a waste of energy. Perhaps even dangerous. You will be safe now. And this baby will be out of reach of a man like Mueller for the time being. That is what matters." He turned the key in the ignition and pulled away. "Mueller will not be going anywhere. The train to Luxembourg is due to pass here in ten minutes. It will finish the job. Chances are the authorities will never know who he was. Better for us. The offensive begins immediately, and who will even think of a drunk on the railroad tracks after that?"

Moments later they were back on the main highway moving through the darkness toward Wasserbillig bridgehead.

The sky was backlit with the glow of predawn pastels. The hilly outline of Luxembourg was peaceful across the river as Horst and Katrina escorted Josie into the customshouse.

Perhaps it was the sight of the decoration on the uniform of Horst von Bockman which made the customs officials and sentries step aside as Josie and the baby were waved through the barrier. Yacov Lubetkin, who had been well dosed with cough medicine beforehand, slept through the inspection at the customshouse.

Josie embraced Katrina von Bockman as if she was a family member. She kissed the major awkwardly on his cheek and thanked him for the enjoyable time.

In an exuberant voice, Horst explained to the early morning shift that Frau Marlow was an American cousin and that the trip with her small son was their very first into the Reich. "She has seen the miracle of National Socialism," he announced solemnly, "and she will carry the good report back to America."

They nodded with pleasure. They did not doubt that National Socialism was the eighth wonder of the world. They simply wanted the world to agree with them.

What Josie had to tell was far more sobering than a glowing account of the Nazi miracle, however. The details of the Wehrmacht's plan she was carrying back along with the contraband baby was enough to have her executed a hundred times. She knew it. Horst von Bockman knew it. The weight of it made her resent the cheerful conversation and the too-long good-byes on the German side of the barrier at Wasserbillig. But for the sake of authenticity, they acted out their family farewell to the last detail.

"Take care of the little one." Horst touched the cheek of the sleeping child. Then he lowered his voice as he leaned close to her ear. "Remember. Do as I told you."

There were tears in Katrina's eyes as she stooped to kiss Yacov. "He will not remember me," she said. "Such a good baby. Mention us to his grandfather, will you, Josephine? Tell him . . . I pray for the baby's mother. I wonder . . ." Then, "Pray for us." The words were no mere scene being played for the Nazi onlookers.

"I will," Josie nodded stiffly, "danke." There must have been something kind to say, some good word to leave with them, but she could think of nothing but the car parked at the bier-stube on the other side of the bridge. She wanted nothing but to put as much distance between her and the miracle of National Socialism as possible.

It was as if she could feel the earth already rumbling from the rolling tracks of thousands of German tanks. What would this place look like by the next dawn?

"Auf Wiedersehen."

The striped barrier pole was raised. The young sentry saluted Horst. Eyes flitted to the Knight's Cross. Then the young Aryan chucked the Jewish baby on the chin as Josie passed by and strode the few paces into Luxembourg.

She tried to control her urge to jog the remaining length of the bridge onto the soil of the Grand Duchy. She heard the clunk of the barrier falling into place behind her. Turning to look back, she saw Horst and Katrina von Bockman gazing after her wistfully. Soon enough the major would be crossing some other neutral border, Josie knew. She did not want to be there to greet him when he arrived.

They waved. The sentry waved. And Josie waved.

⚜ ⚜ ⚜

"Tell me everything you saw, ma chérie! Everything the major said!" Andre gripped the hands of Josie as she recited the details of what lay beyond the West Wall.

"Thousands of soldiers . . . And he told me I must not to back to Paris."

"They mean to bomb Paris, then."

"He told me to take the baby right on to England. The train from Luxembourg to Ostend today and then the ferry across the Channel tomorrow."

Andre glanced at his watch. "We've missed the train. The next is not until tomorrow." He raised his gaze through the double doors of the suite to where Juliette played on the floor beside the baby boy. She was happy for the first time since they had left the home of Abraham Snow. Had he found her only to let her go so soon?

Josie recognized the anguish in his eyes. "Come with us, Andre," she said in an urgent whisper. "Come with us to England."

Considering her with a sad smile he shook his head. "It was you who spoke of courage, chérie. Could I run away for the sake of love?"

"Yes!" Her vehemence surprised her. "Please, Andre! There is Juliette to consider now . . . and me! I don't want to say good-bye again! You once said you had found something worth living for . . . We can marry. Go to America and . . ."

He opened his mouth to reply when the telephone rang. Andre held the receiver to his ear. Who would be calling him here? He recognized the voice of Bertrand instantly.

"We have passed Lewinski's information to the King in Brussels. German fifth columnists disguised as tourists are poring across the borders of Belgium and Holland. They are being mobilized at this instant. You are needed at our embassy in Brussels tonight."

Did Bertrand not realize that the telephone lines might be tapped? That to mention the name of Richard Lewinski was not only foolish but dangerous?

Bertrand did not wait for Andre to respond. "Do you understand?"

"Oui."

"Go now. Tomorrow will be too late. Good luck."

The line clicked dead. What additional news had Lewinski gleaned from the dispatches? Andre replaced the receiver in its cradle and then gave Josie a hard look.

"I will drive you as far as Brussels. Then you must take both children to Ostend by train. Then the ferry across to England . . ."

"But Andre!" she protested.

He cupped her chin in his hand. "My sweet hypocrite. I cannot go with you. I do not know if I am honored by your request for my desertion or insulted that you really thought I might go."

"Then I'll stay with you. Stay in Paris. The Nazis will never get as far as Paris."

He directed her gaze to the children. "Have you forgotten Warsaw, chérie? Warsaw, where perhaps the parents of that baby have been murdered. Paris will be bombed. Look at them . . . They are your duty. Yacov. Juliette."

She embraced him. Tears stung her eyes. "But to leave you, Andre! Knowing that maybe . . ."

"To think of maybe will make us both cowards. The hour has come for France. Some to fight. Some to say farewell. I will not say which is harder. But as for us, we will follow whatever course is charted for us."

❧   ❧   ❧

The sun was high above the hills and canyons of Luxembourg as Andre took the road north across the frontier into Belgium.

Yacov perched wide-eyed and attentive on Josie's lap. Juliette sat sad and solemn in the back seat of the Citroen as the familiar sights of the Grand Duchy fell away. A single sentry checked Andre's papers at the Belgian

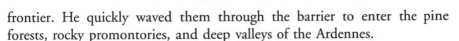

frontier. He quickly waved them through the barrier to enter the pine forests, rocky promontories, and deep valleys of the Ardennes.

The Ardennes: Belgium's natural Maginot Line. Swift rivers ran past castles and tiny slate-roofed villages. Summer houses and stone-walled inns and taverns lined narrow, twisting roads that reached out from Liege like the thin strands of a spider web. Idyllic, storybook beauty could not conceal the vision of coming horror in Andre's mind as he sped through lonely forests and past high cliffs which dropped away into the river valleys below.

This vacationer's paradise, this seemingly intractable wilderness, was Hitler's biggest secret weapon.

Behind the peaceful woodlands, Hitler's Panzer Korps waited for the signal to explode across the border into Belgium.

There was little sign of any Belgian military presence on the twisting highway. A Belgian motorcyclist roared by, followed by a group of young men on bicycles who pedaled toward the heart of the forest. Were they among the thousands German "tourists" being sent across the neutral frontiers of the Ardennes in advance of invasion? Dressed in camping clothes suitable for an outing in the area, they were nonetheless grim faced and hard looking. They did not look like young students out for a holiday.

Andre kept his suspicions to himself, but he pressed his foot down harder on the accelerator.

Josephine must have felt his urgency to reach Brussels, and yet, for the sake of Juliette, she pretended that this was nothing more than a lovely excursion. Yacov slept in her arms as she taught the child American songs. "Bye, Bye Blackbird" and "Happy Days Are Here Again!" The latter seemed a ludicrous sentiment to Andre, considering that this might well be the last happy day in Europe for a long time to come.

They stopped at a small inn and purchased sandwiches made from famous Ardennes ham. Juliette picked out a half dozen pastries to take along with them. That and a bottle of cold, fresh milk provided the makings of a picnic. But they ate their meal as Andre drove too fast along the treacherous highway which led into the lowlands.

The sun was setting as they swooped out of the foothills. Here, they came upon a long line of rumbling troop lorries and camouflaged trucks followed by small artillery pieces mounted on rattling tractors.

Only now did Josie dare to look at Andre and compare the Belgian defenses with what she had witnessed on her journey through the German lines facing Luxembourg.

"Is this the best they have?" she asked him with dread.

"It is," he replied curtly. "And it is headed away from the Ardennes, as you see. Entirely in the wrong direction."

FIFTY-THREE

Word arrived that the patients at the Charity Hospital were to be evacuated south so that space might be dedicated to the future victims of bombing in Paris. If there were any.

Uncle Jambonneau was very pleased. He had always wanted to spend time in Southern France with its balmy climate and vineyards and such. He dictated a message of farewell to Marie and Jerome.

> *Perhaps I shall learn to paint! A new experience for me! Landscapes by a blind man. Ah well, maybe not. Next to seeing the sun, the best thing is to feel the sun warming one's face . . .*

Promising to send notes often, he gave the address of the sanitarium for soldiers of des Grandes Armée outside of Marseilles. As a parting gift, Uncle Jambonneau bequeathed Papillon to Jerome forever. It was very touching.

There were ninety children staying at la Huchette on May ninth. Madame Rose had managed through the assistance of friends in high places to obtain tickets to the matinee performance of *Snow White* for everyone.

Jerome had been to only one movie in his entire life, and of all impossible things which Madame Rose and God had arranged, this seemed the most miraculous of all.

Columns of children passed to the Right Bank over Pont Neuf. Pushing Henri's chair, Jerome pointed out the *Garlic* moored below. The boat looked very fine now. Madame Hilaire and her Thief had fixed it up. There was a For Sale sign on the end of the gangway. The rudder was in place. The sails and rigging were repaired and tied off neatly. Smoke from the engine sputtered up as the Thief worked on it.

"My sister and I used to live there," Jerome said to Henri.

"Why do you not live there now?" Henri looked at the boat and then down to admire the shine of his boots.

"It was stolen from us. But it does not matter. It was a good thing they stole it because Marie has glasses and we are very happy with Madame Rose and Madame Betsy. I think when Papa meets the sisters he will see what a good thing it is we did not stay with Madame Hilaire while he was gone."

Jerome meant what he said. He did not even feel angry about the *Garlic* anymore. He had friends and lots to eat these days. He did not have to worry about Marie. He was going to see an American motion picture with dwarfs and witches. And it was spring. There would be flowers blooming at the Maginot Line for his Papa to see. Soon the war would be over. How much better could life be?

❧   ❧   ❧

There was in all the world nothing so wonderful as *Snow White,* Jerome thought. He conceded that the seven dwarfs were greedy little capitalists who should have distributed all those jewels from their mines to the poor, but Jerome liked them all the same. He hoped that one day the dwarfs would meet up with Madame Rose and their hoarded wealth would become potatoes and shoes and eyeglasses and even tickets to the cinema.

He would like to be around to see it!

The air raid siren erupted just as Jerome pushed Henri's chair onto Pont Neuf. There were a few squeaks and squeals from the girls. Everyone craned their heads up to search the sky for German bombers. Madame Betsy was calm. Madame Rose was calm. A few German bombers? Nothing to worry about. Walk to the nearest shelter and wait until the all-clear.

Below the stone wall of the bridge the piercing voice of Madame Hilaire echoed.

"MON DIEU! HURRY! TO THE SHELTER! WE MUST RUN TO THE SHELTER! YOU KNOW WHAT THE FIREMAN HAS SAID! THE BOCHE WILL BOMB BOATS ON THE QUAY TO BLOCK THE RIVER FIRST OF ALL!"

Jerome leaned over the rail and looked down at the crazed anteater as she ran in circles and waved her arms at the Thief who moved slowly, wearily, toward the gangway. She dragged him toward the stone steps which led up to the street level. Poor fellow. He thought he was only stealing the *Garlic* and he ended up with Madame Hilaire. A fate worse than death. She was louder than the siren, Jerome thought, as he pushed Henri's chair toward the nearest shelter.

❧   ❧   ❧

Federov nodded and tapped his patent leather shoe in time to the tune. Mozart was one of his favorites, and the student ensemble performed most credibly.

Having offered to cater the light refreshments for the noontime recital, the wine merchant was naturally offered a seat in the front row. The Église de la Sorbonne, where the concert was being held, was a pleasant setting, especially with the white marble tomb of Cardinal Richelieu providing the backdrop for the string quartet.

The midday gathering was well attended, despite the restrictions imposed by the war. Federov was certain that since the majority of those in attendance were either poor students or underpaid instructors; perhaps the refreshments were as big a draw as the music. Sugar for fancy baked goods and German Rhine wines to accompany them were almost impossible to obtain at any price. Several of the university officials made a particular point of thanking Federov personally.

"Completely my pleasure," Federov acknowledged to Professor Argo of the mathematics department. "But tell me, are we missing a few familiar faces?"

"Ah, yes," Argo agreed, smoothing back his white hair and stroking his pointed white beard. "The Americans have all gone home, as have the Swiss and the Belgians. It seems that our colleagues of the neutral nations have scurried away."

"Well, it has happened all over because of blighted politics," Federov pointed out. "Fascist beliefs and intellectual life cannot coexist, it seems. Of course, some consequences are more drastic than others. Look at what happened to university life in Warsaw," he shook his head. "Tragic." Then as if a sudden thought struck him, he snapped his fingers. "Say, I wonder whatever happened to that eccentric genius who was Polish. You know the one I mean . . . what is his name? His father was a professor here and he is a wizard at numbers."

Professor Argo thought a moment. "You must mean Lewinski."

"That is it, exactly. What do you suppose happened to him?"

"It is odd you should mention him," Argo said. "A promising advanced level student of mine: female, great mind for numbers theory, higher order equations, that sort of thing . . . where was I?"

"Lewinski," Federov encouraged, trying to not let his impatience show.

"Yes, well, this student, who had heard Lewinski lecture on his arcane theory . . . something about a universal machine that can speak to other machines . . . anyway, this student thought she encountered Lewinski and mentioned it to me."

"Encountered him where?"

"Here, that is, in Paris somewhere."

"What did she mean, she *thought* she met him?"

Argo held the tuft of his beard as if squeezing the recollection out of it. "It has been some time ago now, but I think she said hello to a man, thinking it

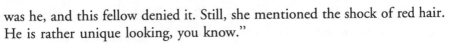

was he, and this fellow denied it. Still, she mentioned the shock of red hair. He is rather unique looking, you know."

"Did she mention where this occurred?"

"No . . . that is, I cannot remember. Is it important?"

Argo, for all his bumbling ways, had a sharp mind. Federov was concerned that he not make the issue seem significant. "Not at all," he said. "Curious how people pop into your mind at odd times, is it not?"

✻ ✻ ✻

"I can only spare a moment, gentlemen," Winston Churchill intoned in his office in the Admiralty building on the afternoon of May ninth. "I am dining at eight o'clock with Mister Eden and Mister Sinclair." Murphy looked at Mac, then asked the question he had been waiting to pose for two hours.

"First Lord," Murphy said, "I wonder if you would care to comment on the rumor that you are about to become Prime Minister?"

"A politician may be in the position of starting rumors or even of being their subject, but he should never comment on them."

"Understood, sir," said Murphy, grinning. "Perhaps you would just comment as to the accuracy of some . . . statements others have made about the present situation."

"I believe that you have phrased it delicately enough now, Mister Murphy. Frame your statements."

"Is it true that Clement Atlee and the Labour party have declared that they will participate in a National Coalition government, only if Mister Chamberlain is not the head?"

"I have heard something to that effect, yes," Churchill agreed.

"Furthermore, they specifically reject Mister Chamberlain's handpicked successor, Lord Halifax."

"As to that," Churchill said, "I do not know. However, Halifax has mentioned that he does not feel he can lead effectively from the House of Lords."

"Meaning he is taking himself out of consideration?"

Churchill pursed his lips and shrugged. "Meaning no more than he intends to mean, I am sure."

"Doesn't that suggest that you are the logical choice; tomorrow you may be Prime Minister?"

"I fear we have wandered back into speculation again, Mister Murphy. Now if you and Mister McGrath will excuse me."

"Just one more thing, please, First Lord," interjected Mac. His question was one he had been pondering for a long time, and Churchill was the one person whose answer was worth hearing. "Is it possible that if you are Prime Minister, it will be because of the *Altmark?*"

Picking at some imaginary lint on the sleeve of his jacket gave Churchill a moment to phrase his reply. "You are very astute, Mister McGrath," he said at last. "I have been debating the same chain of events myself. If the *Altmark* had not been run to earth in Jossing fiord, then perhaps Herr Hitler would not have stretched out his angry little hand against Norway, or at least not at the time that he chose. In such a case, the present cabinet crisis might not exist, and all the speculation about its outcome would be moot." He withdrew a cigar from a leather case and studied it as if he found a message written there. "It is strange," he said, "upon what small hinges great events often turn."

✣ ✣ ✣

Andre drove into the parking area of the Brussels North Train Station just after nine o'clock on the evening of May 9. The city was brightly lit in spite of the fact that Belgian military mobilization was in full swing. It was a strange contrast to Paris and London, and proof that in spite of intelligence information to the contrary, most Belgian civilians did not believe that Hitler would violate their neutrality. The echoing hall of the terminal was filled with soldiers and crowds of men and women who had come to see them off.

Andre left Josie with the children on a stone bench beneath the clock and hurried off to purchase passage to Ostend and then on to Dover. He returned a half hour later with tickets but also with grim news.

"No trains to Ostend tonight." He picked up Juliette, who had been sleeping on the bench. Cradling her against his shoulder, he brushed his lips against her cheek.

"My daddy used to hold us like that," Josie said gently, lapsing into English. "On the way home from barn dances back home my brothers and sisters and I would pretend to fall asleep in the back of the pickup. All six of them and me. Just so he would carry us into the house." What a time to think of such a thing. She put a hand to her head and chuckled. "I must be remembering someone else's life. It could never have been so easy . . ."

"It is not supposed to be this hard, ma chérie," he replied wearily. How long had it been since he had slept?

"She is a beautiful child, Andre. Really. And someday . . ."

"I cannot think of someday." He shot a hot look at the huffing train, which was packed with soldiers leaning out the windows and shouting their farewells. "I can think only of tomorrow; of you and Juliette safely away from here. The next train leaves at nine in the morning. It is nearly sold out . . . second-class tickets only. It seems a number of wealthy Belgians developed a sudden desire to see England. I should drive you to the Channel myself except . . ."

"Except you may be needed here tomorrow."

"I am needed here tonight. At our embassy. Paris telephoned ahead. They are expecting me there now. A meeting with the military attaché to the King. I would like you to tell him what you saw in Germany. They will make up a room for you and the children to stay tonight. As for the morning? We will just hope the train leaves before the arrival of the Luftwaffe."

FIFTY-FOUR

It was just after midnight on May 10 when Sergeant Fiske shook Horst by the arm. Horst bolted upright, reaching for the Luger in the holster that hung over the back of a chair. "It is me, Major. Fiske. Coded Enigma message from headquarters."

"So? What is the time, Fiske? Could this not wait until morning?" Horst switched on the light beside the bed and groped for the wristwatch that he had knocked off onto the floor.

"It was marked *Urgent. Highest Priority,* sir."

"All right, Fiske. I am awake now. Where is the dispatch?"

"It did not seem necessary to bring a copy, sir, for just a one word message."

Horst felt a sudden chill even though the room was warm. "What is it?"

"The word, sir, is *Danzig.*"

"Wake the company commanders," Horst commanded. "Tell them to order their troops to fall in and stand by their machines. Have the men draw rations for three days. Then tell them I want them here, reporting complete readiness, in twenty minutes."

When Fiske had saluted crisply and left on his errand, Horst slipped into his uniform and pulled on his tall boots. He was buttoning his tunic in front of the mirror when he stopped and studied his reflection in the glass. So it had happened. The signal to launch Blitzkrieg against the west had come. Horst knew that he would be summoned to General Rommel in a very short time to hear how soon his units would be rolling across the border to engage the Belgians.

He felt oddly calm. Now that the order was given, the time for introspection was past. He owed it to the men, *his* men, to offer them the best leadership possible. No second thoughts, no troubling doubts. They were counting on him to help them survive, to live through today and the days that followed, until the ordeal was over.

An hour later Horst was sitting with the other officers of Seventh Panzer as their division commander briefed them. General Erwin Rommel was impeccably dressed in his best uniform, his boots polished to a high gloss. A Leica camera hung around his neck, and he looked more like a wealthy Berlin staff officer on holiday than a field commander preparing to go into battle.

"We push off at dawn," Rommel informed the group. "The spearhead of each of our assigned routes will be a reconnaissance team, accompanied by Brandenburgers to deal with any demolition charges which the Belgians may have left behind. The main body will follow. Keep the formation tight, gentlemen! I will sack any commander who does not keep to schedule. I have personally promised General von Rundstedt that the Seventh will reach the Meuse River before any other unit in Army Group A. I intend for us to keep that promise."

Colonel Neumann, one of Rommel's tank commanders, raised the question all of them were thinking. "And what weight of opposition do we expect to encounter from the enemy?"

"At the same time as we move out, General von Bock's Army Group B will move into northern Belgium and the Netherlands. Their attacks will race toward Rotterdam and Brussels. These actions, together with airborne landings behind the enemy lines in Holland, will convince the Allies that we are doing exactly what they expect and repeating the frontal assault of 1914. Therefore, they will weaken the forces facing us to reinforce the north. To answer your question, Neumann, there will be no serious opposition until we reach the Meuse, and we will be there the day after tomorrow. That will be all, gentlemen. Be ready to move out at 0500."

⚜ ⚜ ⚜

Hôtel des Flandres on the Place Royal in Brussels, Belgium, was listed as the second best hotel in Mac's *Baedecker's*. The establishment which received the highest rating was the Bellevue, noted in the guidebook as "frequented by royalty and the noblesse; high prices."

Even the location of the two hotels seemed to reflect this snootiness; the Bellevue and the Flandres were adjacent, but the more expensive lodging preempted the view of the park.

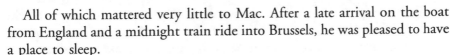

All of which mattered very little to Mac. After a late arrival on the boat from England and a midnight train ride into Brussels, he was pleased to have a place to sleep.

He was up in the early morning hours of the tenth of May, poring over a map staked out between a silver coffee pot and a creamer on his breakfast table in the dining room. Mac was plotting a route that would take him to the Belgian fortress of Eben Emael east of the town. His assignment was to film the Belgian counterpart of the Maginot Line at what was reported to be the most modern defensive work in the world, completely impregnable.

The white-uniformed waiter appeared to take Mac's order for toast and marmalade, bacon, three eggs, and a grilled chop. With a raised eyebrow he asked, "And how many will be joining you for breakfast, Monsieur?"

Mac waved him away impatiently and returned to studying the map. Newsreel cameramen, like old soldiers, learn to eat whenever the opportunity exists; who knew what would happen between this sure thing and another meal?

The distance to where Mac expected to find his story was not far. The map's inch of space translated into no more than sixty miles.

The bacon, eggs, and toast had arrived at Mac's elbow, but the chop had not yet appeared when the air raid alarm on top of the Bibliothèque Royale began screaming out its warning. Mac's waiter dropped a cup of coffee into the lap of a man at a nearby table, adding a different note to the wail of the siren. The service staff all dropped whatever they were carrying and disappeared through the doors to the kitchen, leaving a dumbfounded group of diners staring at each other.

The crump of bombs falling in the distance joined the clamor of the alert. The bass-voiced bells of the cathedral across the park were harmonized by the tenor accent of those at the Church of St. Jacques just around the corner.

Mac was already under his table. "Get down!" he urged the man who was still standing, cursing the waiter, and mopping his trousers with his napkin. Other early diners appeared to be more concerned with looking foolish than being protected.

"Surely this hotel cannot be threatened," remarked a tall, aristocratic woman who had not budged from her tea. She sounded as though the Germans had a better sense of social propriety than to bomb the second-best hotel in Brussels.

"Get down!" Mac said again as he crawled away from the windows and toward the kitchen entrance. "The Boche may be hitting the airport, but their aim is not always perfect!"

As if to punctuate his words, the antiaircraft guns on top of the nearby Palais du Comte began their rhythmic pulse. A second later the drone of airplanes was heard and then the whistle of bombs.

The first explosion in the downtown area hit a building only three blocks away. The sound of the detonation was followed by a rushing wind, and the plate glass facing the blast blew in. Shards from the broken windows scattered across the dining room floor, and the concussion knocked down an entire shelf of stemware with a crash that was the loudest noise of all.

Mac scooted across the tile and into the kitchen where he discovered stairs leading down to a basement pantry. He sprinted to the shelter, finding it already populated with the cook, waiters, and dishwashers. Right behind Mac down the steps were the heavy man, the society woman, and the rest of the breakfast guests.

"I hope you turned off the stove," Mac said to the cook. "I do not want you to burn my chop." Then addressing the assembled group he added, "Ladies and gentlemen: say good-bye to the Phony War."

✾　✾　✾

Was it a nightmare? Once again the too-familiar dreams of Warsaw returned to trouble Josie's sleep. She struggled against the images of carnage and then her eyes opened wide and she sat bolt upright in her bed.

It was not the drone of Heinkel engines that tore her from a sound sleep at the French Embassy in Brussels, but the wail of tiny Yacov Lubetkin. This was no dream!

Like Josie, the infant had heard the rumbling before. It was followed by the undulating scream of air raid sirens and then the distant whine as a stick of bombs was released; finally the dull crumps rattled the windows and jingled the prisms on the lamp shade like sleigh bells.

Juliette, asleep on a little bed on the far side of the room, miraculously did not stir. Josie grabbed up Yacov and held him close to her. In spite of the clamor in the streets, she sat on the edge of the bed and rocked him in an attempt to calm him. Did he feel her trembling?

Shouts of other occupants of the embassy sounded up and down the corridor. She could hear the patter of bare feet on the polished wood floors.

"L'Allemand attaque!"

There followed a light, yet frantic, knock at her door. Paralyzed, she could not force herself to answer or call out. Yacov, red-faced, was blue about the lips because the force of his sobs kept him from drawing a deep breath. He pushed against her as if in instinct of flight. To hide. To shut out the terrible sounds! What must this tiny person have witnessed in Poland?

He would not be comforted. Juliette still did not wake up! Unable to move, Josie sat with the baby in her arms.

There was a long, long whistle and a deafening explosion which nearly shook the windows from the frames. The knocking was drowned out. The door flew open. Andre, barefoot with only his trousers on, stumbled in as plaster dust fell from the ceiling. He picked up Juliette as a bomb pierced the roof of a three-story building across the park. The walls puffed out, hung in midair for an instant, then spewed glass and wood and stone and people into the manicured green of the little park.

Juliette screamed and buried her face in his neck. Andre grabbed Josie by the arm and jerked her to her feet.

"To the cellar!" he shouted over the roar of Heinkels and explosions!

Then every nerve came suddenly awake. She grabbed up her robe and dashed out the door with Andre as the bedroom window shattered from the force of a bomb at the center of the block. The smoke, the terrified cries of the servant girls in the cellar, were things she remembered too well. It was all happening again, she thought as the masonry walls of the cellar cracked and swayed and a curtain of dust covered the crouched occupants.

"The war is finally here!" A pale, dark-eyed secretary laughed hysterically. "The waiting is finished!"

❈   ❈   ❈

By eight in the morning the leading elements of Seventh Panzer were already fifteen miles inside Belgium. The resistance had not been light; it had been nonexistent. Despite the enormous buildup of German forces, or perhaps because of it, the expected opposition by the Belgian troops had failed to materialize.

Horst stood up in the hatch of his Kfz 231, a fast, agile, six-wheeled armored car. The morning sun was warm on the back of his neck and the day had a pleasant feel. Below him the radio crackled to life and a moment later Sergeant Fiske called up to him. "Major, Captain Gruhn reports a group of men with weapons at the highway intersection in Pepuister, about one-half mile from his present position. He wants to know if he should open fire."

"Ask him if the men have bicycles."

Fiske knew better than to dispute his commander's questions, no matter how odd they might sound. He relayed the inquiry and then said, "Gruhn says yes, all have bicycles."

"Tell him to advance without firing, cautiously, of course. If the cyclists neither shoot nor flee, then they are ours."

So this much of the plan had worked completely. For several days before the launch of the invasion force, groups of German "tourists" had cycled peacefully into Luxembourg, Holland, and here in Belgium. Since dawn this morning they had been holding key intersections in advance of the Panzer Group.

Horst saluted the infiltrators as his command vehicle rolled through Pepuister. The men threw off their civilian clothing and, now wearing Wehrmacht uniforms, stood proudly at attention. One of them waved a red *Baedecker's* guidebook at Horst and grinned.

The Belgian civilians who awoke on an ordinary market day looked at the parade of motorcycles and armored cars with astonishment. Horst studied a group of women and children standing near a table displaying strawberries. They huddled together in a frightened knot, intimidated by the German onslaught and not knowing what to expect.

"Pull up in the market square," Horst ordered.

He got on the loudspeaker and in his most authoritative tone issued an announcement. "Attention! All civilians are warned that this city is a military target. It will be bombed. You have one hour to gather your belongings and depart to the west. Do not disregard this warning; we do not wish to harm you, but leaving is your only chance for safety."

There was a moment's hesitation, like a frozen frame in a newsreel, then pandemonium. Mothers screamed and snatched up small children who an instant before had been playing in the dusty street. Larger children were dragged away by their wrists or herded into houses with sharp words and slaps.

Doors slammed shut and the street was deserted, a conjuring trick. The citizens of Pepuister began to reappear almost at once, bearing precious things and loading them into wagons and wheelbarrows.

Sergeant Fiske tugged on Horst's pantleg. "Begging the major's pardon. Do we have the authority to order an air strike on a purely civilian target?"

"No," Horst shook his head. "But if they believe me, Fiske, and flood the roads across the border in France, perhaps it will *save* their town from being bombed for real."

✤　✤　✤

The early morning wedding between Miss Bremmer, the English nurse from Jersey, and Jules Sully, the chemistry professor, took place in the chapel of the École de Cavalerie.

Father Francois Perrin, the priest from Lys, conducted the ceremony. The cadets provided the honor guard. Sepp, Gaston, and Raymond led the troop in a military salute.

The marriage had the same effect, Paul thought, as some ancient royal union of children from warring nations. Here at the École de Cavalerie, at least, France and England were finally friends!

Blessed event.

There was a lovely reception in the gardens, which were blooming with red roses. It was attended by the BEF medical staff from the surrounding countryside as well as by French cavalry officers.

Paul, surrounded by Sepp, Gaston, Raymond and a half dozen other

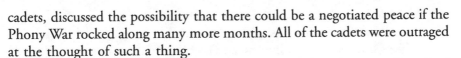

cadets, discussed the possibility that there could be a negotiated peace if the Phony War rocked along many more months. All of the cadets were outraged at the thought of such a thing.

And then came Sister Mitchell. She had not spoken three words to Paul except of necessity since that cold night in the stable some months before. Now she raised her champagne glass slightly and gave an almost Gallic shrug to indicate that he had been right and she wrong.

It was gratifying. The cadets murmured as she approached, bowed stiffly, and dispersed. Paul supposed that they were afraid of being rounded up to collect the dirty dishes or help the caterers distribute hors d'oeuvres.

Paul was left to face her alone.

"A lovely wedding, don't you think, Captain Chardon?"

"If one likes weddings. Which I do." He sipped his champagne.

"So do I." She raised her chin as if to challenge him to dispute her.

"Only a cold, unfeeling individual with antiseptic in the veins could . . ."

She stopped his jibe with a hand on his sleeve. "Please, Captain. There is no person with whom I have so enjoyed conflict as you. Animosity between us has been quite . . . stimulating. However . . ."

"I see what you mean. Something exciting to think about during the long lonely hours in the empty and sterile CCS?"

"Something like that." She looked past him to where the happy couple was being congratulated by the cadets. "I was wrong. About a lot of things. I wanted to apologize."

"In that case." He raised his glass in salute. "I will tell you something I wanted to say since the first moment I saw you."

She grimaced. "It sounds terrible."

"Yes. Terrible, only because you do not let anyone say it to you."

"Then say it."

"All right . . . You are beautiful."

She laughed and put her hand self-consciously to the top button of her uniform.

"You are beautiful," he continued, "and," he leaned close to her and inhaled, "today you smell like Chanel."

"Borrowed."

"You should have a bottle for yourself. It is much better than camphor."

"I suppose I should say thank you."

"Yes."

"Thank you." She lowered her eyes shyly. "Is that all?"

"No. Some months ago I considered asking you to dinner. But I was afraid you would inspect the kitchen of the restaurant and scrub the cook before we ate. So I did not ask."

"If I promise to behave myself?"

"Then we should be friends. Or we should dine together at least once to see if it is possible for one so English and one so French to remain civil for an entire evening. Yes?"

"Yes."

"In that case I must ask you if you possess anything to wear besides the scarlet cloak. I am a bit intimidated by it, you know."

Miss Mitchell's response was interrupted by a sudden droning overhead. All the military personnel ran outside to look, as the sky darkened with flight after flight of German bombers.

❊   ❊   ❊

The fanlight above the door of the French Embassy lay shattered across the sidewalk as Josie and Andre loaded luggage and children into the Citroen. Juliette was frantic about her grandfather in Luxembourg. The Nazis were coming. Were they not the same men who had taken her mother away?

Andre assured her that Monsieur Snow was likely on his way to Paris. But that she must go to England and be safe and happy when he came. This comforted her. Clutching her doll tightly to her, she did not cry, but Josie thought there had never been such sad and knowing eyes in a child.

Except for broken windows and the bellied out building across the square, there was very little damage evident in the streets of Brussels. Red Cross ambulances clanged by, heading in the direction of the airport. For the moment, there had been no news of the North Train Station. Had it escaped the raid unharmed? Would the train to the Channel still be running?

Josie secretly hoped that the train would be delayed or canceled altogether. She wanted to go back to Paris with Andre when he left this morning.

But that was not to be. North Station was untouched by German bombs or stray Belgian antiaircraft fire. It resounded with the babble of confusion as panicked citizens pushed toward the green train which chuffed impatiently at the siding.

Andre carried Juliette on his shoulders safely above the crush. He parted the sea of bodies ahead of Josie using a suitcase as a shield. Coming at last to the open door of a second-class car, he held other people back and jerked a frightened French poilu from his seat and threw him from the train.

Josie and her charges safely seated, he gave the man a shake. "The war is in the opposite direction. French deserters will be shot!"

The soldier scrambled to his feet, and the instant Andre turned back to Josie, he skittered off into the packed crowd.

The train whistle shrilled. Andre stooped to kiss Josie.

"You always were good at controlling riots in train stations." She touched his cheek and tried to smile up at him. "The first time I ever saw you . . ."

"Be safe. Remember I love you," he replied, kissing her again. Then to Juliette, lodged between Josie and a hefty grey-haired woman with a green parakeet in a cage, he said, "Well, Juliette, I hope we will meet again very soon."

"Oui, Monsieur," she nodded, and then, "Maman used to say I have your eyes, Monsieur Chardon. Your eyes are so very sad when they look at me."

"It is only because . . ." He could hardly speak. "My eyes long to look at you always because you are so beautiful . . ." She smiled shyly at his compliment. "But you see, Juliette? Sometimes we cannot have everything we wish. And so I am sad."

The child threw her arms around his neck and embraced him. "Tell my Grandpapa when you see him in Paris I am having a very exciting time. I have never been to England. Tell him I will see him soon."

"I will do that, ma chérie."

The whistle shrilled a second time. The shout of the conductor sounded over the racket. Andre backed out of the car and slammed the door. He reached through the open window and held the hand of Juliette until the train chugged slowly out of the station.

❧   ❧   ❧

Andre's black Citroen rounded a curve at high speed. Blitzkrieg had released the terrors of war on the population of Western Europe, but everyone experienced the horror a little differently.

Now that Josie and Juliette were safely headed out of harm's way, a panic over failed duty engulfed Andre. He had put his personal concerns above his obligation to France, if only briefly. Lewinski was alone in Paris—Lewinski, who might hold the key to unraveling the German plans and stopping the Wehrmacht steamroller.

Pressing harder on the accelerator, Andre raced out of Brussels toward Lys and the cavalry school. There was still one more personal duty that could not be ignored. He wanted to see Paul to tell him that it was past time to get the boys away.

Fifteen kilometers outside of the town he spotted the first flight of Heinkels. A squadron of twenty stubby twin-engined planes passed overhead, followed by another group of twenty. Andre ignored them. He suspected their target was in fact Armentieres, just ahead of him on the road, but there was something he could do about that. He veered to the east to take a smaller country lane around the town, planning to regain the main highway after he had passed the zone of the bombing.

Topping a small hill, he could see smoke rising ahead, though he was still too far away to hear the thunder of the bombs. A flight of French Morane fighters streaked into view from the south, climbing to intercept the German bombers.

Not able to help himself, since the show was right in front of him, Andre's eyes flicked upwards. He watched the aerial combat briefly, then glanced quickly back to negotiate the curves of the narrow two-lane road.

The overhead display got more interesting by the minute. A cloud of tiny black dots that were airplanes at a very high altitude began dropping out of the sky. Suddenly the blue canopy was filled with white streaks as Me 109's engaged the Moranes.

A French fighter, streaming black smoke, dove away from the battle. A parachute popped open, the canopy rocking as the pilot floated earthward. Two more 109's circled another Morane. Andre saw a wing torn from the warplane and saw the crippled fuselage spin crazily out of control.

Andre's eyes snapped back to the roadway just in time to avoid crashing into an oncoming convoy of trucks. The three-quarter-ton army vehicle in the lead was well over the center, leaving Andre just a tiny space. He jerked the steering hard to the right. The wheels of the Citroen dropped onto the shoulder of the road, spurting gravel from under the tires. The rear of the car fishtailed, heading toward the ditch.

Jerking the car back to the left, Andre overcorrected the skid. For an instant it seemed that the auto would straighten out, but the sideways momentum of the slide was too much for it to hold the road.

Andre felt the loss of control, and through the windshield saw the world starting to spin. Instinctively, he lunged toward the passenger side, forcing his body into the tiny space below the seat. The driver's side flipped upward, the Citroen rolled over, bounced in the air, and rolled again. It came to rest right side up just off the shoulder of the road.

Unconscious when a medic in the passing convoy pulled him from the wreck, everyone was amazed that Andre wasn't dead. The medic whistled when he saw the insignia designating Andre as a colonel. Detailed out of the unit to act as an ambulance, a truck carried Andre to the military hospital at the École de Cavalerie at Lys.

❦   ❦   ❦

Despite the cramped accommodations, the trip from Brussels to Ostend proved to be an interesting one for Josie. Twenty kilometers west of Brussels, the train to Ostend was shunted onto a siding as a troop train sped by headed in the opposite direction.

Juliette and Yacov did not mind the delay. Both were fascinated with a green parakeet, named Petit Chou, or Little Cabbage. Petit Chou chirped in the small cage held by its portly owner, Madame Hasselt. To Josie's delight, the old woman entertained the children by putting the cage in front of her moon-like face and pretending that she was trapped inside the bars like the bird.

When she chirped and cheeped, Petit Chou responded. Even little Yacov laughed a great baby belly laugh, but Josie noted that his eyes were still swollen from a morning of hysteria.

There was no tea trolley on the train and no dining car, but Madame Hasselt shared black bread and cheese. Josie tried to pay her for the food, but she would not have it.

She was going to Ostend to catch the ferry to England, where her son worked in a Belgian shipping firm. She had been planning the journey a long time before today, and so it was an unpleasant surprise when the Germans finally broke their long silence. But Madame Hasselt believed with every certainty that the Boche would be turned back this time; they would not have their way with Belgium as they had done in the last war. Madame Hasselt did not like the Boche, she confided to Josie. They were dark-hearted beasts. But she would not say more, lest she frighten the little ones.

As the train to Ostend finally lurched forward again, Madame Hasselt allowed Juliette to put her hand in the cage. Petit Chou perched on her finger. Little claws tickled her knuckles and she giggled. When Juliette laughed, so did Yacov—uproariously! His joyous howls were infectious, making Juliette laugh harder. This was perhaps the first happiness in an otherwise dreadful day, much to the delight of all the other passengers in the compartment. It was assumed that the two children belonged to Josie and the French colonel. Everyone commented that most certainly this pretty little Juliette looked like her father. There was no mistaking, they noted, that Juliette had the eyes and coloring of the handsome Frenchman.

"My maman always said that," Juliette agreed; although the implications of the statement did not seem to register with her.

And as for Yacov! Madame Hasselt said she had never seen such a good-natured baby. And after such a terrible day!

Josie agreed that Yacov was a delight and silently wondered what desperation must have forced the child's mother to send such a remarkable little boy so far away.

The playful atmosphere on board the train came to an abrupt end with the arrival of a German Heinkel. Returning to its base from having completed its bombing mission, the warplane was looking for targets of opportunity when it spotted the train.

Josie barely noticed a dark shape heading for the tracks like an arrow flashing toward its target. She looked back at Yacov as he burst out with another peal of laughter, when the significance of the onrushing plane crashed in on her.

The bomber opened fire with its machine guns, raking the length of the train forward from the compartment just ahead of where Josie and the children were riding. The sound of shattering glass and a loud pounding noise as if someone were swinging a hammer against the metal of the train's skin mingled with terrified screams.

The Heinkel roared over, pulling up on the far side of the tracks. The engine's whistle gave a long-drawn-out cry, as if the iron beast had felt the damage inflicted on it.

The bomber made a lazy turn, in full view of the passengers, then swept back toward the train again. Josie pulled a sobbing Juliette down to the floor and covered the girl and Yacov with her own body.

This time the bullets clattered into the car just behind Josie's, killing two people and wounding a third. When the Heinkel climbed into the sunlight after the second pass, it soared away toward Germany.

Incredibly, the brakes on the train squealed and the forward movement slowed, even as all the passengers were urging it to speed up and get them away from the killing zone. A pair of train conductors came through the cars, asking for doctors or nurses to help with the wounded.

"But why have we stopped?" Josie pleaded. "Can't we go to Ostend and find medical help there?"

"Regrettably, madame, what you suggest is not possible," said one of the trainmen. "Attention, everyone," he continued in a louder voice. "The train has stopped because the engine has been damaged. It is impossible for us to continue onward. Everyone must get off."

"And what will we do then?" Madame Hasselt asked.

The conductor shrugged. "I, myself, will walk back to Brussels. I suggest that you do the same."

FIFTY-FIVE

David's squadron had moved to a new aerodrome near to Reims to provide air cover for the headquarters of the Advanced Air Striking Force located there. The transfer had only been completed late on the night of the ninth of May and *A* flight was supposed to have the morning to sleep. It was with irritation that David found himself being awakened.

"What's the idea, Corporal?"

"Beg pardon sir, but the balloon's gone up. Jerry is attacking in force, and the squadron is ordered to cover our bombers."

Two flights of Hurricanes climbed through a thick mist to twenty thousand feet, heading northeast toward the Meuse River. The shadows cast by the early morning light and the swirling ground fog made picking out landmarks difficult. As the sun grew higher and the mist cleared some, David could see the bend of the river and the town of Sedan on the east bank of the Meuse.

"Where are those sodding Blenheims we're supposed to be protecting?" Hewitt questioned over the radio transmitter.

"Perhaps they didn't like the odds and went home," Simpson replied. "No matter. We'll find plenty to occupy ourselves. Dorniers at twelve o'clock, angels five."

"Cheeky buggers, flying so low," Hewitt muttered. "Don't think much of French antiaircraft fire, do they?"

The formation of forty pencil-shaped bombers plastered their target, the French artillery emplacements west of Sedan. David scanned the skies, locating the fighter cover he was sure accompanied the Dorniers. "Two flights of Messers flanking the Does, angels five," he said.

"Roger that, Tinman. And more fighters at angels thirty orbiting north of the town and just waiting to pounce on us."

In all, there were more than one hundred enemy aircraft facing a dozen Hurricanes. "Slash and run is the ticket," Simpson ordered. "*B* flight to engage the 109's flying low cover, *A* flight to bust through and have a go at the Dorniers. Good hunting, chaps. We're off!"

In contrast to the tactics practiced earlier in the war, the enormous disparity of numbers meant that the RAF rarely had the luxury of ganging up on a single German bomber with a whole section of fighters. As soon as red section swooped into the middle of the Luftwaffe formation, it was every man for himself.

David selected a Do 17 to attack. He curved in toward it from above and commenced firing at three-quarters deflection. The angle of his assault propelled *ANNIE* over the bomber from its port side. The Hurricane's machine guns drew a double line across the German plane's left engine, which began spewing a white cloud of vaporized glycol coolant.

David's pass carried him toward the tail of the next bomber in the formation, which had seen the attack coming and was turning away, climbing into the sun. He had just an instant to loose a burst into its tail surface before he was below the elevation of the Dorniers and had to regain some altitude.

The Hurricane pulled out of its dive and mounted upward when the Me 109's jumped him. A pair of fighters attacked from above, and a burst of machine gun fire jolted the fuselage in back of the cockpit. The first enemy plane flashed past him, and the second came in fast. David kicked his fighter into a climbing turn. He could not get around quickly enough to face the oncoming Messerschmidt, but the move got him out of its sights. By now however, the first attacker reversed his dive and was on David's tail.

Bullets whistled by the cockpit as David banked sharply left, then dove, attempting to shake off his pursuer. The Hurricane's slower speed meant that it would take superior maneuvering to get away, and it had to happen soon or the partner of this pair would return. The two Germans could play him like a pair of foxes driving a rabbit back and forth between them.

"Tinman!" came Hewitt's urgent voice. "On two, break hard left. One! Two!"

David was in no position to question Hewitt's instruction. As soon as the word *two* was pronounced, he yanked the spade grip over, pulling the fighter's right wing up and throwing his plane into a tight left-hand turn at the same moment. This gave an instant in which he was free of the 109's guns, and provided Hewitt, who was on the German's tail, a clear shot.

Hewitt's gunfire converged at the optimum range of two hundred and fifty yards, raking the fuselage of the Messerschmidt from its tail all the way forward to its engine. The Luftwaffe plane rolled over and dove belly-up toward the River Meuse.

Hewitt laughed over the R/T. "You're my witness, Tinman. Scratch one Messer, and you owe me a . . ."

He never had a chance to utter the word *drink*. Pulling out of his spiral,

David saw the second 109 rejoin the battle from below. The Messerschmidt's gunfire tore the right wing off Hewitt's Hurricane. It dropped sideways out of the sky, like a duck falls after being blasted by a shotgun.

"Get out of there, Hewitt!" shouted David.

There was no response. David never saw the hatch open and no chute appeared as Hewitt's plane dwindled to a falling speck.

David and the remaining Messerschmidt fired at each other twice more as the aerial combat carried them far north of Sedan, then David's guns were empty. He put *ANNIE* on the deck and swept away toward the base to rearm.

✼ ✼ ✼

The arrival of Blitzkrieg on Mac's doorstep changed his plans some. He was stuck in Brussels all day on the tenth, unable to get transport toward the front as the trains were all requisitioned for troop movements and the roads were packed with military convoys. The Belgian authorities would not give him a pass to ride with their soldiers.

The news Mac heard on the morning of the eleventh of May, as he finally managed to hitch a ride with a passing BEF troop lorry, was good and bad at the same time. It was good because the Wehrmacht was doing exactly what they were supposed to do. According to the Allied plan that had not changed since 1918, the French and British troops would advance rapidly into Belgium to meet the invaders head on.

But if the good news was good, the bad was fearful. The Nazis were slicing through Holland like a sharp knife through Dutch cheese. And the mighty fortress of Eben Emael which had been Mac's destination the day before? Its unprotected roof received a glider load of German paratroops who blasted their way in. The fortification already surrendered.

Mac was not even sure how the Allied advance was progressing. "We was held up crossin' the border from France into Belgium," remarked a private wearing the unicorn emblem of the Fiftieth Northumbrian Infantry Division. "Them border guards wasn't told that we was invited!"

"How'd it work out?" Mac asked.

"Sergeant Major Quinn pointed a Bren gun at the guards and told 'em that the lorries could either go around 'em or over 'em, their choice. The barricade got moved double quick!"

The area assigned to the BEF was a length of the Dyle River just east of Brussels. The troops were supposed to arrive there in one day, but with the road packed with fleeing refugees, it did not look like that could possibly happen.

There was a roar of airplane engines over the highway. Mac's experience in Poland made him jump up, ready to stampede from the lorry into a nearby ditch. The Northumbrians pointed at him and laughed. "What's the matter, mate? Got the wind up already?"

The heavily lumbering warplanes were not Messerschmidts or Stukas, they were Fairey Battle bombers and Blenheims belonging to the RAF.

Mac's face was red as he sat back down, but his mind was still churning an observation. Why wasn't the Luftwaffe challenging the Allied advance? Where were the dive-bomber attacks that had so paralyzed the Polish military movements? It was almost as if the Germans were allowing the Allies an opportunity to get moved into position. Such consideration on the part of the Nazis worried him.

❊   ❊   ❊

Josie and Madame Hasselt started their trek toward safety in tandem and remained together. Juliette, clutching her doll in one hand and carrying the cage of Petit Chou in the other, tried to keep pace but she tired quickly. Their little group split off from the larger group, seeking shade beneath the leafy plane trees. In a ditch beside the road they found a small child's wagon, and soon Juliette and Yacov were being pulled along among the hundreds of thousands of civilians attempting to flee Belgium. But where to go?

All the ports of Belgium and Holland were under heavy attack from the Luftwaffe. Ostend had been bombed. Refugees streaming back from the coast reported that ferries to England had sunk, with many drowned. And Brussels? Bombing increased at such a rate that those fleeing the capital predicted it could become another Warsaw. The Nazi strategy of civilian panic was working with complete success. After the initial advances, French, British, and Belgian troops on the highways were slowed to a crawl as they faced hordes of frantic people on every lane. Little Luxembourg had vanished into the Nazi maw. The Grand Duchess Charlotte fled to France.

It was this final news which shifted the movement of the frightened herd of refugees south toward the border of France. The human tide along the main road swelled and overflowed.

❊   ❊   ❊

The roads into the interior of Belgium were filled with traffic going in both directions. Mac's ride, the troop lorry of artillerymen, stopped on the road from Brussels to Leuven when a Bren gun carrier in front of them broke down. Bren gun carriers always reminded Mac of toy tanks with the turret torn off. As capable as they were at crossing fields or traversing marshy ground, when the tracked vehicles stalled on roadways they were almost impossible to push by hand.

The four soldiers who traveled in the small open-topped machine jumped off. When their attempt to shove the machine proved futile, they appealed to the men in the lorry for help.

"One try, mates," the artillery lieutenant warned, "then we use the lorry to push her out of the way."

While the British troops moved toward the front, still another family of refugees headed the opposite direction. Their dusty shoes evidenced travel on the unpaved dirt lanes. They threaded between the troop lorry and the stalled Bren carrier.

Leading the group of civilians caught amid the warring armies was a young man carrying a baby. The youth might have been in the army himself; he looked old enough. As he passed, he yanked his cloth cap low across his forehead and turned away, as if fearful that the soldiers might challenge him for being out of uniform.

But the Bren gun crew focused its attention on the second figure in the eastbound parade. A pretty blonde woman in her early twenties pushed a four-wheeled pram loaded with blankets and clothing. She looked tired, but determined. All the British would have loved to offer her a ride, and they hoped that the fellow carrying the baby was her brother and not her husband.

That the family had been prosperous before the war was demonstrated by the figure who came next. The head of the household, wearing his best suit coat and tie, also pushed a baby carriage loaded with belongings. This pram sported a double chrome bumper and a satin lining, but its rightful occupant had been displaced in favor of a gramaphone and a mahogany mantel clock.

Beside the man walked a woman in a heavy, expensive coat, even though the day was warm and the May sun bright on her grim face. Mac wondered how far they could have walked in the two days since the war started and where they would end up before they were through.

A pair of servants in plain black dresses completed the cavalcade. The cook and a maid perhaps? They had carpetbags over their shoulders and toted two suitcases apiece as they trudged along. From the sour expressions on their faces, it seemed that they had started to wonder whether they would still be paid for all the extra effort.

There was a whistling sound high overhead, and a German artillery round blasted a crater in the vineyards beside the road. The shell exploded with a roar, and Mac's three-quarter-ton ride leapt forward as its driver popped the clutch. "Time's up lads!" the lieutenant shouted.

The troop lorry rammed the Bren carrier as the soldiers trying to shift it tumbled out of the way. "Come on! Get aboard!" the officer ordered. It took no further suggestion, as a second and a third high explosive shell slammed into the roadway, bracketing the travelers. The refugees scattered into the vineyard, throwing themselves away from the highway and deserting their possessions.

Mac swung onto the truck as it backed hastily up from its collision. The soldiers jumped for the sideboards, using the motion of the vehicle to swing themselves up, like trick riders in a rodeo. The lorry roared off, carrying four new occupants.

When Mac looked back, he saw no bodies lying in the road. Maybe there were no casualties this time. One of the prams was overturned and tumbled in a ditch. The other had been crushed by the wheels of the truck. Pieces of smashed mahogany clock and splintered phonograph littered the ground in silent company with the abandoned Bren gun carrier.

That the Germans were close enough to shell the road to Leuven meant that they were already across the Dyle. Whatever defensive positions the British finally adopted would surrender a huge chunk of Belgium to the Nazis.

❊   ❊   ❊

The last of the tinned milk was used, and Josie and Madame Hasselt were making no progress. With only a word of agreement between them, they left the main highway and, entering a wooded glen, came upon a dirt track which led to a deserted barn. That night they slept in a hayrick. Here, the war seemed only a bad dream. The star-streaked sky and the scent of hay reminded Josie of her childhood back home. Madame Hasselt prayed quietly and sang the children to sleep, and Josie drifted off with them.

Before dawn Josie was awakened by the munching of an abandoned Jersey cow whose udder was swollen with milk. She had a halter on her head and a lead rope dangled from the leather buckle. What had happened to her owner? Josie simply reached out and grasped the line and captured the cow. As Madame Hasselt held the grateful animal and Juliette stroked the velvet muzzle, Josie milked her. The foursome breakfasted on sweet warm milk shared from a small tin pot which Madame Hasselt had carried with her. The old woman still packed a variety of fine cheeses and two pounds of ham as well as chocolate which she had intended to present to her grandchildren in England.

"A few miles across the border in France there is a boy's cavalry school," Josie said. "I know the headmaster. Paul Chardon. He will help us get to Paris if we can make it that far."

"It will take us several days if we stick to back roads. You see we are alone here. But look . . ." Madame Hasselt gestured to a thick plume of smoke billowing up over the treetops a few kilometers to the east. "If we are careful, our provisions will last." Madame Hasselt soaked her feet in a shallow stream at the edge of the pasture. "And this cow? She is sent from heaven." The old woman winked at Juliette. "My dear child, how would you like to ride to France like a princess, on the back of a pretty brown-eyed Jersey cow?"

Juliette conceded that she would like it very much, so Josie placed Juliette and her doll atop the sweet-tempered creature. Yacov perched in front of her. Juliette wrapped her arms around his middle. Josie set the cage of Petit Chou between the jutting hip bones of the cow where the bird chirped back at other birds in the trees.

"Very well!" the old grandmother declared, cheerfully loading the rest of their belongings into the wagon. She pointed at the dirt lane meandering through the pasture and into a deep wood. "France is that direction, I am certain."

FIFTY-SIX

The view of the Meuse River valley was anything but encouraging to Horst von Bockman as he stood beside his half-track just north of the Belgian town of Dinant. Since his reconnaissance teams had first arrived at the river, French artillery had been bombarding the east bank. Horst had no weapons powerful enough to silence the guns and had ordered his men to pull back while he studied the scene and mentally prepared a report for General Rommel.

On the twelfth of May, after two days of offering no opposition to the Wehrmacht's sweep across Belgium, the German forces had finally reached a position that the Allies intended to defend. Small-arms fire crackled from the far shore, shattering the peace of the Sunday afternoon. The Belgian and French soldiers were dug in along the water's edge and prepared to deny any Panzer unit crossing. Dynamite destroyed the bridge across the river; a fact Horst was not looking forward to recounting. Rommel wanted that crossing intact; needed it if he was to keep his vow to von Rundstedt that Seventh Panzer would be first across the Meuse.

Without the bridge, the Meuse in spring was no small obstacle. Draining waters from the Langres plateau in France all the way to the North Sea, the Meuse at Dinant was deep enough and broad enough for commercial vessels.

Tanks got bogged down in marshy ground; in water deeper than their treads, they sank like stones.

Horst signaled for a fast scout car to pick him up for the journey rearward to locate General Rommel. The driver took off at high speed, expecting to find the division commander back near the center of the Panzer column advance which stretched for five miles back from the river.

Instead, they sighted Rommel's specially equipped command vehicle bristling with radio aerials before Horst had traveled even a mile. Unlike most division commanders, Rommel wanted to see the battlefront first hand.

"Report, Major," Rommel ordered tersely.

Horst explained the situation regarding the bridge and the French artillery, then waited while Rommel pondered. "Engineers and infantry to the front," he said at last. "We will attempt a crossing by rubber boats. Major, you send a company upstream. See if there are any other suitable openings. Speed is important, and not only because of our present need. Great things are happening. Our paratroops have landed in Rotterdam and the fortress of Eben Emael is ours. We must not miss our share of the glory. We must have at least one unit across the river tonight!"

✿ ✿ ✿

On the French held side of the Meuse, north of Dinant, a rifle company commanded by Captain Hugo Ney was dug in beneath the willows overlooking a flood control weir and an island. The rushing water was soothing, and the shade had made this a pleasant place to wait for the war.

Jardin, whose head was too small for his helmet, looked like a turtle peering out from his shell. He leaned back against his cumbersome pack and lit a cigarette as Captain Ney paced and lectured and gestured in the direction of the booming French artillery.

"Listen, men! It is the sound of French victory! Two miles from where we sit, our Armée is beating back the Boches! History in the making! And here we sit!" The captain, who claimed to be a distant descendant of Napoleon's great General Ney, was a strutting, irritating young fellow. Every man but Sergeant Blanchard considered him a fool. Today the Grand Captain Ney was unhappy that his company was missing the glory of battle.

Jardin leaned close to his friend Furfooz, whose eyelids were heavy in the warmth of the spring day. "This is what I do not understand," Jardin whispered. "Why is it that a French poilu is paid only fifty centimes a day and the English soldier is paid seventeen francs a day? I have two small children in Paris who must live on such poor wages. Do they eat less than the English brats?"

"It is the British who got us into this war, and they sent only ten divisions!" Furfooz jerked his head at the ranting Captain Ney. "And for that we must endure this!"

Jardin nodded. "Our Grand Captain," he scoffed. "Even seventeen francs a day would not be pay enough for this!"

Ney raised his hand and pointed at the weir. His voice was tremulous with lust for battle. "Perhaps we will not miss everything! If we are lucky, we will be able to pick off a few stray Boches. If they would only try to cross the river here! They shall not pass!"

Jardin shrugged. "They shall not pass? That is what they have been saying at the Maginot Line. On the Maginot the poilus sleep indoors. They eat hot food at tables. They have huge guns pointed down the throat of Germany. But this is not the Maginot, Furfooz. This is a river. Suitable for fishing. For eating a picnic. For making love with a woman beside the rushing waters. But I do not fancy shooting across it at someone who might shoot back."

The eyes of Furfooz narrowed into hostile slits as he eyed Ney with contempt. "I tell you who we should shoot first . . ."

Ney took a stance imitating the great Napoleon: head lofty, legs slightly apart, fingers slipped between the buttons of his tunic . . . "We shall hold the Boche here, men!"

"He is posing for a bronze," Jardin remarked. "He hopes to die a hero's death."

"Paris has too many statues already," Furfooz commented.

Ney's eyes were alight with imagination as he spoke to the backdrop of the distant booms of artillery and the fire of conflicting tanks. "I say to you, loyal French patriots . . . they shall not pass!"

"He is repeating himself."

The volume of Ney's speech increased. His eyes were wild. His face was flushed with patriotic ardor. "We shall stand our ground here! We shall die to the last man before we let the Boches get by our rifles! France shall revere our memories."

"That is a new thought," Furfooz said glumly. "Now it is not only that the Boche shall not pass, but the Grand Captain adds that we are supposed to all die to stop the Boche from crossing the Meuse."

Jardin wagged his head beneath the shade of his helmet. "I am not for that part of his plan, Furfooz." He drew deeply on his cigarette. "What is the point of that, after all? If we die for France, then what good is France to us?"

Ney stood on a fallen log. ". . . And so, my brave soldiers, remember what it is you fight for! Vive la France!"

⚜　⚜　⚜

The scream of a French artillery shell made Horst duck down inside the hatch, and the concussion of the explosion rocked the armored car as it sped away. North of Dinant, the river gorge was narrow, with no possibility to deploy the division in strength along a wide front. The terrain west of the river was higher than that held by the Germans. Allied artillery could, by raining down from behind the shelter of the far line of hills, make it impossible for the column of tanks to remain.

"Pull up," Horst told the driver. Through his field glasses he inspected a flood control weir built across the Meuse. A narrow path topped the rock dam. It led from the near shore to an island in midstream and then carried on across a still intact bridge to the far side. It was far too small to support vehicles, but it might work for men. If enough firepower were moved quickly across the stream, a bridgehead could be established from which infantry could circle behind the French artillery.

Horst radioed Rommel to explain his plan and request additional motorcycle troops sent forward. "Approved," Rommel's voice crackled back in agreement. "Pass the coordinates and we will lay in some mortar fire."

"Any chance of Stukas?" Horst asked, remembering the effectiveness of the dive-bombers in the Polish campaign.

"Negative," came the reply. "I already asked. Enigma transmission from von Rundstedt says the air support has all gone to General Guderian. Even so, I depend on you, Major. The first wave of inflatable boats has been thrown back. Get across!"

Below a concealing rim of willow trees, Horst assembled his troops. A great spiral of 750cc BMW motorcycles gathered in a clearing like the coils of a lethal snake preparing to strike. The men were armed with rifles, Mauser machine pistols, and MG 34 light machine guns. "There will be no further reason for reconnaissance if the division doesn't get over the river," Horst said. "So we are going to dismount and make a dash for the island. Once there, we will dig in and probe the defenses on the other bank. There is only room to go single file; who will volunteer to be first?"

Captain Gruhn raised his hand. "I claim that privilege, Major."

The explosions of the French artillery shells continued downstream. It was plain that the direct attack by boats was not going well and the day was winding down toward late afternoon.

"Go!" Horst shouted.

Gruhn led off, Mauser in hand. He was followed by five men carrying a pair of machine guns and ammunition boxes. Horst himself led the second wave. The old stone weir looked like a rotting jawbone with some teeth sticking up and many empty sockets. Horst felt naked as he tried to hurry across the slippery rocks, watch his footing, and keep an eye on the far shore, all at the same time. With every running step he expected the rattle of machine guns and thought he would see the west bank of the river erupt in a blaze of rifle fire.

Amazingly, no shots were fired at all. Horst's men slipped into the scrub brush and trees that marked the halfway point. They set up MG 34's at the far ends of the rocky island and another pair behind an old lockgate that controlled the outflow of water past the weir.

At a signal from Horst, Gruhn waved his arm for his men to follow him across to the other shore. The instant he stood up on the edge of the riverbank, a machine gun began to chatter from the French-held side, and Gruhn was cut down without making a sound.

The battle of the weir was joined. A line of bullets stitched the ground beside Horst, and he flung himself behind a pile of boulders at the water's edge. He fired his Mauser through a gap in the rocks until the clip emptied, then reloaded and emptied it again. Fragments of stone rattled off Horst's helmet as the French fired back.

The first rush of firing stilled as both sides realized that their targets were well concealed and protected. Horst studied a map and scribbled some coordinates on a piece of paper. This he handed to Sergeant Fiske, who had been at his elbow throughout the assault. "Get this to the mortar squad."

Fiske jumped up and ran back across the weir. He jogged from side to side as bullets traced his progress, slapping into trees and kicking up dirt beside his path. When he disappeared from view, the firing stopped again. Horst watched him go, turning when Lieutenant Gelb spoke to him from behind the wall of the lockgate. "Major? Gruhn is dead, sir."

"What other casualties?"

"Two wounded, neither serious. What next?"

"Sit tight and wait. We'll see if some mortar rounds won't stir things up a little."

Five long minutes passed, and then a shadow flitted back to Horst's side. In the gathering darkness the returning shape of Fiske drew only a single shot that ricocheted against a rock and whined off down the canyon. "Fiske! I did not tell you to come back across!"

The sergeant grinned. "Nor did you tell me not to, Major. Where else should I be?"

The deep cough of the first launched mortar shell was joined by others in quick succession, and then that noise was drowned out by the detonations of the high explosives landing among the French positions.

The Grand Captain Ney continued to exhort his company as another round of German mortar fire found its mark on the French side of the Meuse. Willow trees exploded, sending huge splinters impaling soldiers on the embankment. Earth and rocks rained down to cover the men. A machine gun on its tripod soared like a rocket into the air to spin among severed arms and legs and shredded bodies. Human debris tumbled back to earth. A booted leg landed between Jardin and Furfooz.

Jardin burrowed beneath his pack and pressed his face into the ground as though trying to crawl beneath it.

"Remember France!" shouted Ney. "Vive la France!"

Between deafening detonations the scene was still not silent. Furfooz covered his ears with his hands and let out one continuous scream, pausing only to fill his lungs with cordite-thickened air.

"They shall not pass!" Captain Ney shrieked. "Stand like men!" He stood among his crouching troops. "Get up! Open fire! Hold the Boche! For France!"

Furfooz, clutching his rifle beneath him, turned on his side, took aim, and fired. The Grand Captain, his hand still high in the air, opened his mouth and eyes as if in amazement. His knees buckled and he fell to the ground.

"SAVE YOURSELF!" Jardin howled as he turned his back to the river. "Sauve qui peut!"

Two dozen men joined Jardin and Furfooz in the mad retreat up the embankment.

Bullets nipped at his heels. To his right, four men were sliced through at the knees by machine gun fire. They shrieked in agony and fell back. Furfooz clawed upward ten paces ahead of Jardin. Suddenly, his torso exploded with red. He spun around and stretched his arms out as if in appeal, then he tumbled past Jardin and slid back to land on the body of Captain Ney.

Jardin clutched his helmet to his head and strained toward the top of the hillside. Behind him the others scrambled over the bodies of their companions in their headlong flight from the Boches and the River Meuse.

✤　✤　✤

Horst saw men running up the far slope of the canyon.

"Now!" he yelled. "Machine guns open fire! Rifle squads, across the river!"

Twenty minutes later, four companies of Seventh Panzer were rounding up French prisoners and planting their machine guns in new defensive positions. Horst radioed General Rommel that the division had its bridgehead on the west bank of the Meuse.

✤　✤　✤

The movement of soldiers and a harsh warning about mines placed along the Lys River toward France put Josie back on the main highway. The little Jersey cow now carried five small children and the parakeet.

The École de Cavalerie was fifty kilometers downriver and across the border in France. Josie looked at the slowly flowing stream which cut across the flatlands and imagined that this same water would be flowing past the École at the exact moment she greeted Paul Chardon. The thought made the journey somehow more bearable.

They passed what remained of the town of Olsene, bombed the night before. The metal girders of the rail bridge across the Lys lay twisted like a giant pretzel. Warehouses, homes, and businesses still smouldered. Old people stood in the doorways of their windowless houses and watched with blank faces as the endless stream of people coursed through their main street. Some citizens of Olsene, with carts and little bundles tied on their backs, joined the great exodus.

Automobiles with matresses flung over their tops to stop bullets bullied through the mass. And then there were the bicycles. Endless thousands of men and women and children who had cycled from Holland caught up with the flow just beyond Olsene.

But no mode of transportation was so fine as the Jersey cow. She not only carried the children, but fed them as well. Yes, the creature moved slowly. Now the Dutch cyclists rushed past. Each evening she was led onto some grassy place and allowed to feed. By morning her udder was near to bursting again. She filled two pails a day, enough for dozens of little ones. She was a four-legged miracle coveted by all.

A few miles from Olsene the long-suffering column met shrieking flocks of British motorcyclists in goggles and leather helmets. They rumbled past, beeping their horns. Giving the thumbs up sign they shouted and waved at the children on the Jersey. The cow gave a low bellow and a little hop, sending all her passengers tumbling onto the ground.

Josie and the Belgian mothers gathered them up again and set them on the cow. They were not hurt. It was nothing at all. What was a little tumble onto the road compared to . . .

In Rotterdam thirty-thousand died in one day of bombing. In Brussels fifty school children perished in one instant when a Messerschmidt emptied his machine guns into them. Beside them the fields were littered with shallow graves of the nameless dead who had done nothing wrong except be there at the wrong time.

The travelers' conversation invariably drifted to the proper position to assume while being strafed. To lay outstretched on the ground meant more body surface exposed to the bullets. Best to stand upright, they decided. Best to lead the cow and its passengers beneath the shade of a poplar tree and wait calmly. The theory was soon to be put to the test.

A white ring of smoke above the trudging column identified a Messerschmidt circling like a hawk. The fighter plane fell from the sky in perfect mimicry of a raptor's attack, and the crowd on the road, agreeing to play the part of the prey, scattered like rabbits.

Bicycles were hastily abandoned in crumpled heaps as their riders discarded them for cover under hedges. Mothers, trying to keep track of flocks of children, shooed some away even while calling others back.

Josie saw a careening, out-of-control car knock down and run over a man pushing a wheelbarrow, all before the machine gun bullets plowed the road for a harvest of destruction.

Trembling all over, Josie tried to sound calm as she grabbed Yacov so he would not take another fall and led the Jersey off the road and under the tree. She motioned for the children riding the cow to plug their ears with their fingers, as if this were all an elaborate game.

Standing perfectly still, with the Jersey behind the tree trunk and out of sight of the carnage on the road, Josie nevertheless peeked around the tree herself. An elderly couple, separated by the initial panic, tottered toward each other from opposite sides of the dusty lane.

The bullets of the Me 109 knit them together even as they touched, and as Josie ducked her head and squeezed shut her eyes, they fell into the embrace of death.

FIFTY-SEVEN

By the thirteenth of May it was clear that the German thrust into Holland and northern Belgium was a device to keep the Allies pinned in a corner. Meanwhile, the real offensive hammered at the gates of France, having successfully navigated the Ardennes and crossed the Meuse.

The Allies were giving ground grudgingly in Belgium, but the clear danger to their southern flank meant the necessity of withdrawing to a less exposed position. There was never any chance of completely breaking free of Wehrmacht Army Group B and going to the assistance of the embattled French troops in the path of the Panzers.

But Mac had no difficulty withdrawing from the battleline; he saw more clearly than the French High Command that the real story of the war was developing between the Belgian town of Dinant and the city of Sedan in France.

He paid a thousand francs for a fifteen-year-old Delfosse sports car. It had no top and the seats showed more springs than the leather, but it also had a 3500cc engine and the ability to cover four hundred kilometers on one tank of petrol. By driving all day, all night, and the next day, Mac hoped to be back in Nancy or wherever the action was on that side of the German advance.

His travel took him south from Brussels to Reims, where he stopped to gulp down some food before going on. The little auberge where he pulled over offered *coq au vin* and an ancient radio that whined and squawked like the ghost of the chicken in the stew as the proprietor attempted to tune in a recognizable sound.

In one of the passes up and down the cracked dial, Mac heard an English voice announce that they were repeating the words of new Prime Minister Churchill's address to the House of Commons.

"One moment, Monsieur," Mac requested. "I would like to hear what Monsieur Churchill has to say."

The measured tones and carefully chosen phrases of Winston Churchill crackled through the warped, dusty speaker, but the power of his character was unmistakable. "I would say to the House, as I have said to those who have joined this government: I have nothing to offer but blood, toil, tears, and sweat. You ask, what is our policy? I will say: It is to wage war by sea, land, and air, with all our might and with all the strength God can give us. That is our policy. You ask, what is our aim? I can answer in one word: It is victory. Victory at all costs. Victory in spite of all terror. Victory however long and hard the road may be; for without victory, there is no survival."

❧ ❧ ❧

It was Juliette who found her. She was only six, and she was weeping in the field beside the body of her mother. Her name was Angelique and she did not know where they were going, only that they had come a very long way from Ghent.

The mother, who had been a pretty young woman in her late twenties, was buried by an old farmer who had an army spade tucked into the pile on his wheelbarrow. And Juliette, who knew about such things as dead mothers, mothers killed by all varieties of Nazis, let Angelique hold her doll.

Now the Jersey cow carried six children on her back. She did not complain. Josie thought of the two sisters in Paris and remembered the joyous laughter of the children at the orphanage at Number 5 Rue de la Huchette. Surely there would be room for one more little girl who would need to learn to laugh again.

And how long would it be before Josie would feel happiness again? She could have wept easily. Raising her eyes from the hilltop, she looked across the miles and miles of road which wound down from Belgium to the border of France. There were the young and the very old and the very rich and the poor and the feeble and the strong, mingled together in one unbroken tide of terror. Numbering two million, this migration of fear marched against the Allied armies, blocking their road to battle more effectively than an enemy artillery barrage.

She glanced back. There seemed to be no beginning to the line. And forward, there was no end to it.

And as she looked, she could see that Death, the very thing they were fleeing, marched patiently beside them all.

❧ ❧ ❧

Only days after the fighting began, the students of the École de Cavalerie witnessed an unusual event. They were turned out of their bunks at dawn and told to form up in companies and march to the train station.

"I knew it!" Gaston exulted. "France needs us! We are going to the front!"

"Being sent away, more likely," Sepp said, shaking his head. "They are not going to let us fight."

A special train was on the siding at the rail platform. The cars were lettered *8 Chevaux Ou 40 Hommes*. "Eight horses or forty men," Gaston read. "We are going to the war in horse cars?"

But it soon proved otherwise. When the sliding doors to the rail cars were opened, down the ramps came two dozen proud, nervous horses. Following the cavalry steeds, a tiny pony pranced down the walkway.

"What is this?" Gaston wondered aloud. "Are we getting fresh mounts to ride into battle? Who gets the pony? Raymond?"

"Be quiet, you idiot," hissed Sepp as a man dressed in the uniform of a Belgian cavalry officer saluted Captain Chardon. "These are not for us. This is the stable of the royal family of Belgium. Look! That is King Leopold's stallion right there."

The boys were detailed in pairs to walk the horses back to the cavalry school. "Brussels is not safe for them any more," Sepp said. "So they have been evacuated to stay here."

"Fine thing," Gaston muttered. "It is not right for trained horses or trained men like us to hide back where it is safe. Captain," Gaston called to Paul Chardon, "will we be exercising these animals for the king?"

"Oh no," Paul corrected. "This is just a rest stop for them until this afternoon. We will be sending them on, just as soon as more cars are coupled to the train to take our own brood mares."

"Take them where?"

Paul looked at his young officers. "Further south," he said. "Where it is safe."

❦ ❦ ❦

There was no missing the Red Cross symbol painted on the roof of the École de Cavalerie. That is what the angry cadets and medical personnel said as they dug through the shattered right wing of the building after the lone Heinkel dropped a single bomb which collapsed two floors and left a gaping wound in the brick. Two hundred wounded were now dead. One British doctor, four nurses, and two orderlies were killed.

Paul Chardon sifted through the rubble with Sister Abigail Mitchell and several hundred angry cadets, who took the attack as a personal insult.

The operating theater was moved to the chapel. Summoned from the village by young Gaston during the emergency, Father Perrin and seventeen nuns from the church at Lys arrived to take the places of the fallen medical staff. There were no more refugees passing through the village. Now it was only the soldiers moving inexorably toward the coast. The civilian population had mostly fled to Paris, Mother Superior told Paul and Miss Mitchell. Was help needed to fight the unmerciful Boches with mercy?

There was no need to ask. Father Perrin was already busy administering last rites. The sisters helped to salvage supplies and set up a treatment room. Raymond, his youthful face showing grief beyond his years, formed a burial squad and helped to lay out the dead in long rows.

That afternoon, a doctor from Ghent who had followed the river back to the village by boat arrived at the docks in front of the town in hopes of acquiring provisions. When Sepp examined his papers and found that he was a physician, he brought him to the chapel at gunpoint.

"But I am an obstetrician!" the man declared.

Miss Mitchell drew herself up in her most formidable pose. She spat the angry words out in English for Sepp to translate in French.

"The most esteemed Sister Mitchell says that you learned to set bones in medical school, Monsieur. You are Belgian and many of the wounded are your countrymen. You will go to work with the rest of us or this young man . . . by which she means me . . . may suspect that you are a Nazi spy and will shoot you as a fifth columnist."

Sepp jabbed the muzzle of his rifle in the doctor's back for emphasis. By evening the Belgian obstetrician was delivering shrapnel from the bodies of French poilus as if he had stopped at the École for that very purpose.

❦ ❦ ❦

The battle Mac witnessed demonstrated that the Allied High Command was not wrong in their assessment of French military muscle after all. After the German tanks rolled out of the forest and through the little town of Longwy, they were met with concentrated fire from French cannons.

Mac stood beside the forward artillery observer, a calm, middle-aged man with a grey moustache and quick, darting eyes. "New coordinates, 75-10 to 78-4," Captain Druot said into the field telephone. Then to Mac, "I'm sorry, Monsieur. Where were we?"

"I was saying that the accuracy of the French artillery is certainly being verified here today."

"Ah, yes," replied the officer modestly, taking credit for the entire operation but showing humility at the same time. "The Germans cannot advance into such a conflagration."

It was true. The eye of Mac's camera registered three PzKw III's turned to flaming wreckage in the field outside the town. The others turned about and scurried back toward cover as fast as their clanking treads could carry them.

The barrage of sharp, angry sounds from the 75mm cannon continued cracking in the noontime sun. As Captain Druot whispered into his mouthpiece, the sights of the bombardment lifted. The fountains of dirt from the rain of shells pursued the German machines with an effect that was almost comical.

"But of course, artillery cannot do it alone," Druot said, waving toward an echelon of French tanks that had emerged from around the base of the hill. "Our guns can keep the Boche from taking a position and can even retake an objective. But cannon shells cannot hold a position all alone, you see." He spoke of the 75's with great affection, and seemed to be apologetic for the fact that artillery alone could not win the war.

The French armored unit, a mixed force of fast moving Somuas, tiny two-man Renaults, and one gigantic, lumbering thirty-two-ton Char, approached the town. They opened up with their machine guns, chasing a pocket of German riflemen out of cover. The Char, carrying a 75mm weapon of its own, launched a round of such force that it demolished the clock tower of the City Hall with one blow.

The German tanks, trying to regroup on the far side of the village, were still being routed by the French artillery. "We have superior artillery, and, as you have noted, clearly equal quality of armor. The courage of our foot soldiers is undoubted. In what respect are we not the match of the Boche?"

The first Stuka dropped out of the sun, followed by three more. Single-minded weapons that carried men on their backs, the dive-bombers fell toward the formation of French tanks. Pulling out of their swoops much lower than the approved height of three thousand feet, the German pilots risked being caught by their own detonating explosives, but the effect was one of firing at point blank range.

The Char, standing out on the bare field like the Eiffel Tower stands above the skyline of Paris, was singled out first. A five-hundred-pound bomb, released at a thousand feet above the tank, impacted directly on the cannon of the Char. The French machine disappeared in a roar of smoke and flame. When the shower of debris had fallen and the fumes cleared, nothing remained but the barrel of its weapon and a pile of charred metal.

In quick succession, the other Stukas attacked the tank formation. Then it was the turn of the French armor to run for safety. But there was no safety. From their aerial perspective, the German warplanes could pick out the tanks wherever they fled. Unlike the artillery barrage, it was not possible for the French machines to retreat out of range. The dive-bombers pursued them wherever they went.

Mac saw the German troops and their armor advance back into the recently vacated town. Druot, still calm and matter-of-fact in the face of the reversal, issued new coordinates to the guns.

As soon as the French 75's opened up again, new waves of Stukas dropped toward the white streamers from the firing cannons. As if tired of chasing tanks, the dive-bombers unloaded their deadly eggs on the French gun emplacements instead.

One after another, the barking noises of the 75's ceased. Although Druot cranked the telephone and called each of four batteries in turn, he received no further response. A Stuka, returning from having destroyed the pride of the French artillery, spotted Mac and the captain in their exposed position on the hill.

The gull-winged warbird flattened out its dive, skimming the hilltop with its machine guns blazing. Mac threw himself into a slit trench as a furious line of bullets stalked him.

The artillery observer's body reclined on the ground as if he had chosen a pleasant afternoon to watch the passing clouds. In his fist he still grasped the handset of the telephone. His sightless eyes stared upward, registering forever a lesson harshly learned: the part of the war in which the French were no match.

❧ ❧ ❧

It was a small village with some unpronounceable Flemish name. Josie did not attempt to say it. Traffic snarled in the center of the square around a fountain and the statue of Jeanne d'Arc. Josie felt an amused revenge against the loaded vehicles that had streaked past them on the main highway earlier in the day. Their horns blared to no avail. They were stuck, while Josie and Madame Hasselt led the little Jersey in and out of the mess with ease.

Some of their larger group had broken off, taking their children with them on a different route to France. Now there was only the cow, Josie, Madame Hasselt, Juliette, Yacov, and solemn little Angelique still clutching Juliette's baby doll.

There were shops open in this unpronounceable place! A miracle.

Madame Hasselt's ham was gone, the chocolate consumed. The cheeses in her pack were moldy. Here was opportunity to obtain food enough to get them to the border at least! It was worth braving the traffic and the reflected heat off the cobbles.

Josie headed to the cheese shop, which still displayed enormous red-waxed wheels in the window. Madame Hasselt was left in charge of the cow and the children. She removed the three little ones from the back of the Jersey and let the beast drink slowly and with great satisfaction out of Jeanne d'Arc's fountain.

A long queue snaked from the cheese shop, but the great rounds of cheese would last a while yet. The proprietor, in fairness to all, allowed only two pounds per customer. Out of fairness to himself he charged exorbitant prices. People paid him willingly—gratefully. Better to sell the stuff now than to let the Nazis have it, the proprietor remarked. At this, men and women looked at one another uncomfortably. Could the old fellow really mean he believed the Germans would get as far as his cheese shop?

Josie took her place at the end of the line. Progress was slow. Past the red-waxed disks and through the plate glass window, she could see little Angelique sitting with the doll on the lip of the fountain. She was cool in spite of the hot sun. Her brown eyes affectionately looked down at the porcelain face. It was a grubby porcelain face by this time, but Josie figured it would clean up as easily as the live children when they all arrived in Paris. But could Angelique be parted from the doll? Josie determined then and there that she would take the child to Samaritaine and buy her any doll she wanted in the entire store.

But where was Madame Hasselt? Josie cast her eyes around the square, finally spotting the old woman with the cow and Juliette and Yacov standing in another long queue outside the public toilet.

Josie had just gotten to the counter and Madame Hasselt had just tied off the cow and entered the toilet stall when the shriek of an air raid siren split the air.

Instantly the square had the look of an anthill stamped on by the foot of a giant. Men and women dove out of their automobiles and fought one another to run to shelter in basements and shops. Then Josie saw Angelique. Fearless, oblivious, the little girl embraced the baby doll and remained on the fountain. Josie cried out and sprinted in an attempt to get to her. But the panic of the mob pushed her back. The terrible snarl of Heinkel engines and the long whistle of bombs was almost drowned out by the screams of the terrified throng. But there beyond the window and the red wheels and the terror was Angelique.

Josie reached the door, only to be thrown back onto the floor as a large man charged in and dove for cover.

The first bomb exploded. Glass shattered, pocking the counter where she had stood. Buildings in the square unfolded like they were made of playing cards. The statue of Jeanne d'Arc collapsed and tile from the church portico slid down on it. The second bomb fell a block away, rocking the shop.

And then there was silence, as profound and terrible as if Josie had gone deaf. No moans. No cries for help. Was it over so quickly?

"Is everyone all right?" The cheese man asked feebly.

A dozen people got up slowly. Josie struggled to rise. The door of the public toilet opened and Madame Hasselt, shaken but unharmed, emerged with Juliette and Yacov into the bright sunlight. The cow had broken her tether, but stood serenely chewing her cud a few paces away.

And then there was little Angelique . . . still beside the fountain . . . still clutching the doll. So very still.

She was dead, of course. Josie knew it before she stumbled, weeping, across the rubble to her body. Sinking to her knees, she picked up the doll and clutched it to her.

A small crowd gathered around her. Someone asked if Josie was the mother of the dead child.

"No."

"What was her name?" a gendarme asked gently.

"Angelique."

"Her surname?"

"I do not know. Her mother was killed on the road. There is nothing else I can tell you."

From around the corner came a blind man, frantically tapping his way across the square with his cane.

"God pity the blind," said the gendarme.

"The blind are blessed," Josie replied.

FIFTY-EIGHT

Since the moment the Seventh Panzer broke out from the bridgehead across the Meuse, it had covered over fifty miles. Not content to be the command that breached the first Allied line of defense, Rommel pushed his men to remain in the forefront of the Blitzkrieg. The French troops reeled backwards in confusion, tangling the reinforcements rushed up to stem the rout. The French High Command wanted to draw a new defensive line along the Sambre River.

But the Panzer advance followed so closely on the heels of the French retreat that key bridges were still intact. Such was the case when Lieutenant Shultz reconnoitered the highway that led to the river crossing at Auluoye, just beyond the little town of Avesnes.

Horst assembled his company commanders, including Lieutenant Borger, who had replaced Captain Gruhn, for an afternoon conference in Avesnes. "Just think, gentlemen," Horst urged his officers, "Paris is only a hundred miles or so in that direction." He waved his hand toward the southwest. "At our present pace, we could be in sight of the Eiffel Tower in four or five days."

"Does the major think that will happen?" Borger asked.

"Unlikely. In my opinion, OKW wants to make the French *think* our objective is Paris, in order to freeze troop movements, while we actually strike westward. If we can completely cut off the Allied Army and trap them between us and our force in Holland, the war will be over in two weeks."

A scout car roared into the village square and an agitated Lieutenant Shultz jumped out and ran to the group. "Major, the bridge . . . the bridge is still intact!"

"Slow down, Shultz. Borger, give him a drink of water."

When the excited outrider had recovered his breath, he explained that he had encountered no enemy soldiers before reaching a point from which he could see the Sambre. "I backed away as quickly as I could to come and tell you," he said. "I did not want to use the radio in case the French intercepted the transmission."

"How many defenders?"

"Only a handful."

"Any tanks?"

"None that I could see. There was a line of trucks crossing the bridge that I think were full of retreating troops. They must not know that we are so close or they wouldn't be so unconcerned."

There was no time to reflect, not a moment to lose. Horst could not even relay to his superiors what he intended. At any moment the French defenders would get news of the German advance and demolish the bridge. "Shultz, you take the lead. Borger, I will ride with you. Gelb, you send all your motorcycles with us while you find General Rommel and inform him about this opportunity. Tell him that I will attempt to seize the crossing. Request that he send reinforcements at once. Everybody move!"

❖   ❖   ❖

"I assure you, Monsieur McGrath, this was all foreseen. It is a most well-planned and orderly retrenchment." The captain, explaining the fine points of how the French army had intentionally given up half a hundred miles of territory, sounded convincing. His performance was somewhat diluted by the fact that he kept looking over his shoulder in the direction of the bridge.

"Then you would not mind if I filmed the movement of troops returning across the Sambre?" Mac studiously avoided using the word retreat. He had been warned that even a suggestion that the French army was in flight would mean the confiscation of his camera and possibly get him barred from the front.

"The passage of trucks is not . . . edifying. Why do you not wait until the Boches come to foolishly throw themselves against our defenses? That will be something to witness."

"And when do you expect this battle to take place?"

"Not for two or perhaps three days. Everyone knows that an army cannot advance without artillery, and it takes many hours to move and set up the big cannons. No, Monsieur, the Germans cannot reach here before day after tomorrow. But then, I promise you, there will be something to see!"

"I notice," commented Mac to the thin officer with the prominent Adam's apple, "that your troops are setting up machine guns and wiring the bridge for destruction."

"Ah yes," agreed the captain. "Our engineers are very thorough. All will be ready long before the Boche arrive."

❖   ❖   ❖

When Horst's column of armored cars and motorcycles arrived at the edge of the hill overlooking Auluoye, the situation had drastically changed. A pair of machine guns flanked the near end of the bridge and the ominous snout of an anti-tank weapon poked out of a brush on the far side. A half dozen men emerged from the shadows beneath the bridge, each carrying a spool of wire. The strands were joined into a single braid and one man began backing across to the western side.

The same tall figure who had stretched the final strand of the demolition cord returned across the bridge and spoke to the gunners. The machine gun crews broke down their weapons and hefted them to carry over.

The armored car of Lieutenant Shultz raced forward, spraying bullets from the gun in its turret. One of the French machine gun crew turned back toward the oncoming Germans and was shot down; the others dropped the tripods and weapons and fled.

The anti-tank gun roared, and a shell shattered a tree trunk beside the road. Horst's column was closing rapidly on the bridge, with less than two hundred yards to go. Rifle bullets pinged off the armor on the scout cars, and a motorcyclist near Horst threw up his hands and crashed as a slug hit him in the face.

The anti-tank gun fired again and an armor-piercing shell sliced through Shultz's vehicle. The armored car slewed sideways in the roadway, then rolled over and over until coming to rest upside down.

"Jog left," Horst ordered Borger at the controls of what was now the lead car. The maneuver was intended to spoil the aim of the anti-tank crew and spread out the targets. The Kfz 231's took advantage of an open area in front of the bridge to move apart, flanking the approach to the span.

The machine guns of the attackers replied to the rifle fire. The anti-tank gun fired again, a high explosive round this time, with deadly effect. The shell missed the front rank of German machines and landed in the middle of a group of motorcycles, killing three men.

The armored car on Horst's right cut back into line with the roadway, attempting to make a crossing while the anti-tank crew reloaded. Halfway over a high explosive round took it squarely in front, flipping the vehicle over backwards in a great gout of flame. Now the bridge was blocked.

✤ ✤ ✤

A bullet went through Mac's camera case where it sat on a tree stump. He dove for cover behind a wood fence, then hastily abandoned the spot when more bullets sailed between the gap in the rails to kick up small explosions in the dirt behind him. Crawling on his belly and pushing the camera ahead of him, Mac wormed his way to the reassuring shelter of a rock wall.

The French rifle fire that responded to the German MG 34's sounded puny by comparison. There was no chance for the poilus to reassemble their machine guns. The only effective weapon the defenders possessed, it seemed, was the 25mm Hotchkiss anti-tank gun. It was keeping up a rapid and potent barrage that had already destroyed several vehicles in the charge down the hill.

Mac's DeVry camera poked over the stones like the periscope of a U-boat. He continued grinding frame after frame of the activity around the scene which his escort had dismissed as not edifying. Mac thought that the film would prove very educational. How was it that the Germans had arrived twenty minutes after the captain pronounced that it would be at least forty-eight hours? And no artillery barrage had preceded this attack. The German motorcycles and armored cars that flung themselves against the defenses of the bridge were staking everything on the speed of their assault, which they had not launched from two days distant.

How had French intelligence failed so badly? Or was it a failure of imagination? The French General Staff had not been in Poland nor were they interested in discussing the tactics of Blitzkrieg. General Gamelin and his cohorts believed that the strength of the French Army could resist the initial German offensive, after which the war would stalemate again until the Allied stranglehold on the German economy dragged them to the peace table.

That idea seemed as likely to explode as the armored car that had reached the midpoint of the bridge before being blown into a heap of flaming rubble. That was the whole picture, Mac decided. The anti-tank gun, like the French strategy, was adequate only if the foe did exactly what you expected. But German tactics, like the armored cars now spreading out across the town square and pouring their flanking fire into the French positions, were not so predictable.

As Mac peeked through a gap in the stones that he hoped was too obscure for a bullet to find, an odd footrace developed. On the near side of the Sambre, the engineer who had been in charge of the demolition detail grabbed up a rifle and sprinted out onto the bridge. Across the river, another armored car slowed to a sideways halt, and a figure in a German uniform emerged to challenge the Frenchman for possession of the bridge.

❋　❋　❋

"Knock out the gun!" Horst ordered Borger. He jumped out of the armored car to lead an attack on foot. Horst expected the bridge to disintegrate in front of him at any second. Surprise was lost and the delay was too great.

That was when Horst spotted the French officer in charge of the demolition detail sprinting back toward the center of the bridge. It could mean only one thing: the charge had failed to explode electrically and the man was going to try to set it off by hand.

Horst fired his Luger and missed, then was forced to duck behind the stonework of bridge abutment as a stream of bullets sought him. When the shooting stopped, he jumped up. The French officer leaned over the center of the trestle, aiming a rifle at the charges below. Horst fired again, hitting the Frenchman in the leg and spinning him around. The man sagged against the railing, but squeezed off a shot that passed between Horst's arm and his body.

Tossing the now-empty pistol aside, Horst leapt for the French officer's throat. The two men wrestled on the roadway while the anti-tank gun roared above their heads and the German machine guns chattered back. Another armored car exploded.

Horst hammered his fist into the Frenchman's face. The wounded man swung his rifle up from the ground, and the barrel hit Horst in the side of the head, knocking him off. The French officer rolled on top of Horst and pressed his rifle across Horst's throat.

A pool of burning gasoline spread out from the destroyed armored car. Horst could see the puddle of fire running closer and closer to his face. He could feel the heat as he struggled to breathe, to dislodge the weight pressing him toward blackness.

Flinging up his legs while grasping the Frenchman's rifle as a pivot, Horst planted both boots in the man's midsection and kicked. The force of the jolt broke the tug of war for the rifle and propelled the Frenchman through the air.

The French officer landed in the pool of fiery gasoline. His uniform blazing, the man jumped up screaming. He climbed over the railing of the bridge and flung himself into the river.

The anti-tank gun exploded in a shattering roar. From back up the hill, a German PzKw 38 tank fired again, and its high explosive round annihilated another pocket of French defenders. Two more PzKw 38's, made in the captured arms factories of occupied Czechoslovakia, moved out of the woods and flanked the scene, their machine guns tearing up the remaining cover on the west side of the Sambre.

A bit of ragged white cloth appeared on the end of a French bayonet. "Enough," cried a poilu. "We surrender. La guerre est fini. The war is done."

❖   ❖   ❖

Mac continued filming when the 37mm shells landed only a hundred feet or so in front of him. But when the tank commanders started aiming the shellfire even closer to the stone wall behind which he had taken refuge, it was time to leave. Mac's captain chaperone was already back in the car waving for Mac to hurry.

"Rejoin your units!" the officer said to a group of poilus surrounding the car. They were demanding to be driven away from the Germans. "Find your commander at once!"

"What for?" one of them growled. "The officers are all either captured or dead already. I have no wish to join them. But you may, since you are so heroic!" The burly soldier grabbed the scrawny captain by the neck and, dragging him out through the car window, threw him to the ground.

"This is desertion! You . . ." the captain began, subsiding when three French rifles pointed at his bobbing throat.

"Be very still and we will not have to shoot you," the chief of the mutiny promised.

"Hold on a minute," said Mac, hurrying up. Two of the rifles swiveled to cover him. He displayed his camera and said, "I am not an officer and I need a ride. How about it?"

"Why not?" the ringleader agreed. "It is time someone reported the truth about this debacle."

"You are betraying France!" shouted the captain in a brave tone, although he had not moved from the ground.

The poilu shrugged. "Our ignorant generals betrayed France first," he said. "We are only following their lead."

⚜ ⚜ ⚜

The distant crumps of artillery sounded like thunder booming out of a clear sky as Josie and Madame Hasselt led the Jersey cow through the ancient stone gate of the Flemish town of Courtrai. Courtrai was situated along the River Lys. Across the border and a few miles downstream was the École de Cavalerie, but the school seemed very much out of reach to Josie this afternoon.

Before the war, Courtrai had been famous for the manufacture of lace and table linen. Today it was the last major Belgian stop before the frontier crossing into France.

Now little Courtrai was overflowing with human flotsam. Old men and women and children all slept in the cobbled square and drank and washed in the public fountains.

The airfield of Courtrai had been bombed on the first day as had the train station. But though the roar of battles was clearly audible, the ancient Flemish town itself was miraculously unharmed. It was clearly in the path of the advance, however.

For now, St. Martin's Church, opposite the sixteenth century belfry of the town hall, opened its doors to feed the hungry. The church of Notre Dame was now a BEF Casualty Clearing Station being filled hourly by freshly wounded soldiers from the front. In the chapel behind the choir men were operated on beneath a Van Dyke painting called "Raising of the Cross." The picture of suffering seemed appropriate in such a place, Josie thought when she was told about it. Rumor was that the Belgian army was being crucified by the Panzers. The Germans had broken through the line at the Meuse and a pall of gloom hung over the place.

Madame Hasselt had a sister in Courtrai. By this she meant that her sister was a member of a lay sisterhood called the Beguines who lived in a grey cloister across the square. Could they stay the night and rest in real beds before pushing on?

Madame Hasselt knocked on the ancient gate, asked to see Sister Madeline, and was admitted while Josie and the children were asked to wait.

Ten minutes passed and an aerial dogfight took place overhead. Josie could not tell which of planes were the Allies and which were Germans. Two spiralled downward in flames, exploding in the flax acreage beyond the walled city. Others made white smoky circles above Courtrai, as if to mark its location for bombers.

Yacov was cranky from a slight sunburn. Juliette, who was quite ragged now, stretched out on the back of her cow and watched the distant air battle without emotion. She held up the cage of Petit Chou and poked her finger through the bars in boredom.

And then the gate opened on the serene courtyard and the orb of Madame Hasselt's face beamed out. "Come in! Come in!" she motioned to them. "Bring the cow!" She applauded herself happily. "There is a BEF medical officer here to discuss the care of additional British wounded at the cloister! I have traded the milk cow to his hospital for a ride across the border to Armentieres for you and the children. I will stay here in the convent with my sister."

❖ ❖ ❖

Bertrand was waiting in the study when Andre arrived home. He seemed not to notice the bandage on Andre's head. After all, what was one little head wound when all of France was getting its brains kicked out?

"It took you long enough." Bertrand was irritable.

"As you can see . . ." Andre put a hand to his head.

"I hope this does not mean you will not be able to think straight. They have changed the codes again you know. At the most critical time. And Lewinski with his miracle machine cannot seem to figure out the riddle this time." Bertrand was clearly impatient with the fiery-haired scientist. "I've got to get back to Vignolles." He stood, then remembering something, he dug in his pocket and handed Andre the yellow envelope of a telegram. It was open.

"What does it say?" Andre asked with a hint of sarcasm.

"Our Anastasie have chopped it up pretty good, but it says that Josephine arrived safely. At least I think that is what it says." He snatched his hat from the coatrack and jammed it onto his head. "Now. If that lunatic in your basement comes up with something, you know where I will be. In the meantime, the new British Prime Minister is flying into Paris tomorrow for an enlightening meeting with our fearless leader, General Gamelin. Be there. For the historical interest it is not something you want to miss, at any rate. Our senile old general lecturing Churchill, who predicted every wrong turn our government has taken over the years!" And then, in a grieving voice, "Why did our soldiers not hold the line at the Meuse, Andre? How did we let the Meuse be crossed? Is our honor dead?"

"Only sleeping," Andre remarked bitterly.

"Yes. Well. We may lose Paris and France because of this little snooze. Good day, Andre. I know my way out." With that, Bertrand hurried out of the house and sped away in his staff car.

Alone, Andre sat down slowly behind his desk and slipped Josie's telegram from its envelope. The paper was filled with black marks, words crossed out by the censors until only the barest essense of the message remained.

DIFFICULTY CROSSING TO THE . . . ALL SAFE AT . . . COMING SOON TO . . . SEE YOU . . . LOVE, JOSIE

Filling in the missing pieces, Andre read the message as he assumed she had written it: She had experienced difficulty crossing the Channel. She and the children were finally safe in England. They were coming to . . . someplace . . . maybe London?

"Thank God they are out of here," Andre sighed. His head was throbbing.

✤   ✤   ✤

Andre met the Flamingo lightplane when it arrived at Le Bourget airport carrying Prime Minister Churchill and his staff assistant, General Hastings Ismay. Andre's head was still wrapped in bandages, and he was afraid he would look foolish.

"Andre, dear boy!" Churchill exclaimed. "How good to see you up and about. I heard about your injury. Clemmie and I were very concerned for you."

Andre grinned ruefully. "Tell Clemmie that she and I now have something in common, and tell her that she did much better with her accident than I did with mine."

The reason for Churchill's decision to fly to Paris hinged on an impassioned phone call from French Premier Reynaud the night before. "All is lost," Reynaud's voice had gasped in Churchill's ear. "The Germans will be in Paris in two days!"

"Tell me the truth, Andre," Churchill urged as they rode in the limousine toward Quai d'Orsay. "Is it as bad as all that? This attack only began six days ago."

"There has been a breakthrough near Sedan," Andre said. "But I am sorry to say that I was not made privy to the details. I will be as much a student at this lesson as you."

Churchill snorted. The idea of sitting while General Gamelin lectured chafed him.

The spacious consultation room on the ground floor was occupied by Gamelin, Premier Reynaud, and Defense Minister Daladier. Near the fireplace stood an easel bearing a map of the French northeastern provinces.

"Mister Premier," Churchill addressed Reynaud. "How sad that our first official meeting as heads of our respective governments should come at such an hour."

The diminutive man with the features of Mickey Mouse wrung his hands. "It is worse than sad," he said. "It is tragic!"

Gamelin lectured with all the pomposity Andre expected. "This black mark which I have drawn on the map represents the front line." Churchill nodded his understanding, as if the chart were not self-explanatory. "And this bulge," Gamelin continued, "represents a breakthrough of German tanks in the area of Sedan."

"How big and how deep a penetration?" Churchill asked.

Gamelin looked unhappy at being interrupted. "As I was about to say," he said peevishly, "the gap is a hundred kilometers wide and a hundred kilometers deep."

"And has it been contained?"

Gamelin nodded. "Surrounded, sealed off. I am afraid our esteemed Premier has exaggerated the danger."

Andre thought that if Gamelin was not worried, that fact alone was tremendous cause for concern.

Reynaud was certainly not reassured. "The German tanks are exploiting the gap. They are racing toward Amiens . . . Arras . . . even Abbeville on the coast. Or perhaps they will turn south and strike at Paris."

Churchill tried to sound reassuring. "But surely Mister Premier, a counterattack launched against the flanks of this corridor would prove efficacious." Turning to Gamelin he asked, "How many divisions are there in reserve for such a counterthrust?"

"There are no reserves," the Commander-in-Chief replied blandly. "Oh, eight or nine divisions can be withdrawn from elsewhere, and I can order another eight or nine sent from Africa in . . . two weeks, perhaps three."

Churchill and Andre were alike stunned at the news. No reserves and the French reeling back before the hammer blows of the Panzer Korps? Churchill pursed his lips and asked judiciously, "And what assistance are you seeking from us?"

"Planes!" Reynaud interjected. "Fighters to deal with the terrible menace of the Stukas and the other German bombers. Our artillery can deal with the tanks if we do not have to face bombers."

Churchill pondered a moment, though he had come prepared for this request. "I can offer four additional squadrons," he said.

"It is not enough!" Reynaud pleaded. "We need more." Gamelin actually looked pleased at his leader's discomfort.

"I will seek approval to release an additional six, for a total of ten," Churchill said at last. "But that is the absolute limit. The rest must be reserved," he laid extra stress on the word, staring at Gamelin as he did so. "Must be reserved for defense. You understand."

Reynaud was almost pathetically grateful. "Thank you! That will make the difference. We will turn the tide now, you will see."

Churchill approved of the return of confidence in the Premier, but he also wanted to know how the French planned to really deal with the German thrust. "And the counterattack?" he quizzed Gamelin.

The Commander shrugged. "We have inferior numbers . . . inferior equipment . . . inferior methods . . ." The rest of the sentence expired in the air and fell to the floor. This was the response from the man who had presided over the training and equipping of the present French Army.

"I am sure you will find a way to cope with the situation," Churchill said with more confidence than he felt. "And now, I must go telephone my cabinet in regard to the fighter squadrons." Passing near Reynaud but close enough for Andre to overhear, Churchill muttered to the Premier, "You must get rid of him."

Reynaud bobbed his head nervously and hurried out of the room. Gamelin was covering the map with a cloth. He had a satisfied expression on his face as if a successful lecture equalled a successful military victory.

A square green object hurtled past the window of the conference room to explode like a bomb in the courtyard. Another followed and another. A cloud of smoke drifted upward in front of Churchill's view, carrying fragments of burning paper on the rising drafts. "What is that?" Churchill asked. "What is going on?"

"The government offices upstairs," Daladier said. "They are burning the secret files."

FIFTY-NINE

It was the second pullback in three days. "Don't return after this patrol," Wing Commander Brown told the flight. "Too much chance of being caught on the ground by another raid. We're moving back again. Your personal effects will come by truck. Good luck and good hunting."

David's Hurricane was orbiting at twenty-five thousand feet when Simpson's voice clicked over the radio. "Right," Simpson said. "A half dozen Heinkels without escort at angels twelve, twenty miles north. Tally ho!"

It was a situation tailor-made for a fighter pilot: slow flying planes without fighter protection too close by to miss and too much lower in altitude to escape. They covered the distance in three minutes. David scanned the space below him for the group of bombers. Then suddenly, there they were. "Fish in a barrel," David muttered.

"They've seen us," Simpson reported as the Heinkels began to break formation and scatter. "I'll take the leader. Jones, yours is the next clockwise, Meyer, the next to port. Watch your six."

David's first pass on the Heinkel 111 shattered the top turret's plexiglass and silenced the machine gunner. He came back on the clumsy aircraft from its opposite quarter, just as the German pilot was attempting a roll away from his attack. The stream of fire from his eight machine guns converged on the underside of the Heinkel. As David rocketed past, a ball of flame shot out and a concussion shook the Hurricane. It was obvious that these bombers had been intercepted before delivering their payloads. Five thousand pounds of high explosive had detonated, disintegrating the German plane in midair.

His altitude down to eight thousand feet, David put *ANNIE* into a steep climb to regain some height. As soon as the nose pointed skyward, David gasped at what he saw and got on the radio. "Simpson," he called urgently. "Forty more Heinkels on the way in from northeast. They have top cover too . . . looks like twenty . . . no, make that thirty 109's."

"Roger that," Simpson agreed. "I'll try to get us some more for our side. Pick out a partner; looks like the dance is in full swing!"

David roared up at the Heinkels from underneath this time, loosing a burst at the portside wing of one as he swept upward. There was no time for a return pass; the accompanying Messerschmidts had seen him and were already beginning their pounce.

At a severe disadvantage because of his lower elevation, and slowed by the climb, there was nothing to do but meet the enemy head on. As the range toward the swooping German fighter closed to under a quarter mile, David fired a short burst and then another. The Nazi pilot was firing back but was more intent on not colliding with David than on his gunnery. The two planes jerked violently apart at a distance of mere yards, without either having damaged the other.

When David came out of his bank and roll, two more Messerschmidts were on his tail. He ducked away from one, using the Hurricane's tighter turning ability. The first enemy attacker hurtled by, and David was able to turn toward the other in another headlong rush.

He took more deliberate aim this time and saw the line of his bullets converge on the 109's nose. An instant later David was rewarded with an eruption of black smoke from the Messerschmidt's engine. It fluttered from side to side, like a dog shaking its head, and then dropped suddenly away.

David followed, loosing another short stream into the tail of the enemy fighter when, with a final burst, his ammunition was exhausted. This was no place to be without a weapon. The Heinkels had taken the opportunity to disappear, but the sky was still full of dogfighting Hurricanes and 109's. Obviously Simpson's call for more players on the side of the RAF had been answered.

One of the latecomers was in trouble. David watched a Hurricane some ten thousand feet above him get into a losing tussle with a pair of Messerschmidts. David was streaking for home himself, but he kept an eye on the damaged British plane as it tumbled like a leaf out of the fight. The Germans must have figured that it was done for, because they left off pursuing it and took out after another Hurricane.

When the falling aircraft reached David's altitude, it regained some measure of control. The pilot was able to level out, even though the plane was trailing smoke. David moved *ANNIE* to join formation with the injured one. He recognized the numbers on the craft as belonging to the First Squadron, together with the identification letter *K.* Who flew the plane designated *K* in First Squadron? David could not remember.

The second Hurricane seemed to be able to fly all right, but David could see what part of the difficulty was; an oil line had been shattered and covered the windscreen with a thick black layer. On the radio David announced,

"Hurricane *K*, this is Meyer. I am formatted on your left wing. I can see your problem and I can help. I'll guide you home. What's your engine temp reading?"

"I . . . I . . . don't know," replied a voice that betrayed near panic barely under control.

Suddenly David remembered who it was that flew the airplane in First Squadron with the letter *K*. He recognized the voice; it was Badger Cross!

"What do you mean, don't know?" David asked, trying to keep the contempt he felt out of his voice.

"When the oil . . . I opened the canopy . . . my eyes and my hands are . . . help me, Meyer! I'm blind!"

"Pop the hatch and hit the silk," David urged Badger Cross. "Get out of there!"

"I tried!" Cross's voice screamed through the earphones. "The hatch is jammed! It won't open any further!"

"Hammer on it!" David shouted back as though the two men could hear each other through the twenty yards of air that separated the two planes.

"My hands are burned. Burned! Do you understand? All I can do is hang onto the stick!"

Swallowing hard and trying to think what to do, David got back on the radio. "All right, Cross," he said. "I'm with you. Just do exactly as I say. You'll be all right."

David knew what had happened. When the Messerschmidt's bullets pierced the oil line on the Hurricane, the hot oil streaming over the engine manifold filled the cockpit with smoke. Cross cracked the canopy to clear the fumes, but the slipstream sucked the boiling lubricant over his hands as he reached up to open the hatch. Now with the canopy jammed, it was impossible for the man to bail out.

David began searching for a suitable field. Without being able to get a picture of the oil pressure and the engine temperature in the stricken craft, there was no way to tell how soon the engine would seize up. It was essential to get down as quickly as possible.

"Meyer!" came Cross's anxious voice, "Where are you? You can't leave me!"

Gritting his teeth, David replied, "I'm right here, Cross, and I'll stay right here. Keep it steady and level for now. I'm just hunting for a clear space."

Over rolling hills and forested terrain they flew, with each passing moment decreasing Cross's chances of survival. Not that they had ever been good. How to talk a blind, crippled flyer down from ten thousand feet, while hurling through the air at three hundred miles an hour in a machine about to break at any minute was not ever in any of David's courses of instruction.

There was a field coming up. It looked flat enough, and there were no obvious ditches or rocks sticking up out of it. "Okay, Cross," David radioed. "Here's your field coming up now. We need to kill some altitude, so when I count three, I want a nice easy dive and a gentle bank left."

Through the oil-streaked glass of Cross's canopy, David could barely make out the hunched-over figure of the other pilot. "Relax," David said. "Pretend this is back in the old Tiger Moth training days, and I'm sitting in the back seat telling you what to do next."

The gradual circuits of the field brought them down to fifteen hundred feet. David maintained a running monologue about routine things, keeping his voice even. "Bring the nose up a touch, Cross. That's it, you're doing fine." If David let so much as half a minute go by in silence, Cross began yelling over the radio. The man seemed certain that David would abandon him.

David moved the *ANNIE* into a direct line astern of Cross.

"All right, now. Pay attention," David said. "You are lined up perfectly with the field. When I say to, cut your engine. Don't move the stick or rudder and you'll glide right in. Got it?"

Silence from the other plane.

"Cross, did you hear me?"

A very meek voice replied, "Don't kill me, Meyer. Don't let me die. I'm trusting you."

"Cut your engine now! Now, Cross, do it! You'll overshoot the field! Trust me Cross, cut it now!"

The engine of Cross's fighter stopped and it began to drop away from David toward the ground.

David put his Hurricane into another gentle circle of the field to observe the result of his coaching. He held his breath as Cross swept down toward the pasture below. The extra moments of power caused by hesitation carried the plane further out than David planned.

At the far end of the grassy area was a hedge and a row of trees. As David watched helplessly, the other aircraft touched down, bounced, and ran on at high speed toward the end of the field. "Brake!" David ordered sharply. "Brake again! Now kick it around to port, Cross. Do it!"

The Hurricane on the ground ran headlong into the hedgerow. David could not tell if Cross had ever applied the brakes or had remained frozen in place. When the Hurricane connected with the brush, the tail flipped up in the air. The fighter plane collapsed sideways toward the ground and ended the crash upside down.

"Cross!" David radioed. "Cross, do you read me?"

There was no response.

David's fuel gauge showed that he had enough fuel to make base, but just barely. He circled the downed plane one final time, looking for any sign of life, and then flew off toward the west.

❊   ❊   ❊

"Are you completely clear on your orders, Major?" General Rommel's question was pointed. With many other commanders a subordinate would have been intimidated into acquiescing whether he understood or not. But Rommel was different—a natural leader. He had personally directed river crossings and had stood his ground while artillery shells rained down, killing men as close as a few feet from him. If there were a remaining question, he would not ridicule a man for asking it.

"No, sir," Horst admitted. "That is, I am clear on the order, but not the intent. I am to spread my entire command into six columns at the extreme left flank of the division. On your signal we are to thrust north and then east around the town of Cambrai. The columns are to remain separated by two-hundred-yard intervals, and we are to make as much dust as possible. Is that all correct, sir?"

"Perfectly," Rommel agreed. "Do you know the history of Cambrai, Major?"

"Just what I remember from the war college classes, sir . . . in fact, I believe it was in one you taught. Cambrai is the site of the first ever major tank engagement. It is recorded as a British victory in the Great War, although they were unable to hold their gains."

"Very good, Major. Highest marks. From that battle came the standard doctrine that tanks must always accompany the infantry and never operate as independent units. The French and the British still believe this, which is why there are no true armored divisions such as our Panzers amongst the Allied forces."

"I am sorry, sir, but I must be failing this class. I don't see the connection between the history and our present plan of attack."

"The chief benefit of tank attack is fear, Major. Fear of being over-whelmed. Fear of facing a steel-hided beast, while armed with a pop gun. The British General Fuller had the right idea, but he was before his time. His tanks could only travel at five or six kilometers per hour. Ours can do close to fifty! Today we will see what intimidation can really accomplish. Go on now. We move out in one hour."

Armored cars in the lead, flanked and followed by motorcycles, Horst ordered the drivers to weave as they drove amongst the plowed fields and country lanes, stirring the dust into plumes.

❊   ❊   ❊

Mac's view of the countryside around Cambrai was excellent, since he and the city's mayor were standing in the belfry of the cathedral. From his perch he could look down on the walls of chalky white stone that distinguished the ancient city of Cambrai from its red brick, industrial-age neighbors.

The mayor pointed out the gateway called the Porte de Paris, built in the 1300s. "And one hundred and fifty kilometers south *is* Paris," explained the short man with the ill-fitting toupee and the warlike attitude. "A great many of the cowardly among our citizens have taken that road in the last week, Monsieur."

Mac scanned the sprawling municipal plaza, over which hovered the cupola of the Hôtel de Ville, the city hall. The large square was crammed with people, thronging the pavement, gawking at the exotic Oriental statues on the clock tower, and leaving behind their discarded garbage. "But your population does not seem to have shrunk, Monsieur the Mayor."

"They are not *our* people," replied the official, shaking his fist. "They are Dutch refugees, Belgian refugees, even . . ." he paused to load his words with disgust, ". . . deserters among the crowd, Monsieur. Men who should be at the front defending France from the Boche!"

Mac panned his camera over the plaza, giving his viewers a high shot of the mass of humans who had run before the Wehrmacht. The truth of the mayor's words were apparent. There were a number of French soldiers in the throng. Some had discarded half of their uniforms and their equipment; none seemed to have weapons. Over his shoulder to the mayor, Mac remarked, "What is the plan for the defense of the city?"

"Defense?" the administrator repeated, one hand holding his hairpiece against a gust of wind. "We have a garrison of infantry here, Monsieur, who will fight to the death. No tanks, no cannons, no planes. But we are a bulwark of the southern line of our army. We will hold the Germans here and give our forces time to launch the counterattack. We will arm the citizens for the love of France!"

Mac raised the camera's view and swung it slowly around the horizon, then turned to study the little man. "I think you'll soon get your chance, Mayor. Take a look there." He indicated the rising pillars of dust that grew in the south and crept closer, encircling the city from the west. Black masses of moving vehicles could be seen below the swirling columns.

"Sacré bleu! They are supposed to go west! They are not supposed to come here; not today!"

Mac pivoted the camera from the approaching German forces to record the mayor's reaction; he expected warlike defiance. What he got was the back of the man's coat retreating abruptly down the stairs and a shot of a forlorn toupee, blown off by the wind and lying on the stones.

❦ ❦ ❦

As soon as the German advance swept toward Cambrai, hundreds of civilians began to appear. They came carrying baskets of clothing, pushing carts loaded with furniture, toting bottles of some precious vintage wines. Among the throngs that walked with heads down, not looking at the invaders, were weaponless French soldiers in dirty uniforms.

Horst looked at the dispirited faces. Once a French soldier glanced up and caught Horst looking at him. The man quickly turned his head to the side, moved to put a horse-drawn cart loaded with children between himself and the major, and shuffled even faster away from Cambrai. Horst thought that for that man and the others, the war was over. He could imagine what the effect would be on French morale when they saw the number of deserters, and they had not even fired a shot.

Nor did they. The mayor of Cambrai advanced to meet the encircling force with a bedsheet as a flag of truce. It was longer than the little man was tall, and threatened to trip him about every third step. "Mon général," the mayor addressed Rommel. "Will you please spare our city? When the garrison saw the immense size of your force and we heard it was the Phantom Division, with your terrible and unstoppable tanks, we knew that resistance was futile. We surrender completely. Only please do not unleash your tanks on Cambrai."

❦ ❦ ❦

Mac moved northward away from Cambrai with a mass of others who did not trust the goodwill of the Germans enough to either remain in the city or try to cross the battle lines by heading south. North was where the Allied Army lay, along with some hope of stopping the Germans before they reached the Channel.

As Mac hiked along the dusty road toward Lille, he fell in step beside a man wearing the uniform trousers of a poilu. The man had no tunic, no helmet, no weapon. He looked at Mac without interest, then returned to staring at his shoes, as if seeking something in the dirt.

"What is your name?" Mac asked casually.

"Jardin," the man said without looking up.

"Where is your regiment?"

"I do not have any idea."

"Are you trying to find it?"

"What for?" the man asked suspiciously.

There was no reply to this that did not sound antagonistic, and Mac remembered the quick tempers of the deserters who fled the battle at the Sambre. "Your rifle?" he said instead.

"Too heavy for this hot weather," Jardin replied. "Besides, it was rusty. And there are plenty more." He pointed to the side of the road where discarded rifles and cartridge belts lay alongside grenades, even a French machine gun.

"Did you fight the Germans?"

"Proudly," said the man in a voice of bitterness and no pride at all. "At Dinant, on the Meuse. And later, at . . . I forget the name."

"After Dinant, did you *see* Germans?"

Jardin frowned. "It was not required. We know they are unstoppable. Someone yelled, 'Save yourself,' and . . . that was all."

"And now?"

Jardin finally looked up at Mac. "It was not supposed to be this way, Monsieur. All I wanted was some money to send home to my children and a pension for my old age. What will happen to them? The politicians have betrayed us. They did not tell us the truth about this war, which they said was no war at all."

❖   ❖   ❖

"Phantom Division. I like that," Rommel remarked to Horst at a conference after the town had capitulated. "How little they know about the accuracy of that statement."

"Sorry, sir. I guess I still do not follow."

"It is all right, major. No reason why you should, but I can explain now. You see, your battalion was the 'immense force.' My tanks are still back east of the town, waiting for fuel and ammunition to catch up with us. Intimidation is a very real and effective weapon."

SIXTY

By the time Blitzkrieg was in its ninth day, the Allies everywhere were falling back, giving ground, abandoning defensive positions. On the seventeenth, Colonel deGaulle had counterattacked near the fourteenth-century battlefield of Crecy. It was a brave attempt to break the Nazi momentum, but failed for lack of coordination. One hundred fifty French tanks were ambushed by, in deGaulle's words, "a forest of anti-tank guns." The promised infantry support failed to materialize. The air arm of the French forces could not hold off the Stukas. In the end, the Panzers brushed DeGaulle aside and swept onward.

On the eighteenth, General Guderian's Second Panzer took the town of St. Quentin before eight o'clock in the morning. Forty of the precious few French warplanes that remained were somehow caught on the ground near Cambrai and shot to pieces. And Cambrai itself had surrendered to Rommel without a struggle.

It was clear that by the end of the day on the nineteenth, all Hitler's Panzers would be in place for the final push to the Channel. General Weygand, a feisty old campaigner, was reportedly in Paris to replace Gamelin as French Commander-in-Chief. But what any one man could do to stem the tide it was impossible to say.

A mood of unrelieved gloom hung over Andre Chardon's home, despite the fact that Lewinski had deciphered the change in the Enigma settings. It took him only ten days to figure out the new substitution, but it was almost too late to matter.

It was anticlimactic. The movements of Guderian and Rommel were not exactly secret any longer. And with the speed of the advance, the Panzers were outstripping their own orders. How could any message decoded in even one day be valuable when towns were being overrun in a matter of hours?

Andre, Lewinski, and Bertrand pondered what was to be done. All knew that the information they possessed was valuable if it could only also be made timely.

When the Wehrmacht reached the sea, as would likely happen in a day or two at most, the Allied forces would be cut in two. The French and British armies that had advanced into Belgium when the conflict began would be surrounded and pressed against the seashore.

The three friends pondered. "When the Nazis went into Poland," Lewinski recalled, "the only thing I could think about was getting out."

Andre nodded, then shrugged, uncertain how that observation helped. "We may all wish to be somewhere else soon," he said. "Especially the soldiers caught in the pocket at the Channel. And they *will be* caught unless they can walk on water." He slapped his hands together, punctuating the importance of the thought. "It is the only solution, of course."

"Evacuation?" Bertrand said.

"Certainly! The British Navy might be able to rescue one hundred, maybe even two hundred thousand men, to fight again."

"But no one in our High Command talks anything but nonsense. They are convinced that the British army is not trying hard enough to break out. It is almost as if they have been watching some other war, still trying to draw a line and dig some trenches!" Bertrand snorted his derision. "I do not think Weygand will have any better ideas, either."

"I bet the British General Gort would listen."

"Even if he did, how could we get the Germans to stop rolling over everything? Can we say to them, 'Excuse us, but would you please stop shooting long enough for us to rescue a couple hundred thousand troops?' "

"What if a major counterattack punched a hole in the weakest point of their lines?"

"At least it would slow them down; make them blink," mused Bertrand aloud.

"And Enigma can tell us where that fragile link is found!" said Andre with rising excitement. "Look at this!" He read over the most recently deciphered messages. "It tells Rommel to expect to be joined on the east by a newly formed SS infantry division."

Bertrand caught the idea at once. "New ground troops, coming late to an operation where the experience and the heavy armor is in advance of them. Rommel's division is already stretched thin, and is the closest to the Allied forces." Then Bertrand remembered something that took the edge off his enthusiasm. "You know the High Command will never go for this."

"I know," said Andre, "but Gort will. His eyes are open to reality." Then to Lewinski, Andre said, "Decode any remaining intercepts and keep doing it as they come in. It is critical that we have the most current information possible about the positioning of the SS troops."

When Lewinski had retreated back down the stairs, Andre drew Bertrand aside. "I know that I am the one who will have to go," he said. "And even if our plan succeeds, I will not be able to get back across the lines. Take care of Lewinski for me, will you Bertrand?"

Bertrand thought about Richard Lewinski and grinned ruefully. "Why do you get all the easy jobs?" he said.

❧ ❧ ❧

Josie and the children rode from Belgium to the École de Cavalerie in the front seat of an ambulance. The officer roared over the road like a demented taxi driver.

He crossed the Lys River at the bridge outside of Armentieres which was already wired with explosives and barricaded on both sides. Which side of the river would the Germans attempt to cross . . . if they came?

"It is a precaution only, Madame," the officer said. "The Boches will never get this far."

But Josie wondered about it all the same.

Yacov slept soundly in her arms as if he had toddled all the way from Belgium and now could not keep his eyes open one moment longer. Juliette, her stubby legs jutting out toward the gearshift, slept against Josie's arm with the same exhaustion.

Josie and the officer talked about the Americans. Would they again come to the aid of France? Josie remembered the songs the veterans sang at Fourth of July picnics at the Fort Smith Electric Park beside the Arkansas River.

"Oh! Madamoiselle from Armenteer, parlay-voo . . ."

This time the Yanks weren't coming. The old songs would not be sung on the banks of the Lys in 1940. Roosevelt had too much at stake with a third-term election coming up to enter a war . . .

The ambulance passed ragged pilgrims with their battered luggage and their bent bird cages and their crying babies and the old people in wheel-chairs. All had tear-swollen faces and bewildered eyes. Now they looked up enviously as the ambulance sped by. What they would give for a lift to anywhere . . .

A short time later, the high elegant walls and the red roof of the École de Cavalerie loomed above the budding poplar trees. A line of lorries and ambulances was stopped at a checkpoint manned by a dozen armed young-sters who wore the dark tin hats of the poilu. They took their duty with a seriousness Josie had not seen anywhere else in the long journey. Beneath the brims of their helmets, their beardless faces were solemn as they narrowed their eyes and studied the documents of each ambulance crew and lorry driver. Teams of youths opened the backs of the vehicles and, rifles at the ready, peered in to search for a secreted enemy who might wish to take the hospital and the school by treachery.

It was an oddly comforting ritual. Even with the ever-present threat of Stukas appearing overhead, she felt almost safe for the first time since the bombs fell on Brussels. How many days ago had that been? Or was it years?

"And this is Madame Marlow," the driver indicated Josie with a jerk of his thumb. "American."

"Papers, please." This boy had a scruffy attempt at a goatee sprouting on his chin. His eyes were dark and earnest.

Josie passed him her precious documents and those of Juliette and the baby as well. The thought occurred to her that the young cadet might wish to frisk the baby before he was finished.

"I am a good friend of Captain Paul Chardon."

The boy's goatee jutted out with new interest. He smiled. "Ah yes! I remember now! You are the . . . the . . . very, very good friend of our Commander's brother, is it not so? I am Sepp." He tugged his beard. "You see. It has grown, has it not?"

Josie laughed for the first time in days. "It" seemed no fuller than last time, but she agreed that it was a most wonderful beard and that he was certainly doing well at his post.

And they were waved through cheerfully.

Paul, looking anything but cheerful, was in his office when Josie knocked at the door. He was on the telephone to Gort's BEF headquarters. He patiently discussed the importance of evacuating the wounded because there were new casualties arriving each hour. There were no more beds and only a few hundred cadets to defend the perimeter should the Germans make their swing toward the coast.

Juliette, clutching the doll, was at Josie's side. With Yacov still sound asleep in her arms, she waited until Paul replaced the handset with a frustrated clatter before she spoke.

It took a moment before it registered who she was.

"Josephine?" He rose quickly to embrace her.

She was crying now as the flood of emotion finally burst. She leaned against him and he patted her back in a clumsy attempt to comfort, like he was patting the neck of a good horse after a grueling race. Dear Paul . . .

"I was going to Ostend . . . Andre sent me . . . Juliette and the baby . . . the train was . . . Oh, Paul! It has been days since we . . . I would like to sleep a while."

"Yes, ma chérie. All the way from Brussels you have walked?" He asked this in English, and then led her to a chair.

Taking her hand, he lapsed back into French and knelt before Juliette. He looked at the doll—his mother's doll. So Andre had managed to get it to her!

He brushed a strand of hair back from Juliette's face. "And you are very pretty, Mam'zelle Juliette." She was ragged and dirty, but the eyes of Andre in miniature looked gravely back at him.

"How do you know my name, Monsieur?" she asked.

"It is a name that fits someone so beautiful, and you are the most beautiful little girl I have seen in a very long time." He laughed as poor Josie continued to weep with relief. "I will kiss your hand, chérie." He did so, which brought a slight smile to the child's lips. Her face was smudged with grime. "My name is Paul and you are quite safe now. I have a chocolate in my desk. I was saving it for someone so beautiful as you are. Would you like it?" She nodded eagerly. The ordeal was finished. "I will see that you are well cared for here at my school. And soon we will see you to Paris."

❧ ❧ ❧

Seventy-three Squadron had received so many combat losses by the nineteenth of May that David was made Acting Flight Leader of B Flight. But he led a unit that consisted of only four Hurricanes. Even worse, the other three pilots were all new replacements, with only limited combat experience.

Jimmy Small was American, like David. Tay Churchman was Australian, and Jeffrey Cameron was a Scot. Small had once attacked a Heinkel off the Thames estuary. Of the other two, Churchman had only seen German aircraft from a distance. Cameron had never seen one at all, only pictures.

Cameron had not even expected to stay in France. He was a ferry pilot, bringing over one of the preciously allotted replacement fighters. Simpson, now the squadron leader, pressed him into service as a combat flier.

"Do you like that Hurricane you brought us?" Simpson asked as Cameron was invited for a drink in the Squadron mess.

"Yes, Squadron Leader. It's a fine machine."

"Any problems to speak of?"

"None. I would say that it is in tip-top shape."

"You had better hope you're right, my lad, because as of right now, it's yours. Tinman, meet your new pilot."

Despite Cameron's protest, David's only discussion with Simpson involved seeing that Advanced Striking Force HQ was notified. "You heard the same story I did," David warned, "about the ferry pilot who got recruited into Number One Squadron, and was sent up that same afternoon."

"What about him? What happened?" Cameron broke in.

"He bought it in the first engagement," David explained. "But no one could remember his name, and since he had not been properly enrolled, well . . ."

"Don't worry, lad," Simpson reassured the Scot. "I'll see to it that you are properly listed as one of us."

Cameron still looked worried an hour later when the squadron was scrambled to provide cover for a mission of Blenheims. The British bombers were attacking the German advance at the crossing of the Oise canal. The intent was to protect the French town of Le Cateau.

Because of the inexperience of his flight, David was to fly high cover only. They would assist if *A* flight got in trouble and then retreat to a high vantage point.

"You'll be all right," David told Cameron. "You fly on my wing and keep an eye on six o'clock and you'll do fine." What else was there to say?

Circling at twenty thousand feet, the Squadron saw neither Blenheims nor enemies for almost an hour. "Stood up again," Simpson broadcast on the R/T. "Pack it in, chaps. Let's head for home."

Clouds extended down to ten thousand feet, and it was while passing a gap in a pair of the towering columns of white mist that Simpson spotted the formation of bombers at last. There were twenty of them, heading east, and they were flying below the base of the clouds.

The whole squadron dove to form up on the bombers, but when the maneuver was only halfway completed, Simpson announced a change. "Correction," he radioed calmly, "those are Heinkels, not Blenheims, and they seem to be unescorted. Tally ho, chaps."

Simpson ordered a formation that swept the Hurricanes back in a diagonal line from Simpson at the leading left-hand end of the line. Because there were no German fighters around, David's flight joined in the attack.

The squadron pounced on the He 111's and caught them unawares. The first pass sent one Heinkel breaking out of formation and spiralling downward. Another was left slowly losing altitude with one dead engine. None of the Hurricanes were hit.

But on the second attack, the Germans changed tactics. The V formations of bombers fought as units, rather than as individual ships. They concentrated their fire on one Hurricane at a time. As the leader, Simpson drew an especially large share of tracers. He shot down another He 111, then white smoke began trailing from his airplane.

"Rotten luck," David heard him say. "Caught one in the engine coolant somewhere."

"Can you make it back?" David radioed.

"Don't think so. Engine's overheating. I'll try to make Le Cateau."

The squadron had racked up three definite kills and possibly five when they broke off the attack and headed for home. David was now leading both flights, and he intended for them to stay with Simpson until he reached the nearby airfield.

"There it is, and none too soon," Simpson radioed. "I'll rejoin you just as soon as I can. Simpson out."

From the formation altitude at ten thousand feet, David watched his friend's gentle descent toward Le Cateau. It looked smooth until Simpson's Hurricane reached five thousand feet, and black puffs of flak began to appear all around him.

"Pull the override and get out of there," David demanded over the R/T.

"It's no good," Simpson responded. "No power. Get the chicks home safely, will you, Tinman?"

A cluster of four bursts of antiaircraft fire erupted directly in front of Simpson. Pieces of his engine cowling and canopy flew off as if the Hurricane were shedding. Then the airframe shattered completely, raining fragments over the airfield of Le Cateau.

When David got the rest of the squadron back to base, he reported the downed Heinkels and Simpson's death. "How could those French gunners be so stupid?" he asked angrily.

"Don't blame the French," he was told. "The Germans were already across the canal and captured Le Cateau before you ever got there."

SIXTY-ONE

Josephine was at least clean when she stepped from the train at Gare du Nord. Her bath at the École de Cavalerie was her first in over a week. That was more than could be said for the masses of refugees who accompanied her and the children on their journey.

Josie remembered how empty and gloomy the station was when she returned to Paris last fall.

A few ragged porters. Old women in felt slippers pushing wide brooms across clean, uncluttered floors . . .

It was instantly clear that Paris had been changed to the very core after only a little more than one week of war. The great station resounded with suffering. Dutch and Belgians and French—so many tragic and innocent faces—faces reflecting confusion and bitterness and loss and rage and weariness now filled the cavernous hall of departure.

Thousands slept beside their baggage on the once-spotless floors. Quaking old grandparents with parchment skin looked after small children. Mothers rested or stared blankly at the gilt clock face as if it could tell them what the next hours would bring. And where were the fathers? And where were the sons?

Little French Boy Scouts provided some order to the chaos. They helped people off the trains and stacked bicycles and issued claim checks for so many thousands that the true owners of the cycles would never be found. Bicycles overflowed the check rooms and lined the walls to tower over the little clusters of refugees who had grown together like little villages becoming one vast city.

There were Red Cross stations at either end of the Gare. Long queues formed for bathing and dressing blistered feet, patching wounds, and feeding the multitudes.

There, in the eye of the storm was Madame Rose Smith, washing the bloody feet of an old peasant woman while she instructed a young, wealthy Parisian volunteer with soft hands to go out and find nipples for the baby bottles and bring back diapers too!

Josie caught her eye and waved, pointing at Yacov, who gaped wide-eyed at the confusion around him. Madame Rose gave her the same thumbs up sign Josie had seen among the soldiers at the front.

"Come by later," Rose mouthed. There was too much going on to stop even for a minute, so Josie headed for the exit of Gare du Nord and the taxi stand.

Once again Josie had no luggage. She carried Yacov on her hip. Juliette, her little fingers hooked in Josie's belt, trailed along. No children were allowed in Foyer International, so Paul had given Josie the key to the Chardon house on Quai d'Anjou. No doubt Andre would be off somewhere with all the other men of his age. They were all somewhere else.

The taxis were also gone. They had been confiscated by the army on the same day that Paris had been declared a part of the Zone des Armée.

They rode the Metro back to Notre Dame. Hoping that Andre would miraculously be there, Josie limped to the house and knocked first.

The flustered face of Colonel Gustave Bertrand appeared at the door.

"Josephine!" he seemed startled by her appearance. "We thought you were in London!"

"As Chamberlain said . . . I missed the bus, Colonel Bertrand. Now, will you let me in, or must I stand here in the hot sun until the Germans come?"

Flustered, he stepped aside. "Andre is gone off to the front, wherever that may be. I have to get to Vignolles. You must stay with Lewinski for the sake of France!" Not waiting for her to reply, he hurriedly scrawled out his private telephone number and gave it to her. "Keep him in the house until I come for him."

"But when will Andre be back?"

"Who can say?"

"When will you . . ."

"I will telephone. You are leaving Paris as well, then?" He glanced at the children as if it were no surprise she had two little ones in tow. There were strays everywhere in the city these days, his expression seemed to say. "The Boches will begin bombing soon, we are certain of it. Most of Paris is sending the children away. You might want to think of doing the same . . . wherever they come from, they will be better off elsewhere. Get them on a train if you can." He called up the stairs to Lewinski, "Madame Josephine Marlow is here to stay with you, Lewinski!"

"Good!" Lewinski shouted down. "Finally a red rose to look at instead of a croaking toad!"

Bertrand grimaced. It was clear the two men did not get along. "Too much! Too much! He is a madman! Good luck, Josephine." And then he left without explanation or apology.

❊　❊　❊

Jerome Jardin and the five Jewish brothers from Austria were not Boy Scouts, and yet they were given Red Cross armbands by Madame Rose and they worked hard at the bicycle racks in Gare du Nord.

Blue-uniformed gendarmes swinging night sticks walked casually among the refugees as if they were strolling through the Tuileries gardens. But the station was no garden. It did not smell of flowers. The gendarmes were checking and rechecking the papers of all the refugees because it was rumored that clever Hitler had sent in many fifth columnists with them.

Jerome felt sorry for the refugees. Even on his worst day he had not been as bad off as these pitiful creatures. It occurred to him many times that he could steal one of the better bicycles and peddle off to the South of France.

Georg, the eldest of the brothers, said as much. "You know we could each steal one of these bicycles and pedal off to the South of France."

Jerome surprised himself with his reply. "Madame Rose would not like it."

"So what?" Georg tossed another tagged bike on the heap.

"That would be stealing," Jerome said. He felt himself pale at such unexpected words.

"Who would know?" Georg put his hands on his hips.

"God." The Name just blurted out! No stopping it! He had definitely been around Madame Rose too long!

Georg wiped his nose on the back of his hand and gave a slight snarl. He

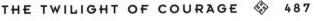

looked very tough, and Jerome thought that it was too bad the Germans did not like Jews because Georg would have made such a fierce soldier. They had missed a good thing, those Nazis.

"Well, well! God, is it?" Georg picked up a bicycle off the vast heap. "You see this? The Nazis melted down all the bikes in Austria after they came so they could make them into bombs! Ha! So what do you think those Stukas are dropping on our heads now?"

"Bicycles?" Jerome chirped. An amazing thought.

"My bike, to be exact! You think we should leave them any more to drop and kill people?"

"Probably not. If you put it that way."

Georg whistled long and loud and made a boom sound. "Gears and spokes and handle bars! Ker-pow! It is immoral!"

Georg was talking himself and his brothers into taking those potential bombs and defusing them by riding off to the Riviera. They might have all done so if it had not been for the sudden wailing which erupted from the young woman holding the baby not far from the stack. A gendarme was speaking quietly to her, trying very hard to take the baby.

"But the child is dead, Madame . . ." The policeman pleaded.

"NO!" She wailed. "You cannot take him! You must not take my baby!"

It was a pitiful sight. Others gathered around and tried to talk her into giving up the dead child. She insisted he was not dead. But Jerome could see plainly that he was. Very grey. Very still. His tiny arm hung awkwardly from the blanket.

Now the mother kicked out at the officer. She drew a knife and held it to her own heart. He stepped back. It was very sad. The five brothers forgot all about the temptations at their finger tips.

"Poor thing," said Georg. "Poor lady."

"Get Madame Rose," Jerome said. And he and the brothers ran the length of the terminal to fetch her.

With a grave expression, Madame Rose left her station and, as if she were marching to war, came with the boys to the scene of the tragic confrontation.

Somehow the crowd of onlookers knew at her approach that she was someone who could help. They parted for her instantly. She turned on them all and growled.

"Get back to your own business! All of you!"

What fierce and angry eyes she had. Even though there was no business for anyone in Gare du Nord to get back to, they all pretended to have other things to do.

Jerome and Georg and the brothers returned to the bicycles. They fussed with the hubs and observed the scene through the spokes.

Madame Rose stuck her lower lip out and waved her hands as though she was shooing the people away like a bunch of dogs.

And then she turned and knelt before the wild-eyed woman. But at a distance.

Jerome could not hear what the old woman said, but all the gruffness melted away. Now she was the Madame Rose who rocked the little children to sleep and told angel-stories to the ones frightened in the dark.

The fear on the frantic face of the mother melted. She looked at her dead child.

Grief!

She looked at Madame Rose.

Help me!

Madame Rose stretched out her square and calloused hand. She shook her head and looked up toward heaven.

Could it be?

The mother touched the infant's cheek. She buried her face against the tiny body. Madame Rose, on her knees, came close enough to put her big strong arms around the mother. The woman leaned against her just like the children at Number 5 Rue de la Huchette. She sobbed and sobbed, and Madame Rose let her cry as long as she wanted. It was a long time. And then it was over.

Jerome read the lips of the young woman as she passed the child to Madame Rose.

"Take him, then. He belongs to God."

❧ ❧ ❧

Lord Gort, commander of the British Expeditionary Force in France, tightened his thin lips into a disapproving line. Colonel Andre Chardon's visit was an interruption. Even in the pale early morning light of the twentieth of May, Gort was already hard at work. All around him on the floor of his headquarters lay discarded maps of northern France. Each was marked with troop movements and enemy positions; each had become outdated and useless in a matter of hours. The speed of the German Lightning War made the concept of a static front line obsolete. "I believe you are who you claim to be, Colonel. Otherwise I would have had you arrested. But why haven't you approached your own High Command, General Georges or General Billotte, with this information?"

"I tried to, sir. I am either ignored or not believed. In the case of new Commander-in-Chief Weygand, I am told that he is too busy getting the 'big picture' to be bothered with 'tactical details.' No one else wants to make a decision this important without testing it for the approval of Weygand, so on and on it goes."

Gort was a hearty, bluff man. Straightforward in his speech and actions, he also was angry with politicians who played at things military, and generals who had political motives. He put his hand to his square jaw and pondered a moment. "I can understand your frustration, Chardon."

The new French Commander-in-Chief Weygand, age seventy-three, had been recalled from the Near East to replace General Gamelin. Since his appointment to the Supreme Command he had issued no new orders and spent his time "acquainting himself" with what was a rapidly deteriorating situation.

"All right, Colonel. What is this urgent secret news?"

"The German drive will pivot north tomorrow. Guderian will continue on to the seacoast near Abbeville. Rommel will swing toward the Channel at the Belgian border to cut off any port of resupply and reinforcement. Wehrmacht Army Group B will pinch in from the northeast."

Gort swung his chair around to study the map that remained on the wall behind him. "At the rate they have been gaining ground, we should begin pulling back immediately to save any Channel port at all," he mused, "even for evacuation . . ." Then despite Andre's presence he said, "It makes sense. They have us in a bag and they would like to draw the string around the top. You must know that a rescue operation may be our only remaining option."

Andre nodded. This was exactly the situation he knew Gort would recognize and the reason he was willing to exceed his authority in sharing the secret Enigma message.

"Here is one piece of good news, from the same source: Rommel's division is stretched quite thin in the vicinity of Arras, General. And behind him in the line is a brand new, untried SS infantry division."

Gort saw the opportunity. "I could order General Franklyn to attack south, try to break through at Arras. But to do so will mean weakening our forces engaged in supporting the Belgians. How can we be certain that your information is correct?"

"I've thought of that, sir. According to our intelligence, Guderian is about to divide his forces. First Panzer will aim for Calais, and Second Panzer for Boulogne. This separation will confirm that our intercepts are true."

"And what is the identity of the new unit joining Rommel?"

"They are called the Totenkopf—the Death's Head division."

"Very well, Colonel. If your predictions are confirmed today, then I will order an attempt to break the German advance at Arras. Perhaps we will force our way out of this box."

SIXTY-TWO

On the twenty-first of May, Seventh Panzer was just south of Arras, the capital of the French province of Artois. Only sixty miles separated it from the English Channel. Rommel was ordered to turn north. The movement would cut off the retreating Allies from possible reinforcement or evacuation through the ports of Boulogne and Calais. The general was not happy about the order because it meant that Guderian's force, heading due west for Abbeville, would reach the coast first.

Seventh Panzer was running low on fuel and spare parts. The tanks in particular were being kept in operation by a supply line that stretched over two hundred miles back to Germany. It was the Luftwaffe domination of the skies that allowed the Junkers transports to keep pace with the advance of the Wehrmacht. Otherwise, many of the machines would have broken down. As it was, Rommel's forces were a thin string that encircled the southern boundary of the shrinking area still occupied by the Allies.

Horst was at the front of a column of armored cars and motorcycles, reconnoitering for the tank battalions. Behind the tanks were the rest of the Seventh and the newly arrived motorized infantry of the SS Death's Head division.

It was midafternoon when the British launched their counterattack, using a mixed force of light and medium tanks. Some of them were the newer Matildas with heavier armor plating. Two British columns emerged from the forest in a surprise movement that struck the line of SS transports.

Horst was ordered to go immediately to the assistance of the infantry. His armored car crossed a hilltop toward the assault, just in time to see a high explosive shell from a British Matilda tank make a direct hit on a troop carrier. The truck exploded with a roar, scattering bodies below a billowing cloud of flame and black smoke. Everywhere over an area of several miles, there were prostrate bodies and burning vehicles.

Pulling up below the brow of the hill, Horst was next to an anti-tank battery. The lieutenant in charge was feverishly working his men, demanding that they reload and fire, "Schneller, schneller!" Even the skinny cannons seemed to be in a hurry as they barked out their eighty rounds per minute.

A line of men passed ammunition up to the Panzerabwehrkanone. The weapon coughed its defiance of the British tanks and, an instant later, the 37mm rounds scored two direct hits on the front armor of the Matilda. The tank paused, like a lumbering bear hit by a tree limb. Then it clanked straight ahead again, its machine gun mowing down more German soldiers.

"The shells bounce off!" the anti-tank lieutenant exclaimed in despair. "We have scored six times on that same machine, and still it comes on!"

The impact of the shell against the tank's steel skin had scarcely damaged it, but seemed to have angered it. A high explosive round from the Matilda arched over the German guns, bursting in the grapevine-covered hillside. A second shot followed, detonating on the ground immediately in front of one of the anti-tank weapons. The gun barrel twisted like a strand of spaghetti, and six crewmen lay in shattered pieces.

There were at least fifty British tanks in sight, and more appearing over the northern horizon. The danger was immediate. If the Allied flank attack was successful, a larger rupture would pierce the German advance, splitting the tanks from the weaker elements. If a way south was opened for the Allies, it would trap the forward component of the Panzers between the enemy and the sea, instead of the other way around.

"General," Horst radioed Rommel. "We need Stukas, and we need them now." Quickly Horst explained the situation and its urgency.

Two more anti-tank weapons were destroyed before the first dive-bombers appeared. In further exchanges of fire, two tanks of the new SS division were reduced to flaming pyres.

At last, black dots appeared high overhead. They fell screaming out of the sky, releasing their deadly burdens. The first wave of four Stukas attacked in a row like a formation of diving pelicans. Each released a pair of bombs that threw up eruptions of earth, showering the tanks with debris.

One of the British machines took a direct hit. Horst watched the bomb release, arc toward the target, and impact. The explosion blew the Matilda apart as if it had been made of tinfoil. Horst blinked at the instant of the burst. When he looked again, only the two treads, looped like giant discarded ribbons, gave any sign of where the tank had been.

But the BEF crews could not hear the sound effects that had been so terrorizing to the Polish and French infantries, and they took no notice of near misses. Even after several waves of planes had destroyed two squadrons of the British tanks, still they rolled forward.

Horst again contacted Rommel.

The general seemed unruffled. "Duly noted," he said calmly. "Do you know the whereabouts of the closest antiaircraft battery?"

"I passed one about a mile back, General. But we have not seen any Allied aircraft, except a few of their fighters. No threat to us."

"Bring the battery to the front, and have them engage the British armor," Rommel ordered. Horst sent Lieutenant Borger back to locate the battery and bring them up at once.

The ungainly Fliegerabwehrkanone weapons had long barrels and cumbersome mechanisms for achieving the elevation needed to shoot down warplanes. Flak guns looked like a poor choice for the flat shooting required to engage tanks. Horst hoped that Rommel's plan was not one born of desperation.

The arrogant captain of the antiaircraft unit was eager to show what his section could do. "Step aside, Major," he said with scarcely any deference to Horst's rank. "Watch what something with some muscle can accomplish."

The 8.8cm shells were more than twice as big as those for the antitank guns, but at one fourth the rate of fire, Horst was still skeptical. The first shot fired ripped the left-hand track off an advancing Matilda. The crippled machine shambled in a clumsy circle as its undamaged tread tried to move it forward. A second shot impacted just under the Matilda's stubby gun, tearing the turret completely off the tank.

The British armor continued to advance. Their gunners loaded and fired with precision and they stayed constantly in motion, making them difficult targets for the slower firing German cannons. They were making for the center of the line of troop transports. These trucks and half-tracks were filled with members of the SS Death's Head Division.

The SS troops cheered the Stukas. They applauded the results of Rommel's novel use of the antiaircraft guns. Now they were stunned. The German army was unbeatable, was it not? The SS in particular thought of themselves as the elite, the unstoppable, the invincible.

A high explosive shell landed in the middle of a circle of SS trucks, shredding the canvas covers and the men inside. All along the line, SS soldiers hid in ditches, took cover behind half-tracks, and bailed out of burning vehicles. They stared in dumbfounded horror at the approaching tanks; many did not even bother to reload their rifles. Horst unpleasantly remembered the lesson of Cambrai: terror and intimidation were fully as powerful as the cannons of the British tanks.

As Horst looked on, the SS division wavered, then broke and fled. Streaming to the rear, their retreat opened a gap in the German line. For the first time since the war began, Blitzkrieg was in jeopardy.

�֍   ✖   ✖

The third wave of Stukas that came over released their bombs short of the line of tanks. Whether by accident or design, the explosives fell in the woods from which the British advance had emerged and in which more units were waiting. The terrible screaming of the dive-bombers made Mac keep close to a ditch or a particularly solid looking tree. He lay in the bottom of a creek bed now, cinching up his helmet strap with one hand and hugging his camera with the other. Mobile artillery. That was how the Wehrmacht used the Stukas. It was the reason that the Germans did not have to wait for their heavy cannons to arrive before launching an attack. It was the factor that had negated the Ardennes as a defense. The planes were used with surgical precision and were almost impossible to shoot down. Mac had never seen one crash because of groundfire, and he had seen no Allied fighters all day.

When the aerial assault ended, Mac was behind a British tank destroyer unit being moved into position. It gave him a panorama of the battlefield of Arras. He could see the spearhead of British Mark I and Mark II tanks rolling over the German opposition in spite of the Stukas and the German antitank weapons.

"Why haven't you Brits done this before?" he asked a gunnery sergeant.

"Blimey, guv, that's what I'd like to know. Mind now, the day hain't won just yet. Them Jerries will be jumpin' on us with their own bloody great tanks. Our job is to keep 'em off long enough for our boys to open a big 'ole; then we can celebrate."

Mac filmed the scene of burning German equipment. Smoldering bonfires made of troop transports and half-tracks littered the nearer fields. At the far edge of the scene he could make out Nazi soldiers running from the advancing tanks.

"See there," said the sergeant, pointing a greasy finger toward the farthest hill. "Them dark spots is Jerry tanks. They aim to 'it us in the flank, same as we done them."

"Couldn't you use some more tanks to get in and mix it up with the Germans? I understand that they don't like to fight tank-to-tank battles."

"Right you are. But the problem is, you're lookin' at all we got just now. Cobbled together on short notice, don't you see."

"Aren't there any French tanks available?"

"I'm sure I don't know the answer to that; you 'ave to ask the Frogs. In my opinion, it's best to leave them out of it anyway. The Froggies got no radios in their tanks. You can't tell them where they are needed. Once they get started, it's just like windup toys . . . they keep rollin' and firin' till they get blown up or run out of things to shoot."

❧ ❧ ❧

Horst watched the SS soldiers streaming away from the Arras battlefield. He felt a curious sense of satisfaction at their precipitate retreat, as if every doubt he had about their vaunted courage was confirmed. Himmler had insisted that they be included in the conduct of the Blitzkrieg so that they would share in the glory. Reichsführer Himmler thought that the campaign was so well in hand that his untried troops could not fail; instead, they now jeopardized the entire operation.

Colonel Neumann, commanding a Seventh Panzer tank battalion, arrived on the scene. He stood upright in the turret of his PzKw IV tank, commenting to Horst on the scene before them. "Look at those dogs run! It seems that enthusiasm for the party one week does not make for heroic actions the next! They would run all the way back to Germany, and perhaps we should let them!"

Neumann was waiting for an intelligence report from Horst's motorcycle patrol before leading his tanks in a flank assault of his own. He was to strike the center of the Allied line, split it, and then chew up the broken halves. The problem was the light. It was nearing seven o'clock in the evening; already too late for more Stuka attacks, and soon too dim for tanks. Neumann did not seem concerned. "We will pierce the line," he said, "then we will pinch the first half into a pocket to destroy at leisure. The rest will certainly retreat." He said something to his driver and the deeply rumbling engine revved up.

"Do you not want to wait for my lieutenant to get back from recon, Colonel? We don't know what else is behind those Matildas in the cover of the trees."

The colonel squinted at the setting sun, then shook his head. "We can deal with whatever it is," he said. "Right now the determining factor is daylight." He gave the order to his column of tanks to attack, and the PzKw IV ground into forward motion, its tracks clanking. Neumann wasted no time; the muzzle of the 75mm gun was already swiveling, seeking its first target.

The tank plunged down the hill. At almost the same moment, Lieutenant Borger arrived beside Horst. "Recon report, Major," he said, saluting. "Warn Colonel Neumann that there are a couple squadrons of French Somua tanks concealed behind the farthest hedgerow and two or three tank destroyer units just emerging from the woods. I do not know if they are French or British."

Horst turned to the handset of the radio that Sergeant Fiske was already offering. Still in Horst's line of sight, Neumann was no more than a hundred yards forward. The tall colonel was still standing; he had not yet buttoned up the hatch.

The first round of anti-tank fire struck the PzKw III immediately behind

Neumann's tank. The projectile shattered against the sloping armor, but the burst reached out in a deadly star-shaped pattern to embrace the colonel. His back was riddled with shrapnel. When he slumped over the hatch, his body pivoted limply and he hung on the edge of the turret. Other rounds began striking the German line. Two tanks exploded in flames.

The entire column halted. Horst ran forward, catching Neumann's body just as it slid to the ground. He pulled the colonel's lifeless form out of the way and jumped up on the hatch. "Go," he shouted to the driver. "You cannot stay here, the advance will be cut to pieces if you do not destroy those guns."

The radio operator looked shaken. "The colonel did not have time to tell us his plan. The second-in-command has just been reported killed as well. What do we do?"

Horst had never directed a tank in battle before, let alone an entire column of tanks, but he had a clear picture in his mind of the terrain and the reported location of the Allied weapons. He jackknifed into the commander's seat. "Radio," he ordered, "squadrons three and four, attack the center of the British line as planned: in column, high speed, fifty-meter intervals. Squadrons one and two, form two waves, fifty meters between tanks and one hundred meters between waves and follow us!"

The inside of the tank smelled of fuel, hot oil, and unwashed bodies. Machine gun bullets pinged off of the steel armor. The sound reminded Horst that if the enemy antitank gunners selected this particular PzKw to target, his career as a tank commander would be very brief.

"Pivot left thirty," he ordered the driver. The man operating the machine gun was firing short bursts, distracting the antitank crews as they sought cover for themselves. But so far the main gun had not fired. "What are you waiting for?" Horst demanded.

"Not in range yet, Major," the gunner replied. "This 7.5cm gun throws a 7 kilo shell, but it doesn't throw it very far."

"Radio, tell tanks two and four in each wave to drop back fifty meters from their present positions. I want to make us as hard to hit as possible."

"Acknowledge," returned the radio operator. "Major, second squadron reports that tank four is out of action with a track knocked off."

Through the periscope, Horst could make out the edge of the woods ahead and the row of antitank guns. He instinctively flinched at a muzzle flash and braced himself for an explosion, but the shot was long and burst behind them.

"We have range now, Major."

"Target left forty-five."

"I have him."

"Fire!"

The high explosive round landed short of the mark, but the concussion cartwheeled the tank destroyer gun twenty feet in the air. Even so, there was no time to exult in a single well-placed shot.

"Target right ninety." The gunner had picked up the next location as quickly as Horst, and the turret pivoted smoothly the instant he finished speaking.

All the rounds being launched were high explosives since their targets were not other tanks but men and equipment without steel covers that required armor piercing shells. Horst was so impressed with the competence and skill of the crew that he was already searching for the next objective even before the last shot had been fired. Just after the gun roared again, Horst commanded, "Reload with H. E. No! Check that! Hard right! Load armor piercing, target right forty-five."

What Horst saw was a line of French Somua tanks emerging from behind the thick row of hedges across the field. The purpose of the Panzer attack was to break through the British line of armor. Even if it meant sacrificing himself, his battle group had to now counter this new threat to the main German thrust.

Somuas were the best tanks the Allies possessed: faster than the German Panzers and more heavily armored. They did not mount as large a cannon but had almost twice the muzzle velocity with greater range and striking force. The only positive thing Horst could think was that he only saw four of them.

"We are within their range already," the gunner reported to Horst, "but not ours."

There was nothing to do but charge ahead, zigzagging in the hope of escaping a lucky hit until able to shoot back.

The leading Somua's muzzle erupted in flame, as did the second and the third. Once again, Horst prepared for the expected shock, but no blow fell.

"Major!" the radio operator said with excitement. "Second squadron reports that the Somuas are firing at the tank destroyers!"

❖   ❖   ❖

Mac's camera watched the approach of the German tanks. He saw them divide their force into a two-pronged attack, one of which aimed for the heart of the British charge. The other was coming right toward him, straight down the throat of the tank destroyer unit.

The gunnery sergeant was very methodical as he went about the business of loading, aiming, and firing. At each recoil, the anti-tank gun jumped up on its rubber tires like a war horse rearing in the excitement of battle.

With an enemy approaching head-on, there was no need to adjust for the speed of the quarry; it was enough to steadily reduce the elevation as the oncoming Panzers roared straight in. The two-pound shells were having a dramatic effect. A PzKw III burst into a ball of fire. It continued rumbling forward for a time, trailing a flag of thick black fumes, orange flames shooting into the evening sky. Eventually it rolled to a stop and the pursuing cloud of dark smoke caught up and enveloped it completely. No one emerged from the pyre.

A second tank was hit low in the lefthand track just as it was at the edge of a slanting culvert. The sudden loss of half its footing made the PzKw III roll over sideways. As Mac watched the machine ponderously revolve, it occurred to him that a viewer seeing this film would assume that it was captured in slow motion. The tank came to rest upside down, its tracks still futilely turning, like an enormous turtle flipped on its back and helpless. Moments later, three men emerged from the carcass. One of them was shot down at the edge of the culvert while the other two huddled below the lip of the ditch.

An approaching PzKw IV fired a shell that fell short in front of the tank destroyers. The sergeant smoothly redirected his weapon to take on the new challenger. The first round sailed over the tank, and he was calmly readjusting the height when another incoming projectile exploded into the British line from the side. Two more followed, tearing through the anti-tank weapons like a scythe through a handful of wheat stalks. The impact tore the first gun into ragged chunks of metal that spun across the intervening yards. One man was decapitated; another looked mindlessly at the stump of what had been his right arm.

"Flank attack!" the sergeant yelled to his remaining squadron of guns.

The next detonation flung Mac into a cavity left from one of the first shells to reach their target. On the theory that lightning would not strike in the same spot twice, Mac stayed in the shallow depression, operating his camera over the lip of the crater. The camera lens and the top of his helmet were the only things that protruded above ground level. Mac thought that an observer could now compare *his* appearance to a turtle.

The tank destroyers fired in a continuous staccato popping. Against the muzzle blasts of the tanks, it sounded weak and almost silly, but when Mac cautiously peered into the eyepiece, he could see that it was effective. One of the attacking tanks was stopped dead, a gaping hole torn in its front surface. Another was still firing its machine gun, but its main weapon was broken off short and contorted from taking a direct hit.

There was something odd about its shape. Mac studied the outline. German tanks from the smallest PzKw I to the new model IV had a similar profile: the turret was mounted directly above the level of the tracks. These machines were built in three stages: tracks, body, and then turret perched on top. They were . . .

"It's the bloody Frogs!" the sergeant bitterly cried. "Our allies have busted us to pieces!"

"Cease firing," Mac yelled, as if he were an officer instead of an onlooker.

"Cease nothing!" corrected the sergeant. "We can't stop shooting unless they do or we'll be blown to kingdom come!"

❧   ❧   ❧

The view through Horst's periscope showed an amazing scene. The newly arrived French armor was blasting away, not at the German tanks, but at the detachment of British antitank guns. The British, not knowing the identity of their new attackers, pivoted their weapons and replied to what was for them a much nearer danger than Horst.

"Turn!" Horst shouted. "If they keep each other occupied, we will hit the British Matildas from behind!"

Squadrons three and four of the German column were mixing it up with the English tanks in tank-to-tank combat. The Brits were still trying to maintain order and complete their breakthrough of the SS division, but the new strike from the rear surprised them.

Tanks are not well protected at the back, and the older British units were especially vulnerable there. The first blast of Horst's 7.5cm gun tore a Mark I in half, scattering debris over half an acre.

The second Mark I targeted received an armor piercing round that must have struck the ammunition hold after penetrating: the turret lifted straight up in the air like the lid of a tea kettle. The chain reaction of exploding shells then ripped the tank to pieces from the inside out.   Horst was indicating the position of the next Mark I when a shell hit the Panzer from behind. The solid shot burst low in the bowels of the tank, killing the driver and the machine gunner instantly. A shrapnel spear sliced into Horst's upper arm. Jagged metal protruded from both sides of his bicep. He stared at it stupidly for a moment, remembering the splinter of metal that had struck his hand during the shelling in Poland. Then he passed out.

When he came to, Horst was lying on a stretcher next to a row of German antiaircraft guns. They were lowered to flat trajectories and blazing away. General Rommel hurried from gun to gun, personally directing the target search of each. He acted as if he wished he could hold each cannon to his shoulder like a rifle.

Rommel paused beside Horst, where a medic was swabbing the wound with something that smelled terrible and burned even worse. "So, you are awake? And what do you have to say for yourself?"

Horst was certain that he was going to be shot. Now that the excitement was over, Horst knew that he had exceeded his authority and botched it. He was sure that he had led the German tanks into a trap and that he would be court-martialed. "Herr General," he said. "I do not know what to say."

"Say nothing! Save your strength. After your brilliant attack, you have left me nothing to do but mop up the stragglers! There will be a Knight's Cross for you in this, Major, and a new job too!"

✳   ✳   ✳

Andre sat in Lord Gort's headquarters waiting for word about the outcome of the counterattack at Arras. Gort was late getting back from a meeting with Supreme Commander Weygand, the Belgian King Leopold, and French General Billotte. When he finally returned, he was in a foul mood. "Did not even wait for me!" Gort stormed into his office and threw down his cap with disgust. "Gave me no notice of this conference until it was too late to reach it on time, then departed before I even arrived! God spare us from allies such as these!"

Noticing the presence of the French intelligence officer did not make Gort apologetic. "I'm glad you waited, Colonel, so you can take a firsthand report to somebody. General Billotte was killed tonight."

"Bombing raid?"

"Killed when his car skidded into a truckload of refugees moving on the highway at two miles an hour! He was the only other officer besides King Leopold who knew Weygand's plans. And I'm not sure how much longer Leopold can be relied on to hold. How can we coordinate any counterattacks now?"

Andre waited patiently while Gort unbuttoned his tunic and settled into his chair. Finally the Frenchman asked, "Is there any news from Arras?"

"Yes, the only positive light in this miserable tunnel. Two columns of our armor hit Rommel hard, scattering the SS division."

"Did they achieve a breakthrough?"

Gort shook his head slowly. "No, but they have punished the German flank and accomplished, I think, part of our purpose. Herr Hitler is full of boundless enthusiasm for war, so long as he is winning. Even a small setback worries him, makes him rethink his plans. Now he will worry about overextended supply lines. He will order his Panzers to slow down for consolidation. He might even force them to halt temporarily."

"And you will withdraw Franklyn's force?"

Again Gort shook his head, even more ponderously, as if a great weight were pressing him into his seat. "Not yet. If they remain where they are, the Germans will have to consume another twenty-four or thirty-six hours mopping up. If Franklyn's force is seen as expendable, it will make the Nazis believe that we have more armor than we do. That deception can buy us some time, time we desperately need." The general pivoted his chair to stare up at the map. "Did you know that Guderian reached Abbeville on the Channel?" he asked. "Boulogne and Calais are next." Andre followed Gort's view of a tiny corner where the French and Belgian frontiers met: a small city and a harbor named Dunkirk. The eyes of the two men met. "Colonel, there is more you should know. You have greatly exceeded your orders in bringing me valuable information and could be in severe difficulty with your own High Command. That I cannot permit."

"I don't understand what you mean, General."

"I have backdated a request to Commander-in-Chief Weygand, appointing you my new liaison officer. Welcome to my staff, Colonel."

SIXTY-THREE

The meeting was buzzing with excited speculation. After the two-day battle at Arras, Seventh Panzer had been ordered to halt for repair, resupply, and reinforcement. With the race to the sea already won by Guderian, even Rommel admitted the wisdom of such a move. After all, his tanks had taken 50 percent casualties, counting dead, wounded, and equipment out of action.

His newest tank battalion commander, Horst von Bockman, had also been grateful for the chance to recuperate. His arm was healing well, though it hurt like the devil whenever he tried to lift anything heavier than a piece of paper.

Horst had tried to dissuade Rommel from giving him the new command. He had pleaded ignorance of tank operation and tactics, but the general was not swayed from his decision. "Anyone who is as good an instinctive leader as you cannot be allowed to go to waste," he concluded. "You handled the columns like an old time Prussian cavalry officer. It was beautiful."

Horst could hardly plead ignorance of cavalry tactics. So here he was, officer over twelve of the new PzKw IV's, together with all their men and machinery.

For four days the division had rested. Now, on the twenty-fifth of May, it was ready to jump off again. The speculation in the meeting of brigade and battalion leaders ran the gamut of possible next moves. Richter, the senior tank officer present, held out for an immediate attack on the BEF troops at Hazebrouck. Colonel Eckberg, the chief of the division's artillery, was certain that the target would be Lille, where the remaining French forces in the north were said to be concentrated. Horst, feeling very junior to the rest, kept his mouth shut, but privately he believed the Seventh would pivot directly toward the Channel. He had heard some rumors from interrogated French prisoners that the British had gotten a belly full and were ready to call it quits. If true, they would certainly fall back toward the coast to attempt an evacuation.

All the men stood when General Rommel entered the room. Before he had spoken a single word, Horst could tell he was seething with anger. Rommel's jaw was clinched and his face drawn in a very uncharacteristic frown. He waved the officers to their seats, but it was some seconds before he could allow himself to speak.

"We are *ordered,"* he said, stressing the final word, "ordered to halt for two *more* days. The division will not advance. Our units which have already crossed . . . *already crossed,"* he repeated, as if he could not believe the words, "the canal will be pulled back. That is all, gentlemen."

As soon as Rommel stalked out, the rising flow of conjecture overflowed its banks. "It is Goering's fault," Eckberg complained bitterly. "He wants to cover his flyboys with some glory, now that we have done all the work. When the Allies in the pocket surrender, he will see that the Luftwaffe gets all the credit."

"I disagree," Richter said. "The ground ahead is marshy, much more so than what we have crossed already. It is belated caution setting in. Or, perhaps the armored units are just being saved for the next phase of the campaign. After all, it is about time that the infantry do some work too."

Horst thought that there was more to this than met the eye. When you have an opponent on the ropes, you finish him as quickly as possible. Otherwise, you risk letting him escape or get his second wind. Making the Allies a present of the time to regroup was not something that Rommel would have permitted, and neither would tank battalion commander von Bockman.

❀ ❀ ❀

Together with British troops from the Second and Fifth Gloucester regiments, Mac found himself on the road to the Channel. Two thousand men were ordered to defend an important stretch of the southern perimeter of the Allied defenses, centered on the city of Cassel.

Mac watched a young lieutenant, who spoke no French, trying to explain to a baker and his wife that their home was needed as a fortification. Eventually they were persuaded to leave, but Mac felt sure that they did not understand fully what was happening. The message became clear to the couple only after the lieutenant ordered a squad to knock a hole in the wall of the ground floor to make an emplacement for an anti-tank gun.

When Mac asked them what they felt about the war, the baker shrugged and said nothing, but the wife took off like a rocket. "What has happened to the Phony War?" she demanded. "What has happened to the Maginot Line? What do the politicians say now? And the vaunted British, is this what they call coming to our aid? *L'Anglais ou L'Allemagne . . . je ne sais pa la nuance.* British or German, I do not see the difference."

A hilltop town only eighteen miles from the coast, Cassel was also in the middle of some of the flattest, best operating country for tanks between the Germans and the sea. That both sides regarded it as crucial was no surprise.

So it was back to business as usual as Mac saw it. The story of this whole campaign for the Allies had been dropping back and trying to hang on to a stronghold. Arras had been the best shot at changing all that, but here it was again.

The lieutenant continued in his efforts to carry out orders. He had another squad of men build a barricade. Soon a pile of milk cans, a horse-drawn plow, and an overturned manure spreader blocked the main road. As a work of art, it would have been titled "Nineteenth-Century Farming." Mac was sure that it did not belong in twentieth century warfare.

The work of fortifying the town of Cassel was as complete as imagination and muscle power could make it. Several homes besides the baker's now sported holes in their walls and protruding machine guns. A Bren gun sat picturesquely on top of a commandeered chicken coop, and the men at the barricade counted a Boyes antitank rifle among their arsenal.

"Fat lot of good it is too," remarked the sergeant who had charge of it, "shells bounce off the Jerry tanks."

"Don't you have anything else?" Mac asked.

"Sure we do," replied the sergeant sarcastically. "Here, Lance. Take this gentleman and show him the heavy artillery."

Mac was led to a fenced depression behind the front row of houses. By its smell the previous owners from whom it had been requisitioned were pigs. The center of the low spot was occupied by a three inch mortar and a crew of three men. The soldiers took turns leaving their position and going to the edge of the hill for fresh air.

At midnight the hum of airplanes sounded from the northwest. Mac guessed there was little chance they would be friendly. Cassel's position on the highest knob of land in the area was particularly attractive to bombers. Long before the sound of the planes arrived directly overhead, Mac and all the soldiers had taken what shelter they could find in cellars and slit trenches.

Mac crouched in a recently dug narrow hole next to his tour guide. Lance Corporal Castle may not have been a religious man, but he kept up a constant litany just the same. "Here they come. We're gonna catch it now. We surely are. What's to stop 'em? They're right on top of us. Here they come . . ."

Mac found himself wishing that something would happen, just to provide a change from Castle's monotonous refrain. When the steady drone of the engines neared the hilltop, Mac and the corporal ducked down below the level of the slit trench. Mac's world was suddenly reduced to a space scarcely one foot wide and three deep.

The chatter of machine guns welcomed the German planes; not that anybody expected to actually down one. It just felt better to pretend to fight back.

A whistling noise announced that the bombs were on the way, and even Castle got quiet. Mac had been through this enough before to know that everyone held his breath until the first explosion. After that you either waited it out, or you took a direct hit and had no more breath to hold.

His count to ten was interrupted by a clanging noise, as if the Germans were dropping milk cans like the ones in Cassel's rampart. Then he heard a fluttering clamor, like a thousand pigeons taking off all at once.

Mac discovered that he was still holding his breath, way past time for the first blast. Cautiously, he poked his head up out of the trench and looked around. Thirty yards away was a new dark lump, sticking in the ground at an angle. And falling through the trees were objects that floated like falling leaves.

Ducking back much faster than he had popped up, Mac thought about unexploded bombs. This object did not look much like a bomb; it looked more like a milk can. Did the Germans have a new type of delayed action weapon, designed to lure people out of safety before it detonated?

Castle still cowered in the trench. He was no help in analyzing this development. Mac reviewed his brief glimpse. There had been no explosions, only the harmless-looking cylinder. And drifting down around it were scraps of something white.

Mac stood up, embarrassed with himself. "Come on, Corporal," he said to Castle. "We've just been attacked by a volley of leaflets."

The canister which had failed to open was full of squares of paper and the ground around the knoll of Cassel was littered with them. By the brief light of a flickering match, each carried the same message, repeated in both French and English:

"Allied soldiers: Look at this map. It gives your true situation. Your troops are entirely surrounded—stop fighting! Put down your arms!"

The map illustrated a tiny pocket around the Channel town of Dunkirk, encircled by a wide band marked "The Germans."

Lance Corporal Castle gathered a handful of the propaganda sheets. "What are you going to do with those, Corporal?" Mac asked.

Castle's voice in the darkness had a smile in it. "Latrine duty," he said.

Mac decided that he really liked the corporal after all.

SIXTY-FOUR

Boulogne flashed past below. Black puffs of German antiaircraft fire reached up toward the pitiful flight of three Hurricanes. Boulogne had fallen the day before and 73 Squadron was flying its last mission. What was left of the group was recalled to England to reform. After today, RAF missions over France would only be flown by Spitfires and Hurricanes operating from Kent.

David found it hard to believe that the entire north coast of France was in Nazi hands. The Wehrmacht invasion had begun only sixteen days earlier. Now the last, best hope was to save as many Allied soldiers as possible. There were those who spoke of holding an enclave on the Channel; of resupply and reinforcement. The truth was a bitter pill: northern France was lost.

Still, he was proud of 73's performance. For the first six months he was flying *ANNIE,* the squadron had shot down only thirty enemy planes; in the last two weeks they had accounted for over one hundred. But hardly anyone was left who shared the memories.

"Close up, Tay," he broadcast to Churchman on his right wing. "Stay tight. You all right back there, Jimmy?" Small was flying as "rear-end Charlie," above and behind the other two, keeping a wary eye out for Messerschmidts.

The instructions for the three pilots were simple: "The British Expeditionary Force is being withdrawn from France by way of Dunkirk; give them all the help you can today and tomorrow you'll be back in England."

Swooping in over Dunkirk, David spotted thousands of men assembling, waiting to be removed. The roads heading into the evacuation area were packed as well. Though outlying units fought rearguard actions as far away as Lille, forty miles inland, the defensive perimeter established around Dunkirk was only twenty miles long and scarcely five deep.

Already the area was being pounded by the Luftwaffe. A flight of Heinkels was unloading thousands of pounds of high explosives on the fortifications and the warehouses. Billowing columns of black, oily smoke curled upward into the sky, towering over the five-thousand-foot elevation of the Hurricanes. David though that the pillars of pitch-dark fumes must be visible from the seashore of England.

Ready to order an attack on the bombers, David stopped when he saw the harbor. A hospital ship, marked with giant red crosses on each side of its funnel and on its deck both fore and aft, was tied up at the Gare Maritime, loading wounded. Six Me 109's were taking turns strafing the defenseless ship, diving in from the east and shooting up the length of the vessel.

"Right. Messers at twelve o'clock." David tried to keep his words steady, but the anger he felt rose up in his throat, almost choking him. His voice quivered with his fury. "Catch them as they pull up from a run," he ordered. "Send them all to hell!"

The timing was perfect. One Me 109 was still reaching for the top of its ascent. The second Messerschmidt was just climbing away from the hospital ship, and a third was beginning its machine gun attack. The other three were only starting their runs.

The Luftwaffe apparently believed that their superiority over the air of Dunkirk was complete. They had left no high cover for themselves and had posted no rear guard.

The three RAF fighters dove out of the sun. David and Churchman aimed directly for where the German fighters were the most vulnerable—pulling out of the attack. Jimmy Small was instructed to get on the tail of the last Me 109 in the line and follow him wherever he went.

David charged the lead Messerschmidt. Some flash from the attacking Hurricane must have reached the German pilot, or perhaps he had a sudden premonition. Across the intervening two hundred yards, David could see the man raise his hand to shield his eyes against the glare. At that same moment, David squeezed the trigger, loosing a burst of .303 caliber fury. He watched the bullets penetrate the glass of the cockpit and saw the German's head explode in a cloud of red haze. One down.

Rolling sharply left and reversing direction, ANNIE roared past where Churchman had just shot the tail off his target. The pilot of the second 109 pushed open his canopy and jumped away from the suddenly out of control ship. Two down.

David dove into the face of the German fighter who just completed its attack on the mercy ship. Out of position for a proper shot, the Hurricane's sudden appearance panicked the Luftwaffe pilot, who rolled his craft into the stream of bullets.

There was no chance to see what the lucky burst had accomplished. David was plunging almost straight down toward the bow of the ship. Just as the next 109 cleared the deck, David fired again. The line of tracers tracked exactly into the fuselage of the fighter. It may have been massive damage, or perhaps just panic, but the German fighter dove to escape, despite its lack of height, and plunged into the sea. Three down.

An excited yelp came over the R/T from Jimmy. "Scratch one for me!" Four down.

Pulling out of his dive, David circled back over the Channel, looking for the remaining two Messerschmidts. He spotted the one he had shot at, now tangled high overhead in a dogfight with Churchman. Where was the last?

The answer came in a stream of bullets that impacted ANNIE's portside wing and left a row of holes. David yanked the plane sharply right, then left and right again, trying to shake off his pursuer. A second burst of gunfire hit the Hurricane's engine. A thin stream of white vapor flowed back from the cowling and up over the glass of the canopy.

The third round of machine gun fire from the 109 hit David's cockpit just behind his seat. The armor in back of the pilot seat stopped two bullets, but another shattered the edge of the plating. A fragment hit the flier in the lower left arm. Just before it went numb, David felt a searing thrust that went from his elbow to his fingertips. His hand fell limply away from the throttle knob, and he could not raise it.

Reversing his direction again, David urged the Hurricane to regain some height as he headed back toward Dunkirk. He expected the German to return at any moment and finish him off. His head spun and he felt close to passing out.

From the radio he heard Churchman's voice. "Number five accounted for, but I'm hit. Losing oil pressure."

"I see you, Tay," Jimmy's voice answered. "Need help?"

Where had the last German gone now? "Tay," David radioed, "you . . . reach England. Jimmy . . . go with him."

"What about you, Tinman?"

"Go! I'll be . . . later."

The flow of glycol fumes was increasing and the cockpit filling with smoke. David crossed the coastline, still reaching for the height he needed in order to bail out safely. Awkwardly, he slid back the canopy, every movement of his useless left arm wracking him with agony. Unbuckling his radio cable and the oxygen tube with difficulty, he readied himself to dive over the side. Three thousand feet of height now separated him from the Belgian countryside. He did not want to travel any further inland, for fear of falling into German hands.

Plunging over the side, David kicked himself away from the airframe. His dangling arm struck the edge of the cockpit as he pushed off, puked into his oxygen mask, and passed out.

When he came to he was floating at a thousand feet, not even able to remember how he had pulled the ripcord. Through vision that was all yellow and black spots, he saw *ANNIE*. The ship now spouted a trail of black smoke as it continued on toward the German lines. Vaguely he hoped that she would explode gloriously, right on top of some Nazi general.

At five hundred feet up he saw the Me 109 return. It chased *ANNIE* at first, then apparently noticed the white disk of the parachute and dove after him. A hailstorm of bullets tore through the silk canopy on the Messerschmidt's first pass. The ground rose quickly and David tried to ready himself for the impact.

He cradled his left arm against his body, but even holding it made him feel close to blacking out again. The fingers of his right hand brushed against an odd jagged lump that protruded near his elbow. The pain reached his senses at the same moment as comprehension. Touching the exposed end of a jagged shrapnel splinter under the length of his forearm, the flier vomited once more.

The impact with the ground jarred him so badly that David passed out again. When he opened his eyes, he was staring stupidly at a diving Me 109 lined up to strafe him as he lay on the ground.

Some unknown instinct urged David to move: roll, crawl, something. The clumsy spin to the right dropped him into a ditch. He landed with his injured arm pinned under his weight, but this time the sudden, sharp pain woke him up to his danger.

A line of machine gun bullets tore up the ground where his parachute lay. David crawled into a muddy culvert and lay there as the 109 came back one more time. The incendiaries in the last burst set fire to his parachute. Then the German left.

A few minutes later, a platoon of British infantry emerged from the refuge of their roadside ditch. They assumed the Messerschmidt was after them. When they saw the smoldering silk of David's chute, they located him and pulled him out from the culvert.

The barrage that arrived at Cassel the morning after the leaflets did not consist of harmless sheets of paper. Just after dawn, German artillery opened up on the town and the battle for the road to the Channel began in earnest.

The Gloucester mortarmen were busy, lobbing shells down onto the

Wehrmacht positions below. Mac filmed the crew in action, loading and firing their weapon. He listened to the hollow ringing sound it made as it tossed the three-inch rounds into the valley. The incoming shells exploded with much greater force than the puny tube seemed to offer.

Running from slit trench to slit trench and hugging the ground when a new barrage whistled overhead, Mac made his way toward the edge of the hill. One jump put him into the same hole he had shared with Corporal Castle the night before. The corporal was there again too. "Hey, Castle," Mac called. "You've got dirt all over you. You're almost buried in it. Why don't you brush . . ." Mac stopped abruptly when he realized that Castle was dead. One of the first bursts had caught him above the level of the ground, and he was pierced with shrapnel. Mac knew that the trench would probably become Corporal Castle's grave.

When Mac reached the position of the forward artillery observer, he could see the progress of the German attack. A half dozen Panzer tanks milled about in the hollow below Cassel. As Mac watched, one of the British shells struck the rear of the lead machine, and black smoke poured out. The tank ground to a halt and the hatches popped open as the German crew hastily abandoned their burning vehicle. Bullets from a Bren gun concealed in a barn mowed them down, all except the last man, who dove headfirst into a ditch.

"Bloody Hun, I hope he broke his neck," the artillery spotter observed.

The return fire from the Germans arched above the spot where Mac peered down from the brow of the knoll. A shell struck the farm building hiding the Bren emplacement and set the barn's roof on fire. The men operating the machine gun continued to fire their weapon, but a trio of young pigs scampered out and ran down the hill.

Moments later, with the barn fully engulfed in flames, the British troops bailed out also. The two-man crew was uninjured, but not all the pigs were so lucky. The smell of cooking pork drifted down to Mac on the morning breeze.

Another shell from the German artillery landed behind Mac's position and the British mortar fell silent. It was possible that the fight had just gotten too intense in that spot and they had moved to another. When some time passed without a resumption of the firing, Mac knew that they had taken a hit. But the British resistance had done its work; the German tanks retreated back into the cover of the trees.

The artillery barrage continued pounding Cassel, leveling the baker's house. It seemed ironic to think that the French woman had fretted about a hole in her wall, when now, not even one wall was left standing.

The bursts of German explosives struck the face of the hill just below where Mac and the spotter lay. The next blow was higher up, and the next almost to the top, as if the shells were climbing the mound to the city.

"Time to go," urged the soldier. "We aren't doing any good here any more."

Mac allowed the rest of the film to grind through his camera. He automatically reached into the pouch at his side to grab another fresh reel. He was already in motion away from the artillery fire, hoping he could find an intact cellar to duck into to change the film.

His fingers fumbled among the cannisters, seeking the sealed edge that would identify the new roll. He found none. He had used every inch of film that he had, and until he got more, his role as a newsreel cameraman was at an end.

"Looks like I'm headed out," he told the lieutenant whose command post was in what remained of the town's police station. "Hope I can catch a ride at the coast."

"Make for Dunkirk," the lieutenant said breezily. "Someone will accommodate you."

"I'll be back," Mac vowed.

"Yes, well, good luck to you." There was a forced cheerfulness in the officer's tone.

"When will you disengage?" Mac asked.

"Really can't say. We have received no other orders than to continue holding here, which we will for as long as we can."

"And then?"

"I suppose we'll be trying for Dunkirk too."

"If you wait too long, this hill will be surrounded," Mac warned.

"I don't fancy German food all that much," the lieutenant said.

❊   ❊   ❊

The whole countryside around David's route of escape was in flames. Bridges, houses, and army vehicles added to the conflagration as the German barrage smashed down. The unending concussions of the shells drowned out the cries of the wounded and dying. David traveled through the wreckage with a group of a half dozen British BEF soldiers on their way to the coast. The name of Dunkirk was on the lips of every man.

At sundown, clutching his wounded arm, David Meyer staggered onto the grounds of the École de Cavalerie. Two youthful sentries on the edge of the wood stooped and questioned them, then following a troop lorry which had been converted to an ambulance, they came to the British Casualty Clearing Station in the school chapel.

The CCS, which had been moved from the bomb-damaged right wing of the school, now held over two thousand casualties.

No matter how swiftly the surgeons worked, long lines of stretchers carrying French, English, and Belgian soldiers continued to grow longer. Lorries filled with wounded streamed in.

David's companions asked an orderly the way to Dunkirk. Without good-byes, they left David on the front steps of the church and hurried on toward the smoking highway which led to the coast. It occurred to David, as he watched their retreating backs, that he never got their names, nor would he recognize their faces.

He tried to hail a harried, blood-spattered nurse in a tin hat who rushed by him with a box of medical supplies.

"My arm is hurt. Badly I think. Shrapnel. Can I get it seen to here?"

She did not hesitate or offer even a word of sympathy. "Injured arm, boy? Look in there," she snapped, jerking her thumb toward the entrance of the church.

The floor of the sanctuary was covered with stretchers. There was not an inch of space between them. Light streamed through the remaining stained glass windows to cover the wounded in a giant patchwork quilt of shifting colors: blue and red on the face of the pale freckled boy with the missing leg and the row of amputees . . . green and yellow over the contorted face of the man who shouted for a nurse to administer some morphine. First it was bright and then dark as smoke momentarily blocked the sun. Once again the shadows broke and patterns grew vivid and distinct on bloody bandages and pale, ghastly complexions. The great, cavernous room hummed with an unending moan. A nightmare of collective agony. Hopeless and angry, the nurse glared at her charges as if she were infuriated at them.

"There are only fourteen nurses here. These men won't escape unless they can walk," she snorted bitterly. "Injured arm? *You* can walk, can't you? The coast is that way."

He could not go on. "I've got to sleep. Can I sleep somewhere?" The world had taken on a sickly yellow pall again. He thought he might throw up if he could not lay down.

"If you can find a spot." She walked past him. "Steer clear of the area behind the altar. That's the only place we have to put the dying men." She scurried into the auditorium, leaving David to find his own refuge. It was obvious that the surgeons did not have time or inclination to cut out a sliver of shrapnel while other men were bleeding to death before their very eyes.

Settling in beneath a heavy table in the foyer, David lay between the support and the cool stone wall. His arm rested on his stomach. Every breath meant a painful movement of the metal which seemed to grate against his bones. He closed his eyes and listened to the distant shelling as it came nearer. He recognized the drone of aircraft engines: Heinkel, Stuka, Dornier, a flock of Messers. But for David, it was over. Suddenly and terribly over.

David gasped as an intense pain shot up through his shoulder. The urge to vomit swept over him again. Swallowing hard, he attempted to stay the violent reaction. He could not. Rolling to the side, he heaved bile onto the stone pavement. Then, he passed out.

❧   ❧   ❧

It occurred to Federov that when the pieces of a puzzle finally fall into place, it is amazing how the completed picture leaps out. He was certain now that he knew Richard Lewinski's whereabouts. Putting Professor Argo's casual remark together with the reports from Oxford and Princeton had led Federov straight to the library of the Sorbonne and a stack of yearbooks. He had no difficulty locating photos of Lewinski's senior and junior pictures. But it wasn't until he examined a staff grouping of stiffly posed academic figures that the information he sought glared up at him, right under his nose.

In the back row of the professorial colleagues for the year 1910 was the face of Lewinski's father. Next to him, according to the caption, was Louis Chardon. Flipping over to the student pictures again confirmed it: Andre Chardon had been a classmate of Lewinski's, and their families were connected as well. And Andre Chardon held some position in French military intelligence.

All that remained was a little snooping, which was what brought Federov to the Buci market on this lovely spring day. From the house on Quai d'Anjou, he had followed Chardon's cook, Jeanette, with a rising sense of excitement that his goal was near.

Federov positioned himself a few feet from the cook and picked up a succession of melons, groaning aloud as he inspected each and replacing it on the pile. His handsome face was downcast and worried when Jeanette caught the sound of another heavy sigh. "Excuse me, Monsieur," she said kindly. "May I be of some assistance?"

"Would you?" he asked with a pleading note. "My wife has taken the children and gone south. My cook has chosen this week to become ill, and I have unexpected guests who have arrived from Belgium . . . you understand?"

"But of course," Jeanette said sympathetically.

"I have hired a temporary cook, but I must do the shopping myself; something for which I am singularly ill equipped."

"But that is the easy part," avowed Jeanette. "I can help you."

Federov flashed his most charming smile. "You are so very kind. This melon," he said. "Is it ripe?"

The cook sniffed the indicated fruit, then set it aside and selected another. "This one is better. What else will you be serving?"

"It may depend on the expense, because of the number who are arriving, you see. How does one know how much to purchase? In your household for instance, how many do you feed and how many melons would you buy?"

"Ours is but a small ensemble," Jeanette said. "Right now there are only two adults, and one of them . . . la!" she exclaimed. "He eats like a stray cat. I put out a saucer of food for him and he dines at midnight when he emerges from his basement lair!"

Federov's pulse was racing, but once Jeanette got started, she provided even more information than he could have hoped. "Alas," she said, "my poor Monsieur will have to cope with the strange one all by himself. I am also leaving for the south."

"Oh?" said Federov, pricking up his ears.

"My son lives in Nice," Jeanette volunteered, "and I am departing soon to join him there."

"Most interesting," Federov assured her. "Now tell me, how many melons this size would be needed to feed a group of ten?"

❧   ❧   ❧

Josie telephoned the house on la Huchette before she took Juliette and Yacov there. Madame Rose was not at the train station today. There were important matters to attend to at the orphanage.

From the exterior everything looked much the same, except that there were many shuttered windows now along la Huchette. People had closed their homes and fled south.

But the big black coach gate and the bell rope remained as before. An echo of laughter drifted up from behind the wall. The gate swung open and Josie, with Yacov and Juliette, entered the sanctuary of the courtyard.

What had changed? Long lines of laundry still waved overhead. The sun was still shining. The faces of the children were still light and happy and alive. Juliette was drawn into a game of hopscotch. It had been a long time since Josie had seen such happy expressions.

Now, however, there were twice as many faces as before.

"One hundred and fifty, give or take." Madame Rose took little Yacov onto her broad hip in a kind of instinctive gesture.

Find a baby, pick him up. All the day you'll have good luck . . .

The old woman waved a hand for Josie to sit. "Well! He is a strong healthy little fellow." She held his arm up like a boxer victorious in the ring. In a baby voice she mimicked, "And that to you, nasty Hitler!" She laughed and kissed him. He drooled and grinned. "A future president perhaps? Or a great doctor who will save us all from . . . something? I always like these guessing games about these precious little lives. You know, Jesus said that their angels are always flying back and forth before the throne of God. I suppose I will be long gone before this little man becomes what he has been saved to be, but I will certainly look down with interest from heaven at the outcome. Now, tell me where you have been."

Josie told her everything. Madame Rose listened with a solemn expression.

"It is time for us all to leave," Madame Rose said when the story was finished. "I have made arrangements with the French authorities. The entire orphanage is to be evacuated. We leave Paris tomorrow from Gare d'Orsay for the south. There are several young women . . . students from the Sorbonne, who will go along to help us. Baron Rothschilds has a villa he has offered for our use near the border of Spain. You and these little ones must come along with us."

This was exactly what Josie hoped for. "What time?"

"You must be there by noon. An entire car is to be reserved for us on the two o'clock train."

SIXTY-FIVE

Rue de la Huchette had never seen such an army since the days of the French Revolution and the Reign of Terror. What a commotion!

Every child wore a two-cornered paper hat made of newsprint. This was because Madame Rose said it would be very hot in the sun at Gare d'Orsay and she did not want any boiled brains or sunstroke or sunburn to contend with!

Jerome felt foolish at first, but he got into the spirit of the thing when the five Austrian brothers made trumpeting sounds and began to duel with sticks. Jerome stuck his hand between the buttons of his shirt, jumped onto an upturned laundry tub. Striking a pose, he declared that he was Napoleon Bonaparte and that Hitler was slime from the nose of a pig and that all Nazis were about to become cannon fodder!

He was cheered by everyone in the courtyard. He doffed his two-cornered hat in a gallant bow and led the cheer for France. Very stirring.

"You are a born orator, Jerome," Madame Rose said.

The hats were quite acceptable after that.

So. The time had come to leave Number 5. One hundred fifty children were lined up ten across and fifteen deep for the march to Gare d'Orsay.

Like the French tour guides known as Universal Aunts, Madame Rose and Madame Betsy held black umbrellas high above their heads. At the end of each row, the women students from the Sorbonne also held umbrellas. Five boys in wheelchairs each carried paper banners of the French tricolor which had been made the same time as the hats. The other children who were lame held the tiny babies and the toddlers and were pulled in handcarts and wagons. Madame Rose declared that these were the captains of the artillery. Jerome pushed Henri's wheelchair.

Papillon, in a high state of rat-excitement, perched on Henri's head, then skittered down his arm and back up again. He twitched his nose with great interest at the four oldest Austrian brothers who pushed the other wheel-chairs. The youngest Austrian brother pulled a wagon. Everyone carried paper-wrapped packages. These bundles contained two pair of clean under-things, two pair of socks, and one change of clothing. It was too hot to wear sweaters, but Madame Betsy would not have them left behind.

"It may be sweltering today," she croaked in her reedy voice when the boys complained, "but you will be sorry if you do not have something warm to wear in the fall!"

Madame Betsy was always thinking ahead and using interesting words. Madame Rose agreed with her.

"Remember it will be cold again some day."

It was hopeless to disagree with both of the sisters at the same time.

One heavy article of clothing, either a coat or a sweater, was tied around the waist of each child. In addition to this, there was lunch. Also dinner, breakfast, lunch, and dinner again. The food was all the same, but there was enough to live on for the journey: cheese sandwiches wrapped in waxed paper, two oranges, and two apples were packed into the pillowcase of each traveler. This was then tied to the belt so it could not be lost.

"If you must abandon anything, leave only your extra clothes behind! But do not lose your food parcels. One may run through the Tuileries as stark naked as the day he was born and still survive. Especially in this weather. But one must have food to survive!"

"And paper hats to keep one's brains from boiling," remarked Georg to Jerome under his breath.

Jerome pictured everyone naked except for the two-cornered paper hats and the umbrellas.

After that there was the very strictest command from Madame Rose that one could only eat when permission was granted and that any soldier who went through his provision without waiting would just have to go hungry.

Jerome had seen the hungry people at Gare du Nord, and so he resisted dipping into his supplies.

Madame Rose, umbrella elevated and tin whistle between her lips, took her place at the head of the procession. Madame Betsy brought up the rear.

Madame Rose puffed out her cheeks and let loose with an ear splitting *FWEEEEEEEEET!* on the whistle.

There was no missing her intention. Papillon leapt up in terror onto Jerome's food sack and then scampered to the top of his paper hat.

"All right everyone! Stick together now! Artillery?" She glowered down at Jerome and Henri and Papillon. "Are you all ready?" She addressed the rat. ". . . *Marche!*"

✣   ✣   ✣

Colonel Bertrand had still not arrived to pick up Lewinski. His tardiness had made Josie late for the rendezvous at Gare d'Orsay. Madame Rose had specified in no uncertain terms that in order to be assured of a place on the train, everyone traveling with the orphanage would have to be at the terminal at least two hours before departure. That mark had passed twenty minutes ago.

She moved the two suitcases to the tiled foyer in preparation for leaving. Where was Bertrand?

She dialed Bertrand's private number, which had been left for Lewinski. The phone at Vignolles rang a dozen times before it was finally answered by a feeble croaking voice.

"Colonel Bertrand please?"

"The colonel? He is gone away long ago. Last night."

"Gone where?" How could Bertrand have forgotten Richard Lewinski?

"I do not know, Madame. They have simply loaded the trucks. Very many trucks, Madame. And they have all gone away. South I think. Like the birds."

There was a knock at the door as she replaced the handset. Josie was pleased. She was sure that it would be Colonel Bertrand. He had come to retrieve Lewinski and he was also apparently running late. Now Josie could leave with her conscience clear, her last duty discharged.

Poking her head through the doorway of the stairs to the basement, she called out, "Good-bye, Richard. We are leaving now." She thought she heard a grunt of acknowledgement, but in Lewinski's case it was hard to tell whether it had been directed at her or was part of some private reverie.

She flung open the front door. "Come in, Colonel," she offered, then stopped awkwardly. The short, dapper man who bowed on the front stoop was not Bertrand. Had he been sent in the colonel's place to retrieve Richard? Josie glanced past him, expecting to see a lorry. There was none. Instead, across the Seine, she glimpsed hordes of people carrying luggage and children and belongings on their way to Gare d'Orsay to catch the train south.

"I was told Colonel Bertrand would call personally," she began. "You are not who I was expecting."

"And you are not Colonel Andre Chardon, but you are a most charming substitute!"

"I am sorry, Colonel Chardon is not at home," Josie said, impatient at this latest interruption. So this fellow was not from Bertrand. Where was Bertrand? "I do not know when Colonel Chardon will return, Monsieur . . ."

"Federov. How unfortunate that I missed him. I am also wine merchant, you see, and a friend of Colonel Chardon." He glanced at the luggage. "I am leaving Paris for Switzerland and only wanted to stop and wish him well. Who knows when we will all return? And when we do, Paris may be filled with strangers." This was an ominous and unpleasant thing to say. Probably true. All the familiar faces were on their way to the train stations.

"When I see him I will tell him . . ." She began to close the door. He put up his hand and held it open, then stepped in past her.

"But of course!" he remarked. He glanced around nervously. "You are Madame Marlow. We met at the Friends of Poland reception."

Josie vaguely remembered him. Had he provided the buckets of champagne? She gestured toward the bags to show that she was in a hurry. "You will have to excuse me," she said, "but we have a train to catch."

"A pity. I would have liked to renew our acquaintance. Perhaps I could just write Andre a note? It will only take a moment. I have a pen," he said, withdrawing one from his jacket pocket. "Could you locate a scrap of paper for me?"

Josie decided it would be quicker to accommodate this request than to try to refuse it. There was stationery in the Louis XIV desk against the wall of the foyer. Turning to fetch the paper, she was stopped by the barrel of an automatic pistol pressed into her ribs.

"Say nothing except what I tell you." Federov's voice was low and menacing. "Where is Lewinski?"

"You are making a mistake. A number of soldiers . . . Colonel Bertrand . . . will be here any minute."

"You are wrong, Madame. The Colonel has been notified by Quai d'Orsay that Richard Lewinski left by plane for England some hours ago. Lewinski has connections at Oxford, we have heard. Bertrand believes the little Jew has flown the coop. No one is coming."

She blurted, "The cook and the housekeeper and the chauffeur are. . . ."

"Gone." Federov jabbed the Czech-made automatic into her side. "There is no time for lies," he said. "The servants are all away and we have already established that Colonel Chardon is out. I will ask only once: where is Lewinski?"

At that instant a roaring sneeze resounded from the basement, identifying the location of Federov's quarry.

"Very good," Federov said. "Then it is to the basement we must go. You will precede me down the stairs, without making any sound."

Three steps from the bottom, the tread creaked and Lewinski looked up from the notes on his worktable. "Who is this?" he asked.

Federov shoved Josie down. She caught her heel and fell to the stone floor. "Richard Lewinski," Federov said. "I bring greetings from your former employer . . . Reinhard Heydrich."

Lewinski glanced toward a wrench laying on the table beside his Enigma machine. His fingers twitched.

"I would not, if I were you," Federov cautioned. "This can either be quick or it can be painful. It makes no difference to me, but it may be important to you."

Lewinski raised his hands slowly and backed away from the table as Josie got to her feet.

Motioning Josie over toward the wall, Federov advanced to stand next to the notebook. He thumbed through the pages. "I see that my assignment was not a waste," he observed. "You are working on an Enigma machine. It does not look like you are successful, but one never knows."

"I beg your pardon," Lewinski said with wounded pride. "It most certainly does work!"

"Really?" Federov retorted as he peered into the cabinet of the decoding devise.

"Do not touch it!" Lewinski barked in indignation.

Federov was enjoying the game. He touched the wheels and smiled smugly at Lewinski as if to demonstrate who was in control. "A fascinating jumble. We will leave it here until the Chief of Security arrives in Paris with the Führer to examine your work." He inclined his head curiously at the two banks of dials and switches on the console. He flicked the top two switches. Nothing happened.

"Do not touch it!" Lewinski roared again. "It will . . ."

With an impish grin Federov flipped the toggle.

His body stiffened in a rictus of electric shock as the voltage coursed through him, pulling him up on tiptoe. An involuntary exclamation of "Ahhhh," started on a low note and ascended the scale to become a shrieking high pitched cry. An electric spark arced from the barrel of the gun to the metal fittings inside the cabinet and the basement lights dimmed to a pale orange glow.

The nauseating smell of burning hair filled the cellar, and Josie ducked her head toward the wall. The lights resumed their normal brightness, and when she looked up again, she saw that Lewinski had separated two electric cords on the floor behind the cabinet.

The gun barrel was welded to the steel of the frame, and Federov was held upright by his grasp on the handle. When the power was shut off and his grip relaxed, he crumpled to the stones.

"I told him," Lewinski said.

Josie reeled back to sit down hard on the stairs.

Lewinski stepped over Federov to examine his machine.

Unable to remain, Josie half-ran, half-crawled up the stairs. She flung the door wide and gulped the air. Across the Seine the crowds had swelled to fill the road from side to side.

Carrying his notes, Lewinski plodded up after her and kicked shut the door to the cellar.

"What a mess," he said glumly.

"Horrible." Josie leaned heavily against the door.

"Worse than that. All the circuits are melted. The machine is ruined."

"You will have to go with us, Richard." Her voice was barely audible. "This man was Gestapo. They know where you are."

"I suppose. And Andre will not be happy to have a dead man in his basement. The whole house will smell." At that, he put on his gas mask. "I told him not to touch it. You are my witness. I warned him."

Right, Josie thought, looking at Lewinski's smiling eyes through the goggles of the bug-like mask. *Just like B'rer Rabbit told B'rer Fox to do anything but throw him in the briar patch!*

Perhaps Richard Lewinski was more practical than she imagined.

"Why build in such a dangerous switch?"

His voice was muffled. "I thought they might come. I thought they might want to play with it a bit before they killed me. It is such a lovely whirligig of a thing. Anyone would want to play with it."

✤ ✤ ✤

Gare d'Orsay, with its rococo ceilings and high arched windows, looked more like a beautiful cathedral than a train station. Yesterday, Notre Dame had overflowed into the square with hopeful Parisians beseeching God to save France. This afternoon, all hope was redirected from the high altar of the church to Gare d'Orsay and the southbound trains. The terminal was packed with the desperately frightened population who prayed to hear the shrill benediction of a train whistle which could save them from encroaching hell.

From the arched porticos to the gilded iron gates, the crowds spilled out to overrun the sidewalks and the curbs and the broad Quai Anatole France. From both directions along the walled banks of the Seine the people kept coming. They arrived much faster than the trains came and went. Little children and belongings in tow, citizens were packed so tightly in the hot sun that when one fainted, the press of the others held the body upright.

Into this throng marched the little army of paper hats and umbrellas. The wheelchairs. The little wagons. The pygmy columns fifteen deep and ten across. Towering at the head was Madame Rose. Tweeting her whistle and trumpeting like the lead elephant of Hannibal's troop, she began to pass through what seemed to be the impassable.

"Pardon! PARDON! We are the orphanage of la Huchette. We have a train car reserved. Pardon! You will step aside, Monsieur! Madame, you must move your heap of baggage. We have children in wheelchairs coming along."

For one moment only she paused and looked back. "Oh, Josephine," Jerome heard her mutter. "Where are you, my dear?"

No time to wait, she forged on.

Hostile, angry eyes stared at the raised umbrellas. Lips curled in disdain at the sight of "cripples," given the places of healthy French children! Comments were muttered at the sight of the lederhosen and kneesocks of the five Austrian brothers. Were these trains not saved for French children? Were the children of foreigners and refugees to be given priority over good, patriotic citizens of the Republic of France?

It was an outrage!

Progress stopped at the closed and locked gates of the Gare. Jerome could hear the angry mutters of the people at the front who said they had been waiting too long to give up their places to the orphans of la Huchette! He heard the indignant bellows of those who pushed in at the sides and jostled behind. What right have these children to crowd ahead?

Madame Rose, stoic and self-assured, passed her paper through the bars of the gate to one of the three gendarmes who stood guard lest anyone attempt to push the gate down or climb over.

"As you see, Officer, we have a car reserved by special order of the Minister of Transportation. It is all there. Very clearly."

Behind her the murmur grew more menacing, the words more harsh. The gendarme looked pale and nervous. The crowds were near to rioting anyway. Did he dare let these pass? Did he dare to open the gate?

"One moment please, Madame," he said, taking the documents away with him.

Now there was a rough shove from a big brassy woman with an enormous bosom and sleeves rolled up like a stevedore. One of the students from the Sorbonne fell down. There was a small scream from Marie. Jerome recognized it. He had heard Marie scream many times.

He peered back to see his sister helping the Sorbonne volunteer struggle to stand. The student's black umbrella swayed back and forth and then slowly rose into its place on the perimeter of the band. Marie looked very angry behind the thick lenses of her glasses.

Jerome stuffed Papillon beneath his paper hat in case there was a riot. He looked around for some way of escape. Jump on the iron bars of the gate perhaps? Then he looked at Henri, stuck in the wicker wheelchair. Jerome decided that even if things got rough he would stick with Henri. They would ride out of the battle together or not at all!

Even Madame Rose betrayed some nervousness, the first ever: her square hands fidgeted.

"Will they let us on the train?" Jerome whispered.

"Pray, my dear boy," she replied, looking past the mob inside the gate who were standing belly to back all the way against the chuffing train.

❊   ❊   ❊

Josie knew they were too late to make the train even before they reached the edge of the ever-widening pool of humans and baggage.

The doll in her lap, Juliette sat on one of Lewinski's shoulders. Her legs were crossed daintily at the ankles, fingers entwined in his wiry red hair. Josie also held Yacov on her shoulder as protection against the ever-increasing pressure building behind them.

Across the thousands of hats and heads between them and the gate, Josie spotted the unbroken square of the umbrellas. The children were not moving forward, but at least they were at the front of the throng.

"Pardon," Josie ventured. "We are meeting someone . . . That group at the front with the umbrellas."

A fiercely dark-eyed woman with bad teeth turned and snarled. "You say you are with them? That group of cripples and foreigners! They have taken our places in line when we have been waiting all day long! *Pardon you!* I will tell you what will happen if you do not get out of here *now* . . ."

Josie backed away, letting a large group behind them inch forward. It was easier to move to the outer edge of the mob than it was to move even one inch nearer Madame Rose. It was hopeless.

They emerged a block away where the bridge known as Pont Royal led across the river to the Louvre. The umbrellas of Madame Rose and her little company were still in plain sight, moving and bobbing now before the entrance of the station. What was happening? Josie thrust Yacov into Lewinski's arms and climbed up on the thick retaining wall at the corner of Pont Royal to see.

❊   ❊   ❊

"Room for one hundred and thirty-five passengers only, Madame." The grim transportation officer spoke to Madame Rose through the gate. "And you have one hundred and fifty plus adult volunteers."

"Our family has grown since the document's issue last week, Monsieur le Chief." Madame Rose called him Chief, even though he was only a second-class official with no gold braid on the sleeve of his blue uniform.

"No matter. We take only what the paper says. There may be a riot all the same, Madame, when we open the gates! So I will tell you the decision which came through this morning: no Jews or children of foreign extraction are to be put before French children."

These words were overheard by people beyond the perimeter of umbrellas and passed back with satisfaction. The news that justice had been served rippled outward as if a boulder had been dropped into a still pond.

"WHAT ABOUT THE CRIPPLES?!" a husky female voice shouted.

The official agreed loudly with the opinion that only healthy and whole children would be transported on the train. A wheelchair would take up too much space. A cripple would require too much care. There were entire trainloads of ill people already transported. Why were these youngsters not in their places? Why had they not gone when they were supposed to go? Now they were here to take the places of healthy children and they were obviously out of turn.

He was a cruel little man to say such things in front of Henri and the others who could not walk. Jerome did not feel so much pity for the five Austrian brothers. Even though they were Jews, they were not hurt by the remarks, they were only angry; they were usually angry about something. Boys like Georg and his brothers were perfectly capable of stealing bicycles from the mountains stacked at Gare du Nord and pedaling all the way to Spain if they had to. But what about the boys who had useless legs? They could not walk across Pont Royal without help. How could they pedal anywhere? Jerome was angry. Madame Rose was angry. But if anything else was done, the crowd would riot and people would be crushed and killed.

"They have all been out in the sun too long," Georg said loudly.

"They should have worn paper hats," Henri said from his chair. He laughed a bit, even though tears were hanging in his eyes.

"Their brains are boiled," Jerome agreed.

Georg eyed Jerome with a bit of resentment. "You are French. You have legs. You can go."

"I am not going," Jerome said, looking up at Madame Rose. "I will not go, Madame Rose."

The anger in her eyes softened. She nodded, approving of his decision, even though he was a small boy and the Germans would soon drop bombs. Jerome knew she would not make him be a coward and go away while his dear friends were made to stay behind. And he loved Madame Rose for letting him be brave.

Marie read his decision in his eyes. "I will stay with you, Jerome!" she cried.

Could he deny her request when Madame Rose had been so kind to him? Yes. "You are going, Marie!"

From her place she wailed and moaned. "Let me stay with you! I will not go! I will not!" It made the crowd restless.

Someone shouted. *"Mon dieu!* Let her stay!"

"All right," Jerome agreed but shook his fist at her. "Now shut up!" Having won, she obeyed.

Now Madame Betsy worked her way up from behind. It was decided what must be done. They spoke in English because they did not want the nasty little official to know what they were saying.

"You must take the others south, Betsy. He will not allow any more than the number on the travel document to board the train."

Betsy smiled and nodded, but her eyes were hard. "He is an evil-looking little creature." Still smiling, she nodded to him. "Look at him, sister. Beady eyes and tiny Hitler moustache. No doubt he will cuddle up with the Nazis when they arrive. Just the type."

"Perhaps the first bomb will land on his head and then we will not have to wonder about it. In the meantime, you and the volunteers get on the train. Take the little ones. I will stay with our special children and the sons of Abraham. I have an ace or two up my sleeve, sister. I'll call Dupont's secretary at the Ritz. He's American . . ."

"He's long gone."

"Whatever. I'll get a car . . ."

"It will take more than a car . . ."

"You need to get on the train, Sister, and pray. God will answer. He always does. I will make it. And if I don't?" Rose enfolded her sister in her big arms. "Well then, remember . . . *There is a river, the streams whereof shall make glad the city of God* . . . I promise you, we shall meet beside the river, Betsy, dear."

And that was that. The gate parted just enough to let Betsy through. Bayonets at the ready, the gendarmes escorted the well children, the French children, inside the terminal.

There was no way to get them through that crowd without the danger of them being crushed. An announcement was made on the loudspeaker that the orphans of French patriots needed to get on the train. The crowd cheered them. One by one, the little children of la Huchette were lifted up and passed above the heads of the people. Hand to hand they floated from the gilded gates of Gare d'Orsay toward the train carriage which had been reserved for them in this needful hour. Likewise, Madame Betsy and the volunteers drifted over the human sea to take their places on the train out of Paris.

PART IV

Heaps of bones once moved by the proud breath of life
Scattered limbs, nameless debris, chaos of humanity,
Sacred jumble of a vast reliquary,
Dust of heroes, God will know you!

—War memorial at Louvremont

SIXTY-SIX

The halt order rescinded at last, the Panzers were soon knocking on the gates of Dunkirk, even as the Luftwaffe battered it from above. Lord Gort ordered Andre to make contact with the French forces holding the eastern perimeter and report back. Gort even loaned Andre his personal car and driver.

Lille was the furthest outpost of the Allied withdrawal. Located fifty miles inland from the Channel, Lille was the toe of the sock into which all the remaining British and French forces were squeezed.

Andre was to confer with General Prioux, head of the French First Army, and Third Corps commander Laurencie. The meeting was held in the massive seventeenth century brick citadel standing high at the west end of the Boulevard de la Liberté. Even as Andre entered the fortress, a German bombing raid ended and another artillery barrage pounded the east end of the city.

The council was one more example of how massively convoluted and inept Allied communications were. General Prioux believed that Dunkirk was to be used as a resupply base to maintain a foothold on the coast. He had not even been informed that the evacuation was underway. Swearing violently, Prioux ordered Laurencie to hold Lille, while he went off to find Gort.

It was near the Belgian border on Andre's return trip that he ran headlong into a Waffen SS reconnaissance unit. Gort's driver had taken a wrong turn and gotten lost on a deserted country lane. While trying to relocate the correct highway, they blundered into the German patrol.

Machine guns opened up on the unarmed Humber staff car, which crashed into a ditch after bullets from the MG 34's smashed the windshield. The driver was killed.

The Germans roared forward on their motorcycles. Andre dropped out of the low side of the upturned car and sprinted rapidly along the trench. Hunching over as he ran, he ducked into a culvert that went under the road just as the lead cycle pulled up next to the Humber.

He could hear their shouts as they examined the car. Andre knew they would find his briefcase in the back seat. Fortunately, it contained nothing of a sensitive nature, but it would tell the soldiers that another occupant of the car had escaped.

Sure enough, a flurry of orders in German sent a motorcycle to either end of a quarter-mile stretch of road, while the rest of the group dismounted to follow their quarry on foot. Andre crawled through the drainage pipe to the far side of the lane and plunged into the densest mass of thorns and brush he could find.

Andre reasoned that a patrol of limited strength, operating on the edge of hostile territory, would not stay in one place for long. He would just wait them out and they would give up the search. Why would they expend great effort for one unknown man?

Suddenly Andre realized that in the minds of the SS troops, his identity was not unknown. The thought was chilling: The Humber was clearly marked as General Gort's personal auto. If the prize was the highest ranking British officer on the continent, they would not give up easily; they might even call for additional troops for the search.

There was not enough distance between Andre and the road. He broke out of the thorn patch on the far side and started running again.

The plot of timber and scrub was only a couple acres in size, and the clearing into which Andre emerged was occupied by a barn and a haystack. He ran across the open space, zigzagging as he went, with the expectation of a shot being fired at any moment. The open ground was too broad to cross at once, so Andre ducked into the barn. He intended to go through and out the other side, using it as cover to regain the woods beyond.

He was met in the cool, dusty darkness with a bayonet presented at his throat. A voice from the shadows demanded in French that he raise his hands. Andre complied, and as his eyes grew accustomed to the dim light, he saw the nature of his captors. They were a ragtag band of ten or twelve men, mostly French army deserters with a couple Belgian soldiers as well.

The leader demanded to know if Andre had come to arrest them. "By myself? Don't be an idiot," Andre replied. "There is a German patrol after me. If you know what is good for you, you will get out of here fast!"

The chief of the deserters laughed at the comment. "There are no Germans within twenty miles of here," he scoffed.

"Suit yourself," Andre said coolly, "but at least let me go, then."

"Maybe he is telling the truth," one of the Belgians observed. "Look at the mud and the thorns in his uniform."

The leader grudgingly admitted that it was unlikely for a colonel to cover himself with dirt just to make a convincing story.

"If you are going to force me to stay here, give me a gun to fight with!" Andre demanded.

More scornful laughter was interrupted by a call from the lookout in the hayloft. "Some more men emerging from the woods," he said, "and they are wearing black uniforms."

The deserters rushed to every crack in the rough boards of the front wall. Unseen by any of them, Andre pushed out a loose plank at the back of the barn. He crouched beside the wall, examining the distance to the cover of the trees. It was too far and the Germans were already too close. The only shelter possible was the haystack. Andre flung himself across the intervening space, hoping that his rush had not been seen. He burrowed into the mound of moldy straw.

A shot was fired by the sniper upstairs in the barn. A German soldier fell, and replying machine gun fire raked the front of the barn. The men inside fired back, a sporadic popping noise compared to the chatter of the MG 34's.

Andre steadily wormed his way deeper and deeper into the pile of hay. Even so, he could hear the shouts of the Germans as they encircled the barn. A fusillade of bullets soon poured into the farm building from three sides. The thin, flimsy panels were no protection for the deserters inside. Andre heard the cries as men were wounded. The feeble rifle bursts coming from the barn were reduced to fewer and fewer returns of the German fire. Finally, they stopped all together.

Andre could hear the poilus shouting for the Germans to stop shooting and they would surrender. The deserters were ordered to come outside and line up along the front wall.

The German officer in charge was obviously disappointed by their catch. He brusquely demanded to know if anyone remained in the barn. Only three dead men and two more too badly wounded to walk out, he was told. The structure was searched and the truth of the statement verified.

The SS commander ordered the prisoners to return to the barn. "You will be kept here," he said, "until arrangements can be made to transport you."

As the last French soldier was herded back into the barn, he turned to ask how soon assistance would be brought for a wounded friend.

"Here is all the assistance you need," yelled the officer.

A French voice screamed the word *grenade!* and blasts of German machine guns began again. The grenade exploded with a roar, and new screams erupted from the barn. Andre heard a window crash as someone tried to escape, and he heard the shriek as the attempt was met by a rifle bullet in the face. The SS troops surrounding the farm building took turns tossing in grenades. They laughed at the frantic efforts of the men trapped inside.

As the explosions died away at last, Andre heard the SS officer say, "Burn it!" There was a terrifying rush of footsteps as the Germans scooped up armloads of straw to dump inside the barn.

The amount of cover on top of Andre decreased. He was afraid to move, fearing that the least squirm would be visible from above. A fragment of hay slid down from his head, and Andre could see out! The toe of one of his boots protruded from the pile. Surely one of the Germans would see it! A black uniformed figure bent over the straw to gather another sheaf. "That is enough," Andre heard the officer say. "Light it and let's get out of here."

For a reason Andre was never able to decipher, the SS troops did not set fire to the haystack too. Perhaps their only thought was to cover up the evidence of their actions. He waited until the barn was a roaring mass of flames, then emerged on the far side of his hiding place. Andre ran into the woods, completely unharmed.

⚜ ⚜ ⚜

Sometime after midnight there was a lull in the shelling around the BEF Casualty Clearing Station at the École de Cavalerie. It was the absence of explosions that awakened David Meyer from a shallow and troubled sleep beneath the table in the foyer of the church. Now the stillness of the night exposed the agonized pleas of the wounded.

Above him came the urgent voices of a man and woman. "Miss Mitchell, the Belgian King Leopold capitulated to the Nazis an hour ago. It is only a matter of time before they move to encircle us here."

"We can't leave our patients."

"You must! Miss Mitchell! There is still time for you to pull your nurses back . . . the coast . . ."

"What about our wounded?" Her voice trembled with the horror of leaving over one thousand wounded soldiers to the Germans.

"We will take all we can! The rest we must leave to German mercy."

"There is no mercy in the Germans, Major!" Her voice choked.

"Then we must leave them to the mercy of God!"

"I can't desert them . . ."

With a groan of agony, David slid out from under the table at the feet of the nurse and the BEF officer.

"I've gotta get out of here," he gasped.

The nurse blinked dumbly at him. "An American? What are you doing under there?" Her eyes flitted to his swollen arm and rigid, purple fingers.

"I stopped to get this splinter out of my arm," David grimaced. "No time for that now."

Miss Mitchell reached down to help him to his feet. "At least you can walk."

The foyer, the nurse, and the officer swam before his eyes. He felt his knees buckle as the dull complaint in his arm changed to a scream.

"You won't get a mile unless we see to that thing," she clucked her tongue. "Nasty." She touched his index finger and he choked off a cry. "Your fingers look like cow teats with a bad case of mastitis."

This was the boss lady, David guessed. He nodded his head in a jerky motion as nausea knotted his gut again. "Cow . . . Yeah. Swell."

"Swollen all right. Quite."

Ten minutes later, the sleeve of his uniform cut away, David lay on a table in a side chapel of the sanctuary. The walls were lined with memorial tablets to honor the dead of the last war who had been trained here at École de Cavalerie. The floor was littered with the wounded of the new generation of an old battle. What would their fate be with the Luftwaffe sinking British hospital ships at Dunkirk? David looked over the carpet of wounded as though they already lay beneath a garden of white crosses. Young men, like him; they had fought, been wounded, received care, and now what did any of that mean to them? They were as dead as if they had been left to bleed to death on the field of battle. Dead men. Boys who had not even begun to live. Back home their mothers watched for ships streaming back to England and prayed their sons were on those ships. Young women like his Annie waited for word and hoped that the names of the men they loved would not be on the lists of dead, wounded, or missing. And what about the troops assembled on the beaches of Dunkirk? They looked over their shoulders and wondered about the comrades they left behind. They looked ahead at the glassy sea and wondered if they would reach the shores of home again. They looked up through the smoke over Dunkirk as the Messerschmidts strafed them on the sand and in the water . . . But at least they had hope. There was no hope for the men left behind in Number 10 CCS at École de Cavalerie on the River Lys. Smack between Dunkirk and the German Panzers, the school would be overrun and the river crossed in the German drive to the coast.

Miss Mitchell still clucked at the enormity of the sliver of shrapnel. "Not too deep though. You're lucky. This will hurt a bit." Chatting cheerfully in an attempt to keep his mind off the pain, she grasped the exposed end of the six inch metal splinter and pulled. It seemed to grind against his bones as she jerked it loose.

The room swam around David. She happily held up the splinter, then tossed it into a metal bowl. David groped for the bowl and threw up for what he hoped was the last time.

"It didn't hurt that bad going in," he gasped.

With a touch of her finger she pushed him back on the table and poured iodine onto the wound.

"An American RAF pilot. My heavens. Thank God we have you. Well, you've done your best. Most important thing now is that you get yourself back across the Channel. Back to Britain. Fly against the Hun again. You'll need to have this X-rayed when you get back. Make sure we haven't left anything in there. Our chaps will fix this properly for you when you get across. Eighty percent of all the wounds we treat are from shrapnel, yours no worse than most. This will do for now. The pain would have knocked you out if we hadn't removed it. What's your name?"

"David Meyer . . . Tinman they call me," he replied through clenched teeth as she wrapped the arm in gauze.

"Tinman is it? Lots of our lads stop in here every hour asking the way to the coast. You can hook up with one of the lot and off you go! To Dunkirk."

Then, from a shadow beneath a Gothic stone pillar, came a muffled cry. "Tinman! Is that you, Tinman?" A figure with hands, arms, and head swathed in bandages sat bolt upright on a canvas cot. He looked something like a mummy sprung to life. "Tinman! Is it you? It's me! It's your old friend, Badger Cross! Am I ever glad you've come along!" Then the explosive joy of Badger crumbled into desperation. He stretched his gauze-mittened arms out in the general direction of David and Miss Mitchell. "Take me with you, Tinman! Get me out of this stinking hell! Please, old chap! I can't see . . . but I can walk. Walk me back across the Channel, will you? Point the way, I'll walk on the water, like Saint Peter! No hard feelings, Yank! Just don't leave me here to the Nazis!"

✳   ✳   ✳

After spending all night in the woods and catching a fitful hour's sleep in the trunk of a hollow tree, Andre emerged into the morning light of the twenty-eighth of May. A small village lay in a fold of the hills just ahead. The smoke from the chimneys curled lazily into the sky. There was no activity in the town and no guards patrolled the streets, but he still crept cautiously along a hedge-line between a dairy and a blacksmith shop. Since he had been lost before the encounter with the SS, and his evasive maneuvers had taken him several different directions, he now had no idea which side of the front line he was on.

A road sign near the edge of town gave directions in two languages. *Ypres* it said, and below that, *Yperen.* That the city was identified in two languages meant that he was in Belgium; from the distance given to what was still an Allied-held strongpoint, everything seemed to suggest that it was safe to show himself.

Andre went to the door of the house in front of the dairy. He had only a few coins in his pocket, but perhaps it would be enough to buy some milk. He had eaten nothing since noon the day before and he was famished.

Knocking twice on the door, he waited a long time before anyone answered. The woman who finally came to see what was wanted looked at his stubbled, dirty face and his torn and stained uniform and screamed. There was a commotion in the back of the house, and a man emerged holding an antique fowling piece. He presented it in Andre's face and demanded that he clear off; leave at once. "We want none of your kind around here," he said.

"My kind?" Andre repeated blankly. Then remembering the way he looked he explained. "I am not a deserter. I had a brush with the Boche and escaped. Where is the local commander? He needs to know . . ."

"Get off with you, I said, before I shoot!"

Andre could not believe his ears. "I just want to buy some milk."

"I said *go!*" the man announced with finality. He cocked the shotgun with a serious air.

Andre raised his hands in submission and walked backwards away from the house. He thought that the man must be crazy. Perhaps the town had been vandalized by deserters and Andre's appearance was too suspicious.

As he reached the main street of the village, the church bell began to ring. It pealed over and over again in a joyous, swelling sound. The doors of the houses flung open and people suddenly appeared where none had been before. They were all smiling and talking in excited tones.

A group of Belgian soldiers appeared on the corner just ahead. They had no helmets or weapons and their tunics were undone. They were laughing as they talked and smoked, and regarded Andre curiously when he approached.

"What is happening?" he asked.

"Have you not heard?" a young, almost beardless private said. "The war is over! It was just on the radio. The war is over!"

"The war is . . . ?" Andre was incredulous. Had he somehow slept more than one night, like a figure in a fairy tale . . . or was he not awake and this was a dream? "The war is over?" he said again.

"Yes, man," repeated the private, laughing. "King Leopold was just on the radio. You can believe it. The war is over!"

"But how? Why?"

A flicker of movement caught Andre's eye from the second story of the house on the corner. A heavyset woman was vigorously waving a white sheet as if airing the bed linen. But then she hung it over the railing and pinned it in place.

Suddenly Andre understood. "Belgium has surrendered," he groaned.

"Sure," the private agreed, looking at Andre as if he were an escapee from a mental hospital. "That is what we said, the war is over."

"Not for me," Andre said wearily. "Not for me."

SIXTY-SEVEN

The sudden and unexpected capitulation of the Belgians created a massive immediate problem for the French and British soldiers in the evacuation corridor. Twenty miles of front from Ypres to the sea, supposedly guarded by the Belgian forces, were now unprotected. It was a gap through which all of Wehrmacht Army Group B could have swept unopposed. If it were not for Lord Gort's willful disobedience, if he had not sent British troops north, in direct contradiction of his instructions, the evacuation would have been crushed.

As it was, General Bernard Montgomery's Third Division stepped smartly into the hole left by the Belgians and took over the guard duties. They made the remarkable maneuver in one night, before the Wehrmacht had time to exploit the opening.

When Andre arrived at Ypres, he found out that General Gort had moved his headquarters from Premesques to Houtkerque. The new command post was out of Belgium and back in French territory. Significantly, it was only a dozen miles from the Channel.

Andre caught a ride with some British artillery forces being withdrawn toward Dunkirk. When he came upon them they were completing a sad, but very necessary project: destroying their equipment. Cannons were packed with explosives and their barrels destroyed. Papers, money, uniforms, and supplies were heaped up and set ablaze with gasoline.

The trucks needed for the withdrawal were loaded with men and lined up for the move. All the other vehicles, like those that had towed the heavy artillery, were drained of oil and water and then left running. It was a strange, weirdly pathetic scene. The great machines shuddered and shook, like the dying convulsions of faithful elephants.

Halfway between Ypres and Noordschote, the column ran into a German tank that emerged without warning from a side road. It struck the center of the convoy, blasting a lorry loaded with men into a flaming heap of rubble.

The front half of the column roared away, leaving the following line of vehicles trapped by the burning debris on a road too narrow to quickly turn around. The soldiers jumped out of the canvas-covered transports and took cover in the ditches as machine gun fire sprayed the bushes.

Once again Andre found himself burying his face in a muddy drainage ditch. The British Tommies had almost no weapons with which to fight back. The rifle fire they used to defend themselves did nothing but bounce off. The PzKw II rolled forward, shoving the burning hulk of the truck out of its way, then pivoted sharply and moved again toward the line of men cowering in the ditch.

Every time its main gun fired, a 20mm shell spelled the end of another truck or troop lorry. Soldiers near Andre, seeing no escape from being crushed by the oncoming tank, jumped up and tried to run into the woods. Every time they did so, the probing fire of the machine gun sought them out and cut them down.

On the other side of the road from Andre, a soldier had somehow located a Boyes anti-tank rifle. This shoulder-fired weapon propelled a shell supposedly capable of penetrating tank armor. As the machine gun mowed down those in front of it, the Tommy with the Boyes rifle popped out. He threw the weapon up and loosed three rounds in quick succession. The impact of the recoil knocked the soldier down, and he lay against the trunk of a tree groaning with the pain of a dislocated shoulder.

But at least one bullet had penetrated a thinner part of the armor. It must have killed or wounded the drive, because the tank's engine gave a bellow like an outraged bull, and it slewed sideways in the roadway.

Next to Andre another panicked soldier jumped to his feet and attempted to run. Even though the PzKw II was temporarily incapacitated, its machine gun was still active. The man had only taken two steps when his body was almost cut in two and he toppled across Andre's legs.

Pushing the weight of the dead man off his knees, Andre's hand came in contact with a heavy pouch that had fallen from the Tommy's shoulder. It was a sack full of grenades.

The tank sat idle in the middle of the road, its engine rumbling. No one moved in the ditches any more and the German machine seemed to be searching for its next victim.

Fifty yards down the road a British truck, mistaking the inactivity for opportunity, roared backwards out of the ditch. The driver frantically whipped it back and forth across the pavement, attempting to turn around and escape.

The slumbering tank snorted and lumbered forward, its snout pivoting to bring the guns to bear. Laying absolutely still as the tank passed, Andre hugged the sack and steeled himself for what he had to do next. At the moment that he was even with its treads, he ripped open the pouch of grenades and began pulling the pins. Two at a time, he yanked the safety rings free until eight live explosives hissed in the bag.

Andre sprinted across the road behind the tank. He threw the pouch as hard as he could underneath the center of the PzKw II, between its treads. Flinging himself over the shoulder of the road, Andre rolled into the ditch. All the time, as the seconds were ticking past, he wondered if the tank would be clear of the pouch before it exploded.

Someone inside the PzKw II must have spotted Andre's dash. The tank turned abruptly, its left tread stopping as the right side clanked ahead.

It was in this position when the grenades exploded. There was a muffled roar that seemed to swell in volume like a peal of thunder heard at first far away then growing as it rolls over the land. Even in its death, the German tank was a lethal weapon. Steel shards, fragments of its corpse, whizzed off into the woods. Several more British soldiers who were unwary enough to watch the explosion tear the machine to pieces were impaled with fragments of its armor. Andre lay curled into as tiny a space as he could manage until the last chunk of metal and detonating shell had whined by.

❧   ❧   ❧

The glorious heroes of France stared down from their portraits at the last gathering of the students of the École de Cavalerie. Even though Paul had not mentioned his purpose in calling the meeting, it was widely known that the subject would be the evacuation of the school.

The hall was occupied by the remaining five hundred cadets of ages sixteen and seventeen. Each was dressed in his finest black dress uniform, as though going to a contest for the pride of the institution.

"Cadet officers," Paul began, "I congratulate you. You have acquitted yourselves with honor as befits the inheritors of the finest traditions of the school and la belle Francais. You have done all that was asked of you and more. The defense of Lys is in hand, ready to be turned over to your successors. The trucks for the evac . . ."

Paul had not expected to be interrupted, and the figure of Sepp, rising politely to stand at attention caught him by surprise.

Sepp took advantage of the silence to ask a question. "Your pardon, Captain, but how many troops are coming to occupy the positions?"

"I have been informed that elements of the First and Third Cavalry as well as a contingent of British . . ."

"Excuse me again, Captain, but will the number reach the fifteen thousand which you yourself indicated are required for adequately meeting the German advance?"

Paul knew that he had been set up. The cadets had planned to use his own words against him, and now they had sprung the trap.

"If you are ordered to leave, you must obey," he said.

Raymond rose to stand beside his friend. "If so ordered, we will obey," he said. "But if thereafter we choose to return and fight beside the others for the preservation of the school, the wounded, and our dignity, is that not our right as free French men?"

Gaston stood to speak. Less sure of himself than the others in front of a large crowd, he nevertheless had practiced his speech beforehand and delivered it boldly. "May I remind the captain," he said, "of the example of the cadets of St. Cyr in the Great War. When one of them said to his commander, 'You are sending me out to die,' the reply was, 'I do you that honor, sir.' Captain, how have we offended you that you would deny us that honor?"

Paul felt a tear start in the corner of his eye and his throat constricted. "It must be understood that no one is compelled to stay," he said, "and no shame attaches to leaving."

The cadets all stood as one and faced him. Paul's voice choked off, and he could say no more. "Captain," Sepp concluded for him, "what can be better for a soldier of France than to live honorably, die gloriously, and to be remembered as faithful to the end?"

Paul could do no more than nod, twin rows of tears staining his cheeks. But that motion of acquiescence was enough to set off thunderous applause and shouts of triumph.

Gaston turned toward his friends, straightening his collar and tugging at his spotlessly white gloves. "What a handsome corpse I will make, mes amis."

❋　❋　❋

"It has always been understood that British forces would be evacuated by British ships and French troops by French ships," Lord Gort pointed out at his early morning meeting with Andre. The general was snipping the ribbons and medals from his spare uniform.

"That may have been the understanding, sir," Andre replied, "but it is not working. Most of the French Navy is in the Mediterranean. The trawlers available are wholly inadequate to the task. How else do you account for the fact that close to fifty thousand British soldiers have been evacuated so far and only five hundred French?"

"Six hundred fifty," replied Gort peevishly. "Why bother *me* with this anyway, Chardon? You should take the matter up with Captain Tennant in Naval Operations, or with my replacement, General Alexander." Gort continued removing any marks of distinction to keep some German soldier from claiming them as souvenirs.

"Sir," Andre said slowly, trying to keep his rising anger from coming through in his voice. "To them I am no more than another French soldier and none of their concern. If you, however, could raise the issue with your Admiralty . . ."

"All right, yes," Gort waved his hand in dismissal. "But my primary remaining task is to see to the defense of the perimeter. If the rear guard is not effective, none of us will be getting off." It was clear from Gort's tone that the discussion was at an end.

"In that case, sir, I request that I be allowed to pursue the matter as your personal representative, beginning with my study of the activities at the harbor."

Gort nodded curtly, anxious to put the matter behind him. "But Chardon," he said, "whatever you do, you must be ready to leave by midnight tomorrow night, if you expect to evacuate with my staff."

"General," Andre replied quietly. "If my countrymen are not provided for by tomorrow night, I will not be going with you."

❧ ❧ ❧

"What day is it, Tinman?" Badger Cross walked with his head thrown back like a child trying to see through a blindfold in a game of blindman's bluff. He grasped David's good arm with one hand. His other hand extended in front of him.

"It's May twenty-ninth, I think," David replied, attempting to reconstruct the events of the last twenty-four hours. By now what was left of his squadron would be back in England. His mind leapt to thoughts of Annie. He wanted to see her again.

Badger muttered, "If it's the twenty-ninth . . . it's almost my birthday. I would be twenty-one, if it was my birthday."

"You'll still be twenty-one, Badger."

"Where are we now, Tinman?"

"Same place we were last time you asked. On the road to Dunkirk with about a million other guys," David replied. "Don't worry about it."

"You know, every year on my birthday . . . at home, I mean . . . since I was a lad, my mother always fixed me strawberries and cream with tea. Sort of a tradition. Lovely it was."

"You never seemed the strawberries and cream type of guy, Badger," David retorted.

But with every mile Badger had become more and more strawberries and cream. Nostalgia for the simple luxuries of everyday life occupied his conversation in unending monotony. The long column of retreating men had

already been strafed twice in four hours. Badger talked as though everything in his life was past tense; already over . . . melancholy drivel for somebody as tough and mean as Badger Cross.

At the sound of an airplane, Cross craned his bandaged head back as if trying to see through the layers of gauze. "What's that?" he demanded. "Ours or theirs?"

This question was important. David searched the sky for the source of the noise. When he spotted the lone black dot high overhead, the answer was clear.

"Dive-bomber!" he yelled. "Clear the road!"

Even though the open ditches that lined both sides of the highway offered no real protection, a thousand men forced their way into the shallow depressions. Those who arrived first were either shoved out of the way, or buried under a pile of bodies seeking to fill the same tiny space. Latecomers burrowed inside the heap, or were roughly pushed away to become tangled in the thorny hedges that bordered the road.

With both hands clamped on David's good arm, Cross stumbled toward the grassy verge. The Stuka was already beginning its run. "Make room!" David shouted. "Blind man! Make way!" His wounded arm was painfully jostled. He made no progress trying to protect it and forced a path while Badger clung to his other arm.

As if sensing the difficulty, Badger lunged past David. Elbows swinging wildly, Cross collided with two soldiers of the Royal West Kent regiment, splitting them like an unstoppable rugby player en route to a goal. "Here, Tinman," he bellowed. "This is our space!"

At the Stuka's scream, terrified men buried faces in the dirt and clamped steel helmets down over their ears. A few raised .303 rifles and fired at the swooping form, as much in defiance as with any real hope of damaging it. At two thousand feet, five objects detached from its undercarriage and the warplane pulled out of its dive.

Bombs whistled downward; a thin, high-pitched replacement for the Stuka's siren. In rapid succession, explosions shook the roadway, blowing large craters in the pavement and spinning out lethal shrapnel fragments. Those nearest the blasts were tossed around like leaves in a windstorm. Hastily abandoned gear flew skyward; packs and canteens sailed into the air. A soldier next to David was struck by a mess kit. He screamed, "I'm hit! I'm hit!"

The plane retreated. Ten men lay dead. A dozen were maimed from two bombs that had landed on the road. Two of the dead stood frozen in upright poses in the thorn bushes. Six of the wounded bled from jagged wounds. Two had lost limbs. These were as good as dead, David knew.

For the rest, most of the injuries were slight. The soldier hit by the tin pan was heartily insulted for his mistake. There was an outpouring of abuse born out of helpless terror. It was as though by making that one man the target of scorn and ridicule, the others could somehow remove the stink of fear from themselves.

Gradually, in jerky movements, as if the column were a single animal stretching and testing itself for injury, the soldiers got up from the ditch. David stood, helped Badger to his feet and pointed him back toward the highway. An infantryman looked at the RAF insignia with disdain.

"Air Force?" he sneered. "What good are you, lousy fly boys? Why do you let that happen?" He pointed to a chaplain administering last rites to a man whose life was pumping out of a ragged hole in his neck.

"Nothing but Nazi planes for days," another chimed in. "Get on, be off with you, worthless . . ."

Badger swung a clumsy right in the direction of the speaker. His gauzed fist connected only with air, and he sprawled awkwardly.

"Leave it," David said to Cross. "Come on, we can get moving again."

"Stinkin' RAF," the call came after them. "A blind man and a busted wing. Good riddance!"

SIXTY-EIGHT

The port of Dunkirk was a mass of ruins: sunken ships, burning warehouses, and the eerie remnants of cargo cranes. The twisted frames of the lifting scaffolds leaned over the waterways like ancient, tired gallows. In short, the inner harbor was unusable for the evacuation. Ships entering were likely to run afoul of submerged wreckage if they were not themselves trapped in its winding leads and bombed.

As early as the twenty-seventh of May, Senior Naval Officer William Tennant concluded that using the inner port was impossible. He also knew that the operation from the beaches east of Dunkirk was too slow. The good news was what he discovered about the two breakwaters that formed the entrance to Dunkirk harbor: two ranks of concrete pilings jutted over a thousand yards out into the Channel and were virtually untouched. Commander J. C. Clouston, piermaster of Dunkirk Harbor, was assigned to make the most of the opportunity provided by the jetties.

When Andre joined Clouston at the eastern mole on the morning of May 30, the evacuation was proceeding better than anyone had hoped. As Andre watched, soldiers marched four abreast along the wooden walkway that topped the breakwater. With the tide in, climbing onto the destroyer *Sabre,* moored to wooden posts alongside the jetty, was a speedy proposition. The heavy, overcast day provided relief from Luftwaffe attacks, and the Tommies embarked as cheerfully as if they were taking a holiday ferry to the Isle of Wight.

In less than an hour's time, *Sabre* loaded five hundred men and pulled smartly away from the mole, bound for Dover. A minesweeper slipped in to take its place and the smooth operation continued. There was just one problem gnawing at Andre: few of the departing troops were French.

"Why aren't more French queued up to leave?" he demanded.

"A lot of reasons," Clouston replied. "Language problems, mostly. The poilus don't understand when told to leave their kit behind, and they don't like it when we break up their units."

It sounded to Andre like an excuse. "Don't you have anyone to interpret for you?"

"Lieutenant Solomon speaks excellent French, but he can't be everywhere at once." Another excuse, but this one could be dealt with.

"Will you let me help?"

"Certainly."

Most of the English officers handling the embarkation had only a limited knowledge of French. Shouting "Allez, allez!" at the poilus produced only contemptuous sneers. But while Andre was able to assist a few of his fellow soldiers, his sense of frustration grew even greater. The real reason no French were being embarked was that there were none in line. The queue that stretched down the length of the breakwater and back into the smoke-filled streets was packed with English soldiers. If French troops joined the end of the line they were roughly pushed aside or told to leave the harbor and go to the beaches. Clearly there was nothing Andre could do as one lone voice in the face of this "English ships for Englishmen" attitude.

From where the unending line of British soldiers tramped down the narrow plank walkway and onto the waiting boats, Andre could look across the mouth of the harbor entrance. There, no more than a quarter mile away was the similar, but unoccupied western mole.

Andre studied the ships tied up at the breakwater. There were three destroyers, two ferryboats, and a dozen smaller craft, all loading at once. But for all the activity, another half dozen boats waited off the jetty for their turn.

Andre approached Clouston with his idea. "Why can't we use the western mole as well and send the French troops over there?"

"No reason at all, except that all the waiting ships think they are to come here."

"Can I use your authority to make them change destinations?"

Clouston laughed. "My authority? You can try. Here, take my pistol . . . it may carry more weight. But, Chardon," he added in a more serious tone, "don't tell anyone I said that, all right?"

Andre located a colonel of the French First Army and told him about the new plan. The officer agreed to round up as many poilus as he could and direct them to the western mole.

Now to find a boat. Andre caught a ride with a motor launch out to the *Bristol Belle,* a hundred-foot-long steamer lying offshore. The ship was practically an antique, a twenty-year-old sidewheeler with a shallow draft and a single stack amidships. She was a jumble of odd angles and curious projections: a jutting narrow prow whose sleek line disintegrated where the great round bulges of the paddlewheel guards stuck out. A canvas-covered flybridge was suspended above her foredeck, looking like a blind duck that had run away to sea.

Andre jumped from the motor launch to a narrow walk that encircled the girth of the starboard wheel. There was no ladder, but by putting one foot on a window ledge he boosted himself up to the rail on the open top deck and clambered over. The *Belle* idled slowly, waiting her turn at the mole. The twin lines that swept up to a single mast on her foredeck were still hung with pennants and signal flags from her last duty before Dunkirk: pleasure boat excursions on the Thames.

Andre found the captain, an anxious-looking man named Pert, nervously pacing the flybridge. "Absolutely not!" Pert insisted. "It's bad enough waiting here. We could be bombed any second. The *Belle* was never made for work like this. Besides, the western approach is in range of those German guns between Dunkirk and Gravelines. I won't chance it, no matter who you say authorized it."

Andre considered taking a launch to another of the transport ships in the hopes of finding a more receptive welcome, but his anger flared at the waste of time. Whipping out the pistol, he snarled, "All right, here is your choice: Either take this ship to the western jetty and risk the guns of the Germans, or be on the receiving end of one Frenchman's gun right now!"

"You can't mean it!" said Pert, backing up against a bulkhead.

"Try me!"

"What's this, Cap'n?" called the *Belle*'s mate. "What's up, then?"

"Do whatever he says!" ordered Pert in a squeaky voice. "He's a crazy man!"

The *Bristol Belle* reversed course, heading out to sea and rounding the harbor entrance to the west. Captain Pert's anxious glances alternated between his navigation, the western horizon where the German artillery lay, and the .38 caliber Webley revolver in Andre's hand.

By the time the *Belle* had steamed around to the other breakwater, a line of men from Blanchard's First Army stretched down its length. They made the *Belle* fast to the pilings and began an orderly filling of all the available space. Andre noticed with satisfaction that when given the opportunity, and orders in their own language, the poilus were as manageable as the Tommies.

Many of the embarking troops paused beside Captain Pert as they passed down the gangplank. Snatching off their helmets, they shook Pert's hand and fervently proclaimed, "Merci! Merci! Que le bon Dieu vous benisse!"

Even the heart of the apprehensive captain was touched. Five hundred men crammed aboard her upper and lower decks and even the iron railings were crowded with perched poilus. Pert looked at the bleak faces of the men left standing on the quay and muttered, "Tell 'em we'll be back, soon as we can." When Andre had repeated this assurance, Pert ordered the hands to cast off and the steamer put about for Dover. " 'Spose you'll make the crossing with this lot," the captain said.

Andre shook his head. "Take me alongside her," he said, pointing to the low form of the opendecked river steamer *Princess Louise*, steaming in lazy circles off the tip of the estuary.

"Make sure you keep your pistol handy," whispered Pert as Andre prepared to leap to the *Princess*, "I know her master. He's a mean 'un."

❊　❊　❊

The knifeblade of *Intrepid*'s bow sliced through the waves toward Dunkirk. She was on her third crossing of the Channel on the twenty-ninth of May. Each load of weary soldiers picked off the eastern mole filled her to capacity with eight hundred members of the BEF spared from the crushing embrace of the Wehrmacht. *Intrepid* was so good at her job that she could unload in Dover in half an hour.

The morning had been cloudy and the sky sheltering from Luftwaffe attacks. But now, after noon, the overcast was burning off and bright blue peeped through.

Trevor Galway was on the bridge beside Captain Collins. Officially second in command, Trevor was actually functioning as an extra lookout. His binoculars scanned the sea for submarines and mines and, increasingly now, had to inspect the sky for planes as well.

Picking out a black dot dancing on the waves, Trevor inspected it, then pointed it out to Collins. "Small boat about a mile distant, sir," he reported. "It appears that it is being rowed."

Intrepid altered course slightly to intercept the route of the sighted craft. Trevor went down to the rail to oversee the loading. Once alongside, twelve soldiers of the Devon Heavy Regiment who were paddling a lifeboat with the butts of their rifles were plucked from the water.

Their sergeant, a portly man named Clifford, protested when he was informed that the rescue vessel would be going to Dunkirk to embark another load before returning to England. "Why didn't you just pick us up goin' the other way?" he asked. "We don't want to go back; it's 'orrible there!"

"Orders," Trevor explained. "When we are loaded, we don't halt to take anybody else, in case we get attacked while we're stopped."

"In that case," Sergeant Clifford blustered. "Put us off again! We'll just keep rowing ourselves. We was makin' it alright!"

"I don't think you want us to do that," Trevor said.

"And why not?"

"Because you were rowing toward Calais when we found you, and it's already in German hands."

✤ ✤ ✤

Mac climbed the flight of narrow concrete stairs that led up from the Embankment toward the Savoy Hotel. Just at the corner, where the steep alleyway met the Strand, was a public house called the Coal Bin.

It was a two-story establishment. Upstairs, in a room of round tables, gathered the office workers and clerks in their starched shirts and ties.

Downstairs, a dark, snug chamber of exposed beams and wooden stools, was the retreat of the men with blue sleeves rolled up above mammoth forearms. It was to the lower compact space that Mac directed his steps.

John Galway was standing under the grimy bowl of a wall lamp. He had a pint of Guinness in one fist and with the other was driving home a point. "I tell ye, the Italians are just waiting to stab France in the back. Mark me words," he said, sloshing dark brown fluid over his listener as he gestured with the wrong hand. "If they think they can do it without risk, those *fascisti* and their goggle-eyed, lantern-jawed toad of a leader will be over the Brenner Pass quick as you can say Musselleeeni."

Mac grinned. "The Duce says 'Italian honor is not for sale . . . ask me about a lease!' Talking politics again, Mister Galway? I thought Annie said it was bad for your blood pressure."

"Ah, McGrath. Right you are, but a pint is a sovereign remedy to keep things level," Galway observed. "Join me?"

Mac and John Galway were soon in a corner of the Coal Bin, each with a fresh pint in hand. "What do you hear from Trevor?" Mac asked.

"Not much. *Intrepid* has been on convoy duty. I did get a curious call from him last evening from Portsmouth."

"Curious how?"

"Couldn't say much on it, but he told me, 'Da, something is brewing. Don't be surprised if you don't hear from me for awhile.' Then he rang off."

Mac pondered Trevor's words for a time. "What do you think it means?"

Galway leaned close to Mac, though there were no nearby drinkers. "I think it ties up with a uniformed bloke who came around *Wairakei* this morning. Said he was from the Small Vessel Authority, or some such."

"What did he want?"

"*Wairakei* is requisitioned. Wouldn't say what for, everyone so tight gobbed these days, but he said to get her down to Ramsgate by tomorrow. Fact is, I'm here, fortifying myself for the voyage, just before shoving off. Care to join us?"

"Us? Is Annie going too?"

"Aye, and the great Duff beast as well. Goin' up agin Ann when her mind is set . . ." Galway pretended to shudder. "I'd druther swim the Channel with both hands tied behind me back!"

❖   ❖   ❖

At three in the afternoon, the torrent of refugees pouring across the bridges into Lys slowed to a trickle. Gaston had been busy all morning directing traffic and gathering what information he could. He was told that the Germans were no more than ten miles away. They would reach the valley of the Lys by tonight.

At one point, an open-topped car loaded with men in French uniforms arrived at his checkpoint. Gaston demanded to see their papers. "Get out of our way, puppet" the fat, swarthy driver sneered. "Stay and play toy soldier if you want, but leave us alone!" The deserter revved up the engine of the vehicle as if to run Gaston down.

Gaston snapped his fingers. From behind the shelter of a pile of sandbags, the snout of an antitank gun rolled forward to poke through a gap in the barricade. It pointed straight at the grill of the truck. "Come ahead," Gaston said calmly.

The driver and the eight men stuffed in the seats lifted their hands into view. "I thought so," Gaston said, yanking open the door. He dragged the deserter out on the pavement by the scruff of his neck. "We shoot traitors here," he said. "Or perhaps you would like to volunteer to aid with the defenses?"

The men hastily nodded their willingness to be of service. "Excellent!" Gaston said. "Lieutenant Beaufort, escort these new recruits to Captain

Chardon. He has a number of empty sacks that need to be turned into sandbags!"

✣ ✣ ✣

The air of the meeting at French Admiral Abrial's headquarters was less than cordial; it was icy. The atmosphere was not helped by the surroundings: Bastion 32 was a windowless concrete bunker. Its chill walls dripped with condensed moisture. About half the time the power supply failed, leaving a candlelit interior that could have been a dungeon.

Acrimony was the order of the day. Despite Andre's efforts at commandeering ships to rescue French soldiers, it was still not close to adequate. And if the discrimination in the rescue effort was not bad enough, General Alexander, who was replacing Gort in command of British forces, indicated that the evacuation would end in the early morning of June 2, only seventy-two hours away.

The French officers, Admiral Abrial and General Fagalde, were aghast. "It will mean thousands of French soldiers abandoned to the Germans," Fagalde protested.

Alexander shrugged as if it were no concern of his. "There are French destroyers lifting French soldiers, are there not?" he said.

Abrial looked to a bone-weary Andre to answer the question. "The *Siroco* is still operating," Andre admitted. "But the *Bourrasque* hit a mine on her way to Dover. She's gone."

Alexander still looked as if the matter were no further concern of his. Abrial and Fagalde exchanged glances, each hoping that the other would have some persuasive argument to be used with the British.

Andre thought about his day's piracy and how effective his use of the pistol had been, though he had never been forced to fire it. Perhaps it was time for coercion on a grander scale. "Is it not true that all the defenses of Dunkirk are now manned by French troops?" he asked.

Fagalde, whose men had defended the line of the Aa canal, nodded. "It will be so after tonight," he said, "when General Laurencie's 32nd Infantry and the 68th division are all in place."

"And if they were to surrender to avoid needless bloodshed, what would that do to the remaining evacuation?"

Alexander sat bolt upright in his chair. "Extortion!" he shouted.

Abrial grinned at Andre and then coolly remarked to the British contingent, "Call it what you will, gentlemen. The fact remains that if from this moment forward French troops are not evacuated in equal number with English, and the evacuation extended as much as possible, we will be forced to seek the best terms we can from the Germans."

"All right," Alexander grudgingly acknowledged. "You have us over a barrel. We will allot future transportation fifty-fifty, to continue as long as possible. Provided," he verbally underlined, "provided the French perform the rear guard duty as planned."

❖   ❖   ❖

Gaston's lieutenant was out of breath when he arrived across the bridge to deliver his message. "Captain Gaston," he said, panting. "Tanks approach the far side of the river!" It was nearly dusk, and no further refugees had crossed the bridge in several hours.

Gaston and Sepp, who had been arguing over who owned the right to place the last of the school's machine guns, stared at each other and then ran over to the island.

Crouching behind the sandbag barricade, Gaston squinted through the narrow gap. Sure enough, two armored vehicles were driving along the riverbank, nearly to the junction with the road to Lys.

"Prepare to fire," Gaston said to the gun crew, even though he could see that the piece was already loaded and aimed at the center of the span. "Wait for my signal," he added.

The first of the machines hesitated at the crossing as if the driver suspected something amiss. The two vehicles circled the end of the structure like a pair of dogs sniffing out a scent. Then the lead machine turned onto the road and started across.

"Steady," Gaston cautioned, even though his own voice cracked as it had done when he was four years younger. "Wait until he gets halfway over."

"Gaston!" Paul Chardon's voice said sharply.

"Captain!" Sepp answered for his intense friend. "You are just in time to see us fire the first shot for the honor of the school!"

"Just in time to save you from a bad mistake," Paul said. "Did neither of you notice that the vehicle you are about to destroy is a Hotchkiss tank, and it is one of ours?"

Paul seized a tricolor flag and waved it over the barricade. A moment later, the hatch of the lead tank popped open. The tank commander waved back, then the two machines rumbled forward across the bridge.

SIXTY-NINE

It was quiet at Number 5 la Huchette tonight, too quiet. The tiny remnant had taken refuge behind the gate and slid the iron bolt in place. Yet still, Josie felt the approach of evil.

How to get out of Paris?

Rose believed in lists.

Seven Special Children: Five in wheelchairs, two on crutches. Five Austrian brothers. Jerome and Marie Jardin. Josephine, Lewinski, Juliette, and Yacov.

"And a partridge in a pear tree," Madame Rose said as she added her name to the column. She looked up at Josie, who sat in the dim glow of a single candle. "That makes nineteen of us altogether. Even two automobiles will not be enough. I can't drive anyway."

"Neither can Lewinski." Josie ran a hand over her aching head. Even if there were three vehicles, she was the only driver. A truck, perhaps? An unused troop lorry? Why not ask for the PanAm clipper or a zeppelin?

"What we need is a transportation prayer." Rose scratched possible modes of conveyance on the list to submit to God. She included everything from a troop lorry to an airplane. "The Lord approves of common sense," she said. "And when common sense fails, then there must be some other course for us to sail."

Hours on the telephone brought no answers. Everyone was leaving or already gone. If some acquaintance had a vehicle, it was already packed or there was no petrol to be had. Madame Rose prayed with the same fervent faith with which Sister Angeline had prayed in the cellar of St. John's in Warsaw that last night.

"We need a true miracle, Josephine." Her words were not fearful, but simply a statement of fact. "You know what will happen to the special children if the Nazis lay hold of them. Their fate will be the same as that of the Austrians—my little sons of Abraham. And your little ones as well. It is a fearful thing, this total war of Hitler's, what it does to children." She shook her head sadly. "They've made war on the apple of God's eye, my dear girl. Pity the German nation. They have made war on heaven, and heaven will not be silent forever."

But heaven was silent tonight, Josie thought glumly as she stood out beneath the star-flecked sky of the courtyard.

The children were asleep now in the corner room of the ground floor where beams and joists and supports were the strongest.

"Just in case . . ." Rose said.

The windows were open. The scent of flowers filled the air. Crickets chirped and the cicadas hummed. But there was no word from heaven.

Josie sat alone for a long time listening, hoping. Rose came out some time after midnight and sat beside her. They gazed up through the patterns of empty clotheslines for a long time without speaking.

And then, from the open window of the corner room a small voice piped, "Sacré bleu! It is the anteater!"

"Jerome," Rose shrugged. "Another nightmare." She got up to see to him.

Jerome croaked distinctly. "Hey, Henri! The Anteater! The siren! The *Garlic*! The *Garlic*! Henri, we have to tell Madame Rose!"

Josie smiled at the muddled nonsense of the dream. Other children moaned with irritation at being awakened.

Rose slipped in quietly. Her whisper drifted out through the open window.

"Jerome, mon petit pêche, you are dreaming again . . ."

The boy's reply boomed like he was shouting across a wide field. "Not a dream! I heard a voice in the siren, Madame Rose."

"There is no siren, Jerome. Very quiet tonight. Peaceful. You see!"

"Wake everyone up! We have to be ready! The siren will go and then we will leave!"

"No, no, Jerome. Only a dream, little one. You must go back to sleep. Shall I sing . . ."

"*Listen to me!* Madame Hilaire! The anteater! She sucked us out the window of the *Garlic*, but . . . she is afraid of the siren!"

"Je comprends, Jerome. But now . . ."

"Listen! When the siren goes it is the only sound Madame Hilaire can hear. She is frightened of it. She and the Thief run away to the shelter, because they are afraid of the bombs from the Boches that might drop on the *Garlic*. But there they stay all night and we all get on the *Garlic* and . . ."

"The boat. You mean . . . the boat? Who told you this?" The response of Rose was no longer patronizing, no longer soothing.

"Oui! Madame Rose! The Voice! I have heard it! We must get up now and be ready for the air raid siren!"

✳   ✳   ✳

Rose Smith was a sailor and the daughter of a sailor. How many times as a girl had she shoved off from the California Coast to sail to Pelican Cove for a picnic on Santa Cruz Island?

What was the wide and gentle river Seine compared to Pacific winds and channel currents and dolphins jumping in a bow wave?

It all made perfect sense, Rose said to Josie.

Of course God did not answer their transportation prayer with automobiles because there was only one driver. God did not send a zeppelin or the PanAm clipper because no one knew how to fly.

But Rose could handle a boat. It was a perfectly logical miracle. A miracle even though it was logical.

They were all ready when the air raid siren wailed into the blackness of the Paris night. The doors of the carriage gates swung back. Guided by the five brothers, Jerome, and a very intense little rat, the wheels of the chairs clattered over the cobblestones. Babies, bundles, little girls, and little boys hurried across the deserted Place St. Michel as the shrieking alert warned anyone left in Paris to get to cover.

Then the high, long whine stopped. There was a sudden and eerie silence as the nineteen souls in need of a miracle turned onto Quai des Grand Augustins. Footsteps and panting breath were loud in their ears as they rushed past the locked boxes of the bookseller's stalls. Only the stars illuminated the dark surface of the Seine. Paris seemed like a ghost town.

And then, in the distance, came the deep bass drone of the Dornier engines approaching from the east. Far beyond the heart of Paris searchlights popped on, throwing wide and beautiful beams of light skyward. Then the staccato cracking of antiaircraft fire joined this terrible and wonderful concerto. The whistle of bombs followed, then the drumroll of explosions as the Renault factory exploded to create a false dawn on the far horizon.

"Do not look back," Rose warned the troop. Heads snapped forward as if by looking they would turn to salt, like the wife of Lot fleeing the destruction of Sodom.

The statue of King Henri on Pont Neuf glowed hellish orange in reflected light. The surface of the Seine seemed to be on fire. The crack of antiaircraft guns rolled toward them. Great pillars of light swept above their heads and the crescendo of battle increased all around.

Steep stone steps led down to Quai de Conti where the *Garlic* was moored. With the help of the five brothers, Rose, Josie, and Lewinski carried the wheelchairs down one at a time as the air trembled and the sound of battle rolled over them like thunder. Marie guided Juliette down the hatch.

Jerome carried baby Yacov into the hold and deposited him inside a coil of thick rope. He wailed a protest, but he was safe unless the boat took a hit.

The Dorniers were directly overhead! Across the river a building on the Right Bank exploded in a geyser of flame and debris. Eardrums compressed painfully.

Jerome clambered belowdecks and cranked the engine. A true miracle! It started willingly. Taking the helm, Rose called for the lines to be cast off.

They had recaptured the *Garlic!*

Jerome, with Papillon on his shoulder, struck a Napoleonic pose at the bow as the peniche shuddered, coughed, and slipped away from the quay to glide away from the ancient stones of Pont Neuf!

❖ ❖ ❖

It took three tries for David Meyer and Badger Cross to actually enter the fortifications of Dunkirk after they reached the city. The first two approaches were heavily damaged by German bombs. The bridges were knocked out. Burning vehicles and the wreckage of earlier attacks blocked the highways.

In contrast to the unorganized, mob-like retreat toward the coast, the third entry appeared businesslike. Despite the brown haze and the spreading black cloud from the burning oil tanks, the entrance had an orderly, confident aspect. Miles of barbed wire ringed the perimeter and a pair of sandbagged machine gun nests flanked the gate.

But giving the lie to this stalwart bearing was a steady stream of civilians leaving the city against the flow of British soldiers. To David, the whole scene looked unreal, like the fragments of a symbolic but confusing dream. A military policeman stopped all newcoming groups and directed the senior officer of each footsore band to the building housing the embarkation officer.

When David and Badger reached the roadblock, the police sergeant looked them over and hummed to himself. "We have no regular RAF organization here," he said. "My advice to you is to ask embarkation if you can hook on to another regiment. Straight ahead, second left. Big brick building with a queue of men straight out the door, I should imagine. Good luck."

The line waiting for the officer in charge of the evacuation ran out halfway down the block. There was much shuffling in place and speculation about what was happening, but no real forward progress. It was like being back in school and being told to line up without being told why. After standing for two hours, David saw a major come out and walk down the row of men. Every dozen places he stopped and repeated the same message. "The embarkation officer cannot possibly get to you lot in the next four or five hours. I suggest that you stay close about this area, but come back this afternoon."

"What about rations? Medical care?" David asked.

The major shrugged. "Catch as catch can, I suppose. Off you go. Jerry has been pounding us pretty regular, so you don't want to be caught out in the street."

"Flaming army," Cross muttered as David led him away toward a hotel at the end of the block. "Exactly why I joined the air force!"

A portly Belgian man with a huge ring of keys stood outside an inn named the Pelican. Having located the one key he sought, he locked the front door and turned to leave. David stopped him. "Is it possible to get a meal, or a room, or both?" he asked.

The man shook his head with a chuckle, jingling the cluster of keys like sleighbells. Then he paused and, as if the absurdity of the request was too great to stand, guffawed. He laughed until tears came, then pulled a handkerchief out of his pocket to wipe his eyes. "There is no one left," he said. "The cook, the maids, the desk clerk. All have gone. And now I am leaving too."

"Can't we at least buy some food from you?"

The Pelican's proprietor gave a negative reply, then stopped and looked at the increasing number of soldiers wandering up and down the street. He turned and studied the glass panels of the door and laughed again. "What am I thinking?" he said, striking his forehead with his palm. "Go in, gentlemen, and thank you for your courtesy. Make free with what you find . . . better you than the Boche. *Bonne chance,"* he said, "good luck!" With that he unlocked the door again and rode off on a bicycle toward the highway.

❆　❆　❆

All through the morning, Andre worked at his improvised evacuation station on the western mole. The official change in British policy was not yet widely known, but even so, more ships were making their way to the line of French troops.

There were setbacks, of course. *Siroco,* a French destroyer, was packed with men and on course for Dover when she was torpedoed. She might have still survived to deliver her cargo of frightened men, but a passing German bomber finished her off.

It was nothing Andre could even think about. He steadied the stream moving down the plank walkway and waved the new steamers, ferries, trawlers, and passenger launches into position as each ship filled and moved away.

The tide was out, and at Dunkirk harbor, that meant a drop of fifteen feet. There were not enough ladders to accommodate the queue and keep the embarkation moving, so Andre walked halfway down the column and singled out a group of French infantrymen. "Take those axes," he said, pointing out a bin of firefighting equipment on the quay. "I want you to chop down every telegraph pole you can find in thirty minutes and bring them back here. Bring the wire too."

"What is in it for us?" a poilu grumbled.

"You will go to the head of the line," Andre promised.

Soon the west end of Dunkirk harbor rang with the sound of axes as if it were a lumber camp. As each pair of men returned with a pole, it was placed on the deck of a waiting ship. The top was secured to the pilings of the jetty with a loop of wire.

Beginning with the ax wielders, the row of evacuees moved twice as fast. The poilus slid down to the decks below, each taking a turn at the bottom steadying the device for the next man.

Andre heard a whistling noise and a fountain of water geysered up. There were still no planes overhead in the dark cloud mass. No Stukas screamed toward the docks, no Heinkels clustered to drop their payloads. What had caused the explosion?

It took a second blast that turned a wooden-hulled trawler into matchsticks before Andre figured it out: these were the incoming shells of the German artillery, just west of the city. The Wehrmacht advance had indeed crept close enough to bombard the harbor. The respite from attack was over.

"Hurry!" Andre demanded. "Move, move!"

Another shell hit the center of the causeway. Andre saw a dozen men shattered and flung into the water. A gap in the mole ten feet wide now opened on the swirling water.

Once again Andre organized a working party. "Bring back all the planks you can find. Drag them out of the rubble or chop them loose from buildings if you have to. Collect any doors you find also . . . anything to bridge the gap!"

Through the shelling the line kept inching forward. All the men realized that no safety would be found by turning back. The only hope lay in escaping from the punished ruins of Dunkirk altogether.

When the artillery barrage stopped after an hour, Andre found that he could continue directing traffic and still think about other things. It wasn't that good a discovery. He began to worry again about Juliette and Josie. And through the day, something nagged at the back of his mind.

Andre was relieved by the First Army colonel who had helped organize the withdrawal. "You have done a magnificent job, Chardon," he said. "Why the Boches gave us this chance, we may never know. Heaven help those on the receiving end of the Panzers now. I would rather be here than face what they are facing."

"What do you mean?"

"Have you not heard? Some of the Panzers have turned around after hammering Lille. They are now facing south, ready to invade the rest of France."

There it was, out in the open at last. Escaping from Dunkirk was not the final answer; the war still continued. Even if Andre lived to flee to England, his war was not done. The secret of Enigma was still vital; Lewinski had to be rescued before Paris was surrounded.

Andre would have to leave with General Gort, if only to return at once to Paris for a different sort of evacuation. The future of France might depend on it.

❧ ❧ ❧

The men boarding *Intrepid* along the Dunkirk jetty double-timed over the plank walkway and swung smartly aboard the destroyer. Trevor smiled as he supervised the loading; it was going so well that they might shave another thirty minutes off the next round trip.

It was almost time to cast off. Eight rows of men were crammed into the deck space between the rail and the ship's superstructure. Stained and bestubbled, they all still wore their helmets and sported smiles of relief.

Trevor signaled the bridge to get underway and the drum of *Intrepid*'s engines increased in pitch. The lines were dropped and the destroyer swung away from the mole.

Glancing around the deck, Trevor noted an exchange between the lookout from his perch on the funnel and the sailor manning the multibarreled Bofors gun just below. The lookout was pointing upward. A single twin-engined shape cruised slowly past, not attacking or hurrying, but loafing along as if on a tour of inspection. A reconnaissance mission, without a doubt. Trevor knew exactly what would get reported: "Weather clearing. Many men and ships concentrated along jetties. No enemy fighter opposition. Very little antiaircraft fire."

Silently, Trevor urged his ship to greater speed, to get clear of the mass of boats moving around the evacuation area, to get out where there was room to maneuver. But it was already too late. Winging in from half the points of the compass were wave after wave of German bombers, Dorniers and Stukas, even some Trevor did not recognize.

The alarm gong pealed and the smiles froze on the faces of the evacuees. The Bofors gunner tilted his weapon skyward, and its rhythmic pounding tore away the last sense of the day's haven from attack.

Clear of the harbor mouth, *Intrepid* began a series of high-speed turns, designed to make her harder to hit. Not so lucky were the vessels still berthed at the mole. The *Grenade* took a hit aft, while another bomb struck a fuel tank. The ship burst into flames. The *Calvi*, a trawler, received a bomb amidships and sank right beside the other two boats to which she was still tied.

Intrepid's antiaircraft fire was weaving a curtain of black puffs of explosions in the sky over her. A plunging Stuka released its load of destruction, which missed the prow of the destroyer by a scant hundred yards. The dive-bomber pilot then returned to his chosen prey, machine guns blazing.

As if sensing what would happen, Trevor was already moving toward the antiaircraft position. He was close enough to be spattered with blood when the Bofors gunner was ripped up by slugs from the strafing run. Trevor grabbed the curved handles of the weapon as the dead man slid out of the harness.

Intrepid made a tight turn away from the dive of the Stuka, which rolled and pulled up after its run. Trevor led the German plane as it climbed, painting a ladder of black smudges of flak directly in its path.

No more than five seconds of this duel took place before the dive-bomber and the shell bursts tried to occupy the same space together. The tail of the plane shattered and it flipped over in the air and fell, the fractured canopy of the cockpit leading the plunge into the sea.

Captain Collins subscribed to the theory that lightning never struck twice in the same spot. As bomber after bomber unloaded sticks of explosives, Collins ordered the destroyer steered toward each towering fountain of water that erupted.

A bomb burst directly alongside *Intrepid* as she made yet another radical twist. It was a miss, but shrapnel from the casing showered the deck with steel splinters. Forty men in the tightly packed front rank were wounded or killed, unknowingly protecting those behind them.

No provisions remained in the kitchen of the hotel. Unwashed dishes crowded the sink. A half-full bottle of wine sat on the counter beside the enormous old-fashioned gas stove. David took a whiff of the bottle, sipped the contents gingerly then passed it to Badger.

"Go easy. That may be all we get for a while."

Badger tasted the sour stuff and shuddered. "Why is it the Frogs can't brew a decent ale? What I'd give for a pint of Newcastle Brown and a ploughman's lunch."

Badger had been conjuring visions of food for days. Strawberries and cream for his birthday. Steak and kidney pie at the Green Man Pub. A pint of beer. Scones. Marmalade. Badger had stopped believing that he would ever touch the shores of England again. The lifelong tradition of strawberries on his birthday was sure to be broken. Badger was convinced that this was the omen of his impending death. So strong was this morbid conviction that David began to believe it as well.

As Badger downed the wine and spoke wistfully of home, David tore through the cupboards, praying that even a spoonful of strawberries remained in the bottom of a pot of jam somewhere. No luck.

David stared dejectedly at an empty hutch. On the top shelf behind a pewter teapot he spotted what appeared to be the molding of a door.

"Hold on, Badger." David repositioned him beside the stove. "I think I've found something."

At that he tipped the hutch forward, sending it crashing down across the flagstones. Bits of pottery shattered and sprayed the room like shrapnel. Badger jumped and shouted, thinking that a bomb had fallen.

Instead, a door opened to a flight of steps that led down to the cellar. After a moment's exploration, David returned and led Badger down into the basement pantry.

A round of cheese was soon divided by David's jackknife, and this was washed down with the remains of the red wine. Cross sat on a sack of onions awkwardly eating and drinking with his gauze-wrapped hands while David continued examining the cupboards and wine racks. Champagne. White wines with German labels. Napoleon brandies. Red Bordeaux of fantastic vintages. All seemed of small consequence compared to the absence of strawberries.

There was, however, one crate containing tins of sardines. David stuffed his pockets full and snatched two bottles of brandy off the shelf. His arm throbbed. This seemed the most logical medication for his pain.

"No strawberries, Badger. But guess what I found . . ."

Badger's guess was interrupted by the arrival of twenty dusty soldiers who gratefully tramped into the cellar as if they had located the promised land. David shoved his discovery into his tunic.

" 'Scuse us for barging in, mates," said a corporal, "but the Hun is fixing to paste Dunkirk right good and proper. We was hunting a good place to go to ground and it looks like we got it. Care to share your provisions?"

The first bombs rained down on the city before the corporal and his men had settled themselves. But with an elaborate air of unconcern, the non-com knocked the tops off twenty-one champagne bottles. As the earth rolled, the beams creaked, and dirt filtered down from the floor above, the corporal proposed a toast. "Your very good health," he said.

That the Germans did not share this sentiment was proven by a sudden explosion which seemed to lift the floor up under the cellar. The walls of the Hotel Pelican shivered and brick dust filled the air. "Hey, Corp," one of the soldiers called, "are we safe here?"

"Safe as houses. This building is three stories tall. Even if Jerry landed one smack on the button, it'd not come clear to us before blowing up, now would it?" The private did not look convinced, but the corporal only said, "Here, have a fig," and he passed around a box of dried fruit.

David thought about the giant gas stove directly above their heads. One well-placed incendiary and they would all be cooked like holiday geese.

The raid seemed to last for hours, and when it was finally over, David and Cross went back upstairs for fresh air. All the windows in the lobby had been blown out. Shattered plaster, overturned tables, and fallen chandeliers littered the carpet.

Outside the Pelican, the street was almost unrecognizable. A brick structure across the street had taken a direct hit and collapsed its upper two floors into the basement. "Give us a hand!" called a captain urgently. "There are fifty men trapped in the cellar." The unmistakeable hiss of gas sounded clearly. One small lick of flame and the whole heap would explode, taking rescuers right up with the fifty men beneath the rubble.

Noticing David's arm and Badger's bandaged face and hands, the captain waved them away. "Get back inside then. The Luftwaffe is not through yet."

They endured a second and a third bombing attack in the confines of the cellar. As Badger placidly waited for his death, a section of wall collapsed on two soldiers, who were dead before they could be dug out. The atmosphere grew more and more foul. Most of the soldiers were sleeping, but a few took on an edge of belligerence with the champagne. "Where is the bloody RAF, anyway?" the corporal slurred. "Glad you two are here . . . get a taste of the real war . . . instead of your la-ti-da fairyplanes." He hiccuped loudly. A bleary chorus of agreement came from the few that remained conscious.

Badger rose and turned his bulk toward the speaker's voice, but David stopped him. "Too many," he said quietly. "Besides, let's go check on our ride."

When they emerged again into the murky sunlight of the Dunkirk afternoon, they ran immediately into the same major David had seen outside the embarkation office. "Don't bother going back there," the major said. "The Germans have been bombing every ship that tried to put in at the harbor. Even if . . . when," he corrected himself, "when some arrive tonight, there are thousands ahead of you. Best make your way over to the beach and wait there. The Royal Navy will be along. You can count on it."

"Ahoy, *Wairakei!*" called a tone of authority over a handheld megaphone. "Can you hear me?" Annie waved a hand to signal her agreement. Mac doubted that her voice could have been heard over the bubble, drum, and purr of the other engines.

From his perch on top of the aft cabin of *Wairakei,* Mac could count fifty vessels of all shapes and sizes. Smelly fishing trawlers followed in the wakes of gleaming white yachts, and barges with rust-colored sails and black hulls idled next to polished mahogany speed boats.

"Form up on the *Triton*," the voice carried over the water. "She's your guide for this trip. Good luck to you."

All afternoon and evening, since *Wairakei* had arrived off Ramsgate breakwater after her daylong journey down the Thames, more and more watercraft joined the strange flotilla. Now, at ten at night, she and her flock mates were setting off on the first leg of the great adventure.

Annie's father was belowdecks, checking the engines. The top of his shining head appeared, framed in the hatchway. "Annie, girl," he bellowed, in a voice that was no doubt heard three boats away, even without a megaphone. "Annie, mind the rev's on number one. She idles a little fast."

"We're shoving off, Da!" Annie shouted back.

"High time it is too! Mister McGrath!"

Mac jumped and almost tripped over the mainsheet.

"Make yourself useful! Haul in those fenders. We want to look shipshape. Lively now!"

Mac was not sorry when the bald dome of John Galway returned below. After hauling in the fenders as ordered, he asked Annie why she was steering instead of her father.

"Oh, Da knows every vibration and sound. He says he can hear one grain of sand in a fuel line. For this stretch of water there's no pilotin' to be done, just follow the leader. He's happier stayin' below watchin' after the engines."

The small armada moved out. Already gaps were appearing in the line as some of the bigger vessels could barely throttle down to match the struggle of the smaller boats to keep up. "How long will the crossing take?"

"Depends on the wind and the currents," Annie answered. "It's not but forty miles and we could do it in four hours if we went straight across."

"What do you mean, *if*?"

"Oh, we can't steer direct over. There's sandbanks and mines between here and there."

"Swell." Mac was beginning to wonder about the wisdom of his decision to join this enterprise. He looked around as the darker hulls of the rest of the fleet faded into the backdrop of night. "Say, I suppose we're all blacked out because of air attacks?"

"Only partly . . . there's the U-boats to consider too."

Mac walked forward to *Wairakei*'s rounded prow, then continued his circuit of the deck to the stern. When his inspection did not answer his question, he again entered the wheelhouse. Duffy raised his massive head from where he sprawled on the teak sole, then lay it back down. "So, where's our arms?"

"Goodness, Mister McGrath, we don't have any."

"No machine gun? Not even a rifle? What do we defend ourselves with?"

Annie laughed and thought a moment. "Da keeps a pair of cutlasses hanging on the wall of the cabin. I think they are used to repel boarders."

"Sure," Mac agreed, "by Nelson at Trafalgar."

SEVENTY

The heavy overcast had become a soupy fog that clung to Mac's raincoat and dripped from the matted ends of his hair. His eyes were strained from trying to make out shapes in the lightless crossing of the Channel. The night seemed endlessly long and the need to keep everything blacked out added to the gloom and apprehension.

The barest gleam from the stern of the ship ahead was all that could be glimpsed of her, and sometimes that too disappeared. How could Mac watch for enemy ships or submarines when he could not even see two boat lengths ahead?

Moving from the roof of the pilothouse, Mac went to the prow of the ketch. Leaning over and peering at the waves just ahead of *Wairakei* conjured up a whole new element of evil. Even the smallest swells seemed to rush down on the little ship, and each carried a sinister, unexplained dark shadow in which it was easy to imagine a floating mine. Mac's mood alternated between gritting his teeth at the expectation of an explosion and a moment's sigh of relief when the wave rushed past.

Mac tried to imitate John Galway's attention to noises: if sight was impossible, perhaps he could use sound. The Channel was anything but quiet, and that was part of the terror. The drumming engines of unseen ships, muffled by the layer of mist, came from everywhere and nowhere all at once. More than once the sound of another ship dramatically increased in volume, as if it were on a collision course with *Wairakei*.

Mac's senses were on edge and his whole body tuned for danger. When a looming black bow appeared unexpectedly out of the fog less than twenty yards away, Mac shouted a warning before the hazard had even fully registered. Annie spun the wheel, more by instinct than planning, and the enormous shape of a freight barge slid past, close enough to touch. A moment later, bellowing fog horns came too late to prevent the screech of rending metal and panicked screams. Mac shuddered at the thought of the victims claimed by the dark water, even without the Nazi killing machines. The blackness and the confusion were enemy enough. He redoubled his efforts to pierce the fog by both eye and ear, still without much success.

Annie steered *Wairakei* through course changes while her father continued to tinker with the engines. During one of these swings, Mac turned around to watch one of the few things actually visible in the night: the wake streaming away from the stern. He was trying to make sense of their new heading and had taken his eyes off the ship ahead when something bumped against the hull directly beneath him. Certain it was a mine, Mac flung himself to the far side of the ship as if he were a child again and the floating bomb an angry dog that could be escaped by running. It was already too late to call out a warning.

No explosion came. *Wairakei* continued on without interruption. Mac wondered if her wooden hull had somehow protected her against a weapon designed for metal ships. Racing to the stern, he looked over in time to see a large piece of driftwood spin away on the wake.

Eventually the fog raised into a grey layer, then hung overhead like a theater curtain drawn up halfway. The change allowed Mac to make out the dim shapes of other vessels that he had not known were anywhere nearby. He checked on the ship just ahead, and on a fishing trawler to port and astern. Ahead and to starboard, a couple hundred yards distant, was the white, sleek outline of someone's private yacht.

As Mac watched the expensive plaything knife through the waves, he saw a vertical dark stripe silhouetted against the momentary brightness of the hull. Something was really there; a solid black pole upright from the surface of the water. It could only be a submarine. "Periscope!" he yelled. "U-boat over starboard! U-boat!"

"Are you sure?" Annie questioned.

"Absolutely! How do we warn the others? Where's your radio?"

"Never had one. Flare pistol? In the locker behind me."

"Quick . . . there'll be a torpedo in the water any minute now." Mac tore open the locker, throwing out rain slickers and life vests to land all over Duffy. The dog sat up with an enormous woof and shook himself free of the pile.

Emerging from the heap, Mac snapped open the Very pistol and checked to see that it was loaded. The gun was already raised and his arm outside the cabin when John Galway emerged from the engine room hatch.

"What's all the noise, then? What are you about there, Mister McGrath?"

"Submarine! A U-boat, Mister Galway! We need to warn . . ."

"Hold on! Where did you see this craft?"

"Not the whole thing, just the periscope! Right over there," Mac said pointing.

Galway took the flare gun from Mac's hand but made no move to fire it. Snapping on a tiny chart light, he consulted a map. Annie's father muttered to himself, "Naw but six fathoms hereabouts . . . not enough water to hide a sub . . . sand bank," he concluded.

"What?"

"What you saw was the mast on top of a sunken freighter. You remember that last turn we made? That was to steer us around the sand bank and the wreck. A good job you didn't fire this thing, Mister McGrath! Might have brought down the whole of Germany right on our heads!"

⚜ ⚜ ⚜

"Keep a sharp eye out!" John Galway yelled at Mac. The cameraman was standing on the canvas-wrapped boom and clinging to the foremast as he strained for the first glimpse of the Dunkirk shore.

The darkness gave up few secrets until it started to get light just past four in the morning. "Wait!" Mac called back. "I think I see something!"

"Where away?"

Mac did not know the correct ship terminology, but he indicated with his hand the direction toward a white object dimly seen against the grey horizon.

"I hear breakers, Da!" Annie said. Duffy sat up and whined, as if he too had heard or sensed some change.

"Can you make out the shoreline?" Annie's father shouted.

"It's just . . . yes! I can see it now!"

The same heavy grey overcast that had protected the little ships from the unwelcome attention of the Luftwaffe, had almost brought the boats to grief on the shoaling sands of the French shore. A thin horizontal line appeared suddenly on the horizon, separating ashen sky from leaden sea.

John Galway spun the wheel in his hands and the boat swung about to parallel the coast. The fog parted just enough for all three to get their first glimpse of their destination, and a ghostly form welcomed them to France.

Mac saw the stern of a white painted sloop directly ahead of them on the beach. It lay high and dry, marooned on the gravel above the falling tide. Mac searched the wreckage for its crew, only to discover the truth: he saw the stern because that was all of the craft that remained. The front two-thirds of the ship had been torn away and destroyed. It was not an auspicious omen to accompany their arrival.

And if the first view was a portent of tragedy, the next vision stunned Mac; it took him some time to remember to begin shooting film. The shore was covered with men. The sands were forested with moving forms, as if animated trees milled about. There were thousands and thousands of them; too many to count. Mac stopped filming long enough to examine the lens with suspicion and then look with his naked eye. The reality just did not seem credible to either man or camera.

"Right," Galway observed tersely. "We've got our job cut out for us then. Mister McGrath! Let Annie take over as lookout. You're the leadsman. *Wairakei* draws five feet, so keep us in a fathom to be on the safe side. We'll load up and ferry the lads to yon great destroyer there."

Mac spun about, still filming as he gyrated. Into focus leapt a warship that had materialized unexpectedly out of the fog behind them. He forced himself to slow down. That piece of film would never be usable; it would make audiences seasick.

"Put away your pretty toy! There's work to be done!"

✳   ✳   ✳

Badger and David and thousands of other soldiers waited all night for ships that did not come. Sometime after three in the morning the bombing raids stopped and David fell into an uneasy sleep. He dreamt of Annie fleeing down a country road, pursued by a Messerschmidt. In his vision, he tried to scream at her to get off the road. But no sound came from his mouth, nor could he run toward her to push her out of the way. She was only an arm's length distant when the tracers from the Me 109 caught up with her.

He awoke with a start to find his shirt soaked in sweat and ashen dawn creeping over the beach. Somehow during the night, the number of men had doubled or even tripled. It looked like the seashore had been thickly planted with low bushes that rustled and moaned despite the absence of a breeze.

"There's a boat!" the artillery captain called. Suddenly the bushes came to life and pursued the retreating tide. The small bobbing white object was a motor launch with a crew of four sailors. As they swept up on the sand, twenty times as many men as the little boat could possibly hold crowded around. "Where is it, Meyer? Help me to it," Badger pleaded.

"Not this time, Badger," David replied, his heart sinking with the words. "It's not our turn."

"No more, no more! You'll swamp it," cried the naval officer, jumping into the shallow sea and wading ashore. "Listen men, we're from the destroyer *Jaguar*. Chin up! We're here to get you off." If the officer expected a rousing cheer of welcome, he was disappointed. The wave of humans who had rushed into waist-deep water looked at the fifty men who received places in the launch with envy and hatred. Then, stoically, they turned about and returned to the sand.

The lieutenant commander stayed ashore. He went from group to group, locating the unit officers and giving them instructions. "Form into proper queues," David heard him say. The artillery regiment brightened at this. Even though the prospect of a speedy rescue was not at hand, the soldiers preferred to be given clear orders. Even when the order has no immediate benefit, just the sense that someone was actually in charge improved the outlook for many. It was the first sign of organization they had seen in days.

Within minutes, serpentine formations of men snaked their way from the dunes down to the water's edge. There was no reason for the lines to curl and loop, except for a very human wish to feel nearer to the front than the actual number of places suggested.

It took the first boat half an hour to return, but with it came two more small launches. The line inched toward rescue in an agonizingly slow process. David kept his good hand on Badger's shoulder as the two moved up, trying to act and sound reassuring. "There's the next boat coming back already. The system is figured out now." Badger nodded without speaking, and David knew that his words were not convincing. A painfully unwelcome, but impossible to prevent mental calculation hit: the three small boats were removing only 300 men an hour from the beach. In the line with David and Badger were five hundred others and there were queues coiled along the beach every two or three hundred yards.

Some of those waiting had a mechanical quality, as if their human consciousness was submerged because of fear. The private in front of David dug a hole in the sand and crouched in it. When the launch returned and the men shuffled forward, the soldier abandoned his shelter, moved up a few feet, and began digging again.

A lone Messerschmidt sized up the beach and found the pickings too good to resist. The fighter plane circled the crowded shore like a fox sizing up a flock of chickens for the fat and the slow.

The artillery captain abandoned the line and ran toward the cover of the sand dunes. Up and down the coast, others also panicked and turned to flee.

"Don't run!" yelled a burly regimental sergeant major. "Stand fast!" The man's courage was meant to be infectious.

But even more convincing in David's mind was the shout raised by the lieutenant commander. "You'll lose your place!"

The 109 flashed overhead. A row of tracers glinted and little bursts of sand flew up on both sides of David as the bullets impacted only a few feet away.

With ample other targets to select, the machine gun fire ceased. Mystified, the soldiers watched the plane waggle its wings and then take off east.

"Respect for our bravery?" Cross asked David.

"Guns jammed," David replied.

✣ ✣ ✣

"There's ten feet . . . nine . . . eight . . . hold it." Mac's voice called out the depth of the water as *Wairakei* slipped up on Bray Dunes beach, east of Dunkirk. The line of men that stretched back from chest deep in the sea numbered five hundred or more. Up and down the beach were similar waiting columns, every couple hundred yards.

John Galway locked down the anchor winch, and the ship hung, stern toward shore, at the end of the cable. The ketch had already made more trips between the shore and the waiting destroyer than Mac could remember. He had long since given up any thought of filming the operation; he needed both hands free to haul waterlogged soldiers over the rail.

As Mac watched, another lifeboat approached the shore. Some of the rescue vessels drew too much water to get close enough for the men to board directly, so life boats, and dinghys, and the captain's launch from the destroyer worked in the surf. Their work was not without hazard. The boat nearing Bray Dunes now was rushed by three times as many men as could really fit it at one time. When the Royal Navy Sub-Lieutenant in charge of the boat warned them to clear off and wait their turn, he was ignored. The already overloaded craft shipped water over the rail, spun broadside to the waves, then flipped over, scattering the Tommies and drowning the lieutenant.

Early on, that same fate seemed destined to overtake *Wairakei*. Wanting to ease the loading process, John Galway had allowed the ketch to almost drag her keel on the sand. Immediately she was surrounded by two hundred soldiers, trying to climb on board from all directions at once. Even the sturdy twenty-ton craft seemed likely to either capsize or run aground.

Mac remembered something Annie had said in jest the night before. Dashing into the main cabin, he pulled an antique cutlass from the pair on the wall. Waving the sword, he raced around the deck like an actor in a pirate movie. When the sight and sound of a giant, barking, slavering dog was added to the mix, the men backed off and agreed to wait their turn.

But in order to take no unnecessary chances, after that episode John Galway purposely kept *Wairakei* deeper than before. He forced the men to swim the last few feet, giving them no opportunity to mob the boat.

Some of the soldiers were so dead tired that they could do nothing to help themselves. In those cases it took both Mac and Annie's father to hoist them aboard. "One, two, three, *heave!*" John Galway called, and another inert body sprawled on the deck.

Galway kept up a running patter of encouragement. "Don't I know you?" he asked. "Song and dance man? No? Picture shows, then?" To others lost in despair or grieving the death of a friend he would say, "Buck up! Never mind this little setback! We'll pay off that Hitler fellow, you'll see."

Mac marvelled at the way Galway not only plucked them from danger, but lifted their spirits. Mac himself got a boost from listening, a renewed belief that everything would work out after all.

Fully loaded with another seventy-five evacuees, *Wairakei* prepared to run up her own anchor line and then steam out to the waiting destroyer. "Propellor's fouled," Galway called when the ship failed to respond to the throttle. "McGrath, take the boat hook and free it. Must be a bit of line wrapped around the shaft."

Picking his way through the clutter of exhausted forms stretched over every possible inch of space, Mac took the gaff and leaned over the rail. There was something down there, near the props. Mac poked it with the boat hook. It resisted at first, then he got a grasp on it and the object floated free, surfacing under his face. It was the body of the drowned lieutenant.

As the tide retreated down the shelf of the Dunkirk coast, the columns of waiting men merely stretched further back before disappearing amongst the dunes. To Mac's eye, this had the curious effect of making it seem that the number awaiting evacuation grew larger instead of smaller with every boatload ferried out to the destroyer.

A mysterious dark column jutted out toward the sea. It had not been there on any of the earlier trips, but it looked like a dock where none had been before. As the ketch got closer to the beach, a swarm of men could be seen crawling around the structure. Soon the nature of the object became clear. As the tide withdrew, a lorry was driven over the hardpacked sand to the front of a line of similar trucks. The groups of soldiers climbing around the vehicles were lashing them together with cables, building an unorthodox but useful pier.

By the time *Wairakei* had completed a few more round trips, the improvised jetty extended several hundred yards seaward. The tires of the trucks had been shot out to settle the machines into position in the sand. An impromptu walkway made from salvaged lumber was secured to the tops of the trucks.

The idea took hold and spread. Several more of the ingenious "lorry jetties" were begun to speed the evacuation of the waiting thousands.

The emotions Andre felt when the launch pulled alongside the destroyer *Keith* were compounded of unspeakable relief and surprise. To be free of the tiny scrap of coastline was to be released from the iron jaws of a trap. The smell of ocean breeze, even tainted with oil and diesel fuel, seemed clean and sweet compared to the pervasive stench that hung over the beaches.

But if the flow of cleaner air carried an aroma of release, his personal safety was still difficult to comprehend. Even while working for the evacuation of others, part of Andre's mind had told him that he would never be rescued. Now the thought of being free to return to the battle became real to him! On the other side of Dunkirk, did lines of French soldiers still hold out against the Germans? Would it be possible for those rescued from the beaches to regroup and enter France from the south to fight for Paris?

He gripped the cold, damp steel of the railing. The sea water and the sand that scrunched in his boots reminded him of what he had left behind. Andre rubbed his hand over his salt-encrusted, bearded face.

A voice at his elbow said something. Andre roused himself from contemplating his escape and turned to find a white-clad steward offering a mug and a silver teapot.

"I said, would you care for some tea, sir?"

"Yes," Andre agreed, "but be careful."

"Sir?"

"I just convinced myself that I am really here; I do not want to start doubting all over again!"

Here and there fires still burned on the dunes from the targets of successful Luftwaffe attacks. In the direction of Dunkirk, an ominous red glow hovered in the sky.

Out on the water, everything was pitch black. The rescue ships went about their duties without lights, to avoid more aerial assaults and to hide from prowling German U-boats and S-boats. Unless a small craft passed close by, the only sign that betrayed the presence of the armada of rescue vessels was the swirl of phosphorescence in their wakes.

On the far horizon, directly in front of the deep crimson bowl that surrounded Dunkirk harbor, a white flare lit the night. The dark outline of a ship, tilted at a crazy angle, was momentarily silhouetted against the brilliance. In a few seconds, Andre saw the shape slide downwards, extinguishing the light as if the cover of a giant lantern had been shut over its beam. "What was that?" he asked the steward.

"Can't say for certain, sir. From the size I'd say another destroyer . . . probably a torpedo got her."

It was one minute after midnight on the first of June. Andre stood at the railing of the *Keith* and marvelled at the course of the last few days. Since reaching the Dunkirk perimeter three days before, he had not slept more than fifteen minutes at a time.

The physical letdown that accompanied release from duty was profound.

Andre leaned heavily on the rail, discovering for the first time that he was exhausted.

Too tired to even worry about U-boat attacks, Andre stumbled below and stretched out on the floor in a corner of the ward room. He was almost immediately asleep.

✳ ✳ ✳

It was nearly midnight when the BEF ambulance screeched to a halt in front of Paul's headquarters at the École de Cavalerie.

A middle-aged British major of the Grenadier Guards dashed into the bomb-damaged school. The man was filthy and splattered with blood. Someone else's blood, Paul thought, as the man faced him in the lantern light.

"The Germans are just beyond the river, Captain," The major exclaimed. "I have been sent . . . that is . . . HQ has heard that there are still English nurses here at the CCS. An oversight. They should have been pulled back days ago."

The man's face was pale. Both he and Paul understood fully what the order meant. The nurses were to be evacuated and as many more of the wounded as the time left allowed.

The remainder of the wounded were to be left to await the arrival of the German Panzers. French. English. Belgian. Perhaps the Belgians would be spared because of the capitulation of King Leopold. It was no secret what the Germans would do to the others. Only a fierce rearguard action could save them now.

Cautiously, guided only by starlight, Paul led the major toward the Chapel. Abigail Mitchell had just come out of the operating room. Her feet were covered with blood to the ankles. In the dim light it looked as if she was wearing high red shoes. Her strong features reflected her exhaustion.

"Sister Abigail Mitchell, QAIMNS," the major saluted. "Orders from HQ. You have twenty minutes to gather your nursing staff and to prepare to fall back . . ."

Abigail Mitchell argued against the withdrawal, but her reasoning was foolish and she knew it.

Twenty minutes passed and she stood at the open back of the ambulance as her staff climbed aboard.

She extended her hand to Paul.

"What can I say, Captain Chardon?"

"Say you will have dinner with me when this is finished."

At his cheerful remark the cold Miss Mitchell melted and dissolved in tears. He put his arms around her in a gesture of awkward tenderness. "If the thought of dinner with me upsets you, ma chérie . . ."

"Oh stop it, Paul. Please. Not now. How can I leave you?"

He cupped her face in his hands and kissed her. "Because you are very beautiful. And strong. And you have given everything here that you can give. Now we must give what we can for the sake of honor."

"I don't know what to say . . ."

"Then say that you will pray for us. Promise you will remember."

She nodded. The major barked an impatient order that they must get to Dunkirk before the Germans. He pointed out that there was nothing between Dunkirk and the Germans but the École de Cavalerie.

"We're already ten minutes late! If you don't mind, Sister Mitchell! I'd like to get home in one piece!" Then to Paul. "If I were you, Captain, I'd pull my men back. You might be able to get on a boat before the German army overruns Dunkirk."

"How long will that be, Major?"

"They'll cross the river right here at Lys in the morning and then . . . whoever is left at Dunkirk is a goner, as the Americans say."

"How much time do you need to clear the beaches?"

"They just keep coming. At least two days for the chaps there now."

Paul nodded gravely. "Then we shall stay. Defend the hospital and . . . we will do what we can to buy you time at Dunkirk."

The major glowered at him as if he was crazy. "You're going to stay and fight? Has it occurred to you that you'll all be killed?"

"Indeed. Perhaps we few may have the honor to die for France."

"You think you can do what the entire Allied army couldn't do? Hold the Panzers here? On the other side of the Lys?"

"We will."

"At least send the boys out. Let the seasoned troops bear the brunt of it."

"These boys, as you call them, are my seasoned troops, Major."

After a long moment the words penetrated. The major drew himself up in crisp salute. He could not speak.

"Hurry now," Paul urged. With one last glance of farewell, he closed the doors of the ambulance and turned back to his task.

SEVENTY-ONE

When Andre awoke, dawn was breaking. The destroyer was still on station off the beach, but Lord Gort had departed for England. Sometime in the middle of the night, the former commander of the now defunct British Expeditionary Force left by speedboat for Dover. The general would be facing an inquiry into how the disaster in France had happened.

But also during the night, hundreds of battered and weary soldiers boarded the *Keith;* men who would now be in a German prisoner-of-war camp if it were not for Gort's leadership during the withdrawal and the French rear guard. In every compartment and companionway, Andre stepped over soggy uniforms that contained worn-out British troops.

The same steward, his white uniform still neatly pressed, offered Andre another steaming cup of tea and a hard biscuit. The servant apologized, but to Andre it was a feast; Sunday brunch at the Ritz could not have been more appreciated.

Feeling refreshed, Andre went back on deck to help aboard men who could hardly stagger and to translate the worried questions of his non-English-speaking countrymen.

The destroyer wallowed in seas that were much heavier than the night before. The rising wind increased the height of the waves. When Andre regained the rail he could see the whalers and lifeboats being tossed around as they made their interminable journeys back and forth. The increasing roughness of the sea and the extra effort required to pull against the wind made the job even tougher for those just now arriving alongside.

As the pale wrap of early morning light replaced the cloak of the night, Andre was startled to look around him at a huge number of ships. From a vantage point at the stern of the *Keith,* he could see destroyers, mine sweepers, and tugboats all within the circle of his view. Each of these larger vessels was surrounded by a flotilla of smaller craft, coming and going, unloading men and leaving again for the shore. It was like watching multiple hives of bees, each with a queen served by hundreds of drones. The activity was astounding.

By eight o'clock the *Keith* was packed full and ready to steam for Dover harbor. Andre helped the last of a platoon of Royal Irish Fusiliers over the side. The small boats headed back for shore to continue the evacuation by ferrying soldiers to the nearby destroyer *Basilisk*.

As the *Keith* got underway, Andre looked toward the southwest. A pall of black smoke had replaced the reddish glow that identified Dunkirk. Andre was reminded of the biblical account of the Exodus, "a pillar of fire by night and a pillar of cloud by day." Still, he was pleased to be going away from, and not toward, that menacing gloom.

A smaller shadow detached itself from the cloud and rose upwards in the sky. As Andre watched, it resolved itself into half a hundred tiny specks. The swarm aimed directly for the *Keith* and the ships around her.

Three Stukas peeled off from the formation and dove for the destroyer. A fascinated horror gripped Andre as he watched their plunge, knowing that nothing he did could possibly make any difference.

A pair of antiaircraft guns began their rhythmic pounding, and black bursts of smoke appeared in front of the swooping warplanes. Andre saw the release of the bombs and shuddered in anticipation of what was coming.

Two bombs plunged into the water near the *Keith*'s bow, raising geysers of water that fountained over the deck. Five sailors were washed overboard just before the third bomb went down the destroyer's smokestack.

There was a tremendous crash, as if the ship had run into a stone wall at full speed. Andre bounced off the armor around a gun housing and was thrown to the deck. He felt the deck plates lift up under his feet, as if a geyser were trying to erupt there too.

The *Keith* gave an agonized groan of twisting steel and failing seams. From his prone position on the shuddering metal, Andre watched a burst of flames, smoke, and steam shoot skyward. The destroyer leaned to port and kept heeling, tumbling Andre against the gunwale.

As the ship settled lower in the water, the shriek of whistles, the bellow of klaxon horns, and the clang of gongs all mingled to scream its death knell. More Stukas dove on nearby rescue vessels, attacking a pair of minesweepers and another destroyer.

"Abandon ship!" came the cry. It was picked up and carried forward and aft and down into the ravaged insides of the dying ship. Those not killed or wounded in the blast swarmed up on deck. Some did not wait, but dove over the side, whether they had a lifejacket or not.

A heap of life preservers piled on the aft deck blew apart and scattered by one of the bombs. As the ship listed, several of these slid across the deck.

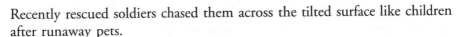

Recently rescued soldiers chased them across the tilted surface like children after runaway pets.

One scooted straight into Andre's hands. He slipped it on, tightening the straps with a savage tug as if his safety depended on the grasp of the device. As he balanced on the rail before jumping over the side, another dive-bomber targeted the nearby minesweeper *Skipjack.* It took two direct hits and exploded with a roar.

The concussion rolled across the water, breaking Andre's grip on the rail and pitching him headfirst into the sea. His head on a floating piece of debris, he just managed to stay conscious enough to fling an arm over the beam. Choking and sputtering, Andre paddled away from the rapidly sinking destroyer as waves continued to roll over him.

❈   ❈   ❈

Smoke from the bombed-out docks of Rouen darkened the sky as the narrow peniche navigated the waters of the Seine.

Just ahead Josie could plainly see that the Luftwaffe had been at work on the river port. It had been an important embarkation point for British and American reinforcements in the last war, and the German High Command was taking no chances.

A thick plume of oily fumes obscured for a moment the castle where St. Jeanne d'Arc had been imprisoned in the struggle against the English in 1430. The black smudge in the predawn sky of Rouen was only one more reminder that, like the martyred St. Jeanne, the soul of France burned on the pyre of war once again. The old walls of the town which had defied Henry V in 1415 had been broadened to boulevards and planted with trees. The ancient vigilance of Rouen had been forgotten, and now the beautiful Gothic city was in flames for a mile and a half along the quays. On the left bank of the river, the two train stations of Gare d'Orleans and Gare de la Rive Gauche were wrecks of twisted metal and charred girders.

"On your toes!" Rose shouted forward to Josie as they rounded the bend and spotted the narrow finger of Ile Brouilly in the center of the river. Just beyond the little island was the larger island of Lacroix and then the bridge across the point where the river narrowed. Was the span still intact? Or had passage down the Seine been blocked by rubble from last night's bombing raid?

"I can't see to the bridge," Josie replied, peering down the right fork of the stream.

"What is ahead?" Rose hailed Lewinski who, with Jerome beside him at the rail, peered through his gas mask from port while Josie and Georg checked to starboard.

"The Pont Corneille still stands!" Lewinski shouted back.

Then Jerome added the warning. "There is a small vessel sunk beside the piling. It will be a narrow passage, Madame Rose!"

Rose chose to navigate down the left branch past the sunken boat which lay, bow up, against the arched piling of the low bridge. Close enough to touch the shattered hulk of the unfortunate ship, the new coat of paint on the hull of the *Garlic* scraped against the iron mooring rings set in the stone beneath the ancient structure.

The river was up. Josie held her breath and ducked instinctively as they slipped through what seemed more a tunnel than a bridge.

Beyond the two islands, the Seine straightened, and in spite of the fact that the wreckage of a dozen larger ships lay half-submerged, navigation became easier. The Gothic towers and chalk hills of the town slid away before the fourteen sleeping children belowdecks awakened.

Long after the sun came up, however, the smoke above Rouen still darkened the sky behind them. Josie was certain that the same planes that had destroyed the ships and quays of Rouen would soon be skimming like hawks over the river in search of new prey.

⚜ ⚜ ⚜

"The sky is clearin' a bit," John Galway observed as the ketch drew alongside the lorry jetty.

The inventive wharf was working well. Both deeper draft ships and shallower ones like lifeboats took advantage of the chance to pick up soldiers without going too close to the shore. There was something more orderly, more military about the process too. Marching down the walkway to climb aboard instead of swimming, and seeing the regular trips made by the little ships took the edge of panic off the men. There was less of the overcrowding that had happened earlier in the day.

Annie's father still kept a watchful eye on the depth under *Wairakei*'s keel. He did not want them to run aground. With Mac assisting, John Galway waved for Annie to let the boat creep forward a little further.

Behind them, a trawler was also coming to the pier. Needing even more depth to operate than the ketch, the fishing boat docked just astern of *Wairakei.*

After a time of almost no challenges by the Germans, the sound of planes overhead was momentarily ignored. Then the skipper of the trawler looked up and saw the flight of Heinkels sweeping in from the north to line up for a bombing run.

In his panic, he shoved the gear into forward instead of reverse and gunned the engine. The collision at *Wairakei*'s stern whacked Annie's head against a spoke of the helm and knocked Mac overboard.

Flying over the rail, Mac had an instant to be glad that his camera was in the cabin on the ship and not slung over his shoulder. Then he hit the water and came up sputtering.

The Heinkels unloaded their bombs further up the beach. One of the improvised jetties took a direct hit and the bodies of men and the wreckage of trucks were blown skyward in company with a Thames river passenger launch. Duffy ran around the deck, barking wildly and knocking more men over the side.

John Galway scooped Annie up and flung her over his shoulder. He shouted "Get by, you daft dog!" making Duffy slink back into the cabin. Then, seeing that the trawler was already steaming full speed astern and the way was clear, he put *Wairakei* into reverse as well.

The little ship shuddered all along her forty-foot length, and green water churned into foam under her props, but she did not move. "We're stuck fast," John yelled. "You men, give us a hand to float her, or she's a sitting duck!"

The German bombers were returning from the last pass and lining up for another run. "Over the side," ordered Galway, "all of ye. We've got to lighten ship and push her free!"

The men already on board obliged. They jumped over into the four feet of water and struggled to help the ketch escape from the sand bank which held her prisoner.

As Mac was already in the water, he stayed there and helped push the boat. "Heave!" he yelled. "Again!"

The engines roared, but still *Wairakei* was stuck fast. "Rock her!" Galway called.

A line of three Heinkels, having already dropped their bombs, opened up on the beach with machine guns. The orderly queues waiting their turn to board were shattered and torn apart, and then the planes directed their line of fire toward the ship.

Some of the men nearest Mac turned to flee. "It's not any safer out there!" he bellowed. "Stay and help!"

Rows of tracers shot up the jetty, flinging men right and left off its length and into the sea. The bullets clanged into the metal roofs and hoods of the trucks, drowning out the screams. "Again!" Mac implored. "Rock her again!"

With the engines at full throttle, when *Wairakei* did break free, she shot backward away from the jetty into deeper water. John spun the wheel, pivoting the ketch away from the dock. The line of tracers plowed into the water exactly where *Wairakei* had been, throwing up a row of splashes. The bomber flashed past overhead, almost close enough to touch.

The ketch headed out to sea, zigzagging as she went. Back near shore, Mac stayed in the water until the last Heinkel had departed. Then he pulled himself out on the jetty just in time to watch *Wairakei*'s stern shrink smaller and smaller out into the Channel.

⚜ ⚜ ⚜

Horst von Bockman stood up in the turret of his PzKw III. Through his field glasses, he studied the outlines of the town of Lys, glimpsed beyond the intervening screen of trees. The orders Horst had received were very simple. They told him that this area was very lightly held by a cobbled together force, including some military school students. He was to punch right through their undoubtedly feeble resistance and drive on to the Channel. Time was of the utmost importance; the Führer, while not admitting that his halt order had been a mistake, was now screaming at the German High Command not to let any more Allied troops escape.

Horst directed his armored reconnaissance patrol forward to scout the bridge and the main road. He moved his tanks to the edge of the river, flanking the highway on both sides.

The lead armored car approached the trestle. Like a chase scene from a silent picture, three Kfz 231's turned the corner in succession at high speed. Each tipped up slightly as it rounded the curve.

Almost at once they were hit by converging streams of machine gun fire. From both sides of the town and from the island in the center of the river, bullets ripped into the scouts.

The first driver immediately lost control of his vehicle, bouncing it off a low stone wall. Then as the driver overcorrected, the car turned in the opposite direction and smashed headlong into the wall on the other side.

The second car following plowed into the first, knocking the already damaged car onto its side. There was a shriek of metal as the force of the impact scrubbed the side of the armored vehicle along the pavement of the bridge.

Machine gun fire continued to pour into the span, and added to this was the sharp crack of a small but well-aimed antitank weapon. The first round punched through the roof of the overturned scout car, passed completely through it, and exploded on the front armor of the second. There was no further motion from either vehicle, both of which now burned furiously in the center of the bridge.

The remaining armored machine did not even turn around. It drove at high speed in reverse back to the safe end of the bridge. But even here, no protection was guaranteed. A round from another antitank weapon located somewhere on the far bank reached out and tagged the scout car and spun it around.

"Covering fire," Horst ordered, and the guns of his tanks opened up on the town's defenders. A building on the island was crumpled by the first blast, and a shot fired by Horst's own tank crashed near the location of the first antitank weapon.

More antitank rounds came toward his position from a slightly different angle. It was clear that the defenders knew well the lesson of how to use mobile weapons: fire and move, fire and move. Horst had only just buttoned up the hatch when a shell splattered against the front plating of the Panzer tank.

"We will have to withdraw," he said, "and bring up the artillery."

❊　❊　❊

Andre's inflated life vest and the death grip he had on the wooden plank kept his head out of the waves part of the time. But the swells that did roll over him covered him with oil and diesel fuel. Opening his mouth to gasp for air at an inopportune moment filled Andre's throat with the guck. He gagged and then vomited.

His eyes, sticky with oil, burned until they swelled almost shut. He paddled with his free arm, peering through blurred vision and hoping that someone would pick him up before his strength gave out.

A tugboat picked its way among the wreckage. It twisted and turned to avoid running over survivors, and it dodged Stuka attacks as it gathered in men who called for help. Andre could barely see its shape looming ahead, but he tried to swim and push his bobbing makeshift float toward it. Once he attempted to wave, but the motion pushed him under the breakers and set off another seizure of coughing and retching.

The plank bumped into someone else drifting in the sea. "Grab on," Andre called in English. "Help me! We'll try for the tug." There was no reply. He nudged the silent form. "I said, grab on," Andre tried in French.

Another wave caused the body to roll over, and a drifting corpse reproached Andre with sightless eyes. Andre pushed away so hard from the body that he ducked himself again and this time lost his grip on the plank. Flailing wildly, Andre shouted, choked, and sputtered. He called for help in every language he could think of, and called on God to save him.

The knotted end of a rope bounced off his head, and the cable fell across his outstretched arms. "Hold on, chum," a cheerful voice called. "You'll be all right!"

The rope slipped through Andre's numb and oily fingers, and he cried out that he was not going to make it. At the very end of the cord, his hands closed around the knot and the motion of the ship dragged him through the water. At any second the pressure of the waves would break his hold and he would spin off astern of the rescue boat.

Andre felt the rope being pulled toward the ship; he felt himself being drawn close to the hull he could only dimly make out. Two pair of strong hands reached down and grabbed him under the arms. He was hoisted aboard the tug *St. Abbs* and laid on the deck. Soaked, oil covered, puking, and half drowned, Andre tried to thank the crew, but they ignored him and went on about their business of rescuing others.

When Andre had recovered some from his own near drowning, he watched the proceedings as the tug's crew methodically loaded and stacked men who were without any ability to help themselves.

Captain Berthon of the *Keith* had been picked up by the tug. A major of the Grenadier Guards and some of his men rowed to the larger vessel in a lifeboat. When they climbed over the side, the rowboat was made fast and towed behind for use in other rescues. Over a hundred men snatched from the embrace of the sea were sprawled on the decks of the tug.

The man propped next to Andre was dying, punctured by dozens of shrapnel holes. His body oozed blood from every surface, as if an overfilled sponge was slowly draining onto the deck. A chaplain bent low over him, murmuring words into his ear. The man's hand gripped the parson's, seeming to cling to the world by that touch alone.

A Stuka appeared overhead. Its siren screaming, the dive-bomber plunged toward the tug. There was no way to fight back; even those who still carried weapons were too tired to raise them.

In the small pilothouse, the helmsman spun the wheel. The tug slithered over the surface of the sea like a mouse avoiding the rush of a hawk. It was all guesswork, really. No way to predict which move would equal safety and which might carry the boat under the falling explosives.

What impressed Andre the most was the way people carried on their tasks. As bombs exploded on both sides and then in front of the tug, a brace of burly seamen went on throwing lines to men in the water, lifting them up, and shouting words of encouragement. A medic moved among the injured, wrapping bloody wounds with gauze and dispensing what comfort he could.

An explosion close astern lifted the aft portion of *St. Abbs* clear of the water and slammed it down again. Several men near Andre panicked, thinking the tug had been hit and was sinking. The chaplain, now hugging the dying man to his chest, ignored the blast and continued to repeat, "I am the resurrection and the life . . ."

The medic asked Andre if he was injured, and gave him a bit of rough sacking to scrub the worst of the oil from his face. A canteen of fresh water was passed for Andre to bathe his face. The cool fluid provided amazing relief to his enflamed and swollen eyes. Andre felt the irony of this oddly commonplace action: washing his face while there was an immediate likelihood of being blown to bits.

Twice more the Stukas attacked the seemingly charmed tug. The old coal burning firebox belched black smoke and cinders from the stack. The wind over the Channel blew the smoke into long streamers, marking the tug's path as it twisted and turned; lines punctuated by fountains of water thrown up by the bomb blasts. Andre heard the terror in many voices as men in the water cried for rescue and men already on the tug cried out in fear of the Stukas.

Like a chronicler of every tragedy, *St. Abbs* was present as ship after ship was struck and sank: the wreckage of the *Keith* slipped below the waves; *Basilisk* went down; and the minesweeper Andre had seen bombed rolled over and floated belly up. Andre shuddered with relief when he remembered that he could have been belowdecks instead of topside and blown clear. Though still in danger themselves, the men on the tug observed with fascinated horror and despair as the minesweeper went to the bottom. Hundreds of men were still trapped inside. The face of every soldier expressed the same thought: *That could have been me.*

The Stukas swooped away to the east. For a time the only sounds Andre heard were the deep, steady thrumming of the tug's engine and the cries for help that still came from every side.

Then a new sound was added to the rest. Faint at first, a buzzing reached Andre's ears that was not the high whine of the Stuka engines but a lower-pitched hum.

A single dot detached itself from the shoreline and rose overhead as if following the plume of the tug's smoke. A lone Heinkel bomber floated lazily into view. There were no fighters to harrass it and no antiaircraft fire to annoy it, so it came forward with no evasive maneuvering at all. Like a sightseer out to view the carnage, it flew straight and level at no more than a thousand feet off the water.

Whether it had really tracked the ship's exhaust or if *St. Abbs* was the only object still moving on its own through the floating wreckage, the bomber was definitely attacking. All those who were able to watch the warplane did so, willing it to pass by. Andre's mind was screaming to be left alone! Hadn't they been through enough already?

Andre held his breath as the Heinkel passed overhead. No bombs fell, no machine guns opened fire. In concert with a hundred others, Andre breathed a sigh of relief. Perhaps the bomber was only an observation mission, to report on the success of the Stukas.

Just past the bow of the tug, dark objects began dropping from the belly of the plane. They hit the water in the path of the ship, but all failed to explode. A soldier near Andre laughed. "Good luck for us at last! A poor pilot and a rack of duds!"

But the skipper of the tug knew better. He threw the helm hard over to avoid the delayed action explosives, but they were too near and the tug too sluggish. The prow swung to starboard and the hull of the ship drifted broadside toward the floating bombs.

The first explosion blew up beside the low freeboard of the ship. A hole was torn below the waterline and the plates buckled upwards. Shards of the hull pierced men lying on the deck and others were dead by the concussion before being flung into the water.

The ship corkscrewed from the force of the first blast, exposing its keel to the full impact of the second. *St. Abbs* broke in two and rolled over as she sank into the Channel. In her dying convulsion, she carried most of her passengers with her to the bottom, leaving in thirty seconds no more trace of her existence than a handful of floundering men.

Tossed upward into the air, Andre was surrounded by a jet of steam that was the tug's last breath. He landed in the water again, while all around him rained chunks of coal and flaming embers from the firebox. For the second time in an hour, he was near to drowning, sucked under by the demise of the tug.

Sinking until he thought his feet would touch the bottom, Andre's lungs were flaming for want of air. He struggled to get back to the surface, endlessly far above. Andre's thoughts ran down sluggishly, like a clock about to stop. Perhaps it was time to open his throat to the sea and get this over with. What was the point of further struggle?

With his last despairing lunge, he strained for the surface but thumped into something floating on the water. His hands scrabbled over a rough exterior and found a trailing cord. Pulling himself upward as if climbing out of the depths on the rope, Andre emerged near the one thing anywhere nearby that was still intact. The lifeboat being towed astern of the tug had blown free of its cable.

It took fifteen minutes of simply hanging on the line before Andre had strength enough to even attempt to pull himself into the boat. Even then, it took three tries before he slumped in the bottom.

The tide and the currents running through the Channel played games with the lifeboat and its barely conscious occupant. After having been blown up twice and sunk twice, his unmanaged craft was drifting east toward the German held shore.

❉ ❉ ❉

"Commander Galway!" called the spotter on *Intrepid*'s bridge, "take a look at this! I think I'm seein' things!"

"After thirty-six hours nonstop, what would make you think that, Lincoln? What is it that you think you see?" Trevor pivoted in the direction indicated and raised his binoculars as he asked the question.

"Over there, sir," the lookout replied. "A mile on the port quarter. It . . . I think it's a dog!"

Peering through the glasses, Trevor confirmed that a large rust-colored canine was poised like a figurehead on the bow of a half-submerged ship. "All ahead full," he ordered, trying to keep the panic out of his voice. "Good eye, Mister Lincoln. That not only is a dog . . . that's my dog, and my dad's ship!"

Wairakei had sunk to her rails. The deck aft of the wheelhouse was awash, and the triangular bow jutted skyward like a tiny wooden island. Shattered windows and riddled hull made it seem as if the Luftwaffe had been using her for target practice. As *Intrepid* idled up alongside, Duffy gave a mournful howl, announcing his readiness to leave his perch as soon as possible.

Trevor anxiously scanned the deck and the water around the ketch for the figure of his father. He was on the point of jumping across to *Wairakei* when John Galway stood up inside the battered remains of the cabin and climbed the slanted deck. "Shut up, daft dog," he bellowed. "So," he said to Trevor, "it's yourself come at last?"

"Da! Are you all right?"

"No, I'm not all right! Look what those bloody Huns have done. Had to stay out of sight to keep them from strafing again, but yon demented beast would not keep quiet!"

Trevor sighed with relief. His father's temper left no doubt that he was in fact unhurt. "Come aboard then," he said.

"Send someone across to help me with Annie."

"Annie? Is she . . ."

"I'm all right too!" Annie Galway likewise emerged from the devastated pilothouse. A bandage was clumsily wound around her head, but the smile she flashed Trevor convinced him of the truth of her words. "Be quiet, Duffy," she scolded. "Look, Trevor is here to take us home."

❧   ❧   ❧

The first shells whistled into Lys at just after nine o'clock at night. Sepp was at his post in the bell tower of the church. There was a rushing sound overhead, and then the night exploded as a house one block behind St. Sebastian took a direct hit. The fragments of roof slates that flew through the air were as deadly as the metal slivers from the artillery round.

A second shell dropped into the square in front of the church. It crashed against the fountain, showering the plaza with bits of stone and a geyser of water.

The third shell detonated on a car parked outside the church. The hood of the auto spun into the air—a glowing, red-hot evil spirit—and swooped down the street, killing two cadets.

These visions created an instantaneous new thought for Sepp: the arms of war turn even commonplace things into weapons of destruction.

"Down!" Sepp yelled at his fellow lookouts. They lunged for the narrow ladder, groping in the darkness for the skinny uprights. "Hurry, hurry!" Sepp urged in a rhythmic monotone. He waited until all the others had preceded him, then swung his leg onto the rungs.

Another 155 millimeter round arrived. This explosion hit the church tower about halfway up. In a thunder of shattering bricks and mortar, the top of the column collapsed. Sepp was knocked off the ladder and hurled to the level below.

Almost by accident, he reached out and grasped the bell rope swinging nearby. The wildly oscillating cord wrapped itself around him as much as he succeeded in grasping it. He slid and fell through a newly created gap in the floor, down to the center of the sanctuary.

An hour later, Sepp was at his post by the river. Despite the pain from his cracked ribs, he had time to wonder why the Germans had not again attempted to cross the bridge. The shelling went on and on, without let up, and no assault came.

He drew a careful breath, since an unguarded one hurt. He thought that the Germans must not know the true strength and disposition of the troops guarding Lys. Perhaps they believed that there were more than actually held the town.

A shadow moved on the far bank. Instantly a dozen rifles and two machine gun positions opened fire. The night was braided into woven strands of light and dark by the flashes and the streams of tracers. The German side of the river responded, the lines of bullets so crossed in midair that it seemed they must knock each other down and fall into the river. Then the crackle of arms tapered off and both banks of the Lys were silent again.

"In the dark," Sepp remarked to Cadet Treville, "they cannot gauge our capacity. The fact that a lucky shot took out that first armored car makes them wary of the bridge."

"Will you tell Captain Gaston that it was a lucky hit?" Treville teased.

"Get back to your post," Sepp ordered, feeling the ache under the yards of sheet wrapped around his middle. "Dawn will change things, and we must be ready."

SEVENTY-TWO

Horst was in the half-track he used as a command vehicle, receiving a reprimand from newly arrived SS General Ruef, "Why are you not across the river already, von Bockman? Here I am with a division of infantry, ready to move on to the beaches and capture fifty thousand Britishers, and I find the road blocked and our armor sitting idle on this side."

Horst tried to remain patient. "Resistance was stiffer than we anticipated," he said.

"Why have you not called in the bombers? Level the entire town, especially that obvious command post up on the hill."

"That command post is a hospital and clearly marked," Horst said, his anger rising in spite of his effort to control it. "Would you bomb a hospital?"

"If it serves the Reich," said the SS officer, with menace behind the words. "In fact, I have already asked for air support but was told that the Luftwaffe is completely engaged attacking the shipping and the beaches. In any case, that is not our immediate concern. Why are your tanks not across that bridge?"

"The fact that the bridge is still intact worries me."

"Worries you!" exploded the general. "Seize the opportunity at once!"

"It should not be intact. It makes me wonder what sort of trap the French are trying to lure us into. I propose sending a flanking movement downstream to Rosier to come in behind the town."

"Nonsense," the general exclaimed. "Major, you will clear the roads of your machines. I will bring up my own tanks, and we will get this advance moving again!"

❖   ❖   ❖

The main building of the École de Cavalerie was rapidly filling with additional wounded for whom there was no more room in the damaged dormitory. Paul Chardon was in his office, meeting with the newly arrived commanders of the British Guardsmen contingent and the French Cavalry detachments.

"With our five hundred men and those that you gentlemen have brought up to the line," Paul said across his heavy oak desk, "our strength is in the neighborhood of two thousand. That should give us the ability to hold out here for at least a day, perhaps two."

"But your five hundred men, as you call them, are schoolboys," protested the senior French colonel. "They should be withdrawn at once."

"My schoolboys have been preparing for this defense for months, Colonel. Your officers would do well to heed what my cadet officers have to say. How many more reinforcements may we expect?"

The Allied officers exchanged a look. "There will be no more reinforcements," the French colonel said.

A cadet, crisply dressed in his black uniform, presented himself at the door. "What is it, Denis?"

"Captain Gaston reports armored vehicles approaching the bridge, sir."

"Tell him to blow the span to the south shore at once," Paul ordered.

Denis saluted and turned to leave when the whine of an artillery shell screamed down. The round came through the roof at the front of the building and burst in the corridor outside Paul's office.

The concussion knocked Cadet Denis across the room. The body of the sixteen-year-old received the shrapnel and the stout oak desk absorbed the blast, saving the life of Paul Chardon. The other Allied commanders were not so fortunate. Exposed to the full force of the concussion, they died instantly.

The artillery fire had raked the town all night long. Shells from the German 155 millimeter guns rained down on Lys. The Hôtel de Pomme d'Or, once-favored haunt of the titled nobility in the nineteenth century, dissapeared in a cloud of brick dust and shattered mortar. The tower of the church took several more hits until it was reduced to a heap of shattered stone.

Explosions also rocked the school, but because most of the barrage was directed at the heart of the city and the buildings on the island, the École escaped serious damage.

The cadets and the other defenders wisely held their fire, knowing that a rifle shot aimed in the dark could scarcely damage the Panzers but would certainly draw a twenty-pound bomb in return. Inside the crypt of the church and the cellar of the Hôtel de la Cité, the cadets bided their time, waiting for the shelling to cease.

At daybreak the shelling lifted. Gaston returned to his command post on the island and under cover of the sandbagged parapets repaired the damaged lines that ran to the demolition charges.

A pall of smoke hung over the town and floated over the river, an acrid curtain of biting fog. Gaston could not see across the river, but the sudden resumption of machine gun fire ripping into the barricade and singing off the stonework into the town let him know what was coming.

The rumble of tanks approached the bridge. A thirty-seven millimeter round shattered the cornice of the building just above him. The raining fragments killed Cadet Lieutenant Beaufort and a chunk the size of a man's fist landed on Gaston's head. It knocked him to the paving stones and left a gash behind his ear.

His antitank crews, seeing him struck down, began to fire without waiting. They loaded and launched cartridge after cartridge of the twenty-five millimeter shells, wasting much of their ammunition when it bounced off the front armor of the Panzers.

More shells landed nearby, tearing apart the gun crew. Bullets from across the river and from the tank weapons poured in, keeping other cadets from being able to take their places.

The forward tank rolled up to the midpoint of the bridge, blocked by the remains of the armored cars. It nosed against them, then pushed them aside. There was a momentary contest between the strength of the tank and the stone wall. Then the three-hundred-year-old rampart yielded. The tank pushed the carcass of first one and then the other Kfz 231's over the edge and into the river.

Gaston felt someone shaking him. He did not know where he was. In fact, he believed that he was home in bed and his mother was trying to awaken him. "I don't have to get up yet," he mumbled. "And I have a terrible headache."

"Captain!" Cadet Plachet urged. "Wake up! The tanks are on the bridge!"

Gaston awoke to the danger. Despite the throbbing in his head and the distraction of seeing everything double, he pulled himself over to the plunger of the detonator. The tanks opened up on the island with their machine guns and cannons, blasting chunks of stonework out of the walls and ripping into the sandbags.

The French soldiers and the cadets stationed on the island and on the Lys shore fired their antitank weapons, but this morning, nothing seemed to be working.

Gaston waved his men back to cover behind the heaps of rubble that had been the buildings on the island. The third tank in the column that rumbled onto the bridge bore the personal pennant of an SS general.

There was not an instant to spare. Gaston twisted the plunger to unlock it, then pulling it up, he jabbed it home. The force behind the blow on the handle made it seem that he was trying to knock the bridge down by the strength of his arm alone.

The lead tank gunner spotted Gaston at the same instant and swivelled the machine gun toward him. Flecks of rock spun into the air from the ricochets, blinding Gaston and lacing his face with fragments.

The bridge erupted with a roar. Beginning at the end nearest the island, the centuries-old arches heaved upwards as if living things were emerging from under the water. Each vaulted span shattered in turn, catapulting boulders into the air. The tanks reared on their treads like startled elephants, then dropped submissively into the river below.

❧ ❧ ❧

The course of the Seine turned south again after Rouen. The farmlands of Normandy spread out in a peaceful carpet of spring color. There was no war here.

"Up on deck!" Rose ordered, when the first stirrings were heard below. She scouted the banks of the wide river and brought the *Garlic* into a lee where a stand of willows dipped their branches in the quiet waters. They moored the boat. Lewinski, Jerome, and the five brothers went to work gathering branches with which to camouflage the dark hull of the peniche.

Personal needs were taken care of on shore. Boys walked or were carried by Lewinski to the bank on the left. Girls all traipsed to the right. Faces washed. Clean underthings put on. Dirty clothes rinsed in the river. Only then were the children gathered on deck for prayer and a breakfast of tinned biscuits and jam. Rose cautiously sniffed a jug of apple juice, then declared it drinkable and passed it all around.

Lewinski, looking oddly happy and at peace, held Yacov on his knee and watched over the congregation from a place in the sun. He did not wear the customary gas mask. His nervous hands twirled a willow branch.

"I will carve whistles if you will bring me sticks," he told the boys and Juliette and Marie.

Then Josie said to Rose, "Even sailors and the daughters of sailors must sleep sometime."

It was noted by those who had lived at Number 5 la Huchette with Madame Rose that in all that time no one had ever seen her sleep. They all assumed that Madame Rose never needed sleep. She had always been up and dressed before they arose, and never to bed before they were all tucked in.

Therefore, it was a matter of great interest when she growled at them to all go away. She placed a blanket on a cotton sack in the bow where the willow branches made a curtain and promptly began to snore.

Madame Rose snoring? It was much more amazing than the sound of bombs.

❧ ❧ ❧

"Send that SS engineer company up here on the double," Horst ordered. When the Captain of Engineers arrived, he looked around for the SS commander. "Your general," Horst informed the man, "is at the bottom of the Lys. You are now under my authority." Whether true or not, the claim worked.

The bridging unit brought up pontoon sections to construct new spans for the river and inflatable boats. Horst ordered the SS infantry into the rubber rafts. "We will supply the covering fire," he said. "Your job is to get across the river and establish yourselves on the island."

The south shore of Lys dissappeared in the smoking roar of cannon and machine gun fire. The defenders on the island and Sepp's troops in the city were reduced to shooting back blindly over the tops of their shelters.

❊   ❊   ❊

Throughout the morning Madame Rose rested while the children played or simply sat and watched from the shelter of the willows. A half dozen times the moaning of aircraft passed overhead. They were too high to identify. French Moranes? British Spitfires? German Me-109s?

Josie did not want to know, but the boys played guessing games. If their conclusions were correct, then four formations out of the six had been Luftwaffe. They were headed in the direction of Le Havre. It was not a good sign.

Willow whistles carved for all passengers, the *Garlic* chugged away from the bank around noon. The Seine snaked south to La Bouille then north to Duclair. One more long *U* brought the *Garlic* to Caudebec, and then the bends began to straighten and the wide mouth of the Seine River opened to the sea and the great Port of Le Havre in the late afternoon. The Canal de Tancarville, fifteen miles long, connected the Seine directly with Le Havre, enabling ships to escape the tidal changes in the estuary. Today, Rose chose not to go to the port city by way of the canal. She guessed rightly that the planes which had swept over them had been heading for the Tancarville and the vessels in the locks. Tall plumes of smoke marked where those craft had been spotted and destroyed in the locks.

"Ducks in a barrel," Rose said grimly as the shallow-bottomed *Garlic* moved easily across the estuary at slack tide.

Entering the bay, it was plain to see that, like Rouen, Le Havre had been hit hard. The grey film of dissipating smoke was visible from miles away. Its ship building and sugar refineries were the envy of all Europe. Eight miles of quays and 190 acres of water-area made the port of Le Havre one of the most important harbors of France. The Bassin de l'Eure was alone seventy acres, and it was there that the great liners of the Compagnie Generale Transatlantique were berthed.

"I had hoped to get fuel there," Rose said. For the first time her voice registered concern. The masts of the peniche were still down, lashed to the decks. Fuel in the tank was alarmingly low, perhaps not enough to reach England, Rose confided to Josephine and Lewinski.

But to chance being in the harbor of Le Havre could be fatal.

"We will sail north along the coast," the old woman decided as she inhaled the fresh salt aroma of La Manche. The color returned to her cheeks. "There is the little port of Fecamp. They might have fuel. And if Fecamp is being attacked, then Veulette. Or Dieppe north of that. And further . . ."

"Calais and Boulougne are fallen," Lewinski said. "This General Guderian captured Abbeville and then swept north to take the channel ports. By now he may have turned south again, Madame. We must be very careful, whatever harbor we enter for fuel."

Madame Rose stuck her lower lip out. Her mouth turned down as she considered the warning. "We have no compass," she said flatly. "Give me a compass and I can sail around the world in a bath tub. But I feel the lack of a compass. Beyond this estuary the Atlantic is a vast place. The Channel current could carry us away if we were to run out of fuel . . . We must stay within sight of the sea coast, then cross the Pas de Calais."

Lewinski's cheek twitched nervously at this remark. The narrow strait between France and England was sure to be filled with battleships, mines, and who could say what else? "Madame," he bowed his head in a gesture like a gawky schoolboy studying an insect. "As I have explained, the entire French coast along the Pas de Calais is in the hands of the Boche. It will be far too dangerous."

"Yes, very dangerous," she agreed.

For an instant Rose seemed undecided. Was that a flash of fear in her eyes? The shouts of Jerome and Henri and Georg pulled her attention as they emerged victoriously from the hold with a cane fishing pole in hand. Wearing his tall boots, Henri rode on the back of Georg, and the boys paraded to where the others sat together at the bow. The wind pulled hair back from newly freckled faces. Big ears stuck out. The boys were grinning; all of them. And the girls? Surrounded by cables and sitting in a pen of canvas, Marie and Juliette shared imaginary tea with the baby. As if it were all simply a great adventure, like ladies on the deck of an ocean steamer, they must have their tea.

"Look how completely they trust," Rose remarked quietly. She flexed her fingers and wiped the perspiration off her sunburned forehead.

The cry of sea gulls sounded as they circled overhead and then spun off toward the north. Her eyes narrowed as if she heard another voice. Some decision was made in that instant, Josie knew. Some thought, some vision, entered the old woman's mind. She brought the *Garlic* about as if to follow the course of the gulls to the north along the seacoast.

"The children may remain on deck. But secure them with life lines," she instructed. "The sea can be rough in the Channel and they will certainly all be sick," she added cheerfully.

❊ ❊ ❊

Mac pitched in to help build still more of the improvised jetties. Since he was not a part of any unit on the beach, he figured that making himself useful would help when it came time to getting out of there.

He and a party of men from Royal Army Ordnance were dispatched to La Panne to round up more discarded vehicles. There had been a Stuka attack a few minutes before their arrival, and the most promising lorries were bombed out and smoldering.

One truck had been overturned by the blast, but it appeared to be whole. If it could be righted, it would take its place as part of a pier.

" 'Fore we go to heavin' on it," an Ordnance corporal said, "what say we look to see it isn't full of bombs or some such?"

The rear doors resisted tugging, but succumbed to the blows of a fire ax. "Blimey," the corporal exclaimed, staring. This is a NAAFI lorry!"

NAAFI was the source of personal items for the servicemen. The truck was loaded with all kinds of food and other treasures. Soon men were loading their arms with cartons of cigarettes, bars of chocolate, and new pairs of shoes.

The corporal passed some jars back to Mac. "Help yourself, mate," he said. "No use leavin' it for the Jerries."

Mac stuffed a handful of chocolate bars into his jacket and added a tin of something without even looking at it. There would be no more work done on the jetty by this party, it was clear. Mac went off to look somewhere else for a ride.

❊ ❊ ❊

How long Andre drifted in the open boat, he could not say. It was the noise of the breakers crashing ahead that roused him, and he saw at once the danger he was in. The lifeboat contained only a single remaining oar. Struggling against his still-overwhelming weariness, Andre rigged the oar as a primitive rudder and used it to aim the bow of the craft toward the land.

A swell rose under the keel of the boat, and for an instant it surfed along the crest, propelled toward the shore. Then the wave outran Andre's ability to keep in position, and he drifted again between the crests.

A vagrant surge turned the boat half round and left it in danger of broaching. Desperately sweeping the oar, Andre forced a correction to the lifeboat's course. It swung ponderously about while Andre divided his attention between the shore ahead and the next wave racing up from astern.

This time the crest of the breaker caught the full weight of the vessel, pushing it beachward as if it had been fired from a cannon. Andre worked his oar with frantic haste, expecting at any moment to be turned sideways and capsized.

The instant that the keel grated on the sand, Andre jumped out, leaving the lifeboat to the rough hands of the sea. He was safely back on shore, but where? He knew that the currents and the wind had driven him east toward Ostend, but how far east? From behind the spit of land on which Andre had grounded, he could not even see the smoke of the ruins of Dunkirk. All he could do was start toward the west and try to find another ship.

Hearing sounds approaching the beach, Andre hid himself in the brush behind the dunes. A German soldier appeared out of a draw and walked toward the water, passing within fifty feet of Andre's hiding place. The soldier was young and had his rifle slung across his back. As Andre watched, the rifleman took off his coal scuttle helmet and wiped the sweat from his forehead. "Fritz! Wo bist du?" the soldier called. Another German within hailing distance, Andre worried. What if there were a whole patrol?

When the German had called twice more, a little white dog burst out of the shrubbery and ran to the soldier. "Fritz," he said. "You bad dog!"

The Wehrmacht trooper knelt down to scratch his pet's ears. His Gewehr service rifle was still loosely hanging across his back. Andre rushed forward, striking the back of the German's neck with his forearm and knocking him face first into the sand. Pulling up on the weapon tightened the strap where it crossed the man's throat and chest.

Andre pressed his foot against the soldier's neck and yanked upward on the rifle. The German's hands fluttered around his throat and then he lay still while the dog bounced around on the sand, yapping and barking.

Andre removed the German's rifle, cartridge belt, canteen, and helmet and faded into the dunes, heading toward Dunkirk. When he looked back the last time, the puppy was sitting on the sand beside the body, pawing his master's outflung arm and whining.

❊   ❊   ❊

One of Gaston's anti-tank guns had been knocked out. He took personal charge of the other, using it to blow the rubber rafts out of the water. The problem was, for every boat that he destroyed, two more seemed to take its place.

An SS sergeant stood on the stern of yet another inflated craft. With one hand he directed the boat toward the island with the tiller of the tiny outboard motor. With the other he fired his MG 34 from the hip. Gaston saw the man snarl as he snapped out orders to the two little rafts on either side. He was resourceful, that sergeant. The two flanking boats contained men with grenade launchers that lobbed explosives toward Gaston's position, even as the sergeant sprayed bullets to keep the defenders from firing back. It was a well-executed attack.

Gaston took particular pleasure in squaring the sights of the antitank gun on the man's chest. The twenty-five millimeter round blew a hole in the sergeant's chest big enough to see daylight through before he toppled into the water. The rubber boat, left without a helmsman, skittered crazily over the river like a spooked horse before being punctured by the hail of gunfire and sinking in midstream. The other two boats turned back.

Gaston called his runner to him. "I want you to carry a message to Captain Sepp," he said. "And when you have delivered it, stay with him. Tell him that that attack here is increasing. I do not know how long we can hold, so I am going to blow the bridge between the island and the town, lest the Germans get it intact."

"Yes, Captain Gaston. Anything else?"

Gaston looked off in the distance for a second. "Tell him to die gloriously," he said.

⚜ ⚜ ⚜

Andre reached the outskirts of the Dunkirk perimeter after dark. On the way, he narrowly avoided two German patrols, but eventually he reached Nieuport Bains near the eastern end of the Allied-held territory. The beach was crawling with Germans preparing for a nighttime assault on the defenses.

Ducking back out to the road, Andre found it to be unguarded. He jogged along the verge, ready at any second to fling himself into the brush.

When he had covered a half mile down the darkened highway without seeing or hearing another person, a shot flashed from the darkness ahead and a bullet whizzed past his ear.

"Halt!" a voice commanded in English.

Andre called back, "Don't shoot! I'm French."

"Come in slowly then," he was told, "with your hands in plain sight!"

Andre was escorted at bayonet point to the field hospital which doubled as the headquarters of the sector's defense. "You are about to be attacked along the shore," he told the lieutenant who interrogated him.

"I have no doubt," said the weary-looking officer, running a hand over his stubbled face and rubbing his bloodshot eyes. "We're trying to evacuate the nurses and the walking wounded."

A tall figure in a rumpled and bloodstained nurse's uniform passed the small cubicle and looked in at Andre's oil-streaked face. Nurse Mitchell turned back. "It is Colonel Chardon, is it not?" she said.

"Ah, Sister Mitchell," Andre recalled. "So you were successfully withdrawn from the school. Do you know where I can find my brother? Has he already taken ship for England?"

"Do you not know?" she asked. "He has refused to leave. He and the students of the École are fighting the rearguard action so that the rest of us can get away!"

✣　✣　✣

North by northeast the compass would have read if the *Garlic* had possessed a compass. Which it did not.

This might have been a disaster had it not been for the resourcefulness of Jerome. An old, water-stained maritime chart was dug out of a musty locker. There was a spot of green mold marking Le Havre, and a tear through the inset map of Dieppe. But every shoal and sandbar which had been in the Channel seventy-five years ago when the chart was printed was marked for Madame Rose to study.

It was after dark. Rose hugged the shoreline. By keeping the sound of the breakers always on her right, she stayed in touch with the coast. It was a trick she had learned in California, she said, to help navigate in fog.

Here and there a wink of light from the shore gleamed out. She steered the ship far enough from the shoals to be safe, but near enough to land that if the wheezing engine of the ancient barge died, there still might be some hope of making it to shore.

Thirty miles up the coast from Le Havre was the tiny fishing village of Fecamp. It was here that Rose hoped to obtain fuel for the *Garlic*. She judged their progress as a tedious six knots. That meant five hours from Le Havre to Fecamp.

Five hours passed and still her scouts had not spotted the lighthouse or the warning buoys which had been plainly identified on the chart as marking the entrance of the small harbor.

Marie, blinking through the thick lenses of her spectacles, caught sight of some small glimmer. She shouted cheerfully that the harbor for Madame Rose had been found. But it was merely the moving lights of some vehicle which, heedless of the blackout, had no covers on the headlamps.

The breakers roared against the beaches to their right. The wind grew cold. Josie took the younger children below and covered them with coarse woolen blankets. They asked if Madame Rose would come to tuck them in. Would she come and sing them to sleep and help them say their prayers?

Explaining that Madame Rose was busy, Josie added that perhaps she would come later. She tried to stand in for the old woman's nighttime ritual, but no one was content.

"Madame Rose is steering the boat. The boat will rock you to sleep. Therefore, Madame Rose is rocking you to sleep."

This explanation satisfied them and they slept.

Six hours passed. No harbor of Fecamp. Then seven. The engine chuffed onward.

"We have missed Fecamp," Rose said. "They blacked out their entrance lights, and we sailed past them."

Josie wondered about the fuel.

Lewinski taught the Austrian brothers and the special children how to play a Polish tune on their whistles. They grew weary. Some went down to sleep out of the wind. Lewinski carried the boys who could not walk. He joked with them and asked Henri where he had gotten such fine boots.

Josie thought that Lewinski was a very human fellow when he was pried away from his machine. He came up and played with his whistle, making a small piping noise like a bird in a thunderstorm.

The noise of the surf was more distant. Madame Rose corrected their course, bringing the vessel in parallel with the roar.

Unable to stay awake any longer, Josie fell asleep against the heap of canvas sails. When she woke it was still dark and the *Garlic*'s shudder had stopped. The engine was silent. The vessel rocked gently on the swells. The crash of the breakers had shifted to the left side of the craft. Had they turned back? Had the engine failed?

"Out of fuel," Rose said to Lewinski when his mellow voice called from the nest he had made for himself beside the anchor.

"Will we be caught in the breakers?" His voice was calm.

"I think not. The current has us. We are somewhere between England and France, drifting very slowly toward America."

For hours the disabled *Garlic* floated in the current of the Channel. There seemed to be no help for it. Josie asked Madame Rose if they could put up the masts and pull up the sails.

"Step the masts and hoist the sails," Rose corrected. "No, dear, I'm afraid not. Even with everyone on board, we are still not enough for a task like that. We will certainly fetch up somewhere. Don't lose hope," Rose told her. "Look how far we have come in this old tub of a ship."

The night itself gave no cause to feel frightened. The engineless boat was never completely quiet. The ancient hull creaked and groaned like a poor old soul with the miseries—definitely a complainer.

Josie found herself wondering how far the barge had travelled in its lifetime; how many ports visited, strange cargos carried. She would bet that it had never seen passengers like this assortment, no matter how exotic its past.

A low hum joined the squeak of the rigging. It grew in volume. The source of the noise was a puzzle. It seemed to come from all around, all at once. "Rose?"

"I hear it too," Rose said.

A grey hull loomed out of the darkness on the *Garlic*'s port beam. Madame Rose clanged the signal bell, the only warning device the barge carried. The sudden, sharp clamor seemed piercingly loud in the stillness.

An angry foghorn bellowed from the new ship. The prow of the vessel swung away from the *Garlic,* missing by fifty feet, but still too close. Josie felt as if her heart would jump out of her chest.

Another horn blasted from the other beam of the barge, then another from astern. "It's a whole fleet!" Rose said. "Light the lantern, Josephine. Now it doesn't matter who they are, we don't want to be run down!"

In response to Josie's lantern, the first ship came alongside. Her bow said that she was the *Lotte,* and the square box of her pilothouse forward of the cargo boom said her home port was Harfleur. "Fishing trawler," Madame Rose remarked.

The children poured up on deck because of all the noise. "What has happened?" Jerome asked. "Are we there yet?"

A spotlight beam from the *Lotte* played over the deck of the *Garlic,* making Josie and the children squint.

"*Quoi?*" a voice said in French. "What is this? A floating nursery school?"

"A kind of Noah's Ark," Rose called back. "We are out of fuel. Can you spare us some?"

"Yes, but if we do so, you must accompany us."

"Where are you bound?"

"Does not everyone know? We are the fishing fleet of Harfleur, bound for Dunkirk to rescue our boys from the Boche!"

SEVENTY-THREE

The dunes north of Dunkirk bore the imprint of thousands of tramping boots.

The tide was out, exposing a jetty made of lorries. A hundred yards up the beach two more piers had been constructed of freight barges run aground and bottoms knocked out. High and dry, they were now out of reach of the swarm of little ships, and yet long lines of men stretched beyond them into the water.

From the hills down to the water, the sand was littered with clumps of newly arrived men. Fifty or a hundred in a group, they gathered around their unit's leader as if they were scouts on a campout.

David and Badger joined a group of half a hundred from an artillery regiment. They were sullen company, having retreated without ever firing a shot. The regiment had moved forward into Belgium on the first day of Blitzkrieg. But because of the refugees clogging the roads, they stopped short of their preassigned position and withdrew in the face of the German onslaught. They had been withdrawing ever since.

Now they had been forced to abandon their weapons as well. An artilleryman who has been trained to fight from behind the breech of a cannon has no purpose in life when he has no artillery to fire. These men felt the shame of never having inflicted damage on the enemy. More than any group David had met, this regiment had accepted the stigma of running away.

David spoke with a captain and asked if he and Badger could join the group waiting for evacuation. "Can't think why you'd want to," the officer replied listlessly. "You and your friend have obviously seen action. Someone should save a place for you at the head of the queue."

The captain returned to staring out at the line of breakers. Some of his men slept. Others scooped out shallow pits for themselves. None seemed interested in talking. It was dusk, and each man was alone with his gloomy thoughts.

A low, incessant drumming of many engines announced the return of another flight of Heinkels to bomb Dunkirk. David counted the heavy-bodied twin-engine planes until his tally reached ninety-nine, then gave up. His arm ached, and he wondered if he had made a mistake leading Badger out in the open and leaving the safety of the shelter.

The bombs whistled down on the docks and the warehouses and the oil tanks of Dunkirk. But the heavy thump and rumble of high explosives was missing, and the objects falling from the German warplanes looked like bundles of sticks.

"Incendiaries," David muttered to Cross.

Orange flames licked at the shattered rubble left from earlier explosions, and the fire soon engulfed the smashed businesses and hotels of the city. Brown and grey columns of wood smoke rose up to join the black fumes from the burning oil tanks.

"Poor sods," Badger murmured, "but it'll be us next." David knew that he was referring to the soldiers who huddled in the cellars, believing they were safe there. Tons of debris piled over their hiding places became massive funeral pyres.

Badger had grown very fatalistic. To counter this despair, David became ever more obsessed with strawberries. He had come to think of Badger's birthday as a symbol of their survival.

The men on the beach did not escape the attention of the Luftwaffe. As the Heinkels unloaded their bombs, each made a lazy circuit of the town and the harbor, ignoring the intermittent fire of a French antiaircraft battery. The planes searched for targets of opportunity to machine gun, and many of their pilots spotted the clusters of men on the beach.

The first Heinkel roared over the dunes, lines of tracers winking into the sand. The machine flashed overhead and was gone.

But that was only the beginning. For the next fifteen minutes, bombers buzzed the beach from every conceivable angle. Some burst into view suddenly from out of the thick smoke over the town. More could be seen turning over the harbor, inexorably charging toward the mass of men.

When it was all over, fifty men were dead and thirty more wounded. As many were struck while running away as were hit sitting still.

"Glad that's done," breathed the artillery captain. "Now if the Navy will just hurry up, we'll get off this bit of shingle before Jerry comes back at dawn."

The blazing town of Dunkirk continued to draw bombs even after dark. David watched the leaping tongues of flame that pinpointed the location for the Germans. He described for Badger the nature of each target by the color of the explosion. Dark red flames erupted over an inferno that had been someone's home or shop. Bright orange was an oil storage tank. The bundles of incendiaries burst with glowing green light. It was an unmatched fireworks display accompanied by rolling thunderous drums.

A new brightness joined the exhibition. High over the beach was the hum of a single aircraft, barely to be distinguished from all the other noise. A brilliant purple light cracked the night sky over the sand. It was followed by another and another and another, until the air blazed with violet torches that swayed as they slowly descended.

"Flares!" came the cry.

It was a time to feel naked. The weird illumination made each man feel exposed—singled out. When even the cover of darkness is ripped away, what hiding place remains? The purple glow reflected on David's arm and Badger's bandaged face and hands, as if to especially mark their owners for destruction. It was possible to be in the middle of twenty thousand men and feel very alone.

Something stirred in the dunes. The instinct to run was almost overpowering. But run where? As if reading the terror in every man's mind, a tall lieutenant in a military police uniform leapt to his feet and cried, "Steady on, lads! Don't move! It'll do you no good to panic!"

Unmoving, David held his breath as the shrill whistle of the first stick of bombs screamed from above the flares. Two hundred yards up the beach, geysers of sand erupted into the air, flinging men like rag dolls and a two-ton lorry like a child's toy.

The officer was right. There was nowhere to run; nothing to do but wait and pray that the next load did not fall on him! David sprawled flat in the sand and covered his head. Badger cringed lower with every blast. The concussions deafened them both, shutting out the screams of the dying.

When the bombers passed, David and Badger were still alive, but a group of twenty men who had waited one dune behind them lay in pieces.

Now, not even darkness offered safety. The Germans, it seemed, were intent on preventing the evacuation of any more troops.

David could not help wondering about the wounded soldiers they had left behind in the hospital at the École de Cavalerie. By now they were probably not any better off than those whose blood leached into the sands of Dunkirk. Had the River Lys finally been crossed by the Germans? How long did the men on the beaches have before the Panzer divisions were blasting them from behind, while the Stukas worked them over from the air?

The defenders of the perimeter could not hold out more than hours longer, David figured, by the numbers staggering to the coast. And that meant only hours were left to escape the carnage of Dunkirk.

⚜ ⚜ ⚜

Before daylight, Andre crept out of the lines, under the noses of a British machine gun crew. He hoped, for their sakes, that they were either more vigilant or already evacuated when the Germans came. Still, he reflected that no one in his right mind was traveling the direction he had chosen. No one was sneaking out of Dunkirk and deliberately heading toward the Germans except him.

Andre had explained the desperate situation of the cadets to as many officers as would listen, but in the final analysis, each had promised nothing. Everyone was done in; none saw the mission as anything other than suicide. All the troops who can possibly disengage are here to be evacuated, he was told, not go back into danger.

That was why Andre was so surprised when he heard the sounds of a jogging cadence being called out in French. Flat on his belly, peering from behind a clump of grass, Andre watched the swirling mist as a group of black soldiers trotted into view.

Like fragments of an odd dream, they emerged from the fog. The men were dressed in baggy white breeches, scarlet vests, and red Turkish conical style hats. There were about fifty of them, and they ran in perfect rhythm, rifles slung, packs on backs, and the blades of their bayonets drawn and carried upright against their shoulders. Shaking himself out of his confusion, Andre figured out that they were Senegalese troops. They had almost passed by when he called out to them.

Instantly they surrounded him. Their leader, a sergeant dark as midnight with a saber scar that crossed both his lips, saluted. "Colonel," he said in pleasantly lilting French. "Would you be pleased to lead us? We have lost all our officers, nor can we find Germans to fight either."

Andre explained that he was returning to the cavalry school for what would certainly be a grave struggle. The sergeant made a sweeping bow. "Direct us, Colonel," he said. "We wish to be of service to France."

With Andre at their head, the contingent of Senegalese troops jogged toward Lys.

An aircraft sputtered. A Stuka, obviously already damaged from its low altitude and slow speed, wavered into view. The warplane nosed over and dropped into a nearby field. It landed mostly intact, and Andre saw the canopy of the plane slide open.

The Senegalese sergeant gave an order, and without breaking stride, ten of his men loped across the field to the Luftwaffe craft. They dragged the occupants from the plane, and Andre shuddered as he saw bayonets rise and fall in short chopping motions.

"Already you have brought us good luck," the sergeant said. "Let us go find more Germans to kill."

❊ ❊ ❊

Far out on the water there was a brilliant flash against a leaden curtain. The weather had closed in around the beaches of Dunkirk, obscuring the view of the gleaming white cliffs across the Channel. The soldiers waiting in the queues groaned when their view of home and safety was snatched away.

At least the lowering clouds prevented the Luftwaffe from renewing their attacks. A brief respite from the constant fear of being bombed or strafed was a welcome relief.

David studied the wall of grey that separated him from England. He stared as if he could pierce it by force of will; see Annie there, waiting for him; see her in his arms. A beam of light broke through the overcast. It danced on the surface of the Channel, highlighting the waves. The ray broadened to become a shimmering band of silver. Like something tangible, it moved across the face of the sea, directly toward David. Halfway to him, it broke in two, and the first patch of glowing light continued his way while the other part retreated to the English shore.

Fascinated, almost hypnotized by the spectacle, David scarcely noticed that he and Badger were now at the front of the waiting column. Waves that ran up on the French coast splashed their feet. A boat was returning again, making its way to shore.

Behind David and Badger, a man broke from the ranks and sprinted forward into the surf. "Take me," he begged, though he came from far back in the mob. "I can't stand it any more!"

A Royal Navy lieutenant commander drew a pistol. "Get back in line," he ordered, "or I'll shoot!"

Sullenly, the soldier returned to his place and melted back into the crowd. There was no outcry raised against him that David could hear, no demand that the man be punished.

The boat grated on the shoal, and this time an officer jumped out and ran to the beachmaster. They held a whispered conference, while David and the others at the head of the line secured the launch against the tide's pull.

The lieutenant commander looked grim as he addressed the crowd. Badger Cross leaned his head forward to listen, as if he had been deafened instead of blinded.

"*Wakeful* has been torpedoed," the officer said, "just after the launch delivered the last lot on board. She went down on the spot. I'm sorry. I have been told that larger ships are now getting into the harbor. My advice to you is to go back to Dunkirk. Otherwise you'll just have to remain here and hope another comes along."

Cross shook his head sadly. "I knew I'd never come away. I've seen my last birthday, Tinman."

❈　❈　❈

Cadet Raymond heard the firing from upstream, but no Germans came near his position. The sound of approaching engines on his side of the river came from the direction of the school. Captain Chardon, his arm in a sling, rolled up in a truck followed by two Hotchkiss tanks. Raymond reported that all was quiet and asked if the time had come to destroy the bridge.

"Not yet," Paul said. "I think we have a use for this crossing still." Swiftly he outlined his plan. "The Germans now know our true strength," he said. "And their artillery keeps us so pinned down that we cannot send Sepp or Gaston any reinforcements. At nightfall the Wehrmacht will cross in force. What we need is a diversionary assault. Perhaps even knock out their guns." He raised his good arm and pointed his thumb at the tanks.

Raymond knew that the two lightweight and lightly armed vehicles were scarcely a match for the Panzers. "We must go at once, before they mount an attack this direction," Raymond said. "I propose sending a troop of our cavalry along as well." He could not believe that he said that. It had just popped out.

Paul smiled at his young protégé. "I thought you'd say that," he said. "Take your force across the bridge and set up a defensive perimeter on that side to keep the road open. Your column of horses and the two tanks will circle toward the battery of German guns, do what damage you can, and come back immediately. Remember," he admonished, "if you are too slow, the bridge will have to be demolished and you will be stuck on the other side."

The oddly mixed column of Raymond's twenty-five horsemen, one hundred British Grenadier Guards, and two rumbling Hotchkiss units spurted across the river on the swaying bridge. Lighter by almost ten tons than any of the Panzer tanks, the French machines were able to cross the creaking structure to launch and attack.

The Guards were detailed off to protect the approach to the bridge, having been given strict instructions by Paul that they were to fall back to the north shore and blow the span at the first sign of a serious German offensive.

The cavalry troop went south into the woods, their horses traveling at a fast walk. The flanks of the line were defended by the tanks. There was no opposition, even though Raymond could hear the continued shooting in Lys.

It was a wide swing away from the river, but one designed to bring them in behind the location of the batteries that shelled the town. Perhaps the German maps did not show the suspension bridge, and so they were unaware of another approach to Lys. Or perhaps they were so supremely confident of their overwhelming force that they felt no need for anything other than a frontal assault. Whatever the reason, Raymond's force met none of the enemy as they pivoted toward the sound of the guns. The Germans were so unused to anyone attacking them since this campaign began that they had not bothered to post any guards.

❖ ❖ ❖

Gaston had been wounded again. Besides the wad of bandage taped behind his ear that looked and felt like a pack of cigarettes, he now had a scar on his chest.

He thought what a close call it had been. The bullet had ricochetted off the brim of his helmet and plunged down into his collar. The steel hat sported a hole just above his eyes and there was an angry red tear that ran along his breastbone.

The little band of defenders shrank rapidly. From over two hundred with which Gaston had begun his defense of the island, only forty remained alive and unharmed. Both anti-tank weapons were demolished, but then they were without more ammunition anyway.

Every hour, the shells of the big guns and the mortars rained down on his position. After a twenty-minute bombardment, the shelling ceased, which was the signal that the waves of rubber rafts would again be crossing the Lys. If it was not so terrifying, it would be tedious.

"They are coming again," Gaston shouted as the firing stopped. The last shelling had taken a further toll of his forces. "Captain," a voice called, "I am almost out of ammunition."

"I also," came the cry.

"And I."

Gaston looked to the sack of grenades and what remained of the box of machine gun ammunition. "Grenades and bayonets, then," he shouted back.

Gaston saw Cadet Francois stand to hurl a grenade; saw him shot down and fumble the explosive onto the ground. Burying his head in his hands, Gaston hid from the blast that erupted over the island. He called out the names of the last cadets he had seen alive; he received no response.

Ammunition exhausted, grenades gone, and reduced to his bayonet alone, Gaston thought about surrendering. He decided he could not give up. Not while Sepp and the others lived and continued to fight.

Racing to the edge of the island nearest to the town, Gaston flung himself off the pilings that remained of the demolished bridge. As he did so, he saw that a handful of other defenders, French cavalry and cadets, were likewise swimming toward Lys. The island now belonged to the Germans, but the battle could be continued from the wreckage of the town.

Rifle shots cracked behind him, throwing up splashes of water. He heard each snap as the round was fired, the zing of the bullet and the hiss as it struck the water. But none found him, and the small arms that replied to the Germans from Sepp's position spoiled their aim.

He continued pulling strongly toward safety. As he swam, the fear struck him that the lump of bandage behind his ear would make an excellent target for a marksman.

As Gaston reached the shore, Sepp dashed down to the water's edge and helped drag him behind the sandbag barricade. Gaston heard his friend give a grunt of pain, and Sepp abruptly dropped his arm.

"Sepp!" Gaston cried out, "where are you hit?"

Sepp's mouth worked, but no sound came. He gestured weakly toward his side.

Ripping apart his friend's tunic, Gaston's hand came away covered in blood. "Help!" Gaston cried. "Help me, Captain Sepp is wounded!" No one replied; no one moved to help. The few who remained alive on the shore fired at the Germans or nursed wounds of their own. For the rest, Gaston could see them fleeing away from the river. "Will no one help?" he pleaded.

Sepp seized Gaston's hand and squeezed hard. He struggled to speak, gathering breath from the bottom of his soul and forcing it out of lungs too weary to go on working. "Gaston," he said weakly. "You . . . must go."

"Never!" Gaston swore, his eyes smarting with tears. "I will stay here and die beside you!"

"Listen to me!" Sepp whispered fiercely, urgently. "France . . . still needs you. Get away . . . une battle perdu . . . n'a pas la guerre." Sepp's voice sighed to a stop, the clock of his life run down.

Gaston took his friend's rifle and tore the badge of his rank from his collar as a memento. "Au revoir," he said. "A battle lost, but not the war." Then he ran away, dodging from a heap of stones to a burned-out vehicle, toward the north.

❧   ❧   ❧

Horst dispatched a column of armored cars along the shore of Lys toward a downstream crossing. The inflated boats had been thrown back so many times that even though the assault continued in front of the town, something else needed to be tried.

The barrage stopped and yet another wave of rafts attempted to cross to Lys. It was difficult to understand how the town continued to resist. The buildings had almost all been levelled, the island was a heap of flaming ruins, and the air was so thick with smoke that breathing was difficult.

How much longer could the Allied soldiers continue to hold?

❧   ❧   ❧

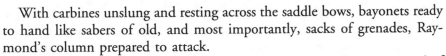

With carbines unslung and resting across the saddle bows, bayonets ready to hand like sabers of old, and most importantly, sacks of grenades, Raymond's column prepared to attack.

The Hotchkiss tanks led the assault, rattling along at their top speed of seventeen miles an hour. But close behind were the cadets of the École de Cavalerie.

The artillerymen were between barrages. The officers smoked in the shade while the soldiers stacked shells in preparation for another bombardment.

The Germans looked up with curiosity as the tanks rolled out of the forest. The armored machines fired their thirty-seven millimeter guns, destroying one cannon and blowing the carriage out from under another. The Wehrmacht troops scattered. Some of the officers futilely fired their sidearms at the attackers but were cut down by machine guns.

Raymond heard one lieutenant yell angrily for his men to stand and form a line, then watched the officer turn with bewilderment to face the onrushing rank of horses. He raised his machine pistol, but Raymond shot him in the chest. The German's gun loosed a burst into the ground as he fell.

The charge tore apart the cannoneers. While the French tanks scuttled in a circle around the perimeter, picking off strays and keeping the Germans from reforming, the horsemen selected out their targets.

Raymond chose the cannon furthest away and galloped the bay horse over to it. Just as he approached, a German soldier who had been hiding behind the gun carriage got up and leveled his rifle. Raymond put the horse into a jump. The front hooves of the bay smashed into the man's head.

With the horse prancing nervously, Raymond watched as his cadets spread themselves out to each of the gun emplacements. Each student took the sack of grenades and prepared for the destruction they had planned.

When all were ready, Raymond pulled the pin on a grenade, dropped it back onto the pouch, and tossed the sack under the cannon. Then he set his mount racing back toward the woods.

When Raymond approached the next emplacement, that cadet did the same maneuver and so on down the line, retrieving the riders and reforming the rank. By the time Raymond had reached the fourth artillery piece, the first explosion shattered the air. The cannon jumped up off the ground, the gun bent in half. Then the weapon flipped over on its side, leaned against the ground, and propped on its now useless barrel.

Horst's tank followed the column of armored cars hurrying toward the downstream crossing of the Lys. Sporadic rifle fire pinged against his vehicle's armor to let him know that the French on the far shore were tracking his progress.

When the line of Panzers had covered four of the five miles, Horst was amazed to see the suspension bridge still intact. The needless sacrifice of men in the continuing frontal assault on the town could cease and a sweeping flank attack substituted.

The next order of business was to secure the crossing and guard it against demolition. Horst knew that for whatever reason the bridge had not already been destroyed, it would be as soon as the German interest in it became apparent.

That he had reached the correct conclusion too late was demonstrated when the lead armored car exploded in a gout of flame, struck by an anti-tank round fired from the south side of the river. Horst ordered his remaining machines to swing into line abreast, taking advantage of the cover of the brush to charge the position ahead. Whatever Allied resources had crossed the Lys, they could not be much compared to the armored unit.

Small arms and machine gun fire rattled off the German tank. His gunner responded by lobbing a high explosive round into the clump of trees ahead. The shot was rewarded with the sight of several bodies in British uniforms flying through the air.

"Major," Horst's radio operator said, "I have picked up a garbled transmission from our battery . . . something about being attacked."

It had to be a mistake. The artillery park was well back away from the river and the Allies had no force across the river unless . . . "Pivot right ninety," Horst shouted to his driver. "All units, watch for flank attack!"

Another armored car, responding to Horst's warning, swung broadside to the British detachment at the same moment that the tank destroyer launched another round. The Sfz 231 was bowled over from the force of the impact, smashing down a tree trunk and ending up on its roof, a smoking ruin.

Ahead was another tank, bearing down on Horst. It was about the right size and shape to be one of the smaller Czech-made Panzer units, but it was coming from the wrong direction. The Hotchkiss tank fired first, an armor piercing shell that narrowly missed Horst's turret and flew across the river before splintering an elm.

"Armor piercing . . . left thirty . . . fire!"

The round penetrated the front armor of the French tank and opened the body of the vehicle as if an opener had been applied to a tin can. "Major," the machine gunner reported, "another Hotchkiss at right ninety."

The gun of Horst's tank was already pivoting to track the new threat when the woods were suddenly swarming with horsemen. The machine gunner fired, knocking a rider out of the saddle and disemboweling a horse when the troop swept past, making for the bridge.

"After them! That is why the bridge is still intact!"

❧   ❧   ❧

Raymond could see the bridge ahead beyond the last screen of brush. Machine gun bullets and high explosive rounds were tearing up the cover on all sides. He urged his horse to redouble his efforts.

The German tanks and armored cars raced along the shore to cut them off. The Guardsmen had abandoned their hopeless position and were retreating back across the span. At any second they might detonate the demolition charges.

Behind him the remaining Hotchkiss tank exploded, victim of yet another German tank. Now there were only a handful of riders jumping over logs and racing death to the remaining link with safety.

Some instinct told him to yank his mount to the side. The obedient horse spun sideways, leaping a ditch just as another shell exploded against a tree trunk along his previous path.

Raymond felt a searing pain in his leg. He looked down to see that a shrapnel splinter gouged a furrow in his leg. But worse, it protruded like a spike from the body of his mount. He tried to pull it out, and the horse nickered in agony.

The bay faltered. It stumbled, recovered, stumbled again. "Not yet," he urged. "Not now! Go! Go!"

The beast responded to this entreaty with a lunge forward, redoubling its efforts to escape the terrible pain.

❧   ❧   ❧

"Left ninety," Horst ordered. "High explosive . . . fire!"

He aimed at the movement he saw on the north bank, knowing that the suspension bridge would soon be destroyed if he could not prevent it.

The guns of the German Panzers reached across the river Lys. Below the fighting drifted the bodies of those who were already done with the battle. German and French together, floating in the amiable comradeship of death, while overhead the machine guns and cannons roared, arguing with each other over the right to claim the river, the crossing, and the fate of France.

❧   ❧   ❧

Andre and his eager Senegalese arrived at the river Lys by the dirt track that led to the suspension bridge and found themselves suddenly immersed in a battle. They unslung their rifles and sprawled forward on their bellies, taking aim across the river.

Below him Andre could see his brother Paul preparing to detonate the bridge. The air was filled with the raining death of the German tank rounds. Andre's arrival had been spotted and his position targeted.

More armored cars and tanks emerged from the woods, an overwhelming assemblage of force.

The Senegalese troops fired back fearlessly, but their small weapons were no match for the cannons and machine guns of the Panzers. They were forced back into a defensive perimeter, dug themselves into the hillside, and prepared to sell their lives dearly.

✤   ✤   ✤

Paul helped a pair of Grenadier Guards who reached the north side of the bridge carry their wounded comrade off the roadway. Behind them, small knots of British soldiers were running back toward the span. They did not bother firing their weapons at the oncoming German vehicles, knowing that the small arms would have no effect on the steel plating.

Paul retreated to the place where the detonation cords came together. "Prepare to fire the charges," he said, realizing as he spoke that he was sealing the fate of Raymond and any of the others who remained across the river.

Suddenly he could see horsemen on the far shore. Behind them shell fire burst among the trees. Paul silently urged them on. He calculated the angle made by the fleeing horsemen and the approaching tanks; knew that the margin was too small, the Germans too close.

Sadly he turned to the engineer standing by the detonator. "Get ready," he said.

Across the river, Raymond came into view. Paul could tell that the bay was injured; it staggered and pitched against the post of the tower that suspended the bridge. Raymond slewed around in the saddle, almost toppling off. So he was wounded too. Paul silently urged horse and rider to hurry, imploring them to get clear.

Raymond had barely reached the north end of the span when his mount stumbled again and fell, pinning the young cadet beneath. Paul started back toward the bridge when the German tank across the river fired again.

"Blow the . . ." Paul's words were cut off as the high explosive round landed close beside him.

✤   ✤   ✤

Paul lay in a pool of his own blood when Andre reached him. Cradling his brother's head in his lap, Andre stroked the matted hair and placed his fingers on Paul's cheek in a gesture of farewell.

Paul, his body shattered, still tried to talk. "Save my boys, Andre," he said. Then he repeated, "Save my sons."

The fighting had stopped. The bridge, the detonation cables severed, had not been blown. Gaston staggered up beside his fallen commander, sinking to his knees at Paul's side.

"Give me a gun!" the boy cried.

Paul shifted his gaze to the row of German Panzer units covering them from the opposite bank of the Lys.

Gaston clutched Andre's sleeve. "Give me a gun! I want to die with honor like the others!"

Paul reached out with a bloody hand to touch Gaston's arm. "It is enough . . . Gaston. Enough."

Andre looked up at a movement across the river. An officer in the uniform of a Wehrmacht major advanced over the span, carrying a flag of truce.

He stood beside Andre and Paul. "I am Major Horst von Bockman, Seventh Panzer. You are the commander?" he asked.

"My brother," Andre replied. "Captain Paul Chardon of the École de Cavalerie."

The major removed his hat and used it to shield the eyes of the dying man. "Captain," he said. "I salute you. Who were the men defending the town?"

Andre replied, "Not men, Herr Major. Five hundred cadets of the École de Cavalerie."

"Kavalleriekadetten . . . Tapfere soldaten . . . brave soldiers." Then to Paul. "Your cadets have resisted the Wehrmacht. You have done all that honor demands. Will you not surrender and stop the killing?"

"No!" Gaston said fiercely.

"Wait," Paul gasped. "Will you . . . let my boys go?"

Andre's eyes seized those of Horst, locked onto them. "I am a colonel," he said. "I will guarantee the surrender of the regular forces if you will let the cadets go."

Horst hesitated only a moment, then nodded and said with a wry smile, "The Führer would not approve . . . however . . . honor among soldiers permits me no other course. A pity you were not born German."

"A pity you were not born French."

"I will allow you a two-hour lead to Dunkirk. You will accompany them. Perhaps we will meet again on another battlefield, Herr Colonel."

Paul smiled and raised his chin. Looking up at Andre he said a last time, "Save my sons for France." Then he died.

❖ ❖ ❖

Lining the road out of Lys, five hundred Panzer troops stood at attention as eighty surviving cadets rode past the body of Captain Paul Chardon for the last time.

In contrast to the depleted supplies of the young defenders, the Germans had a full complement of ordnance: grenades, ammunition, and MG-34 machine guns. As the departing warriors filed by, the Wehrmacht soldiers presented arms.

At the head of the troop, Andre glanced down at the body of his brother, then at Major Horst von Bockman. A look passed between the two men; for a moment, the expression of the German officer softened.

SEVENTY-FOUR

On the morning of his twenty-first birthday, Badger Cross gave up his hope of strawberries, of rescue, and of life.

David also had a growing sense that the Dunkirk miracle would not be a miracle for him and Badger. The defensive perimeter was shrinking as rearguard troops were pulled back and evacuated. As the German lines crept closer to the men on the beach, the Wehrmacht artillery shelled the enclave at will. When the grey skies cleared and Luftwaffe returned in force, it was rumored that the end of the rescue effort was very near.

For the moment the skies above the sand were empty of hostile aircraft. The shelling fell silent.

David had not mentioned the strawberries to Badger or the fact that his birthday had finally arrived. Maybe Badger would not remember the date, David hoped. If they could get on a ship, any ship, and back to England, David would buy Badger a field of strawberries!

"It's quiet," David said. "They've let up."

"I'm twenty-one," Badger replied. "Interesting thing, that a bloke could die twenty-one years to the day after he is born."

"You aren't gonna die." David's tone was firm, but he was thankful Badger could not see the doubt on his face.

"I'm sure of it." Badger raised his nose as if to sniff the air which smelled of cordite and rotting flesh.

"Sure? All this over strawberries. You're looney, that's all."

"No matter about the strawberries. Today is my day."

"Shut up, Badger!" David said hotly. "It's bad luck to talk that way."

Badger paid no heed to the rebuke. "I saw it. Plain as anything." He paused and raised his right hand in the air as if he could see a plane circling above him. "I wonder what time of day I was born?"

"Late," David said gruffly. "Near midnight. Probably it's not even your birthday yet. Probably you still got hours before you have to have those stinking berries."

"Doesn't matter." Badger turned his head away toward the low conversations of a large group of French soldiers who sat in the sand a few feet away.

"What are they saying?" Badger asked.

"How should I know?" David was angry. Angry at Badger. Angry at whoever was in charge of the evacuation. Angry at himself for being stupid enough to get shot down.

"They're saying something about the Panzers moving in on us. The SS shoot anyone wounded. You'd better leave me when they come."

"It would be better if I put my fist in your mouth and knock a few teeth out if you don't knock it off."

"I'm just saying . . ." Badger exhaled loudly. "You've been good about all this, taking me with you and all. I wish there was some way I could repay you."

"I'll think of something. You putz, when we get back to England, I'll think of something. Now shut your trap. We're gonna make it."

Badger did not reply. He turned his head toward the poilus. "I just wish I knew what they were saying."

At that instant an American voice spoke from behind the two men. "They're talking about women. The women they left at home."

David turned slightly to see an oil-covered, stocky-built man, wearing the uniform of an American correspondent.

"You American?" David asked.

"Mac McGrath." The man stuck out a sand-covered paw and pumped David's hand as if they were meeting on a peaceful street corner in Paris. "Some mess we're in, huh?"

David jerked his thumb at the press patch on Mac's shoulder. "You're neutral, unless you know something I don't know. Did Roosevelt decide to join our crusade?"

"Not hardly."

"So what are you doing at Dunkirk? You newsguys go wherever you want on both sides of the line, don't you?"

"I like it better on this side of things," Mac replied with a bitter laugh.

"You've got a death wish. Is that it, pal?" David brushed the sand absently from his hands. "Or are you here for the story?"

"Just not real fond of Nazis. So, what's your excuse for being here?" His brown eyes were ringed with soot, giving him the appearance of a bandit with a crooked nose.

"I wanted to fly Hurricanes," David shrugged. "This is my pal Badger Cross. It's his birthday."

"Lousy place to celebrate." Mac shielded his eyes against the glare of the sun on the water.

"I'll say," David said glumly as Mac moved closer. "The army is not real happy with us RAF guys. Can't say I blame them. They put us at the back of the line. But worse than that, they run us all over the beach and the harbor. We may be the last ones out of this dump."

"We're never getting out of here," sighed Badger. "I told you, Tinman. My birthday . . . and no strawberries."

Mac snorted. "Real cheerful fella."

David shrugged. "Never mind him. He's crazy."

Badger wagged his head. "I'm doomed, Mister McGrath, and you too if you stick by me."

The other solitary souls edged away from Badger at this thought, and shortly, Mac, David, and Badger found themselves a very small group indeed. David explained Badger's preoccupation with strawberries and cream. "I got the tin of milk," he said. "I've been carrying it around with me. But you can't find strawberries anywhere around here. But today is your birthday, and it isn't over yet."

"Would a chocolate bar do?" Mac offered, patting his pockets for the food pilfered from the NAAFI truck. "Or how about . . ." and he withdrew a jar of strawberry jam from his jacket.

It was probably cruel, but David could not resist opening the jar under Badger's nose. The gauze twitched, and the big man said mournfully. "I must be a dead man, mates. Or I'm dreamin'. I can smell strawberries!"

❧   ❧   ❧

The forty lather-flecked horses from the École de Cavalerie carried double riders. Raymond and Gaston shared the bay gelding which had belonged to Sepp. Andre rode a black stallion that had been Paul's.

Two horses abreast in a column of twenty, the defenders of Lys approached the rubble of Dunkirk. The heads of the last footsore stragglers turned to stare after them.

"Cor! Hit's a lot uv li'l boys! Brought their 'orses fer a bit uv polo wif Jerry!"

Andre only heard bits of the English conversation, but he understood clearly the derisive laughter which followed.

Two sentries at the barricade stepped out in the road as the troop reined to a halt. The dress uniforms of the cadets were torn and bloody, giving mute testimony to the action at the river, but these were still not like any livery the sentry had yet seen passing through Dunkirk.

"Colonel Andre Chardon," Andre saluted. "Accompanying the rearguard detachment of the École de Cavalerie."

The BEF sentry rocked forward in surprise. Again the words were in English. "Looks like Napoleon's chaps after Waterloo. S'pose we got us a bunch of ghosts, Bobby?"

"Jack! It's those schoolboys who held Jerry off back at the river . . . At the hospital!"

"Ghosts. Like I said . . . Thought they was all dead!"

"What do we do with them?"

"We can't stop ghosts. Let 'em pass, I s'pose. Let 'em all pass."

The sentry saluted Andre smartly, then as the squadron trotted by he remarked, "Right. The new motto of the French Army. *Let them pass.*"

❦   ❦   ❦

"You have to report your arrival so you can get on the list." A sergeant at the western mole turned back the eighty cadets. Andre bristled at being shunted aside from the rescue site he had himself organized, but the sentry was insistent.

The young soldiers of the École de Cavalerie assembled outside the headquarters. While the other cadets waited, Andre and Gaston were escorted into an office where a short, stocky British colonel was engaged in conversation with a subordinate.

At the sight of the two he roared. "Good heavens! What are you supposed to be? Napoleon's cavalry?"

Andre shook his head and gestured for Gaston to step forward. "This is the acting commander," he said. "You had better listen to what he has to say."

"Cadet Captain Gaston Corbet. École de Cavalerie. Ordered by Captain Paul Chardon to report for duty, sir!"

"The Cavalry School? I thought you were all dead." His French was very bad.

"There are eighty of us, sir. We will fight the Boche again if we can get out of here."

The mocking smirk of the colonel vanished. He pulled himself to attention and snapped a salute.

"Do you know you are heroes, Cadet Corbet?"

"No sir." Gaston's eyes brimmed with emotion. "The heroes are the men who are still beside the river Lys."

Minutes later, accompanied by the British colonel, Andre and the eighty cadets marched to the head of the column of soldiers boarding ships on the western mole.

Small vessels were ferrying men from the mole to the larger craft beyond the harbor. Three British fighter planes passed in formation overhead. Seconds later, two more followed.

Andre, Gaston, and Raymond stood together silently on this last point of French soil jutting into the oil-coated waters of the Channel. How long would it be before they could come back to France? When would they face the German Panzers again?

All hoped it would be soon.

The cadets, conscious of the need to uphold the honor of their fallen comrades, marched proudly aboard the tug that carried them out to HMS *Intrepid* for the trip across the Channel.

❖   ❖   ❖

The high-pitched scream of an incoming artillery shell sent every man on the beach diving for cover.

Every man except for Badger Cross.

Clutching his precious jar of strawberry jam, he stood and faced the sea as the wails of the French poilus were drowned by the boom and rumble of the explosion. A hail of sand and shrapnel fell down on the prostrate forms of the soldiers. The angry buzz of hot metal passed close by David's ear to hiss into the dune. Then silence. The moans of the wounded. Choked sobs and the sounds of men retching with fear.

Then there was Badger. David rolled on his back to see who was alive and who was dead. Badger's shadow fell across his face.

"Well, that was a close one," Badger said calmly.

"Idiot!" David pulled Badger down onto the dune.

Badger was nonplussed. "I won't eat it on French soil, and there's an end to it." He stood again and held the jar of berries heavenward as if to offer thanks for a holy sacrament. "For what we are about to receive, may the Lord make us truly thankful. Amen."

"What's he talking about?" Mac McGrath peered at the blind man suspiciously.

"I told you he's nuts," David said.

"I won't have my birthday tradition here with these Froggies. Tinman, get me out on the lorries. Out on the jetty there."

"Tide's coming in."

"No matter. I won't have my strawberries on this stinking beach. The roof of a sturdy British lorry. That's the place for tea and cakes."

Mac and David exchanged looks. Tea? Cakes? Mac touched his finger to his temple. "Bonkers."

"I heard that." Badger stretched out his hand and began to walk unescorted toward the sound of water. "I'll have my birthday out on the lorry jetty. And I'll eat my strawberries and die a happy man. On English trucks.

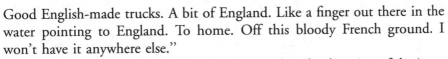

Good English-made trucks. A bit of England. Like a finger out there in the water pointing to England. To home. Off this bloody French ground. I won't have it anywhere else."

David let him weave toward the shoreline and in the direction of the jetty.

Leaping to his feet as the whistle of a shell approached, David shouted, "Down, Badger!" and he grabbed the blind man by the arm.

Badger resisted him, strengthened by determination. Shoving David back to the ground, he waved his hands and pressed on in the general direction of the makeshift pier. "They can't see me, Tinman," he roared. "I'm invisible . . ." The last few words were lost beneath the shriek of the shell.

The sand erupted close by. Badger walked on, unharmed, through the lethal rain of debris.

David jumped up and followed, suddenly filled with the eerie belief that blind Badger Cross, clutching his strawberries, had indeed become invisible to harm. An instant later they were joined by Mac, who muttered over and over, "Nuts. He's nuts. We're nuts. Nuts!"

David and Mac took Badger's arms and guided him toward the jumble of troop lorries and equipment heaped up in the water to make Badger's little bit of England.

Behind them, geysers of soil and pulverized men leapt skyward in a dozen places along the dunes. In front of them was the lorry jetty, deserted and dismal, being swallowed by the returning tide. There were the remains of sunken ships, derelict and abandoned, and the drifting wreckage of men and machines.

A succession of explosions erupted one hundred yards up the beach. While David and Mac ducked and cringed, Badger pressed forward. There was a momentary lull.

"No worry . . . home today." Badger raised the jar toward the Channel. "What's that noise?"

David saw nothing; heard nothing. He looked over his shoulder, anticipating another barrage. "Your imagination."

"No," Badger insisted. "It's there!" He stretched out a gauze-wrapped hand now ragged and grey with dirt.

David followed the line of the arm along the jetty. Far beyond the end of the tide-washed equipment danced a dark speck.

"There is something . . ." David's voice trailed off.

Mac stripped off his jacket and waved it overhead.

"They're still too far to see it." David warned.

"The boat will come straight here." Badger stepped into the water ahead of his companions.

The boat approached bow on, aimed unerringly toward the wharf. A black hull swelled into view and a boxy superstructure reared itself above the swirl of the sea.

Far away thunder announced the nearing of another barrage, but David paid it no mind. The three waded into the surf and climbed onto a three-quarter ton truck. David looked back to see other men staggering after them. Half-running, half-crawling, they emerged from the dunes until a new queue of several hundred snaked towards the water's edge.

The lashings that secured the lorries were worn by the waves. The nose to tail formation of dark green metal beasts swayed with each new surge. A plank walkway, improvised from fenceposts and scavenged driftwood, wobbled under David's feet. In constant danger of pitching into the water, he helped Badger as they lurched from roof to roof.

"How many ships?" Badger cried.

David raised his eyes to count the formation of small ships which seemed to suddenly materialize on the horizon behind the black hull of a river barge. How had Badger known there was more than one vessel coming?

"I count a dozen!"

"How many men behind us?" Badger called the question over the tumult of artillery and the clanking of shifting metal against the tide.

From the veil of smoke wafting across the dunes still more ragged soldiers stumbled out until the number in the queue was perhaps half a thousand. They crept forward struggling to climb onto the shifting pier.

"Five hundred, about," Mac shouted back as he leapt from the hood of one truck onto the swamped bed of another.

"How far to the end of the jetty?" Badger asked as David helped him across the gulf.

"We're almost there. Two more lorries ahead and we're home!"

The jetty groaned beneath the weight and movement of the troops. For an instant the roar of the German guns fell silent, only to be replaced by the more ominous hum of approaching aircraft engines.

A collective moan rose up from the jetty. Faces craned skyward in dread. A few men jumped into the water and began to swim back toward the beach.

"Home today, boys!" Badger braced himself on the wood plank walkway and raised the jar of jam as if it could somehow ward off imminent death.

David crouched and tugged at Badger, who swatted his hand away and faced the oncoming buzz head on.

"Get down!" Mac cried.

Badger laughed and began to sing,

> *The Son of God goes forth to war*
> *A Kingly crown to gain!*

His blood red banner streams afar,
Who follows in its train?

Then exclamations of joy resounded up and down the line.

"It's the RAF!" A spontaneous cheer as a trio of Hurricanes roared in low from the sun and dipped their wings in salute as they passed overhead.

Guardian angels with Merlin engines, they circled above the beach as the school of French fishing vessels moved in.

David, Mac, and Badger reached the end of the jetty as hundreds more crammed in behind them.

"Here we are, Tinman. At the head of the line at last!" Badger opened his strawberries and dipped one unbandaged finger in to scoop out the red goo and sucked it off.

"Happy birthday, Badger."

They sat on the half-submerged hood, their legs dangling in the water. "I had this vision." Badger licked his fingers. "It was the ship . . . you know? The boat . . . the lady of Avalon who carried off King Arthur. Always loved that part of the legend. Now, Tinman, tell me what you see."

"I only wish I had my camera," muttered Mac. "Nobody's gonna believe this." The newsman stood and shook his head.

"I'm not sure I believe it!" David whistled low at the incarnation of Badger's vision.

"Well?" Badger croaked impatiently.

David clambered to his feet. "She's not a magic boat from Avalon. More like *Tugboat Annie,* but she'll do." David waved broadly as a low, broad-hulled barge chugged up to the jetty. It was piloted by a thickset woman with a scowl on her face which would have made the Führer cringe. On her shoulder perched a black and white rat who studied the approach intently.

"Give a hand!" The woman's voice was as gruff as a stevedore. "You think we've got all day? Lewinski! Step lively with those ropes!"

Tending the bow rope was a gangly, red-haired apparition wearing a gas mask. At the stern was a slim, pretty, sunburned woman who shouted at Mac McGrath.

"Where's your camera?"

He shrugged, pointed at the water. "Thought you'd never get here." He laughed with relief, then caught the cable, tying it off to the grill of the lorry.

As the Hurricanes boomed overhead, the faces of a half dozen children popped out of the hatch. The old woman at the helm scowled down at them until they vanished again, then waved to the assembled troops to begin embarking, and Arthur Badger Cross led the men on board.

❧ ❧ ❧

The Royal Navy motor torpedo boat MTB 102 cruised slowly by the Dunkirk shore, even as dawn broke on the ninth day of the greatest military rescue in the history of the world.

Over the loud hailer the sailors called out in both French and English, "Is anyone still there? There will be no more boats. Is anyone there?"

A pudgy figure emerged from the cellar doors beside a demolished house. In one hand he waved a bottle of champagne. "Here," he said. "Do not forget me!"

When he was hauled aboard he smelled of brandy, wine, and paté de fois gras. Over his shoulder he carried a bag that jingled suspiciously like silverware. "Poilu Jardin at your service," he said. "I was a guest of the mayor of the town. Perhaps you know him? A great capitalist, but a friend to the common man!"

❊ ❊ ❊

While the others slept in heaps of exhaustion, Gaston and Andre sat quietly together in the stern of the destroyer.

What disturbed Gaston most were his thoughts about the heroes who remained behind: Captain Chardon, Sepp, the other cadets . . . They would not be remembered long. Perhaps in fifty years the battle of the École de Cavalerie would be a forgotten fragment of the story of Dunkirk—lost in some dusty archive.

"So many . . . who will know them?" Gaston asked bitterly.

Andre sat without speaking for a long time. "Dust of heroes," he whispered at last. "God will know you."